The Wicked Fae Series

BOOKS 1-4

AMELIA SHAW

WICKED FAE

1

THE SHIFTER'S STOLEN FAE

USA TODAY BESTSELLING AUTHOR

AMELIA SHAW

The Shifter's Stolen Fae

CHAPTER 1
Aurelia

I sprinted through the city center, passing the wards into the witch market. My kind weren't welcome in this part of Dallas, but I had little choice in the matter. I pulled my hood lower over my face and did my best to steer clear of the other patrons. The apothecary was my target, and I had no time to waste. As I approached the shop, I pushed open the door, then scurried inside. The woman who owned the store ignored me until I walked up to the counter with my purchase.

"You don't belong here, girl," the woman sneered. "I only serve witches, not filthy beasts like you."

"I need this for my mother," I said firmly with as much calm as I could muster, pushing the item across the glass counter toward her.

She knew exactly who my adoptive mother was and wouldn't question the fact I was here to buy something for her. But the shop owner loved to look down on me and hassled me at every opportunity, anytime I came in on behalf of the woman who'd taken me in.

It's the same song and dance every time.

"One of these days, you won't have her to hide behind, mutt," she grumbled but rang up my purchase all the same.

Anger rose in gut, making my fingers tighten into fists and my jaw clench tightly.

I'm not a shifter, I wanted to scream but it was easier and safer for everyone to think that. The alternative was far too dangerous for me to even fully contemplate. My wings fluttered at my back quietly, thankfully still glamoured from the sight of prying eyes. I took the bag the woman thrust back at me, then exited the shop without delay.

I need to get home.

I wove through the crowd, careful to keep my wings from brushing against any unsuspecting witches or shifters.

"Watch it," I said as a man bumped into my back. I shivered at the strange pain that came with the contact.

Shit, my wings are sensitive today.

"Well, hello there, pretty. I didn't see you there." The man turned to stare at me with a sinister smile as he sniffed the air around me. He was trying to work out what I was, and I couldn't have that.

Not today. Not any day.

I bowed my head and skirted around him, cursing my temper. I should have just kept moving, remaining silent.

The man's hand latched around my arm in a bruising grip, stopping me from going any further.

"I don't want any trouble," I ground out between my teeth as a familiar panic welled up inside of me.

His eyes trailed over me as he pulled my hood down. "What are you?" He drew me closer to him.

"I'm none of your concern," I spat like a desperate alley cat and wrenched my arm free of his grip.

"I think you are," he drawled as he reached for me again.

I raced away before he could catch me. Shouts followed me as I pushed through other patrons of the market to escape.

Does he know what I am? How the hell could he smell me like that?

"That shifter girl stole from me!" the man bellowed, accusing me from behind. "Stop her!"

Shit, shit, shit.

I rushed through the market, wanting nothing more than to blend in and disappear from sight, but the stranger had caused a stir, and more and more witches pointed at me to aid in my capture. There was no love lost between the witches and me, that was for sure.

"I didn't steal anything! He's crazy!" I shouted as I passed several women who glared at me and then started screaming to draw attention to me and help the man.

"Freaking witches," I grumbled under my breath before ducking into an alley just as several men in black uniforms ran past the opening.

With no other option, I hid behind a large dumpster. The scent of rotting garbage made me retch.

Gods, that's disgusting!

I gripped the bag from the apothecary tightly as I stepped out from behind the dumpster and scanned the area for the closest threat.

How the fuck do I get out of this mess?

The man who started the chase stepped into the mouth of the alley and grinned at me, blocking off a potential escape route. "You really are a pretty one. You're going to make me some good money." His eyes twinkled with dark mirth as he stepped closer.

"I'm not going to make you anything," I growled at him as I scanned the alley for a second possible exit. There was a fence immediately behind me, leading to an alternate alley.

Can I fly over the fence without being seen? He obviously already knows what I am, but what's on the other side? Will humans see me? I can't risk it. Can I?

Something flashed in the man's hand and my eyes widened at the silver weapon.

Is that a gun? Is he going to shoot me with iron?

I shuddered. "Are you going to shoot me?" I asked with a raised brow and a quaver of fear. Being pumped full of iron was not my idea of fun. In fact, for my kind, it could prove lethal.

"This thing?" he asked, flashing me a grin as he waved the gun around. "No, it won't kill you. It will just make you nice and sleepy so I can get you where we're going."

"I'm not going anywhere with you." I sneered and unfurled my wings. He couldn't see them, but it made me feel better to know I could act.

I need to get home. Time is running out!

My mother was waiting for the medicine that I'd bought, and I needed to get it to her before it was too late.

"Oh, but you don't have a choice. Do you know what will happen if the witches see your wings?" he asked with a grin.

My stomach fell as I pulled my wings back to my body in a defensive manner.

He knows what I am, and what the witches will do if they figure it out. Shit.

"You can threaten me all you want, but I can take care of myself," I said, crossing my arms over my chest.

"What if I'm not threatening you?" he asked with a raised brow, not unlike my own. "What if all I'm doing is promising you a better life?"

I laughed at his words and pointed to the metal object in his hand. "That looks like enough of a threat to me. I don't need your help or a better life. I'm perfectly fine where I am."

He raised the gun with a frown as if disappointed I'd refused to believe his words.

My gut warned me he had no intention of letting me go. Without further thought, I unfurled my wings. I had to take the risk. My freedom was more important than wherever he thought I would have a better life.

Even if I'm outed to the witches, it's still likely a better fate than whatever plans this mercenary has for me.

I crouched down, ready to jump into the air. My wings weren't used to flying since I had been forbidden from using them my whole life. But I would use whatever advantage I had to get away from the tranquilizer gun that was pointed squarely at my heart.

"Stop!" he shouted and cocked the gun. "I would rather take you in willingly. There are things you should know."

"Bullshit," I said shaking my head. "There's nothing you can tell me that I don't already know—or that I want to know, for that matter."

"Really?" He chuckled. "I would have to disagree on that. My employer would very much like to tell you the truth about who and what you are."

I burst into a fit of laughter at his bravado as I bounced on the balls of my feet and jumped into the air.

"Stop!" the man shouted, and a soft click sounded a heartbeat later when he pulled the trigger of his weapon.

I soared up above the chain link fence behind me and even higher when a pinch to my shoulder made me flinch. An iron-laced dart.

Shit.

I landed on the dirty concrete at the other end of the alley and stumbled, my head spinning as I leaned against the wall for support.

Don't stop. You must keep going. He knows where you are.

The mental pep talk barely helped as I desperately tried to shake away the fog from my brain. I took a few unsteady steps forward before gaining my bearings and remembering where I was. I was still inside the wards and only a couple of blocks away from home. I ripped the dart from my shoulder and tossed it aside. The puncture wound would heal soon enough. I'd always healed quickly. I just had to act fast.

I can fucking do this!

I pulled my hood back up over my head and slipped out into the bustling crowd, hoping to get lost in the shuffle. I couldn't afford for the man to catch up to me again. I couldn't let him find me—too much was at stake. I needed to get home with the medicine for my mother or I'd be alone in this cruel world. And I sure as shit did not want that.

It only took about fifteen minutes before I finally laid eyes on the quaint little Italian restaurant our apartment sat above. I swayed on my feet as I rounded the corner, heading for the back alley where the fire escape waited. Hauling myself up the ladder, I was barely able to keep my eyes open. I blinked groggily as the poison of the iron coursed through my system.

How am I going to give Mother her medicine when I can barely keep my eyes open?

With immense effort, I made it onto the small balcony outside our downtown apartment and crawled to the window. My arms were as weak as jelly when I lifted the window and chaotically plunged into the living room. The plush carpet broke my fall, and I groaned wearily as I pushed myself to my knees. I held my head in my hands momentarily as I rubbed my eyes to clear the black spots from my vision.

Just a little while longer. Come on! I need to get the tincture to her.

I dragged myself across the beige carpet of the living room, my sole focus on the door at the end of the hall. My arms shook with exertion, and I slumped to the floor just outside my mother's door.

I'm so weak. I need to sleep.

My vision swirled again as I battled with all my might past the fatigue and strained valiantly for the door handle. To my dismay, I came up short and lost the battle. My eyes closed again and then there was nothing.

* * *

The sound of a muffled moan woke me up, and my eyes shot open.

How long have I been asleep, and why am I on the floor in the hallway?

My brain was fuzzy as my gaze hit the cream-colored door of my mother's bedroom, and my fist tightened, crinkling the small plastic bag in my hand.

The tincture. Shit. Is Mother, okay?

I winced, pulling myself to my feet. "Mother?" I called through the door as I managed to crack it open. The room was dark, just as I left it.

My mother's still form was on the bed.

I took two large steps in her direction holding out the medicine for her but stopped short.

How long was I out because of that tranquilizer? Is she okay?

Mother's chest wasn't rising and falling like it should and pain lanced through my chest, sudden and sharp, stealing my breath away.

No, she can't be gone! She's the only person I have in the world.

Tears blurred my vision as I sat heavily on the edge of her bed, my shoulders sinking. She hadn't been a great mother to me by any stretch of the imagination. Truthfully, I'd been little more than a slave to her, but she had shielded me from those who would have wanted me dead—or for even more nefarious purposes.

Like that man in the market.

I hunched over her body, her skin cold to the touch, and whispered the words of the witches last rites. I hated that she was gone, and it was my fault. If I hadn't gotten caught by that man in the market, she still might be here.

If I ever see him again, I will kill him where he stands.

As I sat gazing at the only mother I'd ever known, it occurred to me she wouldn't have wanted me to waste time. In a circumstance such as this, she would have encouraged me to run from those who would suspect me of foul play in her death. She'd often told me that if something were to ever happen to her, I needed to run far and fast.

As tears coursed down my cheeks, I resolved myself to action. It would not do to dwell here and grieve. It would achieve nothing, yet risk everything.

Mother might not have given birth to me, but she had found me and saved me. She'd given me a roof over my head, food, and clothing, and I would not dishonor her memory. I refused to be caught, killed, or used. I would run for my life. I would finally be free, because that's all she had wanted for me. So, for both of our sakes, I had to try.

I wiped the tears from my eye as I whispered one last prayer, hoping it would take her into the afterlife, before turning and leaving the room. I didn't know where I was going or how I would survive, but I would. I would do it for her, the one person who ever cared that I could be more than I was perceived to be. Or I would die trying.

As the last of the tranquilizer wore off, I jumped to my feet and marched into the small room that I called my own. It wasn't really a bedroom, it was more of a closet with blankets and some clothes stacked on the floor... but it had been mine. With renewed determination, I packed my bag and got ready to leave.

Someone pounded on the front door.

Bang! Bang! Bang!

Shit. Did someone see me? Are they here to take me away?

My head swiveled, and I glanced between the front door and my bedroom window, indecision warring within me. In no time flat, my own self-preservation won out just as Mother would have wanted. As swiftly and as quietly as possible, I opened the window, climbing down the narrow old fire escape and toward an uncertain freedom.

With nowhere to go and little clue of what I was going to do to sustain myself, I had no choice but to run for my life. I could only flee and hope that I'd figure it all out along the way with a wing and a prayer.

CHAPTER 2
Grey

"What do you mean, you lost her?" I growled at the half-Fae bounty hunter standing in front of me.

"She flew out of the alley. She was unwilling to come with me." He paced back and forth in front of me, grunting and muttering and generally carrying on like an idiot.

The scent of his fear permeated the room, nearly making me gag. I leaned back in my chair and tilted my head back, trying to evade the odor so the smell wasn't so bad.

I need patience to deal with idiots. I can't just kill my best bounty hunter.

"Explain to me how an untrained girl got away from you?" I

demanded as calmly as possible. I just couldn't wrap my damn head around it. My people were all well trained. I made sure of it when I brought them in. I didn't waste time with recruits that showed a lack of potential or didn't have some innate ability worth honing like a sharp blade.

"She's not just any untrained girl, boss. She looks like she's been hiding in plain sight her whole life," he said on a groan.

"How is that even possible?" I wondered aloud.

How does a powerful Fae go unnoticed for years, especially among witches and shifters?

"No clue, but I watched her enter an apothecary shop, talk to the staff, and come out with a bag before I was able to confirm what she was." He took a seat, flopping down into the leather chair across from my desk.

Shit. Who is this girl, and how do we find her?

A knock sounded on the door.

"Come in," I called, annoyed at the interruption.

"Boss, they're ready for you in the ring," Layla my second-in-command said as she opened the door into my private office.

I stood and buttoned up my suit jacket with a sigh. "Find out everything you can about that girl. I want to know where she's been and who she is by the end of the day," I barked at the bounty hunter before he scurried from the room to complete his mission.

"Possible new recruit?" Layla asked as she walked by my side through the door.

"Not a possible recruit. She evaded Dan, of all people. But she'll work for me one way or another." I stabbed at the button to the elevator.

"You really think you can force her hand?" Layla asked with a raised brow.

The elevator dinged, and I stepped inside, clenching my fists.

She will work for me. I won't take no for an answer.

"We'll make sure she is so desperate that she has no other choice," I grunted, crossing my arms as I leaned back against the gleaming wall of the elevator.

"Are you sure that's wise?" Layla pressed, hitting the button for the basement level.

"Are you questioning my authority, Layla?" I turned my glare of annoyance on her. No one was allowed to question my authority. *Ever.*

Layla's back stiffened, and her fear filled the small elevator. "No, boss. I'm just wondering if that's the right choice, especially if you want the girl to trust you and remain loyal to you."

I sighed, repressing my last nerve. "What do you suggest then?" I asked.

"Have Dan watch her for a couple of days and learn more about her. Then pursue her from there. You don't want to jump the gun and go off half-cocked," she answered as she stepped out of the elevator.

The florescent lights of the basement made me wince. My eyesight was too keen for such harsh lighting, but I needed to be here. It helped boost morale when the boss showed up for challenges.

The large group of supernaturals in the underground space grew quiet at our entrance. Whispers filled the air, but at least the noise level was now bearable to my over-sensitive hearing.

"Who do we have today and what's the grievance?" I asked, my tone one of business-like boredom.

"One of the trolls was disrespected by a shifter and called the challenge." Layla sighed.

"Why am I here over something so petty?" I grumbled and moved closer to the ring.

It's going to be an absolute bloodbath.

Trolls were notoriously stupid and had little magic of their own at their disposal, but what they lacked in magic, they more than made up for with brute physical strength.

With my octagon canceling out magic, it affected them the least of all the supernaturals.

"It will be a good fight." Layla shrugged, viewing it from a purely logistical standpoint.

She wasn't wrong there. Shifters could still shift inside the ring, so the two would be somewhat evenly matched.

Layla stepped forward and into the ring, then put her hands up to get the attention of the supernaturals in the room. "You know the rules. Once you step into the ring, you will not be able to use your magic. If you step out of the ring, you lose the challenge. We don't need anyone to die today, but we go until someone is unable to continue or until someone steps out of the ring," Layla called to the gathered crowd, then waved both contestants inside.

I took a seat in the front row, resting my elbow on the armrest and propping up my chin. I should have been out searching for the fairy that had managed to elude Dan, or up in my sleek office planning the next job. I had artifacts to find and no one who was qualified enough to locate them for me.

The troll and the shifter stepped into the ring, and the troll roared out his challenge. The crowd erupted in cheers as the shifter turned into a Siberian tiger.

"The troll challenged Karma?" I asked Layla as she sat down next to me. "Interesting." I leaned forward in my chair, a little more intrigued by the fight now that I recognized our best fighter. The troll *had* to know what he was getting himself into—facing off against a half-witch-half-white-tiger shifter. And if he didn't, he'd soon learn the hard way.

The troll charged, clearly tired of the formalities, one meaty fist raised in the air as he swung out at the tiger.

Karma easily dodged the blow with her feline grace and flexibility and slashed at the troll's side, opening him up with her razor-sharp claws.

He bellowed in pain as his blood sprayed all over Karma's glorious white fur.

She backed away, skulking then dodging the troll's grasp as he attempted to wrap them around her neck.

"He's too slow." I sighed. "How did he expect to beat Karma with nothing but brute strength? I was hoping he might have a brain cell in that thick skull of his, an idea for tactics perhaps."

Stupid troll is going to die because of his ego.

"We don't need supernaturals like that in the Syndicate," I finished telling Layla with a frown.

"He's a good bodyguard for hire." She shrugged, never taking her eyes from the fight.

A roar filled the air, bringing my attention back to the fight.

Karma shook her head as if to clear it and leapt away from the troll's hands once more. She'd clearly copped a blow, but she was just toying with him, like a cat with a mouse.

"Karma just needs to end this already," I said, increasingly irritated, my mind straying elsewhere. I glanced down at my watch, bored with this game she was playing. I didn't have time to burn.

Dan better have information for me soon.

I snapped my gaze back up to the fight as yelling broke out, filling the arena.

Karma had the troll's head lodged firmly between her huge jaws, her enormous, bloodied canines clamped down around his skull, ready to finalize the kill.

The troll was slapping the ground, tapping out.

Ugh. Weakness.

I shook my head in disgust and rose from my seat, waving to Layla. *I was done with this bullshit.* "Take him to the cells. He needs to understand the punishment for showing weakness in the Syndicate," I said with venom. I kept only the best.

Layla gave me an affirmative nod as she ran off to do as I commanded.

I dusted imaginary lint from my jacket and turned back to the elevator, checking my phone along the way. We didn't actually get service in the basement, even with the amount of magic we had down here, but if I didn't have a voicemail from Dan by the time I arrived back up in my office, we were going to have a *problem*.

I stabbed at the button for my private elevator and walked in the doors, which had silently slid open. Inside, I pushed the button for my floor and rode it to the top of the building. The elevator's *ding* caught my attention just before the doors opened. I strode down the hall to my office and slammed the door behind me, releasing a breath of relief. Silence. Blessed, beautiful silence. My oversensitive hearing could only take so much. The cheering and hollering had been headache-inducing.

The shrill ring of my phone made me groan, the irony not lost on me, and I picked it up. "What is it, Dan?" I asked shortly, pinching the bridge of my nose between my fingers.

"I went to the apothecary and asked about the girl," he informed hesitantly.

"And?" I ground out. I didn't have time to dance around the truth.

Get to the point! I need this girl working for me. I need her now.

"The apothecary said that she's the foster kid of a well-known witch. She gave me the address, but..." he trailed off.

"Dan, if you don't fucking get to the point I'm locking you in the cells for a bloody week on principle," I growled.

"I went to the address," he said quickly. "But there were cops all over the place and a woman was being taken out on a stretcher—dead."

I grinned.

I don't even have to make sure she's desperate. She's already lost the only person who ever cared for her.

"And where was the girl? Was she there?" I asked.

"She's not here, boss. I think she got spooked when her caregiver died," he said with a disappointed grunt.

"Do you have a name?" I growled.

"I'll, ah, I'll just text it to you, boss," he said, a note of worry in his tone.

Is he being watched? He better not let anything come between me and this Fae girl.

"Find her. She can't have gotten far. I doubt she has money or anything of value that could help her. She's going to need the Syndicate, whether she likes it or not," I said and hung up the phone.

I sat in the chair behind my desk smirking to myself as I opened my laptop. The news about the passing of an influential witch and her ward going missing would already, no doubt, be hitting supe social media.

As soon as Dan texted me the girl's name, I could put out an official order. No one would ignore the king of the Syndicate, that was certain. My word was beyond reproach.

A text came through within seconds.

Aurelia.

I almost salivated as I read the name, tasting it on my tongue like a fine liqueur.

Aurelia is an exquisite name.

I loved it. Without a further second to lose, I got to work on social media. It wasn't regular social media, where just anyone could join. It was my very own encrypted network of supes who would put the word out for me quickly. If anyone saw her, I would be informed. And I made sure that *no one* would dare offer her work or a place to stay. She was mine.

I grinned and sat back in my seat with a self-satisfied smile. It paid to be the king of the Syndicate, but I'd earned my position with blood and an iron will. No one would cross me, especially not when the stakes were so high. No one would be that foolish. No one who valued their life, at least. The Fae girl would soon be mine. I could almost feel it. And I would ensure she remained so—one way or another.

CHAPTER 3

No one in the supe areas of the city would help me. Shifters and witches alike could sense that I was different somehow, but couldn't pinpoint what it was. It made them feel uneasy around me and bred a natural suspicion that I wasn't able to change. To say it was beyond frustrating to live this way was an understatement.

I walked into yet another supe run motel, this one seedier than the last few I'd tried, and prayed to whatever gods were listening that they would deign to give me a room for the night.

"We don't serve your kind here," the man behind the counter grunted, his face down in a book. He was a shifter, but I couldn't tell what sort.

"And what, exactly, is my kind?" I asked indignantly as my patience wore thin.

Surely, this shifter can't tell what I am.

"Your kind means pampered princesses who aren't shifters," he sneered at me. He sat forward in his chair, his hawk-like nose turned up in disgust.

"Pampered princess?" I scoffed.

What is his deal? Pampered princess? Yeah, right. I've been practically a slave to my foster mother.

My eyes watered at the thought of her lying cold in her bed as I escaped out the window. I wish I'd had more time to attend to her.

I hope someone gave her the rites that she deserved.

"That's all you heard, girl? You didn't hear me say you aren't a shifter?" He shook his head and waved me off without further argument.

I turned to leave, crestfallen, angry, and tired as all hell.

Turned down again. Rejected again.

He spoke up again unexpectedly as I turned my back. "Wait, come here," he sighed. "What's your name, girl?"

"Aurelia," I answered even though it was probably a bad idea to be truthful. Who knew if people were looking for me to ask questions about my mother's death?

"Aurelia, huh? Okay Aurelia, this one night I'll make an exception for you." He nodded and grabbed a key from the wall.

I frowned in confusion at his sudden change of heart, but stepped forward anyway, not about to turn down the offer of a place to sleep for the night.

Is this a trap? Am I going to wake up to police at my door or other bad characters like the man from the market?

Shaking my head, I attempted to clear the intrusive thoughts. I couldn't keep thinking about all that *could* happen when my eyes were drooping. I was running out of steam fast and desperately needed somewhere to sleep. This was the only place that would give me a room, so I had little choice in the matter if I wanted some semblance of safety.

Sleeping on the street is not an option.

Tomorrow, I would have to make money somehow and find a new

place to stay, because I doubted this offer would be extended, and remaining in the same place when I was being hunted was not a wise move. But at least for tonight I could have some rest and grieve my mother and the sense of security I had that went with her.

I handed the man some cash to cover the cost.

He accepted it with a grimace before handing me a key. "Checkout is at eleven. I better not see you again until then. Keep a low profile, you hear?"

I grabbed the key with a curt nod before heading back out the door and around the building. It was a normal door key, the kind that had been used for decades, and not one of those fancy electronic keycards most places used these days. I followed the numbers on the wall until I found a room with the number that matched mine.

The key stuck in the door, and I had to jiggle it carefully so it didn't break. When I finally managed to get it open, the musty aroma of closed-up, badly needing a remodel motel room washed over me, and I sighed heavily. It wasn't the best place I'd ever stayed, but I couldn't fathom whether it was the worst either, since I had so few memories of where I grew up before coming to live with Mother.

The bed was bigger than I was used to, but since I was used to sleeping on a pile of blankets on the floor, it came as no surprise. I flopped down onto the bed—exhausted—and sneezed as dust flew up from the comforter.

If the place is this unused, then why'd he get so huffy about my kind being here? You'd think he gladly take my money at the first opportunity.

I shook my head. There really was no point in trying to figure out other people's prejudices and motivations, especially when it came to what I was. I just needed a place to rest and regroup.

Surely, someone will be willing to help me until I figure out what I'm going to do?

Standing up again, I pulled the comforter off the bed and dropped it in a pile on the floor in the corner before cranking the air-conditioner. It was hot even in the evenings in Dallas during the summer, and I had no intention of suffering any more than I absolutely had to. I'd already paid for the room, so its amenities were mine to use.

I sat back down on the bed and pulled my small bag closer. Everything I had in the whole world fit into one small backpack.

Pathetic. I am pathetic.

I fished out an old T-shirt to sleep in. It was far too big and easily covered all of me in case something happened, and I was forced to run. Pushing the thought from my mind, I wandered into the cramped bathroom and turned on the shower, eager to be rid of the sweat and grime of my panicked brush with danger and my very fortunate escape.

Even turned all the way to scalding hot, the water only achieved maybe lukewarm at best.

It will have to do.

I stripped down and stepped under the tepid spray. It does little to help unlock my tired, tense muscles the way it would have if I was at home, and the thought brought tears to my eyes. The only mother I had ever known was dead. She may not have been particularly kind to me. She may not have even loved me, but she had protected me.

I let the tears fall, allowing myself the emotional release of crying for tonight. I permitted myself to be weak in this tiny, dingy motel room because when I left here, I would need to be strong. This sad, musty hovel would be the only place that bore witness to my weakness and fragility. After this, I'd pull it together—somehow—because I had to.

I tilted my head back into the spray, wetting my hair, only to realize I hadn't thought to pack my shampoo or other essentials when I left in a frantic hurry.

Damn it.

Cleansing myself as best I could, I shut the water off and reached for the thin, scratchy towel, eyeing it with disdain and cringed. I didn't trust it and decided to use my air magic to dry myself instead. Warm air caressed my skin, and I sighed in relief as my hair dried almost instantly. It was a little wild without any of my hair products, but I couldn't do anything about it.

I pulled the large T-shirt over my head and twisted my hair up into a messy bun..

An unexpected knock on the door made me jump, then freeze on the spot.

Who could that be? The shifter at the front desk was serious when he said he didn't want to see me until morning.

I moved instantly into action and shoved my meagre belongings back into my bag without a second's hesitation and scanned the room for another viable exit.

Do I have to jump out another window today?

I slunk quietly around the room and over to the drab curtains in front of the window. I peeked out the side and into the darkening night. It was eerily still outside but another knock came at the door, more urgent and insistent this time.

Shit. What am I going to do?

Reaching for the window, I tried and failed to pull it open. The damn thing was stuck tight, the old wooden frame no doubt swollen into place with age and humidity. Could I use my magic to force it open? What if I broke it? Would I have the motel's landlord chasing me then, too?

"Aurelia, I know you're in there. I just want to talk," someone shouted through the locked door.

I would recognize that voice anywhere. It's the man from the market.

I clenched my fists and pushed down the sudden surge of rage that threatened to boil over. This wasn't the time to lash out at the man who'd inadvertently caused my mother's death. Revenge wasn't worth the risk of being recaptured. I blew out a breath to control my heaving emotions and drew my air magic to me in an attempt to push the window open, but it still wouldn't budge.

Fuck!

"No point in trying the window, Aurelia. I have the place surrounded," the man called out again, clearly ahead of the game.

"Why surround the motel if you just want to talk?" I shouted back at him, angry that he'd somehow found out not only who I was, but also where I was staying.

"You have proven slippery, but it doesn't have to be this way. Open the door so we can talk. I know what happened today," he said, his tone softer this time.

Who fucking cares if I break out a window?

There was no way I was trusting that guy. And every second I delayed my escape was a step closer to becoming who knows what?

Someone's slave or whore? Worse?

A shudder rippled through me. I wasn't about to hang around to find out. I let my magic fill me like a storming tempest and a cyclone of air smashed at the window, answering my summons. Shattering glass filled the air around me and shards hit the grimy floor like tinkling diamonds.

"Shit!" the man yelled and shouldered his way through the door. "Aurelia, don't! You have nowhere else to go."

"Anywhere is better than wherever you want to take me!" I spat before directing the cyclone toward him. It tore through the room, upending furniture as if it were nothing more than kindling and kicked up all the dust as it barreled at its intended target with surprising velocity.

He dove to the side at the last second, narrowly escaping major injury.

I clambered up on the windowsill and leapt out into the humid night air. He was right about one thing. I had nowhere else to go, but I would die before I went with him. My bare feet slapped against the concrete, a jarring sensation racing up my leg. Pain sliced through my tender flesh as glass crunched beneath me.

Fucking ow!

I feverishly brushed the bloodied glass from my feet and sprinted into the night, my poor feet throbbing with each desperate lunge toward freedom. I didn't dare attempt to fly like last time. I would be drawing enough attention to myself simply running through the shifter side of Dallas in an oversized T-shirt without shoes.

My wings fluttered uselessly at my back, and I tucked them in tighter to me so they wouldn't slow my pace. I ducked down a side street and paused briefly to catch my breath and listen for anyone following me. The night was uncomfortably silent, and the offensive odor of rotting garbage hit me like a freight train, causing me to gag.

Where is he? I know he's still following me.

With my heart pounding in my chest, I chanced peeking around the corner and scanned the street. It was silent. There wasn't a single soul in sight, but I couldn't allow myself to lower my guard or be fooled into a false sense of security like I had at the hotel. I had to keep moving.

Like a thief in the night, I rushed down the side street as silently as I could. It was urgent I reached the human part of the city. No supes would bother me there, and I'd heard humans were oblivious to what was right under their noses—so I'd likely be able to fly under the radar there, to speak. The only problem was I had never left the supe side of the city.

How do I even get there?

At the end of the street, lights blared overhead, and I winced. It would be safer to escape from the man who was chasing me, but my clothing, or lack thereof, would raise all kinds of red flags to anyone who was around and gave me so much as a second glance.

I quickly stepped behind a dumpster and dug through my bag for a pair of leggings and flip flops. They would be hell to run in, but at least they were shoes. I put them on as fast as I could and peeked out into the brightly lit street.

There were people milling around and a bar down the block with patrons spilling out on to the street, talking and laughing among themselves. It would be the perfect place to get lost in the crowd and plan my next move. It would afford me the luxury of a little time, at the very least.

I drew my wings in even tighter to my back, making sure that my glamour was still firmly in place. Then I took a deep breath and stepped out onto the busy street, weaving my way through the crowd and trying my best not to let my wings brush against anyone like I had earlier today.

Continuously peeking over my shoulder and scanning the area behind me for any sign of danger, my nervous gaze searched for the man who had ruined my life. The stranger who refused to give up his search for me.

What the hell is his deal? Why does he keep looking for me?

I turned around too late and walked right into a brick wall. Well, not an actual brick wall, but the man's chest that I faceplanted into sure as hell felt like it.

"Ow," I said and grabbed my sore nose to soothe the smarting hurt.

"I'm sorry," a rich voice apologized.

I glanced up and into the most mesmerizing blue eyes I'd ever seen. "No, I'm sorry. I wasn't paying attention," I said and chanced a peek over my shoulder again.

As a familiar face pushed through the crowd, my eyes widened in shock and dismay.

"Are you okay?" the handsome man inquired, his eyebrows creasing in concern.

"Yes, I'm fine. I'm sorry, I have to go." I tried to rush past him, but he sidestepped into my path.

"What's the rush? Are you in some kind of trouble?" he asked, looking me up and down.

Damn it! Yeah, my clothes completely give it away. Fuck.

"No, I'm fine. I just really need to go." I glanced over my shoulder again, my heart ready to leap into my throat.

My pursuer was stuck in the crowd but getting closer every second.

I turned back to those bright blue eyes and groaned. His eyes weren't on me, but over my head, no doubt seeing the man pursuing me most likely.

"I'm sorry. I really need to go," I stressed.

But the blue-eyed brick wall refused to budge. "Let me give you a ride. It's dangerous to walk the streets at night," he said, stepping closer to me.

"I'm tougher than I look," I said with a small smile and turned away, my cheeks heating with a blush.

Why am I embarrassed? He's just a man. A gorgeous man with ebony hair that's a little too long and the bluest eyes I have ever seen, but still, just a man.

"Please, I insist. I can't in good conscience step aside. My name is Grey," he offered with a dazzling grin as he touched my arm.

"Aurelia," I said as if in a daze, and to my own shock, I allowed him to lead me away. He seemed protective and well-mannered, and he wasn't *that* guy. What choice did I have? Perhaps the devil I didn't know was better than the one I did?

Shit! What am I thinking? What am I going to do now? He's going to know within minutes that I have nowhere to go! Then what?

So much for having time to figure out my next move...

CHAPTER 4

My shoulders stiffened and I drew a surprised shallow breath at the shocking realization of just *what* this fairy was to me. My mind reeled, and my whole world view shifted in a single, powerful heartbeat.

Mate.

I peered over my shoulder at Dan and gave him an imperceptible shake of my head as I moved my hand from Aurelia's arm to the small of her back.

She shivered at the contact but didn't step away.

What is that all about?

I couldn't see or feel her wings. Were they out all the time and simply glamoured? Or was it my touch that made her shiver?

"Aurelia. That's a beautiful name," I said with a what I hoped was a comforting and trustworthy smile. "Where are you headed?"

Chewing her lower lip, Aurelia stared at the ground, clearly uncomfortable. She fidgeted with her hands, wringing them together as if anxious. "I don't know," she whispered. She blinked her big, beautiful green eyes up at me. Tears filled them in an instant, but she set her expression and refused to let them fall.

Our mate is strong, my wolf said in my head.

"Were you just going to wander around the streets of Dallas all night?" I asked, the edge of a growl in my tone unmistakable. I couldn't bear to think she'd be out here alone, unprotected, and without simple amenities such as food and shelter. It made my stomach lurch.

"I hadn't planned on it. I *had* a place, but I can't go back there now." She frowned, then glared at me with indignation. She wasn't about to stand being called stupid, literally or otherwise.

Her honest reaction made the edges of my lips curl in amusement. It had been literally countless years since anyone had dared to look at me like that. "What happened?" I asked.

I know exactly what happened because I sent Dan there to find you. I should have known I'd have to do the job myself.

She was a tricky little thing, far more adept at taking care of herself than I'd given her credit for, and after what had happened in the market today, I should have expected she would try to run from Dan again.

That fucker needs more training. So much for being my best! He's about as subtle as a sledgehammer...

"Nothing," she sighed, licking her lips. "I just can't go back."

"I know of a place that helps people with nowhere else to go," I offered with a shrug, playing at nonchalant. In reality, I was hanging on her every word. I needed to play this just right if I was going to win her trust. And my wolf would never forgive me if I fucked that up.

"No, that's okay. Really. I'll find somewhere else to go. I'm nothing if not determined." She shook her head and stepped away from me.

I dropped my hand and shook my head, taking my lead from her body language. "I can't leave you out on the streets to fend for yourself.

You might be stronger than you look, but the shifters will smell the desperation on you, nonetheless."

Aurelia's eyes widened, and she gasped, her face paling. She turned her head left, then right, scanning the area for an escape route.

My nostrils flared, and my wolf beat at my chest from within, excited for a chase. Her instincts screamed at her run, and her fear smelled divine—not *rank* like that of my underlings. With a decidedly concerted effort, I schooled my expression to be as neutral as possible, but with my heart hammering away in my chest and adrenaline zinging along my veins with the power of unbridled lightning, it wasn't easy by any stretch of the imagination.

"You're a supe," Aurelia breathed, wringing her hands together more aggressively as her panic reached a fever pitch.

"I am." I nodded, taking a tentative step toward her. I could almost feel the betrayal in her eyes. She'd been hoping I was human—someone safe, oblivious, and easy to brush off when she saw fit.

"Are you with the man chasing me?" she demanded, her voice shaking as she took another step back, which only served to excite my wolf more.

"Stop, Aurelia. I'm barely holding it together, and if you run, my wolf will give chase." I held my hands up in mock surrender, willing her listen, to comply with my wishes. I took a large step away from her even though it killed me to do so, affording her the illusion of choice.

"Are you with him?" she bit out between gritted teeth, determined to ascertain the truth.

She's bold. I'll give her that.

"No," I lied. And technically, it wasn't a lie. My bounty hunter hadn't known I would be here, and I genuinely hadn't planned on running into the beautiful fairy either. I'd either gotten lucky, or there was an element of Fate at play.

"But you knew I was being chased," she pressed. "I watched you look at him over my head." Aurelia crossed her arms over her chest, innocently pushing her breasts up in her ratty, old, oversized T-shirt.

I swallowed a groan at the sight of nipples peaking against the washed-out fabric. My cock stiffened to the point of pain as she stood before me, oblivious to the effect she was having on me. The leggings and baggy T-shirt did nothing to hide her generous curves from my hungry eyes.

My wolf howled his agreement in my head. He wanted to sink his teeth into her and make her ours. In fact, he wanted to devour her—and in more ways than one.

Not yet. We need her. Don't scare her off! We must exercise restraint.

"I *did* know you were being chased," I admitted. "I'm not blind, nor am I an idiot. I make it a point to be an observant man. It's why I can't let you roam Dallas by yourself tonight. Let me help you," I said softly. I stared down into her eyes and hoped she would be able to recognize my plea.

Please, do not make me chase you.

I didn't want to be the monster she saw Dan as being. And if my wolf had anything to say about Aurelia's role in our future, she would become much more to me than just a means to an end. She would be our mate.

Shit. This is not how I saw all this playing out.

"I can take care of myself," Aurelia said curtly. "I've escaped him twice today already and I'll do it again if I have to."

"But why is he after you?" I asked.

"I don't know," she admitted more softly.

"Why would you run if you don't even know what he wants?" I asked with a frown.

He never got the chance to tell her what he wanted? Which meant she wasn't running from the Syndicate, specifically...

She stared at me like I was a goddamned idiot.

That's new.

No one dared look at me the way this fiery woman just did. Not only was she tricky and determined, but she also had real courage. She was at every disadvantage there could be right now, and she was still doing her best to doggedly hold her own.

"I'm a woman, for starters, which is a peril in and of itself," she quipped. "And on top of that, no one seems to know what I am, so when someone figures it out, I bolt. It's safer that way." She shrugged as if that explained everything and turned away from me. She quickly scanned the signs on the cross street we were standing at and stormed down the street to our right without so much as a glance back.

"Aurelia, wait!" I jogged down the street after her.

We're not letting go of her that easily, I promised my wolf when he started rumbling his concern at her rapid departure.

"What did you mean by that?"

"Nothing," Aurelia called over her shoulder, never slowing her pace.

Tamping my wolf's possessive instincts down was trying my patience by the time I finally caught up and touched her arm. Tingles of undeniable pleasure erupted up my spine, sizzling like electricity, and I groaned. "Just let me help you," I bit out. "I can give you safety and a job."

"I don't need your pity *or* your charity, thank you," Aurelia said with surprising anger as she spun to poke me in the chest.

"It's not either of those things," I growled in frustration.

Gods, this woman is stubborn!

Aurelia flinched away as if stung, her eyes flashing.

I hung my head, breathing deeply to calm myself and my desperate wolf. If I let my alpha dominance out too aggressively, she'd run for the hills. I had to rein it in—fast—or I'd lose her.

"Bullshit, Grey. I'm not a charity case, and certainly not yours. I can do this on my own." She spun on her heel and rushed away again.

This fairy was seriously beginning to try my patience. But what choice did I have? My wolf had recognized her as our mate. So, I did the only thing I could... I ran after her. Blocking her path, I planted my feet and raised my hands in a placating gesture. "At least let me take you somewhere safe to explain my offer. You can think about it overnight and if you are still genuinely not interested, then you can go. Simple as that."

I had no idea what possessed me to offer such a deal to her. There was no way in hell my wolf would ever let her go now he'd caught her scent. I might need her for a job, but he needed her for very different reasons entirely.

Aurelia chewed her lip nervously and her shoulders slumped, dark circles of fatigue visible under her lovely green eyes. "Do you swear that you won't call the police or sell me to someone who will run tests on me?" She crossed her arms over her ample breasts, again awaiting my answer.

I had to avert my gaze before lifting it back to meet her eyes.

This is going to be an exercise in restraint.

"Why would I sell you to be experimented on?" I frowned at her.

Who has been filling her head with this rubbish? We don't experiment on our own people. And if anyone does and I find out about it? They'll be shut down immediately!

"That's why I have to hide!" she said with exasperation. "People hate my kind." She looked away, obviously not wanting to elaborate further on exactly what she was.

"Supes don't experiment on each other, at least not that I've ever heard." I shook my head, equally exasperated. "That would be a disgusting breach of faith between the supe species, and I wouldn't sentence my worst enemy to such a fate."

Aurelia's green gaze slammed into mine at the vehemence behind my words. "All right," she conceded with a heavy swallow. "But I *will* leave if I don't like what you have to say." She raised a brow at me as if to test my oath.

"Of course. I would never hold you against your will. I just want to make sure you're safe tonight and then we'll go from there." I nodded and steered her back the way we came.

"Why do you care?" she asked, moving away from me so I couldn't touch her back.

"I told you. I help supernaturals that have nowhere to go. It's what I do. I give them purpose." It wasn't the whole truth, but she didn't need to know the nitty gritty details until she chose of her own free will to join me.

We walked the several blocks to the high-rise that housed my penthouse apartment. The doorman opened the exterior door for her and I put a hand on the small of her back and led her inside, instinctively reaching for her.

She shivered at my hand on her back but kept an artfully blank mask in place.

My wolf whimpered inside me as I contemplated just what kind of life our mate had led up until this point to be so closed-off and independent. I pushed him back down and pulled my keycard from my pocket. I absently slid it over the scanner of my private elevator like I'd done thousands of times before.

She raised an eyebrow at me but stepped inside without protest. A second later, Aurelia frowned as the doors closed us in, confining us to the intimate space. There was nowhere she could run. For now, she was trapped, whether she liked it or not.

I hit the button for the penthouse, and we rode the elevator in silence.

Aurelia jumped, spooked by the sound when the elevator *dinged* in the quiet space. She smelled like literal heaven, but the scent of her was causing my cock to harden again.

The mate bond between us could be strong, my wolf panted as desire swelled within us.

Heel. We must wait.

I needed to focus on what lay ahead but being in such forced proximity with her made me want to shove her up against the wall and fuck her until we both shattered into a million jagged pieces, like a chandelier smashing into diamond shards on a gleaming ballroom floor. I wanted to fuck her so hard that we'd be picking up the fragments of ourselves for weeks.

Her eyes widened as we stepped from the elevator and directly into my living room.

I led her to my plush black leather couch and waved a hand dismissively for her to sit.

"What am I doing here, Grey?" she asked, scanning my apartment with furtive eyes, like prey assessing an area for potential escape opportunities.

My head spun with the possibilities just hearing my name on her lips. Her lilting tone made it sound exotic. And in an instant, I knew I wanted nothing more than to hear her crying it out, again and again, as I drove myself deep inside her fairy warmth.

My name will be her prayer.

I cleared my throat and the sordid imagery from my mind by sheer force of will. "I thought you might be more comfortable here while you decide whether to take me up on my offer." I shrugged before I made my way over to the oak bar in the corner of the living space and poured us each a stiff drink. "I have an idea of what you are," I said carefully. "But I want to hear it from you." I casually set one of the glasses in front of her.

Aurelia frowned at the amber liquid in the glass and licked her lips, a sign of her anxiety. "I've never told anyone other than Mother what I am." She chewed her lip as she picked up the glass and sniffed it tentatively. With a grimace, she set the tumbler back on the table untouched.

"It's just something to help with your nerves. Would you prefer something else? Water perhaps?" I asked.

She nodded with a small smile. "Thank you," she said as she blushed and looked away, as if somewhat disarmed by the small demonstration of kindness.

"I understand how difficult it must be for you to trust anyone with what you've evidently been told about supes," I said, moving back to the bar and fetching a bottle of cold water from the mini fridge.

"Everything she ever did was to protect me," she whispered in response, so low even I almost didn't hear it.

"Did?" I asked strolling back to the couch and handing her the water.

"I didn't come here to give you my life story," she said, raising her defenses once more. "You said you had an offer for me," she continued, deflecting the question.

I would have been surprised by her reaction except for the fact that I knew the truth. Her mother had just died yesterday. The turmoil she was going through was obvious and still very raw. "I do, but first I need you to tell me what you are." I sat back on the couch and swirled my drink, happy to wait her out until she broke and divulged.

She took a long drink of her water, clenched her jaw, and glared at me as she set the bottle back down. "Fine," she snapped. "Have it your way. I'm an evil, spiteful fairy. Is that what you wanted to hear? Are you going to turn me over to some supernatural testing facility now so they can tear off my wings and siphon my blood for its magic?" She jumped to her feet and rounded the table to the elevator.

Jesus-fucking-Christ! What in the sweet fuck?

"No," I said sternly. "I already told you that such hellholes don't exist, and I *don't* think you're evil, Aurelia. You simply have a specific skillset that I need. So, I would like to offer you a job." I stood and blocked her path. "This was not our deal," I reminded her. "You promised to hear me out."

"Fine," she huffed as if she rather be anywhere else in the world. "What kind of job do you have for an evil, trickster Fae?" She planted her hands on her hips in a silent, attitude-filled challenge.

"Only the trickiest," I retorted with a grin, knowing I had her undivided attention for what felt like the first time.

"And what does that mean, pray tell?" She frowned.

This fairy has a quick temper!

"Have you ever heard of the Syndicate?" I asked, cocking a brow in question.

She gasped, taking a step back. "Do you work for the Syndicate?" she asked warily, her gaze back to scanning the room for any possible escape beyond the elevator.

"I don't work for the Syndicate, Aurelia."

She relaxed slightly at those words, but it was a false sense of comfort at best.

I dropped the truth on her like a bomb nailing its target. "I *am* the Syndicate."

"Explain," she demanded in a shaky voice as she took yet another uncertain step back from me.

My wolf perked up again, begging for a chase.

"I told you. My name is Grey, and I own the Syndicate. And the truth is I have been looking for you for a *very* long time—for a job that only *you* can do." I held her gaze as her eyes widened in surprise.

This has to work. I need her to do this for me, or I'm back to square one. And I refuse to be this close to my goal and have to start all over again.

My heart raced and my mind whirled. This was it. The pinnacle of my destiny. The point of no return upon which all my hard work hung, precarious as a knife edge and as fragile as a butterfly wing.

She has to agree... because I really don't want to have to force her.

My inner wolf howled.

CHAPTER 5
Aurelia

Shit. Shit. Shit! I knew I shouldn't have come here.

My anger and panic spiked, and my magic rose to the surface unbidden as my wings spread wide behind me. "You're just like everyone else!" I cried, my voice breaking with emotion.

He just wants to own me... use me! What happens when I'm no longer useful? Will he sell me to the highest bidder? Turn me over to face the communal justice of the witches or shifters who loathe me with every fiber of their being? I can't trust him.

"Aurelia, you need to calm down," Grey said softly, his brilliant blue eyes wide as he held out his hands in placation.

I frowned.

Why is he acting wary suddenly?

I followed his line of sight and glanced down at my own hands. "Shit! What that the hell is this?"

A blazing purple ball of living magic swirled just above my palm, and my heart leaped in my chest at the startling and unexpected sight.

How do I make it stop?

"Your magic is reacting to your anger and fear. Just focus and breathe with me. In and out. In and out. I need you to calm down before you burn down my apartment with us in it," Grey said in a deliberately soothing tone.

I'd never had this happen before in my life—and I'd *definitely* felt anger and panic before. These feelings were not new to me, not by a long shot. They were basically my bedfellows and constant companions. Fear, anger, and panic were all I knew. How could I know anything else when I'd spent my life hiding from those who would use or harm me?

"You know that telling someone to calm down is the last thing you should do when you want them to actually calm the fuck down, right?" I shrieked as I began to hyperventilate. The ball only grew bigger the more I yelled, the more emotion I allowed to run unchecked.

What the fuck is happening? Where has this magic suddenly come from? And why now?

Grey breathed deeply in through his nose and waited for a beat before he blew it back out of his mouth pointedly. "Match my breathing, Aurelia. Focus on my voice. Look into my eyes."

The way he said my name sent a pleasant shiver through my soul and had me feeling slightly calmer. But how the hell was that even possible? He was a shifter and the leader of a corrupt organization, the Syndicate.

Overwhelmed and drowning in panic, I had no choice but to defer to his instruction. While a shuddering effort, I managed to match his breathing, sucking in one huge lungful of air after another before blowing it out in time with his. Slowly, *so* painfully slowly, despite the tremble in my bones that refused to abate, I felt a sense of calm descend upon me like an intangible mist.

"Good girl. You're doing so well, princess. Keep going," he coaxed.

I glared at him.

What a stupid nickname!

My magic flared again at his words, undoing my efforts at calming myself.

Grey chuckled.

And though it should have further provoked my anger, the sound was like a soothing balm on my skin.

"Okay, okay. No nicknames. Just focus on your breathing and the sound of my voice." He kept his breathing slow and even, coaching me through the storm of fear and anger that threatened to surge up again and swallow me whole.

I matched his breathing once more, listening to his soothing words, losing myself in the deep blue of his incredible eyes, until the magic finally fizzled out, snuffed out like the light of a candle as wet fingers pinched the burning wick.

"You're going to need some serious training to learn to control that, Aurelia," Grey said sternly. "You could accidentally hurt someone—or worse, yourself—with that kind of unchecked magic."

Now, despite the fact he'd just helped me step back from the edge, I desperately wanted to smack him in his smug, gorgeous face. "You think? But there's no one else *like me* to train me though!" I threw my hands up in frustration before raking my fingers through my long hair.

"Well, what did that woman teach you? Your mother?" Grey shook his head in exasperation.

"Not much of anything, to be honest. I was lucky she even taught me to read and kept me fed," I said narrowing my eyes at him. Did he think I was some kind of pampered princess the same way the shifter from the motel seemed to?

"She wasn't your real mother, was she, Aurelia?" he asked with a pointed stare.

"She was the one who counted," I snapped back, turning my back on him. "She didn't *have* to raise me, but she did. She was the only one who ever showed me a scrap of kindness in my whole life as far as I can remember!"

"So, you've never even seen another Fae before?" he asked, placing a hand on my lower back and leading me to the couch again.

"There aren't any other Fae here." I shrugged. "I'm the only one."

Am I wrong? Did Mother lie to me all this time about everything?

The very thought that nothing I potentially knew was real rocked me to my core and left me shaking.

"You're not the only Fae in the realm, technically," said Grey with a wince as he trailed off.

"What do you mean by that?" I asked and sat down heavily on the couch, no longer able to support myself under the weight of my emotions and fatigue.

"Full-blooded Fae are notoriously elitist snobs. They send their half-Fae children to the mortal world more often than not. The Fae like having their freedom, but then treat the half-bloods they birth with disdain." Grey sighed and sat in the reclining chair opposite me.

"So, you're telling me that I'm likely only half fairy?" I asked furrowing my brow.

What else could I be? Mother would have told me if I was anything else right?

But the more this night dragged on, the more convinced I was that I knew almost absolutely fucking nothing, not just about myself, but the workings of the supe world too.

"No, you're definitely a full-blooded Fae. With the amount of magic you almost just unleashed upon my living room, there can be no doubt. You summoned that kind of power without even thinking about it, without intention. Half-bloods don't have such gifts, such strength. You're the real deal, Aurelia." He picked up his glass and took a long sip, eyeing me over the top of it.

"Then why was I left here alone to fend for myself? Why am I not in the Fae realm?" I asked, unable to hide the hint of sadness and rejection from tainting my voice.

Did my real parents really just abandon me to the human realm? And if so, why? What could I have done to make them not love me? Was I truly bad?

"I don't know," Grey said with a shake of his head. "But I wish I did."

Licking my lips, I grasped at straws, at any sense of normalcy, something upon which I could ground myself. I needed a port as much as a ship lost at sea. I needed somewhere to be, to figure all of this out before it spiraled well and truly out of control. "So, you want me to come work for the Syndicate?" I asked, prompting Grey to pick up the threads of the conversation we'd begun earlier.

"I do. I have half-Fae who can help you learn control. Not only that, but you'll have a place to stay and money in your pocket for whatever you need." He put his glass down on the table and the ice tinkled against the sides as it settled.

Can I really do this? Mother warned me about the Syndicate. She told me they were the worst of the supernaturals... but Grey has been nothing but kind to me. Is it merely an act to gain my trust? A ploy to get what he wants and nothing more?

Either way, I was stuck between a proverbial rock and a hard place. I had nowhere else to go, and that was the stark reality of my situation. I had no one and nothing. My choices seemed limited at best. "I would just have to work for you. That's the catch, right? I'll be your full-blooded Fae on staff and will have to do whatever you want me to do, even when I don't agree with it." I said, grabbing my water.

"The jobs I need your magic for are dangerous, I won't lie to you. But you'll have to train for a while before we can get you started on missions. It will give you the time to learn the skills you need to protect yourself," he said, staring in my eyes.

Well, shit. How can I argue with that? It sounds entirely reasonable, all things considered. And I need to learn to protect myself. This world doesn't like my kind.

I just had no idea why. Parched, I cracked the water bottle open again and took a long sip, swallowing slowly. I didn't want to answer too quickly, especially when I wasn't even sure what I wanted. I could definitely use the self-defense skills and the magical control training... but what if he wanted me to do something illegal? Something truly nefarious and wrong?

"If you have half-Fae that can help me learn the skills I need, why don't you have them already assigned to these jobs?" I asked with a raised brow. If he didn't have a good answer, I was leaving. I didn't care that I had nowhere else to go.

He said he wouldn't lie, and I want the truth. I'm tired of not knowing.

"They have passed careful and extensive vetting, and none of them have the kind of magic it will take to get the jobs done, Aurelia. If they had, I wouldn't have been searching for a full-blooded Fae in the first place," he said.

Wait, what?

"Is that why you bumped into me outside the bar?" I asked. "Were you on the hunt? You knew what I was from the beginning? How?" I asked angrily and stood again, my temper lending me the strength to leave.

"I was not on the hunt, as you put it, and I was certainly not expecting to bump into you tonight. It was a fortuitous coincidence, but I'm not one to look a gift horse in the mouth. I will always seize the opportunity to get what I want," he said before moving to block my exit again.

"That's not a good enough answer for me," I bit out angrily and attempted to dodge past him for the elevator.

He gripped my arm lightly, his eyes imploring me to see reason, to give him a chance. "Please, Aurelia, just stay the night. I'll show you where you can sleep, and if you still want to leave in the morning, I won't stop you. But don't make me watch you walk out into the dark with nowhere to go. I couldn't bear the thought of what might happen to you."

Something in his gaze and the earnest tone of his voice had me softening, relenting to his wishes. Fatigue weighed heavily on my shoulders, and he was right, I had nowhere to go. What could it really hurt to stay just one night in an apartment that was fancier and no doubt safer than any place I'd ever been? With a sigh, I nodded. I was strong, but the truth remained that I'd be better able to protect myself and run if I were well rested.

Grey smiled in response and it was devastating.

No, Aurelia. You can't be attracted to the leader of the Syndicate. You are a means to an end for him. Do not *get attached. If anything, even if I accept, this is just a job. A means to an end for myself as much as it is for him. It will be a game of give and take.*

Grey held his hand out to me, his long, dark hair gleaming beneath the mood lighting of the penthouse.

Damn, he is gorgeous.

I grimaced, hesitating for several heartbeats before taking it.

You really shouldn't be doing this, whispered the only instincts I'd ever known—the ones that had kept me alive and fighting this long. But as I placed my hand in his, all thoughts of running away again evaporated like dew in the sunlight. My spine tingled at the flesh-on-flesh contact, and I gasped, unable to stop myself.

Grey sucked in a ragged breath and led me down a hall.

Did he feel that weird electricity between us too? What was that? I've never felt anything like it.

"That room is mine. It's off limits," he said, pointing to a door on the left. Then he indicated toward the room in front of him. "You can stay here for tonight. Please, think about what I've said, and I'll see you in the morning."

"Grey?" I asked as he turned down the hall in the direction of the room that was off limits.

"Yes, princess?" He chuckled at my glare.

"What's so important about this job?" I asked, my curiosity getting the better of me.

"It's a project of mine that I've been working on for a very long time," he answered.

With no further clarification forthcoming, I nodded. "Goodnight, Grey," I said. I closed the door behind me, not waiting for a response and not sure if I even wanted one. I flopped onto my back on the large four-poster bed. The comforter beneath me was the softest thing I'd ever felt in my life. It felt like I was being swallowed by a cloud.

Don't get used to it, Aurelia. You won't be staying.

Even if I decided to accept his job offer, I doubted his employees lived in his home. My stomach roiled and my heart thumped. I didn't want to contemplate *why* that fact made me sad, but I had an inkling it had something to do with his touch... with the electricity we shared.

I crawled up the mattress and snuggled in under the covers. It felt like a heavenly nest made of angel feathers. My exhaustion stormed in, catching up with me, and I was almost asleep when ringing sounded from another room down the hall.

Why would someone be calling so late?

I frowned as I pushed the covers off and made my way on silent feet to the door and pressed my ear to it.

"Hello?" Grey's voice rang out clearly in the hall.

I nearly jumped, scared he would catch me spying on him after he offered me such hospitality.

"No, I can't come out there tonight." His tone was surly and grew louder as he came closer to my door. "I don't give a damn if there's been a challenge, Layla," he barked. "There has been a development."

I nearly raked my fingers down the door at the name Layla. What woman was calling him so late?

Stop it, Aurelia. You don't have a claim on this man, nor do you want one. You are a means to an end.

"This isn't up for debate," he snapped on the other side of my door.

I jumped away from the door with a squeak as Grey threw it open, barely missing me in the process. "What are you doing in here?" I yelled, startled and with no reasonable alternative.

"Did you get the information you desired by spying on me, princess?" He smirked and prowled further through the door.

I backed up until the backs of my knees hit the bed frame, but he just kept stalking closer.

"I'm a predator, Aurelia," he all but purred. "I heard your heart rate pick up when I said Layla's name. Are you jealous of my beta?"

"N-no," I stammered and would have facepalmed right then and there if he hadn't been right up close, invading my personal space.

"You don't sound too sure of that," he said, his eyes glowing with his inner animal as he trailed his nose up my neck, taking a long, deep breath.

Did he just sniff me?

My throat ran dry, and I licked my lips, overwhelmed by his closeness.

His full lips skimmed my jugular, and he growled deep in his throat.

I shuddered beneath him with undeniable desire. "What are you doing?" I groaned and attempted to half-heartedly wiggle away.

I should stop this...

He pushed a little harder, until there was nothing but him.

I fell backwards onto the bed, my eyes wide.

He followed me down, his huge, hot body coming down on top of mine. "You smell like cherries and sunshine. It's intoxicating," he whispered against my skin.

"Grey," I groaned and wiggled my hips, though I some part of me knew that I wanted this, a more prideful part was loathe to admit it.

Something hard grew against my belly as he peered into my eyes. "If you want me, princess, just know that you don't have to be jealous of my second. She's nothing but business, whereas you will be mine in every conceivable way," he said and nipped my shoulder.

What the hell is he talking about? I can't possibly want this man who is in charge of the fucking supernatural underground, can I?

I rubbed my thighs together, still pinned beneath him. What was going on with my body? I'd never reacted like this to anyone.

With my wings pinned beneath me on the bed, he reached his hand up over me, as if he could see them ran a hand down their delicate membranes.

My back arched, and I pushed my breasts against his chest. "Grey," I breathed.

"Get some sleep, princess," he crooned. "I have a feeling tomorrow is going to be a very busy day," he said and was suddenly gone, closing the door behind him with a *click*.

With my heart still racing, my breathing ragged, and the depths between my legs aching, I pressed my palms to my eyes and whined in frustration.

What the fuck have I gotten myself into?

Groaning, I rolled over to bury my face in the plush pillows where I prayed fervently for sleep to claim me. This was bad. *Really* fucking bad.

CHAPTER 6

What the fuck was I thinking?

I'd heard her heart rate unexpectedly pick up last night when I'd admonished Layla, then promptly lost all sense of propriety. I wanted her. Badly. I craved her more than I needed air. Knowing she was my mate and not being able to immediately mark her as mine and claim her in the flesh was driving me to distraction.

I still want her.

My wolf was riding me hard to claim her and I'd lost all control when he'd scented her arousal. I could still recall her scent. She smelled like lush, ripe cherries and warm, radiant sunshine. Reliving the memory of last night made my mouth water, but I could only thank the heavens that I'd been able to pull away when I did. The timing wasn't right—not yet.

"Boss?" Layla's voice drew me back to reality as she called from the other side of the phone.

"If this is about last night's challenge, then I don't care. I have bigger things to worry about right now," I said with a growl.

"It's not," she assured me. "We have a job for the troll, but he's currently in punishment," she explained, sounding exasperated.

"So, send a different bloody troll." I tightened my hand around the phone, nearly snapping it in half.

"He was requested specifically, boss." She groaned.

"Fine! For fuck's sake, Layla. Let him out for this job. But if he shows any sign of weakness or an ego the way he did before, then he's gone. Got it?" I shook my head.

Why am I the one who has to be interrupted to make this decision? She is perfectly capable of handling this on her own. That's why she's my damned second!

"Next time there's a special request, just handle it, Layla. I have bigger problems than weak trolls." I hung up the phone with a snarl, agitated.

"Why does she call you so often?" a sweet voice asked me from behind.

I told her she doesn't have to be jealous, so why has her scent changed?

"She's my second-in-command, but certain things need my attention," I said as I turned to face Aurelia.

She was adorably rumpled from sleep, her green eyes still groggy, and her blonde curls wild. She fidgeted at my inspection, no doubt recalling the events of last night.

I smirked. "How did you sleep?" I asked her.

"Very well, thank you." She ducked her head shyly and bounced lightly from foot to foot as if filled with pent up energy.

"Come, then. Let's have some breakfast and then we can talk." I rose from my chair and led her into the kitchen where Freya my sprite had left breakfast for us. I pulled her chair out for her with a subtle, gentlemanly smile.

She smiled at me in return, her gaze downcast as she mumbled a thank you and sat down.

"Have you gotten a chance to think over my offer?" I asked casually as I scooped up a forkful of fluffy, seasoned eggs.

"I don't know," she answered as she chewed on a piece of bacon. The fact she was purposefully avoiding my gaze did not bode well.

Don't jump to conclusions. She's been through a lot of trauma.

"You don't know if you thought about it, or you don't know if you should take it?" I asked, keeping my tone conversational.

Gods, please. She can't say no. I need her in more ways than one!

"I don't think I should," she clarified, staring at her plate.

Fuck. How do I convince her?

I wracked my brain for an angle of attack. "Can I ask why? Maybe if you can tell me all the reasons you shouldn't, I can provide you counter-balances as to all the reasons you should," I said, picking up my cup of coffee. I took a long sip as I waited for her answer. This had to happen. Now that I'd met Aurelia, now that my wolf and I recognized her as our mate, I really didn't want to have to force her to do what I needed. Ideally, I wanted her to join me willingly. It was the only way I could see all outcomes satisfied.

"I won't be doing anything illegal, will I?" she asked, her tone plaintive and concerned.

I kept my poker face in place, revealing nothing. I needed to be honest with her about what she would be doing, but in the same breath, I didn't want to scare her off either. My wolf couldn't stand to lose her. "There are many rumors about the Syndicate and many of them are true. I didn't get to where I am today without breaking a few laws." I shrugged and took another sip of my coffee, never taking my eyes from her. She needed to know that I was not a good man, but nothing I did was ever without good reason.

"See, that's the thing. I was always taught to respect the laws and fly under the radar. I don't think I can do that working for you." Aurelia turned her gaze on me, finding strength in her conviction.

"Genuinely, what's the alternative, Aurelia? You have nowhere else to go, and the witches will be investigating your mother's death." My fingers drummed on the table. I took another long sip of coffee, watching her with keen eyes.

Her expressive features ran the gamut of emotions, from desperation and worry to sadness and despair, and then finally settled on anger. She clenched her fist around her glass of fresh orange juice as her gaze hardened. "I don't know, okay? Maybe the witches just want to ask me what happened. Maybe they won't see a need to investigate me too deeply, and I won't be a damn pariah anymore." She threw her hands up, sloshing orange juice across the table. "All I've ever done was obey my mother and assist her in all that she asked. Surely, the witches will realize that much. I'd never have harmed the only one who ever cared for me!"

"It won't look good that you ran, Aurelia," I said calmly. "In fact, it'll prompt questions that will be difficult to answer."

"No, it won't," she agreed. "But it wasn't my fault. That man hit me with a tranquilizer dart in the market, and I have no idea why. He said something about how I'd make him good money… I had no choice but to flee. And the truth is that I made it to the hallway outside Mother's room before I lost consciousness." She shook her head, her eyes beginning to water as she relived the memory.

Dan is in some serious shit for pulling that. What the hell was he going to do with an unconscious female in the middle of the market?

I barely contained my growl. "And when you woke up, you found her?" I pulled my phone from my pocket and scrolled through the supernatural news articles. "Shit," I breathed as I found the article I was looking for, the one that would force her to play the only hand she had. "This just got really bad for you, Aurelia." I turned the phone in her direction so she could read the headline.

Her eyes widened in horror, and she blanched, the tears she'd been fighting back so valiantly trickling down her cheeks. "But I didn't do it!" she confessed, the lilt of her voice tainted with panic and bordering on desperation. "I was trying to buy her medicine to help her," she whispered roughly, wiping at her eyes.

I moved closer to her and placed a comforting hand on her shoulder, then squeezed it gently. "The article goes on to say she was hexed. Her illness wasn't what killed her... someone else did." I allowed my declaration to hang ominously between us.

"Do you think it was the man who was chasing me?" she whispered as another tear slid down her cheek.

I brushed the tear away with my thumb, hating to see her cry like that. I wanted her to join me, but I didn't want to her hurt any more than she already had. When it came to the woman who would be my mate, I might be manipulative but I would not be cruel.

I don't think Dan would've killed her mother, but who else would have known what she was and would want to make her desperate?

"I don't know who did this, but the witches aren't kind to outsiders and will want this crime answered for in blood. And unfortunately, rightly or wrongly, you're their prime suspect. It's not safe for you out there, Aurelia. You can't go back. You don't deserve to be targeted for the actions of another." I gripped her chin, turning her eyes to mine. I didn't need to explicitly mention that the blood they would desire was hers, but the inference was there.

She nodded and licked her lips, her shoulders trembling. "This changes everything," she whispered. My mother always told me to be wary of them, but this?" Aurelia's green eyes shimmered with unshed tears. "It looks like your job offer is my only option, after all. No one else in this city is going to offer me a safe place to sleep or self-defense training."

My wolf howled in triumph.

She's ours.

"We can start an investigation of our own into who really did this and clear your name," I offered, squeezing her shoulder lightly. "If there are answers to be had, we'll find them."

"But only if I come work for you." She shook her head in denial. "Maybe I should just leave the city. I doubt they'll look for me outside the witch part of town."

My poor, beautiful, naïve fairy.

"Aurelia, someone is clearly after you. And until we know why, your safest option is here in the Syndicate. You can learn to protect yourself, how to control your magic, and how to fight. Then we can search for your mother's killer," I said, hoping she would see this from my point of view.

"And all it will cost me is my soul, right?" She laughed without humor and shook her head again as she fought a war within herself.

"You will have to come work for me, yes, and it will be dangerous. But not more danger than you currently face alone in the city," I said honestly. I needed her to understand the gravity of the situation. Yes, I was working an angle, but we had no supernatural police force in the city. The witches *would* get blood without a trial. There would be no justice.

"I understand the risks here, Grey, but I'm still not sure. I mean, it's a damn criminal organization! How can you be so at peace with what you do?" The chair screeched loudly across the marble as she stood abruptly, clearly needing space.

"It's not *all* criminal activity," I said as I gripped the arm of my chair. I was doing my best to hold myself back from just shaking some damn sense into her. She wasn't understanding the gravity of the situation. Her pure white morals would not serve her in our world. The supernaturals as a whole were fickle, distrusting, and used to doing whatever it took to preserve their way of life. She would not be shown mercy or kindness if she dared venture back out into Dallas alone.

"Really?" she asked exasperated, her tone one of clear disbelief.

"We hire out trolls as bodyguards and provide protection for both humans and supernaturals," I said, standing and moving into her path.

This minxy fae isn't escaping on my watch.

"And what would I be doing?" She crossed her arms over her chest and tapped her foot impatiently.

My eyes moved to her chest and back up quickly. Now was not the time to focus on the way that posture pushed her breasts up deliciously. "For now, you would be training and learning your magic, and once you're ready, I'll give you an assignment." I reached out and dared to push a golden lock of hair behind her ear.

"You want me to agree to this without even knowing what I'll be doing? You want me to join you, practically blind? Not very likely, Grey." She shook her head and scowled, stubborn as ever.

"Fine, how about this? You come and train. You learn your magic and control, and when the time comes... if you don't like the job, you can turn it down." I shoved my hands in my pockets, biting the inside of my lip as I waited for her response.

This is risky as fuck.

"You'd really let me do that? You'd train me and then let me turn down the job that you specifically wanted me for?" she scoffed.

"Yes." I nodded, my mask solid.

I'll just have to make sure that by the time she's trained and ready, she won't want to turn it down.

She didn't trust me. The evidence of that shone in her eyes, but I would make sure when the time came, she would have to trust me. One way or another, I'd win her over. I'd achieve my goals *and* secure my claim on my mate.

Aurelia paced the room, her brows deeply furrowed and her mouth pinched as she mulled over her limited options. "Okay," she finally said slowly, turning to face me. "I'll train and when the time comes, I'll decide if I want to do this job for you or not."

I kept my stoic mask in place even as my wolf howled his victory in my head. Relief flooded me as I placed a hand on her lower back and led her to the table. "I'm glad to hear it, Aurelia. Let's finish breakfast and then I'll give you a personal tour of the facility." I smiled my most charming smile as I took my seat.

The cat is in the bag!

After breakfast, I strolled into my home office while Aurelia went to shower and change. There was one last thing I needed to handle. One particular detail that could see this all blow up in my damn face.

"Hello?" Dan picked up the phone on the first ring.

"You shot her with a fucking iron tranquilizer dart?" I growled low.

"She was getting ready to fly away, boss. What was I supposed to do?" he asked.

"You've made everything exceedingly more difficult," I said rubbing a hand over my face.

"What do you mean? You have her, right? So, no harm was done," he said warily.

"She was the perfect scapegoat for whoever murdered her mother when she was passed out in the hall. The witches are out for blood, and she blames *you* for this." I tapped my fingers on my desk in agitation.

"Fucking hell," Dan hissed.

"Exactly. Which means all communication needs to be done over the phone from now on. She's smart, and if she sees you at the facility, she will put it all together, and we'll be fucked. You'll be the damn reason my carefully laid plans went to shit!" I sat back in my chair.

"What do you want me to do? I've been trying to hunt down a Fae for a long time now. Isn't my debt paid?" he asked hopefully.

I scoffed. I couldn't believe he'd dare ask that after what he pulled. "You almost ruined everything with this. Like I'm letting you off that easily when I am the one who ended up getting the job done."

"Then what do you need from me?" Dan asked with a sigh.

"I want you to investigate her mother's murder and find anything you can about how she came to live with the witch in the first place." I gripped the phone. Something didn't sit right with me about the story she'd been fed her entire life, and if I was going to get her to trust me, I needed to get her real answers.

"Why would you want me to investigate the witch's murder?" he asked.

"They are blaming her death on Aurelia, you fucking idiot. She will never be safe from them until her mother's real killer is brought to justice." I clenched the phone in my hand tighter.

"Doesn't her being in danger somewhat suit your purposes?" he asked, confused.

"Are you questioning my orders, Dan?" I growled. "Do what you are told and find the killer! Call me when you have the information I need." I hung up the phone and buried my face in my hands.

For fuck's sake! Do I need to start being a ruthless asshole again? Have I been slipping lately?

My oversensitive wolf hearing picked up the shower turning off, and I grinned to myself. Everything was in motion despite the hiccups, and soon I would have exactly what I wanted.

Those who wronged me will pay in blood for what they've done.

I would make sure of it.

CHAPTER 7

A*m I making a terrible mistake?*

My stomach roiled with a storm of butterflies, and I couldn't help but wonder what the hell I was getting myself into as I sat in the back of the sleek, black town car.

Grey sat in the seat next to me, his eyes on his phone, no doubt attending business as we rushed through the city traffic.

I shifted in my seat restlessly, trying in vain to swallow the intangible lump forming in my throat.

"Are you nervous?" Grey asked, resting his hand on my knee to keep me from fidgeting.

My spine tingled at his touch, making my restlessness even worse and bringing back flashbacks of last night. It was hard to banish the sensation of his hard cock pressed again me and the way he scented my neck. With a shake of my head, I cleared my throat.

Do not fall for the boss of the Syndicate, Aurelia! Seriously.

"I just don't know what to expect, I guess. I've never been out of the supe side of the city," I admitted.

"We're actually going outside the city. It's the only place where I'm able to keep my people off the radar." He didn't so much as look up from his phone as he spoke.

"Maybe this isn't such a good idea," I said, twisting my fingers together. "Am I going to put your people in danger by being there?'

Maybe I can get out of this if he thinks I'll be a threat to his employees? Surely, he wouldn't want the witches attacking his building to find me, right?

"No, you are not going to put my employees in danger," he said and finally peered up from his phone.

"Are you sure?" I asked.

He sighed. "Aurelia, this is the best thing for you until we find your mother's killer and you learn to protect yourself. Just trust me on this." He squeezed my knee reassuringly.

Little *zings* of lightning danced across my skin and my heart beat faster.

Can I trust him though? He's the head of a criminal organization. It would be stupid to trust a man like that, right? So, why am I so damn drawn to him? His touch is practically electric...

I shook my head to clear the unhelpfully sexy thoughts as we drove out of the city and were soon surrounded by countless trees, from horizon to horizon. My eyes widened as the city was blocked from my view, nothing more than a memory as the world took on a new form. An innate sense of peace washed through me, and I couldn't help the infectious grin that spread across my face. I had *never* felt like I belonged anywhere before, but surrounded by nature, I felt calmer than I ever remembered being.

I just wish I could get out of the car and enjoy it! I bet it would feel so wonderful to touch, to be connected to it.

My gaze was fixed firmly on the trees as they rushed by us when something like thousands of ants crawling over me made me shudder. I immediately realized it for what it was. It was much stronger than the wards at the witch market. "That's some seriously powerful magic," I said rubbing my arms to rid myself of the strange sensation lingering on my skin.

"It's a little more extensive than a normal ward," Grey said, observing me.

"It doesn't feel very good." I groaned, rubbing my hands up and down my arms some more.

"It does take some getting used to, but it keeps everyone safe from the outside world as long as they stay inside the wards." He squeezed my knee again, his hand lingering.

It wasn't lost on me that he specifically said we were safe from the outside world and not safe from inside.

"Is there something you're not telling me?" I frowned, subtly adjusting my position so that he moved his hand.

"It can be intense in the facility," he offered. "But just keep your head down, train, and you'll be fine." He shrugged and returned his attention to his phone.

What the fuck is that supposed to mean?

I shifted in my seat again as the large metal and glass building suddenly rose up into view. A wave of nervous energy spiked in my chest, and I tapped my foot and wrung my hands to avoid what felt like a freak-out just waiting to happen.

"I really think this is a bad idea now," I mumbled mostly to myself.

What exactly am I getting myself into here? Is it too late to change my mind? Maybe I can flee into the forest where it's safe? I could live off-grid, wild and free.

Grey laughed.

The sound had shivers rolling over me again, and my nipples tingled beneath my shirt in response. I nibbled on my lower lip and waited for the sensation to pass. Why did that carefree sound make my body react so violently?

Is there something wrong with me? Or is this how all Fae feel around other supes?

"You'll be fine, honestly. Try to stay calm. You have more power than any of them, and as soon as you learn to harness it, they won't want to fuck with you," Grey said turning my face to his. His gaze flicked down to my lips, and his blue eyes glowed with hunger.

I squirmed under his intense scrutiny. My breathing became shallow as instant heat blossomed between my legs and an undeniable ache grew there.

Holy shit! What is he doing? Is he thinking about last night? Is he about to kiss me? Am I a horrible person because I secretly want him to?

A throat cleared from the front seat.

I'd forgotten all about the driver being there.

Crap.

"Sir, we're about to pull into the garage," the driver said.

Grey reluctantly released me and locked his phone.

I anxiously straightened my spine, desperately trying to ignore the fire the shifter had sparked within me. This was it. I was heading into the unknown.

What was I thinking? This is a fucking terrible idea!

The sun was blocked out by a deep cement garage. The dark stone structure was ominous as we rolled slowly through the space.

Grey put his hand on mine in my lap and threaded our fingers together as if it were the most natural thing in the world, before giving them a gentle squeeze. "You're going to do great here, princess. I just know it," Grey whispered in my ear, his breath warm against my skin.

I shivered in response and squeezed my thighs tightly together as my heart hammered in my chest.

Fucking fuck! I'm glad one of us is confident. Did I just sign up to live with a bunch of criminals who could very well murder me?

"But if I don't, I can leave, right?" I asked, my knuckles whitening.

Grey stiffened. "Once you're out of danger, if that's what you want, then I won't keep you here. I told you I won't hold you against your will." He waved his hand dismissively. But the way he had stiffened at my question told a very different story.

What if he's lying and he never lets me leave? What if all I am is a tool or some kind of weapon to him? How can I trust he'll honor his word?

I scanned the garage for an escape route but came up empty. The place was sealed up like Fort Knox.

What was I thinking?

The memory of the article on Grey's phone came back, hitting me like a sledgehammer. I couldn't go back to Dallas even if I wanted to. I'd draw the attention of the witches in no time, and they would be out for my blood. They wouldn't care that I was innocent. They wouldn't even spare me the time to try to explain. The fact was that I was different, and they didn't like or trust outsiders.

My mother had been the only thing shielding me from their wrath and prejudice. The witch side of the city was no longer home, and I had to come to terms with that.

I have no home.

The truth smarted like a bee sting, and I gritted my teeth together to prevent a sob escaping my throat. I needed to make the best of this new situation and hope to the gods that I hadn't made a terrible mistake. For now, I was alive. I had to focus on that. Every day I spent above ground or not incinerated by witches was a good one.

The car slowed to a stop outside a large, matte finish metal door. The driver opened his door and exited the vehicle.

I reached for mine.

Grey squeezed my hand and shook his head. "Let him," Grey whispered, and my door opened.

The driver smiled as he held his hand out to me to help me exit the vehicle.

"Thank you," I said shyly as I allowed him. I wasn't used to such treatment and didn't feel worthy of the pampering.

The driver nodded with a small smile.

Grey squeezed out of the car behind me, brushing my wings as he did so.

I had to bite back a moan at the sensation.

"You know, you don't have to keep them hidden here, Aurelia. You can be who you were always meant to be," he whispered close to my ear.

Wait, I don't have to hide anymore?

I glanced back at Grey with a frown. "Are you sure? That seems dangerous. I've hidden my whole life."

"You are far more powerful than you realize, Aurelia. Now it's high time that you see it too." Uninvited, he kissed my neck.

I shuddered and clenched my fists by my sides. How was he able to make me feel like I was on fire? My stomach flipped as his hands landed on my hips, squeezing them gently as he guided me forward.

"It's time to go inside, princess." Grey chuckled.

I scowled at him but let him lead me to the elevator. This was it, the next chapter of my life if I wanted to survive, and I had no choice but to face it head on.

I plastered a grin on my face and followed Grey into the elevator. My stomach dropped as we ascended into the rest of the building, but I ignored it. I would do this, and I would do it with a smile. I would stand as bravely as I could and try my best at whatever was asked of me. If Grey needed me this badly, I must be worthwhile, whether I saw it or not. And whoever I encountered would soon discover the same. I hadn't managed to stay alive this long by being a complete idiot.

The elevator *dinged,* and a tall woman with dark brown hair and gleaming amber eyes stepped in. Her eyes were hard as she looked me up and down, inspecting me like a breeder inspects a pedigreed pup.

"This is her?" She chuckled. "You want to train her to protect herself? She doesn't look as if she's done a single hard day's work in her *life.*"

"Layla!" Grey barked.

I narrowed my eyes at the woman. She was his second, the woman who called him so damn much.

"Boss, honestly? I doubt she can be trained for anything battle-centric. She would do better in the breeding center," she said, crossing her arms over her chest full of attitude.

Grey moved faster than I'd ever seen anyone move. He became a blur before he re-materialized and picked the woman up by the throat, slamming her into the shiny elevator wall.

I gasped at the unexpected display of violence, but I couldn't blame him. She didn't even know me, yet she'd judged me and determined I was no more than a pretty sow to birth pigs for the benefit of the Syndicate. My hands balled into fists at my sides as I stared at the woman gasping for breath. I would have dearly liked to throttle her myself. Her level of disrespect for me, as Grey's newest recruit, was abominable.

"If you ever speak the words *breeding center* when mentioning

Aurelia again, you are gone!" Grey roared in her face, his inner beast rising to the surface and lending his voice to the threat. He dropped the woman with disgust, his rage scarcely contained.

Layla landed lithely on her feet, then bent over coughing and rubbing at her throat.

Grey turned to me and his eyes widened as if he'd seen a ghost. "Remember what we practiced, Aurelia," he said, his voice dropping to a soothing tone. "You need to breathe." He glanced down pointedly at my hands.

I frowned.

What is he...? Oh shit! Not again.

I nearly shrieked at the purple swirling magic that covered both of my clenched fists.

"What the fuck?" Layla coughed as she looked at my hands with bulging eyes.

"Don't fuck with me, bitch," I said through panicked breaths, surprised by my own anger.

Grey grabbed my chin and turned my face toward him. "Eyes on me, princess. Listen to my voice and match my breathing, just like I showed you."

The magic was making me twitchy, and I yearned to release it, but I couldn't do that in the small elevator we were in. I didn't need to guess, I knew I'd likely kill us all. I felt it in the blaze of my power. And I wasn't ready to die, especially not by my own hand. I slammed my gaze into his and took a deep, shuddering, and cleansing breath.

"That's it. Good girl. Breathe for me, nice and slow. That's it," he soothed, rubbing his hands up and down my arms.

I followed his instructions, listening to his soothing voice and matching my breaths to his. It came a little easier this time, and I felt my magic simmering down.

"What the fuck was that?" Layla shouted, interrupting.

I turned my gaze to hers and the surge returned, sparking back to life like gas poured on a bonfire.

Fucking bitch!

"No, princess, look at me," Grey said, pinching my chin and turning my gaze back to him.

I defiantly glared at the woman for another second before flitting my eyes back to his baby blues. Distantly, the *ding* of the elevator chimed, but I didn't react, I stayed put right where I was, letting Grey's soothing presence calm the raging magic within me.

"Get the fuck out of here, Layla," Grey said, not raising his voice from the gentle cadence he used with me.

"But, boss!" Layla screeched, clearly indignant and enraged at having been put in her place.

"If you don't want to listen, I'll *let* her test her powers on you. Now get the fuck out of here," Grey snarled.

The sound of shuffling feet met my ears, and I grinned. That bitch had pissed me off, sizing me up like I was less than nothing.

I can't believe she dared imply I'd be good for nothing but breeding!

"I think you may be a little bloodthirsty after all, princess. And that is something we can definitely work with." Grey grinned as he released my chin.

"I don't like her," I grumbled, glancing away now that my magic was back under control.

"That's going to be a problem, princess. She runs this place when I'm not here." Grey shook his head, chuckling again.

"She runs the place?"

Shit! Have I just painted a giant target on my back? What will I do when Grey's not around to tell her to back off?

"She does," Grey said with a nod.

"Okay, that does it. I've changed my mind. I'll take my chances with the hateful witches instead." I folded my arms over my chest, not missing the way Grey's eyes slid to my breasts at the movement.

"You're going to prove Layla right? You're going to wave your white flag and admit that you're not cut out for this?" He sighed and shook his head with disappointment.

Fuck. I don't want that woman to think I'm weak and can't take it, but I have no idea what to expect of this place. I'm like a fucking fish out of water!

I grimaced and huffed out a breath like a frustrated bull seeing red flags.

"Come on, let's get you settled in," said Grey, obviously determining correctly that I wasn't about to play dead, not even for his second-in-command. He placed a hand on my lower back and led me from the elevator.

The hall we emerged in was clinical white and there were doors every few feet. We strolled down the hall to a set of doors at the very end.

I furrowed my brows, glancing up at Grey. All the other rooms had only one door, but the set he was currently opening for me was more elaborate. "Grey? What is this?" I asked.

"It's your room," he answered. He frowned down at me as he opened the double doors. "Is it not to your liking?"

"It just looks different... bigger than all the others." I chewed on the inside of my bottom lip, glancing inside the open doors.

"All of my most valuable employees get rooms like this. You'll get used to it." He grinned and ushered me into the room.

Most valuable employees? Right. I have to remember that he wants me to work for him—and that's all he wants—no matter how he toys with me or how he makes my body feel.

"Won't people think I'm getting special treatment or something?" I asked, wringing my hands together as my anxiety reared its ugly head once more.

"You are. Have you forgotten? I have to find a way to get you to stick around once you learn everything you need to know." He nudged me further into the room.

I turned to survey roomy new living space. It was utilitarian, but the bed in the center was large, and two doors stood in the far wall, probably a closet and a bathroom.

Don't forget that, Aurelia. He doesn't want you. He only wants what you can do for him. He's just teasing, trying to sweeten the pot. As he said, he's just trying to sway me to stay.

"Grey, I have a feeling that if I stay in this room, I'm going to be a target." I planted my hands on my hips, feeling well out of my depth. If Layla had anything to say about it, that would definitely be the case.

Fuck me. What was I thinking coming here?

CHAPTER 8
Grey

"How is she doing?" I eyed Layla as she lounged in the chair in front of my desk.

"Aurelia?" she asked with a snide chuckle. "She's far too sunny and happy for this place."

I frowned. That didn't seem right. She was as distrusting as anyone I'd ever met. "But how is her training coming along?" I asked impatiently but kept my tone even and nonchalant. I didn't have time for Layla's bullshit.

What is her deal with Aurelia, anyway? She's almost acting jealous, but that's not possible. That's not the Layla I've always known.

Then again, it seemed more and more of my elite team were acting up and speaking out of turn than usual since Aurelia came into the picture.

"The others are getting irritated by the amount of time she spends in the gym. They're complaining that she's getting special treatment." Layla sneered.

"She is the *one* person who can get me what I have worked for all these years. Of course, she's getting fucking special treatment!" I slammed my hand down on the desk, making Layla jump.

Resettling herself, Layla grumped, "So, what? Am I just supposed to tell them that straight up and watch the challenges roll in? She can't hack it."

"If anyone, and I mean anyone, threatens her, I will gut them," I growled, the threat clear in my tone. My wolf would not suffer fools when it came to our mate.

Not even Layla will escape punishment if my mate is harmed. She is literally fucking everything.

"They've always aired their grievances that way. You can't put that kind of target on her by saying she's above the rules," Layla argued.

She's right, as much as I hate to admit it. I can't put that kind of target on Aurelia. These are ruthless criminals trained to kill, and the slight will only make things worse for her.

"Fine," I growled. "But keep an eye on her and tell me how the fuck her training is going! If further challenges are forthcoming, we'll deal with them then," I said.

"She's a quick learner," Layla grumbled, like the thought of Aurelia actually succeeding physically pained her.

"Good. I want weekly reports on her progress." I rose to my feet, buttoning my jacket as I went.

Layla stood and followed me out of the office to the elevator.

"I need to take care of something. Call me if there are any problems." I ordered. The words *with her* were left unsaid. Layla knew now not to damn well bother me with anything else but Aurelia. I hit the button for the garage and waited for the doors to close on my grouchy-looking second. I needed to get to the witch side of the city and meet with Dan. He had information for me and was adamant that I see Aurelia's former home with my own eyes.

Truth be told, I was dreading it. Seeing how my mate used to live, after the things she'd told me, and after the things the witch had taught her about herself... I was certain her life before me was best left forgotten. And I would do everything in my power to ensure it was wonderful from now on, just as soon as she finished her training.

I took my own car instead of bothering my driver. The less people that knew where I was headed, the better. The witches wouldn't appreciate a shifter's interference in their sham of an investigation. But my unwavering need to know what happened to bring her to the human realm in the first place—not to mention what happened to her caregiver—overrode any concern about what the witches might do to me.

Aurelia is a puzzle I need to solve.

I followed the GPS to the Italian restaurant in what the mortals would refer to as downtown Dallas but had been claimed by the witches long ago. Dan stood at the entrance as I parked my car on the street and got out. "This is the place?" I asked with a frown.

"It is. The apartment is above the restaurant. Beware though, the building is predominantly..." He made eyes at the people walking by as he trailed off.

"Got it." I waved to him to go ahead.

He didn't need to say *witches* for me to get what he was saying. Supernaturals did not allow their existence to be known by humans. The fallout of such knowledge would be disastrous. Though, there were a few select humans who closely guarded our secrets.

I followed him up the narrow stairs to the second floor of the building.

We wove our way around until we came to a plain, unadorned door at the end of the hall. There was nothing there to suggest that this was an active crime scene or that foul play was involved.

"It looks so normal," I said with a small shake of my head and a perplexed frown.

"She was hexed, boss. I just can't figure out how someone got in. Everyone I spoke to said she was bed-ridden. And if Aurelia was at the apothecary, then how did she answer the door?" Dan scrubbed a hand over his face.

"So, they either had a key or they didn't use the door," I said thoughtfully before pushing the door open. "Are there any signs of forced entry?" I asked as an afterthought.

"Not that I've seen."

The apartment was small but neat. A threadbare sofa sat in front of an archaic box television that belonged to the early nineties.

"She died in here," Dan called out, having wandered down the hall.

I trudged toward him, remembering what Aurelia told me about how she finally passed out in the hall, just outside her mother's room.

So close to delivering the medication...

"And that's where Aurelia passed out," I said aloud as I glared at Dan, still pissed off that he thought shooting her with a damn dart like that had been a smart fucking move.

"I was just trying to get her delivered in one piece. I thought if she was asleep... I mean, how was I supposed to know she would still fly away even with a tranq in her? That dose would knock out a half-Fae cold," Dan grumbled.

My wolf growled in my mind at the thought of her stumbling through the city, ready to pass out, a dreadfully easy target. He wanted to tear into Dan, but we still needed him *and* there was the small matter of a debt owed.

Dan opened the door to the bedroom and the scent of death still lingered in the air. It had been a week since the witch passed, but the dark presence of finality filled the room like a blanket of suffocating despair.

"She was in her bed when she died." Dan pointed to the rumpled sheets.

"I'm not interested in where she was when she was murdered. What did you actually call me all the way back down here for?" I asked, irritated.

"I thought you might want to see this," he said and grabbed a small vial off the bedside table.

"It's the medicine from the apothecary. So what?" I took the vial from him and inspected it.

"It was never used. So, the witches are accusing Aurelia of hexing her mother." He crossed his arms over his chest.

"Explain," I barked, growing impatient with this detective bullshit.

"The woman she bought the medicine from said she left with this specific vial the day of the murder, giving Aurelia a means to kill her." He shook his head and walked past me.

"But it's not poison," I argued. "What was she going to do? Overdose her only caregiver with medication? And if that was her plan, why would she abandon it and use a hex instead? It doesn't make sense. But even if that were the case—and it's a damn stretch—what's her motive?" I asked as I followed him into the hall.

He opened a door to a room that was no bigger than a closet. There were threadbare blankets piled on the floor and a few sets of worn clothes piled in the corner. "They are saying she was being mistreated by the witch and that she had reached her limit. They're suggesting she lashed out when she couldn't take anymore. This was her room," Dan finished with disgust.

This was her bedroom? I hate the fucking dead witch even more than I did before! Fucking hell.

The room was barely fit for a dog. I couldn't believe that a supernatural had treated another supe so poorly, especially one as powerful as Aurelia. "What else have you found? Anything that tells us how she came to live with the witch in the first place, or how she learned to glamor her wings her whole damn life?" I rubbed my temples in consternation.

"There are some legal documents from the human authorities, but that's about it." Dan shrugged as if that were that.

"Show me," I growled.

Obeying my command without question, he wandered from the closet.

I scanned the tiny room again to see if there was anything that she had left behind that she might want. I crouched down next to the pile of clothes, but nothing there was as good as any replacements I could procure. I stood and followed Dan into a small office. The room was still bigger than the closet that Aurelia had lived in, and I growled, my wolf rearing his head in rage at her evident mistreatment.

Shelves with books and spell ingredients lined the walls and a metal safe sat in the far corner.

"Did you crack the safe or was it like that when you got here?" I questioned.

"It was like that already. Someone got away with whatever they wanted, probably before Aurelia even woke up." Dan crouched in front of the safe. He pulled out a manilla envelope and handed it to me.

This couldn't have been all the witch had on her ward, surely? Was someone else looking for information on Aurelia, and if they were, why leave her passed out on the floor? If she was valuable to another party, why wouldn't they have seized the opportunity themselves to take her?

"None of this makes any sense," I grumbled. "The whole situation is like a tangled ball of yarn." I pulled the papers from the envelope and scanned the topmost one. I frowned at the page as I read the printed words.

"I know," Dan said warily. "How does a small child just show up out of nowhere?"

"I don't know," I answered. "And why would this particular witch take in a child of unknown origin? What was her motive to protect her? This was the first and last time she ever fostered a child. Something just isn't adding up." I shook my head.

"Whoever killed the witch knew what they were looking for and exactly where to find it. Do you think it could it have been a seer?" Dan asked.

I didn't look up from the papers in my hand. "A seer?" I asked. "They are incredibly rare. Almost as rare as Aurelia."

"I know, boss. But nothing else makes sense. They would have seen every possible scenario involving your fairy and are trying force the future they want into motion." He sat heavily in the chair behind the desk with a frown.

"Well, shit," I said, my skin prickling with unease.

Are we dealing with an evil seer who wants to force us into a situation over which we have no control?

"Yeah, this may be bigger than we expected." Dan sighed at the lack of solid truth to be found.

I pulled my phone from my pocket and dialed Layla. We needed to get someone down here to perform a mimic spell as soon as possible.

"Yeah, boss?" Layla answered on the first ring. She sounded like she was busy, but she could drop whatever she was doing. This situation took precedence.

"I need you to send Karma to witch side," I said vaguely. "I need her abilities."

"I'm a little busy breaking up a fight at the moment," she grumbled.

"This is more important than a couple of delinquents fighting over the gym!" I yelled, annoyed by Layla's recent spate of incompetence yet again.

"Is it more important than me trying to calm your girl down so she'll put the shifter down that her magic has pinned to the damn wall?" she huffed in response.

I grinned instinctively, unable to help it. The mental imagery of my mate kicking ass was just too good.

Aurelia has someone pinned to the wall?

She was learning rather quickly. "The shifter probably got what they deserved. Just send the damn half-witch to the address I'm texting you to meet up with Dan. I'll be back at the facility soon." I hung up the phone.

Dan shifted in the chair, pulling the papers on the desk close to him and pretending to read them. "Aurelia got into a fight with a shifter?" he asked with a grin that mirrored my own.

"She has And I need to go. Karma will be here soon to do a mimic spell. Get her whatever she needs and see if you can get a look at the person who killed the damn witch," I said and turned to leave.

I took the papers with me, hoping after closer inspection I might find something that would give us a clue. I needed to get back to the facility because there was a very real possibility that the shifter—whoever they were—would be stuck to the wall until I arrived to calm Aurelia down.

The very idea that Layla thought she could even attempt to calm Aurelia down was laughable. Neither woman liked the other.

As fast as I could get away with, I drove back to the facility. My mind was loaded with more questions than answers and it royally pissed me off. When I got off the elevator at the training center level, I found Aurelia standing in a swirl of her own magic, surrounded by a pack of angry shifters.

They've ganged up on her. On my mate! My wolf roared.

And I lost it. My wolf took control, bursting through my clothes and shredding them to pieces. I jumped at the nearest wolf with a snarl.

"Boss, what the fuck?" Layla yelled as she tried to step between me and the shifter.

I took stock of the room, snarling at any shifter that dared get too close. They would *not* gang up on my mate and get away with it.

I will make them pay.

I agreed with my inner wolf whole-heartedly. Aurelia was mine, and no one was going to take her from me.

CHAPTER 9
Aurelia

"Oh look, the boss's pet is hogging the training room *again*," a snide voice called from behind me.

I plastered on my best smile, desperately hoping I could calm this problem down like the others I'd already dealt with. I had been at the Syndicate for a week, and Grey had scheduled time for me to practice everything I needed daily, but the other employees were getting upset about how often I had the gym to myself.

I turned to face the guy, ready to talk this out.

Hopefully this won't escalate...

He was probably a foot taller than me, and his muscles had muscles.

"I'm sure that there's enough room for us both to train," I said politely. I'd learned during the week that kindness was often the best way to deal with most of the people in the facility. They were so used to being hostile that my friendly disposition disarmed them.

"That's the thing though. The boss doesn't want anyone bothering you while you train," the shifter sneered.

Well, crap. Grey just painted a giant-ass target on my back. Thanks for that, boss.

"The boss isn't here, so I won't tell him if you don't." I offered him a smile then shrugged before I turned around to return to my breathing exercises.

The shifter growled. "You dare disrespect me by giving me your back?" he roared.

My eyes widened and I mentally slapped my forehead, realizing too late that I had inadvertently made everything so much worse. I just thought we were done with the conversation—I hadn't meant to insult him. "I'm sorry," I said turning back to the huge man.

Layla stormed into the room, ever the watchful eye.

Immediately my shoulders stiffened. There was no love lost between us.

"Connor, what are you doing in here?" Layla barked, asserting her authority as second.

"The boss' pet just disrespected me," he said as he took a threatening step toward me.

My hands started to tingle with rage. Being called a pet to a shifter was the worst kind of insult, so Connor had my magic flaring.

"Aurelia, stop!" Layla yelled.

I turned my gaze to my hands.

Does she think that's going to help? Her presence alone just makes me angrier.

Purple magic swirled around my hands as the shifter took another step toward me. I threw up my hands in defense, meaning only to fend him off, but my magic seemed to have other ideas. A gust of air blew the shifter back into the wall, sparkling purple light wrapping around one of his ankles, then flipping him upside down.

"You stupid bitch, put me down!" the shifter roared, spittle flying as his eyes became bloodshot.

I snapped my gaze back at him, glaring hard even though on the inside I was freaking the hell out.

How the fuck do I put him down? What is even happening?

"Aurelia!" Layla yelled again. "Put Connor down, now."

"That's not helpful," I gasped out between heaving breaths. My hands shook as I tried to remember Grey's breathing exercises, but Layla screaming orders at me wasn't helping at all. In fact, it was only making things worse. In the next instant, a breeze slammed into her, driving her away from me.

"You're attacking me now?" she roared in umbrage.

"I can't control it!" I shrieked back as panic and anger surged within me.

"What have you been practicing in here all week, then?" Layla yelled.

I squeezed my eyes closed tight, attempting to block out Connor and Layla so that I could focus on Grey's breathing techniques when a howl cut through the room.

"Connor, if your friends come in here and gang up on Aurelia do you think the boss is going to be lenient?" Layla said, raising her voice.

My eyes popped open at her words as a new group of shifters prowled into the room. My turbulent air magic blew them back several paces, but they just pushed against the swirling vortex until they were all standing in a semi-circle, acting as a barrier between me and Connor.

"What the fuck are you?" the shifter in the middle of the group growled.

My glamour fizzled out as my powers swirled in overdrive ,and I knew the moment my iridescent wings became visible by the gasps that echoed throughout the room.

Well, shit, I didn't mean for that to happen!

"Wicked Fae," someone whispered.

I closed my eyes, blocking out the words. My mother had always warned me that people would call me that. That I was somehow inherently bad simply because of my species. So, I never revealed my wings to anyone.

"Stop fucking around and get her to let me go!" Connor yelled.

The shifters began circling me, but every time one lunged, my air magic protected me, pushing them back again.

I just needed to figure out how to stop the flow of purple magic and put the dickhead bully down. I took a deep breath, trying to center myself, but movement out of the corner of my eye gave me pause.

Layla managed to break free and charged toward me, probably intent on knocking me the fuck out.

I snarled, reacting without thought, and threw her back against the wall too.

"For fuck's sake! Just stop!" Layla yelled.

My gaze went back to the shifters circling me like a school of sharks. "If you want me to put him down, maybe stop threatening me and let me calm the fuck down!" I threw my hands up in frustration, and Connor flew up to the ceiling, smacking into it with a resounding *crack*.

I winced. That did not look good for me.

The shifters roared and their bodies started to shake, their bones cracking and reforming as they shifted into their wild animals, ready to take this to the next level.

Shit. Only I could piss off an entire pack of wolves by accident!

My magic flared even brighter in response, and a shield of transparent, shimmering purple formed around my body.

The wolves circled me, snarling and snapping at the purple shield to no avail.

Without warning, a huge snow-white wolf leaped over the others and stood with its back to me, creating another level of protection between me and the angry mob.

Holy shit, he's beautiful.

His head was almost to my chest and his coat was the purest white as he howled at the wolves surrounding me.

"Boss, what the fuck?" Layla shrieked.

Boss? Is that Grey? His wolf is absolutely breathtaking. But why is he standing between me and the others? He's a shifter just like them—they're his employees. Is he protecting them from me? Or me from them?

I frowned in confusion at the bizarre and surreal turn of events, but his presence alone soothed me. I took a deep breath, calming my emotions, before I ran my hand through the fur at his back, reveling in its thickness and softness.

I could snuggle up against his coat and dream.

He whined in response.

"Layla, get them out of here. I can't drop the magic if I'm not safe, and Grey is just about ready for a bloodbath," I commanded.

"Are you ordering me around?" Layla yelled back. "I'm the second, here!"

"And all you're doing is making things fucking worse, bitch. Now, get them the fuck out of here!" I screamed as my magic whipped around me with even more fury.

A purple strand of magic lashed out at Layla like an intangible whip, and she yelped in pain.

But I didn't care, I couldn't. She had no interest in helping me personally. She fucking hated me. What I needed was for Grey to shift back so he could help me with my breathing. And he wouldn't do that until these wolves were out of the room and no longer presented a threat —that much was clear.

The shifters circling growled angrily as Layla hit the wall with a *thump*.

"Grey, please shift back," I managed to gasp between breaths. "I can't stop it. I need you."

The white wolf turned his arctic blue eyes on me and whined as he glanced back and forth between me and the threat. Then he growled, staring each of the wolves down one by one until they all showed him their throats in a display of subservience. He *was* the Syndicate, and he was reminding them.

I gripped his soft white fur to keep him from following them as they slunk out the door of the gym.

Grey's wolf shivered under my hand before he shifted back into a man.

A very naked man.

A shudder ran through me as I realized my hand was on the smooth, buff skin of his muscular back.

"Aurelia, eyes up here, princess." He lifted my chin.

My gaze locked with his.

"See something you like?" He smirked.

"I need your help, Grey. I can't put him down," I answered in a panic, too overwhelmed to dwell on just how incredibly sexy he was, standing there bare as the day he was born, in all his masculine splendor.

"Just keep your eyes on me, listen to my voice, and match my breathing," he coached. He took a deep breath through his nose and out through his mouth, his intense gaze never leaving mine.

I struggled, but eventually matched his deep breaths and my shoulders relaxed slightly.

"That's it, princess, listen to my voice," Grey said soothingly.

"What the fuck is going on here?" Layla shouted, butting in at the most inopportune moment yet *again*.

My gaze snapped to hers and I glared, my shoulders stiffening, and I growled.

"Hey, ignore her. What did I tell you, princess? Don't worry about her. You keep your focus on me and try and drop the shifter." Grey pinched my chin once more, turning my gaze back to his.

I focused on him, and my shoulders relaxed again. I ignored Layla's scoff and finally succeeded in releasing the magic holding the irate shifter. My eyes widened in horror as the man started to fall. My hand flicked up instantly and my air magic cushioned Connor's fall.

Thanks to my instinctual reaction, he landed safely on one the mats.

Grey stood in front of me, glaring at the rowdy shifter and Layla.

I stepped in front of him, wanting to protect him from his insubordinate underlings and their misdirected rage.

He chuckled softly behind me as his hands found my hips. "How could you fucking react like that?" Grey scolded Layla over my head. "She was already angry. The way you handled that was reckless!"

"But, boss, she..." she trailed off.

"She is no longer your concern," he growled. He wrapped his arm around my waist, moving to my side and pulled me along with him.

"What is that supposed to mean?" Layla shrieked, moving toward me with unbridled hatred in her eyes.

"It means exactly what I fucking said. She is no longer your concern. Now back off, Layla." Grey said peering down at my hands.

They started to tingle with magic again, but I continued my deep breathing. I would not let her get to me again. I needed exercise as much control as possible and get away from the psycho bitch.

"Where are you going to take her? Everyone who lives here is my concern!" she spat back, stomping in front of us like she owned the place.

Unwise move, bitch.

Grey glared down at her, unflinching. "I said, *fuck off*." Without sparing Layla another moment of his time, he scooped me up and carried me to the elevator like he was some kind of jungle man from a storybook.

"Grey! Where are you taking me?" I asked, squirming in his arms.

"My office. I need clothes before I take you home," he grunted and stabbed at the button on the elevator.

"What do you mean, take me home?" I pressed, wiggling in his arms defiantly. My hip brushed his hard cock, and I froze as he groaned.

"Don't move, or I can't be held responsible for what I do in the elevator once we're inside," he whispered close to my ear.

My eyes widened, and I stilled my squirming, swallowing hard.

Grey chuckled as the elevator doors opened. He stomped inside and glared at Layla as she attempted to follow. "Round up those wolves. They are all to be punished for the shit they just pulled," Grey barked at her and hit the button for the top floor. His arms tightened around me protectively, and he pulled me closer.

"Grey? What's going on?" I asked, rubbing his arm soothingly as the doors closed.

"I'm taking you to the penthouse and will arrange for you to be trained there," he said and carefully lowered me to my feet.

"But why?" I asked softly, frowning in confusion.

"When I saw you surrounded by those wolves, my animal lost his mind and took over." He pulled my back to his front and leaned his chin on my shoulder.

Something hard poked into my back, and I squirmed in surprise.

"Princess, I told you what will happen if you keep rubbing up on me." Grey's moan made liquid heat pool through me moments before he spun me around and slammed my back into the wall of the elevator.

I stared up at him, my heart in my throat, wanting him to kiss me more than I'd ever wanted anything before.

Grey's lips crashed down on mine so hard they bruised me, but in the most wickedly delicious way imaginable. His hands squeezed my hips hard, possession clear in his every move.

I kissed him back, opening my lips to his tongue and moaning as he ground his erect cock against my stomach. I should have been embarrassed by his attentions, but since that first night I'd met him, all I'd been able to think about was how he made me feel. And now, after he shifted to protect me, I felt more certain than ever that I wanted him. King of the Syndicate, bad man, or criminal, it didn't matter. Our intense connection was unmistakable.

He broke our kiss to set his lips near my ear. "See what you're doing to me, princess?" Grey groaned loudly now, making shivers course down my spine. "This is why my wolf freaked out when you were in danger. We need you."

Oh, my gods. Aurelia, you fucking idiot! How could I forget that he needs me for something?

I stiffened in his arms at the thought that I was nothing more than a commodity to him, a valuable commodity, but nothing more than a means to an end.

His head snapped up, his glacial gaze revealing confusion.

"What's wrong?" he asked, pulling me closer and bending down to kiss my neck.

"Is this because of the job?" I whispered.

Could he really just be doing all this for me because of the job? Or is there a different reason behind it? Does he want me like I want him?

I scarcely allowed myself to hope for such a thing.

"No! What? Why would you think that?" he asked, kissing my shoulder. "Do you think I get like this for someone who is nothing more than a job to me?" He rubbed his cock against my hip to prove his point.

I moaned, my heart racing.

The elevator *dinged,* and the doors opened.

A second later, he lifted me up by my ass and carried me from the elevator.

I wrapped my legs around his waist eagerly, knowing this was probably a terrible idea, but when his lips met mine, all thoughts of protest left my brain.

I wanted nothing but Grey and if he truly desired me too, I didn't care what I had to do to get him—and keep him.

I might be his fairy, but he's my wolf.

CHAPTER 10
Grey

"Gods, you're beautiful, Aurelia," I groaned as I carried her down the empty hall toward my private office.

My wolf howled in the back of my mind. He wanted her just as much as I did, and I wasn't sure I could hold back much longer.

I kicked open my office door and grimaced at the lack of available space to fuck my mate.

Maybe I should just get dressed and take her home? It would be the gentlemanly thing to do... Fuck it. Chivalry be damned! It's not like I'm a knight in shining armor. She knows what I am, and I know what I want.

My lips landed on hers with crushing intensity, and I thrust my tongue into her mouth, reveling in her sweet taste and delicious heat. I took two more steps into the office before swinging my foot back. The slam of the door didn't alter the passion of our kiss and only served to make me more desperate.

I set Aurelia on the desk and broke the kiss, my eyes blazing with desire. "For what do you crave, princess?" I asked, pressing my forehead against hers, my breathing heavy.

"I want you but..." she trailed off, her eyes wide and searching as she gazed up at me.

I reared back. "But what?" I asked, sinking my teeth into my lower lip.

What could she possibly have reservations about?

"I'm a... well..." she turned her head away, her cheeks turning a perfect shade of pink, reminding me of the serene blush of cherry blossoms in spring.

"What, Aurelia?" I pressed, skimming my hands up her hips to her ribs.

A tiny groan escaped her.

"I've never done this before," she said, chewing her lip, her furtive gaze finding mine once more.

Fuck, that's so hot! My tiny fairy princess is a virgin? Could I get any luckier?

"You've never had sex?" I asked with a grin, my cock aching all the more. "You're really a virgin?"

I raised her face toward mine, letting her know with my smile how happy that made me. I would be the only man that my mate ever knew intimately. It was a gift beyond value. I could have never dared dream the woman I ended up with would truly be *all* mine—completely.

My wolf shivered inside me. An untouched mate appeared to be to his liking too.

"Yes," she said, dragging her gaze to her knees as her cheeks burned a brighter shade of crimson.

"Do you have any idea how sexy that is, princess?" I asked. "I desperately want to fuck you right here on my desk, but that's not the first time you deserve. So, we'll save that for later, and I guess I'll just have to make you come instead." I dropped to my knees in front of her without another word.

"What are you doing?" She panicked.

I just grinned and wrapped my hands around her hips before sliding them up under her shirt.

A tiny moan left her as she rolled her head back against her shoulders.

"I'm going to make you come on my tongue and fingers," I growled, the need to brand her, possess her so fucking impossibly and uncomfortably strong, I could scarcely see straight!

I pushed her shirt up over her head and let it fall, my eyes feasting on her perky breasts. She made my mouth water, and my wolf salivate like the beast he was. I leaned forward, taking one of her nipples into my mouth and swirling my tongue around its rosy peak.

"Oh, gods, Grey," she moaned and squirmed on my desk.

"You like that, princess?" I all but purred as I moved my hands down her sides to the waistband of her leggings.

"Yes," she groaned. "So much."

"Then you will like this even more," I promised and pushed her back on the desk.

She winced momentarily and arched her back, pulling a stapler out from under her before giggling at the ridiculousness of the moment. "Maybe we should have cleaned off your desk first," she suggested, but when I pulled her leggings down and discarded them on the floor, the laughter died on her tongue, and she held her breath.

I ran my hands up her thighs, savoring the silkiness of her flesh and leaned in, running my tongue over her soft inner thighs as I pushed them wider.

"Grab the edge of the desk, Aurelia, and don't let go," I commanded, allowing my hot breath to whisper over her pussy.

Aurelia shivered and wiggled her hips with need, her voice plaintive. "Grey, please," she begged.

"What do you need, princess?" I grinned against her skin and moved up, peppering her pretty flower with teasing, feather-light kisses.

"Touch me, Grey. Please," she moaned, arching her back again, but she didn't release her firm grip on my desk, just like I'd told her.

Good girl.

I ran a finger up her moist slit to her clit and circled it as I nipped her inner thigh with my teeth. The groan that escaped her had my cock hardening more than I thought possible.

Her pussy juices were soon oozing down her lips, and I lapped it up like it was spilled from the holy grail. The taste of her burst across my tongue, igniting every inch of me with fire as my wolf howled in my mind.

Mine. Mate.

My wolf and I were on the same page. There was no way we were letting this delectable virginal female get away. She was ours and we would do anything to keep her—to claim her. And the first part of that wicked plan was to make her come so many times she could never even imagine being with anyone else.

I kneeled on the carpet between her beautiful open thighs and circled her opening with one finger reverently, memorizing its perfection before pushing it slowly inside her.

Her wet pussy enveloped and squeezed my finger as she gasped softly, her knuckles white as she gripped the desk.

Her readiness had me chomping at the bit like a stallion rearing to race. I needed to sample her heavenly taste again. Leaning forward, I licked at her clit, circling it lazily with my skilled tongue.

"Fuck, Grey," she groaned, before pursing her lips tightly, her eyes closing in ecstasy.

"Do you like that, princess? I asked. "The way I worship you with my hands and tongue?"

She didn't answer, her expression one of intense concentration.

I didn't expect her to, honestly. And I was just getting started. I grinned before wrapping my lips around her glorious clit and drew it between my teeth, suckling forcefully like she was the fount of ambrosia —the essence of immortality and the food of the ancient gods.

Aurelia screamed, writhing on my desk as her entire body shook with her first orgasm. Magic flared at her fingers, purple and electric.

But I knew it wouldn't hurt me, so I continued my relentless mission, sucking at her clit.

She wailed for me throughout her entire release, her reactions genuine and unhindered by thought or manipulation. Wave after wave of sensation rippled within her, until finally her body began to relax, and the shivers and shudders of her pleasure subsided.

I sat back on my heels to gaze upon her. She truly was magnificent. "You are perfect, Aurelia." I grinned, the taste of her still slick on my lips as I licked them clean. With a heavy sigh, I stood up once more, my cock fucking aching for release. I reached for her hands and pulled her up from the desk and into my arms. "Let's go home."

"What?" she asked with a frown of surprise as she stared down at my cock. "We're stopping?

My cock jumped at her eyes on it. Her gaze held a hunger that I wanted to explore, but not on my desk. Not for her first time. I wanted her first time to be something she'd remember forever, something that staked my claim on her very soul beyond a shadow of a doubt. "We're going home, princess. Get dressed." I offered her a knee-weakening smirk and then turned to the closet next to my desk.

"But... what about you?" she asked softly looking unsure.

"Trust me, there will be plenty of time for that. But for now, I need to get you away from here," I said glancing at the door.

"Why?" she asked with an adorably naive pout.

"Why do we need to get you out of here? Or why won't I fuck you on my desk?" I asked with a raised brow, pulling a pressed button-down shirt from a hanger. I peered over my shoulder at her, and pink tinted her cheeks as she slowly stood and gathered her clothes from the floor.

"Umm," she said ducking her head with a shy smile. "I guess the first?"

"You've seen how cutthroat this place can be. If we don't go, someone could issue a challenge, and I won't be able to stop it," I answered as I pulled my trousers up over my hips.

"But if I'm not staying, then how will they be able to do that?" she asked softly.

"You're still in the building," I said and held out my hand to her. "It's technicality, but they'll demand it be honored. This lot has a code of their own when it suits them."

"What about my things?" she asked, her lips pinched in concern.

"I'll have them sent to the apartment later, but we will get you new things. Don't worry, princess." I squeezed her hand in mine to reassure her, wanting her to feel my strength and confidence.

We would get her better clothes than she'd ever had before. She would want for nothing. I would treat her like a real princess. But even as I dreamed of spoiling my fairy rotten, rage tinted my vision red as I remembered where she lived before, in a fucking closet. I wanted to bring the witch back just so I could interrogate her and kill her myself.

Pushing the darkness to the back of my mind, I focused on Aurelia. Leading her through the door and into the hallway, I stabbed at the button for the elevator as we approached. I quickly ushered her inside and pressed the button for the garage. I tapped my foot as we passed the training floor, but thankfully no one got on. I might be the boss, but my people would absolutely riot if I denied a challenge, even if Aurelia was nowhere near ready for such a battle.

Best to get out of here before a challenge is thrown down and shit starts unravelling quickly.

The doors opened at the garage level, and I placed a hand on her lower back, leading her to my car. There was no time to wait for the driver. The faster we made it out of here, the better. I opened the door for her and ushered her into the car when the sound of a distinctly feminine throat cleared behind me. Drawing in a deep, frustrated breath, I closed the door and turned to see Layla watching me, her expression as unreadable as a mask.

"What exactly is going on here, boss?" she asked, crossing her arms over her chest.

"You forget yourself, Layla. I don't answer to you," I growled.

"So, you're just going to ignore that there's been a challenge issued against her and leave me with a bunch of enraged criminals?" She scoffed.

"Tell them I've already left," I said, and made my way around the car.

"Half of them are shifters and will smell the lie!" She threw her hands up.

The car door shut with a click and Aurelia got out and stood with her arms folded. "There's been a challenge? Did Connor get his panties in a twist because he got stuck to a ceiling?" Aurelia asked, one defined brow cocked.

"It wasn't Connor," Layla sneered. "Someone else heard about your stunt today and decided they wanted the chance to put you in your place."

"In my place, huh? Considering I'm not staying, I guess they wouldn't know where that is anyway." Aurelia glared and she took a step toward Layla.

I grabbed her arm, halting her forward momentum. "Not a good idea, princess. You've only been training a week," I said pulling her back into my chest.

"Karma is going to start a riot," Layla said and turned back toward the elevator with a nasty smirk.

Karma challenged her? I didn't think the half-witch half-white-tiger-shifter even liked the wolves that much. Why is she defending them? This must be an ego thing. She's been top cat for so long, she probably can't stand the thought of someone being better than her.

"Karma challenged me?" Aurelia asked, her voice softer as her face fell.

Did she think she'd made a friend during her week here? There was no loyalty to be found among thieves and criminals.

Layla burst into laughter.

Aurelia's shoulders stiffened in response and her expression hardened once more.

"Aww, what's wrong, little fairy? Did you think you made a friend only for them to have betrayed you?" Layla mock pouted with a wicked gleam in her eye.

"Fuck you. I'll accept the challenge!" Aurelia took a step from my arms toward Layla again.

What the fuck is going on with my second? She is usually so much more professional with the employees than this, even the worst of them.

"Aurelia..." I started but trailed off when I saw the determination blazing purple fire in the depths of her green eyes. She needed to do this.

"They think I'm a weak little girl that can't take it just because I smile and don't let bullshit get to me, Grey. I need to prove them wrong." Aurelia stared into my eyes, pleading with me to see her point of view.

"Very well, but *I* choose the date. You're not doing this without more training." I glared pointedly at Layla.

Layla knew how important Aurelia was to my overall plans, and I would be damned if her bitchy behavior was going to get in the way of that. She needed to get over whatever the hell this was and focus on being my damn reliable second.

"Fine," Layla spat. "I'll let Karma know." Then she stomped back to the elevator, looking every bit as ridiculous as a toddler having a tantrum.

My shoulders slumped in defeat. How long could I put this off for? Karma was a beast in every sense of the word, and a long delay of affairs would be met with considerable outrage. "All right, let's go." I opened the door for Aurelia and helped her into the car. Closing the door behind her, I rounded the car again. Falling into my seat, I hit the ignition and then the gas, pulling out of the garage. "Are you sure about this?" I asked.

"I have to prove myself," she said absently as she stared out the window at the trees all around us.

"Why? You aren't staying there. You don't owe them anything," I said.

"Do you think I'll feel good about myself and my worth to *you* if I just run away? I'm no coward, Grey, and I'm powerful." She shook her head as if answering herself.

"I know you're powerful, princess, but that won't matter in the ring." I pursed my lips and sighed. She had no damn idea what she'd just gotten herself into. She may be strong magically, but she was only *just* learning how to protect herself and fight in a physical sense.

"What do you mean that won't matter in the ring?" she asked glancing at me.

"The ring cancels out magic, creating an even playing field for everyone. You won't be more powerful there. Layla shouldn't have baited you the way she did," I said with a growl.

"Motherfucker!" she cursed, clenching her fists in her lap until her knuckles turned white. "That bitch did that on fucking purpose."

I could only nod. I didn't know what Layla's deal was lately, but she was acting *off* and extremely unprofessional. Something had changed, but I couldn't put my finger on what it was.

It couldn't be something as petty as jealousy over Aurelia, could it?

"Can we please stop?" she asked suddenly through a heaving breath.

"Stop?" I asked, confused. "Why? We're in the middle of nowhere."

"I need air," she gasped, her eyes wild and panic stricken.

I stopped the car just inside the wards.

She tore her seat belt off and pushed through the door without another word and ran into the trees, disappearing into the forest, her wings fluttering at her back.

For a terrifying second, I lost sight of her, my heart racing. I practically threw myself from the car and took off after her, my wolf howling in my head all the while.

I can't lose her now! I just fucking found her.

And I wasn't sure if I could ever let her go.

CHAPTER 11
Aurelia

I couldn't breathe, and panic swelled within, threatening to choke the life from me.

Karma wants to fight me without magic? What does that prove to anyone?

The leaves crunched under my shoes as I ran through the trees, the earthy scent of the forest blazing through my senses. I had no idea where I was going. What was I even doing? What would this achieve? As I barreled through the dappled sunlight, a breeze whipped against my face, caressing my skin and easing some of my panic. I slowed to a jog before coming to a complete standstill, took a long, drawn-out breath, and let my shoulders slump.

It was peaceful here. More peaceful than I had felt in maybe... forever. I tilted my head back to the sky and let the tiny bit of sun that peeked through the tree branches warm me.

"Aurelia?" Grey whispered from behind me.

I hadn't even heard him coming. "I have never been outside the city before," I admitted. "And when we came to the facility last time, I wanted *so* badly to get out of the car and experience this," I whispered. "It feels so good to be in nature like this. I feel connected, somehow."

"Why didn't you say something then?" Grey asked.

I turned to peer at him over my shoulder.

He closed the distance between us.

"I didn't think you would care." I shrugged and turned back to the tall trees.

I reached out to touch the one nearest to me. The rough bark was scratchy beneath my palm but felt like home. Something rippled within the tree, and I sucked in a startled breath at the pulse of life flowing beneath the bark.

How is this possible?

"What is it?" Grey asked, moving in closer to my back to observe.

"I can feel the life in it," I answered with a curious frown.

"How do you mean?" Grey placed a comforting hand on my hip.

"There's like... a *pulsing* inside of the tree when I touch it. Something almost akin to a heartbeat or like the cadence of blood flow." I shook my head in wonder and grabbed his hand, resting it palm down on the bark. "Do you feel that?" I asked, glancing at him over my shoulder.

He shook his head, his lips pursed as he concentrated. "I don't feel anything, princess."

"That's strange. Do you think it's a Fae ability?" I asked, my brows furrowing.

"It might be. It would make sense that the Fae possess an affinity with nature beyond other supes." He paused a moment in thought before looking me in the eye. "Do you want to try something?" he asked, moving beside me.

I raised a skeptical brow at him. "What do you mean?"

"Put your hand back on the tree and push your magic into it with intention." He grabbed my hand, laying it against the bark once more.

I tilted my head to the side, listening to the river of life within it. Then closing my eyes, I dug deep into the well of magic swirling at my core.

Grow more leaves.

I pushed a trickle of magic into the tree and instantly felt the pulse grow even stronger. I opened my eyes as a surprised gasp slipped from my lips as I gazed above me. Pink flowers bloomed and fresh green leaves sprouted, fueled by the trickle of magic.

"Wow," Grey said with wide eyes. "That is definitely not like any magic I've seen before."

"What did I do?" I asked rhetorically as I reached up, trailing my fingers over the silky petals of a blushing bud.

"You made it grow and gave it new life," Grey said in awe and squeezed my shoulder.

"I knew I had elemental magic, like air... but this?" I asked, shaking my head.

It was all just incredible. Words failed me. And what did this mean? Could I heal sick plants? Is that why I felt so compelled to run into the forest in the first place?

"Come on, I think we should go practice this in a more controlled environment," Grey said as he pulled me away from the tree gently.

I went with him reluctantly, glancing over my shoulder with one last, longing look at the bright pink flowers that continued to bloom by the minute.

What the hell else can I do?

Grey opened the door for me as we got back to the car and pulled his phone from his pocket and spoke quietly into it before getting in the driver's seat. "We will get a lock on what you can do and then get your combat training started once we get to the apartment," he said as he revved the engine to a mechanical purr.

The drive back was silent, as if we were both lost in thought. My chest ached from the moment we left the forest and made it back into the iron and stone of the city. Maybe there was something to that, like Grey suggested, but I knew very little about Fae.

The wicked Fae ...

Before long, we pulled into an underground parking garage, and Grey reversed into a spot with a plaque that read: *Penthouse.*

I opened the door before Grey could make it around to my side and stepped out.

He glared at me.

"What?" I asked with a frown, perturbed by the unexplained emotional response.

He rounded the car and crowded me against the closed door. "When you're in a vehicle with me, you will wait for someone to open the door for you," he commanded with a deep throated growl.

"Holy shit. Did you really just growl at me?" I asked, shocked.

"Don't get out of the car without someone opening the door," he reiterated, then pushed me against the car until I was plastered against it and looking up at him, our bodies crushed against one another. "Understood?"

"Okay," I whispered breathlessly, my heart hammering in my chest at the sudden and aggressive sexual tension that whispered between us and the heat of our bodies. "Understood."

"Good. Now, let's get inside. I want to show you something," Grey said and wrapped an arm around my waist, pulling me along to the elevator like he hadn't just stolen my breath away.

We rode up in the elevator in silence and when the doors opened to the penthouse, I couldn't help but grin. It was *so* different from the last time I was there.

"You didn't have to fill your apartment with plants," I said with an appreciative sigh.

"They're purely for training purposes." He shrugged and walked over to the couch with his arm still around me and sat in front of a slightly wilting plant.

"Are you sure it's just training and not because I felt at home in the forest?" I asked, teasing him a little.

"Heal it," he ordered without preamble. "Do what you did with the tree again."

I raised an eyebrow but sat down next to him. I held my hand out to the withering plant and stroked one of its sad little leaves that were turning brown.

The leaf perked up immediately at my touch, but the pulsing in the plant was slow and almost labored.

My shoulders slumped at the desperation of the plant. It was dying and unable to do anything about it. It couldn't help itself. "It's so sad," I whispered as I wrapped my hand delicately around the stem. Focusing my intention, I pushed a trickle of magic into it, willing it to live and thrive.

The pulses became noticeably stronger as the leaves slowly perked up. It pulled at my magic a little harder, drawing from me like a baby from the breast.

"It's desperate for life and has latched onto my magic," I said in an awed tone, a gentle smile quirking my lips.

"It what?" Grey demanded and snatched my hand away from the plant roughly and unexpectedly.

I glared at him. "What are you doing?"

Why would he stop me from helping the plant? It's already doing so much better!

My heart went out to it. "I'm healing it, just like you asked me to!" I folded my arms defiantly, irked by his sudden change in temperament.

"It would suck you dry if you allowed it, princess. You need to learn to control the flow of magic, and not let the plant control it." He shook his head and moved the plant away.

At least the plant looked better than it had when I first sat down.

All the same, my shoulders slumped in defeat as the poor plant had no option available to it but to continue to struggle. I wanted to reach out to it and push more magic into it, but irritatingly, Grey was right. I wasn't stupid. I wanted to heal and help, but I needed to learn to control this new gift before it took advantage of the source unwittingly.

"There will be plenty of time to learn to heal it without putting yourself at risk," he reassured me more gently, squeezing my shoulder.

"Why did you bring so many plants into your home then?" I asked with a confused frown.

"You seemed so at peace in the forest, and since we can't be out there, I thought bringing some plants to you would help." He shrugged.

If he just wants me for a job, then why does he care how comfortable I am? It doesn't make any sense.

"Thank you," I said with a small smile. "The plants really do make me feel a little better. I appreciate it, Grey."

"Good. There's another thing I wanted to show you as well." He rose to his feet and held out his hand to me.

"What else could there possibly be?" I asked almost to myself and placed my hand in his.

"Come on, and I'll show you." Grey grinned and led me down the hall, past the room I slept in the last time I was there. Then he turned down another hall I hadn't seen before and walked until we were in front of a large pair of metal double doors.

Iron.

I shivered in recognition and took an involuntary step back. It had never bothered me too much before. But after my time in the forest and the way the dying plant had sapped overzealously from me, I could feel the bite of the iron as it pulled at my magic as well and making my shoulders slump. "What is this?" I asked with a frown.

"It's a controlled environment much like the ring at the facility you'll be fighting in. It will make it easier for you to learn to fight and adjust without the use of your magic." Grey opened the doors.

How does he have something like this smack bang in the middle of the city? The power radiating off it is intense. It's already blocking my magic from outside the doors...

I took a tentative step inside, and my limbs felt disturbingly heavy. The oppressive magic-neutralizing effects of the room pressed down on me from every side. It felt almost suffocating.

Is this what it feels like in the ring? I'm damn glad Grey put a stop to the fight happening immediately then. I'd be dead, no doubt about it.

"How do you feel?" Grey asked, resting a palm on my lower back.

"I understand what you were talking about now. I would have been at a huge disadvantage if I had gone into the ring without knowing what it felt like." I nodded as I walked around the giant training room and trailed my fingers over the handles of a few gleaming and deadly-sharp throwing knives.

The longer I stayed within the confines of the room, the less oppressive the feeling was, and I took a deep, cleansing breath. At least it looked like I'd get used to it. "So, what's the plan? I train in here until I'm ready to fight and then I go to the ring?" I asked staring at a bow on display. It was beautiful, with stunningly intricate designs carved into the smooth wood.

"That is part of the plan, but you are going to be doing a lot more training than just this." Grey's hot breath washed over my neck.

I hadn't even heard him move until he was right behind me.

Sneaky wolf.

"What else?" I asked breathlessly. Shivers skated down my arms at his close proximity. How did just his warm breath on the back of my neck make me feel so achy and needy? It was as delicious as it was frustrating.

"I have another training room that doesn't have the same magic-canceling wards. You will train with your magic in there, that way you're covering both bases." He wrapped his arms around my waist.

"Will I get to work with the plants too?" I raised an eyebrow at him over my shoulder.

"Yes, I have some employees who will help you with your plants. They will teach you how to stop the plants from draining you," he said and steered me away from the beautiful bow. He led me from the room and my magic came back immediately.

I rolled my shoulders and pulled them back in relief, the iron no longer pressing down and stifling my magic. I breathed a deep sigh. "That feels much better."

We walked into the kitchen together, and I blinked, mentally questioning what I was seeing.

Two tiny, little glowing sprites were flitting around the space. They were positively enchanting.

I took a tentative step forward, squinting at them. They were glowing green, and their iridescent wings fluttered at the same speed as a hummingbird's wings.

"Fiona, Freya, this is Aurelia," Grey said, addressing the adorable sprites.

Both creatures spun around, and bright smiles bloomed on their faces as they zoomed over to see me. They flew in close, and the flutter of their wings tickled my cheek as one picked up a lock of my unruly hair and tugged on it playfully.

"Hello," I giggled, marveling at their speed and beauty.

Grey grimaced. "You will be helping her with everything she needs, including training, *not* claiming locks of her hair for treasure," he chastised.

The sprites pouted and released my hair.

"Although sprites are known to be mischievous, wicked, little Fae creatures, they are *very* good with plants and earth magic in general. They will be helping you come to grips with your healing and plant magic," Grey explained.

"You have plants?" a tinkling voice asked excitedly as both sprites zoomed out of the kitchen like streaking balls of glowing light.

A high-pitched squeal met my ears a second later, and I laughed.

"They are going to keep you plenty busy during training sessions." Grey shook his head, but a handsome smile tugged at his lips despite the seriousness of his tone.

I didn't care how busy I was. As long as I learned the skills I needed to protect myself and gain some semblance of freedom, I would do whatever it took and then some.

I can't let Karma win.

CHAPTER 12
Grey

"What do you have for me?" I barked into the phone.

He better have something. It's been hours since I sent Karma to work the damn spell.

"The half-witch-shifter took her sweet-ass time getting here," Dan grumbled in response, referring to Karma.

Fucking Layla did that on purpose. She knew I needed Karma for a job, and instead, used that opportunity to tell her what Aurelia did, causing no end of problems.

Fuck, I really don't want to kill my second.

But she was becoming more and more troublesome. "Yeah, there was a bigger issue than I anticipated," I said with a growl. "Did you get anything from the room?"

"Not really. Whoever it was, wore a hood covering their face and never looked up from the book they grabbed out of the safe," he said.

I tightened my hold on the phone to the point where my knuckles were almost white. "What book?" I grumbled with a frown.

"As much as I don't like Karma, she's good at mimic spells. I got *so* much detail," Dan said, rambling on.

"Get to the point," I growled.

I didn't have time for this. I needed useful, tangible information and to make sure my sprites didn't wear Aurelia out too much while working with the plants. They were overzealous with their desire to train her, and it might ultimately wind up doing more harm than good if I didn't keep an eye on them.

"There was a note on the book. It was in Aurelia's possession when she was found as a child, apparently. I couldn't read the title of the book. It was in a different language, one that I'm not familiar with," Dan said and then sighed in annoyance.

I sat forward in my seat and my back straightened. Could this be what I'd been looking for all along?

How the hell are we going to find it now, though? And how did it end up in Aurelia's possession in the first place?

"This doesn't give us any more answers, Dan. Only more questions!" I growled, dragging a hand over my face in frustration.

"I wonder if you should have Karma do it again for Aurelia? To see if she recognizes anything herself," Dan suggested thoughtfully.

"That is not the best idea right now." I grimaced.

Putting the two of them in the same space with the challenge looming overhead was a supremely *bad* idea.

"It may be the only way to find out some real answers though," Dan grumbled right back.

I stood and strolled to the closed door of my office before opening it. A giggle met my ears that had a grin spreading over my face before I could stop it. Aurelia sounded so happy and carefree working with the plants. I didn't even care if I walked into my living room and it resembled a rainforest, to be frank. "Look, just see what else you can find for now. Let me know if you have anything for me, and we might address your suggestion later if there's no other option," I said and hung up the phone.

I walked out into the living room to the sound of buzzing wings and tinkling laughter. I blinked at the plants that had all grown twice their original size and had different flowers budding on them that couldn't possibly exist in our world. "What's going on here?" I groaned.

All eyes turned to me, and the sprites tittered.

"Isn't it amazing? Aurelia knows the plants of Faery!" Fiona said, clapping her hands excitedly.

My eyes widened, and I turned to my mate in surprise.

How could she possibly remember the plants of Faery? She was only a child when she was found. Was she born there? And if so, who were her real parents and why was she left here?

"You know the plants of Faery?" I asked with a frown of consternation.

"No, I mean not *really*. My magic just does it, like it has living memory. It happened with the tree in the forest today, too. Those pink flowers I encouraged it to grow were not like any of the others." She chewed her lip, shuffling from foot to foot as if plagued by anxiety.

I nodded and moved toward her, placing my hands on her shoulders and bending to peer into her beautiful green eyes.

"Are you sure? Fiona seems to think you know these types of plants. Magic works with knowledge, after all," I said.

Her brow furrowed. "How do you mean?" she asked, confused. "I just focus my intent and that's what comes of it. I'm not thinking of any specific flower or design. It just occurs."

Freya flew over in between us. "You have to have *seen* something in order to recreate it, Miss Aurelia," she sang excitedly before she tapped my mate on the nose and shook her head as if the answer were obvious.

"So, wait... you're trying to tell me that I've seen these things before?" Aurelia asked, her eyes widening. "But I've never seen anything like these in Dallas. Nothing so beautiful and magical grows there."

Fiona landed on my shoulder, and I grimaced at her before answering Aurelia. "You must have been in Faery at some point, because these don't grow here, as you said."

Fiona was excited, but I needed her to tone it down. They were the only ones who knew the full extent of my plans, and if they let them slip, Aurelia may never want to help me.

"I was there? When? How is that even possible?" Aurelia asked softly, furrowing her brow in concentration.

Is she trying to dredge up a long-forgotten memory?

"We'll figure it out, princess. Don't worry. There may very well be a block on your memory," I said and pulled her into my arms without hesitation.

Freya flitted away, chittering at me angrily for almost squishing her between us, but Aurelia needed reassurance, and Freya had lightning-fast reflexes.

"Is that where I came from, do you think? And if so, why didn't anyone ever come looking for me? I'm sure a child can't just wander between worlds alone, right?" she asked, whispering her questions against my chest.

"No, a child wouldn't be able to wander between realms on their own. There's a reason you are here, and I'm going to find out what it is, one way or another." I patted her back and then stepped away with a small nod.

I couldn't call a witch on my normal payroll to investigate this new development. Karma was the only one with enough skill, and I refused to put her in the same room as Aurelia or give her information she might then use against her. "I'm going to make a call." I sighed and pulled my phone from my pocket.

Freya's wings fluttered excitedly. "Yay! We can work on the plants some more!"

"No. Give Aurelia time to rest. You two are plenty capable of healing the plants without her help." I glared at the sprite. They were overzealous to a fault.

The light around her dimmed at my admonishment, but she nodded her tiny head in understanding.

I didn't want Aurelia to overwork herself, especially if we were going to attempt to work on her memory block.

Is it even a memory block, or was she just too young to retain any memories of her home? Did she even have a home?

There were just too many unanswered questions surrounding my mate, and it was looking more and more like they all revolved around my plans...

How will she react when she finds out what my plans are?

I was under no illusion that she wouldn't eventually figure them out. She was my mate and a huge part of what I had planned, but I didn't want her to find out the wrong way, or too early, before she was ready.

Fiona jumped from my shoulder and flew right in front of my face. Hovering there, she opened her mouth, probably to say *too much.*

I shook my head. "Don't, Fiona." I pinned her with a hard glare. Without further discussion, I stepped around the sprite and headed back to my office. This new development brought nothing but *more* questions, but maybe I would get some answers once we unlocked her memories.

That is, if it's even possible.

I closed the door behind me then sat at my desk. I leaned my head back against the chair just as my phone buzzed in my hand. I glanced down at the screen.

How does she always know when I need to speak to her? It's kind of creepy.

"Magna, how did you know?" I asked into the phone.

"Know what, Grey?" she answered cryptically.

Is she a seer? She can't be, right? She would never go against me...

"How do you always know when I need your help?" I asked with a muted growl.

"You know that old wives' tale about your nose itching when someone's thinking about you?" She chuckled.

"Um, sure" I shook my head and rolled my eyes. The woman was eccentric, to say the least.

"Think of it as something like that, only imagine it ten times stronger," she said. "Now, what do you need, darling?"

"I found someone who will be able to help me, but I think she has a block on her memory." I rested my head on my hand and blew out my breath.

"This is surely something the hybrid can handle?" she asked, her tone filled with venom at the mention of Karma, my half-witch half-white tiger-shifter fighter.

"Not this time. Karma has a massive chip on her shoulder. She's threatened by Aurelia and has already issued a challenge against her, so that option is not available to me as far as I can see." I grimaced. It would have been much easier if I could have just called Layla to send Karma, but I couldn't take any chances with this. Too much rested upon it.

"She challenged her?" Magna asked with obvious distaste. "If this fairy is as important as I believe she is... you can't let that stand."

"What do you know about her, Magna?" My spine straightened at her words.

She's telling me what I can and cannot allow now? How much does she really know about me? This isn't good at all.

"Nothing for certain," she said cryptically. "It's just a gut feeling, but I'm sure we will find out if I'm right soon enough, won't we?"

I sighed again. "How long until you can be here?" I asked, refusing to answer her cryptic question.

"What exactly do you expect me to do, Grey?".

"I think she has a memory block on her. I want you to lift it and see what she can remember." I stood from my chair and began pacing.

"Very well. I will have to gather a few things, but I will be there within the hour," Magna said and hung up promptly.

"What the hell?" I stared at the phone in disbelief.

I should have been used to Magna's eccentricities by now, but that still threw me off. *I* was the one who hung up on people without a word, not the other damn way around. I leaned against the wall in my office, my gaze glued to the ceiling. What the fuck had I gotten myself into? What things did Magna need to gather to remove the block?

"Grey?" Aurelia's sweet voice came from the other side of the door before she knocked.

I took a fortifying breath and pushed off the wall. "Yes, princess?" I opened the door, staring down at her pink cheeks. She was so beautiful when she blushed.

"I just got this funny feeling that you needed me. It's weird, I know.

I'm sorry for bugging you," she said and turned back toward the jungle that was apparently my living room.

I reached out and pulled her back into my chest. "You aren't bugging me at all. I just got off the phone. I have someone coming to meet you within the hour," I told her, squeezing her hip.

How the hell did she feel that? Magna is half-Fae, so is that intuition a Fae trait or a witch trait?

I shook my head to clear it of questions I wasn't likely to get the answers to any time soon. Magna was always cagey when it came to answers about herself, but I wouldn't let her be about this. Aurelia meant too much to me to let Magna get away without divulging absolutely every answer she might find.

"Who is this person? Are they like me?" she asked.

I shook my head.

There is no one in this world like you.

I led her back into the living room and chuckled at the green space. "Did you do *all* this, yourself?"

"Um, I'm sorry. I should have told them to stop. They were only trying to make me happy. Fiona and Freya may have gotten a little carried away." She glanced away, her cheeks becoming pinker by the second.

The leather couch and chairs were covered in a vibrant green moss dotted with bright pink and purple flowers, while lush vines twisted their way elegantly around most available free-standing objects.

"Fiona. Freya. What the hell?" I groaned. "I told you to go easy with this!"

That damn moss better not ruin my furniture.

Fiona buzzed into the living room. "What's the matter, Grey? Don't you like it? Miss Aurelia said she's never really been out of the city, and we thought this would feel better to her. We like her smile!"

Fucking sprites. Well played, Fiona. Well fucking played.

I could do nothing but sigh and pull Aurelia into my side more tightly as I surveyed their Faery-inspired decorative flair. I couldn't blame them, not really. I'd move fucking mountains to see my mate's smile, too.

CHAPTER 13

An unexpected knock at the door made me jump, and I gasped. Turning to look, my gut tightened.

Grey smiled at me as he strode to the door confidently. "Don't worry, princess, it's just Magna. She's the one I've been waiting for."

My shoulders slumped in relief, but I was still on edge. What would the woman think of the way the sprites and I had redecorated Grey's living room? What would I remember if she was able to remove the memory block?

Is any of this really important? Why does it even matter that I probably lived in Faery as a child?

I squared my shoulders and exhaled a steadying breath. It would matter, somehow, I knew. Even if I didn't yet understand quite how all this pieced together. Ultimately, I would have answers as long as this Magna woman could remove the block.

Grey opened the door wide and invited our guest inside.

A wizened old woman hobbled in, her gaze raking over me.

This is Magna? How is she supposed to help me?

Grey reached out a hand to help her into the living room, but she pushed a huge bag at him instead. Grey let out a breath in a *whoosh*, almost as if his patience was already worn thin.

"You must be Aurelia," the elderly woman said as she ambled nearer to me. Her blue eyes were so light they appeared almost milky white. Then she moved closer to me quicker than should have been possible at her age, taking me by surprise. Her hand wrapped around mine, and she began to hum.

What in the world is going on here?

I glanced up at Grey with wide, questioning eyes.

"Yes, there is strong magic here," Magna said with a hum of what sounded like disapproval.

I frowned at the woman.

What is she?

"What do you mean?" I asked softly. Was she talking about my magic and how strong it was, or was she saying someone had placed strong magic on me—like the memory block Grey mentioned?

Why would anyone do that to me? What purpose would it serve to make me forget my origins?

"Not your magic, darling." Magna smiled at me and patted my hand like an old friend. "Though, your magic is immense as well."

"Immense?" I asked with a grimace.

My magic sure as hell does not feel immense.

Magna scanned the living room and chuckled at the new living decorations. "You think your magic isn't incredibly strong when you have plants thriving all over poor Grey's furniture?"

I scrunched up my nose at the two sprites whose light dimmed only slightly as I turned my focus on them. "It wasn't *just* me," I said.

"I can feel your magic in every plant in this room, so I don't believe that for a moment. Perhaps you don't realize quite how much you gave of yourself." Magna shook her head and hobbled over to the mossy couch.

The sprites beamed at her and flitted to land on her shoulders.

Cheeky little shits!

They could have at least admitted their part in this green mischief.

Grey set the giant bag Magna had brought on the coffee table and crossed his arms over his chest. "Fiona and Freya, I think there are other things you could be doing?" Grey raised a brow suggestively.

The two sprites tittered between themselves and flew off into the kitchen. It was clear they weren't going to argue with their boss when there was company around.

Magna smiled to herself and leaned forward to open her bag.

Grey sat down next to me and rested his elbows on his knees. "So, what do you need to do this?"

Magna peered over at Grey. "I need space, and I need time with Aurelia. I'm sure you can find other things to occupy yourself with too?"

Grey's gaze snapped to Magna, and his lips pinched at her sass.

She raised an attitude-filled brow at him and waited.

They sat in a silent stand-off, each regarding the other until Grey finally huffed out a breath and stood. "I'll be listening from my office. Let me know if there's anything you need for your spell, Magna." Grey mumbled and left the room.

"There, now that we're alone, how are you holding up, my dear?" Magna turned her perilously light blue gaze on me.

"Holding up?" I asked with a frown. "I don't know what the hell is going on with anything. The only mother I have ever known was murdered, and they're blaming me for it! *Holding up* isn't something I can really wrap my head around right now."

Magna patted my hand and smiled with sympathy. "It is a lot that has been laid upon your shoulders, but I think it's the way it must be," she said cryptically.

What does she mean by that? Why would any of this be the way things were meant to be?

I frowned as my confusion only grew. "Can you tell me if I have a block on my memory?" I asked, pushing those thoughts aside to get her back on track. How did she know so much, anyway? A part of me wanted to move away, but at the same time, I also felt a strange kinship with the woman.

"Yes, you have a strong block on you, Aurelia. It's one I'm not even sure I can remove with my magic alone," Magna said with subtle shake of her head.

"Then what are we doing here?" I tried to remove my hand from her grip in frustration, my temper fast fraying with disappointment. Maybe I was going to get no answers after all?

Magna only squeezed tighter, keeping my hand firmly in her surprisingly strong grip. "I may not be able to use my magic to loosen the block just yet, but maybe I can do something to jog your memory of the time before you were sent to this world." Magna suggested sternly.

"So, how do you think we can loosen the block, then?" I asked, my chest tightening with apprehension.

If her magic can't do it, then what can she possibly do?

"Never underestimate the power of stories, child." She squeezed my hand anew.

"Stories?" I asked softly, my curiosity piqued. "What do you mean?" I flopped back into the soft moss that covered the back of the couch and waited for her explanation. Could she tell me something about Faery?

"I am much older than I look." She grinned. "I remember a time before Faery was closed off from us."

Wait? What the fuck is she talking about? Faery closed itself off from who?

Magna shook her head with a sad smile. "I am but half-Fae, and any supernaturals that called Faery their home that weren't pureblooded were expelled and abandoned to hide in the mortal world."

"And you were there?" I asked, my gaze locking with hers.

Surely that would make her ancient, right? How can she possibly be that old?

"Please, darling, ask the burning question I see festering in that beautiful head of yours," Magna said with a gentle woman-to-woman shoulder bump.

"There's *way* more than a single question in there," I said and wrapped my hand around hers once more.

"Tell me the most pressing," she prompted.

"Well, for starters, what are you, exactly?" I blurted. "And what did you mean by *they kicked us out*?"

"I knew that was the question you would latch on to." She squeezed my hand in understanding. "I am a half-breed, child. The Fae did not look kindly on those of us who weren't pure like you," she said, her words without malice or censure.

"But if I am full Fae, why not blame me for what was done to you?" I asked, anxiously chewing my lower lip.

"Were your actions the ones that resulted in us being kicked out of our home-realm hundreds of years ago, child?" she asked as she wrapped her arm around me.

I shook my head.

"I didn't think so either", she said, her tone warm. "I would have remembered a pretty face like yours if it were that full of hatred and malice."

"Are my kind... evil?" I asked, giving the question that had plagued me my whole existence. Could I really be the wicked Fae my mother always told me I was? My stomach knotted, and I grimaced.

Why did my people make them leave? And are the Fae really as bad as everyone says they are?

"Maybe they are not all the wicked Fae they have garnered the reputation for, but there are those who went out of their way to actively purify their realm of all half-bloods, shifters and witches included. They are the ones who are wicked, not you, darling." Magna embraced me with her frail arms.

It did little to make me feel any better about the way my kind had treated the others. It was appalling. Why should any supernatural be cast out of the only home they've ever known? Blood purity, of all things!

Do I want to know about my home anymore? Do I even care?

"It's important to know where you came from, darling. If you don't know that, then you won't know which is the correct path forward," Magna said sagely.

"My people are awful. They kicked you all out of your home

because you weren't pure. Why would I ever want to go back there?" I asked.

"Maybe you can be the one that changes things for the better, darling." Magna's gaze bored into mine with a frightening intensity.

"Why would I matter in any kind of change?" I asked.

She just hummed in response.

What the fuck was I missing here? I was nothing more than a grown-up foster child with a questionable past and an even more uncertain future.

"I think a story is in order. It may help you with your memories, darling," Magna said and shifted on the moss-covered couch beside me.

"What kind of story?" I asked with a raised brow. I loved books whenever I could get my hands on them, but that wasn't often.

"A story about Faery," she said happily. "A story about the goodness in the realm and the ancient tales."

"All right." I nodded, opening myself to any chance at regaining my memories. "I would love to hear them."

"Millennia ago, Faery was a glorious place where all the supernaturals that live in this realm lived out in the open, in peace, in Faery. They didn't have to hide. In fact, there were always grand dances and parties, both in the wilds of nature and at court. The Fae courts were very similar to what you hear about in human stories," she said with a faraway look in her eyes.

I shifted as I listened to her talk about the beauty of the realm that I was beginning to hate. I glanced at the budding plants that were far too beautiful to belong in this world.

Could they be right, and I have been to Faery, and because of whatever block is there, I just don't remember?

"It was a beautiful place and a beautiful time. But as with all history, it didn't stay that way. The courts were always squabbling, and wars broke out. The Fae Elders' Council determined among themselves that the other supernaturals of the realm were to blame." Magna shook her head.

"How were the shifters and witches to blame for the courts warring?" I asked, my brow furrowing.

"The shifters and witches got along about as well then as they do now, and they were members of rival courts as well." Magna pursed her lips at the memory.

That makes sense.

Even I had seen how shifters and witches reacted to each other with utter distrust and general disdain.

"These courts bordered each other, and every time a scuffle broke out along their borders, war would soon follow," Magna said with a sigh.

"So, basically they gave the Elders everything they needed to blame them for the wars that continuously broke out," I reasoned as I rested my elbows on my knees and sat forward. I'd always loved learning about any precious scraps of my history that I could, but this wasn't helping me remember anything. Still, I kept my silence as she continued her story.

"Eventually, the Elders' Council decided that the Fae were the only ones who deserved to live in their homeland and searched for a way to expunge all others from their realm. It was, after all, *Faery*."

My whole focus was trained on Magna as she kept me on the edge of my seat with her story. "And they eventually found a way?" I asked and shook my head in dismay.

Of course they did.

"They did, and the supernaturals who were not full-blooded Fae were ejected from the realm forever." She shook her head sadly, as if it pained her to this very day.

"And perhaps the worst part of all is that it's not even a one-way deal." Magna sat back against the couch.

"What? They can come here, but we can't go there? That hardly seems fair." I covered my face with my hands and closed my eyes tightly. There was something *there*, niggling at me, just out of reach... but the more I tried to grab for it, the farther away it seemed to slip.

"Nothing about being kicked out of our home was fair, child," Magna said.

"Right. Well, I don't think this is working, Magna." I shook my head in defeat.

"Close your eyes again and clear your mind, darling. And just listen to the sound of my voice," she coached softly.

I can do that.

It was much like Grey had taught me to do when I was calming down to control my magic. I took a deep breath and focused myself, preparing for whatever was to come.

"Think back to your first memories," she said, her voice soothing.

I did as instructed, and the memory of being found walking the streets of Dallas hit me like a speeding freight train, and I shivered as I remembered the chill in the air and the utter sense of despair that had plagued me like a shadow.

"That's good," she coaxed. "Now, push back farther."

I concentrated, but there was a wall there. I couldn't go back any further. Grimacing, I tapped at it in my mind, testing its permeability with tendrils of my magic, but it was rock-solid. "I found the block," I said aloud, and then with all my mental strength, I punched a fucking hole straight through it. No one was keeping my secrets from me, not when I had the power to do something about it.

CHAPTER 14

A strangled, hair-raising scream tore through the apartment, chilling my very soul. I jumped up from my seat behind my desk and rushed from the room, practically knocking over everything in my path in my haste to reach my mate. "What the fuck happened?" I asked Magna with a protective growl, my urge to shift almost overwhelming me.

"I don't know," she said, her voice tinged with concern. That spoke *volumes*. The old half-Fae had scarcely revealed her true emotions to anyone in all the time I'd known her. She was a woman of mystery and hidden truths, and always kept her guard high. "She told me she had found the block and mere breaths later, she started screaming." Magna's face crumpled with a deep frown.

"I thought *you* were supposed to be removing the block?" I hissed as I kneeled on the mossy floor next to her.

"It was stronger than my magic could overcome, Grey. So, I tried another tactic." Magna held her hands over Aurelia's head, and a faint green glow emitted from her palms as she focused, her eyes closed.

I trailed my fingers down the side of Aurelia's cheek and pushed an errant lock of hair behind her ear.

What the fuck happened, Aurelia? Why did you just start screaming? Are you all right?

"The block appears to have been damaged," Magna sighed, before directing her words at my mate. "What on earth did you do, child?"

"What do you mean?" I asked turning my glare on the old woman.

"She did something to the magic maintaining the memory block. I didn't tell her to do that," Magna whispered in response, her lips pinched as she sat back, the glow leaving her hands.

"What does that really mean, though? Does it mean you can't heal her?" I asked, pulling my unconscious mate into my arms from the moss-laden couch.

"She's not physically injured." Magna shook her head. "And no, I can't heal her mind. That magic is beyond the reach of a half-blood. We have our limits."

"Are you telling me that she's somehow fractured her damn mind, and you can't do a thing to fix it?" I growled, cradling my mate.

"I don't think it's fractured, but *she* will need to heal herself and face whatever is in her past before she wakes again," Magna said with a shake of her head.

What the fuck does that even mean? Face what's in her past? I fucking hate it when she talks in riddles!

"Now, the time has come for you to tell me what you think Aurelia *is* to you and your plans," Magna said with a raised brow.

"You know I can't tell you that, Magna. Neither of us can risk it. It could paint a target square on your back. I don't need that complication, nor do I want you lost as collateral damage. You don't deserve that,

Magna." I held Aurelia closer to my chest, and her soft, unconscious sigh tickled my neck.

"She may not be happy with your plans, Grey, once she realizes the role she is to play in this game of revenge. Are you prepared to face that?" Magna asked, her eyes shining with an air of knowledge.

This Fae woman always knows way too fucking much.

I sighed. It was fucking vexing at the best of times, but even more so, given the circumstances. "What do you know?" I asked.

"I know that she thinks she's evil because of what her people did to us all, and she doesn't want to go back to the Fae realm because of it," Magna said, shocking me. "She's taken the guilt of an entire people, who came long before she was ever born, upon her shoulders. I can only imagine that weight feels crushing."

"I don't know what you *think* you know about my plans, Magna, but that won't be a problem." I rose from the floor with my precious burden and stormed down the hall, my temper fraying as I tried to keep myself in check.

The sprites flitted around me in bursts of bright pink and green, their wings fluttering furiously as they darted to and fro.

I kicked open the door to Aurelia's room and laid her gently on the bed with a grimace.

"Miss Aurelia's room needs plants!" Fiona gasped, clapping her hands together.

"Not now," I grunted and sat next to Aurelia on the bed, my heart aching as it twisted in my chest. I brushed her wild hair away from her face with my fingertips. She was *so* beautiful—even in sleep—that it hurt.

I can't believe she's mine.

Mate, my wolf simpered.

"Master Grey," Freya interjected softly. "Is she going to be okay?"

"According to Magna, she's just working through her memories, the ones that came before we met her... but I don't know what that will ultimately mean for us." I scrubbed an anxious hand over my face.

Fuck! What if she wakes up and remembers who she is and how to get back to Faery? She's a full-blooded fairy. There would be nothing to stop her from crossing over. Will she leave us all here to rot once she rediscovers herself?

Hiding from humans in plain sight all the time was painful beyond the ability of words to accurately explain. Especially when many of us still remembered what it had been like to be free of all of that. We could shift out in the open without fear, cast magic, and travel as we wanted. We lived our best lives—and then it was stolen away from us. I couldn't imagine what it would feel like to be able to reclaim that...

And what if truly Aurelia can? She may well be the key in more ways than one if we mean anything to her at all. But who knows how she'll feel when she wakes... I stood abruptly and stomped back into my redecorated living room, pushing a curtain of greenery aside as I went.

Damn sprites.

"How long do you think it will take for her to wake up?" I asked Magna.

"I don't know, honestly." Magna pursed her lips and wrung her hands together. "It could be minutes or hours. Maybe more. There's no way to know how she will fare on this journey of the self. It is hers to walk alone."

I slumped down on the couch next to the wizened half-Fae woman with a frustrated huff. "You know more than you are letting on," I accused, crossing my arms over my chest.

"I always know more." Magna smiled.

Could she be the seer that took the book from the witch's house?

I had to find out. Sitting up straighter, I interlocked my fingers and licked my lips. There was no beating about the bush, here. "What do you know about Aurelia and her past?" I asked with a raised brow, hoping I didn't come across as confrontational as I felt.

"I know she's important, Grey. Far more important than even you know," she said quietly. "She is a rare creature."

"Do you always have to be *so* fucking cryptic?" I grumbled. "I *need* answers."

"How would you like me to be, darling? If I tell you *anything* it could potentially change *everything*." Magna stood, her expression terse. "The future cannot be jeopardized."

"You are a seer!" I jumped to my feet, my tone triumphant. I had been right all along!

Fuck, yeah.

My inner wolf howled, his hackles rising.

My suspicions had finally proven true, and vindication never felt so sweet.

Her nearly white eyes turned on me with an intense glare. "That's not common knowledge, Grey," she said evenly, her gaze suddenly more dangerous.

"Were you at her home the day her witch caretaker was murdered?" I marched over to the door and blocked her exit. There was no way she would leave without answering me.

There are too few seers for this to be a coincidence.

"No," she growled, affronted by the mere suggestion. "I would never!"

"Do you know what book was found?" I asked, pressing forward with determination.

"Book?" she asked, confusion contorting her face as the edges of her anger instantly softened. Her eyes clouded over, and she swayed on her feet before her knees buckled and gave way.

I lunged for her on instinct, my reflexes as an Alpha wolf shifter comparable to lightning. She didn't weigh much, and I lifted her with ease, laying her down on the mossy couch from which she had just risen.

What the fuck is happening right now? Is she okay? I can't have her unconscious too!

The sprites buzzed into the room frantically, their voices high-pitched and shrill.

"Don't touch her, Master Grey!" Fiona fluttered in front of me, her eyes wide and worried.

"Why the hell not?" I asked, frowning. "I had to catch her!"

"She's having a vision right now," Freya whispered to me, her tone filled with awe.

"Have you seen this before? What could happen?" I asked, taking a step further away from Magna.

"She could accidentally pull you into her vision," Freya warned and wrung her tiny hands together, her entire being riddled with nervous energy.

"And, after what she just said, if I know what she sees… it could spell disaster." I nodded.

Fucking hell. I can't catch a break here!

I understood, but the not knowing had an irrational anger bubbling to the surface of my mind. It was a toxic feeling, so I pushed it back with a concerted effort. That would serve no one right now, least of all Aurelia.

Anger makes you stupid.

And when your head wasn't in the game, you fucked up and there were some fuck-ups you could never take back. I took a steadying breath and allowed the roar of my anger to simmer down.

I need to save my anger for those that deserve it…

A groan filled the quiet space, snatching me from my thoughts.

I turned away from the frantic sprites and back to the wizened woman. "Magna, did you see something?" I asked as her eyes cleared of whatever she'd just witnessed in her vision.

"Not much, I'm afraid," she grumbled and rubbed her forehead as if in pain. "There's another seer blocking me, I can feel it. And I worry they're after Aurelia."

"Who's after me?" came Aurelia's sweet, familiar voice from the hall.

Startled, I spun around with a broad smile. "You're okay!" I rushed to her and cupped her pale cheeks in my hands.

My wolf was pushing at the surface, ecstatic that our mate had awoken, but he was threatening my control as I stared into her eyes.

"Yeah, I think so. What happened?" Aurelia asked with a shaky sigh.

Magna sat forward with a glare, again shocking me with her uncharacteristic forthrightness. "You weren't supposed to touch the block."

"What are you talking about?" Aurelia asked as she rubbed at her temples.

Strange.

"Princess, what did you do when you found the block on your memories?" I asked, guiding her back to the couch. I sat her down beside Magna and took a seat in front of her on the coffee table.

Aurelia frowned and closed her eyes in concentration, as if searching for something internally. "It's gone," she said, her voice barely above a whisper.

"What do you mean, 'It's gone'?" I asked. "Does that mean you remember everything?" I needed to know about the book and how it fitted into this bizarre puzzle that was Aurelia's life. It could have ramifications for my plan, and it was obviously important. A seer would never have risked exposure for something that wasn't.

"It's still a little fuzzy," she admitted. "But the block is gone." She opened her green eyes and stared directly into mine.

"Do you remember anything about a book?" I asked, leaning forward.

"Grey," Magna warned me with a glare, her tone like cracking ice.

"I was just asking a question, woman." I shook my head at the old woman and pursed my lips in annoyance, probably giving me the appearance of someone who'd just sucked on a wickedly sour lemon.

"Forcing her memories to the surface before she's ready isn't good for anyone," Magna scolded before patting Aurelia's arm like she was a small child.

"Hello? I'm sitting right *here*!" Aurelia threw her hands up in exasperation. "Can you please not talk about me, when you can talk *to* me?" she stressed.

"What's the first thing you remember, Aurelia?" Magna queried gently, squeezing her arm in a more familiar and comforting gesture.

Aurelia sighed, then closed her eyes again.

I leaned closer. I wasn't going to miss a single thing. Anything could be worth noting at this point, even if my mate didn't yet realize it.

"It's cold," she said with a tangible shiver. "And I'm huddled in an alley that I don't remember seeing before. A person in a long, dark cloak with a hood approaches me."

Shit. Could it be the same seer Dan and Karma saw in the mimic spell?

"I say something to them in a language I don't even know if I understand," Aurelia continued as she scrunched her brows together in deeper concentration.

"You don't know what language it was, or what you said?" I

prompted and turned my surprised gaze toward Magna as we observed Aurelia's memory recall.

"I think I said that I want to go home," Aurelia whispered. She opened her eyes and stared at me, her gaze plaintive and confused. "How did I understand that when I have never heard it before? It's so strange."

"What did the cloaked person do when you said that?" Magna coaxed, keeping the track of discovery on the straight and narrow.

"They shook their head at me and said something." She shook her own head as if warring for understanding. "You can't. I think they said I couldn't go home."

"How old were you?" I asked squeezing her knee, piecing the timeline together.

"I look to be maybe six or seven years old? But how is it that I forgot all this? It's not like I was *that* young. That's school aged... I *should* be able to remember." She slumped back onto the couch, her face a conflicted array of emotions.

"Aurelia, there was a block on your memory," I said. "It's not your fault. They were purposely hidden from you."

"Why would that person tell me I couldn't go home? They seemed familiar to me in the memory, like I knew them or something," she said and tilted her head back to stare at the ceiling.

"You knew them? If you saw them again, do you think you could identify them? Point them out, maybe?" I asked, getting excited that we had straws to grasp at.

Could she tell us who this person was and how to find the book? This could be the lead we've been looking for, and it's all just been locked away in her mind!

"I probably could, eventually, but my head is still fuzzy. I feel like I'm trying to remember a dream, the way you do when you're waking and it's slipping away with every second your eyes are open." Aurelia shook her head, her lower lip trembling.

"Not to worry," Magna said and patted Aurelia's hand. "You can't push too far, too fast, or you could hurt yourself, darling. It's not worth the pain." Magna shot me another stern glare to make her point.

My wolf growled angrily in my head, but not at the half- Fae seer woman. He was growling at *me*.

I was putting our mate at risk by being so impatient. I couldn't hide my excitement. I might soon have the answers I needed and be closer to my goals than ever before. But where was my fucking game? I was a master of my damn poker face, and I was forgetting myself. Getting swept up in the thrill of learning like a child.

"I feel like I'm failing you, Grey... by not being able to remember," Aurelia said softly.

I could hear her heart in her throat. "No," I growled. "You are not failing me, princess." I cupped her cheek and pressed my lips to hers softly, regardless of our present company.

"Are you sure? I could try harder" she said, breaking the kiss, her eyes shimmering.

"No, I don't want you to hurt yourself. You've had a long day. It's time you rested. Your trainers will be here early in the morning, anyway. You need to recover." I kissed her forehead and stood, pulling her up with me. I shared a covert look with Magna and nodded toward my office.

I moved through the hall to Aurelia's room and opened the door for her.

Her tinkling laughter filled the space as she scanned the room I'd given her.

"Fiona and Freya," I growled, wanting to smack myself in the head.

Overzealous sprites! I told them not to go crazy.

The blanket was a lush expanse of soft moss draped over the bed, and there were garlands of fragrant, blooming flowers draped around the headboard. They wanted Aurelia to feel at home and at peace.

I shook my head and kissed Aurelia on the cheek. "I need to have a chat with Magna and some overzealous sprites. Get some sleep." Strolling from the room, I closed the door behind me. I needed to talk to Magna. She once again knew more than she was letting on. And even though the future could be at stake, I couldn't be left in the dark. Aurelia was in my care, after all.

I raced down the hall to my office and pushed through the door. "What do you think is happening, Magna?"

"I think we need to tread very carefully here," she answered without preamble. "Whoever was in the witch's apartment is going to come after

Aurelia. That is the truth, Grey. She's not safe." Magna turned to raise an eyebrow at me, no doubt wondering as to my next move.

"I know that! It's why I'm getting her trained to use her magic *and* protect herself without it. I knew she was special the moment I met her, Magna. I felt it in my bones—literally." I sat behind my desk, my fingers steepled.

"I don't think you quite understand what I'm saying. The future is uncertain. This person could be a danger to her as much as a danger to your own carefully laid plans." Magna had a faraway look in her eyes as she spoke, seeing or feeling who knows what.

"So, you're saying that she could still take the other side on this? The potential exists that we could wind up as enemies?" I asked shaking my head as the wind was knocked from my sails.

I can't let that happen. I can't let this fucking psycho seer near her.

There was no way in the world I was going to lose my mate. Losing her would be akin to having my heart torn from my chest and thrown in a blender. I'd never recover from it. There was no healing to be had when your destined mate was lost. I'd be no more than a husk, a shell of myself.

And I can't let that happen, either.

CHAPTER 15

"Again!" the mammoth of a man training me roared from the other side of the makeshift ring, his expression darkening with intimidating intensity as he took up his stance once more.

This guy is absolutely relentless!

"Water," I gasped, small stars dancing before my eyes as my head swooned with the fuzzy onset of dehydration. He'd been working me like a fucking juggernaut in Grey's magic-canceling room for hours, and it felt as though I was fast approaching my limit for the day. I'd never felt so physically sore or fatigued—not even after being tranqed by that bastard back in the alley the day Mother died.

"When you're fighting for your life do you think your opponent will let you stop for a water break?" Max shouted with a cocked brow. "Again," he repeated sternly and without apology.

He's really not going to let this go. Fuck!

Sucking in a deep breath, I scowled and crouched back into a fighting stance, mirroring my trainer. Allowing my frustration and anger to lend me strength, I waited for Max to come at me again. Having been at this for hours I was basically one giant living, breathing bruise. I had muscle aches in places I didn't even know I had muscles, but I kept going. I had to. My challenge fight with Karma was fast approaching, and I was damned if I was going to lose to that bitch. There was no world in which I could live with that shame.

I'll prove myself and make her rue the day she decided to fuck with me.

As Max closed the distance between us, faster than I'd anticipated, I slammed one fist into the pad on his hand and spun in a circle, executing a pretty impressive roundhouse kick.

Max's other hand blocked my foot effortlessly and he pushed it away with a disapproving smirk. "You're slow," he taunted.

"I'm not used to this much exercise," I growled back, every fiber of my being crying out for reprieve as my muscles burned with agony. I had never exercised much in general, but over the last week since my mother's death, Grey had insisted on a rigorous and grueling training schedule. My hours of proverbial torture had been steadily increasing by the day, and Max wasn't about to let up on it either. He knew what was at stake just as well as I did, and he wasn't about to fail his employer or allow me to fail myself, either.

"You need to get used to it," he snarled. "You are a sitting duck in a fight. Try harder, be faster!" Max shook his head, clearly tired of my bullshit excuses.

"In a fight I will have my magic," I huffed, scrunching my nose as my brows furrowed in annoyance.

"Will you have your magic in the ring?" Max glared at me, making his point clear. This wasn't about surviving in a general sense, it was about somehow overcoming Grey's best fighter in a ring that suppressed all magic. "Again!"

I kicked out at him again and spun, bringing my elbow down hard on his side,

Max blocked it easily.

I jumped back, ready to go again, forcing my body to obey my will.

He swiped out with the pad, swatting at me as if I were a pesky fly and no more than a mere annoyance. "You need to start a daily run to help increase your stamina," Max said with a shake of his head. "In this room. Make it five miles before I get here every morning."

My face fell, his words almost like a tangible slap to the face. "Are you fucking kidding me? You want me to run five miles *before* the ass crack of dawn and *before* you beat the crap out of me?" I stressed with a scowl and moved to snatch up my water bottle.

"I'll make sure Grey is aware of the adjustment to your training program and you won't have a choice. I heard the sprites can be very convincing," Max said.

"You wouldn't!" I spun on him, my jaw falling open. "You sure like to play dirty."

"One day, you will thank me for it. You need to be fast. Karma will use everything she has at her disposal, including her ability to shift. And if you hadn't already noticed... that kitty has big claws. Now, grab a weapon. You're going to need to be proficient." Max pointed to the weapons wall.

With a renewed surge of energy like a second wind, I bounced excitedly on the balls of my feet. I had been just dying for a chance to learn a weapon. I eyed a beautiful bow, intrigued, and took a step toward it.

Max stopped me with a cluck of his tongue. "Not the bow, at least not yet. You need to learn close combat first," he warned. "Karma isn't going to allow you're the mercy of distance and time."

My shoulders slumped as I ran my fingers over the glittering selection of small knives on display. "What about this?" I asked, watching my reflection shift and distort over its polished blade as I passed.

"No. Not that one, either. That's a throwing knife and you never want to throw away your only weapon," Max snarled as if that should have been damn obvious to a beginner like me. He stomped over to the rack and pulled a sturdy looking dagger from it before placing the perfectly balanced blade in my hand.

I gripped it tightly. The dagger felt good in my grasp, and I slashed out with it experimentally. It felt like a natural extension of myself. "It's perfect," I murmured mostly to myself. The metal glinted under the harsh and unforgiving fluorescent lighting, its beauty as stoic as it was cruel.

"Come at me with it," Max ordered gruffly.

I raised an eyebrow at his empty hands and instinctively twirled the blade in my palm as if it were something I'd done a thousand times before. I'd never really worked with a blade, but it just felt *so* natural. I widened my stance and slashed out as fast as I dared.

Max twirled away from me, too quick for me to strike him. "You must be faster than this! Karma will *not* go easy on you. I expect better. I demand better. Again!" he barked.

I crouched down once more, adopting the fighting stance Max had so ardently spent two hours perfecting. He'd knocked me on my ass so many times that he finally drilled it into my head. Taking a chance, I faked left and then corrected, slashing at him from the right.

Unfortunately for my thinly veiled sense of hope, Max was smarter than that. "You drop your weight to your right foot before you feint to the left. It's a tell, and any opponent worth their salt will pick up on it immediately," Max said as he spun behind me and jabbed me firmly in the kidney with his elbow.

I dropped onto the mat with a cry of frustration and pain.

Fucker isn't pulling his punches. That fucking hurt!

The blade pressed into the mat beneath me as I caught my breath, prostrate on my hands and knees. A towel dropped down next to me, signaling the end of the foray with weaponry for the day. I picked it up gratefully and swiped at my forehead and neck as I sat back on my heels, hurting all over again.

Fucking hell. I need to get fitter.

"Time for a cool down, or your muscles will seize up and you won't be able to crawl out of bed in the morning. So, get on it. I want a one-mile jog on the treadmill," Max ordered, and he stomped out of the room.

The door slammed shut behind him, and I fell back on the mat like a starfish, stretching out my aching limbs. I felt fucked and the only sound to be heard in the whole training room was that of my own heaving breaths. "Why the fuck did Grey hire such a sadist to train me?" I mumbled to myself, permitting myself a micro pity party.

"*Now*, Aurelia!" Max barked from the other side of the thick iron door.

"Motherfucker has super hearing, too," grumbled as I shook my head and peeled myself bodily from the mat. With a half-hearted sigh, I ran the towel over the back of my neck and trudged over to the treadmill.

This fucking sucks.

I pushed the buttons, programming in a slow jog with a subtle incline, and my muscles screamed in protest as I started my one-mile cool down.

Grey's going to pay for this. What does he expect me to do? I'm doing my best, but this is murder.

I gulped down water as I did what I was told. I wasn't going to give up or quit training, but I sure as hell not going to show up with a smile on my face and a kiss-ass attitude. Aside from discovering my magic and Grey, so much of my situation sucked. My humble life had become dangerous and complicated overnight, and if I were being honest, most days I still found myself reeling with the whiplash of it all. I'd gone from being an outcast fairy hiding in plain sight, to being more powerful than I knew how to handle—and that painted a *big* target on my back with neon lights.

As I mused, my muscles slowly worked free of their stiffness. I jogged for about ten minutes, completing my mile, and sighed in relief when it was done and dusted, taking a breather before drinking the last of my water.

Grey had been even more adamant about starting my training off strong after the revelations of the old fairy's visit. I still couldn't remember much from before the alley, and I had no idea what language I'd been speaking in that memory. The only thing that made any sense was that I was speaking the native tongue of the Fae.

I turned the treadmill off with a sigh and stretched my arms over my head before trudging out into the hall beyond, relieved to be outside the heavy, anti-magic wards of the training room. I really needed a shower, but it didn't make sense to do that until after I'd finished all my training for the day, which included my magic session. Exhausted, I flopped into a chair by the kitchen island as the sprites flitted around.

How do they cook when they are so tiny?

They flew about the kitchen glowing a beautiful bright green that reminded me of the forest. Magic trailed behind them in their wake, sparkling like the tail of a glittering comet.

Fiona turned to me with a tiny grin. "Miss Aurelia, how was your training?" Fiona asked.

Freya gasped and turned to me, startled from her activity.

"Terrible," I said shaking my head, before resting my chin on my upturned palm. A tall glass suddenly appeared in front of me with something thick and green inside it, and I grimaced in response, heaving a heavy sigh.

"Don't look at me like that!" Freya wagged a finger at me. "It will help heal your sore muscles."

"What is it?" I asked, picking up the glass and sniffing at its suspicious contents. I didn't completely trust the mischievous sprites. They were good-natured, but could have very well given me something that tasted like ass just to titter and joke about the prank they pulled off. It didn't smell terrible though. It smelled like berries and something vaguely floral.

Both sprites gazed attentively at me, waiting.

I took a tentative sip, and warmth washed through me like a river of sunshine and honey. I groaned in gratitude and gulped it down without further fuss. My muscles relaxed instantly, uncoiling like the tension on a spring released, and the pain from my bruises mercifully ebbed away. "Thank you." I grinned at them, emptying the glass.

"That will teach you to trust us, Miss Aurelia. We would never give you anything that would harm you," Freya whispered, the tone of her voice belaying horror at the mere thought of such a thing.

"I'm sorry, girls. I just had a *really* tough training session with Max." I pushed the empty glass across the counter feeling a hundred times better already.

"Here," said Freya. "You need to refuel for your magic training after being in that gods-awful box for hours!" A moment later, a plate full of sandwiches appeared on the counter in front of me.

"How do you do that?" I asked, picking up a sandwich. My stomach let out an unholy growl, and I grimaced in embarrassment.

"Magic," Freya giggled by way of an answer and flitted away without another word.

I shrugged and bit into the sandwich. Clearly, I wasn't getting any more of an explanation than that.

Grey strolled into the kitchen, bent down, and kissed my sweaty cheek.

"Ew. Don't touch me right now. I'm all gross!" I leaned away from him in an effort to escape his affections.

"Did you have a good training session?" Grey asked, chuckling and shaking his head.

"No," I huffed. "You hired a complete sadist." I scowled at him.

"He's the best trainer available." He took the stool next to me and reached for a sandwich too.

Fiona smacked his hand away without hesitation.

Grey took a leaf out of my book and scowled back at her.

"Those are for Miss Aurelia. She needs to refuel, or she won't be able to perform." The sprite waggled her finger at Grey with a stern expression, reminding me of a nanny swatting at a naughty child trying to steal another cookie from the cookie jar.

"I can't eat all of these, Fiona!" My eyes widened. There were several rounds piled high, all filled to overflowing with the works—fresh meat, cheese, lettuce and tomatoes, coupled with a variety of pickles and spiced relishes that smelled absolutely mouth-watering.

But there's so much! Do they really expect me to eat all of them? They can't be serious?

My stomach growled again at the thought, and I shrugged. I wasn't going to argue with my body. I trusted it to know what it needed.

Well, shit. Maybe I can eat it all, after all.

A plate appeared in front of Grey a heartbeat later, and he nodded with approval, the scowl turning to something that definitely teased at affection for the sprite.

"Yes, Miss Aurelia. You must eat to refuel. The Fae eat *a lot,* especially after having their magic drained the way that awful box does!" Fiona glared at Grey to make her point.

"Hey, don't glare at me. She was the one who agreed to the match with Karma. This is all just helping her learn to fight without her magic." Grey threw his hands up in surrender.

The sprite shot back a stern glare, obviously unimpressed with his answer. She didn't like the training sessions or the aftermath any more than I did.

I snickered at the little sprite's loyalty, touched that she'd stand up to a great big and powerful shifter like Grey, the Syndicate itself.

"Please eat, Miss Aurelia. You need your strength. The Fae burn through their energy rapidly." Fiona nodded to the plate of sandwiches.

She's not going to let me leave the table until I have cleared my whole plate, is she? Bossy little thing.

I finished the sandwich with a dramatic sigh and picked up another, realizing I really was far hungrier than I'd thought.

"Is Magna coming by today?" I asked after swallowing my mouthful, reveling in the heady mix of flavors assaulting my tongue. "I wanted to talk to her about the block on my memories again sometime."

"No," Grey said, but didn't elaborate.

I unconsciously tapped my foot. "Do you know when she might be back?" I asked. I needed answers, and Magna seemed like the one most likely to get them for me. She was ancient and knew more about Faery than anyone we knew—at least that I was aware of.

"She's working on finding the cloaked individual you met as a child," he said cryptically.

My shoulders stiffened at his words. Why did I not like the sound of that? The person had felt somehow familiar in my memory. They had felt almost like family.

It feels like a bad idea to let Grey anywhere near that person, but why? Who am I trying to protect—Grey, myself, or the hooded figure?

"What's wrong?" Grey asked, not missing my reaction.

"I guess it's just... do you think it's a good idea to look for them? They could be dangerous," I said, the white lie leaving my lips before I could think better of it.

Grey sniffed the air, then frowned at me. "You don't believe the words coming out of your own mouth, princess. Why don't you want me to find them?" He turned me to face him in the chair, his level gaze pinning me down with its intensity.

I shoved the last piece of my sandwich into my mouth and then grabbed the last one from the plate, attempting to buy myself time.

What the hell do I say? I don't even understand what I feel... it's confusing.

"Aurelia?" Grey asked, directing my eyes to his.

"I'm not sure," I began hesitantly. "Whoever they are, they felt familiar to me. But I have this horrible feeling that if the two of you were to ever be in the same room as each other, it would be bad for everyone." I shrugged and glanced away, unable to express more clearly what I was feeling.

"We need to find them," Grey said with a sigh. "I have reason to believe they killed the witch who raised you."

I gasped at his words and turned my gaze back to him. He wasn't lying, and the way he didn't refer to her as my mother wasn't lost on me. Could he know how I lived before? And what more did he know?

But that's not possible. He would have had to have gone to my old apartment.

"Grey, what do you mean?" I asked slowly, swallowing the lump that threatened to swell uncomfortably in my throat.

"I had a witch perform a mimic spell to help clear your name of the murder. But the figure revealed in the apartment by the magic was cloaked. They wore a hood over their head, like they had something to hide. Then they stole a book from the witch's safe. One that was meant for you," he finished.

What book could he be talking about? I don't remember any damn book.

"What was so special about this book?" I asked, my brow creasing in consternation. Mother had never mentioned any book, and certainly not one I was supposed to inherit.

"There was a note that the book was with you when you were originally found. Whoever the hooded figure was, I think it's the same person that abandoned you in that alley all those years ago, before the witch fostered you." Grey steepled his hands on the counter in front of him, allowing me time to make sense of it all.

Something about that explanation didn't sit right with me, though I wasn't sure why, and I closed my eyes in thought, dredging through what few memories I possessed.

Could I be wrong about the hooded figure? Could they be out to hurt me?

The intangible feelings of familiarity pulled at me. Who was this mysterious figure and why did they leave me to a life of hiding among the witches? A strange sensation fluttered in my belly, and an intense heat flushed through me, though I couldn't pinpoint why or from where the sensation originated.

Ultimately, I wasn't sure of anyone's true intentions, Grey's included. But I knew somewhere deep down, in a place I couldn't quite reach, that I didn't want to think that Grey would hurt me. But if was true and I trusted the wrong person... everything could be destroyed. My future wasn't the only one at stake. After what Magna had revealed, I felt connected to Faery in a way that almost frightened me.

I don't know what part I'm to play in all of this, but something tells me I'm at the center of something big.

I just needed to find out what it was before it was too late to take action, and I certainly wasn't going to be able to do it alone.

CHAPTER 16
Grey

Without warning, Aurelia slumped to the side, almost taking a tumble from her stool at the kitchen island.

Thanks to my lightning-fast shifter reflexes, I managed to grab and stabilize her before she fell to the marble tiles.

"Don't!" Fiona shouted, her voice shrill as she darted forward.

But it was too late. My eyes closed, and suddenly I was mentally whisked away to an unfamiliar place—a dark alley, cold and alone, huddled on the ground in nothing but a thin coat with rain pelting my skin.

"Are you listening, child?" My eyes widened as a male voice that was somehow strangely familiar sounded in the dirty alley nearby.

Is this Aurelia's memory? How am I seeing this?

"I want to go home!" I pleaded, but it wasn't my voice. It was that of a child's, crying because she was cold and afraid.

"You can't go home. You have a part to play in all this," the hooded man said firmly as he shook his head.

"I don't care about my part. It's cold and lonely here," the girl whimpered.

I knew the Fae were cruel, but this is some next level shit. They abandoned Aurelia. For what, some unknown mission or greater plan?

I growled but the sound never left my mind. I wasn't here to change things. It was just a memory, and I was merely as observer of the past.

Maybe this is the reason she forgot her past. Did I inadvertently make her relive this past trauma by pushing too hard? She clearly blocked all of this out for a reason.

"You must remember your purpose, Aurelia. A small amount of discomfort now will all be worth it in the end," the hooded man assured her.

She was a small, delicate child starving and freezing, exposed to the cruelty of the elements, and he wanted her to remember some grand purpose?

What fucking bullshit!

"I hate it here! How am I supposed to live like this?" she asked in a small, panicked voice, cowering away from the man as he remained utterly impassive.

"Do you have the book?" he asked, completely ignoring her outburst.

The bastard was unfeeling and cold and didn't seem to give a damn that Aurelia was suffering. This wasn't some minor discomfort. Human, Fae, shifter, or witch… if something didn't change, she would die on these streets, cold, alone, and without even the smallest of mercies.

I tried to remind myself that something *did* happen, and she went on to survive the elements. But my wolf was snarling in my mind, instinctively wanting to curl up around her and keep the child warm until help could be found, or we could get out of this place. He didn't understand this wasn't real—all he could see was that our mate was suffering, and we were doing nothing to protect her.

"Yes, I have the book," she answered. Little Aurelia shifted, pulling the thin coat tighter around her small shoulders.

"Do you remember what to do with it?" the man pressed.

"I need to hide it until the time is right," she said, her voice almost a whisper.

What the fuck is that supposed to mean, and how did it eventually end up in the hands of the witch? Did Aurelia hide it in the safe herself? And who wrote the note Dan saw?

"Good. Do not fail me, Aurelia. Everything hinges on this. You must be stronger than you've ever been before," the man said cryptically, and the memory faded.

I still clutched Aurelia tightly and squeezed her a little tighter as she began to stir in my arms.

"What happened?" she asked with a frown, blinking her eyes open. She pulled away from me cautiously and sat straighter on her stool.

Fiona flitted around the kitchen in a frantic buzz and then another plate of fresh sandwiches appeared in front of Aurelia, this time in an array of sweet marmalades, chocolate spreads, and jams.

"Eat, Miss Aurelia! You need sugar, fast. Using so much magic just after having been in the training room is draining," Fiona fussed.

"What do you mean?" Aurelia asked, still a little dazed as she came back to reality but picked up another sandwich as she'd been told to.

"You relived a memory," I told her as evenly as possible. "But once again, it just leaves us with more questions than answers." I clenched my hand into a fist on the counter. I needed to calm the fuck down, but rage bubbled up inside me after seeing the memory for myself. I'd gotten to know my mate in the present, as an adult, but having witnessed her plight as a child, served only to make me and my wolf even more protective and possessive than ever before.

So much conflicting information. How do I protect her and execute my plan?

"Wait, what do you mean? How do you know?" Aurelia asked, rubbing a hand over her forehead.

Freya settled on the counter, her eyes full of empathy and concern for my mate as a cold glass of water materialized within Aurelia's reach.

"You pulled me in, princess. I saw the memory for myself, as if it were my own." I reached out and tucked a lock of hair behind her ear.

"What was the memory?" she asked with a confused frown. "I don't remember that." She shook her head and took another bite of her sandwich before taking a sip of water.

"I think it was more of the same memory you saw previously. You were freezing in the alley and talking to the man in the hood."

My wolf growled in my mind. He still didn't like that one bit, but neither did I.

"How was I able to do that?" She stared down at her hands, fiddling with the bread.

Fiona fluttered closer. "By touch, Miss Aurelia. I tried to warn Master Grey, but it was too late. He wouldn't let you fall!"

I pursed my lips and continued. "You don't remember anything about your purpose or the part you're supposed to play?" I asked. "The memories aren't ringing any bells for you yet?"

She shook her head. "I don't know. It's all still fuzzy. I can't help but wonder if there's a reason I can't remember though, and perhaps it's for the better that I don't." Aurelia chewed her lip nervously.

Indecision warred within me as I pondered if she could be right. In response, my conversation with Magna came back to haunt me.

So, you're saying that she could still take the other side on this? The potential exists that we could wind up as enemies?

"I need to make some calls." I stood from the island and pushed another lock of hair behind her ear affectionately, admiring Aurelia's strength and beauty before taking my leave.

I can't allow her to change her mind. I can't lose my mate and my plans all in one fell swoop. I don't think she would leave us here to rot, but can I really be sure about anything?

I needed to talk to Magna as soon as possible. Careful not to panic or stress her further, I rushed down the hall on light feet and quietly closed the door to my office. My phone rang immediately, and I shook my head as I picked it up.

She really does know more than I ever will.

"Magna," I sighed into the phone as I took my seat, drumming my fingers on my mahogany desk.

"I don't have anything more than you do, Grey. The future is still uncertain. I can't tell you what to do," Magna said sounding just as exasperated as me.

"I know you can't, but have you seen anything that can point me in the direction of the book?" I asked running a hand down my face. The book was meant to be in her possession. She should have hidden it, but somehow the witch had gotten hold of it.

"Just focus on her training and try not to intrude on any more of her memories, that's all I can say," Magna warned.

"It was an accident, for fuck's sake! Should I have let her fall?" I growled at the old seer.

"No, of course not. Your wolf never would have allowed that," she said, then went quiet for a moment. "Grey, speak with Dan. I believe he has something that may be of help."

The call ended, and I growled. The old woman was getting on my nerves, hanging up on me like that all the time.

She has some seriously big lady balls.

I slumped into my chair and dialed Dan, my angst making me feel unreasonably snappy.

He picked up on the first ring.

"Report," I barked into the phone, wincing at my own tone.

"I think I have a lead. Meet me shifter side, boss," Dan said excitedly.

"Shifter side? But the woman murdered was a witch," I reminded him, shaking my head and rolling my eyes.

"I know, but there's been another murder that matches the same MO," Dan said with a groan.

What the fuck? There's been another murder?

"How does a shifter getting offed have anything to do with Aurelia?" I asked, sitting forward in my chair as I tried to piece the puzzle together.

"It's the guy who ran the motel," he explained. "That cheap shithole that I chased her from. He was a hawk shifter, and he was murdered in the motel not long after she was there. There's got to be a connection," Dan said.

Is someone murdering supernaturals who dared show her a scrap of kindness? What purpose would that serve?

I'd have to wait and see. "I'll be there in twenty minutes," I grumbled and hung up the phone. Rising from my comfortable leather chair, I stormed from my office and into the kitchen, but Aurelia wasn't there. Changing direction, I made my way toward the training room where she'd likely be focusing on her magic lessons.

She stood in the middle of the room, purple magic pooling in her hands as she closed her eyes in concentration.

"Sorry to interrupt. I need to head out for a while," I said.

Aurelia spun on me, and her magic went wild, bursting out in all directions, but before it could touch me, it fizzled out, losing its momentum.

"Grey! You scared the fucking shit out of me!" Aurelia yelled in exasperation, throwing her hands up in the air.

"Sorry," I apologized, offering her a sidelong grimace. "I have to go. Don't open the door for anyone." I raised a brow at her to make my point.

She nodded and heaved a sigh, turning her back on me to return to her training.

At least she's showing some serious dedication. She's going to need all the training she can get before she faces off against Karma.

I rushed out of the apartment and within ten minutes was striding up to the skeezy motel where Aurelia had paid for a room. I grimaced. The place was as dingy as motels came and not fit for a human let alone shifters, and especially not my mate.

What had she been thinking, opting for a place like this?

I flinched at my own judgmental thoughts when her memory played out behind my eyes again. She likely had no choice. I sighed with a shudder, and my wolf whined.

She's stayed in worse than this.

"Hey, boss."

Dan's voice startled me from my thoughts.

"Where was he found?" I asked and moved toward him.

He had dark purple bags under his eyes, and he looked somber. He was clearly exhausted. "It's bad, boss. I know she didn't do it because she was with you, but no one in the supe community does, and they are calling her a wannabe serial killer." He shook his head.

"Show me!" I barked, just about ready to start slitting throats.

Dan led me into the motel lobby and through a door that went out to the back. He pulled a key from his pocket. He stopped in front of a door with a boarded-up window. "This is the exact room she was in when I found her. There was a note of her name and room number at the front desk, too." Dan put the key in the lock and wiggled it until the lock clicked open.

"Get hold of management after we're done here and make sure this place is closed down until upgrades can be made. This is a right fucking shithole." I shook my head and stepped inside behind him.

"Yes, boss. I'll see it's done," Dan said and followed me inside.

"What the fuck?" I asked with wide eyes as I stared at the macabre sight that greeted me. "I thought you said it was the same MO, Dan?" I folded my arms across my chest.

"Blaming Aurelia is the same MO, right?" he answered. "Last time they left her on the floor to take the blame... and this time, well *this*." He grimaced as if the situation explained itself.

Aurelia's name was written in blood above the headboard on the wall.

Why the fuck would the shifters assume this was done by her, when it was clearly left as a warning directed at *her?*

"That wasn't done with the intention of blaming her, Dan. It's a warning *to* her. She's not safe. Whoever murdered the witch and the shifter are dangerous. This is no coincidence." I took a step deeper into the room and pulled my phone out of my pocket.

I don't care if calling the facility is ill advised, I need to know what happened here right fucking now, and I only know one person who can do that.

"Boss?" Layla asked when she picked up the phone.

"I'm sending you an address. I need Karma to do another mimic spell and if I have to wait as long as the two of you made Dan wait last time, then you'll both be punished for your insolence, and it won't be pretty," I said and hung up the phone promptly.

I scanned the room, engaging my keen wolf senses, and walked around to the other side of the bed. My gaze immediately locked on a small slip of paper that was on the floor, partially hidden by the shadow of the bed in the dim lighting. I bent over and picked it up. The flowing script was in a language I recognized but had never learned how to read. Aurelia's name was written on it in, but that was all I could make out. "Whoever did this, is Fae," I growled, my gut burning with a smoldering rage.

Could it be the same hooded figure from Aurelia's memory? What purpose would this stunt serve when he was the one who abandoned her to our realm in the first place? Or at least I think he's the one who sent her here... but why?

I pulled the camera up on my phone and snapped a quick picture of the note, sending it to Magna instantly. Maybe she would be able to read the language better than I could.

Dan wandered out twenty minutes later to await Karma's arrival.

She and Layla walked in minutes later with shocked expressions on their faces.

"What is that?" Karma, the half-witch half-white-tiger-shifter asked, pointing at the name drawn in blood.

"What does it look like, you fucking idiot?" I barked. "Just do what I asked."

Layla raised a brow at me in response, but I was beyond over both of their bullshit.

Karma wandered around the room shaking her head. "Shit," she said. "I can't believe she did this."

My temper flared even brighter. "For fuck's sake, woman. She didn't do it! Have shifters lost their collective common sense over night?" I crossed my arms over my chest, simmering.

It's clearly a threat directed at Aurelia! Why the fuck would she write her own name in blood?

"Are you sure?" she retorted with more attitude than was wise. "The signature is the same. It smells like her in here, too."

Layla took a step forward, following Karma.

"She hasn't left the fucking apartment, and before that she was at the facility. It wasn't her!" I shook my head.

I've really got to tighten up my vetting process. What good are strong fighters to the Syndicate when they're morons?

My phone buzzed in my hand, and I peered down at it with a curse.

It was Magna.

SOS. You need to get home! Now.

My back straightened, and I growled low in my throat, my hackles rising. Something was wrong at the apartment. A chill shivered up my spine, and a sense of foreboding dread slithered into my soul.

Fuck.

If I didn't get there soon, would I lose my mate forever? There was no way on fucking Earth I was going to wait around to find out. Without a word of explanation to my crew, I turned and ran like the very fires of Hell were on my tail.

CHAPTER 17

Aurelia

My instructor for magic control training was not as much of a sadist as Max was.

Thank the gods.

I didn't think I could put up with being butchered for a second time in one day—physically then magically.

Talk about punishment.

"Center yourself, Aurelia. Remember, you control the flow of your magic, not your emotions," Reah offered softly.

She'd figured out pretty quickly that if she raised her voice at me when my eyes were closed, that it didn't go so well. It turned out that I lost control with more than just Grey and his shifters, and it was something that needed to be remedied.

I took a deep breath and pulled my magic back. I wasn't sure how this would help me in a scuffle, though. If I was fighting with my magic, I wouldn't be able to close my eyes and center myself to control it.

I should be learning how to manipulate my magic on the fly. I should be able to wield it no matter how I feel. Angry, sad, panicked, elated—it shouldn't matter. What use is my magic if I can't use it at will, whenever I need to, no matter the situation? This is frustrating as hell.

"Aurelia, you're losing focus. Concentrate," Reah said, calmly interrupting my train of thought.

I banished the thoughts from my mind and tried again to focus on the flow of my magic. It had gotten out of control again. Reigning it back in, I allowed myself to adjust to how it felt. The way it flowed through me, sparking like lightning before whispering along my veins to erupt in my palms.

Shit. Don't lose focus. You've got this, Aurelia. I need to do this for me, and I need to make progress for Grey and the Syndicate. I help him and he helps me...

"Okay, now I want you to attack me with your magic," Reah instructed.

I cracked an eye open, my brows knitting as I tried my best to maintain my focus while also holding a conversation. "Um, are you sure about that, Re? Shouldn't I use a target or something instead, first?" I asked incredulously. "I don't want to hurt you."

"Don't worry, sweetheart. I'm a lot faster than I look." She smirked, looking like an absolute bad-ass with a case of serious over-confidence.

She's not a sadist! She's a damn masochist. What was Grey thinking when he hired these people? They are both freaking insane.

Sucking in a deep breath, I sighed.

All right. Have it your way. Let it be forever on the record that I tried to warn you!

Narrowing my focus to a pinpoint, I let my magic pool in my palm and stared down at the crackling purple spark of magic, willing it to grow and expand. My powers answered my summons eagerly, and the glittering mass grew to the size of a golf ball before I flung it at Reah.

The woman disappeared just before my magic would have connected with her chest, likely searing a blazing hole straight through her—though I had no way of knowing what the effects of my magic were just yet. I hadn't had an occasion to use it that way to find out.

"Too slow!" she taunted.

I spun around at the sound of her voice, almost throwing myself off balance in my haste.

Damn it. How the fuck did she do that? She literally just disappeared right before my eyes and then reappeared like a rabbit being pulled from a magician's hat!

"With enough practice, you will be able to do the same," Reah assured me with a bright grin. "It's early days. You're only just beginning to learn what you're capable of."

"Can you read my mind now, too?" I asked in frustration.

I'm in so deep over my head here.

Refusing to permit my failure to drag me down, I threw another ball of magic before she could answer me.

She disappeared again without a trace, without so much as even a blur of motion, and her giggle soon met my ears from somewhere to the left.

"No, I can't read your mind, Aurelia. But your question was written all over your face," she called. "You're going to have to practice your poker face, too!"

I turned to her and faked a throw, keeping the sizzling spark of my purple magic firmly in hand.

Just as I had hoped, she disappeared from sight, reacting to my move, preempting my strike.

I spun around to my other side and launched my magic in the opposite direction, releasing it as it grew with my intent.

Reah reappeared, only to throw up a shield-wall in front of her at the last second, my magic shattering against the glowing forcefield like purple diamond dust.

"Good!" she sang with a smile. "You're starting to think like a real fighter and you're anticipating my next move. It's not something that can be taught that easily." Reah nodded to me, happy to bequeath her approval and congratulate me on my fast learning.

I'd literally almost just lit her up with magic and she was praising me? What the hell.

She really is insane.

"Um, thanks?" I answered, though it was more of a question.

"Let's go again," my instructor encouraged as she placed her hands on her hips.

I funneled magic into both hands this time, willing it to blaze strong and waited for my opening, but she anticipated everything I tried. I faked left and went right, but she was probably noticing the same tell as Max had. Desperate to land a hit, I dodged left at the last second, trusting instinct alone. With everything I had, I threw my magic just in front of her, going for a direct hit.

To my sick delight, she wasn't able to stop her momentum in time and slammed right into my shimmering magic. She was flung back several feet through the air before she disappeared mid-flight. Then she landed in an ungainly heap on the mat in front of me.

"What the fuck! Oh, my gods! Are you okay?" I asked, rushing to crouch down next to her.

Reah burst into a fit of raucous laughter as she held out a hand for me to take. "That was fucking brilliant, Aurelia! You've got some serious power, there. We can work with that."

With a relieved smile, I helped her up from the mat just as a *crash* like broken glass sounded from the living room. I immediately tensed.

Would the sprites be so clumsy as to break something? Surely, they would be able to avert any slip-up with their magic?

Reah took a step in front of me, and her silver magic coated her palms. "Hide, Aurelia. There's an intruder in the house." She squared her shoulders bravely, never once glancing back to see if I obeyed.

Who the fuck would be stupid enough to break into Grey's penthouse? Do they have a death wish?

My mind boggled at the thought of someone raising the wolf shifter's ire intentionally.

"Aurelia, hide now. That's an order!" Reah hissed under her breath.

I didn't want to leave her—she'd fast become the friendliest person I knew—but what could I do? I wasn't battle-ready yet, not by a long shot.

Who the fuck is in the penthouse and why?

I backed away from Reah but the room we were in was void of anything I could possibly hide behind. "Reah, there's nowhere to hide in here," I whispered back, filling my palms with magic.

"Fine. Follow me out the door and as soon as you're clear, run to the magicless training room and stay there." Reah moved to the door, anticipating action.

"Why there? I won't be able to use magic!" I asked, confusion furrowing my brow.

"If they go inside to look for you then you will have an advantage as they won't have magic either," Reah said, exasperated.

"All right, but you haven't seen me fight without magic." I shook my head but followed in her wake toward the closed door.

She pressed her ear to the door to listen, but our ears were met by silence.

What is going on out there? Where are Freya and Fiona? Are they okay?

"Focus, Aurelia," Reah snapped at me.

I glanced at my hands and breathed in deeply.

Fuck.

The magic in my hands had grown much larger than it had been before. With conscious effort, I stopped the flow of magic but kept the glimmering purple projectiles the size they were. I was sure as hell wasn't getting rid of my only available weapon.

Reah frowned, opened the door a crack and scanned the hall. "On three," she said.

"What?" I asked.

"Three!' she announced with a cackle and jumped headlong into the hall like a Valkyrie from human legend.

"What the hell happened to one and two?" I grumbled as I sprinted out behind her, taking my chance.

Reah lobbed a gleaming silver ball of magic down the hall.

I gasped as I barely caught sight of a hooded figure ducking out of the way.

Is that the man from my memory? What is he doing here?

"Now, Aurelia, go!" Reah screamed.

I shook my head to clear it and ran for the heavy metal door of the magicless training room. I needed to get inside, just as Reah instructed. It would be my only advantage against whoever was after me.

A crash sounded nearby, followed by a feminine grunt and I prayed to the gods that Reah and the sprites were okay as I pushed through the door with all my might. My knees nearly buckled beneath me as my magic fizzled out instantly, snuffed out by the wards of the room like a candle in a storm. I took a handful of calming breaths as I straightened my shoulders, adjusting.

I scanned the room for a weapon and cursed Max for not letting me practice with the bow. Now wasn't the time to opt for a close-range weapon. I'd already proven time and time again that I wasn't fast enough just yet. And I sure as hell didn't want to get close and personal with the intruder if I could avoid it. Taking my chances, I ran to the weapons wall and grabbed the bow down. A tingle ran down my spine with a strange sense of familiarity.

My instincts took over then and I nocked an arrow, pointing it at the only entrance to the room. I started at another crash that sounded closer than the last. Licking my lips, I altered my stance and prepared for the worst.

What is going on out there? Should I risk looking?

I took a step toward the door when the handle suddenly turned, and my stomach dropped.

A hiss filled the air as the hooded figure took a step inside.

"Who are you?" I demanded, pulling back the string of the bow, ready to fire.

"What? You don't remember me?" the intruder asked, his tone one of hurt.

Why the fuck would he sound hurt that I don't remember him? Who is he to me?

Pushing the questions plaguing me aside, I tried again. "Did you kill my mother?" I barked ignoring his initial response.

The hooded figure stepped back out of the room, loitering on the threshold with his hands raised. "That witch was not your mother," he snarled.

It wasn't lost on me that he failed to answer my question.

"How did you know I was talking about the witch?" I growled, stepping forward as a sense of purpose and strength filled me.

He was in the hall now.

Will he be able to subdue me with magic from the outside?

"You have the wrong idea, Aurelia. I don't want to hurt you. I'm here to rescue you. It's finally time to go home," he said, his tone taking on a pleading quality, as if willing me to understand.

"I'm not going anywhere with you!" I yelled back with fire in my heart. "You were the man who left me freezing in the alley, weren't you? I told you I wanted to go home, and you left me there! I was just a child!" I accused bitterly.

"I was, yes," he answered, sounding somewhat remorseful.

But I refused to buy into his bullshit. I had no reason whatsoever to trust this asshole. "You need to leave now. Grey will be back soon, and if you've hurt any of my friends, I will fucking hunt you down!" I held the arrow steady and took another step toward the door with conviction.

Please be all right, girls.

"You need to remember, Aurelia, and if you refuse, I will make you." The man lunged suddenly through the door, taking me by surprise as he knocked the bow from my hands.

The weapon slid across the mat, too far away for me to reach. The air all but rushed out of me in a violent *whoosh* as he tackled me to the ground.

I brought my elbow up, intending to smack it against his temple, hopeful it would disorient him for a moment or two, allowing me the opportunity to clamber to my feet.

He dodged my maneuver with uncanny speed, thwarting my plan.

Pain crashed through me as my blow landed on his shoulder instead.

"You have to remember!" he grunted. "If you don't, all is lost."

"I don't want to remember!" I shouted. "I don't want to remember being left in the cold or the fucking reason behind it!"

Shit. I'm talking too much. Just fuck this guy up!

My assailants hood never moved as he pinned me to the mat, his identity still predominantly a mystery to me. "You don't have a choice, Aurelia," he spat back as he swung his fist at my head.

I blocked him easily and it buoyed my inner pride. My training was paying off!

Where the fuck is everyone? Are they okay? If he hurt them, I will find a way to fucking kill him.

I blocked another hit aimed at my face and managed to get my legs around his middle and bucked my hips, trying in vain to dislodge him. He felt like a lead weight on my body.

He pushed down into me again, dominating me with the clear advantage of his physical strength.

I lashed out with my fists, punching wildly, anywhere I could connect with.

His hands caught mine in a bruising grip and forced them above my head. "You are mine. You were promised to me!" he snarled in my face.

I laughed mirthlessly. "And you left me to die in the fucking cold, asshole. I don't care about whatever claim you think you have on me. I will *never* be yours and I will never help you. Fuck you!" I snarled, thrashing bodily against him in frustration and rage.

"Remember me, damn it!" he roared and pulled the hood from his head with his free hand.

Without warning, memories assaulted me, and I gasped, my eyes growing wide. This man was with me in a vibrant, never-ending green field picking breathtaking wildflowers. Then he was sitting beside my bed, reading me stories from a book I didn't recognize. The memories shifted again, and he was taking me from my bed, throwing his cloak over me as he stole me away from the castle.

What the fuck? Hold the hell up here! The castle?

I could hear the hounds being set free as he ran with me in his arms, shielded by his soft brown cloak.

"I wasn't given away by my parents?" I asked in horror through the memory, breaking through into the present.

He took me from them, then brought me here and left me to die?

"No," he said and loosened his grip.

Wrong move, asshole.

I broke his grasp on my wrists and punched him square in his overly pretty face. "I trusted you, Malcolm!" I hissed. "You were my friend and then you kidnapped me from my bed and left me to die. What the fuck?"

"You once understood why," he said, nursing his jaw. "Our kingdom will never be safe if the other supernaturals are allowed to return. You understood what your role would be as a child." His words left me in shock, and he took the opportunity to wrap his hand around my wrists again before he lifted me and slammed me back down onto the mat.

Pain accompanied by dancing stars exploded behind my eyes, and I found myself winded and reeling as darkness closed in all around me.

At the same moment a shout filled the air, originating from the living room.

"Go to sleep, my love," my once friend soothed. "I'm taking you home, and then we will finish what we started all those years ago," he promised, sounding like an absolute fucking deluded psycho. Not a heartbeat later, Malcolm smashed his fist into my cheek.

Pain blinded me, and my entire skull vibrated, the world tilting violently sideways before I was sucked into the welcoming embrace of sweet oblivion.

CHAPTER 18
Grey

The elevator doors opened, and smoke billowed inside, making my eyes sting and my nose tingle.

What the fuck happened? How did someone get past my wards?

The usually lush and green moss-covered couch was covered in still-smoldering scorch marks, while vases and pots lay smashed, their water and soil spilled from asshole to breakfast. My heart twinged, and as much as I loathed the way the girls had redecorated my penthouse with plants, I missed the fragrant and colorful flowers that dotted the space. They made this lavish place feel like a home, while the odor of charred furniture and acrid smoke coupled with the devastation before me raised my ire and made me feel violated.

"Aurelia!" I shouted into the eerie silence of my smoldering high rise home, but there was no answer, and my stomach lurched.

Has she been taken?

My wolf growled in my mind, his fury boiling to the surface like a geyser waiting to explode. He would hunt down the bastard who took her if that's what turned out to be true—and he would not rest until our mate was found.

Neither of us will.

"Fiona? Freya? Hello? Where is everyone?" I yelled and pushed through the destruction of my home, panic rising by the second.

A groan from the hall filled my ears and I raced to the lump on the ground, recognizing who it was immediately. "Reah, where's Aurelia?" I asked, dropping to a crouch by her side. The distinct scent of blood flooded my senses. She looked like she'd taken a brutal beating, which meant she'd done her job. She'd been loyal when it mattered most and tried to protect my mate with her own life.

"Safe, I hope," she groaned as she tried to sit up.

I pushed her shoulder down, encouraging her not to move, and pulled out my phone, dialing Magna.

"On my way now," Magna answered.

"Hurry!" I barked.

Blood continued to gush from Reah's head, and though she was one of the strongest half-Fae's I had ever met, she could still bleed out.

Shit.

"Where is Aurelia?" I asked again, removing my shirt and pressing it to the wound to try and staunch the blood flow until help arrived.

"Magicless room," Reah slurred, blinking repeatedly as she fought to remain conscious.

I propped her up against the wall and guided her hand to take hold of my now bloodied shirt. "Keep the pressure on as best you can," I instructed and nodded my thanks. "Help will be here soon."

It was a smart move, sending her to the magicless training room since no one else would be able to use magic against Aurelia while she was inside. She'd have stood a fighting chance, at least against an older and superior magic user on a levelled play field.

The destruction continued down the hall, but there was no sign of an intruder or my mate. I roared as I raced to the door, but just as I burst through, it was clear no one was inside the room. The bow lay abandoned on the mat, and Aurelia was gone. I could smell her. She'd been here, and it was still strong. I'd only just missed them.

If only I'd been faster!

A string of unholy obscenities spilled from my lips, and my inner wolf howled in my head, pushing his way forcefully to the surface. My hands turned to anthropomorphic paws ending in lethal claws. As I clenched them into fists, they dug into my palms, and I felt the telltale warmth of my own blood. I punched the wall in frustration and rage. Blood coated my knuckles as they split, but it didn't stop me from punching it again and again, until my hands were a macabre, scarlet mess.

A throat cleared behind me, and I spun to find Magna. I glared at her with the rage of a thousand suns as I turned. "You knew this would happen!" I roared, unable to hold back the pain. "You *knew* and you still told me to go meet with Dan."

The seer was fucking lucky that she was more powerful than me and that we had a working friendship, or I'd have painted the walls in her entrails.

Why the fuck did she tell me to go?

"No matter how uncertain the future, this was always going to happen. It was a trigger point in the timeline." Magna shook her head regretfully.

"And what is that supposed to mean?" I fired back, shaking my hand out to ease the pain. Blood still oozed from my battered knuckles, but they were already healing, thanks to my shifter.

"It means that no matter our actions or choices leading up to this moment, this event was always meant to happen. The rest is up to Aurelia and what she decides to do," Magna explained with a sigh. "This acts as a catalyst for a great change."

"And you think I'm just going to let this fucking psycho keep my mate?" I scoffed.

There's a better chance Hell will freeze over. She's mine!

"Think about this, Grey. How did he know that Aurelia was here without you?" Magna asked.

"He's a damn seer!" I threw my hands up in the air, my expression contorted.

"Is he? Are you sure? Or was he simply following Aurelia all this time and knew where to find people she had interacted with?" Magna raised a questioning eyebrow.

He's not a seer? Then how did he know that I was gone? Fuck!

"Someone told him," I snarled as the realization slammed into me with the force of a fucking truck. "Only a handful of people knew I wasn't here. I've been betrayed!" I stomped past the old woman and back to the hall where Reah was propped up against the wall where I'd left her.

The half-Fae's eyes widened at my angry glare and heavy approach.

"Did you tell the psycho that you were alone with my mate with only a couple sprites for company?" I raged, wrapping my hand around her throat and cutting her air off.

Reah choked, her eyes bulging in fear as she struggled against me in her already weakened state.

"It wasn't Reah, Grey," Magna called out from behind me, her voice firm.

I released Aurelia's magic instructor spun on the seer. "Well, that leaves you, Dan, Layla and Karma. And if I find out *you* did this, playing God for some favorable future outcome, I will find a way to end you, Magna!" I crossed my arms over my chest, my gaze narrowing into blazing pinpoints of gold as my wolf tried pushing through once more.

"I've already told you it wasn't me, Grey. And it certainly wasn't Reah. She tried to protect your mate. If you pause and allow your logic to overcome your emotions, you'll realize that deep down in your gut, you know who it was." She shook her head with a frown at my denial.

No. I refuse to believe it's who I suspect. It can't be! She's been with me forever, since I began the Syndicate.

"You have to be wrong, Magna. It can't be Layla. I won't believe it. She might have her faults, but she has been my second since we were exiled here!" I said and punched the wall nearest me. Plaster rained down, covering the floor in fragments and dust as I pulled my fist from inside the wall.

"I didn't say it was Layla," she answered calmly. "She would make the most sense though, wouldn't she?"

"She's been acting strange since I found Aurelia. She seems almost jealous, but would she really be willing to sell us out in exchange for Aurelia to be kidnapped?" I ran a hand through my hair, matting it with my own blood. "Or, if it wasn't Layla, it has to have been Karma. She hated my mate from day one. She issued the challenge, for fuck's sake! Or perhaps they're working together on this? I don't fucking know."

"This is all how it should be, Grey. And now is the time that you figure out the path you want to walk. Everything you do from here on out is shaping your future," Magna said, almost as though she were in a trance-like state.

"First, I need to find the sprites. Then we need to formulate a plan to find my mate and bring her home!" I stomped off and into the living room, kicking debris from my path. I turned over the coffee table that was on its side and scorched with elemental magic. A few of the plants were still smoking, and as I walked past them, dread pooled in my gut. If the sprites were unhurt, Aurelia's plants would have already begun the process of healing.

This does not bode well.

"Fiona? Freya? Where are you?" I called out as I sifted chaotically through the rubble, worried I'd find them crushed like fragile dragonflies beneath the ruin.

Maybe they were in the kitchen when the bastard came in and were simply hiding?

I pushed through the door into the kitchen, only to discover that everything was in perfect order. My brow furrowed in consternation. Why had the intruder come through the hall and not even bothered with the kitchen if he wasn't a seer? How could he have known where to look for Aurelia?

Fuck. It has to be Layla, doesn't it?

I growled at the betrayal. How could she do this to me? Was she really so damn jealous that she would have organized to have my mate kidnapped? What was her angle? What did she want? My attention? My affection?

What the fuck! I've never been interested in her that way!

I opened the door to the pantry in frustration but there was still no sign of the sprites. I spun around and marched back to the hall to find Magna tending to Reah.

"Reah, did you see the sprites?" I asked as I rounded on her for the second time.

She was still slumped against the wall, wincing as she received care. "No, I didn't see them. I just figured they were in the kitchen."

"They aren't there," I grumbled.

"Did you look in all the cabinets?" Reah asked, her shoulders barely rising as she shrugged.

I turned around and stormed back to the kitchen. If I didn't find them hiding in the cabinets, I didn't know what I would do. I'd already lost Aurelia, I couldn't lose them too. I loved those flitty little critters more than I cared to admit. I flung open every cabinet in the kitchen, pushing aside pots and pans and dishes As I called out to them to let them know it was safe... but there was no answer.

"They aren't hiding in the kitchen." I hung my head as despair clawed at my insides.

Magna rushed to join me in the room as fast as her old bones could carry her, and a grin parted her lips.

"What is it?" I asked, a part of me hopeful she'd seen something that could help us in this shitshow we'd found ourselves in.

"Those sneaky sprites," she chuckled. "They're with Aurelia!"

"How the fuck did they manage that?" I ran a hand through my hair as I paced.

"I'm not sure, but they are safe. And when the time comes, *that's* how we find Aurelia!" Magna said.

"What do you mean 'when the time comes'?" I growled.

I can't sit back and let them stay with that madman! What is she thinking?

"We have no way of knowing where he's taken them," Magna answered all too reasonably. "What do you suggest we do but wait until the sprites are able to escape and lead us there?" She planted her hands on her hips, her gaze stern.

She was right, of course, but I was loathe to think about what might happen to her while she was with that psycho hooded freak. He could hurt them. He could do anything, and I wouldn't be there to protect them.

My wolf snarled in my mind and thrashed inside my chest. He was *very* close to the surface and ready to shift right here and now.

I took a huge cleansing breath through my nose in an effort to push him back, and a scent caught in it like a butterfly snatched up in a net. "That scent," I started. "Why is it similar to Aurelia's?" I asked as I followed it down the hall and into the magicless room.

"He's Fae. They have similar scents," Magna called after me, returning to her injured charge.

"This is different," I called back as I investigated further. "It's like their scents are tied together somehow. I'm not sure. I can't make sense of it." I shook my head as I walked over to the bow on the floor and picked it up. I placed it back on the wall where it belonged and sighed as if the small semblance of order might somehow soothe my raging beast.

This fucking blows! I can't just sit here, idle and do nothing... and why would their scents be tied together? Who is he to her?

My wolf snarled again and beat desperately against the cage in which I kept him. There was no reason to allow him to lose control when there was no one to punish. It was pointless. No matter how much I hated this, I had to try to keep a clear head on my shoulders. I was the Syndicate. I was better than this.

Keep it together, Grey. For Aurelia.

Magna's soft footsteps followed me to the door but stopped short of crossing the threshold. She hated this room just as much as any magic user did. The wards were oppressive, heavy, and suffocating until you adjusted to them—and even then, it felt like a tangible burden.

"Dan needs to come and check this out," she said, a hint of anxiety seeping through into her usually stoic and wise voice.

"I'm not bringing any of them into my home! They caused this, and my wolf will go *insane*." I shook my head vehemently, clenching my fists at my sides.

My wolf already adamantly wanted to hunt Layla and Karma down and destroy them, along with the hooded Fae who'd stolen our mate from us. He wasn't the only one, but we had to do this in such a way that none of them would ever see it coming. I couldn't have my prey fleeing before I had the chance to sink my claws into them.

They owe me blood, and I will have it.

"Grey, are you sure it's wise not to call on them when you need help with something like this? You could end up making them suspicious. They may suspect that you know what they are up to. You'd lose the element of surprise." Magna raised a brow.

"They wouldn't be able to do anything here, anyway. It's a no-magic zone. Karma's mimic spell won't work in this room." I scanned the room with a frown, my gaze roaming over the empty space that should have safely contained my mate.

"It may be worth it to find out where he entered the property from and what he did in the moments before he came down the hall," Magna suggested thoughtfully.

She wasn't wrong, again, but I hated the thought of having traitors in my space. How was I going to keep my wolf from tearing them apart when they came in here? And how could I keep them away from Aurelia's surviving plants and flowers? They didn't fucking deserve to enjoy her magic when they were the reason she was gone.

But she's right, damn it.

"Fine," I huffed and pulled my phone from my pocket like it was a lead brick covered in thorns. I really didn't want to do this.

"Boss?" Dan asked on the first ring, sounding surprised.

"Are Layla and Karma still there?" I asked, keeping my tone as even as my emotions and inner wolf would permit.

"Yes, they wouldn't leave until you returned," he grunted back.

Like that's not fucking suspicious.

"I need you all to come to the penthouse. There's been an attackm and Aurelia was kidnapped. I need some kind of lead if I'm going to find her."

"We'll be right there." Dan hung up the phone before I could respond.

I punched the wall again angrier than ever.

Fuck! People need to stop doing that before I let my wolf out, and he takes a chunk out of them.

"They're on their way," I growled, informing Magna and Reah as I paced the room. I was careful not to touch anything else until they arrived, and Karma started the spell, in case it hurt our chances of finding anything useful.

Fifteen minutes of pacing was getting on my nerves when the elevator door dinged and finally opened, revealing Dan and the others.

"What the hell happened here, boss?" Dan asked with wide eyes.

"I told you, we were attacked," I answered tersely as I turned and scanned the room. I had to turn my back on the women. My wolf was snarling at me, pushing his way to the surface, ready to tear both those bitches a new fucking asshole.

"Not that... I mean, yeah, your penthouse is wrecked, but is your couch covered in moss?" Dan covered his laugh with a cough.

"Aurelia has been learning some new skills, and the sprites got a bit overzealous in supporting her." I shrugged, a pang of loss painfully needling its way into my heart again.

"Where is Aurelia?" Layla asked from behind Dan as she gazed about, drinking in the destruction.

"She was kidnapped," I growled, rounding on her.

"What?" she asked with wide eyes. Clearly, Dan had not communicated the details of our call. That, or she was playing fucking dumb and insulting my intelligence.

"What about my challenge?" Karma shrieked, her eyes flashing, startling us all with the intensity of her vitriolic venom.

I glared at her, barely able to keep my wolf from launching for her goddamn throat. "She's been fucking kidnapped. What do you think?"

Is this shifter-witch for real? She's making this about her? Seriously?

"You're here to do a job and you will do that job without complaint, or you'll find yourself no longer welcome at the facility or employed by the Syndicate." I punched the wall again to demonstrate my point.

They were quite happily pushing every button I had and doing a shitty job of convincing me they weren't involved in her disappearance. The women were just lucky I was biding my time for the moment, but their luck would run out soon enough.

Their days spent breathing and above ground are officially on fucking countdown.

CHAPTER 19

"Miss," a small tinkling voice whispered next to my ear insistently with an edge of fear.

My eyes felt heavy and sticky, and I couldn't open them easily. I groaned in response, grimacing as I struggled to regain a firm grasp on consciousness.

"Aurelia, you have to wake up!" The shrill voice was followed by a small hand tapping on my cheek.

What the hell?

I cracked one eye open, blinking myself awake with all the energy I had.

Wait? Why was I asleep?

As if on cue, my skull throbbed, and I winced. Everything seemed so hazy. "What happened?" I slurred as I fought to sit up. Someone had laid me in a bed and even tucked me in, but the room itself was unfamiliar. I forced my other eye open and rubbed them hard, trying to shed the sense of fatigue that clung to my mind.

Where the fuck am I? And why are the sprites staring at me with concern?

"Miss, you were taken from our home," Fiona said, wringing her tiny hands in her lap. "It's not safe here!"

I shot up at that, and the room spun violently, lurching like I imagined the crew on the deck of a ship at sea might during a storm. It made my stomach heave, and I swallowed hard to keep the sour bile in my belly where it belonged.

Fuck. That was stupid.

My brain felt like mush as I glanced between each sprite. "What are you doing here?" I managed, the memory of my fight with Malcom surging back to me with dizzying clarity.

"We couldn't let him take you all alone!" Freya planted her hands on her little hips and glared at me like I'd asked the single most ridiculous question in the world.

"It's too dangerous for you," I argued. "Malcolm is delusional. He thinks the Fae are in danger if we let the supernaturals back into Faery. You need to get back to Grey as soon as you can. He's going to worry about you." I shook my head as I pinched the bridge of my nose, trying to center my focus.

"But we are here to help," Freya said adamantly.

I couldn't let them do this. If they got hurt or killed, Grey would never forgive me. We all joked about the sneaky sprites, but we all loved them fiercely, Grey especially. "You can't help me," I said with a sad smile. "Grey will be devastated if anything happens to you two. He needs you."

"He will never recover if we don't make sure you come back!" Freya snarked before she flew up in my face and flicked my nose.

I swatted at her lazily. "That's bullshit. He just wants me for a job. For some plan of his." But even as I said the words, I didn't believe them myself... not entirely. The way he looked at me and the way that he touched me showed me how he really felt, even if he hadn't told me in so many words.

Both sprites glared at me with renewed fervor.

"That's not true, and you know it, Miss Aurelia!" Freya planted her hands on her hips and Fiona followed suit.

"Fine, but still you shouldn't have hitched a ride with me. It's dangerous." I threw my hands up. We had no idea what this guy wanted or what he would do to them if he found them. I touched my head and winced at the throbbing pain there.

Ouch. Did the fucker knock me out?

The sound of light footsteps alerted me to someone coming, and I widened my eyes at the sprites to alert them of the approaching danger. "Quick! Hide," I whispered.

They buzzed their way into the open closet and hid as I'd instructed.

The door opened, and Malcolm stood there with a radiant smile. He didn't have the cloak on now, his face was clearly visible, and he was just as I remembered him. His was an ethereal beauty, but I noted it as if from afar. I wasn't attracted to him at all. In fact, I scowled at him. If I ever had a soft spot for this guy, I certainly didn't anymore.

"You're awake," he said, his tone bright before his blond eyebrows drew down in a frown.

I continued scowling and remained silent.

Fuck you, Malcolm.

"Come on, Aurelia. Don't you remember me?" he asked.

"I remember you, but I don't know why you brought me here," I answered tersely and crossed my arms over my chest defensively.

"I brought you here because it's almost time for us to go home," he said and took a step into the room.

I scooted back on the bed trying to get away from him—trying to put as much distance between us as I could. I didn't want to go wherever he thought was my home. I barely remembered anything about this man. He was no more to me than a few disjointed memories at best.

He left me for dead. I can't trust anything he says.

"You hit me in the head and then kidnapped me from Grey's. Not to mention the fact you left me in a cold alley to freeze to death as a child. And now you want me to trust you?" I scoffed.

"It was all for a good reason. I wish you could remember our plans," he said and sighed. "What did you do to block your memories, Aurelia?"

"What do you mean, I blocked my memory?" I asked with a frown that mirrored his own.

Could I have done this to myself? Why would I do that? How does a child have enough power to create a block like that? Even Magna couldn't remove it!

"There's no way that pathetically weak witch successfully put a block that strong on you. Your old friend would have removed it easily if that were the case." He took another step closer.

"I don't want you to come any closer," I said as I leaned back into the headboard defiantly, denying him what he clearly wanted—to be near me.

"You are meant to be mine, Aurelia. We were tied together at your birth," he growled in frustration, losing his beautiful and treacherous mask of calm.

What the fuck? He can't be serious! Just no. There is no way I'm going to be with this psycho. I mean, what the fuck... an arranged marriage since infancy? Fucking gross. What is wrong with these people?

"Good thing we aren't in the Fae realm then, huh?" I snarked back, crossing my arms over my chest.

"Get up and follow me," Malcolm ordered as he skulked back to the door. He glanced over his shoulder, waiting for me to comply to his wishes.

"Where are you taking me?" I asked, refusing to move.

Like hell I'm going to make anything easy for him.

"Your magic is out of control and it's time to train. I can't believe you thought that mutt and his half-blood colleagues could teach you magic." He shook his head with a dark smile.

How bad would it be if I threw a ball of magic at this asshole?

"Mutt? How dare you? You think I'm going to do anything to help a fucking wanker who insults my friends, the people I care about, at every given opportunity?" I jumped from the bed, glaring at him. My hands shook with the need to release my magic upon him. It was pooling readily in my hands, and this time, it didn't scare the hell out of me.

I wanted that magic at my disposal. I wanted to hurt him with it. He was just as prejudiced as the Elders who kicked the shifters, witches, and half-bloods out of their homes in Faery in the first place.

Elitist fucking prick!

"Aurelia, stop!" Malcolm yelled as he encroached into my space.

"No, you are just like the rest of them. Fuck you. I won't help you!" I shook my head, trembling with the power of my rage and indignation.

"You won't have a choice, I'm afraid." He crowded me and reached up, pinching my chin like he owned me, the move far too intimate.

I ripped away from his bruising grip. "I will *always* have a choice. For the first time that I can remember, I had friends and a place that felt like home, and you just stole that away from me."

"Your parents will be so disappointed in you," he said with a bored sigh as he took a step back out of my space.

I laughed so hard it almost came out like a wild cackle. "Are you for real? Do you seriously think that I would give a damn about what the parents who I don't even remember think of me? They obviously sacrificed me for some *supposed* greater good like I was a tool to be used and implemented at the right time, rather than their daughter. If they're disappointed in me...fuck them, too."

"What happened to the girl that knew what her job was?" he asked.

"She died when you left her freezing in an alley. She learned the true meaning of cruelty and became someone else!" I shouted back as if that fact weren't fucking blindingly obvious.

Where has he been this entire time? Not sleeping on a pile of blankets in a closet. being little more than a slave, that's for damn sure.

Based on the comfy bed I just woke up in, I would say he'd never suffered a day in his life.

Arrogant prick. He doesn't understand me at all, and he's about to learn his actions have consequences.

"You understood it was for the best," he said, running a hand through his white-blond hair.

"Did I really?" I snarked. "Because I obviously did something to ruin your plan after that night. It's the *only* memory that comes easily to me. I can feel the chill in my bones when I remember it." I raised an accusatory eyebrow at him.

"What happened to you, Aurelia?" he asked softly, as if altering his demeanor was going to somehow successfully manipulate me or change how I felt.

I wasn't born yesterday, buddy.

"What happened to me?" I laughed without humor. "You have been in this nice warm house this whole time while I was either freezing in an alley or sleeping on the floor of a closet with threadbare blankets and scarcely enough to get by. What the fuck do you think happened?"

He reached up to cup my cheek.

I slapped his hand away without a second thought. "You don't get to fucking touch me," I snarled, the purple, shimmering magic in my grasp flaring with my emotions.

"Fine. If you want to be a brat, you can stay locked in this room until you remove that block on your memory and remember the stakes!" He turned on his heel and slammed the door behind him, leaving me once more with the sprites.

A soft click filled the room followed by the subtle but unmistakable buzz of magic. He wasn't taking any chances with the possibility of my escaping him.

I slumped back on the bed and put my head in my hands.

How the hell am I going to get out of this?

I refused to help him. I'd never submit to doing whatever it was that would ensure no shifters, half-bloods, or witches could ever return home. It was beyond cruel that they were exiled from Faery in the first place. If Faery was a place of magic, a realm especially for supernaturals, then we all belonged there, as far as I was concerned. No one should be excluded. It was a racial prejudice, just like the humans demonstrated so often against others of their own kind. It was sickening.

The sprites buzzed out of the cupboard and back into the room, their glows dimmed more so than usual. Were they sad? Or was that to appear less obvious in the face of danger?

"He wants you to keep us all out of Faery?" Freya asked in her tiny voice.

"Yeah," I sighed. "For whatever reason, that's his master plan, it appears."

"Why? I don't understand?" Fiona asked, adding to the conversation.

"I don't know why exactly. It doesn't make sense. He says it's for the greater good, and that I used to understand. And that just makes me not want to remember the child I used to be." I shook my head and flopped on my back, staring up at the ceiling blankly.

Not having answers is infuriating...

"But why you?" Freya asked buzzing in front of my face. "Who are you?"

"I don't know that either, unfortunately. I'm afraid though. I mean, I caught glimpses of a memory of where I lived in a castle. What do you suppose that could mean?" I covered my face again.

What if I push through what's left of the block, and I start to believe what I did before? I can't risk that. I don't want to believe that the pure-blooded Fae are any better or more worthy than any other supernatural. That's not who I am.

"Knowledge is power, Aurelia," Freya said as she landed her tiny feet on my stomach. "You need to have all the facts before you can decide what to do."

"I don't think you would follow him blindly just because you get your memories back," Fiona offered, tapping my hand with her own.

"But how do you know?" I asked, peeking through my fingers and swallowing hard. "I don't want to become like him."

"You may have been raised to hate other supernaturals, Miss Aurelia, but you've learned through experience that we aren't all bad. And we certainly aren't as bad as that man who has locked us in here," Fiona said.

I closed my eyes and sighed. She was right, but I still hadn't had the best of experiences when it came to the supernatural world either. But one truth remained. No race of people was inherently bad or toxic. Just like with humans and animals, there were always going to be bad eggs, those who did the wrong things, and hurt others with malicious intent. But they were far and away in the minority. And other whole races of life didn't deserve to be tarred with the brush of hatred and prejudice because of them.

Shoving my fears aside, I pushed into my mind with a renewed sense of purpose and went back to the first memory I possessed that wasn't too fuzzy. There was a castle in the distance as Malcolm ran with me across the grounds and into the forest.

Malcolm?" I asked softly. "What are you doing?" I could barely see past the cloak he'd thrown over me.

"Shh. The hounds will hear you, little one." He squeezed me tighter to his chest.

A familiar blue glow lit up the night, and my eyes widened in instant recognition. Everyone in Faery knew what that was. Did he really intend to take me through it and into the mortal world? I panicked and struggled in his arms as the portal drew closer.

"Aurelia, stop," he whispered. "We must go to the mortal world. It's not safe for you here anymore."

What does he mean it isn't safe here? This is my home, and we have the best guards in the realm!

"But why?" I asked, pulling the cloak down so I could see his face.

"There was a prophecy, Aurelia. A prophecy that puts you directly in danger if you remain here," he said in a rush.

"A prophecy? What kind of prophecy?" I pushed as my eyes widened in fear.

Malcolm's expression was hard, but I could tell he was scared too.

He was my best friend, and I trusted him… but what if he was wrong, and I was in more danger in the mortal world?

How can he be so sure? Leaving Faery is dangerous. Everyone knows that!

"I'll tell you everything, little one. I promise. But for now, we must go." He covered me back up with the cloak and stepped through the glowing portal.

Pain shot through me as soon as we made it to the other side. I cried out at the terrible feeling that threatened to burn me alive.

Malcolm squeezed me tighter in an attempt to alleviate my panic. "You'll get used to it, Aurelia. The iron is draining, but it will hide you from the others who would seek to use you," Malcolm whispered in my ear.

Why would anyone want to use me? What isn't he telling me?

"Iron?" I questioned. "But that's a poison to us! Where have you brought me, Malcolm? It hurts." I sobbed through the unfamiliar pain that seemed to permeate me to my very core.

Malcolm whispered and kissed my forehead softly in a final goodbye. "It will be okay. You will be safe. And when the time is right, we'll go home—together—I promise," he said. And the memory ended there like a cliffhanger, leaving me none the wiser and infinitely more frustrated. I needed to backtrack and summarize and figure this all out.

Who am I, really? And what do I know so far?

I was a full-blooded Fae who lived in a grand castle with guards and the daughter of a couple Malcolm was obviously very well acquainted with. He was my best friend, and they trusted me with him... even promising him my hand if he were to be believed. And then on top of all that there was a prophecy—one that threatened my very life—and spurred my childhood friend to spirit me away through the portal and into the mortal realm where I'd suffered to survive ever since.

My existence was like a great big fucking puzzle, and I was missing a bunch of integral pieces...

CHAPTER 20
Grey

I growled at the women, my temper fraying and close to snapping.

This is ridiculous. They're toying with me!

"Have you found anything yet?" I snapped.

They were taking their sweet-ass time with this and the longer they took the less clear the picture would be. Memories, scents, and auras only lingered so long before they faded into the ether and were irretrievable even to magic.

Dan patted my shoulder, a grimace on his face. "Let them work, boss. We aren't likely to find anything anyway."

My gaze ripped to his, and another feral growl escaped my lips. My wolf was *so* perilously close to the surface, my eyes were probably already glowing golden with his very aggressive presence.

Dan took a step back and held his hands up in immediate surrender. "Sorry, boss. I didn't mean anything by it. This is all just a long shot. I think you know that."

"It's not a good idea to challenge me right now," I said and exhaled in frustration.

Layla turned to me with a raised brow. "Why is your wolf freaking out?" she asked and crossed her arms over her chest, adopting a stance of authority and power.

"I need her back. Now," I spat, glaring right back at her.

"And it's just for the job, is it?" she scoffed.

I just told Dan not to challenge me, and now she's doing it? How fucking dare she. Layla's lucky I haven't shifted and let my wolf have her. He'd tear her limb from limb inside of three seconds flat.

"Are you questioning my motives? I don't have to explain myself to you or anyone else, for that matter." I stepped forward menacingly, closing the space between us until I towered over her.

"No, sir," she answered, dropping her show of bravado as she looked down and away in submission, once more deferring to my leadership without further question.

"Good. Now, I want you all out of my damn house as soon as possible, so go help Karma with her spell." I turned on my heel and strode into the kitchen, my rage lending me its strength.

"You're being overly hostile toward them," Dan noted, following me into the kitchen.

"Someone told that hooded Fae bastard that I wasn't here. It's the only thing that makes sense," I retorted as I spun to face him.

"What?" he asked, eyes widening in apprehension and shock.

"Only a select few knew that I left suddenly, and Magna suggested it was likely a mole. Someone has betrayed me, and the list of suspects is fucking short." I sat down on a stool at the kitchen island, interlocking my fingers.

"And you think..." he trailed off and glanced to the living room. "Holy shit."

"Karma was supposed to be headed to the witch's house when she challenged Aurelia in the first place. That was why it took her so long to get there. Layla told her what happened, and together they devised a plan to get rid of her." I untangled my fingers and clenched my fist on the counter at the treachery. I was almost ready to go off like a bomb, but instead of fire and ash, it'd be raining blood and flesh.

Dan strolled to the fridge and opened it, grabbing two bottles of water and tossing one to me. "They thought they could control when the challenge took place and get rid of her quickly," he said, rationalizing it out and shaking his head as he cracked the lid on the bottle.

"And it didn't work," I added. "I told them it would happen when I was ready, when Aurelia had time to train. But it looks like they came up with a new plan to make her disappear on their schedule anyway." I set my bottle on the counter and leaned back on my stool.

"What do you want me to do?" Dan asked, his gaze hard and unwavering.

Maybe I should make him my second. He's much more loyal than Layla, apparently. He might fuck up from time to time, but we all do. At least he's actually on my side.

I stood and moved back to the living room as Karma's chanting filled the air. "Keep an eye on them while Karma performs the spell," I whispered.

Dan nodded surreptitiously and moved closer to the women.

Karma wandered around the space almost in a trance as she continued her chant.

Wispy figures took form around us and appeared to be fighting with magic. Balls of silver light shimmered to and fro, sizzling through the air.

I moved closer to the hall to follow their progress as the memory of the penthouse was relived in real time, thanks to the spell.

The man in the cloak threw magic at Reah again, and Aurelia ran away from the intruder and toward the magicless room.

"Coward," Layla mumbled under her breath, but before I could react, Reah was in her face.

"She was following orders!" Reah hissed and pushed Layla roughly in the chest.

"Whose orders?" Layla growled, and her shifter eyes glowed in response.

"Mine, fuckwit! She was not ready to face an attacker with her magic. It's not quite stable yet. I made the choice, and she tried to argue with me." Reah glared at her and took another step forward, ready to defend my mate's honor.

"Easy, Reah," I said and grabbed her arm.

"No! Why is this bitch so quick to judge?" she fired back before turning her gaze on Layla once more. "What do you know about her kidnapper?" Reah asked before she ripped her arm from my grasp.

"What are you talking about?" Layla shouted with wide eyes.

"Don't you think it's strange that he showed up here within an hour of Grey leaving the penthouse?" Reah crossed her arms, correct in her deductions. But now was not the time.

Shit, she's going to blow everything to Hell.

"Reah!" I shouted, feigning outrage.

"He left unexpectedly. So, how did this Fae know where to find Aurelia when Grey was gone?" Reah continued with a sneer, determined not to let her suspicions of Layla escape her.

"I got something!" Karma shouted, changing the subject.

I spun on the woman who was several feet away from the magicless room.

The intruder had removed his hood, and Aurelia stared up at him with wide eyes as she was pinned beneath him.

My inner wolf snarled in outrage, and I completely concurred with his stance. Seeing that fucker on top of my mate had me trembling, the fuse on my temper almost spent.

We couldn't hear what Aurelia said, unfortunately, as the spell only mimicked what could be seen. But Aurelia fought back and thrashed before she was punched in the head and knocked out cold, going limp. Freya and Fiona buzzed into the room, but I didn't see where they hid before the man turned like he knew we were going to watch this very moment in the future.

Fucking prick!

Magna gasped as we all watched, holding a hand over her mouth in shock. "By the gods of Faery... I know him."

"What do you mean, you know him?" I asked, turning to her sharply.

"You don't recognize him?" Magna asked softly as she stared ahead.

The mimic spell cut out then, but his face remained clear in my mind's eye, and I thought about the long white-blond hair and slate-gray eyes. "Fuck. The Captain of the King's Guard."

"What do you mean?" Reah asked with a frown. "What king?"

"The Fae king. But what does that make Aurelia?" Magna whispered in horror as the impossible truth settled upon us like a fine mist of doom.

No! It can't be true. She can't be the Fae princess. The king that Malcolm serves is known to be calculating, brutal, and cruel beyond reason. Fuck!

Had Malcolm brought her here to save her from him, or was there a more nefarious reason for it? Either way, it changed nothing right at this moment, and time was of the essence. The longer Aurelia was with that asshole, the more likely she was to come to harm, and we would not fucking allow it—not my wolf or I—not while we still had strength in our bones and breath in our lungs.

She's everything to us.

"Dan!" I barked, turning toward the living room.

He jogged over, quick to answer my summons.

"I need you to dig up everything you possibly can on Malcolm."

"Does Malcolm have a last name, or is this like a Madonna thing?" Dan asked, chuckling. Fucker sure as hell didn't know when to keep his sense of humor in check despite his unwavering loyalty.

"Fae don't have surnames!" I growled.

Dan raised his hands up in surrender for the second time since he arrived in my penthouse. "All right, boss. I'll ask around about a weirdo Fae in a cloak named Malcolm. Got it." Without another word, he ran to the elevator and stabbed at the button to get on with his mission.

"You two." I pointed to Layla and Karma. "Get this shit cleaned up and get back to the facility."

"You don't want my help to locate this Fae?" Layla asked, frowning.

Not in this lifetime or any other.

"Dan has it under control. Do what I ask. I know where to find you, should I need you." I waved them both off, dismissing them from my sight.

"You think I did this, don't you?" Layla asked angrily.

I couldn't answer without her smelling the lie, so I turned on my heel and walked away. "Magna, Reah, my office please," I called over my shoulder, maintaining my pace, my shoulders and head held high.

"Looks like someone is no longer the boss's favorite!" Reah said with a laugh.

"Watch it, Reah. You filled his head with some fucked-up bullshit. He knows I would never betray him!" Layla said.

I took a deep breath through my nose and smelled the lie in her words. I turned sharply, but instead of letting her know I'd caught onto it, I called out to Reah instead, "Move it."

Stomping feet followed me to my office, and I held the door open while both women walked in. I slammed the door shut behind them and stormed over to the chair behind my desk, sinking into the leather cushioning with a small measure of gratitude for the comfort it offered. "Magna, can you place a ward, please? I want privacy." I rubbed at my temples, the new information regarding my second giving me a tension headache.

I just got fucking clear confirmation that she would betray me... but did she? Why would she do that? Is it truly petty jealousy? Have I mistaken her loyalty all these years?

Magna waved her hands and chanted softly under her breath.

I waited for her nod and rounded on Reah. "I'm trying to keep Layla's deception quiet for now," I snapped and glared at her.

Magna took a seat in the chair across from me and raised an eyebrow. "So, you're sure it was her?"

"I scented the lie when she said she would never betray me." I sighed bitterly.

Rhea's face reddened at the confirmation of Layla's betrayal. "What are you going to do about it?" she yelled, outraged.

"I appreciate your loyalty, Reah, but I have to play this smart. They could spread lies through the facility about me wrongly accusing them to get Aurelia out of the challenge. It would cause mistrust among all my employees." I clenched my fists.

And I know they'd fucking do it, too.

"That's smart," Reah conceded. "I'm sorry. I can't imagine how angry you were just being in the same room with them. I was practically about to lose my shit, and when she called Aurelia a coward..." The half-Fae magic instructor snarled.

I could clearly feel my wolf's approval of her reverberating through my veins. True loyalty was hard to find, and couldn't even be bought for any amount of wealth. So, the fact Reah was standing up for Aurelia meant *a lot* to us both.

"We just need to play this smart, like I said. I don't want her figuring it all out and pulling shit at the facility," I said. "The last fucking thing I need a coup or a riot on my hands."

"I'm sorry to interrupt, but we need to talk about Malcolm," Magna said as she stared at me with trepidation. The mere hint that she was afraid meant we were in deep shit. Magna was ancient. If the King's Guard scared her...

"What do you know about him?" I asked, suppressing a shudder and leaning back in my chair.

"He's a brutal killer. He protects the royal family with his life, and before we were kicked out of Faery, he never would have been caught dead in the mortal realm. He hates humans just as much as he hates all other supernaturals..." Magna trailed off, staring off into space as if lost in thought or memory.

"So, what would he need Aurelia for, and how does she know him?" I asked mostly to myself.

"I think you already know the answer to that." Magna raised a knowing and suggestive brow. "The truth is always straightforward, Grey. The most obvious answer is the often the right one."

No! I couldn't believe that the daughter of my greatest enemy was my fated mate, and also formally bonded to his greatest enforcer. It was beyond comprehension. It was the worst possible outcome of all.

Fucking fucker's fucking fucked!

"She can't be," I mumbled, a tight knot forming in my gut. "She just can't be."

"What if she is, Grey? You will have to figure out how to feel about that. She doesn't remember her family right now, but what happens when she does?" Magna asked sagely, always one step ahead.

"I will deal with it when I know for sure, but who her parents are means nothing to me." I shook my head. I couldn't allow it to mean anything.

She is what I want and need, nothing else. Finding your fated mate is everything... it happens once in a lifetime. There is only one and no replacing them. If Aurelia is mine, so be it. I will not jeopardize our union. We must find a way to save her!

I would even give up the plans I'd been formulating for decades for her if she asked it of me. I know my wolf would certainly demand it and there would be no denying him on that crossroads.

"What is this Malcolm dickhead even doing here?" Reah asked as she leaned against the wall.

"I don't know what his ultimate game plan is. I wish the mimic spell did more than just let us see. They were saying something to each other, but I couldn't read their lips." I slammed my fist against the desk in frustration.

Magna narrowed her eyes at me and leaned forward, an intensity to her that belied her old age. "About twenty years ago, there was a rumor of a prophecy," she whispered. "I can't help but wonder if that has something to do with Malcolm and Aurelia being in the realm."

"A prophecy?" I asked, raising my gaze to meet hers.

How does she know about the prophecy? Who am I kidding, Magna knows way too much about everything.

"You already know what I'm talking about, don't you?" Magna asked.

"And you already know the answer to that." I couldn't hinder the grin that split my face at our banter. The prophecy was the reason I had been looking for a Fae in the first place. I needed her to help with my plan—the only problem was she would have to *want* to help me.

What will I do if Malcolm convinces her that she belongs in Faery and we don't?

"According to the prophecy, there will be one who can either free us, or keep us trapped here in the mortal realm forever," I said with a fateful sigh.

This is some heavy shit.

Reah straightened. "And you think Aurelia is the only one who can bring us all home to Faery?" she asked.

"I'm not sure if she's the one or not, but why would Malcolm bring her here if she was? Wouldn't they all want her to grow up in Faery where that kind of prejudice reigns? From there, she could close the portal without ever knowing the difference."

"Probably, but perhaps not," Magna said thoughtfully. "They may have seen the possibility as more of a risk than they were willing to take."

"Do you mean to say that they would have killed a child because there was a *possibility* she might one day open the portal for us?" Reah asked, flabbergasted by the mere suggestion of such an atrocity.

I couldn't imagine killing a child, no matter what any damn prophecy said, even if there was one that threatened me personally. It was just pure evil, and despite my life of crime and questionable choices, it sickened me to my very heart.

"They aren't nicknamed the wicked Fae for nothing, Reah. Any threat to their status quo must be eliminated... even a child who hadn't even yet made a mistake." I stood and started pacing.

It still didn't make any sense in a broader sense. He'd brought her here and then abandoned her. He told her that there was a reason for it, and she had understood it at the time. What was I missing? It felt crucial.

What if she gets her memories back and decides that he's right after all, and we never get to go home?

My chest hurt, my heart squeezing as if a damn elephant were sitting on top of me, crushing me with its weight. The thought of never returning to Faery *and* having to live without Aurelia—our mate—was too much to bear.

CHAPTER 21
Aurelia

I closed my eyes tightly and focused, trying not to allow desperation to overwhelm me. "We need to get out of here, girls."

Freya scoffed in despair. "The door is locked and sealed with magic!"

"You were able to sneak out the window. Did you see anything familiar?" I asked, then blew out a breath.

Stay calm, Aurelia.

I needed to center myself. If I let my magic get out of control, I was afraid of what Malcolm might do to me.

Who knows what he's capable of. I just need to breathe, like Grey taught me. In and out. Focus.

"No, nothing seemed familiar, and I couldn't explore far either," she said with a sigh.

"Is there a ward keeping us in?" I asked, cracking an eye open. "Is that really a thing?"

"Yes," Freya said. "Of course. Wards can keep people in or out, the same way they can allow or mute magic," she explained. "I can probably get through it now that I know it's there, but it's going to take some time."

"Time isn't something we have, Freya," I answered as I flopped onto my back once more in frustration. "He's going to start growing impatient soon. It's already been two days."

Fiona tapped her foot on my knee to get my attention. "What if we all go out the front door?" she suggested.

"Fi, you know that's not possible," I said, pressing my hands to my head.

"Hear me out," Fiona pressed. "All you need to do is pretend that you are ready to train. He will open the door, and we can use that opportunity to attack him."

"You want to attack a pureblood Fae who is much older and more experienced with magic than me?" I sat up again, wringing my hands. That was a seriously bad idea, but I didn't have a better plan to offer, and I'd been wracking my mind for the past forty-eight hours straight.

Freya chewed her lower lip anxiously. "If we catch him by surprise, it just might work."

"You are both insane. I mean... our chances of success are almost painfully non-existent!" I threw my hands up.

"What do we have to lose? He won't kill you—he needs and wants you. You are his promised. And even if you can't get out, maybe one or both of us can. Then whoever makes it can fly back to Master Grey," Fiona argued. "We could lead him to you and organize a rescue, Miss Aurelia!"

"I can't believe that I am actually going to agree with this," I huffed in exasperation.

Am I completely out of my head? Grey will never forgive me if the sprites get hurt... but can I just sit here and not *do whatever I possibly can to get back to Grey?*

Fiona clapped her tiny hands together in triumph and flew up to sit on my shoulder.

Freya did the same, alighting on the other.

"So, all you have to do is get his attention, and then when he opens the door, we will fly up in his face and distract him. Then you hit him with the biggest blast of magic you can, and hopefully that will knock him out, and we can make a run for it," Fiona said with a comically malicious grin.

"Actually, that just might work," I admitted with a heft measure of admiration. The sprites might be tiny, but they were like pocket rockets where their pluck and courage were concerned. They were loyal to a fault, and I couldn't help but love them for it. I nodded with a small burst of hope filling my belly. "All right, so when are we going to do this?"

"There's no time like the present!" Fiona announced as she flew up next to my face.

I stood from the bed and stretched my back in preparation for our escape attempt. I'd been in this damn room going stir crazy for two days. The only time the door ever opened was when a servant came in to feed me. Even then, the magic held firm, like it was made specifically to keep me in. Whatever ward was on the door would only be lifted if Malcolm believed I was coming out and ready to give into his demands. I shuddered at the thought.

Just as well this is nothing more than a ruse!

The mere notion of agreeing to fulfill his wishes and likely becoming his wife was enough to cause a hot surge of bile racing up my throat.

Fuck that for a joke. I'll never join him—not in this lifetime or the next!

"All right, girls. Wait for my signal and stay out of sight until he opens the door," I whispered. I approached the door and sucked in a deep breath before banging on the door loudly. "Malcolm. You win! I'm ready to start training. Please just let me out of here!" I yelled. I was met by nothing but silence, so I tried again. "Malcolm! Let me fucking out!"

Footfalls sounded from the other side of the door. "Aurelia, what are you screaming about?" Malcolm asked, stopping on the other side of the door, though there was no indication that he was moving to open it.

I glanced at the sprites out of the corner of my eye.

They were hiding behind where the door would open, fluttering silently and preparing for action on my signal.

"I'm ready to train. Let me out. I feel like I can't breathe in here!" I said again, my voice raised.

"Are you really? You are willing to come home with me, finally?" he asked, sounding almost hopeful.

Crap!

I couldn't believe it. I felt almost bad for my deception.

Can I lie about this when he has that painfully hopeful note in his voice? I don't want to go anywhere near Faery.

And then I remembered my Grey. His beautiful, ripped human body, his intense gaze, the way he made me feel, and even how soft his incredible snow-white fur had felt under my hand when he defended me at the facility. My sense of resolve strengthened at the memories, and I focused on my mission to get home, back to the penthouse and Grey, with the sprites safely in tow.

"Yes, I will go back to Faery with you." I grimaced and glanced at the sprites. "I'll go," I added, "but I'm not making any more promises than that. I still can't remember much..."

They both gave me encouraging nods even though the lie made me feel every inch the wicked Fae that Malcolm was.

"All will be well, Aurelia. If you will only just trust me like you once did, everything can return to normal," he said, his voice soothing and encouraging, as if he were talking down a jumper who might change their mind at any second.

The familiar sound of buzzing magic could be heard on the other side of the door as the ward was lifted, and I breathed deeply as I took a step back.

This is it. He's taken the bait. It's now or never. Please let this fucking work...

I put my hands behind my back and let my purple magic pool in them before I nodded firmly at the sprites, giving them the signal.

The doorknob rattled before clicking open and the smile on

Malcolm's face was brilliant—he almost looked as beautiful as I remembered him from my time spent in the castle—until he was dive bombed by the sprites.

"What is this treachery?" he shouted and covered his head with his hands, swatting at Fiona and Freya in annoyance.

While he was distracted, I seized my chance and pulled my hands out from behind me, hurling my magic at him with the intent of knocking him the fuck out. The shimmering purple blast struck Malcolm in the chest and sent him soaring back until he crashed into the wall at the opposite end of the hall.

All the breath left him in a shocked *whoosh* just before his eyes rolled back in his head and he slumped to the floor.

"Go, go, go!" I yelled to the sprites, and we all took off down the hallway. I had no idea where I was going, but based on the view through the window, we were definitely on the second floor at least, so looking for stairs was going to be my best bet.

"This way, Miss Aurelia!" Fiona urged as she tugged at my hair.

I changed direction on a dime and followed the sprite to a long stairway. Without hesitation, I sprinted down the stairs, taking them two at a time as a roar filled the air. "Shit. He's awake already! We need to find a way out of here, *now.*" I pushed myself faster down the stairs, glancing backward over my shoulder at Freya who was watching my back.

"I don't think he is up yet, Miss," Freya squeaked as she watched the landing above. "I'll stay and hold him off!"

"Oh no, you won't Freya," I hissed as I snatched her out of the air much to her displeasure. I would fucking take her with me!

"Miss Aurelia, please! I must protect you. The master is probably out of beside himself and out of control without you!" Freya's tiny fists beat against my hand.

I ignored her as the front entry way came into view, relief flooding through me.

"Aurelia, where are you?" Malcolm roared from the top of the stairs, before he spotted us.

"Miss, let me go hold him off! There's no time," Freya pleaded.

Fiona glanced back between us before she zipped past me so fast, I didn't have time to catch her. It was clear she had every intention of sacrificing herself for her sister and me.

"Go, Miss. Get out of here. Take Freya! Hurry!" Fiona cried as she flew up the stairs directly toward danger.

"No, Fiona. Come back here!" I cried out as I lobbed another purple ball of magic at Malcolm where he stood at the top of the stairs.

He dodged out of the way at the last second and landed on the floor by the stair's banister with an *oomph*.

I spun on my heel. "Come on, Fiona," I screamed. "Let's go!"

Malcolm shot up faster than I could have anticipated, and a wicked smile crossed his face as he vanished from sight. A second later, he reappeared right next to Fiona, only to snatch her roughly from the air.

"No!" Freya screamed with a yelp, biting my hand in desperation and forcing me to let her go. She flew back to her sister, buzzing angrily around Malcolm, but he just snatched her from the air too.

"Let them go, Malcom," I demanded and held up my hands as I pushed magic into them. Purple swirls filled the air, and my wings fluttered to life at my back. He would *not* take my friends from me. I refused to let the asshole hurt them.

Not on my watch, bucko!

"I'll let them leave," he bargained. "But you must come home with me. You have to train to use your magic and then you must close the portal once and for all."

"No, Miss Aurelia!" Fiona cried out as Malcolm shook her roughly.

"Don't do it. You are not allowed to sacrifice everything for us!" Freya shook her head.

Malcolm's fist tightened around her, crushing her small body and making her choke.

"What is your answer, Aurelia?" Malcolm boomed before he cocked his arm back and threw Freya against the front door like he was pitching a baseball.

I cried out in agony, tracking Freya's body as she slid down the door into a little heap on the ground. Her glow dimmed and a tear trailed down my cheek, hot and filled with emotion too heavy to bear.

She's not dead. She can't be dead! No!

I turned back to Malcolm with a scowl.

Fiona was thrashing furiously in his hand. Failing to break free, she bent her little face down and bit into his finger with all her might.

"Fucking vermin!" Malcolm shouted in disdain. "How about I pluck your pesky little wings to show you your place among purebloods?"

"No, you said you would let them go!" I screamed back, my magic flaring in response to my panic.

I couldn't bear it if he took her wings.

What kind of monster is he? How can he be so deluded as to think that I would have ever helped him?

"That was before they showed what pests they truly are. Being here so long, I almost forgot what vermin sub-Fae are." Malcolm sneered, viciously handsome and wicked all at once as his blond hair spilled over his shoulders.

"You said you would let them go. So, just let them go, and I will do whatever you want." I held my hands up and took a deep breath, willing my magic to disappear. To my utter shock, my magic dissipated, and I breathed a sigh.

Finally, my magic has learned to listen to me even when I'm panicking.

"No, Aurelia. Don't do it. I'll be okay!" Fiona shouted, but the terror in her eyes mirrored my own.

Malcolm shook her and pinched her wing with unbridled cruelty in his gaze. He raised an eyebrow at me. "Perhaps I should keep them, so I know how to keep you in line." He grinned. "That would be most convenient."

"If you don't let them go, I'll never help you," I growled in response, my face burning with anger.

Fiona yelped as the pressure on her wing increased.

I glared at Malcolm, allowing my magic to fill my palms once again.

He tugged sharply on her wing, delighting in the tiny sprite's pain.

With nothing on my mind but preventing the tiny Fae's destruction, I threw a ball of blazing purple magic at his head, willing it to fuck him up in any way possible.

He flinched, but not fast enough, my magic singeing his ear.

The odor of burned flesh reached my sensitive nose and I smiled with dark satisfaction in return. It wasn't a perfect hit, but it had landed, nonetheless.

Fuck you, asshole! I hope it hurts.

"Fuck," Malcolm yelled and cupped his ear with his free hand. "Fine, I'll let them go, but you're staying with me, or I *will* kill them! And I'll make you watch."

Malcolm stormed down the stairs and grabbed my arm in a bruising grip. He dragged me across the foyer where Freya was still lying in a heap by the front of the door.

I cried out at the sight of Freya's broken little body, praying to whatever gods were listening that Fiona would be able to get Freya back to Grey before it was too late. Surely, he had a healer at his disposal.

Or perhaps Magna can help?

"I'm not leaving you, Miss Aurelia," Fiona shook her head vehemently, still in Malcolm's unforgiving grasp.

"You have to get Freya to Grey," I said through my tears. "She needs you."

Fiona glanced at her sister with sadness and then back to me, obviously torn on what to do. She was so loyal that my heart broke for her.

"Make up your mind quickly, vermin. I don't have all day." Malcolm shook her again. and

I gritted my teeth to the point of pain and clenched my fists by my sides. This motherfucker was going to pay dearly. I didn't know how or when, but I was going to find a way to destroy him for what he'd done. He was the very definition of a prejudiced, wicked Fae. And now I truly understood why we were named the way we were, especially if the majority of my kind acted and thought the way he did.

"Go, Fiona. Please, get her out of here," I begged. "I'll be okay."

"Fine," Fiona sighed, miniature glimmering tears staining her cheeks.

Malcolm opened his hand at hearing her response, keeping his word and releasing the tiny sprite.

Fiona flew down to her sister, picking her up gently in both arms and cradling her against her chest like a mother would clutch her precious child.

I felt so incredibly proud of her at that moment. She was truly a little hero.

They are lucky to have each other. Fly strong, little one!

Malcolm squeezed my arm even harder as he shoved open the front door.

I lunged forward in a desperate if not futile attempt to break free of his grasp and run.

At the last second, he wrapped his hand around my throat and pulled me back roughly to his chest.

To my revulsion, I felt something distinctly hard pressed into me from behind as I squirmed against him.

Sick fucking psycho!

"No," Fiona's tiny voice cried, but then she was gone from my sight.

Malcolm slammed the door closed with his foot, gripping me even more tightly and without a shred of remorse.

"Can't breathe," I gasped. Panicking, I clawed at his hand and tried to loosen his grip. I needed to get air into my lungs, but it was no use. He was physically too strong, and soon I could see stars, and several heart racing moments later, darkness began to encroach on the corners of my vision as my pulse throbbed in my ears.

Malcolm laughed, his breath hot against my ear. "You shouldn't have tried to run from me, Aurelia. This is only the beginning, my love. You are mine now."

What have I gotten myself into? What is he going to do to me? If this is how he treats the woman promised to him, I can't imagine what he intends for his enemies...

As fear warred with revulsion, I could only hope the sprites would make it back to Grey before this insane asshole choked me to death... but I wasn't counting on it. So, with my last conscious breath as Malcolm lewdly ground against me and ran his tongue down my ear, I thought of Grey and focused on recalling the time we'd spent together.

If I die today, he was the best thing that ever happened to me.

The beauty of the simple truth bolstered the fragile flame of hope burning in my heart and offered me a small measure of comfort as oblivion surged in to claim me. Whatever took place now was beyond my control, at least for the moment...

CHAPTER 22

"Any news?" I asked Dan as I impatiently paced my office.

It's been two days since Aurelia was taken, and I'm losing my fucking mind here!

"Nothing at all, boss. How did that fucker just disappear with her, anyway?" Dan asked and scrubbed a hand over his face. We were all tired but wired, and it showed. We'd barely slept a wink in forty-eight hours.

"You have never been to the Fae realm before so you wouldn't know," I explained. "Pureblood Fae have the ability to sift as long as there are no wards preventing it." I ran a hand through my hair trying to maintain my hold over my growing frustration. I'd never thought to ward my home against the ability because there were so few pure-blooded Fae around outside of Faery itself.

"Sift?" he asked with a frown. "Is that what they call vanishing like that?"

"It's like teleporting from one place to another, basically, but they *have* to have been to the place before," I said. "They can't just sift somewhere they've never been."

"Well, shit. They could literally be anywhere. If this guy is as ancient and powerful as Magna fears, then he's likely been fucking everywhere in his time." He sat back in his chair with a scowl on his face.

"Exactly. And I have no damn idea of where to even start looking. They could already be through the portal and in Faery, for all I know." I clenched my fists at my side, my lips pursing in irritation.

Please don't be in Faery, Aurelia... that's somewhere I won't ever be able to follow you.

Magna had said we would never find them without the sprites' help, but my wolf was thrashing inside me. He was losing control of himself, and I was losing control of him.

"Fuck. It's been two fucking days and there's still no sign of Freya and Fiona yet. I know Magna said we would need them to find her, but I want her back now!" I stopped pacing to glare at Dan. It wasn't his fault, none of this was, but our general inaction and inability to do anything fruitful was eating me up inside.

"I'm doing everything possible, but there's nothing more we can do. I've gotten all the information I can, and we're just coming up at a stalemate." He straightened his spine, clearly not willing to take my shit lying down when he knew he'd done all he could, just as I'd asked.

"It's not enough!" I roared, gripping my head.

My wolf thrashed in my chest desperate to get out and go look for her himself, but he couldn't. A huge white wolf wandering around the streets of Dallas trying to sniff out his mate—shifter, witch, or mortal side—would raise some eyebrows. My phone buzzed on my desk. I stomped over and picked it up. "What is it, Magna?" I asked, putting her on loudspeaker and trying to keep my temper in check.

"The Fae note just held a warning. It simply said that he was coming for her and that it was time," she said in confusion.

"That doesn't help us." I growled.

Dan shook his head. "Nothing makes sense though. If she was passed out in the hallway at the witch's apartment when he came to get the book, why didn't he just take her then? He would have been able to avoid everything that went down here in the penthouse. He would have had no opposition whatsoever and Aurelia was tranqed, so it would have been easy for someone like him to just sift her out of there."

"The bit that confuses me is that he assumed she would know how to read the Fae language," Magna added.

Did she know how to read the language? Was that something she's forgotten with the block?

"in the memory I was pulled into, it was clear she knew the man. She spoke in Fae to him, so maybe she also knew how to read." I proposed and scrubbed a hand over my face in a fresh wave of frustration.

"Dan has a good point as well," Magna said. "Why didn't he take her before? What was the purpose of him leaving her on the floor and endangering her further?"

"What was the purpose of leaving her starving and freezing in a dirty alley when she was just a small child?" I yelled, unable to bite back the remark. Nothing this asshole son of a bitch did made any sense at all.

He is bound to her in some way, and yet he knowingly and willfully allowed her to suffer. I could never let her suffer like that.

She was mine and I was hers—we were fated mates—and if I had to kill the wicked Fae to get to her then I would.

"That's a good point too," Magna agreed. "Though he may have needed something else to happen, or had something else to do before he could take her."

"Have you seen anything at all that will help us find her?" I slammed my fist onto the desk. I needed to get her back, like *now*. I couldn't take care of the fucking moles in my organization until I did.

"No, the sprites are still our best bet for rescuing her, but you need to be ready, Grey." Magna sighed.

I paced over to the window and stared out into the cloudless night sky. We didn't see many stars in the city, given the ambient light, but the full moon hung high in the sky, and the sight made my heart hurt. I missed Aurelia terribly.

Is she okay? What does that psychopath want from her?

Dan and Magna's voices turned to white noise in the background as I stared out the window, lost to thought. Before I realized what I was seeing, a faint green glow caught my attention in the distance, and I squinted, leaning closer to the glass. "Dan! Come here. Is that...?" I asked, trailing off, not daring to hope that I could be right.

"It's definitely a sprite," he said leaning closer to the window beside me. "But I can't tell if it's them. Plus, there only appears to be one."

"Fuck!" I growled and slammed my open palm against the window. The glass rattled in its frame, and I flinched. It probably wasn't the best idea to go smashing windows.

"Wait a minute! It looks like it's carrying something," Dan said as the sprite continued to move closer toward the building.

I squinted into the darkness and called upon my wolf vision, my heart skipping a beat. "That's Freya!" I announced, recognizing her instantly.

What the hell happened to them?

Fiona was flying in a tired and chaotic zigzag pattern, like she was barely managing to maintain her altitude as she held her sister in her arms.

I raced from the room and into my bedroom, flinging open the doors to the balcony wide. "Fiona!" I called down to the sprite, my heart in my throat as hope blazed within me. She needed to fly higher to reach me, but I wasn't sure she had the energy left in reserve to achieve it.

"Master Grey!" she yelled excitedly, her tiny voice like music to my ears. She flew a little higher but fell again, unable to stay up with the precious burden clutched to her chest.

Fuck, she's not going to make it.

"Dan," I yelled into the penthouse. "You're going to have to go downstairs and get them. Careful that they aren't seen."

"I'm on my way," Dan called back and rushed down the hall without a moment's hesitation.

"Fiona, it's going to be okay! Just stay there. Dan is coming for you, okay?" I called out, beyond relieved to see my sprites again.

"Okay," she said her voice fatigued as she jerkily maintained her hover.

How long has she been flying with her sister in her arms and what the hell happened to them?

If I wasn't already planning on killing Malcolm—which I was—this would have been the nail in the coffin that would put an end to his miserable fucking life. I raced back into the office and picked up my phone. The call with Magna was still connected. "I think I'm going to need your help," I said. "It looks like Freya is in pretty bad shape."

"I'll be there shortly," she said, and the line went dead, and this time I wasn't even annoyed someone had hung up on me.

I wandered into the living room to wait for Dan. My eyes caught on the black leather couch, free of all traces of Aurelia. I'd nearly strangled the meddling bitches, Layla and Karma, when I'd realized they'd destroyed the last of Aurelia's plants that had survived the home invasion and magic battle between Malcom and Reah. Even if the moss had irritated me at first, they had no right to destroy the plants. This was my home, not theirs, and if nothing else, it proved just how petty they were and how much they truly hated my mate—which would be dealt with in future. I wasn't going to keep people in my employ who were a danger to Aurelia.

I clenched my fists at my sides and breathed deeply to calm myself. Being angry wasn't going to help Freya and Fiona. Turning on my heel, I paced the living room for several long minutes before the *ding* of the elevator alerted me to their arrival. I spun to face the door, my heart lurching in my chest.

Please be all right, my little sprites.

Dan stepped out of the elevator with his jacket bulging with his precious concealed cargo.

Magna stepped out from behind him a moment later wearing a worried frown.

I ate up the space between us in two giant steps, holding my hands out to him.

He opened his jacket, and an exhausted Fiona flitted out.

"What happened?" I asked, swallowing the lump in my throat as I waited to hear what had transpired after what felt like the longest two days of my entire life.

She wobbled in the air then landed on my open palms. "My wing's a little torn." She grimaced and glanced away. "We tried to escape with her, Master Grey, but she was caught. I'm so sorry. I wasn't given a choice—he was going to kill us or hold us hostage to control Miss Aurelia." Fiona hung her tiny head in shame, a single tear trickling down her rosy cheek.

She just flew who knows how long carrying her unconscious sister with a torn wing and she's apologizing to me? What the actual hell is going on here?

"And I bet Aurelia told you to leave her, didn't she?" I asked, shaking my head.

My mate is far more courageous than she gives herself credit for.

Fiona swiped at her eyes and nodded. "He was going to start torturing me... he almost ripped my wing off, and he threw Freya into a door! Aurelia bargained with him to save us, to let us go free."

"What?" Dan barked as he laid tiny Freya out on the leather couch to be attended to. Her small body was broken, was a miracle she was still breathing. Malcolm was a fucking monster, that was for damn sure.

"You did the right thing, Fiona. Now, we'll be able to go and rescue her." I ran a hand through my hair as I pondered my next course of action.

What kind of sociopathic bastard tried to rip the wings off a sprite and slamed another into a solid door? I would *really* enjoy killing the bastard now. The sprites were just as much my family as Aurelia was destined to be. They were my chosen family, those loyal to me, those who cared for me.

And no one fucks with my family and gets away with it.

"Magna, can you heal Freya?" I asked spinning to the half-fae woman.

"I'll do my best," Magna said with a nod before sitting next to her on the couch.

I looked away sharply, gritting my teeth and clenching my fists until they shook at my sides. The sprites had been with me forever, and seeing Freya like that burned all the way to my damned shifter soul.

"I don't know how long we have before they leave, Master Grey. It's bad! She only agreed to train and help him so that he would let us go," Fiona babbled in panic.

"What is he planning?" I asked with dread, my insides twisting.

"He wants Miss Aurelia to go with him to Faery so she can close the portal. He wants to make sure we can never get back!" Fiona cried.

"It can't be done, can it?" Dan asked with wide eyes.

Magna hummed softly by Freya, the green light of her healing magic glowing over the sprite. "I think it's the prophecy," she answered. "Aurelia must be the one the prophecy is all about. She can either set us free or leave us to rot, forever exiled from our home. Malcolm played into her purity and used her kind heart against us." Magna shook her head in exasperation as her hands completed slow circuits in the air above Freya.

"But she only did it to save us," Fiona said softly and sniffled. "Maybe it would have been better for us to—"

"No!" I snapped. "It would not. Don't even think such a thing! Aurelia's not going to close the portal. We know her better than that! We're going to get her out of there, no matter the cost. And we're not going to let this asshole succeed." I turned to Dan, filled with renewed purpose.

"What do you need, boss?" he asked as his shoulders straightened.

"I need you to go keep an eye on Layla and Karma. I need to organize a team that I can trust to help me get Aurelia back, but I can't have those bitches alerting Malcolm that we are coming for him," I ordered.

"But, boss! I want a piece of this guy too," Dan complained.

"I can't have Aurelia seeing you, Dan. Remember the whole *you shot her with a tranq dart* thing and got us all into this mess?" I raised a questioning eyebrow at him.

"I didn't mean to fuck up... but fine," he grumbled. He turned and stalked to the elevator without another word.

It was time to call in some reinforcements. I would show Malcolm what happened when he stole what was most precious to me.

He's going to fucking pay. Big time.

"Fiona, you need to rest while I get a rescue team together," I said.

She followed me into my office. "I can't rest knowing what is happening to her, Master Grey. He had his hand around her throat and was choking her when he slammed the door in my face." Fiona chewed her lip nervously, fear in her eyes.

"He what?" I yelled, rage bursting within me like an erupting volcano.

The bastard was already on my shit list for punching Aurelia in the head and kidnapping her... but leaving Fiona to wonder if Aurelia was still alive as she worked desperately to save her sister made him worse. He wasn't just a wicked Fae.

He's a dead Fae.

"He hurt her a couple times, and I'm afraid of what he will do to her if she doesn't do as he asks," she said, her lip trembling as she landed on my desk, slumping down on the smooth surface.

"We won't let that happen, Fiona. But we can't find him without you. We're relying on your help, so I need you to rest until my team gets here," I said sternly. "That's an order, little one."

Fiona's face fell but she nodded and took off, still flying in a chaotic zigzag, due to her damaged wing.

"If Magna is done healing Freya, ask her to fix your wing. You can't fly like that!" I called out after her. With my heart thumping in my chest, I picked up my phone and opened a text conversation that I'd hoped I wouldn't have to engage until my end game plans were well underway. But drastic times called for drastic measures, and time was not on our side.

Aurelia needs me, now more than ever.

And every supernatural, whether they knew it or not, was counting on me to stop that fucker from sealing us out of our true home forever. It was time for the big guns.

I need your help.

I typed into my phone and hit send, pulling the trigger. Then I turned the device off and slumped back into my chair, exhaling a deep sigh. I wasn't expecting a response. I knew I wouldn't get one from them.

It's done. There's no going back now.

A moment later, I grinned maliciously, the flames of my ire rekindled with blazing glory. Malcolm had *no* fucking idea what was coming for him. With the Riders of the Wild Hunt after his ass, not even Faery would be safe.

I will do whatever it takes to rescue Aurelia, even if it means calling on Death himself.

My wolf howled inside my head in triumph. He was just as ready for blood, carnage, and revenge as I was. And one way or another, we were damn well going to get it.

Soon. Very soon.

CHAPTER 23

"No," I said defiantly, crossing my arms over my chest and glaring at Malcolm.

"You said if I allowed the vermin go free you would do whatever I asked," Malcolm reminded me through gritted teeth.

"I lied," I said with pleasure, and I shrugged out of his grip. "Well, I wasn't raised by Fae, and who's fault is that?" I raised a brow in silent accusation.

"You will do what I ask, Aurelia, or you will be punished!" Malcolm roared, quickly losing his patience. He grabbed me again and dragged me behind him, his rage buoying his stride to a near run.

I tripped over my feet just trying to keep up with him and fell to my knees, my breath whooshing out of me with an *oomph!*

Malcolm let go of my arm in frustration and fisted my hair, pulling me roughly up with it. "You don't get to be a brat when you don't even remember who you are! You will help me, or you will learn the true meaning of suffering, my love."

"You taught me that already when you stole me from my bed in the castle," I snarled back at him as fire danced across my scalp at his grip. My eyes widened at my own words.

Shit, I lived in a castle.

I'd known it since I attempted to retrieve my memories and relived Malcom spiriting me from my room. But knowing it and *saying* it aloud were apparently two very different things. This time, the fact really registered with me, sinking into my consciousness, and I my mind reeled at the impossible.

Who am I?

And it seemed there was only one logical answer to that question. I'd been in quiet denial of it, but now the truth was unavoidably clear.

Holy shit.

"My parents were the king and queen, weren't they?" I asked in no small amount of horror and disgust. My parents were the elitist, prejudiced, wicked Fae who hated all other supernatuals. The realization made me feel sick to my stomach in the space of heartbeat.

"Your parents *are* the king and queen, and you will meet them as soon as we close the portal," Malcolm said, tightening his fist even more tightly in my hair.

"I don't care to meet them, asshole. They never looked for me, so I why should I fucking care about them at all?" I yelled and thrashed, not expecting an answer.

"Is that what you think?" He shook his head, his eyes hard as they stared down at me. "They sent warriors looking for you for years! And even though you were hidden with the witch, they never gave up on their search."

My real parents actually searched for me? That doesn't sound right. Why wouldn't they have been able to find me?

It didn't make sense. Aside from a bit of glamour to hide my wings,

I wasn't living underground or skulking about like a shadow. I avoided trouble, but I was out and about. I ran errands for Mother, I brought home groceries. I partook in daily activities like everyone else. I was despised and unwanted, but people saw me around.

Surely, elite Fae warriors would have been able to find me?

I stopped in my tracks and glared at Malcolm. My head screamed in pain at the pressure on my hair, but I didn't care.

Malcolm stopped and loosened his grip, watching the emotions flash behind my eyes.

He had to be lying. He was trying to make me *want* to go back, but I would never willingly return to a people so prejudiced they purged entire races of people from their realm based on nothing more than some fucked-up notion of blood purity.

"Your plan backfired, asshole," I said. "I will never condemn the supernaturals to a life of hiding if I can help it. They deserve their home back! We had no right to do what we did."

"Why do you care so much about them, anyway?" Malcolm asked with another shake of his head. "Your friend, Grey's most trusted beta, is the reason you are here right now. They can't be trusted. They sold you out at the first given opportunity."

What? Layla is the reason he knew when to come after me?

My gut roiled with hate, and I fumed with an instant desire for revenge. She was the reason I was in this fucking mess, not to mention the sprites being harmed.

I'm going to kill that bitch.

Malcolm grinned at the defeated expression on my face. He obviously assumed that meant I would help him. Unfortunately for him, he couldn't be more wrong.

I hadn't met many benevolent supernaturals in my life, but there were a precious few, and I wouldn't want to condemn them. Having never had a stable home of my own since early childhood, I knew just how much losing one could mean to someone. Living in exile, hiding among humans was not what we were destined for. It couldn't be!

"It doesn't matter. She has hated me from the day she met me. I would expect nothing less of her." I slapped his hand away.

"They are a scourge, and you would bring them back to our realm?"

Malcolm ground out. "Your parents will be so disappointed." He wrapped his hand around my arm again and flung me through an open door.

I crashed to the floor but held in the cry of pain that threatened to pry its way from between my lips and expose me. I wouldn't show weakness. Not now and certainly not to him. My back screamed from the brutal landing on the stone floor, and I blinked back tears, unwilling to let them fall.

Fuck him. I'm going to get through this.

This wasn't the room he'd locked me in before when I first arrived. It was musty and dark, and a chill ran down my spine as he slammed the iron door closed.

"I showed too much kindness to you before, apparently. So, you will stay here until you agree to do as I ask," Malcolm snarled through the door. "I've waited this long to fulfil our task. I can wait a while longer."

I scooted back, away from the door, until my back hit a wall. The room couldn't have been bigger than six feet wide. There was a small, dirty cot in the corner, and the only light in the room slipped in from under the door. Otherwise, he'd left me in complete darkness. I brought my knees to my chest and wrapped my arms around them, praying that the sprites had made it back to Grey and that they were okay.

I quietly attempted to call my magic to me, so that I could attempt to blow a hole through the damn wall, but it fizzled out as quickly as it was summoned. The iron in the cell was draining my magic, like water through the many holes of a colander.

"Shit. This isn't good," I said to myself and rested my chin on my knees once more.

"Who's there?' a rough voice asked unexpectedly, startling me.

There's someone else in here? How the hell did I miss that?

"Oh, just Malcolm's latest prisoner," I groaned.

"I'm no prisoner, girl. He dumped you in my living quarters," the voice answered.

It was too dark to see more than a small shadow on the other side of the tiny space. Scuttling sounds filled the tiny room, and I flinched back.

A small man stood about three feet tall in front of me, and by what scant light there was, I could see he wore a scowl.

"What?" I asked and reared back in surprise, hitting my head against the wall.

"What did you do to the master to make him to throw you in here?" He raised a huge, bushy eyebrow, his face mostly hidden in shadow.

"I refused to be his pawn," I said simply, raising my chin in defiance.

I don't owe this little man anything.

The small man gasped and leaned forward, suddenly more inquisitive than perturbed. "Who are you?" he asked.

"I'm a prisoner and that's all you need to know." I straightened my spine and sighed, not willing to cave and divulge my life story to this nosey little goblin.

"You're the princess!" The miniature man gasped. A second later he snapped his fingers, and a flame sparked to life in his hand.

"I don't know what you're talking about," I retorted.

"By the gods. The master has been looking for you for years. Why would he put you in here?" he asked, almost speaking to himself.

"I don't care. He's an asshole, and I just want to go home," I said, glancing away into the darkness in the corners of the room.

Home? Is that what Grey's penthouse has become in such a short time? I've never really thought of anywhere as home. But it is...

The realization floored me. Grey and my small group of acquaintances had come to mean more to me than anything or anyone else I'd ever known in a very short space of time. But the feelings, the love? They were real. I knew it in my bones.

"If you want to go home, I'm sure the master will take you to the portal," he said and patted my knee.

"You misunderstand. I *don't* want to go back to Faery. That's not my home." I shook my head and pursed my lips.

The little man gasped and took a step away from me, his face a mask of horror and confusion. I could practically see the questions on the tip of his tongue. "You... how? Why?" he stuttered out. Clearly, he was on the wicked Fae's side of the argument if he thought I was the one in the wrong.

I sat in silence, refusing to answer his questions. I didn't owe this man my history. He could come and go as he pleased, while I was a prisoner. He worked for Malcolm, and for all I knew, Malcolm put me in here so the little man could get information on me or convince me of the virtues of Faery.

He stared at me, waiting for a response, and when I didn't give him one, he huffed. "Fine, keep your secrets," he grumbled and walked away. "You would do better to do as the master asks. He's not terrible." He laid on his cot and snuffed out the flame in his hand.

As a result, I was plunged into darkness again, but it didn't bother me. I liked the dark. I'd dwelled in the dark my whole life and it hadn't broken me. Hell, I was used to living like this. There was no way Malcolm would be the one to break me.

Not a chance.

I curled into a ball on the grimy floor and closed my eyes. Grey would come for me. I had to believe that. And when he did, I would tell him what a traitorous bitch Layla was.

He'll have a fucking field day with her!

* * *

I must have dozed off at some point, because a shout had me straightening in the darkness and I was instantly alert. "What was that?" I asked the small man, assuming he'd been woken by the noise too.

"I don't know," he answered as he shot up from the cot. He peered at me for a moment then vanished into thin air.

Soon after, there was another shout and then a crash. I jumped up from the floor and took two long strides toward the door and beat my fists against it, hope swelling inside of me.

Yes! It's Grey. It has to be. He came for me.

"Grey, I'm in here!" I yelled at the top of my lungs, still beating against the door.

"Step back," a gruff voice answered from the other side.

Who is that? Did Grey bring reinforcements?

I sidestepped away from the door just in time and ducked, holding my arms over my head as the door flew across the room and hit the opposite wall with an almighty *thunk*.

The man on the other side of the door was so wide I doubted he could even fit through the door without having to turn sideways. He had a long, scraggly beard and a scar above his left eye. He was obviously a man that had seen many battles.

"Who are you?" I asked, taking a wary step away from him.

"I'm an acquaintance of Grey's. Come, we need to get out of here." The man turned on his heel and stormed away, expecting me to follow.

I wasn't stupid. No matter who this guy was, he was huge, strong, and he'd broken me out of Malcolm's clutches. He was without doubt the better option. Without hesitation, I jogged to catch up to him and followed close to his back, keeping my eyes peeled for danger as we went. As soon as I was out of the iron-laced room, my magic came back, and purple shimmering glory crackled across my palms.

"Where's Grey?" I whispered. Was I stupid for following this surly man that I knew absolutely nothing about?

Probably, but he got me out of that poison-laced room, so perhaps it's a case of looks can be deceiving.

"He went after Malcolm, but we need to go." He grabbed my arm far more gently than I would have expected from a bear of a man and nothing like the way Malcolm had treated me. It was an urgent gesture, but guiding and protective at the same time.

"Asher!" a man yelled in the near distance. "Did you find the princess?"

I stiffened and glared at my rescuer, immediately on edge.

How do they know that I'm a Fae princess?

"Don't look at me like that, Princess. Grey figured it out quickly because of Malcolm's involvement," the man, who I now knew to be Asher, said as he led me to the entryway of the building.

Tears misted in my eyes as I looked at the front door, recognizing it immediately. My gaze dropped to the floor, and I swallowed hard. "Freya?" I ventured softly.

"She's healing," he answered before putting his hand on my back and leading me out into the early dawn light.

I squinted as my eyes adjusted and breathed in a deep sigh of relief. I hated seeing her like that, crumpled and dim, unconscious with the shock of the sudden impact. I shuddered at the thought as I relived it in my mind. Just knowing that she was healing lifted a huge burden from my shoulders.

I scanned the forest with a smile, my heart filling with relief until I saw the motorcycles parked in the driveway. "You want me to get on one of those?" I asked in shock, pointing at the huge hunks of metal on wheels. I'd never been a fan.

Asher grinned and nodded. "Are you scared, Princess?" he teased.

"No," I shot back and stomped my foot. "Those things are just fucking death traps, and I have a healthy respect for my life."

"Well, it's either that or you walk back to Dallas, but that's nothing short of a recipe for disaster if Malcolm isn't caught." Asher shrugged. "Your choice. Far be it for me to order about a princess," he added.

Shit, he's right. I don't really have a choice. Fuck it. Smart ass...

"Fine," I sighed. "Let's go then."

The truth was I didn't even know which way to go to get back on my own, and there was no telling where the hell Grey was at this point in time.

Is it even safe to head back to the penthouse?

I moved toward the motorcycles with trepidation, when out of nowhere, pain shot through my back, and I was knocked face first into the hard-packed dirt. A surprised, clipped shriek escaped me as I hit the ground. I tried to move the fucking boulder of a man off me but couldn't. I was pinned.

"Stay down, princess," Asher warned. "Looks like Malcolm is back." My burly rescuer rolled off me, staying low to assess the situation.

"What the fuck happened?" I asked against the ground, gasping for air.

"He attacked you with his magic, but I tackled you before it could touch you," he said, scanning the trees intently.

What the hell? I thought he needed me to close the portal. Not to mention the psycho wants to claim me for his own. Why would he try to kill me now? And where the hell is Grey?

Malcolm stepped out from the trees and there was a shimmering quality to him. He was using some kind of magical shield. "I killed your wolf, my love!" Malcolm taunted, his eyes blazing with malice as his blond hair whipped around him in the morning breeze. "Now that mutt is out of the way, you have no reason not to help me."

"No!" I screamed, unable to hold back my instant, natural reaction.

He can't be dead!

Magic erupted in my palms as I jumped to my feet, pain and rage fueling my power like too much gas poured on a bonfire.

Asher was on his feet in an instant and stepped in front of me, ready to take a hit for me.

But I wouldn't be stopped. I stepped to the side, twirling around him to throw everything I had at Malcom. I screamed in defiance when it bounced off without harming him. His shield shimmered on impact, but otherwise, there was no outward sign of any damage.

"He's lying, Princess. He's trying to bait you. Ki... *Grey* is much harder to kill than that!" he said and stepped in my path again, acting a physical shield of flesh in my defense.

This man was truly willing to give his life for mine, and though I was humbled, I couldn't help but frown at him.

What was he about to call Grey? What doesn't he want me to know?

"Am I lying, hunter?" Malcolm asked with a raised brow and took a step closer. "Why would I lie about killing that mongrel? It serves no purpose, because after I kill the rest of you, I'll take her home anyway." Magic, unlike anything I'd ever seen before, blasted from his fingers like bolts of raw, unbridled lightning.

I gasped and once again hit the ground with a jarring *thump* as I was tackled to the ground by Asher.

A bolt of Malcolm's magical lightning struck a tree, and it exploded into an inferno of flames before falling on the motorcycles, totaling them in a heartbeat.

"Shit! That bastard is going to pay," Asher snarled as he got up into a surprisingly swift crouch. "That was my favorite fucking bike." Shadows suddenly gathered and swirled around Asher out of nowhere like they were living, breathing entities. His arm shot out and the shadows hurtled toward Malcolm with frightening speed.

Malcolm's eyes widened as the shadows broke through his shield like it wasn't there at all. They slithered and wrapped around his body, pinning his arms to his sides, as a rustling sounded in the bushes from behind him.

"Grey!" I whispered, tears of relief pooling in my eyes as an absolutely beautiful white wolf lunged for Malcolm, his maw wide and his teeth bared.

Malcolm smirked, seemingly unperturbed. "I'll see you again soon, Aurelia," he promised, and then disappeared from sight.

"How did that fucker sift with my shadows on him?" Asher growled, scratching his beard.

Grey's breathtaking huge, white wolf raced forward and nudged my cheek with his wet nose.

I wrapped my arms around his furry neck and sobbed my heart out in relief, unwilling to let him go. He felt so soft and strong and smelled like mine—like home. Everything about his presence instantly comforted me and soothed the ache that had steadily grown like a thorn in my soul over the past two days. "He said you were dead," I cried, burying my face in his thick coat and breathing deeply. A pair of pants hit the ground beside me, and I startled, before looking up into Asher's kind eyes.

"As touching as all this is, we need to find a way out of here," he grunted. "This shit isn't over."

My handsome, brave alpha wolf whined but backed away from me and started to shift.

I shivered when he returned to his human form, naked as the day he was born. Without shame I scanned his tan, toned body, nearly groaning at what I saw. He was beyond mouth-watering, and an ache bloomed to life between my thighs in response. Biting down on my lower lip, I teased it between my teeth and sighed aloud.

"There will be time for that later," Grey assured me with a chuckle, following my obvious gaze. "But right now, I need clothes."

My cheeks burned with embarrassment as I crouched down and grabbed the pants from the ground and handed them to him reluctantly.

He was just *gorgeous*, and he made me feel all kinds of things I probably shouldn't, given how little I truly knew about him. Was this likely a recipe for disaster? Probably, but as I peered up at him, the fire in his eyes matched mine, and I decided that I could deal with a disaster just fine. We were fated mates after all, and given the benefit of time, I was sure there wasn't anything we couldn't overcome together. He was my wolf, and I was his goddamn fairy princess.

CHAPTER 24
Grey

Thankfully, after Aurelia's immediate rescue we hadn't encountered any further complications. With the bikes smashed, we'd had to call in alternative transport, but the main thing was that we made it back to my building in one piece. We bid our friends a good night, offering our thanks and gratitude for all their help, and then headed for the only home we had outside of Faery.

I picked Aurelia up in my arms as soon as the elevator doors opened to the penthouse. I knew there were others there who wanted to see her, those who had helped and were now waiting... but I didn't care. They could wait. It had been hell on earth without my fated mate for days, and my wolf had reached the limit of his patience. He had been going absolutely mad with panic and anger in her absence and he now that we had Aurelia back, there was no way he was waiting a moment longer. Though I wondered how it could feel like that for us after only having known her for such a relatively short time.

It has to be the fated mate bond we share.

It was the only feasible explanation. The only thing that made any sense at all.

"What in the gods... What happened to my poor plants?" she asked with a frown as she surveyed the remains of our once lush and green apartment.

"Later," I grunted, inhaling the scent of her as I stomped past Magna and the sprites. There would be time for words, but that time wasn't now.

Magna opened her mouth to say something, the words dying on her tongue a heartbeat later.

I glared at them. She wasn't stopping me. No one was. My wolf was thrashing inside me to get to his mate. We'd suffered long enough.

"Hi!" Aurelia called back to them apologetically as I whisked her away. "Grey, where are we going?" she asked with an amused giggle, the sound like music to my ears.

I nuzzled her neck and kicked open my bedroom door, which slammed into the wall with a loud *thunk!* I stopped just inside the room and set her down on her own two feet. Her body slid against mine in the most delicious of ways, and I licked her neck possessively. "I need you," I groaned. "I need to feel that you are here and *mine.*"

She shivered at my touch, her stunning emerald-green eyes gazing up into mine.

I gripped her hips, pulling her back against my body with feral desire. My already rock-hard cock rubbed through my clothes and against her belly.

Shit, I don't know how long I'm going to last with these wickedly tempting curves.

Aurelia reached up with a smile and wrapped her arms around my neck, standing on her tiptoes to plant a sensual, drawn-out kiss on my lips.

The door clicked shut behind me and I broke the kiss to glance over my shoulder and raised an eyebrow at her.

Did she just do that with her magic?

"I've been practicing," she said in response to my unspoken question, a grin on her beautiful face.

I slid my hand around to her back, then underneath her tank top. The skin-on-skin contact made me shudder with anticipation and yearning.

Her lips came up to my neck, and she kissed and licked her way back to my mouth, pulling me down to her. "Grey, I want you," she whispered, rubbing her thighs together, no doubt heightening the pressure of her need.

I pulled her tank top up and trailed my fingers over the exposed skin before I ripped the shirt over her head. Staring down at her voluptuous, lace-covered breasts, I groaned.

She's fucking perfect.

Her hands tightened in my hair at my touch, and a moan slipped from her lips.

I leaned in and licked along her collarbone, then trailed kisses down to the swell of her breast, reveling in the taste of her flesh as I nipped the sensitive skin there.

Aurelia's back arched, her warm body pressing against mine with obvious desire.

"Go lay on the bed and take the rest of your clothes off." I took a step back, waiting for her to do as I commanded.

Heat tinted her cheeks a breathtaking shade of pink as she reached behind her back and unclasped her lacy bra. She slid it from her arms and let it fall silently to the floor, averting her gaze as she sucked in a deep breath.

Fuck. And I thought she was beautiful before. Her curvy body is a work of art and it's all mine.

"Wait," I objected.

She stopped with a frown, her fingers looped into the waistband of her leggings.

I prowled toward her like a wolf ready for the kill, or more accurately a wolf ready to claim his mate. I picked her up and threw her over my shoulder, racing to the bed with her.

She giggled and flailed playfully, pummeling my back with her fists. "Grey!"

I tossed her onto the mattress and leaned over her glorious body, taking a nipple into my mouth.

Her giggle soon became a moan as she dug her fingernails into my shoulders, her head thrown back in ecstasy.

I nipped at her luscious flesh and attended to her other nipple, lavishing it with the same level of attention before slowly trailing kisses down her soft belly. And then I moved on to the waistband of her leggings.

"Grey," she whimpered, her voice breathy and ripe with need.

"What is it, princess?" I asked with a wicked grin. Unwilling to wait for her response, I tugged on her leggings, pulling them slowly down her creamy, thick thighs. She was fucking perfection incarnate, and I was dying to be inside her. One taste of her wasn't enough. It would never be enough.

With a casual flourish, I threw her leggings on the floor, adding them to the pile along with her bra and shirt. Then turning back, I trailed my fingers up her inner thigh. Eagerly I followed my finger with my lips, keen to pepper her beautiful skin with my hot lips.

Aurelia's hands sank into my hair, and she cursed under her breath at my languid, slow, and purposeful ministrations.

I shuddered at the sting of pain as she gripped the strands of my hair too tightly, trying to forcibly tug me up her body.

Aurelia wriggled her hips in frustration and attempted to rub her thighs together, no doubt to expel me from my position of power of her.

I gripped her hips, holding her firmly in place as I ran my nose over her panty-covered center, breathing her in. She was soaked through, and the delicious damp scent of vanilla and jasmine filled my nose.

I need to taste her. She's so fucking perfect. She literally even smells like a fucking fairy princess!

I glanced up at her flushed face with a dark smile and brought my hands to her hips. Gripping her panties in a tight fist, I ripped the flimsy fabric down the middle, destroying them in a single brutal moment of passion.

Aurelia gasped and tightened her grasp on my hair, her whole body trembling with wanting.

I lunged forward, plunging my face into her heaven, and licked her all the way up her slit and to her clit and sucked on it, savoring the sweet flavor of her slick.

Her back arched, her muscles tight, a scream tearing from her throat as she held me to her soaking pussy.

I couldn't breathe, but I didn't give a fucking damn if she smothered my face into her dripping wet pussy. If I died right here and now, it'd be the way to go—a death worthy of a king.

"Oh, my gods, Grey," she breathed as her thighs fell open. Like a cut snake, she squirmed and thrashed beneath my touch as if fighting her desire, unwilling to succumb to the deviant pleasure afflicting her curvy form.

I thrust my tongue inside her, scooping up her desire and lapping at it greedily before making my way back up to her swollen and sensitive clit. Without warning, I thrust a finger inside her, my digit gliding in effortlessly and without resistance into her tightness.

She thrashed her head from side to side, biting her lip all the while until I saw blood bead there. "Fuck, Grey!" she shouted, her voice trailing off into a needy whine that made my cock ache. Her whole body shook as she climbed higher and higher toward her inevitable climax. She was so fucking responsive.

I'm going to fuck my golden princess every day for the rest of my damn life!

Smiling wickedly, I curled my finger inside her at the thought as I pushed a second finger inside her pussy, pumping several times hard and fast as I flicked her clit with my tongue.

"Grey!" she screamed my name like an anguished prayer as she shattered, unable to hold herself together under my relentless onslaught.

Her sweet cum coated my fingers and tongue as I devoured her like a man starved, feasting upon her until she finally stopped bucking and swearing at the ceiling, her fists tangled in her own hair.

When she finally relaxed, having come down from her orgasm, I crawled up her body, trailing kisses along her stomach and over her breasts until I was directly above her. Her expression as I leaned down and sealed my lips to hers was priceless.

She moaned into my mouth and wrapped her leg around my hips, pulling me toward her. Aurelia broke the kiss, frowning in confusion. "Wait, why the hell do you still have clothes on?"

I chuckled at her delicious enthusiasm and kissed her again before sitting up and scooting back off the bed. I removed my pants with ease, and my mate's gaze burned into me, setting my insides on fire.

"Like what you see, princess?" I grinned as I crawled back over to her.

"That stupid nickname isn't so much of a nickname anymore," Aurelia growled, twisting her lips into a delicious pout.

"Shh, we aren't talking about that right now," I soothed as I leaned down and kissed her roughly, stealing her breath away and bruising her lips. I would need to know what she'd learned while in that bastard's clutches... but not now. Now, I just needed to make her scream for me again. I wanted her to scream my name until it was engraved on her soul.

I rolled on top of her again and gripped her hip tightly, fitting our bodies together while rubbing the head of my cock against her wet entrance. But I stopped short of burying myself inside her. With her warm breath against my face, I simply rocked my hips, just dipping in and out of her puffy, slick lips.

"Grey! Are you teasing me?" she demanded, thrusting her hips up at me.

I gripped her waist, maintaining my control—keeping her my prisoner—and trailing my lips down her neck, nicking her flesh with my teeth. "I would never dream of teasing you, princess," I drawled, enjoying the scent of desperation and need a while longer. To be so desired was a heady and delectable drug indeed, and I wanted more. As much as I could possibly get.

"Then please!" she cried, begging me for a reprieve. "I couldn't bear it if you stopped again." She threaded her hands into my hair and tugged my mouth back to hers in a bruising kiss. "Just fuck me, wolf," she whispered, breaking the kiss to breathe against my lips.

I growled, the demand turning me and my shifter on even more. "As you wish, princess," I snarked softly, overwhelmed by desire. With a satisfied grin, I positioned myself at her entrance. Then, calling upon all my resolve and self-restraint, I pushed in slowly, remembering that she was a virgin. And the last thing I wanted to do was to hurt her in my need for her.

Damn.

It was almost like mission fucking impossible. She was hot and wet and so tight that every inch of me yearned for nothing more than to be hilt deep in her.

She hissed in pain and arched her back, biting down on her lip from the inside, her brows knitted.

I froze, studying her face as I hovered, not daring to move another muscle until she offered me some indication that she was all right to continue. I wanted her, but after everything she'd been through, I'd fucking *kill* myself if I hurt her. I never ever wanted to be the cause of her pain. I couldn't bear the thought, and neither could my wolf.

"I'm okay, Grey," she whispered, suddenly cupping my cheek and breaking through my reverie. She pressed her lips softly to mine, encouraging me to claim her, to make her mine.

And so, I did. I didn't need more than that. I pushed forward, forging inside her, leveling out until my sac rested against her thick ass.

Fuck me.

She fit me like a glove, and my body shuddered from the tips of my fingers to the ends of my toes at how *perfect* she felt. She was mine now. Forever. I'd claimed her and taken her virginity. My cock was the only one that would ever taste the heaven that resided between her luscious thighs.

And I'll kill any fucking man or woman that tries to take her from me.

I rocked my hips forward and grunted as I reached the deepest parts of her again and again.

"By the gods," she breathed, arching her back, her fingers tightening in my hair.

I gripped her hip and withdrew to my head before slamming back in. "Fuck, Aurelia, you feel *so* good," I groaned as I thrust in and out of her hard and fast, pumping her so forcefully that I felt the wicked sensation of our pelvises colliding with each stroke. “I don’t know how long I’m going to last,” I hissed before I shifted my weight onto a forearm so that I could trail my fingers down her belly to her clit and circle it roughly.

Her legs tightened around my hips as her body thrust back against me, desperate to feel everything all at once. Our bodies moved in sync, and she gave as good as she got. She was without doubt the keenest and most earnestly passionate lover I’d ever had.

My spine began to tingle with my impending orgasm, and I pinched her clit between my fingers, making her yelp aloud. “Can I mark you, mate?” I asked, my wolf shining through my eyes and his husky gravel taking over my voice.

“Yes,” Aurelia moaned as her back arched and she willingly and instinctively bared her neck to me.

There would never be anything sexier than my beautiful mate submitting to my bite. I licked up the column of her neck, my wolf howling in my head like a beast on crack.

Mine.

“Grey, please, make me yours,” she moaned, the unmistakable note of desperation not lost on me.

I’d never heard anything sexier in my entire life. I lunged forward, my heart in my throat as I sank my partially shifted fangs into the spot on her neck that met her collarbone. I froze as euphoria unlike anything I’d ever experienced before tore through me, triggering my orgasm. It hit me hard and fast, almost knocking the sense out of me. I came on a roar, unleashing my hot load deep inside her, filling her with my shifter seed.

Aurelia screamed in ecstasy, and her pussy rippled around my cock, milking me until there was nothing left to give.

I released her neck and lapped at my mark on her skin. My shifter saliva had healing properties and would encourage the wound to heal faster. Exhausted and sated beyond my wildest dreams, I pressed my forehead to hers and took a deep, steadying breath. “Are you okay, princess?” I asked as I disengaged and rolled carefully to my side, then pulled her back to my chest.

“Yes. That was incredible,” she whispered.

I squeezed her tightly and nuzzled her neck. I’d missed her so much when she had been gone from the apartment. But my wolf was finally calm with my mate in our arms. As protective as I was feeling, a deeply disturbing and unsettling thought washed over me in our post-coital bliss. “Did he hurt you?” I growled, my voice low as I pulled her closer.

“It was nothing, Grey. Nothing I couldn’t survive. I’m stronger than you think.” She shook her head and turned in my arms to face me.

“I will fucking kill him one day,” I said as I glared into her eyes, unable to hide my passionate desire and fervor for revenge. My declaration was a promise and it was one I would keep no matter what. I would have Malcolm’s damn head even if it fucking killed me.

“I know you will, my love,” Aurelia soothed. “And then we will go home to Faery, together, and take our place back in the world.” She kissed me softly, her lips lingering on mine as our hearts beat as one.

And I could only hope that she was foreseeing the future, because there was nothing more I wanted than to make her my queen.

CHAPTER 25

Grey paced the room, anxiety clear in his every move as I got ready for the challenge, or at least what was supposed to be the challenge. “Are you sure about this?” he asked softly for the third time.

“Yes, this is the only way.” I reached out to him and laid a hand on his arm, halting him..

“But what if everything goes to hell? They are all my employees, but Layla and Karma know them much better than I do. They’re there with them on the ground every damn day.” He gripped my arms, his brow creased as concern and love for me warred on his features for pride of place.

Asher stepped into the locker room and shook his head. "The princess has the makings of a fine and brave warrior. Stop being the nagging mate, Grey," he chastised. "It doesn't suit you."

"I'll kill you next, hunter!" Grey growled, his lips downturned.

I smacked Grey on the arm and groaned at the feel of his taut muscles beneath my palm. We hadn't left the bedroom for *days*, but we needed to deal with Layla and Karma sooner rather than later. "Asher saved me. You will not kill him, wolf." I frowned at Grey in playful warning.

My mate sighed and rolled his eyes. "As you wish, my love." He grinned and kissed me softly in return.

Asher coughed. "Sickening," he remarked with a wink at me. "All this affection is enough to turn the stomach of even the most seasoned soul."

I put on a brave face and smiled at the hunter's joke, but inside I was nervous—really nervous. What would happen if they found out that I was aware of what they had done, or their betrayal of not only Grey and me, but the Syndicate itself?

Did Malcolm tell them what he told me? Has he given them a heads up so they can cause chaos at the challenge?

I hoped not. So far, there didn't seem to be any unrest that was out of the ordinary and everything was quiet, but I'd certainly learned that in the world of supernaturals anything could change at any moment. Ours was a world of survival, deceit, underhanded dealings, and crime and that attracted a certain type of individual—ones with flexible morals and loyalties.

"Are we sure that Layla doesn't know anything?" I asked, chewing on my lower lip.

"As far as we can tell, based on our work inside the facility, she has no clue what's about to go down," Asher confirmed with a grin.

"You were spying from inside the facility?" I raised a brow, intrigued.

"No one in the facility or anywhere else in this realm would question the Riders of the Wild Hunt." He crossed his arms over his chest, clearly more than a little proud of his prestigious position.

I couldn't see what everyone else saw. He didn't seem that scary to me. The other Riders didn't seem that scary either, to be honest. Sure, they were big, imposing, and lethal, but... they had hearts. They were kind to those deserving of it, and fiercely loyal.

But I guess it's all just a matter of perception. Perhaps others have not seen the side of them that I have?

"Are the guys in position?" Grey asked Asher. "It's almost time."

I bounced on the balls of my feet nervously, buzzed with equal measures of energy and fear. This was the challenge everyone had been waiting for. And even though I'd been working relentlessly with Max to hone my physical prowess, my anxieties remained.

Karma was the best the Syndicate had. She'd been a point of pride for years... until she chose the wrong side and revealed her true colors.

What if she tries to kill me?

A challenge was only meant to end in defeat, but sometimes things went too far. Deaths happened in the ring, and I knew that had been Layla's plan all along. It was why she sold me out to Malcolm in the first place. The cocky bitch thought we would never find out.

Dumb bitch.

She thought she was so good and had played the long game so successfully that no one would ever guess, let alone believe that she would betray Grey. But she was wrong, and she was about to find out just how fucking wrong she was.

I checked my knives were secure on my body and ready for action before I blew out a breath to steady myself.

Grey squeezed my shoulder and sent an encouraging smile my way that made my heart skip a beat. "You're going to be great, princess, don't worry." He wrapped an arm around me and pulled me against his chest.

It was beyond comforting. I *loved* it when he touched me. His lips on my neck made me shiver. "Thank you," I whispered. With stoic resolvem I stepped away from him and gave him what I hoped was a confident smile before doing exactly what Reah had encouraged me to do. I schooled my features into an unreadable mask, adopting my poker face.

In this battle, I will not allow my enemy to read me like a book. I will give away nothing. I will be hard, strong, fast, and smart. You can do this, Aurelia.

The crowd outside the locker room started shouting. They were already baying for blood. Their feet stomped on the ground, causing vibrations to shiver through the floor. I took a cleansing breath. This was it. They would be savagely thirsting for a bloody battle, and I would do what I could to give them what they wanted without actually killing anyone... even though a part of me wanted it to go that far. I wouldn't become what they said I was. I'd leave the outcome of their lives to Grey or Fate—whichever came first.

"All right, let's get this show on the road," I said with more confidence than I felt. I mentally pumped myself up and stomped to the door and stood there, waiting until Grey came to open it. He'd drilled into my head the importance of him doing that for me in this fight. We had to present a united front, or I would be seen as weak and without allies. It needed to be seen that I had the Syndicate's favor, that it was me who was in the right. It us against the traitors.

I am not weak. I am a damn fae princess, as weird as that is to say.

I strutted out the door with my head held high with Grey and Asher at my back. The room was practically an industrial-sized basement with bleachers for blood-thirsty spectators set up next to a ring. The magic pouring off the ring made my stomach flip-flop. It was just like the warded, magicless room in Grey's penthouse that I used for training for this very moment.

Layla stood next to Karma on the other side of the ring and smirked at me, her eyes narrowed and expression rife with venom. She thought this was a done deal and that I would be gone shortly, her problem erased and out of her hair. The dumb bitch really, truly believed that she'd won. That she'd walk away from this the victor.

I grinned menacingly at her obvious challenge and nodded subtly to Grey.

Grey squeezed my hand before stepping in front of me—my love, my man, my wolf, and my shield.

My mate.

"It's come to my attention that we have traitors in our midst!" Grey shouted over the screaming voices looking for a fight, his voice carrying a terrifying air of authority and power. It was clear he was in his element. He commanded obedience like he was born to it.

All the yelling ceased, and the employees of the Syndicate whispered among themselves as they glanced around at the people nearest them.

"What are you talking about, Grey?" Layla asked, stepping forward.

Yes, please step into the ring!

There was nothing I wanted more than to take Layla down a peg or two, but this was technically Grey's battle. She'd fucked with me, but she'd betrayed him.

"Someone in this room betrayed me," he repeated and raised a brow at her, daring her to deny it.

"Who would dare betray the king?" she sneered aloud and scanned the room, as if it was really anyone else's at fault but her and Karma.

King? What the fuck is she talking about? Does she mean the King of the Syndicate... or something else?

I peered over at Asher, remembering his near slip outside Malcolm's house of horrors, and something inside my gut twisted, but I maintained my poker face. I wouldn't forget Reah's training.

Is Grey a king of some kind? If so, why didn't he tell me?

"Cut the bullshit, Layla!" I spat, pushing the thought aside for the moment. "Everyone knows you've hated me from the day I set foot here. You're jealous as fuck."

"You bitch. What are you accusing me of?" Layla screamed back, her eyes blazing.

"Betrayal, treachery, handing me over to the enemy, and getting Reah and the sprites injured just for starters," I quipped with a nonchalant shrug.

"That's a lie!" Layla screamed.

"Is it?" Grey asked as he stepped menacingly forward. "Because that sure as hell smelled like a lie to me."

"What?" she asked in shock.

"Step into the ring, Layla. If you really are innocent, step inside the ring. You should have nothing to fear." Grey crossed his arms over his chest, standing tall, broad and handsome. He was an absolutely imposing figure.

Layla took a step back and bumped into one of the Riders of the Wild Hunt. She wasn't going anywhere.

He glared down at her with his arms crossed over his chest like am immovable fucking mountain.

The crowd sat in complete, sterile silence now as they watched the betrayal unfold before their eyes. This was no doubt a far juicier show than even they had hoped for. But who were they most loyal to?

Will they retaliate against us when this is all over?

They thought they were getting a bloodbath, namely mine. But they were getting an entirely different kind of show instead.

Karma took a step away from Layla. It was kind of cute how she thought she was off the hook.

"Where do you think you're going, Karma?" I asked sweetly as I felt the thrill of justice surge through my veins.

"What do you mean? I didn't betray the boss!" Karma spat as she crossed her arms over her chest.

"You see, I know that's a lie, kitty cat." I grinned. "Layla may have been second-in-command, but at the end of the day, she is still *just* a shifter. How could she have possibly known who Malcolm was or where to look without the half-witch who performed the first mimic spell in the first place?"

"No, you're wrong! I had nothing to do with this, you lying bitch!" Karma screamed, as clearly guilty as her partner in crime.

The lady doth protest too much!

She tried to turn and flee, but was caught easily by one of the Riders.

Grey stood next to me, his hands clasped behind his back as the two women started bickering with one another. It was pitiful to see. Even at the end, they couldn't present a united front. They were truly traitorous to their filthy fucking cores.

"You all know what happens to traitors, do you not?" Grey shouted over the shocked gasps of the crowd.

"No, Grey!" Layla turned her pleading eyes toward him. "We've been together forever, and you're going to throw all of that away over some fucking wicked Fae?"

"Yes. You should have known better than to move against me," he said flatly. "I might be your boss, but you know I'm so much more."

"I wasn't moving against you! I was just trying to get her out of the way!" she shouted back desperately before she lunged, making another escape attempt. But again, she was caught by the ominous Rider behind her.

"At the expense of your own people?" I asked, my brows furrowed.

What a selfish, fucking cow. She can't see past her own damn nose!

Layla sneered at me. "My people have nothing to do with it. How could sending you to Malcolm hurt the shifters at all?"

"Did Malcolm share his plans for me with you? Did he inform you that he wanted me to seal the portal forever and leave you *all* stuck here?" I asked. "Of course, he didn't. Otherwise, I don't think you would have done this. No matter how much you hate me and the rest of the Fae, I doubt your petty jealousy would have won out over your desire to go home to Faery."

"You lie! You're an evil, wicked Fae, and I wish you were dead!" Layla screamed and thrashed in the arms of the Rider behind her. In the next instant, her body convulsed, and bones cracked and reformed as she shifted into the form of a huge black wolf. The Rider holding her lost his grip on her, and she jumped forward into the ring, stupidly daring to thwart justice and attempt to prove herself innocent with a lie.

Just as quickly as she had shifted and landed inside the wards, she was forced back into her human form. Her naked body convulsed violently as blood spewed from between her lips, painting the floor in a ghastly splash of bright crimson. She writhed on in her own blood as more crimson leaked from her ears and nose, the spell upon the ring slowly boiling her from the inside out.

The acrid metallic scent of blood and the odor of cooked flesh filled the large space, and I turned my face into Grey's chest, not wanting to witness any more of the carnage. Guilty or not, it was a truly horrific and fucked-up way to go.

When her whimpers faded, and silence again descended upon the oppressive training grounds, I glanced up and saw someone I never expected to see at the facility. "You!" My eyes widened, and I tore myself out of Grey's arms.

The man who shot me with the tranquilizer and started this whole mess was standing a mere ten feet away from me.

His eyes widened as my purple swirling magic lit my palms.

If he hadn't shot me, the witch might still be alive! Malcolm never would have been able to kill her and set me up.

I turned to Grey, and the first night we met played over again in my mind like a broken record. He hadn't found me randomly. That man was there. And the pieces of the puzzle finally fell into place. They had been working together from the start. *Grey* was the reason everything had changed. He sent that man after me because he needed me for his grand plan.

Betrayal sank into my stomach like sour rot as I took another heavy step away from the man who had become so much to me. The whole situation was played out on his order all along. It was all a lie. My heart lurched and my insides ached.

You'd lied to me...

Grey reached for me. It was clear he understood exactly what I was thinking. I'd finally figured it all out, and the penny had dropped. And now he was going to try to smooth it over.

I shook my head, my nose scrunching in anger. "Don't fucking touch me!" I said through gritted teeth.

Grey turned to the man I was staring at, then back to me. "Fuck, princess. I can explain all of this. Don't go jumping to conclusions." He made to reach for me again.

My magic reacted to the feelings of my betrayal and threw up a shield between us. "You had him follow me!" I accused. "The only mother I remember is dead because I was passed out from being shot with a fucking tranquilizer dart. You're the cause of all my suffering these past weeks! How could you? I thought you cared about me."

"Just listen, Aurelia, I can explain. I didn't know that he shot you until you told me. That was never a part of the plan. I'd never do that to you. I just wanted you for a job at the time and asked Dan to bring you in—that's all. And I honestly ran into you by accident on my way back to my penthouse. I wasn't trying to corner you, but my wolf claimed you as his mate immediately. So, I kept Dan away until I could find the right way to tell you." He reached for me again, but my shimmering shield knocked him back ten feet, right into his buddy, Dan. They could have each other.

Betrayal threatened to drown me along with a new fresh sense of despair. I had no idea where I was going to go, I just knew I had to get out of there. Again, everything I loved was gone, taken from me between one breath and the next. And I was fucking sick of it.

I don't want to hurt anymore! Why can't anyone just be honest with me? I'm not a fragile fucking flower. I deserve better.

"I don't ever want to see you again, Grey," I said with a finality that chilled my soul before I made a run for the elevator. No one stopped me as I hit the button and stepped inside.

But Asher suddenly appeared and stepped in beside me. "Going down?" he asked.

"What are you doing?" I asked with a frown, struggling to hold myself together as the doors began to close.

"I was going to offer you a ride," he said with a shrug of his enormous shoulders.

"I don't need a fucking ride," I mumbled. "I don't even know where I'm going." Pain lanced through my chest, sharp and cold, and I gasped.

Why does it hurt so much?

It was like the betrayal was a physical weight crushing my body, and I had no idea how to relieve it.

How could he do this to me? How?

My mind reeled, and I began to hyperventilate as panic overwhelmed me. I'd trusted Grey—I'd loved him. How could he be behind it all? I met his gaze once last time and I felt everything and nothing all at once. My heart was a cacophony of raw emotion, and I didn't know if I could take it. As Grey's expression crumpled, so did my future. I never imagined I'd be forced to reject my fated mate. It hurt so much, I thought I would die.

Asher patted my shoulder as the doors to the elevator closed with an insulting and ridiculous *ding*. "I know of a place you can stay," he said as he pushed the button for the ground floor of the building.

I didn't want to have to accept the kindness of a stranger again, let alone a stranger that had such close ties to Grey. But ultimately, what choice did I have? I didn't have anyone else.

I had no place to go. I had no friends. And now I was losing the few people I thought I cared for and cared for me in return. It seemed like my whole life was a vortex of nothing but lies, deceit, and betrayal. This was the third home I'd lost inside of two decades. How was I supposed to go on? Where did I belong?

And who am I, really?

An exiled princess? A nobody mated to a traitor? Just a young woman who'd grown up to discover the world was truly as dark, remorseless, and fucked-up as she'd always believed it to be?

Maybe the supernaturals are as bad as Malcolm says. They call us wicked... but they have shown their true colors time and time again! Witches, shifters, half-Fae... the whole fucking lot of them!

With my heart racing and fury clouding my judgement, I wracked my mind for hope. For something, anything to grab onto. An anchor in a sea of turmoil and despair. A glimmer in the dark to guide my way.

Maybe I should just go back to Faery and see what happens? Sure, it can't be worse than here, surely?

Perhaps I could rediscover who I was. Maybe I could meet and hear my birth parents' side of the story. I could return home—to my real home—and become who I was born to be, the Princess of Faery, the daughter of the reigning king and queen.

I swallowed the lump in my throat that seemed intent on choking me and took several calming breaths the way Grey had taught me, the irony not lost on me. Licking my lips, I stood tall once more beside the Rider of the Wild Hunt as we waited for the elevator to reach the bottom.

Maybe I'll find the happily ever after to my fairy tale in Faery...

It was a desperate hope, but I clung to it like a lifeline. Come hell or high water, I was going to face the next chapter of my life with courage and an assload less naivete than I'd done so far.

I might not be the fastest learner, but I learn, and I sure as shit am not going to be burned again!

* * *

Aurelia's story continues...
in Book 2 - ***Shadow Fae*** and is AVAILABLE NOW: HERE!

WICKED FAE
2
SHADOW
FAE
MAGIC
USA TODAY BESTSELLING AUTHOR
AMELIA SHAW

Shadow Fae Magic

CHAPTER 1

Could I trust the man I'd left with? I wasn't sure and had no idea if he would tell me the truth anyway.

Probably not.

Even so, there was no harm in asking. I chewed my lip nervously and stared up at the huge guy beside me. "You won't tell Grey where I am?"

Asher peered down at me incredulously, his eyes wide and eyebrows raised. "Of course, not. There's obviously a reason you're running from him."

I wasn't running, was I? And even if what Asher said was true, I had every right to run away from a bad situation. Betrayed right from the beginning, Grey only ever wanted me for a job, and he'd done whatever was necessary to bring me in, including all the lies he'd told me. I was done with it all, him and his half-truths.

"I appreciate the offer, Asher. I really don't have anywhere else to go." That was the truth, but with that thought came a crushing loneliness. Was I making a terrible mistake going with him? The Riders were friends with Grey, not me. So why was Asher being so nice?

None of it makes any sense.

I eyed him warily. "Why are you helping me run from him, anyway?"

The elevator doors dinged open, and Asher put out his arm to make sure it didn't close on us. He gestured for me to go out ahead of him in a very gentlemanly manner, but he didn't answer my question, and that fact wasn't lost on me.

The receiving room was completely empty. Everyone was obviously still down at the ring watching the end of the horror show. Layla's gruesome death flashed in my mind, and I shuddered. She deserved what she'd gotten, of course, but that didn't make her demise any less disturbing or gory.

My footsteps upon the pristine tiled floor was the only sound in the empty space as we moved through the receiving room with purpose and out the front doors. The sun beat down on us, its light unforgiving and blinding me after having been so long in the dark. But I took several deep breaths of the crisp air and sighed as happiness began to filter through me. I'd loved the forest from the moment I saw it for the first time. It felt like home, or at least reminded me of someplace like home.

Maybe I could just run into the forest and live out my days on the land. That wouldn't be too difficult, right? I sighed. *Who am I kidding?*

I scanned the outside of the facility and groaned at what I saw there. Asher seriously wasn't expecting me to get on the back of that death machine, was he? Fate had already intervened once. Again was surely too much to ask. I blinked at the motorcycle as the hulking guy moved toward it, shaking my head as I stood there. There was no way in hell I was getting on that thing. I'd already shared my dislike with him the last time he'd expected me to get on one, when we'd narrowly escaped Malcolm.

"If you want to get out of here, this is the only way, Princess," Asher said as he strode toward the bike, throwing the words over his shoulder.

Well, shit.

I moved slowly, taking careful, tiny steps toward the motorcycle. My heart was pounding, and feelings of fear and anxiety were quickly tinkling along my nerves.

Asher, the big brute, mounted it like it was the easiest thing in the world, and pushed up the kickstand as he waited for me to climb on too.

It's this or face Grey again.

My choice became no choice, ultimately. "Fine, then," I huffed. I could die on a motorcycle, but at least death wouldn't break my heart again.

"Here." Asher grabbed a helmet and handed it to me.

I pulled the helmet on but fumbled while fastening it, quickly becoming flustered.

Asher chuckled before turning on his seat and securing it under my chin with his thick, steady fingers. He tightened it with a final tug, ensuring it was on properly.

"Thank you," I said, still unsure of the huge machine and its rider. "How many motorcycles do you have? Don't you have a car?"

"No, I don't have a car," he said, rolling his eyes "And I have several bikes. Though one less, since we rescued you."

We both knew I was stalling, but I needed to psych myself up to get on the two-wheeled vehicle of doom. My hands were shaking, and my breathing was more reminiscent of panting. "I'm sorry about that," I said, glancing away. He'd lost his favorite bike to a fireball when they'd come to rescue me from Malcolm's house of horrors.

"It's fine, Princess, but we're running out of time if you want to get out of here before Grey comes after you. He's your fated mate, he can only hold out against his wolf for so long." He raised an eyebrow at me and revved the engine for effect.

The bike rumbled ominously, the sound shivering along my spine and causing goose bumps to break out over my skin. I blew out a shaky breath.

It's now or never.

I moved to the bike and threw my leg over the huge machine then I grabbed onto the back of Asher's shirt, trying to keep a little distance between us. We weren't *that* familiar, after all.

He reached back and wrapped my arms around his waist. "You need to hold on tight, especially if you're scared." He chuckled.

His ribcage was so wide, my hands couldn't touch as I wrapped my arms around his waist. So, instead, I gripped the only thing I could—the front of his t-shirt.

A moment later, he started the engine and without warning me, he took off down the dirt road.

A girly squeal escaped as I plastered my front to his back. "A warning would have been nice!" I yelled over the roar of the engine and *whoosh* of the wind.

Asher's deep laugh was his only response.

The trees flew by at high speed and the wind continued to rush by, whistling loudly past my ears. The air beat uncomfortably at my face until I had the common sense to hide behind Asher's broad back, his enormous body acting like a windshield. I breathed in deeply, attempting to calm my racing nerves.

Asher's back suddenly tensed beneath my touch, alarming me further.

He was relaxed until now. What's wrong?

"Hold on, Princess!" Asher shouted, a note of panic clear in his voice.

The fact he was worried made me tense up too and grip his shirt even more tightly. "What's going on?" I shouted back and peeked up over his broad shoulders to see a roadblock up ahead, but we weren't slowing down in the least.

Malcolm stood in the middle of the street on the other side of the ward.

I flinched, my heart beginning to race anew.

What the fuck? How did he find me again?

An iridescent shield wove its way around Malcolm and blocked any kind of escape.

I glared at him when he smiled cruelly.

He no longer cared what happened to me. It was obvious by the way he stood there, ready to witness me crash headfirst into his shield.

The second we crossed the wards, I screamed, "Stop!"

Asher skidded to a stop, heading my command just inches from Malcolm's shield. The bike slid out from beneath us, kicking up dust in our enemy's face.

I rolled across the dirt road chaotically, gravel digging into my skin, but other than a little road rash, I was largely unharmed. I jumped to my feet, magic lighting up my palms instantly, answering my unspoken summons.

"Run, Princess!" Asher boomed, clearly ready to take on Malcolm on his own in an attempt protect me, in order to buy me time.

"No!" I growled back.

I can take care of myself this time. I'm not helpless.

I glared at Malcolm as purple magic swirled with life, glowing in my hands. "Why are you here?" I yelled.

A smirk lit Malcolm's face and he shook his head as if the answer were ridiculously obvious. "You are mine, and I have come to take you home… by force, if necessary," he answered simply.

"I would rather die than go anywhere with you." I threw my magic at Malcolm's shield, fueling its momentum with my anger. It struck the shield and ricocheted off, the magic pitifully crackling a few feet away from him. It fizzled out without causing any damage.

Asher rose to his feet and put himself between me and Malcolm. "Run, Princess," he repeated, more sternly this time.

"You sound like a broken record, Asher. I'm not running away." I shook my head and stepped to the side so I could see my enemy once more.

"Infuriating woman! I swear you'll be the bloody death of me. You have one choice here, Aurelia. You run *now*, because in a few minutes Grey will be done with the assholes at the facility and then he'll be on his way here," Asher growled.

Shit. What will I do when I'm forced to confront Grey and Malcolm at the same time?

Malcolm stepped forward and held up his hand. It crackled with energy. "You will not leave here, Aurelia. I'm taking you home with me."

"I'm not going anywhere." I threw another ball of magic, only to achieve the same result as earlier.

Goddamn it!

"You know, this would be a fair fight if you'd stop being such a fucking coward and actually dropped the shield."

Malcolm laughed. "Why would I do that when I can get the same result from behind the safety of my shield?"

"There's no honor among the Fae," Asher growled.

Malcolm let his electric power crackle over his palm once more before he lobbed it in my direction with shocking precision.

Asher shoved me out of the way at the very last second.

I rolled across the dirt road again, tearing more skin and landing in a crouch, an enraged scowl upon my face.

"You can't get past his shield. It's pointless. You need to run now!" Asher yelled.

He was right. I needed to try a different tactic. Trying the same shit over and over again wasn't going to result in a better outcome. Scanning the trees, I searched for a good place to get lost, but couldn't see a viable path that Malcolm wouldn't be immediately able to follow.

With an angry sigh of frustration, I scrambled up from the dusty ground and crouched low, making up my mind.

I have to try.

As fast as my legs would carry me, I raced to the tree line, taking off like a horse whose stall door was left open. I had *no* intention of being caught by Malcolm again. He'd treated me horribly when he'd kidnapped me before, and he clearly had plans for our future that I would rather die than endure or be a part of.

I will not allow him to capture me again. I'm no one's slave.

The trees swayed in the breeze with an ethereal quality as I ran. It was almost as if they were directing me the way I needed to go. It was a strange sensation, but it really felt like they were tangibly guiding me. I didn't stop to think about it, of course, I just ran, trusting my instincts and nature. The sounds of fighting and shouting faded the longer I fought my way through the underbrush, following the trees' direction.

What was I thinking? How could trees possibly be telling me where to go? It didn't make sense. But then, I was a fairy, and not everything in my life made a hell of a lot of sense to begin with, anyway. And at this point, I was flying by the seat of my pants.

Maybe the Fae can communicate with nature? Is that what I'm experiencing?

"Where are you taking me?" I whispered before I stopped to catch my breath, laying a hand on the nearest tree for support. The bark pulsed beneath my touch with a palpable sense of urgency.

How do I know that it's trying to warn me? What if this is a trap?

The tree pulsed again, and the urgency increased. I felt it flowing through the life that dwelled beneath the bark. Someone was following me, and the tree didn't know whether the presence was friend or foe, so it urged me onward. Yet again, I didn't seem to have much choice in the matter but to do as it demanded. It was connected to the wider world around me in a way I wasn't. I had to trust its intuition.

But what about Asher?

My steps faltered, and my heart ached in my chest. Could he fight alone against the seasoned Fae warrior? I wasn't sure. In a fair fight, I believed he could hold his own. He was a Rider of the Wild Hunt. But as it stood, he wouldn't be able to get past Malcolm's shield any more than I could. So why did he stay behind? Did my life truly mean so much? Glancing back, my lips twisted in anxiety, and I made up my mind. Whether he lived or died, it'd all be for nothing if I didn't keep moving.

With renewed determination, I followed the trees deeper into the forest, but the skin on the back of my neck prickled all the while with unease. The tree was right. I *was* being stalked and I didn't know if it was by a desperate friend or a malicious foe. All around me the trees pulsed with more urgency, triggering a deep and primal fear. Stumbling heedlessly in the direction they swayed, I picked up my pace until I was running flat out, the forest around me no more than a blur of green and dappled shadow.

Soon, I'd completely lost track of where I was going. I ran until my chest ached and my heart felt ready to explode. I panted for breath, and I imagined myself all but frothing at the mouth.

I need to stop. I can't keep up this pace much longer!

My knees finally buckled beneath me, and I crashed to the ground on my hands and knees, sucking in huge, heaving breaths. I really wasn't in the best shape to be running like this for my life. A twig snapped in the nearby distance, and I flinched, scrambling to my feet and summoning magic to my palms, ready to defend myself despite my overwhelming exhaustion.

"Easy, Princess," Asher said, stepping into view, his hands raised before him in a placating gesture. "It's just me."

I released a shaky breath, relieved to my core that it was only him. "Asher."

"Don't get too comfortable," he warned. "Malcolm is still out there somewhere. The bastard eluded me. He doesn't like to play fair." He clenched one large hand into a fist at his side. His face was dirty and there was a hefty cut above his brow that was trickling blood.

"Are you okay?" I asked, taking a tentative step toward him. He'd gotten hurt because of me. He'd stood against a powerful enemy for *me*. A deep sense of humility thrummed through me at the stark realization that all of this was so much bigger than me—but that I was somehow at its center, like planets rotating around the sun.

"I'm fine, but we need to move." He turned back toward the direction he'd come, expecting me to follow.

"Wait, the trees want me to go this way," I said, chewing my lip at just how absurd that sounded. Even as a fairy mated to a wolf shifter talking to a Rider of the Wild Hunt, it seemed ridiculous.

Asher raised a brow in question but thankfully didn't ridicule me or ask if I was losing my mind. "Okay then, we follow the trees," he answered simply as he stepped forward and peered up at the swaying trees. His innate trust floored me and honored me at the same time.

"Don't ask me how." I shrugged with a sheepish smile by way of an explanation. "I just know they want me to go this way."

"Some of the Fae have elemental magic that helps them communicate with the Earth. It's rare and mostly relegated to the royal bloodlines, though." He put a hand on my back, encouraging me to trust myself.

Oh, great. Just more proof that I'm a royal Fae. Just what I needed!

"So, what happened back there?" I asked, changing the subject and not wanting to talk about the elephant in the forest. I was still futilely holding onto the hope that I wasn't who everyone said I was. It seemed selfish, but the last thing in the world I wanted was to be a princess and rule realms. I just wanted to live in peace. Was that so much to ask? Did the fate of Faery have to rest upon my shoulders? I sighed and exhaled, waiting for Asher's answer.

"Malcolm lost his shit when you ran. He tried to go after you, but don't worry. I still have a few tricks up my sleeve." He winked at me with a broad grin.

I was never going to know all that the Riders of the Wild Hunt could do, that much was clear. They were a secretive bunch, it seemed, and ancient. They wouldn't even tell me how they knew Grey. But even so, I was thankful for whatever tricks he could pull out of his proverbial hat to help me.

My chest tightened at the thought of the shifter who'd betrayed me. He'd known from the beginning who it was that had caused all of this, and he'd kept it from me willfully. He'd even lied to me about the role he'd played in my adoptive mother's death. How could I still miss him? How did I still want to be with him?

I must be mad.

I stomped through the forest with Asher by my side in diligent silence until a tingle ran down my spine, alerting me to something, though I wasn't sure what. "Do you feel that?" I asked. There was some kind of magic present here and it felt strangely familiar.

"Magic," Asher breathed, his eyes scanning the forest. "It's Fae magic, no doubt about it."

What was Fae magic doing out in the middle of the forest not far from Grey's facility? Had Malcolm found us and gotten ahead to spring yet another trap? Magic crackled in my palms as I continued gingerly through the trees, mentally preparing myself for whatever was about to come.

The trees around us parted suddenly, and a clearing came into view as I stepped beyond their safety. A shimmering portal of pure, pulsing magic stood at the center of the green space, and I frowned. "What is that?" I whispered, mesmerized, though in my gut I thought I already knew.

Asher's gaze snapped to mine before strafing in the direction of the magical door, his eyes unfocused. "What is it? I don't see anything but more trees, Aurelia."

I grimaced in confusion. "There is a shimmering purple door of some description *right* there." I pointed and took another step forward. The door was calling to me, drawing me inexorably toward it, like a moth to a flame.

Asher reached out and grabbed my upper arm, halting me. "You see a door?" he asked slowly, his whole posture stiffening. "It must be the door to Faery."

"But why can't you see it?" I asked, frowning as I pulled my arm from his grasp and stepped even closer to the buzzing magic.

"Aurelia, I wouldn't get too close," he warned, just as the magic wavered.

A gloved hand reached out of the door impossibly fast, catching me off guard, and latched onto my arm with a vise-like grip.

A scream tore from my lips—Asher's name—as I was pulled through the sparkling, misty door and into the unknown.

CHAPTER 2
Grey

I spun on the half-Fae. "What the fuck are you doing here?" I demanded.

Dan's face paled as realization dawned on him.

What the fuck was he thinking, coming down to the ring when he knew Aurelia would be here? I wrapped my hand around his throat and lifted him to his toes, cutting off his airway.

His brown eyes widened.

"You better have a really good reason for being here right now." I shook him roughly. How dare he defy me and mess up my carefully laid plans?

He's fucking ruined everything! And now my mate wants nothing to do with me. I should kill him.

My inner wolf growled his agreement in my mind.

Kill. Kill. Kill.

The fact my wolf was so ardently on board with killing Dan was seriously concerning, but I still had use for the fairy. I couldn't let my emotions rule me. Common sense and logic had to prevail. I dropped him to the ground as I would a piece of trash.

He stumbled back, rubbing his throat. "The artifact!" Dan coughed as he bent over, sucking in huge gulps of air.

"What about the damned artifact?" I snapped. Why would he even bring that up? Especially since I no longer needed it. Aurelia's presence in my life and scheme had changed everything. Old plans were no longer in play. I'd adjusted course.

I just need figure out how to get her back.

"It's being moved," he croaked.

"Does it even fucking matter now? Idiot. You drove away the only person who could have retrieved it anyway!" I bellowed. I threw my hands up and spun away before I did more than simply choke the moron.

How could he be so stupid?

Catching movement from the corner of my eye, I grinned. Karma's attempt to slink away failed dismally.

"Where do you think you're going?" I growled, storming around the ring, careful not to cross the barrier. Zeke, one of the Riders, was a master when it came to nasty little enchantments like this, and I wouldn't venture inside the ring until he removed it—not unless I wanted to end up like Layla.

He wrenched Karma back with his big hand on her arm and pulled her into his chest. "Where are you going, little witch?" Zeke grinned, echoing my question.

Karma thrashed against him desperately like a rabbit caught in a trap.

I prowled over to her, rage bubbling within me. "Did you think you could get out of being punished?" I grinned maliciously.

"It was *all* Layla!" she replied through gritted teeth as she continued to thrash against Zeke's hold on her.

"We already know there's no way that's possible, so just give it a rest. Your voice is giving me a fucking headache," I said dismissively.

"I didn't do this, boss! You can't kill me. Please! I didn't betray you!" Karma wailed.

Zeke dragged her toward the elevator as if she weighed nothing at all.

"Put her in a cell. I need to go after my mate," I growled and stepped up to my private elevator. I stabbed repeatedly at the button in frustration until the doors opened.

Dan boldly stepped in next to me.

I raised an eyebrow, a low growl rumbling from my throat. My wolf was not impressed. "And where do you think you're going?"

"It's my fault Aurelia is gone and I'm going to help you find her." He crossed his arms over his chest, as if that were the end of the discussion and the final word was his to have.

"You really think I'm going to let you anywhere near my mate when I'm trying to get her back?" I barked in disbelief. "She fucking hates you."

Dan shrugged. "That may be, but I'm the best tracker you have," he reminded me as the elevator doors closed and the lift started to move.

He wasn't wrong, but he'd also failed to track down my mate in the beginning. It was probably for the best, ultimately, or I wouldn't have had the time that I did with her. "You caused all this, and she would sooner kill you than go anywhere with you." I shook my head and ran a hand through my messy black hair. It wasn't the sleek style I normally wore, but that was the result of running my fingers through it repeatedly since Aurelia had stormed out.

"I caused this problem, as you said, and I will take the princess' wrath if I must. She is Fae royalty, and I am half-Fae, boss. I owe just as much loyalty to her as I do to you," Dan said solemnly.

"Just like that?" I asked, taken aback.

He finds out she's the princess of the realm that threw him out and he's suddenly loyal to her? What the fuck?

I threw my hands up and huffed. "Fine, but don't come crying to me when she beats you to a fucking pulp and uses you for magical target practice." I shook my head again. A moment later the elevator *dinged*, and the doors slid open to reveal the pristine lobby of the facility. All was eerily quiet in the large, open floorplan office. The reception desk stood empty, the receptionist probably still downstairs waiting for an elevator to bring her up and back to work.

My shoes squeaked on the tiles as we raced toward the front doors. Outside, the sun was far too bright for my liking and made me wince. My wolf didn't like it either. I scanned the area and groaned. "Fuck it! Asher's motorcycle is gone."

Where is he taking her and what the hell is he playing at here?

I pulled my phone from my pocket and called the Rider, but his number rang out and went to voicemail. "He'd better not be trying to poach my mate, or I will gut the motherfucker. I don't care who he is!" I gripped my phone tighter, my rage simmering.

"Asher would never. He's probably just giving her the space she needs while keeping her safe." Dan clapped me on the shoulder, offering the most likely of assurances.

He was right, of course.

Damn him.

I was just seething with anger, and it was making me illogical. Asher would never get in between a mate bond. I knew that. He was probably protecting her from herself and our enemies, just as Dan said. She'd be in too much danger if she were allowed to run off on her own. At least with him there, I knew I'd find her in one piece—whether she wanted a piece of me or not when we found her was an altogether different matter.

I nodded. "All right. Let's go after them." I jogged to the car I'd left out front for a quick getaway. It always paid to be prepared and I did my best to stay one step ahead of the game whenever I could.

We jumped in and took the dirt road at high speed.

They couldn't have gotten too far away just yet...

"Keep an eye out for anything suspicious, just in case. I wouldn't put it past Malcolm to try something else. He's a sore loser, it seems," I said, never taking my eyes off the dusty road.

"What's that?" Dan pointed to something in the middle of the road, just on the other side of the ward.

Orange embers danced off gleaming metal, and I cursed. The black insignia of The Hunt gleamed under the flames.

"That fire is seriously close to the gas tank," Dan warned.

"That's Asher's bike. Where the fuck are they?" I asked as I cut the engine and kicked open the door.

"Boss, I don't think it's a good idea to get any closer."

"I need to make sure my mate isn't trapped under the fucking motorcycle!" I raced to the edge of the ward, but the heat flared a second later and ignited the gas tank. A deafening boom filled the air as I leapt away into the forest just in time, taking shelter behind a tree. Twisted metal rained down onto the dirt road in a hail of flames and ash. I'd never been so grateful for my shifter reflexes. Being barbequed was not on my list of things to do today.

"Grey!" Dan called out from the other side of the inferno. "Are you okay, boss?"

"I'm fine. I'm going to search the woods. I can't scent her here. I don't think they lingered long," I called back and turned to the forest. Shifting was the most effective way to pick up and track my mate's scent. My wolf would recognize her scent anywhere, but with him wanting to tear Dan's throat out, I wasn't sure that unleashing him was the best idea.

The breeze whispered by me, carrying the faint scent of lilacs and smoke. My wolf whined in my head, clawing at my mind to be free. He had a better nose than I ever would, so with little choice in the matter, I stripped out of my suit and shifted.

I took off, bounding through the trees, my mate's fading scent stronger than it had been while I was in my human form.

What the hell happened? How did they crash just outside the wards?

Asher was a Rider of the damn Hunt. He could drive or ride anything with killer speed and accuracy. So why was his bike now sitting in pieces in the middle of the road? My ears drew back as another scent filled my snout. Asher was following her and was just a couple minutes behind. His scent was a bit stronger than Aurelia's.

The trees swayed in the cool breeze and blew some of her scent away. If I wasn't careful, I would end up lost and running in circles. I had to concentrate and stay on track, and continued moving in the same direction. There was no way of knowing how much time had passed, but there was no trace of my mate except for the faint scent of lilacs and Asher's musky scent tinged with magic.

Where are they going?

The trail just kept moving deeper into the forest. Had someone been chasing them? Did they have a confrontation with Malcolm at the wards? Malcolm was a pureblooded Fae, and he surely could have gotten past my wards. So, if it was him, then why did he wait until they were outside to strike?

A twig snapped, and my wolf snarled at the potential threat. Who the hell thought it would be a good idea to sneak up on the Shifter King? I growled low in my throat, but whoever was coming toward me was moving fast and clumsily through the foliage. There was no way it was anyone trained at the facility. They would engage stealth no matter how fast they were moving. Whoever it was wanted me to know they were coming, or they weren't trained correctly. Either way, my hackles were up. I crouched low, ready to pounce.

Ten feet to my left, Dan crashed through the trees, his chest heaving.

I growled, low and menacing. The idiot was louder than a herd of elephants! My wolf lunged at him, snarling a warning. He was still just as shitty about this whole avoidable situation as I was.

Dan held his hands up in surrender. "Easy, boss. I'm here to help."

My wolf snarled again. The man was the sole reason my mate had left me, and he still clearly wanted to tear him apart.

Easy, I tried to calm my wolf. *He's a friend and he's trying to help...*

My wolf snarled one more time for good measure. He didn't want Dan anywhere near our mate and hadn't ever since he'd shot her with a tranquilizer dart.

I couldn't blame him, but we needed his help right now. And I wasn't too proud to admit that a king needed his men behind him to succeed and stand strong.

My wolf relaxed but growled when Dan got too close.

"I brought your clothes with me," Dan said. He pulled a bag over his shoulder and dropped it on the ground in front of me.

I shook my head and picked the bag up off the ground with my teeth before bounding forward again. Her scent was growing colder as I ran through the forest with Dan hot on my heels. Out of nowhere, I finally broke through the trees into a large clearing. The scent of my mate dissipated on the breeze here, and my wolf growled angrily. He sniffed at the ground as he trotted around the clearing until all he could smell was the spicy scent of raw and immense Fae magic in the air.

My human self finally took control of my body once more, and I quickly shifted, dropping the bag at my feet. Crouching low in my human skin, I opened the duffle bag and dug through it, dressing quickly and scanned the clearing. "There's something here," I said, on edge. Magic tingled against my skin even though I couldn't see anything.

I circled the entire clearing twice, just as my wolf had, but there was no sign of my mate. Her trail had gone cold *here*. It didn't lead in any direction and there was no exit trail to pick up on. Aurelia simply wasn't in the forest anymore and wherever she'd been taken, Asher was with her.

Fuck!

CHAPTER 3

I screamed into the void, the cosmos spinning around me in a kaleidoscope of stars and impossibly disorientating beauty. The hand still latched firmly around my arm was bruising my skin with its unrelenting grip, and I pulled against it, wanting to be released. For a sickening, heart-racing moment, I was suspended within time and space. Then a bizarre and unsettling sucking sound grew loud in my ears until it became a deafening roar. Without warning, I re-entered the world and fell in an ungainly heap on soft, vibrant, green grass.

"What the fuck?" I growled aloud, pressing my fingers into the lush ground for purchase. Forcing myself to sit up, I scanned my surroundings with an eagle eye.

Where the fuck am I?

The trees were different here, prettier somehow. A brighter green than anything I'd ever seen before. It's like they weren't just green, they were the definition of green. The living essence of the color itself.

Asher groaned from where he was on the ground next to me. His hand was on my arm, opposite to the one the strange, gloved hand had seized. "Are we—"

"Are we what?" I frowned. "Alive? I ventured without humor.

"I haven't seen colors this bright in centuries," Asher said with awe, slowly sitting up and gazing around as I was.

"What do you mean, centuries? Where exactly are we, Asher?" I chewed my lip, fearing I knew the answer. It was the one I'd known in my gut all along. The one I was so desperately in denial of.

A gloved hand thrust itself in my face, and I reared back. "Who the fuck are you?" I asked, peering up at the offending owner of the hand.

The armored, blond-haired man's brows drew down as he cocked his head to the side curiously. "Princess Aurelia, do you not remember me? I have been searching for you for years." He crouched in front of me with a frown on his strangely pleasant face.

I swallowed hard.

He's a fairy.

Asher tensed beside me, answering my question in not so many words. "How am I *here*?"

"Our princess willed it," the man answered softly. "I just want to know why."

"Oh, I don't know," I began. "A strange hand grabbed me through a bloody magical doorway, and I didn't want to get myself dragged into yet another kidnapping situation without protection." I glared at the stranger. Just because he seemed pleasant enough and was eerily pretty didn't mean I could trust him—not by a long shot. I'd learned that lesson. "Now, who are you and where am I?"

"My apologies, Princess Aurelia. My name is Fenrick. I was your personal guard as a child, and I have been searching for you all this time." Fenrick grinned as though he'd won the lottery, and while he must have felt like he had, I certainly hadn't.

"Where am I?" I asked again, more softly this time. I didn't want to hear it. I really didn't. But I had to know.

Shit. Did we seriously just get dragged into Faery? How is that even possible? I thought the gateway to Faery was closed!

With a sigh, I turned to look at Asher, who was glancing around the space in awe.

"You're home. Finally," said Fenrick, further sealing the truth with a grin. He held his hand out to me again as if I would instantly accept upon learning such "wonderful" news.

I peered at Asher. I could definitely trust the Rider more than this supposed ally looming above us. He'd pulled me through the door without my damn consent and was appealing to a previous relationship status I couldn't even recall.

"Are we in Faery, for fuck's sake?" I asked the giant beside me.

The hulk of a man simply nodded.

Well, shit.

"I was banned, just like everyone else," Asher whispered. "How am I here?"

Fenrick huffed out a breath in what plainly seemed like annoyance. "Like I said, you are here because our princess willed it. She has the ability to close our realm forever or open it up for the witches, shifters, and half-bloods to return."

"Wait, what?" I'd thought all along, since learning about this from Grey, that there was something I had to do. Something *more*. He'd needed me to retrieve something he couldn't... It couldn't be this simple. It didn't make any sense!

The book.

I jumped to my feet, my heart pounding. After all I'd done to elude my royal fate, I was exactly where I didn't want to be, surrounded by those who claimed to know me but didn't truly know me at all. It was a very one-sided advantage, and I had only one true ally.

Asher.

"You just have to will it, Princess Aurelia. It's always been so. It's why you were taken away, I suspect. The Elders will not be kind to you, I'm afraid," Fenrick said. "You wield far too much power for one being, and they don't like it."

I just had to will it? Is he serious?

"Then why did you bring her back here?" Asher threw his hands up in exasperation, finally coming to the party with his wits about him.

I waved a hand at the huge man to calm him down. "It's fine. I know about the threat of the Elders and how they feel about their dwindling control. But if they're a danger to me and you were my protector, why am I here? The Rider's question stands."

"It's Malcolm," Fenrick answered flatly. "He was never supposed to abduct you as a child. As a result of his actions, I was tasked by your parents to bring you back to them." Fenrick ran a hand through his blond hair, adjusting the helmet tucked under his arm.

I puckered my lips in consternation and thought. "He said repeatedly that I was his when he kidnapped me recently. What did he mean by that?"

I don't belong to him or anyone else. The Fae are deranged. I'm not fucking chattel to be traded or bought or sold!

Fenrick frowned, the expression in his eyes one of guilt.

He knows.

"You were betrothed to the Captain of the King's Guard as a baby. There is a connection between you."

"What does that mean? Is that how and why he keeps finding me?"

Fenrick closed his eyes and sighed. He clearly didn't want to tell me what I feared. That I would never escape Malcolm completely.

Asher scratched the back of his neck as he addressed my so-called protector once more. "Well, does he know where we are?"

"No, not right now, he doesn't, and it will be a while before he thinks to look in Faery," Fenrick said. "Especially given the princess' reluctance to return."

"So, how does the princess even know she can trust you? She has no memories of this place or you from the sound of it." Asher crossed his arms over his barrel-like chest and glared at the blond man.

For the second time today, I was glad for the Rider's overprotective instincts.

Fenrick didn't seem fazed at all as he shrugged. "I was tasked with bringing the princess home and keeping her safe. If Malcolm has become a danger to her, then I will be forced to deal with him."

"That doesn't answer my question," Asher growled. "Speak plainly."

"What do you want from me, Rider? Do you want an oath?" Fenrick stepped boldly into Asher's space despite the intimidating size difference.

Are they about to fight? What the hell is even happening here?

"Would you even be able to keep that oath? What happens if your Elders order you to kill her or bring her to them? You can't disobey them, and then your oath would kill you anyway!" Asher yelled.

Fenrick sighed before glancing away and taking a step away from Asher.

"He's right, isn't he?" I asked. "The Fae will do anything to keep the others out of Faery." I shook my head in disgust. The more I learned of the Fae, the more I despised them. They were my people, but they also were a bunch of privileged monsters.

No wonder they're called the "wicked fae".

"Come on, Princess, we need to find a way back to the human realm. It's not safe for you inside Faery," Asher said, offering me one of his immense hands.

"Am I safe anywhere? I mean... this is too fucking much. I don't want to be the one everyone craves to control! I don't want to be the reason why people never get to go back to their homes. I don't want *any* part in this." I threw my hands up in dismay. I spun around instinctively at the sound of a twig snapping. Magic filled my palms as several fairies in gleaming silver armor bearing purple crests across their chests marched into the green space.

"What is this?" I asked, the hint of betrayal in my voice.

Fenrick's royal guards surrounded us.

"We had a feeling that after all these years you would not be amenable to coming back to the palace. So, I took... precautions. And it seems they were warranted." Fenrick lowered his gaze to the ground.

"I knew we couldn't trust you," Asher said in a lethal whisper.

One of the soldiers stepped forward with a sneer. "You brought a Rider of the Wild Hunt through the portal?" Whoever he was, he glared at me through the thin slits of his medieval-style helmet.

"Yes, I brought him through the portal with me. So?" I squared my shoulders, refusing to back down.

"He's a dangerous criminal, Princess." The soldier unsheathed his sword, pointing it in challenge at Asher.

"By whose reckoning?" I retorted. "He's the only person that has never lied to me or tried to use me for his own plans!" I raised an eyebrow at Fenrick who'd already proven his true colors.

My protector, my curvy ass!

He lowered his eyes in shame, but he would do it again in a second if he was ordered to.

I needed to remember that I couldn't trust anyone in this world or any other. It seemed the hard lessons just kept coming. Ultimately, it seemed like I'd be alone. A singular creature destined to be used and abused, no more than a pawn in a multi-realm war.

"Honestly," Asher chuckled. "You needed ten of the king's men to bring in a tiny princess?"

Swords unsheathed all around us, pointing squarely at Asher.

"We will not be disrespected by someone who was banished along with the other *undesirables*." The soldier angrily poked Asher with the tip of his blade to further his point.

Fenrick stepped in front of me and waved the weapons of his party away before turning to face me. "Come with us, Princess Aurelia. There doesn't need to be bloodshed." He held his hand out to me expectantly.

I eyed it like a snake about to strike. "Right. You're just a glorified errand boy, aren't you? I love how you act so nobly, Fenrick, like I have some sort of a choice?" I growled, indicating all the soldiers ready to take me and my only ally in by force.

"I would much rather you come willingly," Fenrick soothed. "But when we were alerted to your presence in the nearby vicinity to the doorway, the king and queen ordered us to bring you in safely... by any means necessary."

Heaving a fucked off sigh, I resigned myself to my only option. Again. "Let's go, then." I waved, gesturing for him to lead on. If I was a damned princess, I wouldn't let these soldiers drag me to my castle after all these years like a pitiful dog fighting against a leash.

The nameless soldier stepped in closer to Asher, getting right up in his face. "Detain him," he sneered, "until he can be expelled from the realm again."

"What?" I yelled, turning on the prejudiced upstart. "You wouldn't dare!"

"He's not supposed to be here, Princess Aurelia, and your parents will adamantly agree. He can't be trusted and *needs* to be detained." The soldier glared at me as if I were an idiot.

Asher stood there unmoving all the while. He didn't struggle at all. Perhaps he knew now was not the time to pick a fight.

Well, I feel differently about that.

The soldiers secured some kind of metal cuffs around his wrists, forcing them behind his back roughly, treating him as the criminal they deemed him to be.

Asher flinched when his bonds clicked shut.

That simple body language spoke to me in a way nothing else could. I knew exactly what it was like to be detained, to be trapped, and to have your freedom stolen from you. "I don't care what you all think of him," I snapped. "I brought him here and I want him to stay with me!" I let magic crackle against my palms again, ready for a fight.

Fenrick ran a palm down his face. "Princess, it is not up to us what befalls your... friend. The king and queen will decide what to do with him."

"This is bullshit!" I yelled. "I'm fucking sick of everyone telling me what to do, what can and can't happen. You talk to me as if I were a petulant child, but I'm not. I'm a grown-ass woman and I'm allowed to be angry! I'm allowed to be fucking frustrated that I'm being pushed and pulled, left and right, against my will. But no one seems to give a damn about what *I* want at all! Which is fucking comical, given how apparently important I'm supposed to be around here."

My magic grew stronger, multiplying in volume to trail from the pools in my palms, up my arms. My beautiful wings beat angrily behind my back as I glared at all the soldiers surrounding us. I was so ready for this fight. I was practically itching for it.

Asher stiffened. "Princess, it's okay, I'm fine. Calm down," he said softly.

"You realize that is not the way to get me to calm down, right?" I asked through gritted teeth.

"Breathe with me," Asher said in a soothing voice, echoing Grey's methods.

I wasn't scared this time though. I was just angry.

How dare they pull me from the forest and then demand that I let them take my friend from me?

It was bullshit, and I honestly didn't know how much more I could take of this push and pull. Where was my damn autonomy?

"Princess, regain control," Asher said with warning in his tone. "Killing the King's Guard will not endear you to your parents or the Elders."

"I don't care. I don't want to!" I growled, unwilling to allow my rage to simmer. I wanted so badly for it to burn and blaze. And for a fleeting moment, the thought of igniting the world and letting it smolder to ashes was enormously appealing.

The soldiers stepped away from me, glancing between each other warily.

They should be worried. I'm done letting assholes push me around. I'm truly over it.

"Aurelia!" Asher shouted, breaking into my thoughts.

I glanced over to him, unable to remove the scowl from my face.

His eyes betrayed nothing but concern.

"They don't get to boss me around and bully me into being who and what they want me to be." I held my hand out in front of me, ready to unleash my weapon, my magic, upon them.

"Stop!" Fenrick shouted suddenly, realizing I wasn't as weak-willed as he'd first hoped or been led to believe. "Very well, you may have it your way. Let him go. Now! We will take the Rider with us, and he shall remain by the princess's side."

The nameless soldier scoffed at us, not liking the command at all, but he nodded to the guards behind Asher, acknowledging his superior.

Doesn't feel good to have no choice, does it, asshole?

The men quickly released him and stepped back, giving him his space.

Taking deep, steadying breaths, I slowly allowed my magic to fizzle out and smiled the way I imagined a true princess would. A pretty smile that adhered to position and tradition, as was expected, but failed to reach my eyes. It was entirely false, and not only did they know it, but they also found it deeply unsettling. "Lead the way to the castle, Fenrick," I said in a polite, but clipped tone.

The blond guardian eyed me warily before taking the lead at the head of his troop.

Asher stepped up beside me. "Are you okay, Aurelia?" my true protector and friend whispered.

"No, I really am *not* okay. This is just one more thing to add on to this already shit day." I shook my head and fell in step, following Fenrick begrudgingly.

"It will be fine as long as we figure something out," Asher replied mostly to himself. He didn't want to be here without his brothers, his fellow Riders.

I knew how close they were. I'd seen it firsthand. We needed to get out of this realm and back to our lives as soon as we could.

But where does that leave me when we do?

The mark from Grey's bite tingled on my shoulder with awareness, and anger bubbled up inside me in response. Violet magic crackled in my palms, and I clenched my fists tightly to suppress it. His betrayal was the most painful thing I'd ever felt in my life. It was worse than freezing and starving in that dirty alley as a child. And worse than all the years I'd felt like no more than a burden to my adoptive witch mother.

As we trudged through the forest in silence, I lost myself in thought. The soldiers still surrounded us, flanking us on all sides creating a shield-wall of bodies, but I ignored them.

Before long, we broke through the tree line and stepped out onto an immense, manicured lawn that stretched before us.

Raising my eyes, my heart leapt into my throat. A gleaming white castle towered above me. Memories flashed through my mind so quickly that I couldn't hope to catch them. The only one that I could grasp by the tips of my mental fingers was the fleeting glimpse of that very same castle over Malcolm's shoulder as he abducted me and took me away from the only life I'd ever known.

I'd lived in this castle as a child. I was now sure of it now. It was just one more thing that proved I was exactly who everyone said I was.

Damn it! Am I the only girl in all of history who doesn't want to be a princess?

"Princess," Fenrick said softly, putting his hand on the small of my back.

Asher growled at the gesture, like an impossibly enormous bulldog.

I cut him off with a look. "What is it, Fenrick?" I sighed and side-stepped away from his hand.

Fenrick let his hand drop to his side, unphased, and turned to the castle looming ahead, directing my gaze.

I froze as if what was about to happen sucker punched me in the gut. What would I find when I went inside? My long-lost parents? The Elders? And did I even care at this point? I felt like a leaf on the wind—lost, helpless, and caged in on all sides by those from another life. People who didn't care for me beyond what I could do for them and their plans for Faery.

"Welcome home, Princess Aurelia," Fenrick said, and led the way across the grand lawn and inside the fairy tale castle.

This isn't my home.

I had no home, and I probably never would.

CHAPTER 4

I slammed my phone down on the desk in frustration. "Where the fuck is Asher?"

Zeke sat back in his chair and ran his hand down his beard in thought, his heavy brow crinkled. "We can't connect with him at all. It's almost like he's in another realm."

My jaw dropped as an impossible possibility dawned upon me. "You don't think?" I asked, my brows rising in surprise as I trailed off.

No... That's not possible. No one has been able to find the portal. No one has been able to get to Faery in centuries.

"He's not dead," Zeke growled, misunderstanding my train of

thought. He clenched his hand into a tight fist on the arm of the chair as his emotions rose to the fore.

"I never said he was dead, I was asking if it's possible that he could be off world." I scrubbed a hand over my face, my fingers alighting upon the scratchy stubble that lined my jaw, adding to my irritation. I hadn't done much of anything but search for Aurelia since her mysterious disappearance.

"But how? We were *all* banished." Zeke shook his head. "There's no way back in. Fuck knows, folks have tried searching in vain for a long time.

"Malcolm abducted Aurelia because she could close off Faery from us permanently. What if she's also able to bring people home?" I asked and flopped back into my chair.

"I have an idea," said Zeke, sitting forward with his elbows resting on his knees.

Fiona buzzed into the room carrying a charcuterie board with her magic and set it on the desk between us.

"What idea?" I frowned, willing to try almost anything at this point.

"Her." The rider pointed at Fiona. "The sub-Fae weren't banished."

"Motherfucker!" I shouted, rising to my feet and shoving my chair back. Why the fuck had I never thought of that? We couldn't see the portal because we were banished, but Zeke was right. The sub-Fae could probably still see it.

"We need to go to the place where they disappeared," Zeke said, standing from his chair.

"What good will that do us, though?" I asked. Sure, we would know where the portal was and where to find Aurelia theoretically, but we wouldn't be able to rescue them. We couldn't go into the portal.

"The sprite can find her and get Ash a message," Zeke answered with a shrug and made his way to the door of my office.

Fiona glowed green with excitement and buzzed chaotically. "You want me to find Miss Aurelia?" she sang.

"Do you think you can do that?" Zeke grinned over his shoulder.

Fiona fluttered excitedly. "If I can see the portal, I will go find the mistress!" she affirmed confidently, despite how viciously she and her sister were treated the last time they went on a rescue mission.

I wasn't so sure about this—given my affection and attachment for my sprites—but it was the best option we had. If Malcolm already had her, I wasn't going to sit around and do nothing. I was going to find a way to my mate and then kill the bastard, even if she didn't want anything to do with me afterward. I had a bone to grind with that fucker, and I wasn't going to let it lie. "All right, then. Let's head back to the facility." I pushed in my chair and grabbed my keys, storming through the penthouse and to the elevator, then stabbed at the button.

Ready or not, asshole, here we come.

"Do you really think this will work?" Fiona asked softly from her place fluttering in front of me.

"I think it's our best shot," I answered as I stepped into the elevator with the others following behind me.

Fiona landed lightly on my shoulder as we rode the elevator down.

"I don't think Malcolm has her," Zeke said suddenly, shattering the tense silence.

"What do you mean?" I asked as the elevator *dinged*. I stepped out into the underground garage and led the way toward my car.

Zeke was quiet for a moment before he answered, "He wouldn't have taken Asher as well, not if he'd successfully gotten his filthy Fae hands on the princess. So, there's something or *someone* else at play here. But how the hell did Asher even get through? Nothing makes sense." He shook his head before opening the passenger door of the car.

"I don't know, man. But I'm going to find out." I slammed the door behind me and turned the key in the ignition, starting the engine.

Did Aurelia unknowingly hop into Faery and take Asher along with her?

How could she possibly do that? If she had, it was a power beyond reckoning. It was almost unfathomable. There was an ancient prophecy that claimed she would either close Faery or open it back up to us all, but I'd thought she would need the book to do that. Could she truly pull off such a feat on her own? And was it through magic or sheer force of will?

The drive to the facility was silent. I was lost in my own head, wishing my mate would return. But could she even come back? Was she in trouble? Had someone other than Malcolm abducted her this time? I pulled off the dirt road just outside the wards and parked not far from where Asher's motorcycle exploded.

Fiona fluttered out of the car before I could even get out. "What is that?" she asked. She cocked her head to the side as she buzzed straight for the trees.

"Fiona, slow down!" I yelled as I leapt from the car. I picked my way through the trees and underbrush, much slower in my human form than my wolf had been only days ago.

Zeke kept pace beside me, staring after the sprite.

Fiona buzzed through the forest ahead of us.

The trees swayed in the breeze, their branches all bending in the direction Fiona was flying. "What the hell is happening?" I stared at the tops of the trees in awe. There was no way that was natural. Something was afoot.

Zeke turned, peering at me as we ran. "What are you talking about?" he huffed.

"The trees!" I frowned, keeping pace.

He turned his gaze up to the trees and his eyes widened. "Are they showing her the way?"

"They aren't Fae trees. They aren't alive in the same way as the Fae trees are." I shook my head at the possibility.

Does all nature respond to Fae, and I've just failed to notice it?

There was no way they were pointing us in the direction of the portal, right?

"That makes me think the portal could actually have been here the whole damn time," Zeke groaned as he pushed a branch out of the away.

We broke through the tree line into the clearing, the same place I'd lost Aurelia's scent days earlier.

Fiona buzzed around excitedly, almost becoming a blur of glowing green motion.

"Do you see anything?" I asked Zeke, slowing to a standstill as I looked about.

He shook his head. "No. Nothing."

"What do you mean?" Fiona squeaked, turning to us and then back to something apparently only she could see.

"It's an empty clearing, Fi," I said. "We can't see anything at all."

My wolf perked up at the sprite's response and growled in my head. Could he sense something in the clearing that I couldn't see? And if that were the case, how had he missed it the first time we'd been here?

"There's a shimmering purple door right there!" Fiona scoffed, rolling her little jewel-bright eyes.

"Where?" I stepped forward. Could I push through the portal even if I couldn't see it? To my knowledge, no one had ever tried. They hadn't even successfully located it to make an attempt.

Fiona fluttered a few feet away and pointed at the empty space. She glanced back at us in exasperation when we shrugged in union.

Zeke ran a hand over his hair. "So, there *is* a portal there that we can't see, and you just happened to buy the land it's fucking on."

"Why do I feel like that's way too much of a coincidence?" I circled the space Fiona pointed to, giving it a reasonable berth out of caution.

"You said there was a prophecy, right?" Zeke stared at the empty space, his brows knitting once more in thought.

"Yeah," I said slowly. What was he getting at? Was he saying that whatever this prophecy was, I was somehow an inherent part of it? I was involved without even knowing?

"The Fates are crazy bitches. I wouldn't put anything past them." Zeke took a step forward and frowned.

He strolled confidently to the spot that Fiona indicated, and a loud buzzing filled the air before he cursed, and his huge body was flung back ten feet.

"Fuck! Are you okay?" I asked as I rushed to his side.

"There's some kind of ward there or something." Zeke groaned then slowly sat up and shook his head to clear it. "I don't think we're going to have any luck."

Fiona's tinkling giggle filled the air. "You can't just walk through a closed door, silly."

"You could have warned me," Zeke grumbled and rubbed the back of his head.

"Oops! I forgot you can't see it," Fiona giggled as she fluttered closer to Zeke.

The Rider bared his teeth at her.

"Back off, Zeke," I warned. No one threatened the sprites. They were under my protection, and he knew that better than anyone.

Zeke shook his head and picked himself up off the ground, dusted himself off, and moved to the invisible portal again. "Can you open the door?" Zeke asked over his shoulder.

"I'm not sure." Fiona frowned and buzzed back to the door.

"I don't know if that's a good idea. What if you can't get back?" I rubbed my neck as anxiety prickled up my spine.

"Well, we don't have many options at this point, Grey. I think its best that we give her a message, just in case she can't return." Zeke shrugged, a master of the obvious.

"You send the message to Ash," I said, stepping away. I knew all too well that my mate wouldn't listen to a message from me—not anymore. She would probably just stay in Faery to spite me. I sighed, my damn heart on my sleeve.

"She may not be as upset now, friend," Zeke offered, clapping me on the shoulder. "It's been a couple days, and we have no idea what's happening to her right now."

I shook my head in defeat. He was right. Again. "Fine. Fiona, tell Ash that we are looking for him if you can't get back. Find out what's happening with them and try to return as quickly as possible."

"I will get any information I can and report back!" Fiona said with a solemn nod. Her determination shone in her tiny eyes. She was not going to let us down. I knew that without a shadow of a doubt. She loved Aurelia just as much as I did. Well... almost.

Ugh! Why the fuck did I lie to her in the first place? I should have told her about Dan and that we were investigating the witch's death from the beginning. This is all my fucking fault, not Dan's.

Fiona buzzed closer to the spot where she indicated the portal was and took one last, long glance at me before flying into it and disappearing with a *pop!*

"She was able to get in," Zeke said, shocked.

I hadn't been entirely sure she would be able to get in there either. I had hoped, of course. Her being a sub-level of Fae was certainly worth the shot. But ultimately, I didn't know how this would help our situation. For all I knew, she loved it there and never wanted to return to a place where she'd always felt she'd never belonged. "Let's see if she can get back before we start celebrating," I said. Running a hand through my mussed hair, I pulled my phone out of my pocket.

Dan picked up on the second ring. "Yeah, boss?" he asked, his voice wary.

"I need you to come out to the clearing with our best guards. I want this place guarded around the clock." I expelled a breath as I made new plans.

"Do you want the trolls?" he asked.

I frowned as something unexpectedly occurred to me.

Can the trolls see the portal?

I couldn't remember if the trolls were expelled along with us, or if they'd left persecution before we were banished. "Just bring one troll for now," I said. "I need to test a theory." I glanced up at Zeke's gasp and nodded. He knew where I was going with this.

"On it, boss," Dan said.

I hung up the phone.

"I don't think they'll be able to see it." Zeke grimaced.

I wandered over to the nearest tree and sat with my back resting against it. "I don't know that for sure, though. I honestly can't remember if they were expelled or not."

"Everyone would know that the portal was here if the trolls could cross over," Zeke replied as he sat down next to me with his knee bent and his elbow resting on it.

"People overlook the trolls constantly. I'm guilty of doing the same myself. No one would think to even ask them if they can sense a portal since they are notoriously private and sometimes seemingly basic creatures." I clenched my fists as the possibilities raced through my mind. I could have had a way in, or at least a means to get goods out of Faery this *whole* time. It pissed me off that I'd been so stupid. It hadn't even occurred to me to hire trolls and sprites to search for the portal.

We sat in silence for a long time, just waiting patiently for Dan to come out with the troll. It would take a while.

I watched the portal, hedging my bets and waiting for Fiona as well.

Would she be able to get back? Or did I just condemn her to being stuck in Faery with no possible escape?

What if she never sees Freya again, and it's all my fault?

I leaned my head back against the tree and closed my eyes tightly. Freya was going to kill me or leave me forever if anything happened to Fiona, and I'd completely understand if that were the case. If she found out that her sister was stuck in Faery with no way to return to her, Freya would come searching for the portal herself to go and find her. They were inseparable. The news would not go over well.

The ground rumbled beneath me, and I stood, turning in the direction of the facility.

They're here.

Dan broke the tree line first, followed by a huge troll.

The troll gasped loudly, his gaze immediately panicked. "What is that?"

"You can see it?" I asked, taking a step toward the troll with hope.

"It's the door to Faery," he said, voicing his realization. "Why did you bring me here?" The ground rumbled as he took a step back.

A light buzzing filled the air, and something flew by my head frantically. "Fiona?" I asked, my eyes wide with shock as I tried to track her frantic flight path.

She was frazzled and speeding all around the clearing.

How had she managed to get so freaked out? She had only been gone a matter of minutes, really. Not even a full hour.

"Master Grey?" she asked in shock. "You're still here?"

"What do you mean? Of course, I am. You've only been gone about an hour," I said slowly.

That same buzzing filled the air once more and Fiona's eyes widened again. "Something's coming through!" she announced, her voice shrill.

I turned to face the direction of the portal and widened my stance, awaiting whatever was about to manifest as magic pulsed in the air around us.

A huge body flew straight toward me, hurled like a giant stone, and I cursed.

Zeke lunged forward to catch the body like a prized athlete catches a ball. He moved much faster than I'd have imagined possible. "Ash?

What the fuck did they do to you?" he growled, assessing his brother-in-arm's condition.

"Where's Aurelia?" I asked warily, still watching the empty space where the portal was supposed to be.

"She's gone," a knight of the Shadow Court said as he appeared out of thin air. "And she's never coming back."

CHAPTER 5

Aurelia

I dragged my feet as we made our way through the castle. "Where are you taking us?"

Fenrick led the way, his gaze focused ahead of him.

I scowled at his back. He'd tried to get me to trust him when he'd been planning on ambushing me from the beginning. Had he even stopped to think for just a second that I might be more amenable to my fate if people like him didn't just keep shoving it down my throat by force?

Fenrick glanced at me over his shoulder, his lips pursed. "The king and queen have requested your presence in the throne room."

"And what if I don't care about what they want?" I asked snidely. I genuinely didn't care. I was sick and tired of it all and wasn't going to hold anything back from these people that were supposedly my own kindred.

"Princess." Fenrick blew out an aggravated breath. He'd clearly had enough of my shit.

Welcome to just a little taste of what I'm having to deal with, jerk!

"Watch your tone, soldier," I warned. "Have you forgotten who you're talking to? Take me to them and then let me go my own way. I didn't ask to be here," I snarked as I held my chin high.

If they want a pain in the ass for a princess, they'll damn well get it.

Everyone wanted a piece of me, but no one wanted to treat me with any kind of respect or cared enough not to betray me. They weren't going to get loving, loyal Aurelia without earning her respect in return, that was for damn sure.

Grey.

I shook my head as my heart skipped a beat, clearing it of any thoughts of the traitorous shifter.

He only wanted me for a job.

I had to remind myself of it again. My heart was a fool for clutching at straws. He'd caused all my problems from the beginning, sending that man after me and then pretending he'd had no idea.

Large, gilded doors stood before me as Fenrick came to a halt.

I glanced at Asher next to me and held a shuddering breath.

He shot me an encouraging smile that belied the softness within the giant Rider. "You can do this. Show them the princess you really are," Asher whispered.

I rolled my shoulders back, held my head high and raised my chin in the air. I was as fucking ready to meet my long-lost parents as I was ever going to be. There was no point delaying the inevitable any further.

Fenrick nodded to the guards on either side of the door, and they opened them.

The room was huge, even bigger than Grey's penthouse. I swallowed the invisible lump in my throat, not wanting to betray any weakness. I hated that I compared everything to *him*.

The room was decorated in bright silver and deep royal purple. And there, centered on a raised dais in the middle of the area were two exquisitely elaborate winged seats—the thrones of the monarchs of Faery.

The room caused memories to flash in my mind like glimpses of butterflies I couldn't quite catch. I saw seats filling the space, and I sat in a smaller chair beside my mother in a tulle-covered monstrosity of a frock as the king and queen held court. Malcolm stood off to one side of my father, and Fenrick stood behind me like a guardian angel in the shadows.

Huh? So, he hadn't been lying about being my protector...

The proof was in the pudding, right there in my memories. But he still had to answer to the king and queen, which made him suspect until I could prove otherwise. As far as I could see, his loyalty would always lie elsewhere, to someone higher up the royal food chain. Those in positions of power could always be corrupted by those who held even greater power.

Shaking my head ever so subtly, I attempted to clear it of the weird and unwelcome memories. I didn't want to have reminders of this place and these people, but I did. And much to my distaste, they were getting clearer by the minute.

I peered at the people on the thrones, both just as regal and ageless as I remembered them. The queen had long, white-blonde hair, and her eyes were a deep, jewel-bright green, just like mine. The king, meanwhile, had caramel-colored hair and sky-blue eyes. My own long, curly, golden locks were clearly the perfect blend of both. These Fae were *definitely* my parents.

If only I could remember what kind of people they are.

"Aurelia?" the queen gasped as she stood from her throne.

I stiffened as she moved toward me gracefully, a hand covering her mouth. "Yes, it's me," I answered and glanced away, unwilling to hold her gaze.

"You truly don't remember us, do you?" she asked softly as she drew nearer. She was impossibly elegant and looked way too young to be my mother, though I knew the Fae aged exceptionally slowly. Her deep purple dress boasted a beautiful, multi-layered, bell-shaped skirt but the bodice hugged her trim waist. Her alabaster skin was flawless and practically glowing, as if kissed by starlight instead of sunlight.

"I remember a little," I admitted. "But not much." I pursed my lips and held my ground even as she moved into my personal space.

"You are even more beautiful than I imagined you would be," the queen whispered as she smiled. She rested her hand softly against my cheek and swiped her thumb tenderly across my cheekbone, her eyes searching. "How are you here?" she asked, her softness disarming.

"Your man, Fenrick, pulled me through a portal," I answered. "Oh, wait. And I can't possibly forget how Malcolm abducted me all those years ago—and was *not* kind. He hurt my friends," I finished, keeping my gaze straight ahead and focused on the foot of the thrones. If I looked into her sad eyes, I would break and be lost.

I can't let that happen. They gave the order to bring me back against my will.

A part of me understood that they were simply parents who missed their daughter, but realistically, I had very few memories of them.

"Aurelia, what did Malcolm do to you?" the king asked, interrupting my thoughts.

Asher fidgeted by my side but remained stoic and silent.

I held strong and kept my chin up. Now was not the time to relent and succumb to memories and weakness. I knew exactly where I stood in this equation. This little family reunion meant little, if anything at all. "He abducted me from the castle, initially, obviously. Then he abandoned me, and a witch took me in. To make a long story short, she was murdered, I had people hunting me, and just when I thought I'd finally found my place in the world, he showed up again—out of the blue—and kidnapped me once more. When I tried to escape, he injured me and held me prisoner in a basement."

The queen gasped, bringing her fingers to her lips again in genuine shock. "Surely, Malcolm would never hurt you!" she exclaimed. "He's your betrothed."

"You mean you tied us together when I was just a child unable to give my consent, and when he didn't get what he was told was his, he lashed out." I shook my head and stepped away from the woman who was my mother. The truth was ugly, but it was the truth.

"Aurelia," the king said in warning. "You will not speak to your mother like that."

"My mother?" I said in disbelief. "The only mother I remember was murdered by Malcolm, and I was left to take the fall for it!" I growled back. "All he has done from one moment to the next is destroy my life. He's taken everything from me."

The king sat forward on his throne at the same time as the guards stepped forward. The king held up a hand, indicating to the guards they needed to stop.

They're worried about little old me? Well, that's entertaining.

"I did not know that Malcolm had stooped so low." The king sighed, at a loss.

"Well, how could you?" I shot back. "He's remained in the human realm all this time and waited for just the right opportunity to abduct me again." I shook my head as anger bubbled inside me.

"What has happened to you, my daughter?" the queen asked, her elegant brows knitted.

"I don't think there's enough time in this visit to tell you both everything that has happened to me since the first time I was abducted." I shrugged, trying to maintain control.

"We have plenty of time to learn all the new things about each other now that you are back," said the queen with a warm but troubled smile.

"What do you mean by that?" I asked, stepping back and away from the queen before bumping into Fenrick.

"Well, you are home now, my dear. We have all the time in the world to catch up." The queen frowned and it did little to mar her ethereal Fae beauty.

"I can't stay!" I objected. "I must stop Malcolm. He will find me and try to force me to close off the portal forever." I shook my head again.

They can't be onboard with his plan, can they?

"My queen," Fenrick said with a bow, interjecting. "I'm afraid the princess has been somewhat affected by the supernaturals of the Earth realm."

The queen gasped, a true look of horror spreading across her features.

The king turned instantly angry eyes upon me, all openness and softness gone in the blink of an eye. "What does Fenrick mean?" he demanded of me. "You wish to let *them* return to our realm?"

"Do you even know what they've all gone through these past few centuries?" I asked just as angrily. "They must hide what they are from the humans! They are miserable and miss their homes, and it's all because the Fae are racist."

"So?" the king thundered in return, unphased by my plight. "They do not belong here. They were banished for a reason."

Asher stepped forward finally, entering the conversation and glaring at the king, bold as brass and every bit the Rider of the Wild Hunt I knew him to be. "We did *nothing* to deserve being sent away!"

"You say you don't deserve to be banished even though you were among the worst we got rid of," the king spat back with venom.

"And how is that exactly?" I shrieked as I stepped in front of Asher, defending my only friend.

Fuck this shit for a joke. Enough is enough!

"The Fae are so quick to judge and label others as undesirable, but what are their crimes? What are they guilty of, other than being different?"

"The Riders of the Wild Hunt are older than time, Aurelia. They cannot be trusted. Step away from him, now." My mother held her hand out to me, beckoning me forward and away from the supposedly dangerous criminal.

I glanced at Asher out of the corner of my eye, but his expression gave nothing away. "I don't care. He has been kinder to me than anyone else in my entire life so far. He's literally saved me more than once, and put his own life on the line for mine!" I crossed my arms over my chest, practically seething. If I wasn't careful, my magic was going to seep out along with my emotions the more out of control I allowed them to get.

"You will learn to care!" the king boomed, outraged. "You don't get to be a petulant child."

"A petulant child?" I bellowed in astonishment and outright disgust. "I have *never* been a spoiled child that I remember. But I know one thing for certain, and that's that my friends don't deserve the fate they have been saddled with!"

"And what fate is that?" the queen asked. Tears rimmed her eyes, so much like mine, but she didn't let them fall.

I felt badly for her. She'd lost her only child, then I'd lost my memories and had ties to the very supernaturals they were supposed to hate. What Malcolm and the Elders had done to all of us was far from fair.

"Their fate is that they must hide from the humans for mere survival! They cannot permit their true natures to run free in that realm. They have been suffering for centuries needlessly, and Malcolm nearly beat me to death to get me to block them from ever returning home!"

"But why do they have to hide?" the queen asked. "Is the Earth realm not of a sufficient size for them all?"

Asher stepped forward and bowed his head. "The shifters cannot shift openly. If they did, they would be hunted by the human authorities and put to death, or worse, they'd be experimented on. The witches? They already knew the humans would fear them from the time of the infamous witch trials. They drowned, burned, hung, and crushed them alive. Humans are hateful, prejudiced beings. We cannot co-exist. We are exiles in exile. Nowhere is safe for our kinds outside of Faery." The Rider shook his head, glaring at the king and queen with obvious disgust.

"That sounds horrific," the queen gasped, her gaze stricken. "At the time, we wanted you gone from our lands… but we did not know of these terrors. Surely, the Elders couldn't have known of this. Husband?"

"Are you really that naïve, your majesty?" Asher asked, a thick, prominent brow raised.

I turned to Asher with wide eyes. That was risky and rude, given his position. I was certain the king and queen wouldn't harm me, but I couldn't guarantee the same for the safety of the Rider. I peered at my parents, awaiting their reactions, but neither seemed to be angered by his comment.

"Asher," I warned, surprising even myself.

Am I seriously being protective of my absentee mother right now?

"No, the Elders knew exactly what they were doing to the rest of us. They knew we would suffer in the Earth realm. They have their own seers, which is how they received news of the prophecy in the first place." Asher shook his head in dismay.

"Asher," I tried to warn again. He was on dangerous ground, and I wasn't sure how far my influence would go in protecting him if he continued to so brazenly challenge the reigning monarchs.

"It's okay, Aurelia," the queen whispered unexpectedly. "We need to know what those old bastards have planned."

I almost bit my tongue as I burst out into a fit of laughter at the regal queen and her gentle curse words. "Mother, what was that?" I asked in a shocked gasp.

Her eyes widened and happiness shone within her green gaze. "Aurelia, I am disgusted that the Elders think they can harm whomever they desire to at will, but at the same time, I'm so happy to hear you recognize me as your mother."

"Wait, what?" I asked, doubling back mentally, my mouth open in disbelief after everything I'd been through. After everything the exiles of Faery had been through.

"Those old bastards have no idea what they are doing and even if they did, we can't let them get away with it, Channing," my mother said and glared up at the king.

I took a step back.

What the hell is going on here? Are my parents agreeing with me about the ban on the other supernaturals?

"Are you serious?" I scanned the throne room, my gaze strafing between my parents. "You don't agree with them?"

"No, of course not!" my mother growled. "If this is what they have done, then they are a bunch of old fools."

"Katrina!" my father bellowed. "You cannot speak such things."

The queen scowled back at him but kept her mouth shut.

A commotion sounded from outside the throne room, and I groaned. What the hell was going on now? Was something happening outside?

"Who's there?" the king hollered.

The doors to the throne room flew wide open, and five old men stormed in with a dozen guards flanking them.

"What is the meaning of this unannounced intrusion?" my mother shouted over the top of their noisy entrance, her voice booming with authority. She waved her hand, summoning their retinue to arms.

The knights around the room all unsheathed their swords, pointing them at the new arrivals, ready to defend their king and queen.

A man with a cane pushed through the crowd and into the throne room, his beady eyes narrowing on me. "Queen Katrina, why have you not told us of your daughter's return?" he demanded.

"She's only *just* returned, literally!" the queen scoffed. "And what difference does it make to you?"

The king stood from his throne and stalked across the room to do the first fatherly thing he'd ever done for me in living memory. He stood between me and the intruding men.

Are these the Elders? Are they a literal, physical threat to me?

I glanced at Asher, wanting to know what his take on the situation was.

Despite being a Rider of the Wild Hunt and bigger than most, he immediately stiffened in their presence.

So, they are *a threat. That's good to know.*

The man with the beady eyes glared at me before turning his focus on Asher. "I think it is of the utmost importance to us. Especially since she had the gall to bring a Rider of the Wild Hunt with her!"

The other old men gasped and started shouting obscenities left and right in indignation.

One man shouted above the rest, "Abominations aren't permitted here. I told you we should have taken care of her as a child!"

"And by take care of her, you mean murder an innocent child?" Asher sneered. "And you have the balls to call *us* the abominations."

"Asher," I hissed, widening my eyes at my defender. He seriously didn't need to be bringing any more attention to himself than there already was. What was he thinking?

"Eliminating the threat to our very way of life is what I meant," the loudmouth barked back at him.

Fenrick stiffened beside me and clenched his sword tighter in his fist.

Is he expecting a fight?

My heart raced as the commotion of my arrival crashed around me like a stack of falling cards.

"That threat is my daughter!" King Channing roared, unleashing his rage without restraint.

All the knights stiffened at the king's tone.

"How do you know that she hasn't brought more abominations with her?" the beady-eyed Elder demanded, smacking his cane on the marble floor as if it would afford him extra authority.

Fenrick stepped forward. "I pulled her through the portal and in her fear, she dragged the Rider with her. There was no one else," he said firmly.

It wasn't lost on me that he'd stepped right in front of me, blocking me from the Elders. Despite everything I'd thought, he was protecting me. He was loyal to my parents, not the Elders, after all.

"She's coming with us!" the beady-eyed fool proclaimed just as the doors to the throne room burst open and guards flooded the room.

I swallowed hard, taking stock of the situation that had just exploded dangerously out of control.

Shit! There are too many of them. What the hell are we going to do?

CHAPTER 6
Grey

"What do you mean?" I growled. My hands shifted to claws as I stared down the shadow Fae. He was practically asking to be murdered unless he told me what happened to my friend and my mate real fast.

"The Elders have her," he said emotionlessly.

"The Elders?" I asked, my stomach sinking at the news.

Shit.

That was literally the worst possible thing that could have happened. We needed to find a way to get her out of there and fast.

"I have been tasked with finding Malcolm," the shadow Fae informed us.

"If I find that bastard first, I'm going to gut him for this!" I ran a hand through my hair in frustration.

"I don't think you will want to do that. He has stolen a priceless artifact from our princess, and it may be the only thing that can save her from the Elders. We need Malcolm alive, or all is lost," said the knight as he sheathed his sword.

Dan stepped forward, his brow creased. "Are you talking about the book?"

"Yes. How do *you* know of it?" The shadow Fae's tone was filled with loathing and there was no need to guess why. Dan was half-Fae and half-human, and there was one thing the pureblooded assholes hated more than anything, and that was their precious bloodlines being tainted by other species. It was one of the primary reasons we were all banished in the first place.

"I saw him take it with the help of a spell," Dan answered, crossing his arms over his chest. He wasn't taking the knight's shit.

Good.

"We need that book if we are to fulfill the prophecy, and you are to be allowed back into Faery." The Fae removed his gloves, surprising me as he reached out a hand. "It's an honor to meet you, Shifter King. My name is Fenrick, and I am Aurelia's sworn protector."

Well, you haven't done a great job so far, have you?

It was a cruel accusation, given the involvement of the Elders, but still. I reached out and shook the Fae's hand. "Call me Grey. I don't advertise that I am the king of shifters. I don't want to until I can get successfully get my people home."

"That's admirable. The Elders will go to great lengths to make sure that never happens, I'm afraid." Fenrick shook his head.

"Then why would you help me with this?" I asked. It didn't make any sense. Why would the Fae want to help us? The Elders banished us, but it looked like the Shadow Court wanted my help.

"Our princess has been threatened, and the king and queen are rethinking their decision to banish you all." Fenrick shrugged, the gesture of a man merely following orders. He was a soldier first and foremost, not a politician.

Asher groaned and writhed on the ground, drawing our attention. His face was bruised and bloody.

What the fuck did they do to him?

"Aurelia," he whispered.

"What about Aurelia?" I rushed over and knelt beside him.

One of his eyes was completely swollen shut and blood trailed down his chin from a cut on his lip. He blinked his one good eye open, but he was still dazed. "How did I get back?" he mumbled, glancing from me to Zeke.

"I don't know, my friend, but you were talking about Aurelia. What happened?" I asked urgently.

Ash's eyes rolled back in his head before he could speak.

"What the hell did they do to him?" I growled, glaring up at Fenrick.

"They didn't take kindly to his presence in Faery and retaliated. I got him out as soon as I was able. The how and what are not important," said Fenrick before he moved away from the group.

"What *is* important, then?" I snarled, rising to my feet. "He's not okay. He's fucking immortal and look at him!"

"The most important thing is finding that book and fast, or something terrible will befall your mate." Fenrick shook his head as if despite my status, I had very little between my ears.

"Fuck. Okay, let's get out of here and regroup." I scanned the clearing, looking for Fiona, but couldn't locate her. "Where's Fiona?" I asked, meeting the shadow knight's gaze once more.

"The sprite has her own part to play. She went back to the princess." Fenrick pursed his lips and stormed through the tree line.

"Where the fuck are you going?" I shouted at the Fae warrior's back.

"I'm getting out of the damn forest where anyone could hear our plans!" he yelled back.

"He's not wrong," Zeke growled, still holding his brother.

I didn't particularly like the shadow Fae warrior thus far, but he was right about one thing. I turned to the troll. "Can you guard the portal?" I asked.

"I don't want to be anywhere near the Fae portal, boss."

"And that's precisely why I want you to guard the portal. You don't want to go back to Faery, so you're the best man for the job. You'll guard the portal and not disappear on me." I clapped him on the shoulder in support. I needed someone to keep an eye on that blasted thing.

"Of course, boss. I will watch it for you." The troll nodded solemnly, even though he was definitely not happy about the situation.

I followed Fenrick from the forest and back to my car.

Zeke carried Asher behind us.

I grimaced when I realized that I would be returning to the penthouse without Fiona. Freya was going to lose her shit in the *worst* way.

Dan clapped me on the shoulder as he sidled up next to me. "What's that look for?" he asked.

"Freya," I said simply and shook my head.

Fuck.

"She's going to be fucking with you until the end of time for this." Dan chuckled. "There's nothing quite like the wrath of a tiny glitter bug."

"You're not wrong," I grumbled with a zing of paternal guilt. I was not looking forward to explaining to the sprite what had happened to her sister. That was going to be a pain in the ass. Sprites were like little firecrackers when their wings were in a twist.

We made it back to the car without further incident, and I pulled the keys out of my pocket. "Dan, organize for a pick-up, and take Zeke and Asher straight back to the facility and get a healer on site immediately. I have to go."

"On it, boss. No problem." Dan dug out his phone and was making arrangements before I'd even taken another step.

I nodded to Fenrick, satisfied, and got in the driver's seat of my car and waited for the Fae.

He climbed in and grimaced as he sat in the passenger seat.

"You get used to the claustrophobic feeling," I told him as I turned the key in the ignition.

"I haven't spent much time in the human realm, to be honest," Fenrick said, adjusting himself to fit more comfortably.

"Did you see my mate?" I asked as I did a slick burnout, coming around one-hundred-and-eighty-degrees to accelerate back toward the city.

"I was the one who pulled her into Faery. But had I known what would unfold, I never would have brought her back." He blew out a breath of frustration, clearly genuinely annoyed at himself.

"You're the reason that she's in this mess?" I growled, glancing over at him.

"I had orders from the king and queen. They wanted their daughter back," he answered without hesitation, never glancing away from the window.

"And it didn't matter what she wanted?" I felt disgusted. Of course, it didn't. My own father never cared much for what I wanted either and we both ended up paying the ultimate price for his ego.

"No, it didn't. They gave her life and have been searching for her for decades," Fenrick said. "What she wanted—though I didn't stop to ask —would have been of no consequence. I am duty-bound to obey them."

"Decades?" I asked curiously. There was no way she had been taken away from them for decades. That didn't make any sense at all. Aurelia was maybe twenty-something, and had been at least seven when Malcolm abducted her.

"Time works differently in Faery, it seems. We have been looking for her for a lot longer than she has been alive in the human realm," Fenrick grumbled. "I cannot explain it better than that."

"How long has it been since you ripped her out of the human realm, then?" I asked.

How long has it been for my mate? Weeks? Months? Does she think that everyone here has forgotten about her?

"It had been two weeks by the time I pushed the Rider through the portal." The shadow knight shook his head in dismay.

"Two weeks isn't a terrible timeframe," I admitted.

It's not great, but it could have been worse.

Hopefully, she knew deep down that I would be coming to save her. I needed her to have faith in that, even if she hated me. I refused to be that man again, and if she gave me a second chance, I would never break her trust. I'd sooner die.

"It is when you consider she was taken by the Elders almost upon arrival, and we haven't seen her in those weeks," Fenrick said softly.

"Then how can we know that she's okay? That's she even... still with us?" I asked.

"We don't. We can't. All we know is that the Elders have her, and we don't have much time to waste," Fenrick said, a subtle quaver in his tone I hadn't expected to hear.

That was not what I wanted to discover. How the hell were we going to find Malcolm, especially if he didn't want to be found and had acted against the king and queen's wishes in the first place?

I sighed heavily. "I think we need to check out Malcolm's house, the place he took her when he abducted her from my penthouse." I turned the car down another dirt road, the directions to my destination clear in my mind.

"You know where he lives?" Fenrick asked, seemingly shocked.

"I doubt he lives there anymore," I admitted. He likely switched up his operations after we rescued Aurelia. It would be too easy for us to catch him if he chose to remain there."

"Malcolm is just arrogant enough to stay there and not care if the Shifter King found him again." Fenrick shook his head at his fellow Fae's bravado.

"You're not wrong on that one. He also might have left some nasty little traps for us and returned to Faery. He could be lying low, waiting for an opportunity to present itself to his best advantage." I gripped the steering wheel tighter in my hands until my knuckles were white. I wanted a piece of that stupid Fae bastard badly, and my wolf was in full agreement.

"That's not possible," Fenrick said bluntly. "He can't go back to Faery without the princess."

"Okay, I'm going to need you to explain that." I glanced at the Fae warrior from the corner of my eye.

Why the hell would he need Aurelia to get back into Faery?

"When he took the princess from our realm, the king and queen formally banished him. And even if he does manage to get back into the realm, there is an order to kill on sight."

"So, that bastard is desperate to find her, but he's also stuck in the same situation, where he'll never get back?" I chuckled.

It serves the stupid son of a bitch right.

We pulled up to the sprawling ranch house, and I cut the engine. I'd never wanted to come back to this place, but if it helped me get my mate back, then I would do anything at all. I'd cross realms for her and burn everything in my path. "There might be some booby traps inside. He is a sadistic prick." I opened the car door and got out.

"You don't become the Captain of the King's Guard without being a sadist," Fenrick agreed.

The pile of twisted metal that was once a motorcycle was still beneath the tree that landed on them. Luckily for all of us, the Riders hadn't been overly concerned about their bikes.

The house had an ominous feel to it that sent a shiver down my spine. No one had been here since that night apparently, as the door was off its hinges when we walked up the path.

"I don't think he's here," Fenrick mumbled as he scanned the house with suspicion, clenching the hilt of his sword.

"No, but we can have a look around and see if he left the book behind." I stepped through the open door a moment later.

"I don't believe he would be *that* stupid," Fenrick said. "The artifact is priceless."

A loud click filled the quiet space. "Fuck. Don't move. I think one of us just sprung a trap." I grimaced and scanned the floor. The tile directly under my foot was depressed a quarter of an inch below the rest and I groaned.

Just my luck.

"I triggered the trap. I'm not even sure what it does or what will happen if I move my foot." I turned to glance over at Fenrick.

He grimaced. "I can't sift." He frowned, concentrating again, but he stayed in the exact same place.

"Malcolm has wards on the place." I sighed. "He would make it so no one else could sift into his home." An unexpected ticking filled the room, like a clock ticking down the time until the trap went off whether I moved or not. "I don't have a choice. I have to move because either way, this trap is going off."

Fenrick nodded and edged back out the front door.

It's only a few feet away. I can make it before anything happens.

I had my shifter speed to count on. "Three, two, one," I said under my breath and pivoting faster than the human eye could see, I bolted for the door. Despite my supernatural speed, an inferno of heat blasted me off my feet from behind. I sailed through the air as a deafening *boom* assaulted my ears from all sides.

I slammed into the ground with a vicious *thud*. My head pounded with the reverberations of the explosion and my body burned, forcing a primal scream from my lungs before everything went black, and I plunged into nothingness.

CHAPTER 7
Aurelia

I gripped the iron chains, tugging hard against them. "What the fuck?" I exclaimed, a sickening mix of worry and fear bubbling within me.

The beady-eyed Elder sneered. "The humans and the undesirable rabble really didn't do much for your attitude, did they?"

"Why am I here?" I asked, scanning the cell and ignoring his snide remark. It was dank and smelled of mildew and rot. Why the fuck did they think I deserved to be behind iron bars and locked in chains? No one deserved to be treated so cruelly.

Aren't I supposed to be important to Faery?

What had I done, beyond showomg a little attitude that could warrant such a response? The stone floors were disgusting, and I was pretty sure the hole in the corner was supposed to be a toilet. The conditions weren't fit for an animal, let alone a princess of the damn realm. And where were my parents? Were they trying to rescue me? And what about Grey? Despite everything, had he given up on me?

My mate.

I sighed internally, pushing such things aside. None of that thinking was going to help me right now, so there was no point dwelling on what might or might not be going on beyond my four walls of filth. All I could do for the moment was focus and survive whatever these old bastards were going to subject me to.

"We need to test you to see if you have shadow magic," the Elder said.

The gleam in his eyes was hate-filled and deeply unsettling. Why would he think I had shadow magic? I had never used such magic, nor had I heard of it.

"That's ridiculous," I said. "I've never used such a thing. All I possess is air magic. You know, the purple, crackling power you saw me with before you had me bound up like a common prisoner!"

"You have yet to come into your full powers. You have no idea what you may possess, but that is why we're here." He shook his head.

What? I haven't come into my full powers? What I have is already terrifying and difficult to control. What will happen when I have my all my supposed powers?

"That can't be right," I argued back before chewing on my lip.

The Elder sighed. "Do you remember nothing?"

"Next to nothing. I had a memory block put on me at one point. Everything from the past is a blur. It comes in fleeting flashes at best." I pulled against my bindings in frustration. I might be indignant and enraged, but I wasn't going to let this elitist bastard's rhetoric faze me. He was not important.

More than anything, I just needed to get out of here in one piece and search for Asher. Fenrick had gone with him, and I hoped against hope that the Rider was okay. It would be all my fault if something bad were to happen to him. Guilt ate at me, making my stomach roil. I hadn't seen either of them in days.

"The Fae do not come into their full powers until their twenty-fifth birthday, and yours just happens to be in a few days' time," he grunted.

What the fuck?

I'd never even known when my damn birthday was, yet this asshole knew it. That was really depressing. How much more about me did these Fae know that I didn't? "So, you're saying I have to be here for a few more days so that you can test me for magic I've never heard of before? Well, that's just great. Bring it on." I shifted uncomfortably, and the chains clanked together, echoing around the dank space.

"Why do you think your parents' court is called the Shadow Court, child?" His beady eyes narrowed on me as if I might be playing with him.

"I don't fucking know! I wasn't even aware that's what it was called. It's news to me, like most of this shit is!" I threw my hands up in frustration, but the chains would only allow me so much freedom of movement.

The chains suddenly pulled tight, no doubt controlled by the magic, and the manacles scraped against my fair skin. I winced in pain.

Fuck. That hurts.

The beady-eyed Elder chuckled at my discomfort, obviously enjoying the show and his pathetic power trip.

"Why are you even here telling me all this?" I asked. "Why don't you just get on with these magic tests?" Truthfully, as far as I knew, I thought they ultimately wanted me dead. They didn't want me controlling who came and went from Faery, so why was he bothering to tell me any of this if they just planned on killing me anyway?

"I just thought you ought to know what to expect before we start experimenting." His grin was malicious as his eyes bored into my soul.

My eyes widened, and my stomach practically sank out my ass.

Are they going to experiment on me?

I couldn't help but laugh darkly. The irony was not lost on me. All these years I'd feared that the humans might discover me and experiment upon me. And yet, now, it was my own people inflicting that fate.

Just perfect. Fears realized. Check. Brilliant!

But beyond the irony and my dark humor, trauma boiled. I did *not* want to know what they planned to do to me to make this crazy magic surface. And I sure as shit did not want to hang around to find out.

I need to get out of here!

"I don't even want to know what you plan to do to get the magic to surface," I said aloud, giving voice to my thoughts and shuddering as I took a step back into the wall to which I was chained.

"You will know soon enough." He grinned and waved a hand over his shoulder.

A signal.

Four Council soldiers stepped forward and unlocked the cell door.

He wants to do this now? Fuck. I thought I was going to be tested, not experimented and tortured!

The soldiers stormed into the cell and unhooked my chains from the wall. The men on either side of me grabbed my arms in bruising grips before they shoved me forward.

I stumbled slightly, their unforgivingly tight hold on my arms the only thing that prevented my fall.

They were not being kind or gentle, though I shouldn't have expected any sense of decency to exist in a hole like this. I ripped away from the Fae on the right with all the strength I could muster.

He merely sneered as he shoved me forward again without a shred of remorse.

"You will want to come quietly, Princess Aurelia," warned the beady-eyed Elder as he glared at me.

"And why is that?" I asked with disdain, temporarily overcome with righteous rage.

"You care for that criminal's wellbeing, do you not?" he asked so casually my stomach dropped.

Asher is still here? I thought Fenrick got him out. So that's how they plan to keep me in line while they experiment on me. Shit. I'm so fucked.

"Where is he?" I demanded angrily but allowed them to lead me from the cell. I wasn't going to do this for myself. There would be no hope for me regardless, unless I was somehow able to escape the Elders. I would do as was necessary to protect Asher. This was all my fault, after all. He never should have been dragged into this. He'd been kind to me and look what it got him!

Bad fortune followed me around like a tangible plague. The people that dared show me any form of kindness always suffered for it.

Is Grey suffering right now? Do I care?

When I searched my heart, I couldn't deny that I did in fact care. I cared a lot. No matter how hard I tried to put him out of my mind and to think of him as my enemy, I couldn't.

The mark of his claim on my neck tingled as I was led out of the dungeon and to a room with sterile white walls and a large, solid table of gleaming stone at its center. There were leather straps at the head and foot of the slab, which were connected to metal D-rings that were drilled into the stone.

Those are supposed to hold me down? Not likely.

A smaller metal table stood off to one side, an array of shining instruments lining the tray. They looked like torture devices.

I struggled against the arms holding me tightly. I couldn't possibly allow them to strap me down and torture me. My every survival instinct fought against it.

"Remember, Princess, your friend will suffer." The Elder strolled to the little table, turning his back on me.

Fuck. What am I going to do?

I didn't want Asher to be further harmed, but it looked like they were about to fucking dissect me or something! Again, I was confronted with a choice that was not a choice at all. Resigned, I straightened my spine and moved to the stone table, sitting down heavily with a sigh.

The soldiers circled me and strapped me to the cold and solid slab.

The leather cuffs had some kind of enchantment upon them, because no matter how hard I struggled, I couldn't break free. This was it. No matter what I did now, regardless of whether I succumbed or fought tooth and nail—it was happening.

"Magic is innately tied to emotions. So, to bring it forward, we will need to invoke some," the Elder explained, his tone one of necessity and boredom. He picked up a scalpel, turning it over in his hand, before a gleeful smile crossed his sadistic face. He ran the dull side of the blade down my neck, toying with me to garner a reaction.

Sweat broke out on my forehead, and I clenched my hands into tight fists. My stomach flip-flopped as he continued to torment me with the blade. Keeping my fear in check as best I could, I held very still and glared at him with defiance. Even if I cooperated, I didn't have to be fucking happy about it. "So, you're just going to cut and bleed me to see if this shadow magic comes out?" I asked.

The Elder was an idiot. Despite being restrained by the leather cuffs, I still had the damn iron manacles on. How did he expect me to access my power with the iron draining me with every passing moment?

"I'll do whatever is necessary to discover what magic you possess." He sneered.

I smirked a challenge at his incompetent ass. "And how do you plan on getting my magic out with this iron draining me?" I raised a cocky eyebrow and pulled at my restraints to draw his attention.

"You imbeciles! You didn't remove the cuffs?" the Elder roared.

The soldiers guarding the room stiffened before springing into action and removing the manacles.

Relief flooded me instantly. The lack of iron touching my skin nearly made me groan with gratitude. Magic tingled in my veins and came easily to my fingertips in a crackling purple heat, though it didn't affect the leather straps still wrapped securely around my wrists in the slightest.

"Easy there, Aurelia. You don't want to cause your friend more distress, do you?" The Elder smiled obscenely.

I took a deep breath and called my magic back to me, willing it to settle. "You want me to let my magic out and then threaten me when I do what you want? That makes a ton of sense," I scoffed.

He turned the knife so the sharp end was against the tender flesh of my throat.

I gulped. Pain blossomed where he nicked my throat, and a small trickle of blood made its way down my neck to pool beneath my chin. My magic flared to life but there wasn't anything new on display. It felt the same as it always did. What was shadow magic supposed to feel like, anyway? Would I recognize it? And would it be different? My usual magic continued to crackle against my palms.

The Elder studied me like a lab rat, his gaze focused on where he'd cut me. "Your healing works much faster when your magic flares," he observed. "There isn't even the tiniest of scars there," he said in awe.

I stared at the ceiling, not even bothering to acknowledge his words. It was good information and I filed it away for later, but I refused to let him see my curiosity.

He huffed an aggravated breath and turned back to the metal table. When he turned back, he had a small hammer in his hand.

Oh, fuck no.

With wide eyes I thrashed on the bed, my hands lighting with magic again. Asher was tough, great big brute of a man... surely, he'd understand. I couldn't let this sicko start smashing my bones. "Let me fucking go!" I screamed, pulling at the straps on my wrists in another attempt to get free.

"Hold her arms down with her palms facing the stone!" the Elder barked.

I kicked out at one of the Fae moving toward me, but the strap on my ankle didn't afford me enough movement to stop him.

Strong hands banded around my arms as the soldiers secured me with their physical strength, squeezing hard.

I nearly cried out, but I bit down on my tongue and held it in, not willing to give the bastards the satisfaction of knowing that they were hurting me. They saw me as nothing more than a threat or a piece of property. I just wasn't entirely sure which one anymore, especially after having seen the gleam in the Elder's eyes when he talked about the possibility of shadow magic.

"You will be able to heal the damage," the Elder assured me with a grin.

"It doesn't mean that I want you smashing my fingers to see if any new magic will surface!" I glared at him.

"You don't have a choice in the matter, dear. You are at my mercy here, and your friend will suffer for any insolence you display." He was *way* too excited to have me at his mercy. These Elders were a breed unto themselves.

What a sadistic asshole.

I kept my mouth shut and gritted my teeth, waiting for him to get on with it. Fixing my gaze, I stared up at the white ceiling, refusing to give him any further reaction or satisfaction.

"You're going to scream for me before all is said and done," he said in a depraved and conversational tone. He was reveling in the anticipation of the torture. He wanted my reactions more than anything.

I squeezed my eyes shut tightly and waited for the inevitable pain that would soon assail me.

The Elder chuckled. "Very well, then. Let's begin," he said, just before my knuckles crunched beneath the weight and momentum of the hammer's blow.

Searing pain filled my hand, tearing a scream from my throat. My magic flared to life and another scream met mine as power sizzled out of me and flowed into the hammer. A dam I never knew existed broke inside of me and magic, unlike anything I had felt before, exploded out of me.

My back arched as the room was flooded with my unrestrained power. I managed to open my eyes just in time to see the hilt of a soldier's sword coming toward me. Pain erupted in my head, and a sickeningly loud crack filled the air, reverberating in my ears as my consciousness faded.

Fuck, this fucking sucks.

CHAPTER 8
Grey

A shadow loomed over me. "Did you think I wouldn't have taken precautions?" sneered a familiar voice.

I groaned as I sat up. What the fuck was Malcolm doing standing over me? I blinked against the dim light and scanned the dank, dark room.

Where the fuck am I?

"What the fuck happened?" I shook my head to clear it.

"You and the protector were stupid enough to walk right into my trap." Malcolm chuckled.

"Where is Fenrick?" I asked. There was a small cot near a window with bars on it. The space was so small that I couldn't stretch out completely. It was maybe six feet wide at best.

"Don't worry about him, worry about yourself, Shifter King. Tell me where Aurelia is hiding." Malcolm crossed his arms over his chest and glared down at me.

"You don't know?" I chuckled right back, amused by the irony. "She's well beyond your reach."

"No one is beyond my reach," he answered smugly.

"So, you really don't know?" I clucked my tongue and snickered. I was going to enjoy taking this bastard down a peg or two. I moved to cross my arms and metal clinked together.

He thinks he can chain me so I can't shift?

There weren't chains that could hold down the Shifter King in this world or any other.

"I know more than you can even possibly imagine, mongrel," he spat.

"Do you know that you've been banished, I wonder?" I smirked.

He narrowed his eyes at me. "Banished? You must be desperate to delay me. That's impossible."

"Is it really, though? You abducted the princess and didn't think the king would retaliate?" The king was a notoriously angry man and could hold a grudge better than anyone in Faery. Did Malcolm think because he was Captain of the King's Guard, he would be exempt from the king's ire?

He's stupider than he looks.

Malcolm's face turned red in anger, and he vanished from the room. Was he going to check for himself if he could re-enter? He would be sorely disappointed when he discovered there was a troll guarding the portal and that he could no longer see it.

I rose to my feet and took two steps toward the door and the chains clanked against the floor. Taking another step, my ankle caught and pulled back.

My wolf growled inside my mind at the chains binding us.

Borrowing from his strength, I gripped the metal in both hands and pulled at the cuffs. At first, they didn't budge but after I twisted hard, exerting even more power, the sound of twisting, grinding metal filled the quiet place as the metal broke off at my ankle. Reaching for the chains that were attached to the manacles on my wrists, I pulled with all my strength once more until one snapped, then I proceeded to do the same with the other. I didn't have time to waste. I needed to find Fenrick and get the hell out of here before Malcolm returned on a rampage.

"Master is going to be very angry," a voice cried out behind me.

I spun to the sound and found a brownie standing with his little hands planted on his hips as he glared at me. "Ask me if I care," I retorted. "Why do you even work for a psychopath like him? Brownies are good and kind and respond best to those who are the same."

"Master bought the house, and I was included in the sale." He shrugged but he frowned at my words all the same.

"So, we're in Malcolm's house. It didn't explode?" I asked carefully. I needed to gather as much information out of the brownie as possible before Malcolm returned from the portal.

"No, it did explode, but the master used his magic to fix it." The brownie waggled his finger at me. "You should not have been breaking and entering."

"I didn't break anything, and the door was still blown off its hinges from before," I said, turning away and back to the door. "All I did was enter." Without hesitation, I gripped the door handle and turned it. The door clicked open, offering no resistance.

"You can't go out there!" the brownie yelled, suddenly exasperated.

"Who's going to stop me? You?" I asked over my shoulder.

The brownie looked down and away, showing submission, knowing full well my wolf was close to the surface. He was no match for the predator inside me and he knew it.

I stepped out of the room and glanced around. There was no sign of Fenrick to be found in the long hall.

Fuck. Where is he hiding the Fae warrior?

We needed to get the fuck out of here. I crept down the hall to the next door and cracked it open, but there was nothing there other than an empty office. Could that be where he hid the book? I pushed the door open even further, and a squeak from behind me had me glancing over my shoulder.

"You can't go into master's office!" the brownie cried.

"Watch me," I said, and stepped into the darkened room.

There was a single lamp on the dark hardwood desk and bookshelves lined the walls. A high-backed office chair was positioned behind the desk, but my eyes returned to the books on the shelves. I didn't get a good look at the book during the mimic spell Karma had performed, so I was going in blind. Ideally, I needed Fenrick. He might have some idea of what the book looked like—he might even recognize it. I turned back to the door and stomped out of the office, determined to find Fenrick before Malcolm returned. "Do you know where the Fae warrior is being kept?" I asked the brownie over my shoulder, continuing my search.

"I cannot say," he mumbled.

I growled and spun around on the twerp, picking him up by the throat. "My mate is in danger in Faery and the Fae warrior is the only one who can help me save her. You will tell me where the warrior is. *Now.*" My wolf was *right* at the surface. I could feel him.

"Your mate?" he wheezed. Coughing as he desperately struggled to breathe, he clawed at my hand.

"Princess Aurelia is my mate. She is trapped, and I need to save her, but I can't get there without the Fae. So, where is he?" I snarled, punctuating each word. I dropped the brownie and

He coughed harder as he sucked deep breaths of air into his lungs. Then, without further loyalty, he picked one hand up off the ground and pointed at a room down the hall.

I raced down the hallway and pushed open the door. Fenrick was on the floor, the skin of his arms flared painfully red because of the iron manacles on his wrists. They were slowly eating away at his magic. "Fenrick," I said softly, and he lifted his head.

His eyes were entirely black and the pupils unfocused.

What the hell happened to him?

"Can you move?" I asked.

Fenrick shook his head but held up his arm.

I gripped both sides of the manacle on his wrist and called on my wolf's strength again to bend the metal. It screeched in protest before snapping free.

Fenrick sighed in relief and offered me his other wrist.

"How did you get out?" he asked. "The last time I saw, you were knocked out from the blast."

"I woke up with that asshole, Malcolm, standing over me," I explained. "My wolf helped out."

"Where is he now?" he asked.

I destroyed the remaining cuff.

The brownie muttered angrily to himself every time a lock broke.

I ignored him. He was being overly dramatic. I didn't give a fuck about what he thought. I just needed to get Fenrick to the office and then get the fuck out of the traitor's house.

"C'mon, you good?" I asked as I wrapped his arm around my shoulder and lifted him.

"Yes, let's get out of here," Fenrick said.

"We need to check his office first," I grunted.

"You think he would leave the book in his office?" Fenrick asked, incredulous.

"Well, we didn't think he'd be here, but he was. He's an arrogant son of a bitch. Whether it's here or not, we have to check." I stormed from the room and back down the hall, Fenrick hardly slowing me down.

The brownie followed closely behind me. "You can't take anything from the master's office!"

"Do you want me to tie you up and gag you, brownie?" I asked.

The creature gasped and stomped his foot angrily, having a mini tantrum.

I opened the door to the office and turned back to Fenrick. "Do you know what the book looks like?"

Fenrick hobbled into the room and followed alongside the bookshelves. "It's gold and priceless. I doubt he'd make it easy to find."

"Okay, let's look around quickly. He could be back at any time." I ran a hand through my hair and positioned myself by the door. I would be of little help finding a book that I had never seen in person, but I could keep watch.

How long will the troll be able to keep him busy?

"How is your magic, Fenrick?" I asked. I had no idea how long it took to recharge after iron sucked the magic out of a Fae. It could be hours.

How long was he locked up back there?

Malcolm was a sick fuck, torturing a fellow fairy that way. He really was a wicked bastard.

"It's returning quickly," Fenrick assured me, still scanning the books on the shelf.

"He must have a safe or something." I turned on my heel to face the brownie with a sinister grin.

"I will not help you steal from the master," the brownie growled before he tried to dart down the hall.

Obviously, I was faster and picked him up by the back of his shirt. "You don't have a choice, little friend."

The bastard screamed and thrashed like I'd cut off a limb.

I shook him angrily, trying to shut him up. His whining pierced my ears, and my wolf whined in my mind.

The little fucker had a good set of lungs on him, that was for damn sure. "Shut up before I shut you up forever. Where is the bloody safe?"

"It's hidden with magic," the brownie said smugly, ceasing his wailing. "You will never find it."

Fenrick strolled over and crossed his arms across his chest. "If you show us where it is, I can get into it."

"No!" the brownie screamed again.

"What should we do with him?" I asked with a malicious snarl. I snapped my teeth at him in warning.

The brownie gulped but kept his mouth shut.

"He's been brainwashed and is harmless," said Fenrick with a shrug.

I spun back to the door as a crash sounded from down the hall.

The brownie laughed. "Master, they are trying to steal from you!" he screeched at the top of those bastard lungs of his.

I shook the little bastard hard. He was about to lead Malcolm right to us. With Malcolm being the only one in the house who could sift, the little asshole would give him exactly what he wanted—our exact location.

Malcolm appeared in the door in the blink of an eye.

I threw the brownie onto the nearby chair.

Mangy little fucker!

"How the fuck did you get out of the chains?" Malcolm growled.

"You underestimate shifters." I smirked. Crouching down into a fighting stance, I grinned.

My wolf growled in my head, thrashing at the barrier in my chest. He wanted to rip Malcolm apart and was just waiting for the opportunity.

"Rabid beasts," Malcolm snarled.

"The only one rabid around here is you." I smirked. "Where did you get that cut on your forehead?"

Fenrick chuckled. "Did you find a nasty little surprise when you went to the portal?"

"Fucking trolls!" Malcolm swore, then narrowed his eyes at me. "How did you know?"

"Who do you think stationed him there, idiot?" I asked. "For an ancient Fae warrior, you aren't very smart."

Malcolm roared a battle call and magic erupted out of him.

Fenrick dove and smashed into me, protecting me without a second's hesitation.

I flew back and hit the wall with a thud as flames poured from Malcolm's hands. Pain erupted up my spine and the breath *whooshed* out of me. The bastard clearly didn't care about destroying his own house when he could just fix it all with magic.

Fenrick stood in front of me with magic of his own lighting up his palms. "Malcolm, you don't want to do this," Fenrick said, widening his stance and readying himself for combat.

"And why would you say that?" Malcolm sneered. "I can take you."

"Don't!" I gasped as I realized just what the princess's protector was about to reveal. If he told him about the book and what it held, there would be no way we could retrieve it and rescue my mate from the Faery.

"Aurelia is in trouble. She's gone," Fenrick said.

Fuck.

The stupid Fae didn't listen.

"Fenrick, no," I groaned.

"So, she's in Faery." Malcolm shrugged. "It's inconvenient, I'll admit, but not impossible to retrieve her."

What did he know that we didn't? Had he seen the book already and knew what needed to be done?

Shit.

"It's more than inconvenient. When did you become the Council's puppet?" Fenrick asked, the insult not lost on the Captain of the King's Guard.

"I am *no one's* puppet. This is what's best for all of Faery!" Malcolm yelled back. He smirked a second later and waved a hand at the only exit. A wall of fire erupted, the heat searing my skin even from the other side of the room.

"Have fun burning alive, gentlemen." Then he sifted away to safety, leaving us to go up in flames.

Shit. What the fuck are we going to do now?

CHAPTER 9

My head pounded behind my eyes, and I ran a hand through my hair, but my fingers got tangled in the mess of caked-up blood. Grimacing as I sat up in my cell, dizziness overwhelmed me like a crashing tide and nearly made me fall back onto the cold stone.

Fuck.

They'd dumped me back in a cell, and I was lying on the disgusting floor, cradling one hand with the other before realizing I couldn't feel any pain there.

Has my magic healed me?

I wiggled my fingers, and they were fine. It didn't seem as if anything horrible had happened to them at all. Not even a doctor would be able to tell I'd just had my knuckles smashed with a damn hammer, I marveled.

"You're awake," a gruff voice said from the other side of the dingy, cold room.

"Who are you? I thought I was alone in here," I croaked, my throat parched.

"No, I have been here a very long time," the man answered. "How is your head?"

"I'm feeling a bit dizzy…well more than a bit, really. What happened?" I asked, shaking my head to clear it and immediately regretting the action as a fresh wave of pain and nausea wracked me.

"I don't know exactly what you did, but they brought you in here unconscious with gushing blood from your head." He chuckled then. "From the talk I heard, though, that Elder got the shock of his life."

I almost laughed in response but fell abruptly silent when I touched my head and winced, the memory of the soldier's sword pommel smashing into my head making me shudder. "I lost control of my magic," I said as I leaned my head back against the wall.

"I guessed as much. The way your fingers looked when they brought you… I can't blame you," he replied. "They looked mangled."

I flexed my fingers again, grateful for my incredible Fae healing. "Who are you?" I ventured.

"Just a fellow prisoner," he replied with a sigh. "I've been gone so long, I doubt you have ever heard of me."

"Why are you here?" I asked.

I may as well get to know my cellmate between torture sessions.

"I am apparently a danger to society as well as the Elders' plans." He chuckled again, though the sound was without humor.

"Fucking Elders!" I growled. I hated the old bastards with my entire being and wanted nothing more than to destroy every single last one of them. It was clear to me now more than ever, that the Elders were the toxicity poisoning Faery from within—and not the others. Without warning, a scream tore from my throat as shadows slithered up my arms out of nowhere.

What the hell?

"What? What's happening?" The man's panicked voice reached me through my screams.

"There's something wrong with my magic!" I cried. I flung my hand as if to dislodge the darkness, but the shadows flew forth and wrapped around the bars of the door. They bent under the pressure and onslaught of the strange, new magic.

"Breathe with me, Princess." My fellow prisoner's calm voice was familiar but somehow different, although soothing.

I focused as best I could and matched my breath to his, doing my utmost to keep Grey's face out of my mind as I made use of exactly the same technique he'd always taught to regain my calm and control. Soon my breathing slowed, and the shadows untangled themselves from the bars, retracting back to me.

Shit. That's going to be noticed.

The shadows slithered along my arms like writhing, intangible snakes, pulsing against my skin. They were foreign yet also an innate part of me.

"Are you okay, Princess Aurelia?" my cellmate asked, concern evident in his tone.

"I have shadow magic," I whispered, my heart racing at the realization.

"Shhh, Princess! You need to control it. They must not see it," the older man whispered back with an unmistakable sense of urgency and panic.

"That's why they were torturing me. They were trying to see if I had it. Why is it so important?" I asked him.

"I'll tell you, but first you must control it. Make it *obey* you." Gnarled, tan hands grabbed at the bars that divided our cell, and he stretched them out just enough that they looked like mine.

I closed my eyes and coaxed the magic back inside me, desperate for the it to listen. It couldn't be seen, that much was paramount. I didn't know why exactly, but the man in the adjoining cell was sure about it, and from the sounds of it, he'd been here a hell of a lot longer than I had. Whatever was going on in Faery and with me couldn't be good. Thankfully, after exerting my willpower over them, the shadows slithered a bit more, almost as if they had a will of their own, before seeping back into my skin.

"Okay, it's gone. It's hidden." I blew out my breath in relief.

"Good. You mustn't let the Elders see it, no matter what pain they cause you," he said, sounding relieved.

"What's your name, friend? How do I know I can trust you?" I asked.

"You should trust none but your mate," he countered emotionlessly, withdrawn once more.

I scoffed. The memory of Grey and his betrayal was still too fresh in my mind and sent a knife of pain through my heart. "I don't have a mate." I shook my head and slid down the wall, leaning my head back against it again.

"You forget that I saw them bring you in, Princess. What do you think that mark on your neck means?" he asked angrily.

I must have hit a nerve, but I wasn't sure that I cared. He wasn't experiencing my pain. He wasn't feeling what I was with every ache of my still beating heart. "I know what it means, but trusting my mate is a bit tough right now, given he betrayed me." I shook my head in hurt, even though he couldn't see me.

"Impossible!" he barked. "Betraying a mate would be like chewing your own arm off."

"Wait... are you a shifter?" I gasped, my stomach roiling.

I thought all the shifters were sent to the human world. How is this man in a cell next to me?

"Yes, though I was too powerful to exile, according to those assholes," he said with a growl.

He's been here since the Exile? How has he not gone completely insane?

"Holy shit," I whispered with renewed empathy.

"That's putting it mildly." He chuckled.

"You've been here all this time?" I asked, not even bothering to hide just how horrified I was. I knew the Elders were cruel bastards, but that was going too far. What about his wolf? His need for the open sky, the moon, and to run free? That would drive him mad, surely...

"But none of this is what you really want to know, is it, Princess? They're not the questions you should be asking."

"What's so important or dangerous about shadow magic?" I asked, agreeing with the old shifter and deciding to get straight to the point. "My parents' court *is* the Shadow Court."

The shifter sighed. "It's been centuries since anyone has developed shadow magic," he revealed. There was a shuffling noise like he was moving closer to the bars again.

"But if they're the Shadow Court, how can they *not* have shadow magic? It doesn't make sense." I curled my knees up beneath my chin and wrapped my arms around them as I mused over the strange contradiction.

"They believe they have been cursed because they failed to stop the Elders from exiling everyone," he said. "They were short-sighted and agreed to their foul plan when they should have stood and fought for all the residents of Faery."

"If they think they're cursed, then why do I have the shadows?" I whispered, squeezing my eyes closed.

"The prophecy says the one who rules the shadows will decide."

"Decide what?" I frowned, looking up. Was I truly supposed to decide who could live in Faery? I didn't know anything about the politics of Faery, but I knew a wrong when I saw one.

"I think you already know, Princess Aurelia," he said.

I flinched. "This isn't a fair exchange," I said. "You know exactly who I am, but I have no idea who you are. A powerful shifter whom the Elders fear? Tell me your name."

"My name is Nickolas, and I am the Shifter King," he said.

My jaw dropped open, and I stared at him through the bars in shock.

The Shifter King?

"What?" I cried. Was that why the Council had locked him up for centuries, simply because of his birthright? Why not let the former king go with the others, with his people? Why did they keep him here? He would have been no trouble to Faery beyond the portal...

"That's why I am stuck here, Princess. I'm far too powerful to be set free. And they know that my son won't come into his full power until my death, so they are purposely keeping me here and alive until they can seal the portal closed forever," Nickolas said with a growl.

"That's terrible," I breathed, tears of unexpected emotion pricking my eyes. "I'm so sorry, Nickolas."

How could they keep another living soul in a cage like this for so long? It's barbaric and cruel!

"It's okay, though, Aurelia. I'm here to meet you and help you escape," he said with a smile in his voice.

"You're going to help me escape? How?" I asked, equal amounts of surprise and doubt creeping into my tone.

"Don't sound so incredulous," he chastised. "I don't know what my son did to betray you, but when we get out of here, I'll be sure to slap him upside his idiot head," he finished, humor in his voice.

"Grey? Grey is your son?" I asked in horror.

Oh, my God... that's why he sounds so familiar!

He had to be talking about Grey. It couldn't be anyone else. He was the only one I'd ever let get close enough to hurt me and he would be the last. He was my mate, and I wasn't ever going to trust anyone again the same way I'd trusted him.

"Is that what he's going by in the mortal world? And yes, I can smell his mark of claim on you."

Okay, that isn't weird at all. He can smell him on me?

I shuddered, not liking the idea of that at all. "What the fuck? You can do what now?" I asked. "Wait, can everyone smell it?"

"No, Princess Aurelia. I'm stronger, and he's my son. My blood," Nickolas assured me.

"That really doesn't make me feel much better." I squeezed my knees to my chest more tightly, as if I could shield myself from all this realm-altering drama going on around me. Drama I'd fast become a part of, whether I liked it or not.

Drama I've always been at the center of.

"Why don't you tell me what he did? I know my son, and he would never betray his mate unless there was no other option," Nickolas said.

"He was looking for a Fae to help him find something and sent a man to locate me. That man shot me with a tranquillizer dart and is the reason why the witch who raised me is dead, and why I had nowhere else to go." I shrugged.

If I tried really hard, I could probably find a way to blame him for this too. If I hadn't been running from him, I never would have been pulled into the portal. The truth was that I was finding it difficult to stay angry at him. I missed him horribly. I missed him in my very bones, and the harder I tried desperately not to miss him, the more I did. My mark tingled at my neck, and I nearly groaned, reaching up to cover it with my hand.

Where is he? Is he looking for me? I've already been gone much longer than I should have been.

"It must have been difficult for him to decide what to do in such a circumstance, Princess. It would be an impossible choice—to choose between his Fated Mate and his people who depend on him to get them back home," Nickolas said so softly I almost didn't hear him.

"Yeah," I said, but frowned at the news. Is that what really happened? Did he only do what he did to save his people? That made him sound exceedingly noble, but did it not matter that I was hurt in the process? Did it not matter that I was accused of murder because of his actions?

The lock on the door clicked. My eyes widened, and I scrambled to my feet, pressing myself back against the grimy, cold stone wall.

Shit. I'm not ready to go back to the torture chamber. Not yet!

A woman in a dress that was practically rags walked in with her head down, with chains connecting to her wrists and ankles so that she was forced to shuffle. She carried two plates in her hands and pushed them carefully beneath the bars.

I opened my mouth to say something but stopped short.

The woman's eyes met mine, and she shook her head almost imperceptibly.

Got it. Do not talk to the help. It could be bad for us all. And the last thing I want is another innocent soul being punished because of me.

A familiar buzzing caught my attention, and I cocked my head to the side, scarcely willing to believe.

No. It can't be, right? That would be too good to be true. The blow to my head must have left my ears ringing.

The woman left the room without a word, disappearing from sight.

I peeked at the food she'd left behind.

Is it safe to eat or would they drug me? I can't use magic without something to sustain it though. Fuck. I'm so hungry!

"It's okay to eat," Nickolas said. "I don't smell anything foreign in there. Your friend is back, though."

"Friend?" I asked as the buzzing started up again and a tiny blur darted forward, and all the air rushed out of my lungs.

Fiona glowed bright green and flew up to eye-level to stare at me. "Oh, Miss Aurelia! You look *much* better than the last time I saw you."

"You've been here before?" I asked.

"She has," Nickolas grunted.

"Do not speak to the princess, Disgraced King," Fiona spat with a surprising amount of venom.

My eyes widened once more. That was another round of questions that needed to be asked, but not now. "Fiona, focus. King Nickolas has been very helpful, but I need information. Have you seen Asher? And where is Grey?"

"Asher is back home but it doesn't look good, Miss Aurelia. And Master Grey is gone. No one has seen him since we rescued Asher." Fiona fluttered about my face, her tiny, frantic wings fanning my hair.

Asher isn't okay and Grey's gone? What the hell are we going to do without them? Do I even want to live in a world where Grey doesn't exist?

My heart sank. This was not the news I'd been hoping for.

Grey... where are you?

CHAPTER 10
Grey

F*uck. We're going to die here.*

Smoke billowed up from the heat of Malcolm's magical fire, choking me. I could barely see my nose in front of my face as I coughed and hacked. Haze clouded my eyes, making them water, and I held my breath as best I could.

My wolf thrashed inside my chest as I crawled across the room searching for Fenrick.

"Fenrick!" I coughed.

Where the fuck did he go? He should be here.

"Grey, I'm here!" Fenrick called, but his declaration ended in a violent, hacking fit.

"We need out," I croaked. This was complete bullshit. How was Fenrick not able to counter the magical fire? What the hell did the Fae have magic for, if not to fight magic *with* magic?

Fenrick appeared in front of me, crawling on his belly. "We need to go that way." He jerked his head in the direction of the door that was still currently a raging wall of fire.

"How the fuck are we going to get out of there?" I asked, exasperated.

"I have a plan, don't worry." He turned around and army crawled toward the wall of flame.

Do I follow him? How the hell is he going to get us past that?

With a shake of my head, I didn't bother commenting again and instead just followed behind the Fae. Could I really trust him? Why was he helping me with my mate, anyway? Could he really want everyone to return to Faery? And if so, why? It didn't make any sense.

Why were the shadow Fae suddenly so willing to let us come back? Was it the shadow Fae, or just Fenrick going rogue? He'd said the king and queen sent him to retrieve the book and help my mate... but then why would they let her fall into the Council's hands? Did they have a choice?

Pushing those thoughts temporarily from my mind, I came up behind him, staying low to the ground. The smoke billowed and continued to choke me as I waited for Fenrick to do something—to pull off some kind of magical miracle.

A moment later, he got up on his knees and faced his palms toward the glowing, orange flames. Water gushed from his hands as if he were channeling a goddamn fire hydrant and hit the wall of fire with a crackling *hiss*. Though his actions afforded us movement, we weren't out of the woods yet. The flames had spread throughout the room and into the hallway beyond.

How long can Fenrick keep up this intensity of magic?

Doing something like that no doubt cost him. "I'm going to shift. Get on my back. I'm faster in wolf form," I said.

Fenrick tilted his head to the side in curiosity momentarily. It wasn't every day that a shifter allowed someone to ride on their back to safety. It showed immense trust.

I didn't yet trust the Fae, but we were both going to die here if we didn't do something and fast, plus if he wanted to protect Aurelia for any reason, we were at least on the same team when it came to that front.

"Okay, thank you, Sh— Grey," Fenrick corrected.

I was just glad he was trying to stop with all the Shifter King nonsense. I would deal with that title when I got my people back to Faery. Allowing my wolf to take over, I quickly shifted, then bent my big body down so Fenrick could climb on.

My wolf growled, not liking the idea of the Fae on his back but didn't react otherwise. He wanted our mate rescued too and he knew Fenrick could help.

As soon as he was securely mounted, I took off down the hall, leaping over the fire wherever it sprung up, making my way to the front of the house. A tiny, wailing voice reached my ears, and I cursed in my head.

The damn brownie.

That bastard Malcolm had just left his loyal little servant behind as if his life was entirely worthless.

"Grey, what are you doing?" Fenrick asked as I slowed. He was still spraying water with his hands at everything in our path, trying to quell the flames and stop the bastard fire from singing the shit out of my fur.

I tilted my head to the side, where the damn little brownie was cowering in a corner.

"Shit," Fenrick whispered.

I trotted over to the mini shithead and picked him up by the back of his tiny coat between my teeth and ran back to the front door.

"Let me go!" the brownie shrieked and squirmed, fighting to be free of my jaws.

"He's saving your pathetic life, brownie. I would be grateful and stop wriggling about before he drops you in the flames!" Fenrick yelled.

The brownie stilled immediately, his protestations dying on his lips as he instead began to babble and whimper.

Fenrick slid off my back and blasted water at the front door, blowing it off its melting hinges.

I waited patiently on tenterhooks, searching for the tile that I stepped on previously to not re-trigger the trap and be thrown into yet another explosion. That son-of-a-bitch Malcolm was sadistic and had zero regard for his house or anyone's life, including his poor misguided but loyal servant. The man made me sick.

When the flames engulfing the front door were extinguished, we sprinted out of Malcolm's house of horrors to the safety of the outdoors.

I jerked my head, motioning for Fenrick to get back on.

"The car should be out here." Fenrick grimaced, perhaps not entirely keen for another wolf ride.

But I knew that the vehicle would be gone after Malcolm caught us. He wouldn't leave anything behind that would aid us in an escape or possible rescue mission. We would have to make it on foot to the facility. It was the closest and safest location. My penthouse was in the city, and I wasn't walking through the damn city without clothes, so I wouldn't be shifting until we arrived at the facility.

Fenrick frowned but climbed onto my back again. He'd never been to the facility, so he couldn't sift us there.

Nope, good old paw power is what it's going to take.

I tightened my jaw around the brownie's shirt. My wolf would just as soon eat the little fucker than permit him the privilege of riding on my back, so that wasn't going to happen.

The little turd whimpered. He probably thought he was destined to be wolf food. "Thank you for s-saving me, but I'm s-safe now and would like f-for you to let me go," he stammered.

"You're coming with us, rodent. You have information we need," Fenrick said.

Good. Glad we're on the same page.

I ran through the forest with speed and stamina the likes of which only my wolf was capable. He raced between the trees without so much as a misstep. He ran for miles and as he did so, I noticed there was a magic to the trees that should not have been. They continued to pass by us in a blur until the magic of the wards washed over me, and I instinctively slowed my pace.

The brownie was still screaming and cursing us, his gratitude for being saved apparently very short lived.

My wolf shook him slightly in fun. He certainly enjoyed terrifying the tiny annoyance for all the hassle he caused.

Zeke, the Rider, met us out the front of the facility, his face drawn and his eyes tired. Without a word, he threw clothes at my feet.

I waited for Fenrick to jump from my back and secure the brownie before shifting back to my human form and dressed quickly.

A few of my shifters raced from the garage.

I nodded toward the brownie. "He has information we need. Lock him in a cell until I can question him."

The shifters reached for him as one.

Fenrick turned to me. "Do you have a magic-canceling cell? He'll be able to get out of anywhere else."

"You heard him!" I barked at the shifters. "Don't let him escape."

The brownie flailed and screamed as they carried him off to the magical cells.

"Where have you been? We thought you were going to the penthouse. Freya and Fiona have been worried sick." Zeke crossed his arms over his chest.

"Fiona's here?" I asked, hopeful and glad to hear she was alive and well.

"She was, but she went back yesterday when no one could find you." Zeke shook his head with a grimace.

Fenrick raised a brow. "What do you mean, yesterday? How long have we been gone?"

"You've been missing for two days," Zeke answered.

"Two days?" I asked, shocked. "Shit."

"Where have you been?" Zeke asked again.

"Malcolm got us. It's a long story. What did Fiona report? Is Aurelia all right?" I stomped into the parking garage, ready to devise a plan and throw myself into action. We'd lost enough time as it was.

Zeke and Fenrick followed closely behind me.

How the hell did I lose two days to that house? I was passed out... but for days? What the hell?

Zeke sighed. "It isn't good."

"Just spit it out," I growled with impatience.

"The shadow Fae have lost all access to their shadow magic since the Exile," Zeke informed.

I turned sharply to Fenrick.

He nodded. "We have been cursed to lose the shadow magic we were created with. The gods were not kind to us after the Exile." Fenrick rubbed a hand over his neck.

"What does this have to do with Aurelia?" I asked. I already had a feeling I *really* wasn't going to like the answer.

"They think she may be the one to bring the magic back to the court, and if she does prove to have it, the Council will kill her," Fenrick said softly.

"They want the shadow Fae to be weak. They don't want them to get their shadows back and they will do anything to keep them down." Zeke clenched a hand into a fist.

"What aren't you telling me?" I growled. If I found out they were hurting my mate, I would tear the fabric of the universe apart to get to her and destroy the Elders once and for all.

"You don't want to know, Grey. I'm one of your oldest friends and I know that look. You need to calm the fuck down and think logically, or I'm not going to tell you." Zeke planted his feet wide, refusing to take another step.

We were stopped in the middle of the parking garage, glaring at each other. He needed to tell me what those fucks were doing to my mate before my wolf freaked out and forced a shift on me.

"I'm not telling you anything until you calm down." Zeke stared me down, his gaze hard but that of a true friend.

My shoulders slumped, and I rubbed a hand down my face, forcing my aggravation and panic down. "Fine. Let's get up to my office and you can tell me over a fucking drink." I shook my head. "God knows I need one." I stomped over to the elevator and pushed the button. It wasn't coming quickly enough for my liking, so I stabbed at it again.

"Easy. That is *not* you calming the fuck down," Zeke warned, clapping me on the back.

"I told you after the last few weeks I've had, I just need a fucking drink," I growled as the elevator *dinged,* and I marched inside. "Just give me a minute." Exhaling my rage, I pushed the button for the top floor and leaned back against the glass wall then turned to Zeke with a grimace. "How's Ash doing?" I asked, feeling like a shitty friend for not having asked sooner, but to be fair, I'd just had a ton of information dumped on me and I was reeling.

"His body is still broken and he's in a coma. It doesn't look good." Zeke sighed heavily, clearly worried about his brother-in-arms and dear friend.

"He will be back to his obnoxious self in no time, just you wait and see," I assured him with a grin.

Asher was one of the infamous Riders of the Wild Hunt, and those bastards were damn near impossible to kill—they were practically immortal as far as I'd witnessed. He wouldn't be taken down by the damn Elders and their pathetic bullshit. He was stronger than that, and I knew it. He just needed time.

The elevator doors opened, and we stepped out into the empty hall.

I led the way to my office and opened the door for my friends. It looked exactly the way I'd left it, but it somehow felt empty. But it wasn't the office that was empty, not really... it was *me*. I was empty without my mate, and it hurt me to my core, like a splinter lodged in my heart, deep and unreachable. Could she ever forgive me once we rescued her? I didn't see how it was possible when I was honest with myself. I'd truly done all the things she'd said, and I was a fool for it. I should have been truthful with her instead of hiding my part in her foster mother's death.

Heaving a sigh and shaking my head to clear it, I grabbed a bottle of aged scotch and three glasses from the drawer in my desk. I poured us generously and handed them out to the others. I took a sip and then glared pointedly at Zeke. "Okay, I'm *calm*. What did Fiona report?" My hand tightened on the tumbler as I waited for him to speak.

"Aurelia doesn't have her full magic as she is yet to turn twenty-five. So, they are trying to pull it out of her," Zeke said as he rubbed the back of his neck.

"Speak plainly, Zeke! I need to know what's happening to her." I sat forward, resting my elbows on the desk.

Zeke eyed Fenrick with a modicum of distrust before he turned back to me with a frown. "Fiona said they were torturing her. The last time she saw Aurelia, she'd been beaten and was left in her cell. She said that she saw a lot of blood." He stood with his hands raised in a gesture of placation that said "Hey, I'm not the bad guy here".

I vibrated with rage, and the glass shattered in my hand, the dark amber liquid pooling on my desk as it mixed with my blood. They were torturing my mate, and there wasn't a damn thing I could do to stop them. "We need that fucking book," I snarled, clenching my wounded hand more tightly and reveling in the pain. "Because I'm going to tear every last one of those fuckers to shreds!"

CHAPTER 11
Aurelia

Sitting in the cell with my back to the bars, I stared into space, feeling everything and nothing all at once, and it left me numb.

This isn't the way it was supposed to be...

"Aurelia," Fiona said, patting my cheek insistently. "You need to stop! Please, Princess."

Snapping out of my vague trance, I peered down at my hands with a frown. Shadows pooled there, silently writhing up my arms. I hadn't even noticed. "Shit." I panicked, and Nickolas's sudden intake of breath gave me pause. Did he smell something? Was someone coming?

Shit. Shit. Shit.

I did my best to call the shadows back inside me as footsteps manifested and keys jingled in the lock on the other side of the door. "Fiona, hide," I whispered fiercely, my heart racing a mile a minute.

She acted instantly, buzzing up to the top of the bars to hide. Sitting there, she kept quiet and silenced the buzz of her tiny wings.

The same beady-eyed Elder from before—the one who'd smashed my knuckles with great delight— strutted like a damn peacock into the dungeon, flanked by three soldiers.

"Leave her," Nickolas growled in warning. "She won't experience a change until her birthday. You can't force the magic to manifest before its time."

"Shut up, Shifter King," the Elder sneered. He spoke Nickolas's title like it was an insult, and maybe to him it was.

"It's okay, Nickolas, I don't have a choice. He knows nothing will happen, but he wants to punish and torture me all the same." I shrugged as if I didn't care, as if I was too strong to fear further pain and rose to my feet. But the truth was, pain was pain, and I didn't want to feel anymore—even if my magic ensured I healed so beautifully there was not so much as a trace of what I'd endured afterward. Sucking in a silent breath to steel my will, I stepped away from the bars.

The Elder jingled the keys, taunting me like a pathetic, power-tripping child.

I kept my carefully bland expression blank, waiting for the inevitable. Whether he wanted me for himself or not, I was beginning to wonder if Malcolm was secretly working for the psychotic Elders behind my parents' back all along. He certainly believed in the same ideals.

The door to the inner cell opened, and the men stormed inside, placing cuffs on my wrists before dragging me back out once more.

"Don't do this, Ronaldo!" Nickolas yelled, rising to his feet in anger. "You have no idea what you are doing here!"

His name is Ronaldo? That suits him perfectly.

I almost smirked at the ridiculously pompous name but held my expression firm.

Nickolas continued to yell at the guards and the Elder as he tried in vain to protect me, but they simply ignored him.

None of that mattered. I needed to focus harder than I'd ever focused on anything in my life. I couldn't let my shadows slither out of me during the torture session, no matter what, even if he broke my hand with that damn hammer again. Regardless of what torment he put me through, I had to be strong. I couldn't let them know I'd come into my shadow magic. It would spell the end for me and all those trapped beyond the portal of Faery.

I'll be dead, and all those I cared about will never see their homes again.

They turned me down a long hallway that I didn't recognize.

I frowned, worry and fear rising within me. This wasn't the way to the torture room. Where were they taking me? Were they going to just put me to death regardless and get it over with? I wouldn't put it past them to lie and cheat to gain ultimate control over the realm, especially where my parents were concerned. I struggled against the guards and tried to drop my weight. Anything to get them to stop their forward march to wherever it was we were going...

The two guards only tightened their bruising grip on me and continued on, forcing me to find my feet or be dragged on the cold, uneven and rough stone floor.

"Where are we going?" I asked, infusing as much attitude into my tone as I could summon. "Tired of the torture already?"

"You will be tried for bringing that *criminal* into Faery," Ronaldo spat with a sneer.

"You're going to charge me with a crime that I couldn't have possibly had knowledge of?" I asked indignantly. I hadn't even meant to bring Asher with me. It had been a desperate afterthought, the simple desire to not be alone and unprotected again. I never meant to come here myself at all!

"You have broken our laws and must be punished accordingly. Your ignorance does not excuse you from the consequences of your actions, Princess." Ronaldo grinned maliciously, obviously enjoying every damn minute as he gloated over my very convenient misfortune.

"Where is Asher?" I demanded. "Will he be at this hoax of a trial?"

"The criminal will not be there," the Elder answered, waving a hand dismissively.

Well, that doesn't make any fucking sense.

"You don't have him anymore!" I said as realization struck hard and fast and as cruelly as lightning. They had deceived me into thinking he was still a prisoner at their mercy to guarantee my cooperation, but he hadn't been.

What happened to him? Did Fenrick manage to get him back home?

I sure as hell hoped so. Even if they succeeded in their farce and decided to execute me, I was glad that he was where he belonged, with his fellow Riders and hopefully in one piece.

"Your assumption is preposterous. *No one* escapes the Council. Be assured, we still have him locked up to ensure your cooperation," he said.

"That's a lie." I could sense it somehow and inside, my soul crowed in triumph. He was gone. He was safe. And now it was my turn to grin. I didn't have to fucking cooperate anymore and as soon as I got the opportunity, I was going to bust out of their damn cell and make a break for it. My shadows had already proven they could bend the bars, so I had a better chance now than ever before.

Ronaldo stopped in front of an ornate door and whispers trickled through from the room on the other side.

How many people were there to see this sham of a trial? Without Fenrick and Asher present they had no solid proof of their claims. Even so, I was under no delusion that the proceedings would be anything but unfair and unjust.

Ronaldo opened the door with a flourish and gasps rang throughout the room.

My parents were there looking as regal and ethereal as ever, and they stood shouting angrily at the collective Elders.

"You dare treat the Princess of the Shadow Court with such disrespect?" my mother hollered, her pale cheeks flushing with rosy color.

"You mean to start a war by treating her as nothing more than a common prisoner?" My father added, vibrating with rage and loathing.

Something dark flickered over his hand, and my eyes widened in surprise.

Did they get their shadow magic back when the Elders tortured mine out of me?

That did not bode well for me. I subtly shook my head at my

parents, willing them to notice my gesture, and directed my gaze pointedly at my father's hand.

My mother caught my expression and glanced down before covering his hand with hers.

To anyone else, it would have seemed nothing more than a gesture of comfort or solidarity, but I knew the truth. She was hiding his magic, *for me*. My mother, the queen, knew the stakes and what would happen if they found out I had shadow magic and awakened it once more within Faery.

Regardless, they may just kill me anyway. I'm the only thing in their way.

"Enough!" Ronaldo roared. "The princess has broken a sacred law that has allowed us to live in prosperity for centuries, and she *will* be treated like the criminal she is!" Ronaldo shoved me roughly into a chair facing the crowd.

My father growled, daggers in his eyes.

My mother caught his ear and whispered something to him.

His face paled as he glanced down at the hand she still held firmly in her grasp. "My daughter will not be put to death for something that was not her fault," he countered a moment later, squaring his shoulders and holding his head high.

"The punishment will be as the Council sees fit." Ronaldo grinned, happy as a pig in shit.

"You will release my daughter to me," the king shot back. "She will not be treated so poorly! Do you want war with the Shadow Realm?" he roared.

"You would wage war over a daughter who remembers nothing of you and has become associates with *undesirables*?" Ronaldo scoffed in disbelief.

"I wasn't given much choice when your puppet took me to a realm, I knew nothing about and left me to fend for myself!" I shook my head, my voice confident but full of derision.

"Malcolm left you to fend for yourself?" an Elder with greasy, dishwater-colored hair asked with a frown. "But you were just a child."

"The same child some of you wanted to kill because I was supposedly too dangerous." I scowled.

"We didn't want that at all, Princess. We voted only to watch you from afar and to wait. Whether you posed a true threat to our way of life remained to be seem," the greasy-haired Elder replied.

"The problem with all of that is you thought you could decide my fate. And ultimately, you chose wrong if all you cared about was safeguarding your precious way of life." I snickered under my breath at the bittersweet irony.

"How were we wrong?" Ronaldo growled.

"If I had grown up here, I may have seen things your way. But you let your fear rule you and now you've inadvertently caused all of this. Everything that has happened up until this point is your fault."

The Elders glanced between themselves wearing expressions of conflict and trepidation.

Old fools. They are all old fools. And they did this to themselves.

"You aren't endearing yourself to us, Princess Aurelia," the greasy-haired Elder warned, narrowing his eyes on me.

"You're going to find me guilty whether I *am* guilty or not. Though you might not have put me to death as a child, your minds were already made up. Your prejudices were already born all those years ago. And all you've done ever since is foster them, feeding them and growing your hate of what you don't understand." I clanked the chains around my wrists as I held my hands up.

My parents' eyes widened, and they shook their heads, wishing me to remain calm. They didn't want me to antagonize the Elders, but I was fast running out of fucks to give.

"You don't believe that we are capable of treating you fairly?" Sir Greasy Hair asked with a frown.

"*Are* you capable of treating me fairly? I mean, not you specifically, of course, because of the way you have spoken to me so far, but do you think the others can put their prejudices aside and listen to the facts as they stand, even if they don't like what they hear?" I asked with a raised brow, already knowing the answer that was to follow.

The Elder with the kindest expression of the lot scanned the other faces in the room and grimaced apologetically. "You are probably correct, Princess."

Ronaldo scoffed, outraged by his fellow Councilman. "Richard, how dare you?"

"The child speaks the truth. Whether she understands our ways and our beliefs is irrelevant, and she brings to light an undeniable quandary. You have *all* become corrupted by your power. I can see that now." Richard shook his head in disgust.

The rest of the Elders rose to their feet as one, most of them screaming at Richard, and from there the courtroom devolved into a chaos of accusations and people raging to keep the old ways.

I sat back in my seat and scanned the pandemonium with mild amusement. They'd done this to themselves. I didn't have to do anything. All along, I'd been nothing more than a catalyst, one that would reveal the undesirable truths and the terrible power imbalances within Faery. I turned to my parents with a small, lopsided smile.

My mother grinned behind her hand and winked at me.

My chest warmed with pride and for the first time in as long as I could remember, I felt her love in a tangible and real way. She was proud of what I had achieved by my wits alone. Turning the Elders against each other had honestly been easier than I'd thought. It just went to show that the Council were not a united front. There were cracks in their precious façade and now they were exposed for all to see.

Three Elders stood with Richard, spitting insults at the three remaining Elders who seemed rabid to get a piece of me.

What will happen if they're split down the middle when deciding my fate? Will I be executed or will they set me free?

I could only hope for the latter, but despite what I'd manage to reveal, I wasn't entirely optimistic. It was nice to get a small win in, though.

"Enough!" Ronaldo roared. "Don't you see what she's doing here? She's become infected by the views of the *undesirables* and is trying to divide the Council."

I raised my brows at the greasy haired Elder. His face was slowly turning an ugly shade of eggplant with his palpable rage.

"Let's just get on with this farce!" Richard said, waving his hand in the air.

"Farce?" one of the elders next to Ronaldo countered. "She has broken our laws by bringing that criminal here."

My father stepped forward, his demeanor more composed than previously. "That is unequivocally untrue. She was brought here at our order and had no idea what was happening when she was pulled through the portal."

Richard raised an eyebrow of his own. "That doesn't sound like she knowingly brought a criminal here *or* that she even returned willingly."

"I didn't!" I interjected passionately. "I was running from Malcolm and stumbled upon the portal. I had no idea it was even there, and I certainly didn't intend to come through or bring anyone with me." I nodded, grimacing at Richard.

"Can you really prosecute her for something beyond her control?" Richard asked, glancing between each of his fellow Elders.

The men closest to him frowned as they stared at me.

What were they thinking? Were they contemplating finding me innocent? There were seven of them in total. Would my future come down to the opinion of one solitary Elder?

"Let's vote," Ronaldo said smugly, unsettlingly sure about the assumed outcome.

What did he know that the rest of us didn't? Could he have one of the uncertain sympathizers in his pocket?

"I vote we release her to her parents." Richard grinned in my direction, causing relief to flood through me.

My parents gasped. They probably had not expected that.

I held my breath, waiting for the remaining votes to be tallied. They could still yet vote to kill me. Richard was just one vote after all, though I was grateful for it.

Ronaldo's eyes bored into mine with skin-tingling hatred. "I vote execution."

Well, that wasn't the slightest bit surprising.

I raised an eyebrow at him, unconcerned as the others cast their votes.

Three voted to send me home and three voted for my execution. It was a tie, just as I had suspected it would be. There was just one Elder was left. He sported a nasty gash on one side of his face, and he stood on Richard's side.

I held my breath as I waited for him to decide, my gut roiling with dread. I wasn't so optimistic anymore. My fate rested in the hands of an old man, one who'd spent all his years surrounded by corruption and an unhampered hunger for power.

Conflict and guilt twisted his features as he did the worst thing imaginable. He cast his vote for my execution.

My mother screamed through her fingers, her expression wrought with anguish.

My father hurled insults at the Elder who had tipped the balance.

The Elder who had sealed my fate hung his head in shame. He was in Ronaldo's pocket. He had to be. That was the only feasible explanation for his outward signs of guilt.

Ronaldo grinned and raised his voice out over the crowded courtroom. "The Council has decided the Princess of the Shadow Fae will be executed at dawn!"

My father roared as shadows crawled over his arms, writhing with menace, ready to obey their king.

Ronaldo gasped before turning his vicious glare at me. "You *are* the girl foretold by the prophecy, and for that you must die!" The evil Elder raised his hand and lightning sizzled in his palm.

The other Elders rushed my father as one to stop whatever he'd planned to do with his shadows, which was likely unleash them upon Ronaldo.

I yanked at my wrists in a desperate attempt to free myself from the magic-canceling cuffs they'd placed on me.

Ronaldo bellowed and threw his lightning at me with all the energy and hate he could muster.

With nothing else to do, I closed my eyes and prayed to the gods that today would not be the day I died.

CHAPTER 12

"Where is it?" I growled at the brownie by my feet.

"You're just going to kill me either way," he whimpered pitifully.

I rubbed my eyes in frustration. I'd been interrogating the brownie for hours, but the diminutive bastard refused to talk. "I have no intention of killing you right after having rescued you from a blazing inferno," I said through gritted teeth. "If I wanted you dead, I would have just left you! But I'm not like your master."

Why won't the little shit just talk?

I leaned back against the bars and stared at the ceiling as I let my nerves settle. Perhaps it was time to try a different tactic. I left the brownie's cell, locking it behind me when someone screamed my name. I turned to the sound and found Karma still sitting in her cell, pressed against the bars. She had a black eye and a swollen, bloody lip. Had she been causing problems for the guards? Is that why she was a bruised and bloody mess? "What do you want, Karma? You're not getting out of that cell."

"I didn't do anything! I had no idea what that man had in store for us." Karma growled.

Yeah, good one, bitch. Growl at the only one with the authority to either have you killed or set you free.

"You followed Layla blindly, and for that, you'll stay in the cell. You knew exactly what she was doing and still pretended to have no idea that she was behind Aurelia's disappearance." I clenched a fist at my side, my heart aching at the mention of my mate's name.

"I didn't know that he was planning to make Aurelia trap us here!" she argued, as if that was what I was mad about.

"Did you know he beat her and locked her in a tiny room like she was some kind of animal? I think your punishment fits the crime," I snarled and turned my back on her.

The jaguar in her growled at the insult, but I didn't give two shits.

I strolled down the hall, to its end, and knocked on the locked and sealed door.

Zeke saw me through the bulletproof glass panel up at eye level and opened it with a nod. "Did you manage to get anything out of him?" he asked hopefully.

"No, he's not talking. The stupid little fuck thinks I'm going to kill him." I sighed in annoyance.

"That makes no sense. You don't kill people who are useful, you reward them." Zeke frowned and closed the door behind me, sealing the prisoners inside.

Maybe he's right. Maybe I should show the petulant shit that I can be nice... and maybe then he'll give me the information I need.

"Have a good meal sent in there for him, and make sure Karma sees that he's being rewarded." I stormed down the hall.

"You're rewarding him for bad behavior while treating her like the enemy she is?" Zeke questioned, chuckling as he followed behind me.

"I'm showing her what disloyalty gets her while showing the evil little brownie exactly what he can expect if he chooses to cooperate," I called over my shoulder. I stabbed at the elevator button impatiently and waited for the familiar *ding*. I hadn't garnered any new information about the book, and they were torturing my mate in the Fae realm. If she lost control as she had so many times before—and she does have shadow magic—she would be as good as dead.

The elevator opened, and Dan stood on the other side. "Good, you're here. I need to speak with you. You have a visitor," he said and glanced warily at Zeke.

Zeke was an intimidating guy to most as a Rider of the Wild Hunt, so Dan's reaction made perfect sense. He stiffened before stepping back to afford us more room to enter.

I stepped in and hit the button that would take us to the floor where my office was.

Zeke followed me into the elevator, a huge and silent sentinel of a man.

"I think this is a personal matter," Dan said softly, clearing his throat.

"Zeke is here to help. He knows everything that we do regarding Aurelia," I said. "Nothing need be hidden from him."

"All right," the half-Fae agreed. "Well, Magna is here, and she and Fenrick are waiting in your office for you." Dan crossed his arms over his chest.

"Good. I need to know what this prophecy is all about beyond Aurelia being able to bring us home or kick us out for good." I stared at the ceiling in the stagnant silence that followed until the doors opened.

"I have some items I need to discuss with you on the business side of things as well, by the way." Dan held out a hand to keep the elevator door from closing too soon when it opened.

"You know my top priority right now is getting to my mate. If you can't handle the job of second-in-command, I'll find someone who can," I said and waved him off.

"That's not necessary, boss. But we do have jobs that need assigning though," Dan said following behind me.

"Then get them assigned. There are employee files and job descriptions in your office. Something as simple as research shouldn't be difficult for you." I growled.

I have more important things to worry about than this!

"Got it. Sorry, boss. I didn't realize I got an office as your assistant," he said.

I whipped around to face him. "What exactly have you been doing, Dan?" Was the facility falling apart while he was my second? How did he not even know he had an office?

"I've been getting to know the staff and looking for Malcolm. This place is *crazy*." Dan threw his hands up.

I opened the door to my office to find Fenrick and Magna whispering quietly, their heads close together as they spoke.

"What's going on here?" I asked.

"You didn't tell me you had a half-Fae seer working with you," Fenrick accused and glared.

"Seers aren't common here. They're a closely guarded secret," I said and moved to my desk. "Plus, she says more cryptic shit than anything that actually helps."

"That's unfair," Magna retorted, narrowing her eyes at me.

"Is it, though? You still haven't told me the details of this prophecy, and my mate is in danger of being executed in the fucking Fae realm." I raised my brow to emphasize my point.

Magna gasped and her eyes widened. "She's in the Faery?"

"Yes." I turned an accusing stare right back at Fenrick.

"I was following orders from the king and queen," he snapped. "We had no idea that the Council would find out so quickly." Fenrick pursed his lips and set his jaw.

"Of course, they did. I'm sure they had an alert spell cast on the portal that let them know the moment the Shadow Princess went through. They've been planning this since the prophecy was first spoken," Magna said with more passion than I was used to seeing from her.

"Magna, it's time. I need to know the exact wording of this fucking prophecy or we're dead in the water." I ran a frustrated hand through my hair for the fiftieth time that day.

"I don't know the exact wording," Magna replied.

"What about you?" I demanded, turning to Fenrick again.

"I haven't been informed of the exact wording, either. The Council of Elders kept most of that information to themselves."

"Then tell me what you do know," I growled, my temper flaring as my wolf grew ever more aggressive and impatient at being parted from his mate.

"The shadow Fae think that there's a curse on us all. Ever since the Exile, we have been slowly losing our shadow magic." Fenrick held out his hand to display his lack of magic, only for shadows to creep over his skin. His eyes widened in shock, his mouth falling open.

"What the fuck?" I asked, my voice raised as I stared at his hands. "I thought you just said you didn't have shadows anymore?"

Magna gasped. "They have brought the shadows out of her!" Magna stepped away from us, her eyes round and filled with abject fright.

"What does that even mean?" I asked, deeply unsettled by her reaction.

"She's the one who can bring us back to our realm... but only if the Council doesn't kill her first." Magna sat heavily on the leather sofa by the window and tilted her head back to stare at the ceiling, seemingly lost.

"They're going to kill her," I breathed. "Hopefully, she knows better than to show them what she can do. Maybe they haven't even realized yet."

"There is a powerful ally with her," Magna said cryptically. "He will tell her what to do."

"Who's the ally?" I asked, turning to her.

Who would defy the Council? Is she talking about Fiona? She's just a little sprite...

"I can't see his face, but he is very powerful. He will protect her as best as he can from a cell." Magna's eyes clouded over, and she withdrew entirely.

I hated it when that happened. She saw more than she would ever tell me, and it pissed me off big time. What the point of being able to see into the past and future if you couldn't fucking benefit or learn from it?

This is growing damn tiresome.

"Have you found the book yet?" Magna asked as her eyes cleared unexpectedly.

"No, the brownie isn't telling us a damn thing." I drummed my fingers against my upper arm as I stood with my arms folded.

"It's in the facility," she mumbled so quietly that I could almost have sworn even my wolf misheard her.

My eyes became saucers, and I turned to Zeke. "Did anyone search the little fucker?" I asked with a growl that shook the room.

"I figured that would be the first thing your people would do," Zeke said, raising his hand to his head is frustration.

Fenrick wasted no time. He raced out the door and down the hall with me hot on his trail.

Those idiots who dragged him in were going to end up in a cell next to Karma if the brownie had that book on him.

How is it that he wasn't fucking searched?

I stabbed at the button on the elevator, momentarily contemplating just taking the stairs but ultimately decided against shifting and running down ten stories. Though more exhausting and perhaps faster, I didn't want anyone to see me rushing through the stairwell. Questions would be asked, and this had to be kept under wraps until we could investigate properly.

The doors opened, and I barely waited for the others to load in before I stabbed the button for the jail floor. "We have been trying to get him to talk for hours and he had it on him the whole time?" I said seething and shaking with frustration.

Aurelia...

"Let's just get down there and get the book from him," Zeke said and double-stabbed the button after I had. He was clearly as pissed as I was that my men hadn't thought to search the little idiot. You *always* did a pat down with prisoners. Always. Even fucking human cops did it to their criminals, it was so damn obvious. You always checked for weapons, valuables, or items of interest!

What if he has something on him that could help him escape a magic-canceling cell? He might have gotten out with the book already.

I shifted restlessly in the elevator. If he got out with the book, we would have yet another problem on our hands, and my mate was likely fast running out of time. When the elevator doors finally opened on the floor with the cells everything was deathly quiet. I breathed a small sigh of relief as I marched out into the hall. Placing my hand on the security scanner outside the door to the cells, I rushed to the brownie's cell.

Karma started screaming at me about food and how unfair I was.

I threw a look at her that that said "Don't fuck with me," and it shut her up on impact. Without delaying a second longer, I opened the cell with the little brownie in it.

He sat there on his small bunk eating and stared up at me in surprise. "What do you want now?" the little turd grumbled.

"You have been holding out on me, brownie. Where is the fucking book?" I took a menacing step into the cell, practically oozing rage.

The brownie gulped. "Your people took it from me!" He glanced away in shame.

"You're lying!" Zeke roared, coming up behind me. "If his people found something like that on you, they would have told him immediately. Don't fucking lie to us!" The Rider strode past me and grabbed the brownie by the back of his jacket and lifted him into the air.

The agitated creature flailed. "Stop! You can't take anything more from me."

"We can't? You're at *my* mercy, brownie. If you had told me where the book was, I would have let you go! You did this to yourself." I nodded to my burly friend.

Zeke shook him violently, letting the little shit know that we meant real business this time. There would be no games.

"I told you!" the brownie wailed. "Your people took everything!"

My wolf howled inside me, his proverbial heckles up as he sensed betrayal.

It can't be true. My people would have informed me!

Zeke patted him down roughly and frowned. "There's nothing here, Grey. Whatever he had, it's gone now."

"Dan!" I barked, spinning on my heel. "Find the shifters who brought the brownie in and search their quarters. If I don't have that book in my possession within the hour, there will be fucking hell to pay."

Dan ran from the cell, a man on a mission, to the chaotic sound of Karma's cackling.

I tilted my head to the side and exited the brownie's cell to confront the bitch of a shifter-witch. With lightning reflexes, I reached out through the bars and snatched her by the neck, picking her up until her feet dangled from the ground. "What do you know, Karma? Tell me now, or you won't live to see another sunrise," I growled through gritted teeth.

"Not everyone here is happy about the Fae princess catching the boss' attention," she managed between gasps.

I squeezed my hand tighter, cutting off her airway. I wouldn't be lenient with anyone who proved to be disloyal. Never again. I had given them everything they could desire in this realm and a way to prosper as long as they were loyal to me.

And this is how I am repaid?

Jealous females in the Syndicate thought they could steal from me to try to get rid of my mate? To try and get their claws into me like I was nothing more than a prized piece of meat? I dropped the bitch to the floor, gasping, and turned to the others, hell blazing behind my eyes with righteous flames. "Find the book and the shifters who stole it and bring them to me. I will take no more disloyalty. They will pay in fucking blood."

CHAPTER 13

When death didn't come, I cracked an eye open, my heart thundering in my chest like a bird frantic to be free. An impossible wall of writhing, living shadows stood between me and my enemy, blocking Ronaldo entirely from view.

Shouts rang out, magnified by the enclosed space, hurting my over-sensitive ears.

In the next instant my mother was beside me.

"Are you doing that?" I gasped at her in shock, shaken.

"No, it's your father giving us a chance to escape," she breathed, her voice thick with anguish before reaching out her hand and helping me from the chair. Purple magic flared in her palms and the manacles clicked open.

Tingles raced over my skin, and I breathed a sigh of relief as my magic flared back to life inside me. "We must go back to the cells. I need to get my friends!" I said urgently. Without awaiting her response, I turned toward the door I'd been dragged through, dodging a fireball that'd been aimed straight at my head. The heat seared my skin as it came dangerously close to its mark.

"She's getting away!" Ronaldo roared.

I glanced at the Elder over my shoulder, rage surging within me with a life of its own.

Again, he threw lightning at me, his eyes blazing with hate.

My magic flared in response, and shadows wrapped around my torso like armor, writhing in anger. In a split second they shot away from me, surging through the air to meet the lightning head on. The Elder's power fizzled out instantly, the threat nullified in a heartbeat.

Is that why the Elders have wanted to get rid of shadow magic all along?

Or was it just Ronaldo specifically? Without shadow magic to challenge him in the realm, it seemed he was the most powerful Fae in all of Faery.

"Mother, do you know a way out through the cells?" I asked over my shoulder as I kept moving. I had no idea how I was going to get out of there, I just knew I had to get to Fiona and Nickolas. I couldn't leave without them. I wouldn't! It wasn't even a possibility.

"We will find a way, even if we have to blow a hole in the wall, Aurelia!" answered my mother, who kept pace beside me.

My gaze snapped to hers and despite the chaos and fear, a fleeting smile lit my features.

My mother is badass. Good to know!

"Okay, but let's try a door first." My smile broadened into a grin as I reached for the lever that would lead us to the cells. Pain exploded in my back and sent me flying face-first into the door. I cried out as agony exploded in my nose and the crunch of bone made my vision blur as blood, hot and sticky, gushed from my shattered nose. "Fuck!" I cried, my hands instantly rising to meet the mess of my face.

"Aurelia!" my mother screamed and whirled on whoever was trying to kill me.

My magic pulsed within me as I turned. Shadows writhed and dripped to the ground at my feet, pooling around me. Unbelievably, my nose was already beginning to heal, spurred on by the use of my magic. I sucked in a breath and hissed as a twinge of pain hit me when my nose set itself back into alignment of its own accord.

My shadows tried to creep across the floor, back through the main doors and toward Ronaldo as my father kept him busy trading one magical attack after another. I wanted that motherfucker to *pay* for what he'd done to me, but we had a small window of opportunity to escape and we couldn't waste it.

"Come on, Mom," I called, waving to my mother. I reached for the lever on the door again and pulled it open.

"Aurelia, watch out!" my mother screamed and shoved me forward, sending me flying through the door.

Instinctively, I managed to tuck and roll, rolling through the hallway just low enough to duck the rogue bolt of lightning that was destined to take me out. "What about Father?" I asked as I scrambled to my feet, a little worse for wear.

"Channing can take care of himself, believe me. But if we want to get to your friends, we need to hurry." She grabbed my hand and pulled me down the hall the same way I'd originally come in.

I took her lead and raced down the hallway to the door of my prison and threw it open.

"Princess, what happened?" asked Nickolas, who stood abruptly in his cell.

"Nickolas?" my mother gasped. "How?" her eyes wide.

"We don't have time for that now!" I interrupted. "Fiona, come on."

Buzzing cut through the shocked silence as Fiona flitted to me from the safety of her hiding place.

I willed my shadows to wrap around the bars to Nickolas's cell and let them do their thing. They seemed to tap into my wants and desires, and reacted as I responded accordingly without the need for explicit instruction.

"I'm guessing they found out about your magic." Nickolas raised a brow.

"It wasn't my fault. You didn't tell me that *every* shadow Fae would get their magic back when I did. My father lost it a bit when they sentenced me to death..." I grimaced, and my magic ripped the bars wide open.

An echoing boom filled the air, rattling up the hall.

"Fuck, time's up," I said and turned to search for an exit.

"We don't have time, darling." My mother focused a moment and pooled her shadow magic into her palms.

Nickolas stepped out of his cell and straightened to full height. He was even taller than Grey, which was more than a bit intimidating. He was an incredible specimen of a shifter.

"Blow a hole in that wall," Nickolas instructed, pointing a finger at the far wall. "I'll watch the door to make sure we aren't ambushed." The Shifter King stepped past me and placed himself between us and the door, a physical shield.

"But we all need to go," I countered, clenching my fists at my sides. "I won't leave you!"

"We will, I'm just making sure you get out first, Princess," Nickolas said with his gravelly timbre, though he never turned to face me.

What was he planning?

He better be coming with us, or I'll come back and drag his stubborn ass out.

I narrowed my eyes at his back. I couldn't leave without him. How would Grey react to knowing his father was still alive and had spent all these years of the Exile confined to a dank cell and that now he was nobly buying us time?

"Katrina, blow the damn wall open!" Nickolas shouted as more screams and blasts filled the air, becoming increasingly closer with every passing moment.

My mother took a deep breath and then hurled her magic at the spot Nickolas had indicated. A deafening roar exploded through the prison as dirt and stone debris blasted me in the face.

I choked on the dust and coughed as I waved a hand in front of my face.

My mother grabbed my arm and pulled me toward the steaming rubble just as Ronaldo and his goons appeared in the cell's doorway.

"Go, Princess Aurelia! I'll hold them off." Nickolas roared.

I dug in my heels. There was no way I was going to let them keep him a prisoner anymore. Anger at the Elders rushed through me hot and fierce as a tornado of my shadows and purple Fae powers combined, billowing around me and whipping up my golden hair. "You will not keep him chained!" I bellowed. The magic surged forward, erecting a wall of shadow and elemental magic between them and Nickolas.

"Let's go!" my mother cried and pulled at my arm again.

Nickolas stared at the wall of shadows that the Elders were trying to beat down with their own attacks for a millisecond longer before turning on his heel and raced back toward us.

My mother stopped abruptly on the other side of the rubble, standing as still as a statue.

I nearly ran into her. "What's wrong?" I asked in confusion. As the dust cleared, my eyes widened. Ten of the Elders' knights stood blocking our path.

How did they get there? What made them think we'd even come out this way? Was it the explosion?

There had been tons of them going everywhere. It didn't make sense. Unless they were counting on my weakness—or my strength—on my loyalty and love for my friends to predict my movements. They'd guessed I'd go back for them.

Nickolas stepped up next to me and removed his shirt, his golden eyes blazing.

"What are you doing?" I asked, shocked, as I turned away. I didn't need to see Grey's father undressing.

"I'm shifting. I'm sure you know all about that, being mated to my son." Nickolas chuckled before he focused his intense gaze on me and gave me a subtle nod.

Is he offering his approval of our match?

My heart galloped with emotion, aching and rejoicing all at once. It was a touching gesture, though I hadn't known the great Shifter King long, I treasured it.

"Mated?" my mother asked softly and shook her head, breathless.

"Now is *not* the time. We have ten Council guards waiting to haul me off to my death," I reminded her.

My shadows slithered up my arms, eager to come to my aid. The more I used them, the more natural it became. It felt like I'd never been without them. They caressed my arms and waited for instruction as we found ourselves between a rock and a hard place—the Elders on one side and their knights on the other.

A wet nose nudged my hip, and I turned. Nickolas's wolf stood almost to my chest. He was a beautiful russet brown color with startling clear grey eyes.

He snarled as one of the Fae warriors stepped forward, ready to launch himself and defend us.

But, why? How have I commanded such loyalty? Is it truly just because I'm his son's mate?

Nickolas leaped in front of me, putting his huge, muscular body between them and me.

The men drew their blades and crouched at the ready in our high-stakes standoff.

I let the shadows and my elemental magic pool in my hands. They twisted and writhed together like lovers in a dance. I didn't want to have to hurt anyone. Well, that wasn't entirely true. Given half a chance, I would have gladly ended Ronaldo's miserable life for all that he'd done to Faery, the exiles, and Grey's father—not to mention *me*.

Nickolas crouched low and snarled, his hackles raised and teeth bared.

My mother stiffened, then screamed. "Guards!"

Three men appeared from out of nowhere, wearing the armor of the Shadow Court and surrounded my mother and me.

We're still outnumbered almost two to one.

One of the Council warriors broke our stalemate and slashed out at Nickolas with his blade, clearly brainwashed into believing Ronaldo's vile vitriol.

Nickolas charged, and chaos erupted all around us as the Council warriors attacked as one, falling upon the Shifter King like vultures hankering for blood.

No!

I blasted shadows at one warrior, and they turned into black, merciless chains that wrapped around his entire body, holding him tight. A second later, I spun as the hair on the back of my neck prickled with unease, narrowly dodging the blade aimed to take my head clean off my shoulders, and channeled elemental magic at the offender.

They evidently didn't care about taking me alive to face their executioner officially. They would likely be rewarded by the Council for killing me in the thick of battle.

Not going to happen, assholes.

Vines raced up the man's legs, bursting through the stone, and he stumbled as they grew more verdant and stronger, binding him to the spot.

I spun around and crooked my elbow before smashing it into the traitorous Fae's nose.

He fell in a heap against the vines, unconscious.

Grabbing the sword from his limp grasp, I turned it over in my hand, getting a feel for it. I wasn't great with swords, but I'd have to make do with what little training I possessed. Pivoting on my heel, I scanned the area for my mother.

She was engaged in the heat of battle, fighting with her magic against two other guards.

Nickolas stood nearby, bloody, over a third.

The queen's summoned warriors were each busy dueling warriors of their own.

A high-pitched yelp full of pain and anguish filled the air, shattering my soul, and I spun to find the last Council warrior standing over Nickolas with a scarlet-stained sword. Without thought, I screamed, and my magic burst out of me in a protective and rage-fueled wave. There was no controlling it this time. It harkened to my deepest fears and desires, spiraling around the man, cutting off his airway and lifting him off the ground by his throat.

I couldn't stop it, and at that second, I didn't want to. I wanted the Fae's blood for what he'd done to Nickolas.

"Aurelia!" Someone shouted my name.

I barely heard it through the roaring in my ears.

Death.

I wanted his death and nothing else mattered. Not even when my mother's face filled my vision.

Her eyes implored me to find myself again. "You got them, Aurelia. They won't hurt Nickolas again," she said, her voice soothing.

I cocked my head to the side, returning from the haze of my blood fury.

The shadow knights all stared at me with wide-eyed horror, ankle-deep in the midst of the sea of bodies. The Elder's warriors were all dead, slaughtered one by one by my shadow magic. Just as I'd willed it. Just as I'd wanted.

I didn't do that, did I?

It was certainly what I'd wanted... to end the fighting, to save Nickolas and my mother... but my shadows had responded *ruthlessly*, obeying my unspoken wants without remorse or measure. I shook my head to clear it.

"Aurelia," Nickolas whispered. He had returned to his human form, a great bleeding gash up his side. "Breathe with me, Aurelia," he said.

It was just like Grey used to do, and I found myself missing him even more in that moment. With hot tears pricking my eyes, I took a deep, cleansing breath and dropped the dead man still suspended in the air by my magic. I matched my breathing to Nickolas' until his started to falter. "What's wrong? Why aren't you healing?" I asked frantically, my voice thick with emotion as tears spilled down my cheeks.

My mother kneeled beside me and laid a gentle hand on my shoulder. "The Council guards' weapons are treated with a poison that prevents the healing process."

"What? No. He has to heal!" I cried out and placed my hands on his chest, willing my magic to heal him. But my magic was depleted and needed time to regenerate. It stuttered out the moment I called upon it. I'd done my dash killing the Elder's knights.

"I'm so sorry, Aurelia," my mother whispered.

"Can you heal him?" I asked hopefully, my voice scarcely above a whisper.

Nickolas grabbed my hand and shook his head. "Whatever magic your mother still has in reserve she'll need for what's to come. It's okay, Princess. But can you promise me something?" He coughed and blood dribbled down his chin and his breathing became progressively more labored.

This can't be happening!

My only companion these last few weeks as I went through hell was going to die and there was nothing I could do about it. There was nothing I could do to save my mate's father. My heart wracked with guilt and pain. Helplessness washed over me as more tears washed down my cheeks. "What is it?" I whispered, my voice shaking.

"Take care of my boy," he breathed. "He deserves all the happiness in the world. He's a good man, I know it in my heart. Whatever he did, I'm sure it was out of duty to his people. He'd never hurt you, Aurelia. You have his heart."

I nodded my head furiously, choking on a sob as the words I so desperately needed to say lodged in my throat, refusing to come out.

Nickolas smiled, gratitude and deep trust reflecting at me from his beautiful gray eyes and then he closed them for the last time.

A heaving sob violently tore out of me, and I let it all out. How was I going to tell Grey that his father had died protecting me? That when I'd needed a champion most, he'd been my hero.

It was *so* unfair.

CHAPTER 14
Grey

I paced the office, running a hand through my hair repeatedly. "Has anyone found the fucking shifters yet?" I growled. My gaze strafed between the men posted in the office.

Dan shook his head. "They signed out half an hour ago, saying they were going on a job." He stared down at his phone, checking over the details.

"Both of them?" I scoffed. "And no one thought it was the least bit suspicious? All jobs have been *suspended* because of Layla's death!" I clenched my fists and continued to pace, every minute that ticked by adding to my aggravation.

A moment later, Zeke stepped into the room with a grim expression. "Asher is awake," he said.

"That's good news. So, why do you look like an angry toddler?" I asked. "Shouldn't we be celebrating the fact he's pulled through?"

"It's not good news, old friend. They told him things while they were beating the shit out of him." The hulking rider folded his arms over his chest, glaring at into the distance.

Fenrick shifted uncomfortably in his seat. "What could they have told him that I didn't overhear?"

"You're not going to like it, Grey." Zeke sighed, refocusing.

"I don't like much of anything these days. Let's go see Ash," I said. "Check the shifters' rooms for the book and report back to me," I added, turning to Dan.

"You got it, boss." He nodded and left the office to fulfil his mission.

We strode from the office and made it to the elevator. I stabbed at the button, which was fast becoming a habit, and waited impatiently for its arrival. "What did Ash say exactly?" I asked Zeke.

"I'll let you hear it from him. He was adamant that I do not tell you." The elevator doors *dinged* opened, and Zeke walked inside.

I followed him in, wondering what could have been so dire they he wouldn't let Zeke share the news.

Fenrick squeezed in just before the doors closed. "I helped get him out of there. I think I should come too. And any information he has regarding the princess could aid us in our rescue attempt." Fenrick shrugged as he leaned against the far wall.

I pushed the button for the infirmary. "All right, that's fine by me. I think he'll probably appreciate the company after being out for days."

The elevator doors opened, and Asher's obnoxiously loud laughter filled the entire floor.

"I guess we can say he's definitely feeling better." I shook my head with a grin as I strolled to the door of his room.

One of the female healers was in there performing a scan, which was why he was in such a good mood.

"Ash, stop flirting with my staff." I chuckled.

"When the only thing I have to look at is your ugly mug, I have to flirt with every pretty girl I can." Asher winked.

The healer blushed a deep scarlet as she scurried from the room, giving us our privacy.

"Now you're embarrassing my staff, you big brute." I rolled my eyes as I made my way to the side of the bed and sat in the chair next to him.

Ash's face fell and his gaze darkened as some unnamed memory hit him. "Grey... it's Aurelia. The Council has her."

"I know. Fenrick told us when he dragged your heavy ass back through the portal," I said, attempting to lighten the mood in the room. And it wasn't just for Ash, but me too. Whatever he had to say, it was nothing good.

Asher turned to the Fae standing in the doorway and nodded to him. "Thanks for getting me out of there."

Fenrick simply nodded solemnly, clearly not wanting to make a fuss. Men were often insular in that way. We were taught very young to guard our emotions and keep everything close to our chest.

I raised both brows. Asher wasn't one to thank people for anything, even when it was warranted, but I guessed it had to do with the trauma he'd suffered at the hands of the Elders.

It must have been horrific.

"What did they do to you?" I asked, leaning forward on my elbows.

"This isn't about what they did to me." Asher sighed. "They have someone else locked up with the princess, Grey."

"Who?" I asked. Why would I care about who else they had locked up with Aurelia unless they were a danger to her? I frowned in confusion.

"King Nickolas is alive," Asher said, his tone wary. He ran a hand over his tired face upon his revelation.

"What do you mean? That's impossible. He was killed as a traitor to the Shadow Fae Crown." I stood and rubbed the back of my neck, trying to process the unexpected information. My father had vehemently opposed the removal of the shifters, witches, and half-bloods from Faery, and the Fae had killed him for being disloyal.

Hadn't they?

"He wasn't. The Elders knew of the prophecy long before the information was leaked. They knew the shadow Fae would lose their magic but still forced the king and queen to accept their decree." He stared at the wall and swallowed hard.

"I don't understand how one thing connects to the other, Ash," I admitted, my brows furrowed.

Fenrick stepped forward and cursed. "A new king can't come into power until the death of the old king. If he's still alive, the prophecy can't fully come to pass." Fenrick balled his hand into a fist, his expression murderous.

"You're telling me that my father has been stuck in a cell for *centuries*?" I asked with wide eyes.

"They kept him alive so you would never become king," Asher said sadly. "I'm sorry, Grey."

The thought of my father being trapped in a rotten Fae cell for hundreds of years killed me. Regardless of our relationship, that was a cruelty of the highest order. He was a wolf, a shifter… he would have suffered incredibly during his imprisonment. Never having the ability to shift and run free, to stretch his legs, or feel the wind on his face and the earth beneath his paws. My stomach flip-flopped, and anger unlike any I'd felt roiled up inside me.

Death likely would have been kinder.

"And I'm stuck here with no way to get him or my mate out of chains?" I jumped to my feet with a roar and punched the wall so hard my hand crumpled it like tissue paper.

Zeke stepped forward as if to stop me.

I shot him a glare. The very same one that had silenced Karma. The one that said, "Don't fuck with me". There'd been too many injustices piled one on top of another for me to settle down now. I wanted to rage.

I want justice and my fucking mate!

He raised his hands up in surrender. "I just think we should all calm down. We don't know anything for sure. All we have is just what they taunted Ash with."

"I need that stupid fucking book. I need it *now* more than fucking ever!" I yelled.

Fenrick clapped a hand on my shoulder. "There may be a silver lining here. Yes, you have been exiled, but the king has not. If you got his power somehow, you might not need the book."

"Yeah, if he dies. That's the only way! But the Fae are keeping him alive in a cell so he can't," I said.

"That's a real shitty thing to say, Fenrick." Asher shook his head with a perturbed grimace.

They just got through saying my father had to die for me to get his power, and I didn't really want it. Not if it meant he had to die. Regardless of our quarrels and issues over the centuries, he was a good king. I knew it in my bones, and I'd never wish death upon a man who stood up for his people and kin.

"From what I know of the prophecy, true royal mates could break the curse on the shadow Fae. I mean, I have shadow magic I never had before. It means things can change." Fenrick crossed his arms.

Asher blinked and frowned. "You have the shadows?" He shifted in his bed. "They were taunting me, saying they were going to use my presence there to force her to cooperate."

"Cooperate, my ass! They were intent on torturing the magic out of her all along," I growled.

My wolf was close to the surface. He hated all this talk of torture when it came to his mate—*our* mate. He wanted desperately to end any threat to Aurelia, but for the time being, we were frustratingly helpless to save her.

All was quiet until the elevator *dinged*, and thudding feet moved toward us from the hall. Dan peeked his head in, breathing heavily. "We have a location on the shifters, but we need to hurry," Dan said between gasping breaths.

"How did you get a location?" I demanded as I spun around and stomped to him.

"One of them left a scribbled note in their quarters."

"If I hadn't planned to kill them both anyway, I'd fire them for such carelessness." Without a glance back, I thundered out of the room and after Dan.

"They didn't leave the book behind, so they must have it on them. I'm hoping they aren't meeting to hand it off," Dan said, pushing the button for the elevator.

"If there is a note about where to meet, then I'm sure that's *exactly* what they're doing." I stepped into the elevator and turned to face the doors.

Zeke and Fenrick followed closely behind, forcing their way into the confined space of the elevator along with us.

"Where are we going?" Zeke asked.

"Witchside, in the city. It's actually not far from where Aurelia lived with her foster mother," Dan said as he leaned back against the wall.

"But why somewhere so public?" Zeke asked, his heavy brows knitting.

"No doubt to stop anyone from starting a fight and taking the book. They're hoping no one would dare risk revealing our world to the humans. But that plan will not succeed," I said.

Fenrick turned to Dan. "Did the note say who they were meeting, by any chance?"

The doors opened to the parking garage, and I strode over to my SUV. Four huge men wouldn't fit in one of my sleek cars. I grabbed the keys and hopped into the driver's seat, barely waiting for the others to get in before turning over the ignition. "Put the address into the GPS and let's get the hell out of here." I turned and pulled out of my reserved parking spot. The tires squealed as I drove faster than I should have toward the main road.

The drive to the city was silent, and I was okay with that, lost in my own head. We were so close to getting the book, but something about this scenario didn't sit right with me about the note, and the shifters taking the book back to Malcolm.

Does he even know the book is missing yet? And if it isn't Malcolm, then who are the shifters working with?

I pulled into the parking garage at my penthouse and decided we would walk from there. The address was close by, so it would be easier to sneak up on the exchange. It was nearly impossible to find parking in downtown Dallas anyway. I turned the ignition off and stared down the men who came with me. "Dan, you and Fenrick go around the back. Zeke and I will go around the front. There should be no escape for them that way," I said and launched myself out of the car.

The streets were bustling with activity as we strolled to the small coffee shop that was mentioned in the note. They had an outdoor patio and every seat was full, but the shifters weren't there.

"I don't see them," Zeke mumbled.

There was an alley along the side of the building, and I nodded my head in that direction. Zeke caught my meaning, and we moved toward the mouth of the alley.

My shifter senses went wild, suddenly on high alert. The scent of rotting food and garbage nearly made me sneeze in revulsion, but the low voices talking were what had my primary attention. The fact that they were in an alley in broad daylight where anyone could see them made me cringe. They were beyond stupid and careless, and I was glad they were as good as dead for selling us out. The Syndicate didn't need shit like this.

"Do you promise we can go home for this?" one of the shifters whispered.

"I've already said as much, mutt. Don't make me repeat myself!"

I stiffened at the voice. I recognized it but hadn't heard it in centuries. I turned to Zeke.

His eyebrows were raised practically to his hairline. He recognized the Council puppet's voice just like I did.

I stepped into the alley and cleared my throat. "I see the Council fucks sent their best errand boy into my city." I held up my hand when the shifters moved to run. "You aren't getting out of here. Submit to me and I'll make your deaths painless."

The shifters gulped and glanced between each other before dropping to their knees. That was the most mercy they were going to get, and they knew it.

"This is a private affair, Shifter King. No one asked you," Erik said and stepped toward me menacingly.

"You shouldn't have come into my damn city and tried to turn my shifters against me." I smirked and shook my head as if admonishing a child.

"This doesn't concern you," he warned, taking another step forward.

"Doesn't it, though?" I asked with a leer. "Your masters have my mate and sent you to get the only thing that could help me get her back. I'd say that makes the two of us intrinsically involved."

The two shifters tensed on the ground, still on their knees as if suffering.

A searing pain exploded in my chest and my wolf howled in rage and agony. I dropped to my knees with a savage roar. My wolf wanted to rip himself from my skin.

The shifters in front of me howled a long mournful sound.

Fuck.

This could only mean one thing. There was no mistaking it. My father had been locked up for centuries and now he was inexplicably and suddenly dead.

How did he die?

Anguish tore through me even as the power passed on from my father fueled me. But it was too much power and far too quick. Headless of the alley in broad daylight and the presence of humans so near in the café, I screamed, locking eyes on the Council's spy. They killed my father, and I would do anything, give *anything*, to make them fucking pay!

CHAPTER 15
Aurelia

A bellow of rage filled the air as the Council descended on us.

I stared down at Nickolas, sadness and anger warring within me. He'd died protecting me, and that would be a heavy weight to carry for the rest of my life. But I'd carry it all the same and ensure his sacrifice was worthwhile.

I'm going to find a way to make all this right! Somehow.

Ronaldo cursed his dead warriors as they littered on the ground at my feet. "The idiots killed the Shifter King!" he screeched. The Elder seemed completely unhinged about the death of the Shifter King—but it wasn't because he cared about the man or the wolf within. His lamentation was entirely selfish.

My father raced toward us, carefully stepping over the fallen, his shadows coiling around him. "Are you okay?" he asked, glancing between my mother and me.

I shook my head, my lips trembling as the pain of what had happened to Nickolas crippled me.

My father followed my gaze and glanced down at Nickolas. A gasp escaped him, and he turned sharply on Ronaldo. "You were holding him prisoner all this time?" the Shadow King roared.

"You don't get to question me, Shadow King. I'm your Elder and you *will* respect my authority," Ronaldo spat back. His focus fell upon me, and mania shone in his eyes.

My father stepped between us, blocking Ronaldo from view. He had become our shield and was fast making up for lost time with his protectiveness and obvious love.

"Step aside, Shadow King."

"Or what?" answered my father through gritted teeth.

"The Council has sentenced the girl to death, and *now* more than ever, she must die!" Ronaldo raised his arms, preparing to defend his staunchly held hate and misguided beliefs.

"Katrina, get Aurelia out of here," my father said too softly.

"What are you going to do?" I cried. "You have to come with us!" There was no way I would lose my parents a second time. Not if I could help it.

"I will, just a second after you. Now go," Father ordered.

My mother grabbed my arm, and a disorientating dizziness washed over me, making my stomach churn. The landscape spun away, and darkness clouded my vision.

What the hell is happening? What has she done to me?

My head whirled as I hit something soft and swayed bodily, confused and taken aback. "What?" I asked as I glanced at the vaulted ceiling above me. "I don't understand."

"I'm sorry, dearest. I should've prepared you before I sifted us, but there was just no time. I needed to get you out of there." My mother stroked my hair back from my face as she gazed down upon me, practically glowing with her love.

Oh, she sifted us. So that's what that feels like. Yikes! I should have figured that out.

"Where are we?" I asked, taking deep, steadying breaths to regain my bearings. I didn't think being back at the castle where they took me from was the best idea and if I were honest, I wanted to go home to the human world. I needed to find Grey and tell him about his father. Anguish ate at my gut and guilt riddled me for not being able to do more for him. If I hadn't used so much power when I'd lost control, then maybe I could have saved him.

Maybe he wouldn't have had to sacrifice his life for mine.

"We are at a secret home of ours," Mother said softly. "It's safe and far away from the Council."

"Safe from the Council? Is there even such a place?" I scoffed with a defeated sigh as I attempted to sit up slowly. I had no doubt the Council would hunt me across realms to keep their way of life as the status quo. My very existence threatened everything they wanted for Faery's future.

"It's as safe as we can make it," she answered, sitting next to me on the fluffy bed.

I nodded and managed to get fully upright without a head spin. I needed information if I was ever going to defeat the Council. I needed to know exactly what was happening to me.

"Why does Ronaldo care so much about Nickolas' death, anyway?" I asked. "Nickolas said it was something to do with Grey, but didn't get into details." I met my mother's gaze evenly, hoping for the truth.

She thankfully obliged. It seemed the time for lies and miscommunications was finally over. "Long ago, at the height of the Shifter King's reign, a prophecy was shared regarding his death. It was believed his death would bring about a new era in Faery. The Elders despise change and want to stop any chance of such a thing eventuating, especially if it had anything to do with the shifters or witches," she said.

"Then why did everyone seem so surprised that he was alive?" I asked. It still didn't make sense. They kept him locked away instead of exiling him with the rest of the shifters and witches.

"Nickolas was originally meant to be executed before the Exile. He was staunchly against the plan to get rid of the shifters from Faery and they charged him with treason." Mother sniffled. "I honestly thought I watched him die. They obviously staged the whole thing."

"So, they faked his death and pretended that the Exile was the new era that the prophecy had spoken about," I said, putting everything together in my mind. "But really, they just wanted to keep him alive as a prisoner to prevent the prophecy from ever coming to fruition."

"I'm starting to think you're right about that," my mother, the Shadow Queen, said.

"But that isn't the same prophecy that's about me, is it?" I asked.

"No, darling, it's different." She shook her head and sighed, clearly at as much of a loss as me as to how all this treachery and pain had blossomed in the darkness, right under their noses.

"Katrina! Aurelia!" My father's voice boomed from somewhere inside the house.

Mother jumped to her feet and ran to the closed door, throwing it open and calling down the hall, "Aurelia's room, Channing!"

"Are you sure that's wise?" I asked.

Surely there are ways for the Fae to mimic voices, wear glamours, or trick wards. We should be extra careful at this point. Friends aren't always who they seem.

Magic pooled in my palms as I anxiously waited to see if it really was my father and if he was alone. They could have forced him into giving up our location.

"Aurelia, are you okay?" my father asked from the doorway.

"Are you alone?" I questioned, craning my neck to peer behind him.

"Of course, you are perfectly safe, Daughter. I would never jeopardize this location. It's our safe house. If I even suspected I was being followed, I would have sifted to several locations to throw the trail." He shook his head and stepped forward into the room.

There was no one else in the hall behind him. I blew out a breath of relief and released my hold on my magic. "I need to get back to the human world as soon as possible," I said softly. Guilt ate me up no sooner had the words left my lips. My parents had saved my life, and all I could think about was getting back to Grey... and of course, figuring out a way for us all to be safe. Because until I did, there would be no peace between the realms for any of us.

"Your mother didn't tell you?" My father smiled as his gaze found mine.

"Tell me what?" I frowned.

Not more secrets.

"The only place in the realms we could ever have a secret house away from the Council's prying eyes that was truly safe enough... is *in* the human world, sweetheart." Father chuckled.

"What?" I gasped. "We're in the human world? How? Where?" I asked as I jumped off the bed and raced to the nearest window. I threw the curtains open to reveal a sea of beautiful green trees stretching for as far as the eye could see.

"We are in the Texas wilderness," my father said, coming up beside me.

We're in Texas?

My heart raced at the sudden and impossible situation. "Did you know where I was when you bought this place?" I asked, my voice breaking as emotion flooded me. If they had known where I was, why hadn't they come looking for me?

"What do you mean?" Mother asked, her brow furrowing as she studied my expression.

"I grew up in Dallas, with a witch," I revealed. "It's right here in Texas."

"You were *that* close this whole time?" my mother asked with tears pooling in her eyes. Now she understood and it hit her just as hard as it hit me.

"I was." I shook my head, trying desperately to hold back the deluge of sadness that threatened to swallow me whole.

It's in the past. None of it matters now.

But past or not, the realization rocked me to my very core. My parents had been a scant stone's throw away, and yet light years might as well have separated us.

How did the witch mask my presence so easily?

My parents were right here at times, almost within reach... and neither of us ever knew it. It was a cruel twist of fate that would take time to come to terms with. "Anyway, I need to get to the Facility," I said, shuffling my feet anxiously. "I have people who need me."

"It's not safe," Father declared, clapping me gently on the shoulder. "I'll go see if I can find this Facility or your mate for you."

"It's warded, Father." I couldn't let fear of the Council stop me from making things right with Grey. Despite his betrayal, I missed him, and I still had a promise to keep to Nickolas. Pain lanced in my chest at the thought of the slain Shifter King. He had done everything he could to protect me, and it had cost him his life. I had to make things right. I owed him that much.

"You don't need to feel guilt over the Shifter King's death, Daughter," Father said as he squeezed my shoulder.

I glanced up at him. How did he know I was feeling guilty over that? It was true, but it wasn't the only thing I was feeling guilt over. If I hadn't run off, then maybe Grey's father would still be alive. But would we have even known he was alive? There was no way of knowing any of that. He could have rotted in Faery for several more centuries. I shuddered at the thought.

"Oh, what is that?" Mother asked curiously as she plucked something from my shoulder.

Fiona buzzed angrily, held between my mother's fingers.

"Fiona!" I gasped. "I forgot you were there."

"Miss Aurelia, I don't like being forgotten and tangled up in your hair!" Fiona glared at me as she struggled in my mother's hold, ever the little spitfire with attitude.

"Mother, Fiona is my friend. Let her go please?" I asked with a lopsided smile.

My mother released her.

Fiona buzzed up to the top of one of the posts on the four-poster bed. "Miss Aurelia, I can take King Channing to the penthouse. Maybe we'll find Master Grey there," she said in her tiny voice.

"That is a wonderful idea," Father beamed. "I approve of this tactic."

"And what am I supposed to do? I don't want to just sit around here and do nothing," I said, shaking my head and pursing my lips. I'd had enough of feeling helpless and was ready for action.

"You could start with a shower," Fiona said in a snarky and disgusted tone.

"Hey, that's not my fault!" I countered. "I was stuck in a fucking dungeon for *weeks.*" I crossed my arms over my chest and mock-scowled at Fiona.

The nerve of that little thing!

"It doesn't mean you stink any less." She waved her tiny hand dramatically in front of her nose.

"Rude," I scoffed.

"I thought you said she was your friend," Mother whispered to me, wearing a look of confusion.

"She is," I assured her. "Social morays are a bit different here in the human world, and friends come in unexpected packages." I chuckled.

"Very strange, indeed." Mother frowned at Fiona.

The little sprite was still sitting on top of the post, swinging her legs back and forth as her wings fluttered behind her.

"But wait!" I interjected, a thought suddenly occurring to me. "I want to know more about the prophecy that I'm involved in." I glanced between my parents.

They shared a look at my abrupt subject change.

"If I'm going to stay behind while you go find Grey, I want to make good use of that time." It seemed they weren't going to let me out into the world without an escort, but why? If the Council never came to the human realm, I would be safer here, right?

"Fine, my dear. Let's go into the sitting room. I have a book in there that may help explain what I know for now." Mother looped her arm in mine and led me from the room.

"I'll bring your prince back, Daughter, you have my word," Father announced and then sifted with Fiona on his shoulder.

Was Grey my prince? I didn't think he was technically a prince at all. Did he know that his father was dead? Did he feel the magic transfer through the Veil? I just hoped my father didn't explain to him what really happened—that Nickolas was dead because of me.

Will Grey hate me forever if I tell him?

My mother nudged my shoulder. "Don't fret, darling. He will not blame you for his father's death, especially if he is truly your mate. He will be glad of his father's noble sacrifice."

"How do you guys do that? You seem to always know when I'm feeling guilty," I said curiously.

"The scent of guilt is acrid. It's a very easy emotion to discern." She shrugged as if that were common knowledge and led me down a set of marble stairs.

"So, I smell? Well, that's not weird at all. Maybe Fiona was right, and I should go start with a shower." I shuddered. The last thing I needed was to be repulsive to my own flesh and blood.

"No, no, dear. It's not a physical scent on your skin. It's rather more like our magic is empathic and the emotions come through with a scent. Not everyone describes it as a scent. Magic is very subjective." She glided away from the stairs, ever graceful, and into a small sitting room. She stepped next to the black, overstuffed couch and sat delicately down on the edge of the seat.

Would I ever be that graceful and elegant? Probably not.

I plopped on the couch beside her and leaned my head back on the cushion. It was so nice to sit on something that wasn't stone or seriously uncomfortable. It had been *so* long, I'd nearly forgotten what comfort and relaxation felt like.

Mother grabbed a book from the side table and opened it wide in her lap. "I'm not sure if the prophecy about the king is connected to the prophecy about you, but it would make sense if it was."

"What are you talking about?" I frowned. "I thought you said they were different?"

"Separate, yes, but *connected*. Think about it. The prophecy foretold that the death of the Shifter King would usher in a new era. An era where *you* would bring back the shifters and witches. Shadow magic would return to us, and we live in prosperity." Mother pursed her lips, never looking up from her book.

In the next second, Father appeared in front of us, a grim expression on his eternally youthful face.

Fiona hovered by his side and was crying softly.

"What happened?" I stood abruptly, every nerve instantly on edge.

"The penthouse was ransacked, Miss Aurelia, and Freya is..." Fiona trailed off, unable to finish her sentence.

My heart broke for her. "Freya is what, Fiona?" I asked, panicked.

"Freya is gone!" she wailed. "I think someone took her," she sobbed.

"Was Grey there?" I asked, but I knew it was a stupid question before I even finished forming the words. If Grey had been there, he would have come back with them. Nothing would keep him from me, I knew that. If he could find a way, he would.

Where are you, Grey? Please be all right.

CHAPTER 16

"He's gone," I said through gritted teeth as I breathed through the pain.

"What?" Zeke asked with a heavy frown as he leaned down to help me up.

My hands shifted to claws as I stared the Council spy down. "They killed my father," I said aloud. On my feet, I was barely managing to hold my wolf back from shifting and tearing into the spy.

He was beating at the inside of my chest with shocking force, baying for the Elders' blood.

Power, unlike anything I'd ever felt before, poured through my veins, and I snarled.

"Shit," Zeke said, taking a step back. "He's dead? I'm sorry, Grey. So, it's finally happening then."

I took a threatening step forward, fighting every emotion and raw instinct within me.

Erik glanced around the alley, scanning it for any possible exit, but he wouldn't be fast enough to escape my claws. "I was just sent to retrieve a book!" Erik revealed and threw his hands up in surrender. "I didn't even know the Shifter King—your father—was still alive."

"No? Then why aren't you shocked by the power surge that's just raged through me?" I sneered.

"I have no problem with you, Shifter King. I just came to retrieve the book, that's all." Erik took a step back but stopped when I growled.

"You two," I snarled as I peered at the shifters on their knees. "Give me the fucking book. Zeke is going to detain you."

"Please, boss," one of them whimpered shamelessly in fear.

"You stole from me, and you will be punished." I glared, holding out my hand expectantly for the book as the sound of running footsteps pounded the ground behind Erik.

Fenrick came into view first with a grimace. "Erik. Of course, they sent *you*."

"Fenrick," Erik countered. "I see you are as much of a traitor to the Council as I always believed you were." The Fae smirked.

"Detain the assholes," I said, turning back to the shifters and issuing a command to Zeke. They were going to pay for what they'd attempted, that was for damn sure. I stomped forward, picking the shifter on the right up by his throat. "Tell me where the book is," I snarled, my wolfish teeth just peeking through with my rage.

He glanced at the other shifter almost reflexively, revealing the book's location.

I threw him on the ground at Zeke's feet, done with him for the moment.

The second shifter stiffened.

I stomped toward him, my anger like a palpable cloud of darkness. "Zeke, detain him!" I called over my shoulder to the rider, referring to the second shifter. Reaching down, I ripped the bag off his shoulder.

"Erik, you don't want to do that!" Fenrick shouted.

I glanced up to see Erik, his magic crackling over his palms. "You want to challenge me?" I laughed. I threw the bag to Zeke so he could check it for the book. If the shifter had lied to me, his death would be even more painful than already promised. I would guarantee it.

"I need that book," Erik growled in challenge.

"You just watched me become the new Shifter King. Do you really think you're fast enough or strong enough to challenge me?" I shook my head at how egotistical and desperate the Fae was.

Erik glanced away, unsure, clearly second-guessing himself, but he was a soldier with a mission and his conscience warred with him. Duty or life?

Fenrick frowned in confusion at my words, having taken up the rear as we'd originally planned. "He's dead?" he asked, seemingly shaken by the news.

"Apparently, something happened. I need to get the damn book now, more than ever before because he was with my mate in those cells!" I growled.

Is my mate dead too? Or did she manage to escape, and my father helped her?

I really hoped it was the latter. Surely, I would know if my mate were dead.

I'd have felt it... wouldn't I?

Aurelia's death would be unacceptable. It would be something I could never accept or forgive. Losing one's fated mate was an agony without end, and I would rage against both fucking realms if something had happened to her.

Zeke clapped me on the shoulder, momentarily bringing me back. "Grey, I have the book. Let's get them rounded up and get the hell out of here."

"No!" Erik yelled, startling me.

I turned just in time to watch him throw crackling electricity right at Zeke. I barreled into my friend on instinct, shoving the Rider hard, out of the way of harm. Then with speed I never possessed before, bolted to Erik, gripped him by the throat and threw him against the brick wall. His head cracked and his eyes rolled back in his head, and I let his body crumple to the ground.

I turned to Zeke to make sure that he still had the bag in his hand.

He did. He had the bag in one hand and the other was wrapped around one of the shifter's necks.

Dan stepped forward from the background, peering down at his phone in concern. "Boss, I received an alert from the security company that oversees the building you live in." Dan frowned.

"What's going on now?" I growled, before offering a nod to Fenrick.

Our Fae ally came to stand over Erik and used his magic to wrap around the Council spy's unconscious form.

"Someone broke into your penthouse," Dan said, his gaze rising to meet mine.

"What the fuck?" I raged.

Can this day get any fucking worse?

I was torn between checking on Freya, securing the book, and dealing with the supernaturals who needed to be punished.

Fenrick glanced at me with a nod of his own, fast proving himself invaluable. "Go, Grey. We can handle things here."

"Are you sure?" I asked. I couldn't handle any more fuck-ups.

"Yes, now that I know where the Facility is, I can sift there." Fenrick reached down and grabbed the magically secured Erik, throwing him over his shoulder before he sifted away.

I turned toward the mouth of the alley. I needed to get to the penthouse as soon as possible. It was urgent that I make sure Freya was okay. She was like family to me. Watching my behavior as best I could, I rushed the two blocks to the building, forcing myself not to run supernaturally fast. There would be no way to explain that to the humans in the area. We needed to keep the humans unaware of us. Gods only knew what would happen if they ever discovered our existence.

The elevator from the parking garage took far too long to ascend. I ran a hand through my hair in agitation as I watched the numbers change with the passing of each floor. I tapped my foot impatiently.

Fuck. I hope Freya's okay.

The elevator finally *dinged*, and I raced into the entryway. My home was in complete disarray... again.

What the fuck? Who would have the balls to trash my apartment?

"Freya?" I called into the room. Furniture was overturned and slashed, feathers and stuffing littering the room. But it was just furniture. It was replaceable. Freya was what I was truly concerned about, and she hadn't responded. "Freya?" I called again, crossing to the kitchen where she would normally spend most of her time.

Where the fuck is she? Has she been kidnapped?

The kitchen was destroyed, just like the living room and entryway. Everything was torn from the cabinets and tossed about carelessly. It seemed the goal was to make as much mess and upset as possible.

Why would someone do this? It's not like I would hide things in the kitchen.

This wasn't simply a robbery, I realized. Someone wanted to send me a message. This was personal.

"Freya!" I yelled again, more desperately, and ran to the hall just as the elevator *dinged* a second time.

Zeke, Fenrick, and Dan stepped out of the elevator and into the hall.

"She's gone." I sighed.

But who would take the sprite from my home?

Fenrick cocked his head to the side as he surveyed the destruction. "Can you smell anything, Shifter King?"

I snarled, because no, I hadn't tried to scent the intruder. I hadn't had such heightened senses long enough to really think about scenting the air for anything. "I forgot my senses are even more enhanced now," I admitted. Calming myself the hell down, I took a deep breath through my nose and growled at the scent. "Malcolm," I rumbled.

"Of course, that rat bastard would come here." Zeke said, his hands balling into fists at his sides.

"How did he know where you lived?" Fenrick frowned.

I sighed.

I should have moved...

"This isn't the first time that fucker has broken into my home and taken someone important to me."

My hands turned to claws and I roared out my anger.

"He's after the book too, boss. I bet he plans to trade Freya for it." Dan shook his head.

"Well, he's not getting it. Freya's stronger than she looks. She would be pissed if I gave up the only thing that could bring us to Aurelia." I shuddered, wondering what kind of nasty pranks she would pull if she had the chance. It would not be pretty. She might be a tiny sprite, but she knew what was at stake. If I gave up the book, not only would be potentially never find my mate, but our hopes for ever returning home to Faery would be lost.

"That sprite does get angry easily. I wouldn't want to be you if she was pissed at you." Dan grimaced.

"So, what are we going to do?" Fenrick asked. "We can't give him the book, but we can't let him keep your little friend, either."

"I don't know. We could pretend we're agreeing to give him the book and then get the sprite back by force," suggested Zeke, crossing his hulking arms over his chest.

"That could be an option, but he's not stupid. He'd expect us to try to double-cross him after everything that's happened," said Fenrick as he ran a hand through his hair roughly.

"You don't become the Captain of the King's guard by being stupid," I agreed.

An unexpected *buzzing* hit my oversensitive ears, and my head snapped to the hall. Was that Freya? Did Malcolm not have her after all? "Freya?" I called, hope filling my tone.

Did she somehow escape the madman?

A buzzing ball of green flew down the hall with a beaming smile.

Fiona!

The sprite crashed into me, excited. "We thought you were gone!" she screeched. "I am so glad to see you, Master!"

"Fiona? What are you doing here?" I asked, confusion knitting my brows. She was supposed to be in Faery, helping Aurelia.

"I can answer that," a male voice said.

I stiffened at the familiar cadence As I slowly turned. How the hell was the King of the Shadow Court standing in my destroyed living room? "Where is Aurelia?" I asked instantly with wide eyes.

I couldn't believe her father was standing right in front of me, especially at a time like this.

"She's safe, but we have been looking for you," the king said.

Fenrick dropped to one knee upon seeing the king.

I, on the other hand, scowled at him—king to fucking king. "Where is she?" I demanded. I was a king too now, and his fucking equal. I didn't have to bow to him.

"She's at our safe house and she's fine. I will take you to her." The Shadow King nodded to Fenrick.

"My king, what has happened since I last saw the princess?" Fenrick asked softly as he rose to his feet.

"Much has happened, but we must leave before Malcolm returns. We cannot have him follow our trail." The king turned.

I eyed Zeke and Dan. "Keep track of the book and don't let *anyone* in the Facility know where it is."

"You got it. But what happens if Malcolm reaches out about Freya?" Zeke asked.

"Try to trade for his brownie, though I doubt he cares about the servant who is so loyal to him. Stall as much as possible and call me if there is a new development. I need to see my mate."

Zeke nodded, and he and Dan walked into the open elevator, ready to carry out my instructions.

"Okay, Shadow King, let's go. I need to see my mate more than I need air to breathe," I said.

My wolf howled in my head, excited about seeing his mate and wanting to shift.

I refused to let him out, even though he was stronger than he had ever been before.

Fenrick wrapped a hand around my arm and sifted. He obviously knew where the king's safe house was, which meant he was someone I could truly trust.

Dizziness washed over me as we appeared in a cozy living room.

Fiona flitted off my shoulder as we touched down.

I followed her progress to the sofa. My shoulders straightened and my eyes widened as I stared down at my mate sitting on the plush, overstuffed black leather couch.

Her green eyes bore into mine.

I stood rigid, scarcely daring to breathe.

Is she still angry at me?

I couldn't tell based on her expression.

What is she thinking right now?

"Grey?" Aurelia whispered.

My wolf howled in my mind, the sound tentative and mournful. He was just as frightened as I was that she would be angry and not want anything to do with us.

"Aurelia," I breathed.

She gave nothing away as she stood slowly.

I clenched my fists at my sides so that I didn't reach for her and overplay my hand. She had every right to be angry with me and accuse me of betrayal.

The Shadow Princess stepped in front of me slowly, not quite meeting my gaze. "You're okay?" she asked quietly before swallowing hard. "Your father…" she trailed off, glancing away, her eyes shimmering with unfallen tears.

"I know. I felt the transfer of his magic. What happened?" I asked, even though that wasn't what I wanted to know.

Her face fell, and the tears pooling in her eyes fell down her cheeks.

I reached up a hand and cupped her cheek, willing her to strength as I searched her glistening eyes for answers.

"He… he died protecting me," she whispered, her voice broken.

My heart ached for her. She seemed shattered and fragile. "I'm so sorry, I can't imagine how traumatic that would have been for you," I said tentatively, daring to draw her in close.

Without another word she let me tug her into the circle of my arms, and I breathed a sigh of relieved contentment. My mate was alive and finally back, and she wasn't pushing me away.

CHAPTER 17

Grey was *here* and holding me in his arms! He hadn't reacted in anger when I'd revealed that his father had died to protect me. He just held me close.

How could he not be angry with me though? It was my fault his father was gone. I was the reason he was no longer here for his son. Pulling back hesitantly, I stared up into his eyes. So many emotions and unspoken questions passed between us.

Am I still angry with him?

If I was honest with myself, I hadn't been angry for a while. I was a woman, not a self-obsessed teenage idiot. Though it hurt, I understood why Grey's actions. He had so much responsibility on his shoulders and the welfare of all those who were expelled from Faery when the Exile took place. It was a heavy burden, and there was so much more to all of this than just him and me and what we felt for each other. I sighed and laid my head back against his chest, listening to the familiar thumping of his heart.

Grey's arms tightened around me as a throat cleared in the room.

"Sorry to break up the reunion, Daughter, but we have things to discuss." My father clapped Grey on the shoulder.

"Right, sorry." My cheeks heated as I took a step back.

Grey refused to let me go and growled softly.

With a regretful smile, I eased myself away from him and sat on the couch beside my mother once more.

He quickly sat down next to me, crowding me and entwining our fingers.

Does he think I'm going to leave?

I had no intention of ever leaving him again. Not only because of the promise I'd made to his father before his untimely death, but because I needed him. He was my mate. His betrayal smarted but was inconsequential in the grand scheme of things. He did what he did for his people and didn't know how to tell me, or if he could even trust me at that point in time. I'd been wary with my own ability to trust, so I could forgive that.

"What do we need to discuss?" Grey asked, tightening his fingers around mine.

My father blew out his breath before turning to answer Grey. "Aurelia is the princess from the prophecy, and has successfully brought back shadow magic to our people—as foretold—but I fear we are going to have a war on our hands with the Elders, as they sentenced her to death."

"They sentenced her to death? For what?" Grey snarled, stiffening next to me. The growl in his tone hinted that his wolf was perilously close to the surface.

I patted his hand to soothe him. "For no other reason than I was a threat to their way of life. They trumped up some ludicrous charges regarding my bringing Asher with me into Faery," I said. My eyes widened and I snapped my gaze to Grey. "Asher?" I asked. "Is he..." I held my breath, my stomach tightening in a knot.

Grey shook his head with a small smile. "He's going to be just fine. He's already being a royal pain in the ass."

I breathed a sigh of relief and grinned.

Thank the gods. I couldn't bare if someone else had lost their life on my account.

"We need to gather our forces," Father said, picking up the conversation where we left off.

"The Syndicate is having some staffing issues at the moment," Grey admitted with a grimace.

"But you do have people trained for battle, yes?" my father asked with a raised brow.

I slumped back on the couch and exhaled. I did not want to go back to that place. Every time I did, something bad happened.

"Yes, but what good will that do us if we can't get through the portal to march on them?" Grey countered, squeezing my hand. He must have seen my reaction when the Syndicate was mentioned.

I hate the facility.

Fenrick ran a hand over his face and groaned.

He'd been so quiet, I'd almost forgotten he was there.

"We have access to the book now. We could probably find a way to get everyone back in through the portal, but the Council watches it as closely as we did," he warned.

"You have the book? Where?" Father asked with wide, hopeful eyes. He turned, glancing between the two men. It was clearly the first bit of solid, good news he'd heard.

"Well, I wouldn't take it with me to my home that had just been ransacked." Grey sat back, his shoulder brushing mine and sending tingles down my spine.

"Fair enough." Father nodded. "But we need it."

"What about Freya?" I asked softly. "Where is she?"

"We fear Malcolm's got her," he said, his heart obviously heavy with regret. "I have people on that already, but I have a feeling the only way we're going to get her back is if we pretend to trade her life for the damn book." Grey sighed.

My heart fell.

Fucking Malcolm!

My free hand clenched tightly into a fist as pent-up rage reignited within me.

"I think we need to go to this facility of yours and retrieve the book. Time is of the essence." My father rose from his chair.

As much as I wanted to save Freya, a flicker of anxiety sprang to life in my chest, making my voice catch in my throat. "Right now?" I asked, glancing out the window at the darkening sky. Every fiber in my body wanted to put off going back to the Facility for as long as possible. Not only was that place littered with bad memories, gory deaths, and pain, but I hadn't even had a chance to talk to Grey privately yet.

"Daughter, we need to do this quickly. The Elders will continue to send their men after you. They will stop at nothing to see you dead." The Shadow King crossed his arms over his chest in a manner that said there were to be no arguments made and eyed me evenly.

"You're right. I know you are... but I just don't like that place," I said, looking down at my hands in my lap as I twisted them. "A lot happened there."

Grey wrapped an arm around my shoulders and drew me in close. "You don't have to go now if you don't want to. You can remain here safe with your mother. But King Channing is right. We need to move quickly on this. Our enemies won't wait for us to be ready."

"No," I said, standing immediately despite my heavy stomach. "It's fine. We should go. I need to train anyway." I hadn't sparred in weeks and still didn't know how to utilize my magic the way other Fae could.

Father smiled at me with pride. "That's the spirit, Daughter." He turned to Fenrick. "You have been there, yes?"

"Yes, my king. I will take you there first so you can help take them there." Fenrick bowed his head to my father. A second later, he clapped a hand on my father's shoulder and sifted them both away.

I strolled anxiously to the window. What would happen when we got to the facility? What was the plan?

"Are you okay?" Grey asked, stepping up behind me.

"I'm fine." I sighed.

"Are you really? Are we good or..." he trailed off.

Is he still afraid to ask that question?

I turned and leaned against him. "We're good," I assured him. "I should have given you the time to explain. I was just in shock at seeing the stalker right there in the facility after the horror show of Layla's death."

"You were so angry at Dan, sweetheart. I didn't want you to leave. It really wasn't malicious, and it happened so fast." He wrapped his arms around me and rested his chin on my head.

My mother stood with a smile on her face. "You two will definitely bring in a new era for all of us."

"What?" Grey asked with a frown.

"It was foretold that your father's death would usher in a new era for Faery." My mother patted his shoulder.

"One thing at a time, Mother," I said, shaking my head. "It's all a bit much, and we haven't even had a moment to talk."

Father and Fenrick sifted back, appearing in the sitting room once more.

I pulled away from Grey. I needed to learn to sift like they could. It would make things so much easier. Besides, as the Princess of Faery, it seemed only common sense I had a crash course in all things Fae. Gods knew I needed it!

Fenrick clapped Grey on the shoulder, and they vanished into thin air.

My father wrapped his strong arms around Mother and me with a reassuring nod.

The room spun out of focus quickly, and I closed my eyes against the dizziness that always took hold whenever someone sifted me. I stumbled as we appeared on the dirt road outside of the wards of the facility.

My father's arm tightened around me to steady me. "Not quite used to that?" he asked with a grin.

"No, I never really had anyone to teach me how to use my magic. I feel a little bit out of my depth, to be honest." I shrugged.

"I'm sorry for that," Father whispered.

Why was he sorry? It wasn't his fault that Malcolm had abducted me and then left me in Dallas to fend for myself. Nor was it his fault I'd been raised by a witch and forced to sleep in a closet. Perhaps he simply felt the empathy of any parent when confronted with the truth that their child had been put at a disadvantage.

Grey stepped up next to us. "We need to get inside the wards before Malcolm shows up again and we have a fight on our hands."

"Malcolm will pay for all that he has done," my father growled.

Without another word, we rushed as one to the other side of the wards.

I breathed a happy sigh as the trees danced in the breeze, bathed in the radiance of the moon's light. It was my favorite place. This forest spoke to me in a way no other forest had, not that I had been in many forests. There was just something magical about the trees that surrounded the facility. I might not like it in within the confines of the Syndicate's compound, but I felt at home among the branches and thick trunks of the forest in a way I couldn't quite explain.

Grey wrapped his hand around mine, probably more for my comfort than anything else.

The previous time I was here had not been a fun experience.

Then, out of nowhere, the last person I expected to see rushed toward us with a huge grin on his face. The mountain of a man grabbed me away from Grey in one smooth move and spun me around as if I were a small child.

"Shouldn't you be resting?" I shrieked at Asher with a startled giggle, hugging him tightly.

Asher gently lowered me to the ground, his chest rumbling with mirth. "Zeke told me you'd escaped the Council, and I've been waiting to see you." He grinned and set me right, revealing just how protective and loving he truly was.

Grey growled and wrapped his arms around me possessively. "Don't do that again."

"We went through a great trauma together, Shifter King. I'm allowed a damn friendly hug." Asher crossed his arms over his broad chest defiantly.

I swatted Grey's arms from around me. "He's my *friend,* and I was worried about him too. Cut this possessive crap out."

Possessive damn wolf!

“Fine,” Grey grumbled but he didn’t let me go. “Where is Zeke, anyway?”

“He’s in your office.” Asher jerked his head in the direction of the parking garage. The Rider glanced between all of us, his eyes widening as they landed on my parents. His shoulders stiffened, and he peered at me with a question, seemingly awaiting my word as to how he should respond.

“They helped me escape,” I said calmly. “They’re with us.”

“I’m just shocked to see them in the human world more than anything,” Asher admitted, his shoulders relaxing before he turned back toward the parking garage.

We walked through the space, dread filling me as we stepped into the elevator.

Grey pushed the button for the top floor and pulled me to his side. It made me feel slightly better. When the doors opened, Grey ushered me out first and we walked down the deserted hall.

I stopped short, stiffening when we walked into the office. The man who shot me with the tranquillizer dart was standing right there by the huge window.

“Shit,” Grey whispered. “I forgot he was still here.”

I took a step back instinctively and scanned the room. What did I want to do? My gut wanted me to run again, to protect myself, and panic tugged at my insides with sharp claws.

“Princess,” the man breathed and dropped to his knee, his head bowed.

“What the fuck?” I gasped, turning to Grey with wide, searching eyes.

“Dan might be my best tracker, but he is also half-Fae,” Grey said. “He’s bowing to royalty.”

“Make him stop.” I panicked, my voice rising in pitch as my nerves thrummed with electricity. I took two large steps back. My mind couldn’t seem to reconcile that this man was in my mate’s employ. All it could focus on was the fact this half-Fae had attacked me and changed the course of my life forever.

I can’t do this. I need to get out of here.

My throat tensed and dried up, leaving me gasping for breath. Shadows slithered up my arms angrily, responding to my panic.

Grey took hold of my upper arms and turned me to face him. "Breathe with me." His tone was so soft, it helped calm some of my distress, but also left a pang of sadness in my heart.

Nickolas had helped me the same way when I'd panicked. I glanced down and away, the loss of the ancient Shifter King still raw.

Grey pinched my chin gently, turning my face to meet his gaze. "Keep your eyes on me and match my breathing." Grey inhaled deeply and blew his breath out slowly.

"You still need to make him stop," I managed, but did as he directed.

"I think it's his way of apologizing, beautiful."

I nodded in understanding. That made sense, given my established title and position now that everything was out in the open. Without further distraction, I continued to breathe with Grey. Slowly but surely, my shadow magic slithered away until it was completely gone and hidden within me once more.

I'd told Grey on more than one occasion that I wanted that man—Dan—dead for what he'd done to me. And now that I knew he was no longer a threat, I no longer wanted to kill him... but I didn't want him anywhere near me, either. Worst of all, I was still mentally freaking out. I needed to find a way to be calm and accept the past, but it was harder than I'd imagined.

Maybe I'm not as strong and brave as I thought.

"I'm okay now," I said with a small smile, though I wasn't sure who I was trying to convince more, Grey or myself.

"Are you sure?" he asked, placing a kiss on my forehead.

"I am," I said and turned to Dan, who was still on the ground. Unable to hide a grimace, I spoke to him for the first time since our fateful engagement in the alley. "You can get up now."

The half-Fae didn't get up right away.

Is he ignoring me?

I turned back to Grey, a question in my eyes.

"Dan, get off the fucking ground. You're making Aurelia uncomfortable," he said with a shake of his head.

Dan finally stood and lifted his gaze.

I breathed a sigh of relief.

This princess shit is going to take some serious getting used to.

"I'm sorry for my part in your foster mother's death, Princess Aurelia. I am, truly. I hope you can forgive me some day." Dan bowed his head.

Anxiety leapt to the fore again at the heady mix of confronting emotions, and I instead directed my attention to what mattered *now*. "This isn't what we came here for," I said with frustration and turned back to my father.

"What did this man do?" Father asked, his gaze narrowing in an accusatory glare.

Dan cleared his throat and regretfully faced the Shadow King. "I shot her with a tranquillizer dart, my king."

King Channing took a threatening step forward and lunged for Dan. He was so insanely fast, no one could stop him—and those that possibly could, didn't bother to try. He had Dan around the throat in a heartbeat and lifted him off the ground.

"Father, stop!" I yelled, surprising even myself as I rushed forward to grab his arm.

"He shot you," my father growled, tightening his grip.

"I know," I stressed. "But it's over now. What is done can't be undone, and I'm okay." I succeeded in getting him to lower the tracker back to the ground, but his hand was still cutting off Dan's airway.

"You're lucky she's so forgiving," my father snarled. "In my court, any slight against my family is punishable by death." The king pushed him away roughly in disgust.

All the while Grey just stood there, arms crossed over his chest, a smirk on his handsome face.

Dan coughed and gasped, bent at the waist, trying desperately to get air back into his lungs.

"It's less than you deserve for that particular stunt," Grey finally remarked.

I turned to him sharply. *He* was the one who'd sent Dan after me in the first place. Weren't they his orders? How could he be saying such a thing? "Grey?" I said with a raised brow.

"I sure as shit didn't order him to shoot you with a dart," he responded. "I only wanted him to bring you to me. I didn't even find out about what he'd actually done until you told me yourself." Grey moved around his desk and sat behind it, pulling me down with him and onto his lap.

My father raised a brow but didn't offer any comment.

I swallowed my anxiety down as best I could and licked my lips. "It doesn't matter now, like I said. We have more pressing matters to deal with," I reminded our odd little resistance team.

Like starting a damn war with the Elders, and hoping we all make it out of this alive...

CHAPTER 18

I pulled Aurelia close and rested my chin on her shoulder with an internal sigh of agitation. I hadn't gotten to enjoy a *proper* reunion with her due to our present circumstances, and it was making my wolf even more possessive and jealous. He wanted me to kick everyone out of my office and greet her properly, in the deeply carnal way only two mates could share.

Unfortunately, we have bigger things to deal with, though.

"You have the two shifters secured in the cells?" I asked Zeke, raising my gaze to meet his.

"They are, and Erik is in a magicless cell," Zeke answered, stepping forward.

I nodded to him, grateful that he was capable of handling all of it while I was busy recovering my mate. "And where is the book?" I asked.

Zeke held up a bag and placed it on the desk in front of me.

They couldn't have found a more secure place for it?

I lifted a brow at Zeke.

He just shrugged. "I've had it the whole time on my person. Do you think anyone in this place would dare cross me?" Zeke grinned.

"I would!" Asher boomed.

"Fuck off, Ash. You're barely healed and you're on our side, you idiot." Zeke shook his head at his brother-in-arms.

Aurelia reached for the bag with tentative fingers, drawing it closer.

I peered over her shoulder into the bag with curiosity.

Aurelia's brow furrowed as she removed the book from the bag. Her hands glowed softly in response, her sharp intake of breath not lost on me. "This isn't the right book," she whispered, her voice quavering.

"What?" I demanded, my volume rising in frustration and anger. "How do you know?"

"I'm not sure," she answered, turning the book over in her hands. "I just have a feeling this isn't what we need. This isn't the key." Aurelia hung her head, her disappointment a tangible thing that filled the room.

"Don't feel that way. This is not your fault. It's the fucking shifters' fault," I growled, pulling her in closer to me to reassure her with my heat and strength.

"Are we sure it was the shifters and not the brownie?" Zeke asked. "The little loyal shit could have hoodwinked even them."

My fist clenched on the desk. That fucking brownie had been the bane of my existence since I'd met him!

"Brownie?" Aurelia asked. "The one from Malcolm's house? How?"

"Yes." I nodded into her shoulder. "We crossed paths when we were looking for the book."

"He's a mean little thing," she said and shivered.

Of course.

She had encountered him when Malcolm had abducted her.

"That he is," I agreed. "I wish you'd heard him squeal when I picked him up by his jacket and carried him out of the burning house." I grinned against her shoulder.

"Maybe he didn't know he was grabbing the wrong book?" she asked, playing Devil's advocate.

"Perhaps. But why did Malcolm bother to destroy my penthouse if he had the correct book already?" I asked, staring up at Zeke.

"Maybe we should go ask our little *friend* that question," Zeke suggested with a grin and turned for the door.

I picked up Aurelia as I stood and set her back on her feet. "Let's go have a chat with an asshole brownie."

Aurelia nodded and stepped aside. She had no idea where she was going.

I wrapped an arm around her waist and led her to the elevator, the rest of our trusted team following us.

She leaned her head on my chest with a sigh as the elevator descended. "What are we going to do without the right book?" she whispered.

"We'll figure it out," I said as the elevator door *dinged* opened and we made our way down to the cells.

"Let me fucking out of here!" Karma screamed as we walked past.

"Shut up, bitch!" I barked at her.

Aurelia scowled at the woman, her anger bubbling just beneath the surface.

"Oh, you got your princess back," Karma sneered.

"She really doesn't know when to shut her fucking mouth," Aurelia muttered. Magic sparkled along her fingers, but she let it subside. She glared at Karma, who was no threat to us now.

"You'll get your shot at her," I promised, wrapping an arm around my mate.

We stood outside the brownie's cell together as we waited for Zeke to open the door. The little shit was huddled in the corner on the small mattress like a mouse.

"What do you want?" he asked, glaring up at us. His eyes scanned our faces until his gaze landed on the Shadow King. His beady eyes widened, and he scrambled to kneel on the floor, immediately humbled. "Your Majesty!" he spluttered.

"Brownie, where is the *real* book?" the king asked, an air of command in his tone.

The brownie glanced up with a frown. "*His* people took it from me," the brownie answered and pointed an accusing finger at me.

"The book they had was not the correct book," I snarled back, shaking my head.

"What? It's the wrong book?" the brownie shrieked. His eyes widened, and he jumped to his feet, his bearing panicked and erratic.

"I could tell immediately," Aurelia interjected. "It's not the one."

"Burned. Burned! The book is burned!" he wailed, gripping his head.

"What is he babbling about?" Aurelia asked with a shocked gasp, turning to me.

"Malcolm's home was in flames when we escaped. The dickhead tried to burn us alive." I scrubbed a hand over my face.

"I barely got to the book before the flames grew too big, then the wolf grabbed me and stuck me here!" The brownie glared at me.

"So, the book is truly gone?" Aurelia whispered, her voice shaking.

"It can't be. This doesn't make any sense. Why would Malcolm search my penthouse for the book if he had it?" I asked.

"Maybe he doesn't have it," Aurelia said with wide eyes.

"Wait. Did he ever have it?" I asked, realization dawning upon me.

Zeke ran a hand through his hair. "Well, what book *do* we have then? It was clearly magical. The princess' magic glowed when she touched it."

Aurelia frowned. "Perhaps he's been looking for it all this time?"

Had Aurelia hidden it better than any of us thought, and then managed to block her memories, shielding and safeguarding its true location?

That would be extensive magic for just a child to perform.

"Have you gotten any more of your memories back?" I squeezed her to me, searching her glorious green eyes for answers.

"Not many," she admitted. "But do you think I'm the one who hid it? Why would I have done that? After Malcolm left me with it, I assumed it was lost or taken by my witch mother..." Aurelia shook her head.

Fenrick shuffled his feet and cleared his throat loudly. "I don't think we should discuss this *here*." He eyed the little jerk in the cell with no small measure of suspicion.

He's right. The brownie is loyal to Malcolm, first and foremost. We shouldn't give him any more information than necessary.

"What other properties does he have?" I demanded, turning to the brownie.

"I only know of the place I have served him from," he answered staunchly.

That was too easy. Why would the little shit be so willing to give us that information? Was it because of the Shadow King's presence or something else?

"All right. Okay, let's go." I moved to the door.

Everyone filed out behind me, and we returned to the office. The book was still on the desk, safe and sound. I moved to it with Aurelia by my side. "Pick up the book," I said to her.

She picked it up, and her hands glowed a bright purple. Her eyes widened as she stared down at the strange sight, which seemed even more intense than the first time. "I think I remember this book," she whispered, her brow furrowed deep in thought.

"What do you remember?" I prompted, hoping that if I spoke softly, perhaps I wouldn't break her concentration.

"I'm not sure. It's more a feeling. I just *know* that I've held this book before today." She flopped into the chair in front of my desk, her expression one of uncertainty as she opened it.

I leaned over her shoulder and cursed. "Are all the pages blank?"

"What do you mean?" Aurelia frowned, glancing up at me momentarily.

"It's blank," I repeated.

Fenrick stepped up to the other side of Aurelia, his brow creasing in kind. "What's the point of a blank book?" he asked.

"You can't see the words?" Aurelia asked. She trailed a finger over the page from left to right as if there were words there only she could see.

"No, there's nothing there." I turned, waving over the Shadow King. "Do you see anything?"

My mate's father peered down at the pages as if trying to discern the intangible, then he sighed. "No, nothing. That is most strange, indeed." He scratched his head in confusion.

Zeke leaned over and shook his head as well.

Why would he think he could see it?

I figured it might only be visible to the Fae, but the king and Fenrick couldn't see anything either. "It must have something to do with the prophecy," I muttered as I sat down next to her.

"I don't think so." Aurelia leaned further over the book, peering at the pages.

"What do you see?" I asked.

Aurelia flipped the page and gasped. "It's me."

"What do you mean?" I leaned over her shoulder again even though I couldn't actually see anything.

"*I* spelled this book," she breathed. "I wrote on these pages... but how?" She bit her lower lip, mulling it over.

How could she have done all of this when she was so young?

My phone buzzed in my pocket, and I pulled it out, recognizing Magna's number on the screen. "Magna, what do you know?" I chuckled despite the tense atmosphere.

"Aurelia is there?" she asked.

"Yes, but you knew that already."

"You're in the office?" she followed up.

"You know that too. You're our friendly neighborhood seer, so just come on up since I know you're here." I sat back in my chair.

What is the seer going to reveal now?

This night was dragging on longer than the limits of my patience. I was tired and wanted a proper reunion with my mate. My wolf needed to feel her soon, or he was going to lose it. I hung up the phone and turned to Aurelia. "Magna is here."

"Of course, she is," Dan chuckled.

Magna walked in minutes later, bringing with her a sense of mystery and expectation.

"Do you know anything about this?" Aurelia asked the seer.

"I do," she said. Magna glanced down at the book and mumbled something in the Fae language I didn't quite catch despite my supernatural hearing. The book glowed and words magically filled the page.

"How did you do that? What have you been keeping from us?" I said, focusing an unimpressed glare at Magna.

"I have kept many things from you for your own protection, Grey," Magna said with a raised brow, utterly unphased by my aggression.

"Of course, you have," I growled.

"I think... I think I knew you before," Aurelia said suddenly, a frown creasing her lovely features.

"What?" I turned to her sharply.

"It wasn't time for you to remember before now, Princess." Magna shrugged before she sat in a spare chair on Aurelia's other side.

"You had best explain!" I barked, crossing my arms over my chest. What had this woman been planning and for how long? If she'd known Aurelia as a child, how and in what context?

"I can see the wheels turning in your head, Shifter King. I found her in an alley as a child and I knew she was special. No matter how hard she tried to hide her wings, she couldn't hide them from me." Magna smiled.

"You were in the alley?" Aurelia gasped. "Are you the reason I ended up living with the witch?"

Was she finally about to get the answers she had been searching for most of her life? Why hadn't Magna told us all this sooner?

"I am the reason for that," she confirmed. "You were so small, and you were freezing, but no matter how many futures I searched in my visions, it never went well for all of us if I had kept you with me."

How horrible that must have been for her to see all those possible futures and have to hand Aurelia over to someone who would treat her as little more than a slave.

The witch had been a monster to her. I gritted my teeth against the memory. "You knew that she would be sleeping in a closet on the floor," I growled.

"You do not get to condemn me for that, Shifter King. We would not even be here today had I chosen any differently." Magna crossed her arms over her chest in silent defiance.

"What do you mean?" Aurelia asked. "How bad could it have been?"

"You would not have met at all, and we would not be in a position where we can finally go home." Magna smiled softly. "I'm sorry for your struggles, Aurelia, but the future will be bright. You'll see."

How can she say that with war so clearly on the horizon? No one is safe.

CHAPTER 19

Aurelia

I sat back against my chair in shock as the realization washed over me, my hand straying to toy with my long hair.

I knew Magna as a child, and she never told me?

"Did you hide the book we need?" I asked softly.

A hand squeezed my shoulder, and I glanced up to find my father's sky-blue eyes staring back at me.

"I did not hide the book—you did," Magna said, her lips quirking.

"You left my daughter, the princess of the Shadow Kingdom you once belonged to, with a woman who had her sleep on the floor of a closet?" my father boomed, coming to my defense.

"Everything I did was so that we could get to *this* moment." Magna stood and squared off with him, clearly not at all phased that he was her king.

"What's so important about this moment?" I asked warily, resting my hand on my father's to calm him.

Magna just smiled. "It's a turning point. I can't tell you the details or it may change the timeline of what's to come."

I covered my face with my hands at her answer. I was *so* tired, and all this back and forth was just making it worse. I yawned. "Do you know where the book is hidden?" I asked.

Magna shook her head. "No, I do not. I refused to let you tell me the location of the book."

Grey sat forward, pursing his lips. "Smart. Malcolm could have tortured the information out of you."

"So, how are we supposed to find it?" I asked. I still couldn't remember anything from my childhood except fleeting bits and pieces. I certainly didn't remember Magna finding me in the freezing alley. I only remembered Malcolm leaving me to my fate.

"This book will jog your memories." Magna tapped the tome with a knowing twinkle in her eyes. "You wrote it to remind yourself when the time was right."

I stroked a finger over the page it was opened to.

I hid the real book and left myself clues in this one?

How was I supposed to figure this all out? Clearly, I was some kind of child prodigy, because right now all of this seemed so beyond me. I sighed.

Grey cleared his throat, breaking the tension in the room. "All right, it's getting late, and I need time with my mate. I think we should pick this up tomorrow." It was a command, not a question.

Magna opened her mouth to argue but closed it and nodded. "Very well. I'll go find a place to settle in."

Everyone filed out of the room to find a place to sleep in the facility.

I frowned. "We're sleeping here?" I asked Grey. I didn't like *or* trust this place, and I wasn't sure I could catch a wink of rest here even if I wanted to.

"The penthouse isn't safe. Malcolm has broken in twice now. I don't want to take that chance again." Grey pulled me up into his arms.

"I get that, but I'm not comfortable here," I said as I laid my head against his chest.

"I know, Princess," he soothed, running a hand through my golden hair. He pulled me closer and kissed my forehead.

Everything felt so right when I was with Grey. "Where are we sleeping?" I asked.

"I don't know how much sleep we'll be getting," Grey chuckled. He tilted my chin up so I could meet his eyes and placed a tender kiss on my lips.

A shiver ran through my soul, and I melted against him.

"I'm truly sorry, my love. I should have told you sooner about Dan, and the book... about everything. I promise my intentions were never malicious," he said, pressing his lips to mine again.

I ran my hands up his chest and wrapped them around the back of his neck as I went up on my tiptoes, pressing my lips harder to his.

His hands slid down my sides slowly until they gripped my ass.

I moaned into his mouth, overwhelmed by the small amount of pleasure after having gone without for what felt like forever.

He took my eager response as permission to deepen the kiss, and his tongue met mine in a heated dance as he lifted me off my feet.

I wrapped my legs around his hips instinctively. "Wait, Grey, I need a shower," I said, breaking the kiss. "I've been in a dungeon..."

"I don't care," he growled and nipped at my neck.

The skin tingled where he'd bitten me before. "Grey, I still have blood on me from my escape," I countered, but he must not have heard me.

My shifter crushed his lips to mine, cutting off any further protests.

I melted into him, our bodies melding like two pieces of a puzzle that were always destined to be reunited.

His fingers skated up under my shirt, sliding up my waist and under my shirt to cup my breast. He groaned and spun us around, pressing my back to the wall and ground his hips into mine. His cock was rock-hard against my center.

I squirmed in his arms, trying to get friction. I still didn't like the idea of having sex with him covered in blood and grime, but this was as wild and primitive as it got, and I was mated to a wolf. Something about

Grey and his hands on me always made me go crazy with need. I couldn't fight it, and I had no intention of doing so.

"I missed you so much, Princess," Grey groaned against my neck as he licked at the mark on my neck.

My back arched with desire, and I pressed my breasts into his eager hand. "We need a bed," I breathed and gripped his dark hair.

"We don't need a bed for me to make you come, baby. I could lay you out on my desk again and lick you until you scream my name." Grey ground his hips into me to drive his point home.

"Grey." I pulled his head back and crushed my lips to his. His dirty mouth alone had me squirming in his arms, hungry with need.

"What do you want, Princess?" Grey asked against my lips, his breath hot and sweet.

"You," I moaned, bucking my hips against his hard cock.

"I was so scared I would never hear you say that again," he admitted, resting his forehead against my shoulder.

I ran my fingers through his beautiful hair, and licked my lips, reveling in his taste.

He shivered in my arms, his rock-solid body craving my soft curves.

"It wasn't until I was in that dungeon that I realized how much I need you," I said softly, my voice full of regret. "I'm sorry that's what it took to recognize that I truly belong with you."

"I'm sorry too. There was just never a good time to tell you." Grey shook his head, mirroring my regret.

I covered his mouth with my fingers, silencing him. "I don't want to talk about this right now."

Grey gripped my ass and moved to the desk. He glanced down at the surface before swiping everything off and onto the floor, including the book, and set me down on it. He trailed his fingers up over my ass and around to my waist, leaving goose bumps in his wake. Ripping my shirt and pulling it up and over my head, he groaned as he stared down at me. "Take off your bra and lay back on the desk, Aurelia," Grey demanded, lust blazing behind his eyes.

I reached back slowly and unhooked my bra, letting the straps slide down my arms.

Grey's eyes practically glowed with his hunger, revealing his inner wolf as I bared myself to him.

I leaned back on my elbows and slowly lowered myself onto the hard surface.

Grey followed me down, taking a nipple into his mouth and sucking it hard.

My back arched, and I pushed my breast further into his mouth, loving the feel of his lips on me.

His hand slid down my side to the top of my panties and stroked the skin there, making me shiver.

"Oh, fuck, Grey," I whimpered.

Grey smiled against my skin before switching out, giving the other breast the same level of attention. "You're going to scream that before I'm done with you, Princess." He reached up and pulled at the waistband of my underwear.

I lifted my ass off the desk to help him slip my pants down over my hips and down my legs.

Grey kissed and licked his way down my body while my hands clenched at my sides in anguished desire.

His gaze met mine as he threw my panties to the floor and kneeled on the ground at the end of the desk, positing himself between my legs. He trailed his fingers up my calf, all the way to my thigh, teasing me cruelly before he pushed my thighs apart wider. Inhaling deeply through his nose like an animal, Grey grinned. "You smell like heaven when you're so wet for me." He kissed my inner thigh before nipping it with his teeth.

My hips bucked up, needing him somewhere else entirely. "Grey, stop teasing me." I groaned.

"I'm not teasing you," he growled. "I'm worshipping my queen." He licked up my thigh until he reached my pussy, then moved to the other leg and gave it the same treatment.

I grabbed his hair in a desperate attempt to pull him up to me where I needed him most.

Grey rumbled, grabbing my wrists and pinning them to my sides. "Don't rush me." He nipped my thigh, taking his time.

"Grey, *please*," I begged. My body tensed as he licked up my slit and my back arched, I clenched my hands into white-knuckled fists before grabbing the edge of the desk to keep myself from reaching out and pulling him toward me.

Having released my wrists, his tongue circled my clit and tingles raced down my spine as he pushed two fingers inside me and groaned. "You're *so* wet for me, Princess," my mate praised.

"Yes," I moaned, glowing with internal pride at his praise.

He curled his fingers inside me, repeatedly hitting that spot that made my toes curl. He commanded my body like an artist commanded a canvas, and it was as sensual and beautiful as it was raw and hot.

Before long, stars burst behind my eyes and tingles wracked my body as I screamed just the way he promised I would.

Grey lapped at my cum, prolonging the orgasm even further, pushing me to even greater ecstasy. Then, crawling up my body, he kissed and nipped a path all the way to my mouth. He kissed me punishingly, thrusting his tongue between my lips with a growl, claiming me with a ferocity that set me ablaze.

I could taste myself on his lips, and that alone was enough to make me squirm. I reached for his belt, wanting him just as naked as I was.

He batted my hands away, completely in control. "Patience, my love." He grinned, standing up to pull the shirt over his head and expose his tanned, toned chest.

I trailed my fingers over his abs appreciatively, my teeth sinking into my lip.

His eyes closed tightly, and he blew out his ragged breath. "Your hands on me make me want to lose control."

"Well, I happen to like watching you lose control," I teased with a grin of my own.

He pulled my hands off him in one fluid motion and trapped them at my sides again. "I need you to keep your hands *there*."

I pouted playfully, wanting to touch every part of him, to sate the separation I'd been forced to endure for too long.

Grey just shook his head and gripped his belt, unbuckling it with ease. He dropped his pants and boxers slowly to the ground and kicked off his shoes as if we had all the time in the world. My mate caressed my hips as he stepped between my legs once more.

I kept my hands at my sides as instructed but squirmed on the desk at the sight of his glorious, naked form.

Oh, gods! I need him.

He pulled me down the smooth, polished surface and rubbed the head of his cock along my pussy lips slowly, but held himself back.

I wiggled my hips suggestively, almost embarrassed by my dire need to be conquered. To feel him inside me after so many weeks of being apart.

His hand clamped down on my thigh in an almost bruising grip. "Aurelia, do you need something?" Grey chuckled.

"I need you inside me," I moaned, my tone bordering on a whine.

His cock slid over my clit, further tormenting me. "Grip the desk and don't let go," he commanded. Spreading my legs wide, he stared down at me before pushing his way inside me torturously slowly.

I held onto the desk with a white-knuckle grip, enduring each inch, all the while wishing I could touch him. But I didn't want him to stop and deny me his physical affection if I misbehaved.

When he was finally buried deep inside me, his sac against my ass, Grey scrunched his eyes closed and blew out a shaky breath.

I wiggled my hips, urging him to move again. "Please."

Pain and pleasure warred within me a moment later when he smacked my curvy ass.

"If that's supposed to be a deterrent, it's not going to work," I said softly with an edge of attitude.

"I need a minute. It's been too long, and my wolf is going crazy with his need to reclaim his mate," Grey growled. When he reopened his eyes, his pupils glowed golden with his wolf perilously close to the surface. Circling my clit with his thumb, he pulled out so slowly, I could have screamed. He was fucking torturing me in the best way imaginable.

It feels like I'm going to die! I can't take this!

Grey pushed inside me hard and fast on the next thrust, rocking my world.

My back arched off the desk, spots dancing behind my eyes.

He thrust in again, and again, gritting his teeth as he fucked me, his wolf gazing down upon me all the while.

As I edged nearer and nearer to my second climax, I wrapped my legs around his hips to grind myself against him, to claim every last second of contact I could.

"Fuck, Princess, I'm not going to last. Can I mark you?" Grey leaned over me then, crushing his lips down on mine with breath-stealing need.

I groaned into the kiss, keeping my hands on the desk even though I wanted nothing more than to tangle them in his hair and clutch as his strong, muscular back like a lifeline.

He broke our kiss and licked his way across my jaw to the mark on my shoulder and nipped at it. "Mine," he growled.

The rumble of his desire flowed through me, and I squeezed my insides tightly, desperate to keep him. "Yes, Grey," I hissed. "Always."

His fangs scraped slowly over my skin, and he ground his hips into mine.

I shivered, tightening my legs around him once more and pulling him deeper inside me, until he hit that perfect, sacred spot. My head thrashed from side to side, and pleasure pulsed through me on impact, triggering my release and taking me higher than ever before.

His fangs slid into the mark on my neck, and he roared like a beast against my neck, slamming himself inside me a final time and spilling his hot seed inside of my quivering pussy.

CHAPTER 20

I rolled over and pulled my mate into my arms, still half groggy with sleep. After our fun on my office desk the night before, I'd carried her to the bedroom I reserved here in case of emergencies and helped her shower before we fell into bed together.

"We have to get up, don't we?" she asked, stretching and yawning.

"Yes, unfortunately. We need to find the place a child would hide a book," I grumbled.

"But I don't want to," she moaned, rolling into me so her head was against my chest.

With a sigh, I stroked her magnificent mane of golden hair, burying my nose in its fragrance.

Aurelia... her name suits her perfectly.

Truth be told, I really didn't want to get up either. I hadn't had nearly enough time with my mate. I wanted to steal more precious moments like this, moments where I could just love, appreciate, and worship her, but we needed the damn book to stop the Elders. "You know what they say. There's no rest for the wicked, my love." I grinned and patted her back, signaling I was about to move.

"I'm not wicked," she griped. "I hate how that term has become synonymous for the Fae."

"I know, Princess. It was a bad joke." I squeezed her to me tighter before releasing her, missing her soft warmth almost immediately.

She sighed and sat up in bed, the sheet pooling around her waist.

The glorious sight was making me impossibly hard.

We really need more quality mating time!

I glanced away reluctantly, knowing that if I didn't stop staring at her, we wouldn't be leaving the bedroom any time soon.

Goddamn it. Duty first, fun later.

"What am I going to wear?" she asked, grimacing at the pile of dirty clothes on the floor.

"I have spare clothing in the closet if you want to take a look," I said, jerking my head toward it.

She jumped from the bed naked and went to investigate.

I stared as she crossed the room, adjusting myself beneath the sheets and sighed. There was just no way to take this time with her, and no matter how much I was resolved to being the king I was born to be, I hated that obligation *always* had to come first. Time was ticking even now, even with the book Aurelia had written to give herself clues. The Elders wouldn't sit on their laurels. They were bound to send more people after her and the book, and they had endless resources at their disposal and no shortage of willing soldiers. We needed to gain ground. We needed a win, desperately.

"You have women's clothes in here," Aurelia said as she peeked her head out of the closet with a raised brow.

"I brought them from the apartment after the first time we were attacked by Malcolm, just in case," I explained as I got up from the bed and moved toward the dresser. I grabbed a pair of black jeans from the drawer and unfolded them before pulling them on. I paused in between one breath and the next when a knock sounded on the door. I turned quickly to make sure that Aurelia was dressed before stomping over to answer it.

I threw the door open to find Dan standing there on tenterhooks, his back rigid and his eyes wide with panic.

"What's wrong?" I demanded as the acrid scent of his fear hit me, overwhelming my senses.

He glanced away. "Someone is tampering with the wards, boss." He fidgeted, moving from foot to foot, unwilling to hold my gaze.

"Have you sent a team out?" I barked over my shoulder as I moved back toward the closet to grab a fresh shirt.

Aurelia stood there with wide eyes, fear rippling off her. Not only was she reacting to the unexpected news, but she was also responding in a very primal way to a fellow fairy's fear, even if he was only half Fae.

"We have, but the individual in question will only speak to the princess. Alone." Dan stressed and scrubbed a hand over his face.

"Absolutely not!" I growled. "No fucking way."

"I figured you would say that." Dan sighed.

"Why do they want to speak to me?" Aurelia asked as stepped out of the closet.

"He didn't say," Dan said shaking his head. "At this point, we're lucky they aren't using brute force to push through the wards.

"It could be anyone, Aurelia." I turned, now fully clothed, pulling her into me.

"But what if it's Malcolm with Freya?" she gasped, her hand flying to her mouth. She was clearly just as attached to the tiny, mischievous but fiercely loyal sprites as I was.

Fuck. What if it is Malcolm?

"Then we trade him the brownie," I said, gently releasing her to cross my arms over my chest.

"Are you sure that's a good idea?" Aurelia asked, chewing her lower lip. "He heard a lot of what we were discussing yesterday."

I growled deeply in my throat. She wasn't wrong. "We don't have another choice. We don't have the book we need, and have no idea where it is," I said.

"Agreed," said Dan, piping up. "And we can't give him the book we have. It may be the only clue we have to finding the actual book." My tracker leaned against the door frame, his nerves settling the longer we spoke.

"Maybe we can just wait it out? It may not even be Malcolm," Aurelia reasoned and laid her head on my shoulder.

She hated this, I could feel it. Freya was once again in the hands of a monster, and all she wanted was to get her back. But at the same time, another confrontation with Malcom was not something any of us was looking forward to. I squeezed her tighter to me, willing her to be calm and glanced back at Dan. "Get everyone together in the parking garage. We're going to take a look." I stepped toward the door, but Dan was still blocking the way.

"Are you sure that's wise, boss?" Dan asked hesitantly as he scratched his head.

This guy is my best tracker. He needs to get the fuck over his fears if he's going to prove useful to the Syndicate.

I bristled with annoyance. "I can't have people tampering with my wards." I stomped past him, pulling Aurelia along with me. Maybe I should have left her with Dan and checked the wards out for myself. But at this point, I wasn't going to let her out of my sight. I pushed the button for the elevator and waited impatiently. When the doors opened, the Shadow King was already inside.

"Where are you going?" King Channing asked.

"Someone is screwing with the wards, and I need to check it out." I stepped into the elevator.

Aurelia followed close behind me.

"Why are you going, Daughter?" her father asked with a furrowed brow. "You should remain here, where it's safe and guarded. I'll go with your king to see what kind of threat is at our doorstep." The Shadow King clapped me on the shoulder as if we were old buddies.

"The person, whoever they are, wants to speak to me. Alone," she said, staring straight ahead.

"All the more reason for you to stay behind," the Shadow King growled.

"Seriously? After all these years apart, Father?" said Aurelia with a hint of agitation. "I'm a grown adult and can take care of myself. I've survived this long at least, and I've escaped Malcom twice now."

"But not without help along the way," Channing countered. "Be it your witch mother, the sprites, your mate, or your friends. This is not something you can—or should—do alone. Your life is precious, Daughter, and there is too much at stake."

"I'm going with her, and we'll be staying on our side of the wards," I assured him, pulling Aurelia into my side to kiss her temple.

"I'm coming too," the Shadow King insisted. "I want to know who dares to call upon my blood and threatens your people in the same breath." He leaned back against the wall of the elevator and fell silent for the rest of the ride, unwilling to take *no* for an answer.

I nodded and pushed the button for the parking garage.

Honestly, the more protection Aurelia has, the better.

When we reached the parking garage, several supernaturals were standing around, their expressions shuttered.

"Where are they?" I asked.

A shifter was shoved forward, their gaze firmly down in an open gesture of submission.

"Boss, he was *adamant* it only be the princess," he breathed, his fear permeating the air.

"I don't care what he was adamant about," I snarled and shook my head. Whoever *he* was, I wasn't leaving my mate alone with him for one damn second, especially with so many threats against her.

"He's screwing with the wards at the road leading to the city, boss," another shifter pointed over his shoulder.

I nodded to the shifter, and marched past him with the king and Aurelia at my back. A second later, someone clapped me on the shoulder, and the world spun around, my stomach along with it.

Motherfucker. I was not expecting that.

"You can't just do that without warning!" I spat at the king as we appeared at the edge of the wards.

But he wasn't paying attention to me. His eyes blazed with the fury of a thousand suns as he stared at someone behind me.

I spun around and growled.

My wolf beat at the cage of my chest, ready to tear the bastard a new asshole.

Ronaldo stood on the other side of my wards with a smug-as-fuck smile on his face.

"What the fuck do you want?" I snarled, scarcely holding my rage in check.

"The princess is condemned to death," he said matter-of-factly. "I'm simply here to take my prisoner back to Faery to be punished for her crimes." He shrugged as if his declaration was entirely reasonable.

"You have *no* jurisdiction here. Fuck off!" I yelled.

"I don't?" Ronaldo asked, his tone far too light and airy, as if he knew something I didn't.

What the fuck is he talking about? Of course, he doesn't. We aren't in Faery.

I hadn't been back in two centuries, and it was my sole mission to return my people to our home realm, and my mate was going to help me do it. I refused point blank to give her to this psychotic, murderous bastard Elder to be executed! "No, this is my property," I fired back. "And you are trespassing. Leave!" I turned my back on the Elder.

The Elder Fae growled at the slight.

Turning my back on him was a major show of disrespect to him, and I didn't give a shit.

"You will give the princess to me before all is said and done! Her *real* betrothed misses her terribly." Ronaldo smiled.

"Real betrothed?" Aurelia scoffed, raising her voice, a flash shining behind the emerald of her eyes.

"Malcolm will pay for the things he's done!" the Shadow King roared.

"He's baiting you, Shadow King," I said, gripping his shoulder. "Don't bite."

I tightened my arm protectively around Aurelia.

She glared at the Elder. "I will *never* be with Malcolm!" Aurelia yelled. "He can rot in Hell!"

"Shhh, I know. You're *all* mine—always," I assured her. "Don't let the old fool rile you up, my love," I said with a shake of my head. I would sooner die than let that bastard touch her ever again.

She is mine.

My wolf snarled in my mind at the merest suggestion of her being with someone else.

Least of all, fucking Malcolm!

Another man stepped forward, revealing himself, and I jumped in front of the Shadow King. "I know how badly you want to kill him," I warned. "But don't go out there, Channing."

Aurelia's father's face flushed red with so much rage that he trembled with it.

Aurelia crossed her arms over her chest and glared at Malcolm, ever defiant. "Where is Freya?" she demanded.

"Nothing he says is going to be true," I said as I pulled her away from the edge of the wards.

"Where is my brownie and the book your lover stole?" Malcolm sneered, completely ignoring me to address the princess.

"Do not speak to her!" the king roared beside me.

This was devolving *way* too quickly. I had to hold the king back. "You want your damn brownie? Then give me Freya. And the book never belonged to you! It was Aurelia's all along," I spat, turning back to face the assholes.

"No," Malcolm growled.

"Fine," I said with a shrug I hoped appeared nonchalant. "I'll *keep* the brownie. You left him to die in a fiery inferno anyway."

"I want the book!" he roared.

He beat against the wards in frustration but was unable to pass them.

No one with ill intent could ever get through them. A very powerful witch had set them up for me long ago.

"You're not getting that book," Aurelia hissed. "You have no right to it!" She unfolded her arms as if ready for a fight and planted her feet.

"I can make you give me the book," the bastard taunted, a malicious grin spreading over his face as he pulled something from his pocket.

Aurelia gasped aloud.

My mate's heart was racing so loudly that my inner wolf howled in warning.

Malcolm pulled Freya from his pocket, keeping her firmly trapped in his tight fist.

Aurelia's hands crackled with angry purple magic before her shadows began to snake up her arms, dark and brooding, ready to answer to her will.

Freya's limp form made me see red.

My wolf snarled in my mind, pushing at my restraints. He wanted to tear the fairy apart for so many reasons, but hurting Freya had definitely skyrocketed to the top of the list.

Without warning, Aurelia launched her magic at Malcolm through the wards, the power behind her shocking us all.

He dove out of the way with a roar, just in the nick of time. His hand opened instinctively, and Freya's limp form went flying through the air.

There was no time to think, I just reacted. Barreling through the ward, I dove to catch her before she hit the ground, and even more damage was done.

Ronaldo shouted something in the language of the Fae, his arms upraised.

I twisted mid-air, managing to get out of the way just as his electricity scorched through the ether toward me. I landed in a heap next to Freya, who lay crumpled on the ground, and scooped her up into my hand.

"Grey?" she breathed with her tiny voice, her body and face bruised. "I thought I'd never see you again."

"Hush. I've got you, now," I whispered. "Hang on."

"Die, Shifter King!" Ronaldo roared.

A scream tore through the air, and I knew it was my mate.

Ronaldo's lightning was met by Aurelia's and the chaotic purple magic exploded around us but didn't hit me. I rolled to my feet, crouched, ready for whatever was coming next.

At the exact same time Malcolm launched himself at me.

I turned fast, Freya still cradled in my hand, and elbowed him in the gut. A crunch sounded and I grinned.

He bellowed in pain, clearly out of practice.

Not wasting a moment, I rolled away, back to the edge of the wards as excruciating pain tore through my back, causing me to stumble. "Aurelia!" I shouted in desperation and tossed Freya to her on the other side of the wards as I fell to my knees. Electricity tore through me again, and my body twitched and convulsed as I fell face down, half inside the wards, half out.

The Shadow King, the man who would one day become my father-in-law, bellowed, his shadows lashing out at the men on the other side of the wards as he came to my defense. He directed a tendril of shadow at me. It wrapped around my body and pulled me back inside the wards and to safety.

"Grey!" Aurelia cried, her heart in her throat as she dropped to her knees beside me. Her hands were on me in an instant, trailing down my body and over my back. Healing magic pulsed between us, offering me an impossible amount of relief.

Turning my head to the side, I stared up at her in question.

If both her hands are free... where was Freya?

Aurelia grinned and jerked her head toward Freya, who was safely resting on our side of the ward, her little chest rising and falling with every breath.

"You did it, Grey. You got her back!" Aurelia grinned.

"No," I said, reaching out to rest a hand on her thigh. "We got her back. And we didn't even have to give him anything. Your reaction was flawless, mate," I commended her, before closing my eyes and resting my head on the dirt road with a groan.

"Maybe we finally have a win," she whispered, but turned at her father's shout of rage.

"Come back, cowards!" King Channing roared in outrage.

But Malcolm and Ronaldo sifted away, knowing they were beaten and no longer had anything to bargain with.

As Aurelia's healing magic soothed my injuries, I rolled to stare at Freya again. She was so small and fragile. I just wanted to protect her, always. She'd been with me forever, since before the Exile.

She has to be okay.

Fiona would be devastated if anything happened to her that was beyond our means to heal. They were sisters. And I would be devastated, too. The sprites were family and always would be. I could not bear the loss of either one of them.

CHAPTER 21
Aurelia

"Someone, help!" I yelled as we were sifted back to the facility and ran straight for the infirmary.

Grey cradled Freya's tiny, fragile body close as we ran.

It would have been a touching sight if I wasn't so scared *for* the little sprite. She looked badly banged up.

A healer peeked out of a room with wide eyes and beckoned us forward to give Freya a visual once over before shaking her head. "We don't have the right healing here for sprites, sir."

"We need Magna," I said with conviction.

If anyone can help, surely she can?

But where was she right now? She always seemed to uncannily just pop up whenever we needed her.

"She should be in my office, I think," Grey said, his tone clipped as he turned back toward the elevator.

"Stay here. I'll go get her!" Without waiting for his approval or consent, I raced ahead of him to the elevator and stabbed at the button. Freya was my friend, and this was the second time she'd been hurt on my account. She'd put herself in harm's way for me, to protect me, to get me help when no one else could. I shuddered with quiet rage.

I'll make Malcolm pay before all this is over.

The doors *dinged* open on the top floor, and I rushed down the hall to Grey's office.

The door flew open at my approach, and Asher stood there, his immense arms crossed over his broad chest. If we weren't already close friends, I'd find him intimidating as hell. "What's happened?" he asked, his brow heavy set.

"I need Magna," I breathed. "Freya's in bad shape!" I brushed past him, not wanting to waste time.

"You got her back?" he asked, shocked as he followed me into the office.

I scanned the faces in the office, my heart racing, but there was no sign of her. "We did, but she isn't well. We need healing powers we don't have. Where is Magna?"

Fenrick stepped forward and placed a soothing hand on my arm. "Calm down, Princess. Take me to her, I can help."

"You can?" I asked, hope bursting to life within me.

"I have extensive healing abilities, just like I imagine you will once you are afforded to the opportunity to practice." Fenrick squeezed my arm.

"I already have some," I said without further explanation. I'd healed Grey when Ronaldo and Malcolm had attacked, but I didn't have time for him to placate me. I spun on my heel and ran back down the hall. Rushed steps followed behind me as I stopped at the elevator and jabbed my finger into the button impatiently.

Asher stepped up next to me. "We'll get her fixed up, Aurelia."

Fenrick flanked my other side.

"How can you be so sure?" I asked, without meeting his gaze. "You didn't see her. She's covered in bruises. She's more black and blue than anything else!" Tears stung the backs of my eyes, and I willed them not to spill.

"She's the strongest little sprite I've ever seen," he answered. "She'll make it through this." Asher offered me a confident grin.

The elevator doors opened, and we stepped inside.

I'm glad someone feels that confident about her recovery chances.

I pushed the button repeatedly for the floor of the infirmary, my nerves aching with anxiety and stress, and my gut with guilt. Shuffling my feet, I stood there waiting impatiently for the damn doors to open again. They finally slid open, and I moved to rush out, but a hand on my shoulder stopped me. I glanced up at the numbers and huffed with annoyance.

Wrong floor. Shit.

"Aurelia, I'm here for Freya," Magna said, appearing out of nowhere before stepping into the elevator to join us.

I collapsed into the other woman's arms with a sob, grateful we'd found her—or she'd found us. Freya needed healing desperately, and with two friends present and capable of substantive healing, my relief was tangible.

She patted my back as the elevator doors closed behind her.

"She's injured badly!" I cried. "And it's all my fault. She's my friend and such a tiny little thing… she shouldn't have to endure shit like this!"

"We will do all we can," Magna soothed. "Breathe deeply and be calm. Panic will help no one, my dear."

The elevator finally stopped at the correct floor, and I straightened my shoulders. Magna was right. I had to be strong for Freya. I swiped at the tears on my cheeks and strode into the sterile hall. I'd secured help, which was the most important thing. Now, it was up to them.

Father subtly nodded his head to a door at the end of the infirmary, letting me know without words where Freya was.

I dragged Magna to it and knocked on the door before pushing it open, too impatient to care about manners at a time like this.

Grey's face softened when he saw me, and he opened his arms for me to step into his strength.

Magna rushed from my side to Freya, her hands glowing green as she immediately began the healing process, calling upon her magic to aid our littlest family member.

I rested my head on my shifter's chest, praying to whatever gods were listening that the tiny sprite would be okay.

Please, she has to be. We love her. We need her.

"We are no good to her here," Grey said quietly as he squeezed me tightly. "She's in good hands now. We need to find that book before the Elders do."

I nodded. He was right. Magna could handle healing Freya, and she would be as good as new soon.

Grey led me from the room with an arm around my shoulders, my father, Fenrick, and Asher following behind.

I had been in a daze the whole elevator ride, just hoping against hope that Magna would be able to heal poor Freya. Her tiny, broken body would haunt me much like when Fiona was injured at Malcolm's house of horrors. They might be palm-sized sub-Fae, but they had the hearts of lions and had been through too much grief already.

Another elevator ride later, we walked into Grey's office.

Zeke and Dan sat waiting in the chairs in front of his desk.

Someone must have cleaned Grey's office because everything was back in its place. I couldn't even bring myself to blush about what had happened there the night before. There was just too much at stake. My mind was a chaotic whirl of emotions and our passionate reunion, while thoroughly rapturous, was the furthest thing from my thoughts at this point.

Zeke smirked but quickly dropped it when he saw the expression on my face. "What happened?" he asked, his usually stoic façade creasing with concern.

"Malcolm and Ronaldo were at the wards with Freya," Grey responded with a sigh.

"The Elders know where to find us now. They probably wanted to talk to me alone because I would have traded myself for Freya. I've done it before. They know I'm a soft touch for those little girls." I ran a hand down my face in frustration.

"Don't beat yourself up about it, Aurelia," said my mate gently. "All we can do now is look for the *real* book and trust in Magna's ability to heal her." Grey squeezed me tighter to him and led me to the chair behind his desk. He sat in the chair and pulled me down into his lap possessively.

I reached for the book and pulled it into my arms before opening it.

Grey rested his chin on my shoulder, reading the book with me.

Where the hell did I hide the damn book? It was so long ago... I was just a child. Would I even be able to find it without my memories? "I don't know if this is even going to have the answers we need," I mused aloud, shaking my head in dismay.

"Why not?" Grey asked, kissing my cheek. "You've clearly always been a prodigy, my love. If anyone can figure out their own game of hide-and-seek, it's you."

I sighed, not quite filled with the same level of confidence in my abilities as my mate. "I went to a lot of trouble to make sure no one could find it. I even blocked my own memories to accomplish it. And yet Magna easily broke the spell on it so others could see what it said."

"So, you're thinking that you need to unlock your memories?" Grey asked. "That didn't go so well the last time."

"I went through that block like a freight train, and I still wasn't able to retrieve everything," I agreed.

"Maybe there's an answer you need in the book." Grey squeezed me. "Just have a read, give it a chance. Something might jog your memory, just as intended."

I glanced down at the words. How did I write in such a beautiful, curling script at such a young age? How was it even possible? I turned the page and gasped, my mind spinning with memories.

I ran through the forest outside the castle giggling wildly as someone chased me.

"Princess, don't run from me! How am I supposed to protect you if you're constantly running way?"

Fenrick's panicked voice made me giggle more, and I ran faster. "You're supposed to catch me, silly." I ducked into the hollow of a tree and hid as he passed. I giggled again as I ran in the other direction, away from Fenrick. He was always so stuffy and never wanted to let me play.

Running into the stables, I hid in one of the stalls with a beautiful mare called Buttercup. Backing into the corner, I plastered myself there so Fenrick couldn't find me. Unexpected voices filled the space, and I strained my ears to listen. It wasn't Fenrick. It was Malcolm, the Captain of the King's Guard. He was talking to someone in hushed tones.

"You know what will happen if we do this," he said to someone I couldn't see.

"You must!" they hissed back. "She is too dangerous to be here. If she knew what she is capable of, she could overthrow everything we have built here. Our plans for both realms could be ruined," the man whispered forcefully.

I didn't recognize his voice, but it sounded strangely familiar.

"The king will hunt me down if I do this," Malcolm growled back in frustration.

"Then dump the girl in the first major city. She won't be able to take care of herself. Maybe she'll die, and it will save us all the trouble of having to kill her later."

Who were they talking about, I wondered. Why would they want to kill a girl? What they were saying didn't make any sense.

Heavy footsteps sounded in the stable, and I peeked out through the wooden slats of the stall. Malcolm and the strange man were gone, and Fenrick stood on the other side of the stall. I breathed a tangible sigh of relief.

I didn't think it would be good for them to see me when they were plotting someone's death. Who were they going to kill, and why would my daddy hunt him down for it? I poked my face out of the stall, the game over.

Fenrick frowned when he saw the expression on my face. "What is it, Princess?" he asked.

"How did you find me?" I asked with a stomp of my foot.

He crouched in front of me, still wearing his frown. "This is one of your favorite places to hide, Aurelia. Of course, I found you here."

Back in the present, I shook my head to clear the memory of the past, my breathing a little heavier than usual.

Everyone in the room was staring at me with matching frowns on their faces.

Grey gripped my chin and turned me to face him. "What happened, my love? I called your name several times," he said. "You were lost, just staring blankly in some kind of trance."

"I remembered something," I said, glad to be safe with Grey. "I was playing a game of hide-and-seek. I ran from Fenrick and hid in the stables. I heard Malcolm talking to someone, nad I'm pretty sure it was Ronaldo." I grimaced.

"You never told me about that!" Fenrick crossed his arms over his chest, his frown deepening.

"That's not the point," I said, waving him off. "Is it at all possible that I might have made it back through the portal as a child and hidden the book there? Where they'd least expect it?"

"That doesn't make any sense, though," Grey said and shook his head. "Why would you have gone back? And how? You were cold and alone in most of the visions you've seen. Even Magna can corroborate that."

"I don't know," I answered, a niggling sensation building in my gut. "But I have a feeling the other book has something to do with it." I rubbed at my temples and pursed my lips as I mulled it all over.

Why was that memory attached to *this* book? It had to be important... but how?

"Princess, what did Malcolm say?" Fenrick growled, interrupting me.

"They were talking about my abduction and inevitable death," I said hotly.

"And all the while you were hiding in the stall," Fenrick said softly despite the flare in my mood.

I nodded. There wasn't much more to say. As a child, I hadn't known who they had been talking about, but after what'd happened in my life up until now, they were *definitely* talking about killing me. "Malcolm tried to play me. He convinced me into thinking he was protecting me from the Council, but it's plain as day that was a lie. He was doing exactly as they wanted."

I sighed in frustration. The more I knew, the less I understood. Every time I learned something new, I just had more questions. I turned my attention back to the book, running my fingers along the swooping letters.

Fenrick cleared his throat. "Perhaps it would be prudent to check the stables, Princess. Gut feelings exist for a reason, and if you feel a connection, we should not overlook the possibility. Even if it doesn't lead us directly to the book, it could reveal more clues."

"I need to know for sure," I said, not looking up from the book. "It doesn't make sense why I would return only to come back, especially when at the time, I remembered the life I had there. Surely, I would have gone to my parents, as any child would?"

"Keep reading," Grey said, gently nudging me. "You might remember more."

I glanced back down at the book, reading the words with intense concentration, but no new memories came to me. Turning the page, I frowned.

"Is this some kind of map?" I asked, showing the page to Grey.

Grey grimaced. "I can't see anything there, mate."

"What?" I asked, my own brow furrowing. "But Magna already took the enchantment off the book." I peered down at the hand-drawn map in the book with a hint of annoyance.

"Maybe this is a different enchantment," he suggested. "Magna might not have known about it."

Fenrick stood and walked over, staring at the book in my lap but shook his head as well. "I don't see anything either, Princess," Fenrick grumbled. "Clearly, whatever you're seeing was intended for your eyes only."

"Is it a map to the book, I wonder?" I tapped the page with my finger, astounded by the lengths I went to as a child to keep the book secret and safe. I turned the book sideways but still couldn't figure out what the map was. Nothing seemed familiar, at least with what limited memories I possessed. "I think we need Magna, but I don't want to disturb her while she's working on Freya."

"In the meantime, can you draw it so we can see it?" Grey asked. "Maybe one of us will be able to recognize it?"

"Maybe. I don't know. I was a child when I drew this. I didn't even know I could draw this well." I set the book back down on the desk.

"You were always drawing me pictures," Father offered with a grin. "You had your mother's artistic gift."

Grey opened a drawer in the desk and pulled out a stack of papers and a pencil and set them on the desk next to the book. "Stop doubting yourself, my love," he said. "If anyone can figure all this out, it's you. We all believe in you."

Nodding, I picked up the pencil and brushed my hand over a clean sheet of paper, ready to begin. I just really hoped I could do this and that my everyone's faith wasn't misplaced. This might prove to be the only way to move forward and put a stop to the Elders' plans once and for all.

As it was, this involved more than Faery. They had plans for *both* realms, and I shuddered to think what those plans would mean for the rest of us Undesirables.

CHAPTER 22
Grey

"Argh!" Aurelia yelled in obvious frustration and slammed the pencil down on the desk.

"What's wrong?" I asked, glancing over my mate's shoulder.

"It keeps moving! Every time I try to draw something, it moves. The paths change. I don't think it's going to let me draw it. Like it won't allow itself to be copied. I'm obviously going to need to learn more, because this is ridiculous!" She placed her head in her hands in defeat.

"Can you read anything else on there? Does it give you any indication of what it might be?" I rubbed her shoulders. She was seriously tense, but I would be too. It wasn't fair that this burden was solely on her. It was a heavy weight to bear, the future of Faery... and it frustrated me to no end, though I did my best to hide it in a show of strength and solidarity.

We are mates. She should be able to lean on me.

"No, nothing here sounds familiar to me." She shook her head.

"Perhaps try reading it aloud. Maybe one of us will know what it's related to." I suggested.

"Motherfucker!" she screamed, slamming her fists on the desk. "All the letters are scrambled now. What the hell! It's like it senses my intention and reacts."

What the hell kind of enchantment did she put on this map that she couldn't share it with anyone? And to think she performed this level of magic as a child was intimidating to say the least.

She'll be a true force to be reckoned with when she gets all her memories back.

"Maybe keep reading the other pages, just to yourself? It might help. You may need to absorb it all before it makes sense," I said, patting her on the shoulder before kissing her on the head.

Dan rushed into the office and frantically waved a hand at me, then stepped back out into the hall.

What now?

I walked out to meet him, frowning.

He held out his phone to me. A video was queued to play.

I hit the play button and cursed under my breath, my hands turning to fists at my sides. It was grainy, obviously from a surveillance camera, but it showed a man shifting into wolf form in full view of the camera before proceeding to attack someone. Then the video cut to a news story. "Where was this taken?" I asked with a growl.

"Right here in Dallas, on the shifter side," Dan answered through gritted teeth.

"Fuck me. Is there a way we can spin this? Debunk it as a Photoshop stunt or something?" I ran a hand down my face. "It's already everywhere, boss. The guy is in a human jail."

"How the fuck did the human police manage to catch a damn shifter?" I groaned.

This was the last thing we needed piled on top of everything else!

"They had to have had help. There's no way a human, or even multiple humans, could take down a shifter—especially during a killing frenzy." Dan shuffled his feet warily.

"Even though this prick has fucked up royally, there's got to be a way to get the guy out of jail. He's going to end up in a fucking lab somewhere and then we all risk being exposed." I unclenched and re-clenched my fists, wanting desperately to punch something.

How could one of my own shifters be so stupid? Our entire existence has been a highly guarded secret for centuries.

Zeke turned to us with a scowl, hearing the commotion from the hall. "What's going on?"

"A fucking shifter went wolf on someone, and it was caught on a security camera," I growled.

Zeke pulled his phone from his pocket and typed something into it. He frowned at the screen a moment later. "Headlines are saying that a bystander subdued the wolf with magic." Zeke tilted his head back to stare at the ceiling in an *oh, fuck* gesture.

"What the fuck?" I roared. "Does it say anything about the location of the bystander? Who the fuck would dare to openly use magic in front of humans?"

Aurelia gasped.

"What is it?" I asked, spinning to face her and stepping back into the office. Was she having another memory? Did she find something out about the real book's location?

"Something they said in the memory... They inferred they had plans for *both* realms. What if this is it? Maybe they're behind this stunt! They're trying to out us to the humans so that they'll eradicate us for them..." Aurelia sat back in my tall office chair, a haunted expression on her beautiful face.

"It's probably even more nefarious than that," I agreed. "But I bet I know someone who has some answers." I grinned, waving for Dan and Zeke to follow me.

"Where are you going?" Aurelia asked.

"I'm going to have a chat. Stay with the book, beautiful. Fenrick will keep watch."

Fenrick nodded, agreeing immediately to maintaining his duty and vigil.

He had been her protector as a child and had guarded her well so far. I trusted him above most to watch her back. With a curt nod of my own, I jogged from the office to the elevator.

"Who are we going to have a chat with?" Zeke asked as he came up beside me.

"Who else but their spy would know the Council's plans?" I smiled grimly.

"You think Erik will tell us anything even if he does know?" Zeke pushed the button on the wall to summon the elevator.

"I'm not going to give him a fucking choice, am I?" I stepped inside the elevator and pushed the button to the level where the facility's holding cells were.

My men followed in behind me.

"He's a Council spy, so he's adept at torture," Zeke said as the elevator *dinged*. "He'll be more than familiar with not only doling it out, but enduring it too."

I stepped out of the elevator and strode down the hall.

As if on cue, Karma started screaming from her cell like a goddamn banshee.

"Shut the fuck up!" I roared back at her. The bitch was asking for execution if she didn't stop annoying the fuck out of me.

"What are you going to do to me?" Karma yelled, ignoring my order.

That's it. I've had enough.

The dumb bitch didn't know when to quit. I stormed to her cell and grasped her by the throat through the bars. "I said, shut the fuck up. You sold us out. You're lucky you're sitting here in a cell, instead of me throwing you in the enchanted ring. You could be dead right now. Is that what you want? To go out the way Layla did?" I squeezed her throat, crushing her airway.

Her eyes widened as she gasped for breath, reaching up desperately to claw my hand.

Yeah, I bet you regret your decision to run your mouth now, don't you?

I tossed her away in disgust, my rage lending fuel to my strength.

Her back hit the bars on the other side of the cell with a bone-crunching *thud,* and she collapsed to the cold, concrete floor.

I spun on my heel and stormed down the hall of cells. I didn't have time for any more of her shit. Erik was in a cell at the very end of the hall, furthest away from all the other prisoners. The cells at the rear were special. They blocked magic just as the brownie's cell did, but I was a lot more cautious about opening this door. Erik was cunning and much larger than the brownie, being one of the pure-blooded Fae. He was also skilled in combat even without his magic.

"Be vigilant. He may try to rush us when I open the door," I said over my shoulder.

Zeke and Dan nodded as one and adopted combat stances.

I rolled my shoulders and grabbed the key from my pocket. It was the master key to all the cells on this level. I was the only person in possession of one. "Stay back from the door, Erik!" I shouted through the door before sliding the key card in the lock and opening the door with a distinct *click.*

Erik sat back on the cot with a smug grin on his stupid face, as if completely unphased.

I stormed in, and the door closed behind us as Dan and Zeke having followed me in. "What do the Elders want with the human realm?" I asked, crossing my arms over my chest.

Erik shrugged one shoulder but kept his mouth shut. There was no way he was going to offer anything up easily, that was for damn sure. But it was worth a try.

I glared at the Fae and took a threatening step forward.

"What are you going to do, Grey? Torture me? Good luck with that." Erik laughed, shaking his head as if I wasn't the Shifter King of Faery.

"Do you know who I am?" Zeke rumbled as he stepped forward, his huge, hulking form threatening as fuck even to the most powerful of supernaturals.

Is he about to use his Rider powers on the Fae?

Erik visibly gulped and nodded, the bravado slipping from his smug face.

"Not so tough now, hmmm?" I asked, raising my brows with a smirk.

Zeke laughed, deep and threatening. "You know I can show you your worst nightmares and feast on your soul while I'm doing it."

"It's why you were exiled, criminal! The Hunt was barbaric." Erik sneered.

"You're going to tell us what you know, Erik, or you *will* be the next victim of the Wild Hunt." I shrugged, reveling in my nonchalance.

In the end it wasn't up to me, but Asher would take my request into consideration and would most likely run the fucker down in the forests of Faery when Aurelia and I got us back home. We had to succeed in getting us all back home, especially now that the humans knew about us.

"I won't betray the Council," Erik spat, finding his courage once more.

I turned to Zeke and nodded. "Did the Council out us to the humans?" I asked.

Zeke walked over to his cot, gripped Erik by the chin and stared into his eyes.

It only took a second before the stubborn Fae started screaming and thrashing. Erik tried closing his eyes tightly, but the nightmare was already playing out.

Zeke straightened and crossed his arms over his chest, a look of dark satisfaction upon his face.

The screams would die down a short while later, so we waited. It would do us no good to try to ask questions while he was hollering at the top of his lungs because he was trapped in his own head.

"Zeke is a scary motherfucker," Dan whispered next to me, his brows raised.

"Yeah, so maybe think twice before you shoot a woman with a tranquillizer dart in the future," Zeke muttered.

It sounded like everyone was angry over that particular situation.

Poor Dan.

"I'm going to ask again, Erik. Did the Council out shifters and magic to the humans?"

Muddy brown eyes turned to me, and he nodded wordlessly.

"And what is their end game here?" I asked.

Erik braced himself for pain and shook his head, refusing to divulge any more.

Fuck.

He wasn't going to give us anything. He would rather live out his worst nightmares over and over again than give us anything more.

"We should just talk to Ash," I said with a scowl. "Once we go home, you can hunt him in the wild as you used to." I shrugged and turned to leave.

"You mean to go back?" Erik called out after me with a frown.

"Yes, we are going home," I growled at him before addressing the rider. "Leave him here and you can do what you want to punish him once we take down the Elders."

"I really want to give him another nightmare." Zeke chuckled.

"Do what you will, I honestly don't care." I waved a hand over my shoulder. "If he gives you any more information, though, let me know."

I walked out of the cell and down the hall.

Karma was blessedly silent.

Meanwhile, Dan followed closely behind me.

I turned to him after pushing the button for the elevator. "Send a team to investigate the human jail. Someone has to be able to get that shifter out of there before he's taken by the human authorities and tested," I said. The elevator doors opened, and I stepped inside.

Dan stepped in after me, his nose in his phone as he typed away on it. "Got it, boss. I'll have our best team on it now." Dan never glanced up from his phone.

"Do you even know who the best team is?" I sighed.

"I've been going through the files in my office. I take my job seriously, you know," he said, affronted.

"About time." I leaned back against the wall, anxious to get back up to my office and my mate. I hated having to wait in the elevator. If only I could sift like the Fae, I could just pop into my office. But not only was it not an ability that shifters had, but I'd also placed wards against sifting within the building. Friends and allies could sift *to* the facility but had to be given permission to enter the old-fashioned way.

The doors opened, and shouting came from my office, the noise carrying down the hall. I didn't even think about it, I just sprinted down the corridor to my open office door.

Fenrick was standing over my mate, his expression distraught.

Aurelia's eyes were wide and unseeing.

I pushed the Fae away from her and snatched her up from the chair. Her heart was beating wildly in my ears, unmistakable with my enhanced shifter hearing. "She's alive," I said aloud. "I just don't know what's happening."

"Is she having a vision?" Fenrick asked in shock.

Why would he be shocked? Some Fae had the gift of Sight, like Magna, and were often referred to as seers. My mate could very well have that gift too. We had yet to uncover everything Aurelia could do with her magic. "Maybe? I don't know. I've never seen her do this," I said.

"She already has so many gifts," her royal protector marveled. "This could place an even bigger target on her back," Fenrick whispered.

I squeezed her to me, holding her tightly, giving her my strength. It wasn't her fault she was chosen or had all this power. She'd never asked for it. It was just who she was.

Who she was born to be...

"Maybe it has something to do with the book?" I suggested hopefully.

"It's possible that it was the book. She was reading it when her eyes rolled back in her head." Fenrick shook his head, watching on with concern.

"What could she possibly be seeing? What's even in that blasted book?" I growled as I sat with her in the chair behind my desk. I ran my hand through her hair and kissed her forehead, rocking her gently. "Wake up, my love. I'm here. Wake up."

She twitched in my arms and moaned softly as she came to. "Grey?" she mumbled, her voice airy and distant. "I know what they are doing... and where to find the book."

Holy shit.

CHAPTER 23

Aurelia

Magna smiled softly as she caressed the book. "You must hide this, child."

"Where?" I asked as I chewed my lip. I didn't know any safe places in the human realm. I only just found someone kind enough to take me in. Where could I possibly hide it?

"No one can know, not even you, until the time is right. The Elders have terrible plans, and if we don't do things exactly right, we could doom us all." Magna sat back in her armchair.

"What am I going to do?" I mumbled.

She reached up and patted my hand. "You must hide it where they least suspect it."

They would never expect it to be at home. Could I go back for just a minute and hide it in one of my usual hiding places? Mommy and Daddy must be so sad. If I had known that Malcolm and that man were talking about me, then I would have told someone of their plans. I would have warned them or told Fenrick!

Magna said it's better that I didn't. That future wouldn't turn out the way it was supposed to.

"How do I get to the portal?" I asked.

"No one has seen the portal in centuries, I'm afraid." She shook her head in dismay.

"But I was brought through the portal into the forest," I answered, fidgeting and twisting my fingers together.

Magna closed her eyes briefly but opened them a heartbeat later with a snap. She moved to a book on the shelf and pulled a different book off. She flipped through the book and grimaced. "You're going to need to use this enchantment, child." She handed me the book that was written in the language of the Fae.

I cocked my head to the side. "If I do this, how will I ever know where it's hidden?" I asked, peering up at the woman.

"You won't remember until the time is precisely right. I know I am putting a lot on your small shoulders, but I promise it's for a good cause. You will be happy one day, and our people—all of them—will prosper because of it."

"I just want to go home. I won't even run and hide from Fenrick anymore if I can just go home." My lower lip wobbled.

"I know." She rubbed my back. "It's not a good idea right now though. It's too dangerous and there are too many chances for the future we need to be lost..."

"What happens if I just go home and stay there and forget this world even exists?" I sniffled, peering up to her with pleading eyes. Why couldn't I just go home? Was it really that bad? Surely, my parents could protect me? They were the king and queen!

"If you go back and stay there, you will die, Princess," she said in a low voice, and her words rang with truth.

I gasped and stared down at the enchantment in the book she'd handed me. Was she telling me the whole truth or trying to scare me into doing what she wanted me to? "You've seen my death?" I asked in a small voice.

"A million different ways," she breathed, glancing away, her face paling, and a ghostly emptiness flitting behind her eyes.

"I don't want to die," I whispered as I straightened my shoulders. I would do what needed to be done, and I would suffer if I had to. I had already suffered the cold and loneliness. How hard could it be?

"I know, Princess. I don't want you to die either. It's why we have to be very careful." She turned away as if to collect her thoughts and sighed.

I picked up the golden book and stood, making my way to Magna. "Can you sift?"

"Yes, I can." She nodded. "Where do you need me to go?"

I thought hard about the place we'd come out in the portal all those months ago.

Magna turned curious eyes on me. "I thought you understood." She crossed her arms over her chest. "Only death awaits you there."

"I do," I assured her. "I'm not going to stay there. I'm very good at sneaking around the palace grounds..." I squeezed her arm.

Magna nodded. "Very well." And then we were swirling through space and time to the shimmering portal.

"Come on," I said, waving her over to the portal.

"I can't come with you, Princess. No one can know what you do with that book. I must remember some things about you but not all." She took a step back.

"Will you be here when I come back?" I asked with a hint of fear in my voice.

"I will see it when you come back, but I fear lingering here too long." She glanced around the clearing as if she was waiting for someone to jump out at us. Maybe she was.

"Okay, I'll be back." I took a step toward the shimmering portal with a small amount of trepidation, before taking a deep breath and stepping through. A sensation like cool water washed over me as I stepped into the glittering portal, but I was dry when I reached the other side. The forest in the palace grounds greeted me like an old friend.

Tree branches reached out in welcome, and a gust of wind nearly pushed me back, as if trying to save me.

I scanned the forest, allowing my Fae senses to wander.

A new urgency fell over the forest that made me tense. The trees were urging me to move. They wanted me to hide—fast.

I ran to a huge oak and just like the many times I'd played and hid from Fenrick, I ducked inside its hollow.

Bushes bent in front of the hollow, hiding me from whoever was coming.

"The king suspects it was me," Malcolm said angrily.

"Yes, I fear what he will do when he has proof." It was the same voice as before that answered him.

I peeked over the bushes carefully and my eyes widened when I saw Ronaldo the Elder, with his squinty eyes standing in front of Malcolm. Why was he there? What did he have to gain from my death? Our Elders were supposed to be wise. Why would I be a threat to them?

"How do we stop him from seeing the truth?" Malcolm growled again.

"We do not. You must stay in the human world to keep watch over the girl from afar. She has something we need. If you can convince her to work with us to take over the human world and make the undesirables our slaves—as they should be—even better." Ronaldo shrugged.

I nearly gasped but covered it quickly. They wanted to rule both realms? But why? They were already the most powerful individuals in all of Faery, so what good would it do them to rule the humans and their world of iron, too?

"If I can convince her to help us, she doesn't have to die, right? I can keep my betrothed?" Malcolm asked with a relieved sigh.

"Fine, so long as she remains ours to command. Now, get back to the human realm. Keep an eye on the princess until she is grown and find the book." Ronaldo waved a dismissive hand at his co-conspirator and sifted away.

I blinked the memory away. Strong arms were wrapped around my body, and I stared up into the beautiful dark eyes of my fated mate. "Grey?" I mumbled. "I know what they are doing... and where to find the book."

"My love, you scared the life out of me and poor Fenrick." He squeezed me tighter to him.

"I'm okay," I said. "I poured all my memories into that book. I put the most dangerous ones to us are in there." I wiggled in his arms.

He refused to loosen his hold, instead he stayed seated in his chair with me cradled in his lap.

"What did you see?" Fenrick asked hesitantly.

"I went back to Faery once, but I had to block out the memories or they might have been able to find it." I pursed my lips.

"You hid the book in Faery?" Grey asked, defeated.

Why does he sound defeated? I can just bring him through the portal with me to retrieve it.

"I didn't know the human realm," I explained. "I thought that was the best place. No one would have guessed a child would be strong enough to get themselves back home and then leave willingly, but the threat was clear." I shrugged as best I could in his tight embrace.

"You hid it in the very last place anyone would expect. Right under their damn noses. There's just one problem, Princess..." Fenrick flopped into the chair across from us.

"What is it?" I asked with a frown.

What am I missing? It's all so simple. We go to the forest, get the book, and come back to figure the rest out.

"You can't sift at all, not to mention between realms, and the portal is being watched closely by the Elders." Fenrick leaned forward on his elbows.

"Fuck," I said and ran a hand down my face. He was right. I wouldn't be able to bring anyone else along if my father or someone else sifted me there. Grey wouldn't be able to come with me.

Would two warriors be enough if the Council guards found us?

My thoughts raced back to Nickolas and his noble death. We'd had only a few soldiers with us at the time, and we were still in trouble and vastly outnumbered. I'd lost a friend that day. A tear leaked from my eye and rolled down my cheek, betraying my thoughts.

Grey wiped it away. "It's okay, my love. We'll figure out a way to get the book. Don't get upset now. You've done so much in such a short time," Grey whispered and kissed my forehead.

He thought I was crying because of the book? I was remembering the blood... and Nickolas' dying request.

Fenrick stared at me from across the desk. "You said you knew what the Elders are up to?" he asked.

"It's terrible and I'm not even sure if it's too late to stop them." I chewed on my lower lip. I patted Grey's arm.

He reluctantly let me sit up but didn't remove his arms from around my waist. "What is it?" Grey frowned.

"They want to enslave everyone, including the humans."

Fenrick stood abruptly, his hands clenched in anger. "They're mad. The humans will wipe the Fae off the face of the planet. They have iron weapons and technology that we don't, and their sheer numbers alone far outmatch us." He ran a shaky hand through his hair.

"That's a suicide mission," Grey murmured as his hands clenched my hips roughly.

"I don't know how long they have been plotting this. They could already have their plan in motion, just like I suggested earlier." I leaned my head back on Grey's shoulder and stared up at the ceiling, allowing a heavy sigh to escape me.

"The shifter," Grey said. "They are behind it. You're right. That has to be it."

I nodded. It was probably true. They'd been infiltrating the human world for a long time, now. They'd had centuries to do so. And now they were setting everything in motion to enslave all the people they perceived as weaker than them.

"So, what do we do?" I asked.

"I have a team on route to rescue the shifter from the human jail as we speak. They will get him out and then we find out what happened to make the idiot shift in public," said Grey as he shook his head.

Fenrick's eyes blazed with fury. "And then we get the book back and find a way to stop them!"

Dan burst into the room, his breathing shallow, as if he'd run up the stairs instead of taking the elevator. "The team is back. They have the shifter in the holding cells," he wheezed.

"That was quicker than I expected," Grey said and stood with me still in his arms.

I wiggled until he put me down. I appreciated the support and love, but I could stand on my own two teeth, literally and figuratively.

His arm snaked from around my waist as he rushed over to the door.

"I had already taken the initiative to send them when you asked earlier. I didn't want to tell you because I wasn't sure how you would react." Dan's cheeks turned pink.

"Good instincts. Your head's in the right place. We don't want our people coming up missing or being experimented on." Grey clapped him on the shoulder.

Together, we raced to the cells, unsure of what we were going to find. The team that Dan had assembled stood in the hall outside, ragged and worse for wear. A couple were even bleeding.

"Report!" Grey barked at them.

The three men glanced between each other warily and shuffled their feet nervously.

What could be so concerning that they were afraid to speak to their own boss and king?

The one in the middle stepped forward. Whoever he was, he had magic. There was a subtle buzz of it around him. He bowed his head in submission. "This was not your average jail break, boss. We barely made it out of there alive."

"Explain," Grey ordered. His hand tensed on my thigh as I stood just off to the side, but behind him.

"That wasn't a human jail," he answered. "The guards there had magic. Every last fucking one of them."

Oh, my gods. We were right... it's already begun.

CHAPTER 24

"What the fuck did you just say?" I growled, every inch of me instantly electrified at hearing the impossible.

That was a typical human jail. How the fuck did a bunch of supernaturals get in there and take it over?

"It wasn't normal magic either, boss. It was stronger and different from mine," the guy said.

"They're Fae?" Aurelia asked with wide eyes. She turned to stare at me in horror.

But why on earth would they take over the human jails when we had our own ways of dealing with our people? Was this a part of their seizing power from the humans?

"How long have they been here?" I asked.

My team of three bowed their heads and offered only silence. They had no answers.

I sighed.

Fuck. All right, there's only one way to get answers then...

I still needed to talk with the shifter who'd shifted in public. Perhaps I could find out how he'd become the Council's target. They'd basically set him up as a sacrificial lamb. But how did they make him shift in front of the camera? Shifters knew better than to snap when being provoked.

Fenrick scrubbed a hand over his face in frustration. "We need to ask the shifter," he said through gritted teeth, echoing my thoughts.

"Where is he?" I asked the group.

The guy in the middle, one of our best and a warlock, pointed to a cell a couple down from Karma.

The shifter was lying on a cot and appeared to be sleeping.

"Was he checked over by a healer?" Aurelia frowned as we approached.

"No, he's been like that since we found him. I think he was drugged," the warlock said.

"For fuck's sake. Someone go and get a damn healer!" I barked.

Fenrick waved me off. "No need. I'm a decent healer by Fae standards."

"I'm not exactly happy with Fae standards at the moment," I said offhandly.

"Watch it," Aurelia warned. "He's on our side, remember. Not to mention the fact you're mated to a Fae, or had you forgotten?" She tapped her foot, one prominent eyebrow cocked at me.

Reaching through the bars, Fenrick held his hands over the shifter's body, and they glowed green with healing magic.

He moaned and blinked his eyes open. "Where am I?" he mumbled. "This doesn't look like the human jail."

"That was no human jail," the warlock said.

Did he really think he was in a supernatural jail of some sort? We just didn't have those, for the most part. "What's your name?" I asked the shifter.

His eyes locked on mine for only a second before he averted his gaze. "Taryn, my king," he said from his cot.

"So, you do know who I am then?" I asked, raising a brow.

"Yes. I am very old even though I don't appear it. I knew your father before his passing all those years ago," he said sadly.

"We will get back to that in a minute," I said as I glanced at Aurelia.

Her shoulders stiffened with his words, but she remained tight lipped.

"What is it you wish to know?" Taryn asked.

"How does someone as old as you get caught on camera shifting and attacking humans?" There *had* to be a good explanation. I didn't want this man dead, especially after the way we retrieved him.

"I don't know. There was something strange about the whole incident." He shook his head.

"What do you mean by strange?" Aurelia asked and stepped closer to the bars.

I pulled her back gently.

She scowled at me. She wanted answers as much as we all did.

But just because I didn't want Taryn dead didn't mean I trusted him so close to my mate.

"I was just walking by a shop and there was a strange scent in the air. It had an almost chemical aroma. I became irrationally angry. I lost control and then shifted." He raised himself up and scooted forward on the small cot.

Fenrick withdrew, his job done, giving us center stage.

"A chemical smell? That sounds more like something pertaining to the humans than the Fae," I said as I rubbed a hand across my chin.

"But why would humans expose us? Even if some small sect of them knew about us, they wouldn't want mass hysteria." Aurelia leaned forward again, shuffling her feet while she chewed her lip in thought.

"What do the Fae have to do with any of this?" Taryn asked with a growl, his inner wolf rising to the surface. He sniffed the air and cocked his head to the side as he looked between Fenrick and Aurelia.

"That is my mate and her guardian, and they will be respected!" I barked at the shifter.

His glare turned to curiosity before he averted his eyes.

Good.

I needed more information from him, and if he thought they were wicked Fae, then he wouldn't be as forthcoming or as helpful as he was currently being.

"We've discovered that the Fae want to enslave us all now," I informed him, leaning my back against the wall and bringing Aurelia with me into the protective circle of my arms again.

"It wasn't bad enough that they exiled us, but now they want to enslave us too?" Taryn scoffed.

"Apparently. And this whole situation has their dirty dealings all over it." I stared the shifter down. "How did *you* come to be on their list?"

"Even after he was disgraced and executed, I was an ardent supporter of your father. I was loud about it, too, and attempted to rise up against our oppressors. They have long memories, it seems." He stood abruptly.

I tensed.

Fenrick did too and immediately took a step to block Aurelia from the shifter's view.

Once a protector, always a protector.

"He wasn't dead," Aurelia's whisper was choked on a sob.

Taryn's gaze snapped to hers. There was anger in his eyes and the scent of his fury filled the space.

I nearly choked on the sour stench.

"You dare lie to me after all this time? I watched his execution with my own eyes!" He took a threatening step forward, vibrating with rage.

"Watch your tone with the princess, mutt. I saw him alive and well and stuck in a Fae prison cell right next to hers," Fenrick snapped, stomping to the bars.

This conversation was devolving fast, and tensions as well as emotions were flaring. We'd gotten almost everything we needed from the jailed shifter, but something just wasn't adding up. "Easy, Fenrick. He can't get to my mate, nor would he. Would you, Taryn?" I raised a brow in question.

"No, never, my king. I just don't believe it," he whispered.

"Whoever they killed was not the king. I made friends with Nickolas in that cell... he saved my life." Aurelia turned and buried her face in my chest as tears filled her eyes.

Grimacing, I redirected the conversation. "This isn't the point." I rubbed Aurelia's back in soothing circles. "What happened in the jail? You were stone-cold unconscious until Fenrick healed you just now."

"I was shifting uncontrollably until they knocked me out with a needle. Then I woke up here. That's all I remember." He glanced around the holding area, his shoulders slumping.

"What the fuck did the humans come up with that could make a shifter go crazy like that and why? Did the Fae have something to do with how that was made?" I asked aloud to no one in particular.

"I think we're getting ahead of ourselves here, and I don't want to discuss plans in front of the other prisoners," Aurelia said raising her face to eye Karma warily.

"Agreed." Fenrick nodded, still glaring at Taryn. "We should head back to the office and devise a plan. We can't really do anything about this mystery right now. We still have our main goal to achieve."

Retrieving the book from Faery...

I nudged Aurelia.

She turned to leave without a backward glance at either prisoner. She was getting the whole royal act down quickly for someone who grew up never having anything for the most part.

I grinned. She would be my queen one day, and I was glad she would live up to the title in every way imaginable. My mate was still her own puzzle yet to be put together in her entirety. But when she came into her full power, she would be a grand and intimidating queen, indeed.

When we got into the elevator, I reached to push the button for the top floor.

Aurelia grabbed my arm. "Can we check on Freya first?" she asked with tears pooling in her eyes.

I could deny my mate nothing. What happened to the ruthless leader of the Syndicate? I used to be so cold and unfeeling. This incredible woman was going to be the death of that image, I was sure of it.

But would that be such a bad thing?

I nodded my head and pushed the button for the infirmary instead.

Face still streaked with tears, Aurelia raced out of the elevator as soon as the doors opened.

I followed behind her to the room in which we'd left Freya in Magna's capable hands.

Fiona sat on the small empty cot with her head in her hands, silently sobbing.

"No," Aurelia gasped. "Please no!"

"What?" I asked, searching the room for the injured sprite. Where was she? She had to be here. And where was Magna? "What's going on?" I croaked. "Where's Freya?"

Fiona sniffled and turned her watery gaze on me. Her eyes were red rimmed from crying, and I swore to all the gods in existence that if this was one of their ridiculous pranks, I would strangle them myself.

"She was injured too badly," she breathed. "Nothing that Magna did helped." Fiona broke down into another wave of sobs.

I was shaking my head, already denying the truth before the words were even fully out of her mouth. "No," I murmured in disbelief.

It can't be.

Magna walked into the doorway and stopped, her expression grave as she met my gaze. "It wasn't that I'm afraid. They tainted her blood with something that would not allow her to heal. They... I'm sorry. They experimented on her."

"They did what?" Aurelia gasped as she sat like a stone on the bed next to Fiona, who was still quietly sobbing.

"It's like the shifter and that chemical, but different, isn't it?" I asked as I ran a hand down my face, my blood boiling inside my own skin.

"It would seem so," Magna said softly. "I'm sorry for your loss, Shifter King."

What the fuck was the Council doing? Why were they experimenting on their own damn people? They were fucking monsters! "I don't care how long it takes, or what I have to do, I *will* see the Council fall," I vowed. I'd lost one of my sprites, something I'd hoped never to face. I'd wanted to return to Faery with both Freya and Fiona by my side... but now that future was lost to us, and Fiona had lost her sister.

Aurelia stared at me sadly, probably already knowing who would make them all pay. This had all been firmly on her shoulders and I had a feeling it was only the beginning of her trials. "I'll kill him for this," she whispered.

"I would rather you not have blood on your hands," I said as I pulled her from the cot and into my arms.

"It's too late for that. My soul is already stained with the blood of my enemies and my friends. I will end them all for this, and for what they did to Nickolas." A single tear traced down her cheek before she swiped at it angrily.

"Let's go get the damn book so we can end this once and for all," I said, reaching down to stroke Fiona's little head, before pulling my mate from the room. We didn't need to be in there anymore. What was done was done. The scent of death there permeated the air and made my over-sensitive nose twitch.

"Fenrick!" Aurelia called out to her guardian. "Find my father. We are going to need his help if there are any problems."

Fenrick nodded and pushed the button to the elevator.

I wrapped my arms around Aurelia and brushed a kiss across her forehead.

"How is it that everything is moving so fast, but it feels like I'm standing still?" She laid her head on my chest, her heart hammering against mine.

Magna walked out of the room a moment later, leaving Fiona to her grief.

"You found your memories, Princess?" she asked, her tone uneven and giving nothing away.

"I did, and I understand so much more now," Aurelia answered the seer with a nod.

"Just by touch alone you can grant access to Faery, child," Magna said with a watery smile.

"What do you mean?" Aurelia asked, her eyes narrowing. "I can't sift at all."

"You don't need to be able to sift. Just touch me and I will be able to sift to Faery independent of you. I have foreseen it, my dear," said Magna, her smile brightening.

"So, I can take Grey?" my mate asked hopefully.

"Yes. You can set out to follow the path you wish to walk," said Magna as she patted her on the arm.

"This changes *everything*." I squeezed Aurelia tighter to me, my heart filled with hope.

The elevator dinged and the doors opened. Fenrick and the Shadow King stood inside, together.

We rushed through the doors with Magna hot on our heels.

"We need to get to the parking garage. We can't sift inside the wards." I hit the down button. We were really going to Faery for the first time in centuries... I knew I shouldn't smile so soon after my dear friend's death, but the thought of going home even for a short time on a mission made me irrationally happy.

Turning to the woman responsible for it all, I crashed my lips to hers in a bruising and passionate kiss.

She's made this all possible.

"Grey, my father," she whispered against my lips.

I wouldn't let her go. "I was just thanking my mate for being the best thing that has ever happened to the realms." I grinned.

"You're crazy," she said, pulling away from me with a small shadow of smile.

I let her go reluctantly.

The elevator doors opened, and we stepped out into the empty garage. We didn't quite know what we were facing at this point, or what would happen when we got there, but we were going home... and I, for one, would have faced the very doors of death to get that chance again.

CHAPTER 25

I crouched behind a leafy bush and stared up at the royal castle. The trees were waving urgently, signaling to me. It wasn't as weird to me now that I was aware that they'd done the same thing in my presence when I was a child.

My father crouched next to me, glaring at the men patrolling the majestic and impossibly grand building. "What are the Council's soldiers doing guarding my castle?" he growled under his breath.

"I don't know, but we need to get out of here," I said just as softly. "The trees are trying to warn us away. We're not safe here."

Grey gazed up at the trees with a frown.

Together, we backed away from the tree line.

The Council was clearly moving to take over anyone that opposed them, and my father's kingdom was firmly in opposition.

"What's happened to my soldiers?" he asked as we moved swiftly through the trees to a safer location.

Fenrick paused and shook his head. "I'm guessing that any who didn't swear allegiance to the Council were either killed or sent to the dungeons, my king."

"That's going to make things exceedingly more difficult for the battle ahead," I mused and chewed my lip nervously.

Grey squeezed my hand, offering me his unspoken and eternal support.

I peered up at him. Even with the grim news of our lack of army and Freya's recent passing, there was a light in his eyes I hadn't seen before. He was happy to be back home, even if the state of it was presently terrible and oppressive.

"We'll fix it," Grey murmured, as if he knew my train of thought. "Let's just get the book first."

"It's close to the portal," I said with certainty. I was *so* glad I'd finally remembered where I'd stashed it, but when we sifted, we'd missed the mark by a mile. Father assured me it was by design—in case any Council soldiers were near it.

Fenrick did warn us earlier that the portal was heavily guarded...

The trees swayed in the opposite direction of the portal.

I cringed.

Damn it!

They wanted us to run the other way, but we desperately needed the book.

"I think they're at the portal right now," I said as I scanned the trees. "They are frantic that we get the fuck out of here."

"We'll have to fight then, Daughter. There is no other choice. We must retrieve the book," my father whispered, his expression stoic.

"I know," I agreed. "I just like having the early warning system. It keeps us all on the same page." I stepped on a twig, and a loud *snap* filled the air, shattering the otherwise perfect silence. I winced physically. That was not what I wanted to do.

Way to go, Aurelia. You could have just alerted the whole forest to your presence!

Fenrick turned sharply and stared at me like I'd grown two heads.

It wasn't like me at all. As a child, I'd moved silently between the trees. I'd been a natural master at hiding and stalking without making a sound or leaving a trace. Now, I was as clumsy as a damn human. With a grimace, I asked the trees to remove the sticks from our path.

They silently agreed before enacting my will. Vines and supple limbs swept and bowed, dragging obstacles out of our way and clearing the path for their shadow princess.

Placing a palm on the trunk of the nearest tree, I briefly closed my eyes and poured a little magic into it as a *thank you*.

They listened to me, not because I demanded things of them, but because I asked them nicely, respecting their natural autonomy, and then thanked them, showing gratitude when they agreed.

The tree pulsed with fear.

I attempted to reassure it, but it was afraid for me. They all seemed to be, as the branches reached for me, urging me in the other direction. "They're scared," I whispered loud enough for my team to hear me. "They are saying there are *a lot* of bad men in that direction."

Grey cocked a brow. "How many?" he asked.

"They have no concept of numbers, just *many*. They're afraid, but they feel angry and violent. They're very protective of me, they always have been." I licked my lips, an anxious tell, and continued on quietly.

We have to keep moving. Staying here is not an option.

"Over this hill," Fenrick whispered, pointing ahead at the small rise in front of us. "The portal is just on the other side."

"We need to keep low. Being on higher ground is where you want to be in battle, but it can also put a target on your back if you reveal yourself before the right time." Father squared his shoulders, which only succeeded in making him appear bigger, not smaller. He was bolstering himself for what was to come. He was the King of Faery, and these were his lands. He would not rest until his realm was returned to peace.

And neither will I.

As we came to the crest of the hill, a clearing was visible below. The Council's guards filled the space.

"What are they doing?" I asked.

They stared at the portal in perfect formation as if they were waiting for something.

"They are preparing for war," Grey said and clenched his fist around the hilt of his sword, still in its sheath on his hip.

I hadn't even known he could use a sword. I'd assumed he would just shift and kill that way, in his wolf form. But it made sense that the King of Shifters, and the Leader of the Syndicate knew multiple forms of combat. He'd had hundreds of years to perfect as many deadly arts as he desired, and they were likely many.

I didn't dare ruin the moment by admitting just how damn sexy he looked in his battle armor. I needed to get my head out of the gutter and back to the task at hand. "What are we going to do?" I asked as I pointed to the tree that once had the hollow close to the portal. "It's in *that* tree."

"In the tree?" Fenrick frowned. "Is that how you always hid from me?"

"So not the time, Fenrick." I grinned.

"I never could figure it out," he mumbled to himself.

I held in my giggle at our countless memories together, but just barely. A second later, I squeaked as the ground rumbled beneath me and a root shot from the earth and wrapped itself around my waist firmly. "What the fuck?" I whispered, but I felt no malice or ill intent from the roots.

Grey had his sword out at the ready and was just about to start hacking at it when a hole opened up in the ground.

My stomach jolted, and as I fell, a scream tore from my lips.

Fuck, that was damn subtle.

The tree root caught me again halfway down, and another hole opened in front of me.

What the hell is going on?

Were the trees helping me sneak past the army at the portal? Calling on my magic, it crackled willingly along my palm, lighting the dark tunnel before me. This was absolutely insane, but I reached out to the root with my free hand and sent my thanks. Dredging up my courage, I traveled down the tunnel quietly, following behind a root that reached out, beckoning me forward.

I stumbled on a pebble in the hard-packed dirt, a small curse escaping me.

A root sprung from the earthen wall next to me and wrapped around my arm, balancing me.

Weird, but very cool!

The clang of metal reached my ears from somewhere above my head, and a mournful howl broke through the din of battle. What the fuck was going on? Were Grey and my father okay? Were they already fighting for their lives?

Panic seized me, and I picked up my pace.

The tree root beckoned me more frantically.

I ran as fast as my feet could carry me, begging the trees above ground to help my family and friends in any way they could, though I was unsure if they could hear me. I had to believe I hadn't put them all in mortal danger with my scream of terror as I fell. I had to remain focused on the task at hand and pray to any gods who might be listening that they would make it out alive.

The root led me down a second tunnel and silence filled the space.

Are they still fighting up there, or have they fled?

I hoped beyond hope that they had fled the giant army that had been waiting at the portal in battle formation. There was no way they could have taken them with the few we had. And I really needed them all to get out of this alive. I'd lost too much already.

At the end of the tunnel there was only a singular root and hard-packed earth awaiting me. The root wrapped around me tightly again and it lifted me into the air, the ground opening up directly into the hollow of the giant oak from underneath.

It was space inside was smaller than I remembered, but then, I was a grown woman now. Thankfully, the bushes still covered the entrance, keeping it hidden from sight. I peeked out of the bush, and my heart stilled in my chest.

Ronaldo stood in front of the large army, and four very familiar people were on their knees in front of him. He grinned down at them with a maliciousness only he could possibly possess.

Grey struggled against his bonds, his eyes surreptitiously scanning the forest and he held his head high. "You will never find her!" he yelled, but a tear was streaming down his cheek.

Did he think I was dead? Is that why he told Ronaldo he would never find me? I sat back on my heels in the confined space and glanced frantically between the others.

My father's expression was thunderous, but he too had his chin up, maintaining his pride and valor.

"The new realm order has already begun," Ronaldo announced smugly. "And you four will be the first of our new slaves!"

"No!" I whispered quietly, my hand flying to my mouth. But no one would hear me over the raucous shouts of victory.

Several soldiers of the army came forward to clamp iron, magic-dampening cuffs on my friends and family.

A root nudged me from behind.

I turned to find an old, gold book sitting in a bed of burnt orange leaves. It was the book I'd had been looking for… but now that everyone I loved was captured, did it really matter? I couldn't sift to save my life, and my only means of transport was a portal currently blocked by the enemy army.

I grabbed the book, and it buzzed with recognition. This was most definitely the right book. I turned back toward the sight of the army, wanting desperately to be with Grey and the others, but I was our only chance of survival now. It was all on me—just as I had feared it would be—as Grey had intimated back at the Facility. The prophecy unfolding was mine, and I was the only one capable of changing the fate of Faery forever.

I eyed the root and jerked my head in the direction we had come. I had to get out of here before I could do anything, and that was the only way. No matter what it cost me, I would get my friends and family back and end the Elder Council's stranglehold on my home… even if it meant I had to die in the process.

"Can you take me to the dungeons without being seen?" I whispered to the root, an idea slowly forming in my mind, blossoming like a shy flower seeing sunlight for the first time. If I was going to defeat an army, I needed to free an army of my fucking own. I would be the princess I was born to be. I would rise against all odds to become their queen and lead them all to victory.

I just need to rescue them from my father's dungeon first...

WICKED FAE

3

CHOSEN BY THE FAE

USA TODAY BESTSELLING AUTHOR

AMELIA SHAW

Chosen by the Fae

CHAPTER 1
Aurelia

I dashed through the tunnels as fast as my legs could carry me, the trees and their roots directing me away from danger.

What the hell just happened? Everyone I care about was just captured by the Council. What's going to happen to them? Will they be tortured the way Ronaldo tortured me?

I grimaced and shook my head to clear the doom and gloom from my mind. It wouldn't help my friends or me to dwell on what might be. It was best to focus on the here and now, and what I *could* do. Pressing on, I followed the tree roots through the tunnels that opened before me like magic. If I hadn't already trusted the trees of Faery, I would have been frightened of where they were taking me. But they'd saved me time and again and protected me from my enemies, so I trusted them implicitly.

A root brushed my arm, urging me on. They clearly wanted me to get away from the hollow, and further from harm.

Unfortunately, I had a feeling they wouldn't like the place I was set on heading. I clutched the precious gold book to my chest, not wanting it out of my sight for a moment. All of this would be for nothing if I lost it.

Can it help me rescue my friends? Probably, but not without an army at my back it's going to take more than magic to win this battle.

All my hopes hinged on this plan I was winging. There was no Plan B, and if I didn't pull it off, both realms were doomed.

No pressure.

I needed to find my army. I couldn't rescue Grey and my father without one. Every chance I had was pinned on the dungeon holding loyal soldiers ready to battle the Council, for my parents, and the good of Faery. I placed a gentle hand on the root in front of me, willing it to understand my desires. "Please, I need a way into the castle dungeons."

The root recoiled at my request, shaking back and forth before surging forward and pushing me back a step. It obviously didn't want me to walk into danger, but I had no choice in the matter. My loved ones and the safety of both realms depended on it.

"I *have* to," I said sternly. "I need an army to fight the Council. I need your help. Please?" I stroked the root with my fingertips, hoping it understood the gravity of our situation.

The root nodded, waving itself up and down in understanding before a tunnel opened up in front of me.

I smiled briefly, grateful that we could communicate effectively, and quickly followed it through the packed, damp earth. All the while, worry clawed at my gut for Grey and the others.

Hold on. I'm getting help!

I needed to stop doubting myself and rise to the occasion. I had to become the princess they all deserved. I would rescue my father's guards and loyalists, then wage war against the Council.

The dirt tunnels around me became more varied in their appearance, the earthen walls mixing with evidence of stones the closer we got to the castle.

The root waved me forward. Nervousness for my wellbeing bled through our connection.

Regardless, I couldn't allow the tree's fear or my own to stop me from accessing the castle dungeons. The ground began to slope down the farther I ventured. The dirt walls of the tunnel shifted to completely cracked stone. A chill swept down my spine. The stone held the cool of the earth in, where the earth had regulated its temperature.

Forging on, I picked my way through the darkness until it came to an abrupt dead end. I spun in a circle, running my hands over the stone, searching the walls for any hint of a secret door or lever, but found nothing. "We're deep underground and obviously close to the castle now, but where is the way inside?" I asked the root.

It pointed up, its tapered end directing my attention to the space directly above my head.

My eyes widened at the sight of the wooden hatch above me, and I grimaced. "That just seems like bad planning." What was I supposed to do? Swing my way up? Without any other option available, I jumped up, grasping at the handle. A loud creak filled the quiet and I flinched at the horrible sound, praying to whatever gods were listening that no one above heard it. I'd be completely screwed if there was anyone from the Council in the dungeon.

The hatch swung down, and the root tentatively wrapped around my body. It pulsed with fear for me but dutifully lifted me up into the open hatch space anyway.

Crates were stacked in front of me as I pulled myself the rest of the way out, hiding me from view. I stroked the root, giving it a trickle of power in gratitude for saving me and getting me to where I needed to be. Reaching into the darkness below me, I pulled the hatch closed. There was no ghastly creaking this time, and I thanked the powers that be for small mercies.

The silence of the dungeon was eerie. Not even the sound of shuffling rodents' feet scratching through the walls could be heard. It was like a tomb.

Where is everyone? Where are the prisoners? Surely, Ronaldo has filled them with those loyal to my parents...

But it was way too quiet, and doubt niggled at me, chewing at my nerves as I went. I crept through the crates stacked high and searched the cells for any sign of life. The stench of rotting food hit me like a ton of bricks, making me gag on the stench.

There should have been prisoners here, but they were gone it seemed. Where had they been taken? Had my father's enemies been released? The torches that lined the walls emitted a spooky glow in the darkened dungeon, throwing dancing shadows that stretched along the walls and floors.

One cell was left wide open, as if the occupant had escaped in a hurry, not even bothering to close it as they ran for freedom.

Is that what happened here? Did the Council free them all to wreak havoc on the realm, or was it something worse?

I jumped when a *thump* sounded somewhere above me. My heart raced and panic clawed at my insides as stomping footsteps raced down the stairs.

Who's in my father's castle, and why would they come down here?

Without a moment to waste, I hurried back to the hatch and hid behind the stacked crates, holding my breath so that I didn't make even the slightest of sounds.

The metal door to the dungeon groaned open, and angry voices filled the space.

"Where is she?" Ronaldo's boomed around me.

I flinched back against the wall, willing myself to be as still and invisible as possible.

"We've searched everywhere for the princess," a male voice replied.

A *crack* filled the air, and a man groaned in pain.

"The princess is in the realm! She's the only person who could have brought the mongrel through the portal. I want her found. Now!" Ronaldo roared, and another *slap* rang out.

What are they doing here? Are they seriously just looking for me? Why would they come down here? Or are they looking for something else?

"My lord," Malcolm whispered.

I flinched, recoiling internally.

What the hell is he doing here?

"What is it?" Ronaldo barked.

"The princess grew up here and was always adept at slipping away from her guards. Finding her will be next to impossible, especially if she doesn't want to be found."

"The princess lost her memories. She can't be *that* difficult to find," Ronaldo growled. "She would be lost in this castle, if anything."

"Do we know for sure that she hasn't regained them somehow? We don't even know how she lost her memories in the first place." Malcolm's voice softened at the end of his sentence as if he were reliving a memory that was fond to him.

"Why are you even here?" Ronaldo barked in response. "You're supposed to be in the human realm enacting our plan already."

"I needed to see for myself that the Shifter King was finally captured. He still thinks that my betrothed is his mate," Malcolm said with irritation, and something hit the wall.

"You could destroy our entire plan, you idiot. Your betrothal means nothing at this point, fool! We have bigger plans than your marriage."

"Yet I'm the person who knew her best as a child. I am familiar with her hiding places. I'm sure I can find the princess," Malcolm answered calmly.

"Did I stutter when I ordered you back to the human realm? Your role there is what's most important right now. Gods help you if you fail, Malcolm. I will destroy you. Go. Now!" Ronaldo's voice rang out with all the authority of the pompous bastard he was.

What are they planning with the humans? Are they really working together with the human government to enslave us all?

The words of the shifter who was rescued from the seemingly human jail came back to me. He didn't even know how they'd made him shift. Something chemical had been used to trigger him. And humans used chemicals, not Fae. But why were the humans targeting us? I could only guess. We'd gone from not existing in the eyes of the mortal world, to being viral tabloid news. It was insane and none of it boded well for the magical world.

The metal door to the dungeon crashed closed, drawing me from my thoughts, before two pairs of feet stormed back up the stairs to the main floors of the castle.

Ronaldo's ego truly knew no bounds. He hadn't even bothered to search the dungeon for me. He really thought his lackeys would find me, and that he didn't need to lift a finger.

Malcolm's assumption that he would be able to find me was correct. He knew about many of the secret passages the castle boasted, just as I did. If Ronaldo had been foolish enough to have allowed him to search for me, hiding from them would have been infinitely harder.

Silence once again rang throughout the stinking space, and I slumped against the wall in momentary relief. They hadn't given me anything new to work with. All I knew was that Malcolm had an important role working with the human government on something.

That doesn't sound good for us at all.

I crept out from between the crates and resumed searching the cells. I tucked the book into the waistband of my jeans and opened the first one. Strangely, none of them were even locked it seemed. My father would likely lose his mind once he discovered his prisoners were all gone.

There was a crude metal tin on the stone floor that held some sort of revolting gruel or something that was well past its expiration date. I plugged my nose against the stink that threatened to empty my stomach and searched the ten-by-ten cell but found nothing that hinted at who had occupied the cell. Without delay, I moved to the next cell, again coming up empty. There was no discarded tin with food to suggest that it had held a captive recently at all.

On swift feet, I searched each individual cell, but only three in total contained any signs that someone had occupied them. A dark thought overwhelmed me and sent a shiver rippling through my bones. What had the Council done with the soldiers who'd refused to bow to them? Were they killed, or had they all defected to serve the Council like traitors? But why would they?

Nothing about this makes any sense.

Had my father's army ever been locked up, or had this been a fool's mission from the start? At the opposite end of the dungeon, mounted on the wall, a torch caught my eye. It looked exactly like the others but was somehow special as well—I could sense that its simplicity belied something more. The gold sconce was unassuming, its flames flickered and danced, casting shadows on the wall. But I wasn't fooled.

With conviction I pulled down on the torch and it moved like a lever. Stone ground against stone as the wall opened in front of me.

A secret passageway! I knew it.

Dust swirled in the air like glitter in the light as the gears ground and the door swung open wider. The musty smell of the passage tickled my nose, and I determinedly held back a sneeze. With a flick of my fingers, I harnessed my air magic, and a cool breeze blew the dust out and away from me.

Very few were entrusted with the locations of all the hidden passages in the castle, but I had found them as a child, simply exploring, much to Fenrick's displeasure. A pang of guilt prickled in my chest. Fenrick and the others were still in very real danger, and I was stuck in Faery with no way out. And to make matters worse, the army I had expected to be on my side was nowhere to be found.

The only thing I could do at this point was to hide and hope for a miracle. I slipped inside the secret passage and blew out a relieved breath when the door swung shut behind me without alerting anyone. My eyes adjusted to the darkness as I crept down the small passage. I remembered them being *so* much more spacious when I was a child. Now, the walls were too close, and I panted quietly as fear ate its way through my gut.

It felt like they were closing in on me, too small now that I was an adult. I hadn't known I was claustrophobic, but apparently I was, and it left me rattled. Taking a deep breath through my nose, I blew it out through my mouth several times to maintain my sense of control and calm.

It's just a small space. It can't hurt you. The tunnels beneath the trees were small too. You've got this!

No matter how hard I tried to convince myself, it seemed apparent that I really didn't have this. How long was I going to have to hide out in the hidden passages until I could figure out a plan? I couldn't be seen or heard inside the castle, or someone would catch on to what I was doing.

The castle was ancient, and things creaked and groaned all too often for my taste, furthering my unease. None of that had bothered me especially when I'd played with Fenrick as a child, however things were far more dire for me in my current situation. If I fucked up, Fenrick wouldn't be the one to find me, it would be my enemies, and the punishment for defying them would be far more severe. I swallowed hard and steadied myself against the stone walls, my heart racing.

The Council had already called for my head on multiple occasions, and if they got their hands on me it would mean my death—whether I was ready to meet my makers or not.

CHAPTER 2
Grey

"The new realm order has already begun!" Ronaldo announced smugly. "And you four will be the first of the slaves."

This idiot has absolutely lost his mind.

On my knees in front of the sadistic fuck, with my hands held behind my back by the guard, I growled. "You realize you're going to doom us all," I hissed as I struggled against the guard holding me until the kiss of cold metal graced my throat.

"Stop fighting, mutt, or you won't live long enough to be a slave. With the High Councilor's permission, I'll slit your throat," the guard at my back whispered.

"I'm not dooming us all. I'm saving us from the destruction that humanity and the unclean bring to the Fae." Ronaldo's voice was high-pitched, and his face flushed red with the force of his anger.

"You *will* doom the Fae," I argued back, the fire of rebellion burning in my veins. "Humans outnumber us ten to one. And you wish to go to war with them? Then you're even more stupid than I gave you credit for." I spat on the ground at his feet.

Just because he'd managed to force me to my knees didn't mean I had any respect for him. He'd never earned that, and he never would. I'd despise him with my dying breath. He was the reason we'd been dumped in the mortal world in the first place. He was the one who'd pretended to execute my father and then kept him a prisoner like a rat in a cage for centuries. Eventually, I would watch him die. I'd make sure of it.

"You wish to die, Shifter King?" Ronaldo chuckled.

The blade at my throat dug in a little, but I didn't flinch at the small bite of pain as a trickle of blood trailed its way down my flesh. Instead, I reveled in it. I would get my revenge, and I would get retribution for whatever Aurelia suffered too.

My beautiful mate.

Where was she? Did she survive the fall? I sent up a silent prayer to the gods as I stared into the eyes of evil and vowed to take him down.

"I'll tell you what," Ronaldo said, tapping his lips with an index finger. "Tell me where the princess is, and I won't torture you until you can't stand."

Aurelia's father, the Fae Shadow King, spoke from beside me. "You know he's a liar, Grey. Don't say a word."

"I know. It doesn't matter though, because I don't know where she is," I said before glaring at Ronaldo.

"Last chance before you're sent back to your cesspool." Ronaldo glanced down at his fingernails as if he were bored, but I knew better. He was very interested in where Aurelia was.

"I told you, I don't know," I growled, my wolf rising to the surface with the need to kill the smug bastard where he stood.

"Take them back through the portal. They will change their tune when I'm done with them." Ronaldo waved a hand and walked away.

Cuffs were snapped on my wrists behind my back, and I groaned as my intrinsic shifter magic was dampened. "What the fuck?"

The Shadow King glanced at me, but the hilt of a sword smacked him in the back of his head and silenced him.

"No talking! Don't even look at each other, or you're dead," a soldier in black armor barked. He was originally one of the king's warriors.

How can he smack his own king and threaten him that way?

"We will get out of this!" the king bellowed. "And when we do, all you traitors will feel my wrath!"

"I don't think you understand, *King*." The same guard sneered. "You are in magic-blocking cuffs and on your way to becoming a slave. You've already lost. We will rule all. The pure-blooded Fae will rise once again."

Is he really that delusional? He won't rule anything. He's a guard. A grunt meant to be cannon fodder.

I kept my mouth shut as my blood boiled.

The guards shoved us roughly through the portal, following Ronaldo's orders without question or hesitation.

My shoulders slumped as I landed back in the human world again. I'd never wanted to return. The chance to go home had been everything—for all of us. It's what we'd clung to. It was the hope that had sustained us all these centuries. With a glance behind me, I physically saw the portal for the first time since being expelled from Faery. It really had been there the whole time. So close to my building as to be heartbreaking, yet I never even knew it.

I scanned the clearing, searching for the troll I'd left on guard, but there were too many Fae around even for a troll. I sincerely hoped that he'd run when the Council took control of the portal.

We were so close to my property, it pained me. And even if I were able to escape their clutches, the last thing I would have done was gone to my people. I wouldn't lead the Council's goons there no matter what. I was their king and still bore responsibility for their well-being.

Who knows what would happen to them?

"Move, Shifter King," the guard behind me snarled as he shoved me in the back.

I stumbled with a growl.

The Fae Shadow King glanced sidelong at me as if to suggest action.

I shook my head subtly. There was no way out of this at present that wouldn't endanger people we cared about. We had no choice but to do what they said and pray to the gods that Aurelia was okay and able to help us out when she could.

Aurelia.

My wolf howled in my mind as I thought about my missing mate. I couldn't shake the feeling that something was wrong. Had the fall into the earth killed her? Or was she simply biding her time until she could get us all out of the mess we were in? I wanted more than anything for it to be the latter. I couldn't exist in a world where she no longer drew breath. The mere thought made my heart stammer with pain, and my soul howl with anguish.

The guard behind my back shoved me again. "What's the matter, Shifter King? You don't have anything cocky to say to me?"

"It'll do me no good to make threats now." I shrugged. "But mark my words, you won't win this war."

The guard laughed as he pushed me yet again, determined to egg me on. "Look around, asshole. We already have."

"And you dare call me a cocky asshole?" I smirked. I glanced at Fenrick on my other side, but quickly turned away before my anger could dissipate, and an unstoppable depression swallowed me alive.

His eyes were haunted. It was clear that he didn't think Aurelia made it.

I could tell that from the stricken look in his eyes, but I refused to believe she was gone. The trees in Faery had helped her before, they responded to her in a way they did for no one else. I had to believe they came through for her again this time. "She's alive," I whispered to Fenrick. "She *has* to be."

My wolf would have felt it if she'd died, I was sure. Even if she wasn't officially mated to me yet, she was mine, and I would know if she were gone. I had to believe it with all my heart. Our connection—our love—was stronger than anything else I'd ever experienced. I had to trust in it or else I'd be truly lost.

The guards forced us to march through the forest and to the main road single file, all of us still shackled with the magic-cancelling cuffs.

Please don't let any of my people drive past us.

They'd try to save us, and there were just too many Fae soldiers. Up ahead, a black van with no windows sat idling on the side of the road as we broke through the tree line.

That's fucking ominous.

And I knew ominous. I *was* the Syndicate, after all. There was no license plate on the back of the van, nothing I could see that would identify where it had come from.

One of the guards opened the back door, which revealed two rows of bench seats inside the completely gutted van. They'd obviously been planning this. I was shoved toward the vehicle first and sat where they told me, at the end.

The asshole guard sat next to me, his sword gripped tightly in his hand as he eyed me warily.

Magna was pushed onto the seat in front of me. She frowned at the man who treated her with such little respect but turned quickly away. Her eyes gleamed with something I couldn't quite name, and a small smile pulled at her features a moment later.

What the hell is up with her? Is she seeing something we can't? How can she foresee anything without her magic?

I glanced back at Fenrick and the Shadow King being manhandled into the van.

The guard beside me brought the hilt of his sword up under my chin.

The blow caused my head to fly back and rattled my jaw. Pain washed through my skull as my head made impact with the metal wall of the van behind me.

"Don't talk, don't look at each other, and keep your eyes on the floor until we get where we're going, mongrel," the guard hissed in my ear.

My wolf growled inside my head at the *mongrel* comment.

I would show the idiot who the real mongrel was, but that would not be today. There was nothing I could do with my power locked down. Even if I could, it was likely the others would be injured in the crossfire. And my mate would never forgive me if something happened to them because of me.

I made a vow to myself then and there to see all the traitors to the crown dead before the end of the war that was coming. It would be my mission in life to watch the motherfuckers burn. If they wanted to hurt my people, they would go through me.

The van made a sudden, sharp U-turn, and I pitched to the side into the guard next to me.

He shoved me off him, loathing in his eyes.

I nearly toppled to the floor and growled at the guard, my wolf riding me hard. But he couldn't come out no matter how much he wanted to. Shifting while wearing the cuffs was impossible..

The guard gulped a heartbeat later at whatever horrors he saw in my burning gaze, likely seeing his death by my hands.

"Grey, easy," Magna mumbled under her breath.

The guard beside her slapped her face hard.

She turned to him and smiled even as a red handprint formed on her pale cheek. That guard had just earned his death as well. Magna was not someone to be trifled with, and the wicked grin on her face was a testament to her power as a seer.

What are you planning, Magna? What have you seen?

She glanced at me like she knew what I was thinking and shook her head imperceptibly.

Right. We can't reveal our hand.

The country roads were bumpy, and with our hands tied behind our backs, there was no way to keep ourselves steady and anchored.

The guard beside Fenrick punched him in the gut for daring to accidently bump into him.

The loyal Fae grunted in response but kept otherwise silent.

Our whole situation at present was a mess, and our inability to sit still was a great excuse for the guards to continually punish us. We jostled over the smaller, unmaintained roads until we finally reached the highway. The road mercifully evened out, but I couldn't see where we were with the solid partition between us and the driver. They'd ensured that we'd remain completely clueless as to our direction and whereabouts.

Where the fuck are they taking us?

The van slowed to an unexpected stop.

I trained my ears on the voice in the front of the van.

"Are these the criminals we were told the Councilor was bringing in?" a rough voice asked.

"It's the High Councilor, idiot. You will be punished just like the beasts in the back if you don't show him proper respect," another deep voice drawled.

Beasts.

That's all we were to the Council. Beasts that deserved nothing more than to be slaves. I would end them all right now if I could. If that were possible without hurting those I cared for.

The individual at the front of the van cleared his throat. "Yes, sir. The *High* Councilor said you had prisoners coming. I'll alert the warden. You know where to go."

My brow furrowed. Were we at a human prison manned by the Fae? How the hell had Ronaldo started working so closely with the humans that they were willingly giving him the use of their facilities to imprison those who had committed no crimes?

The van started moving again onto another bumpy gravel road, and we all lurched at the motion.

I groaned as a buzzer sounded too loud in my ears and startled when the *clang* of metal on metal sounded.

That had to have been the gate.

We were locked in, and if Ronaldo had anything to say about it, we were never going to get out.

The van stopped and the doors opened, letting the too-bright sunlight filter into the cramped space.

I was yanked by my arm out of the vehicle and stared up at the intimidating building before me with bars securing every window. It was exactly as I feared. They'd brought us to a maximum-security human prison.

Shit. Where are you, Aurelia? I hope you have a plan to get us out of here...

CHAPTER 3

Memories hit me like a sledgehammer to the chest as I picked my way through the secret passageways in the castle. I'd had such a happy childhood until it all went wrong. Until Malcolm abducted me and set me on this path. My days had been filled with sunshine, beauty, fun, laughter, and luxury… and then I'd lost it all. I'd been forced to live in poverty and destitution, unwanted and unloved.

One day he would die for his crimes against me, but for the moment, I needed to find someone—anyone—still loyal to my father. I couldn't do this alone, that much was clear. I didn't have a savior complex and was open to all aid I might be able to obtain. The sooner I rescued my father and mate, the sooner Faery would be free of Ronaldo's insanity and tyranny.

The passage curved up, and I followed it to its end where I found a small door. I needed to get into the actual castle if I was going to have success in finding anyone. I pressed my hand against the door and pushed. Metal scraped unnervingly against stone as the door opened into a child's bedroom.

My bedroom.

"Well, shit," I whispered.

They'd kept it exactly the way I'd left it. But why? And why did a tunnel even exist that led from the dungeon of all places, directly to my bedroom? It boggled the mind. I crept silently to the four-poster canopied bed with its bright pink comforter and ran my hand across the stunningly soft and luxurious silk. I'd always secretly hated pink but never had the nerve to tell my mom.

She would have been so disappointed, I remembered thinking, and I didn't want her to ever be disenchanted in me or my choices. But the things you think when you're a kid can be funny. She wouldn't have been disappointed, I saw that now as an adult, myself. She would have happily changed the color for me to whatever my childish heart desired, I was sure.

The dresser still had my classic silver hairbrush sitting on it, just below and in front of the attached vanity mirror. I ran my fingers over the white dresser remembering all the times my mother would reprimand me for not taking better care of my long, golden hair and smiled. It was wonderful to have my memories back and not thinking that I was unwanted and thrown out on the streets.

I set the brush back on the dresser carelessly, and it thumped against the wood louder than I'd intended. I froze, my breath hitching in my throat as my heart instantly pumped with fear and adrenalin.

"Hey! I heard something," a man's voice announced.

Startled, I jumped back from the dresser and raced back to the hidden door.

"Do you think it's the princess?" another male voice asked excitedly. "Princess, it's okay. We want to help you. The king's looking for you," the other man said through the main bedroom doors. while

The first one snickered.

I rolled my eyes in disbelief.

They must know I'm not that dumb!

I crept back into the secret passage and closed the door as quietly as I possible behind me.

A moment later, the footsteps stopped and the doors into my bedroom opened. "I swear I heard something in here," the first voice said.

"It might have been a rodent or something."

"Rodents can open and close doors now, can they, asshole?" the first man scoffed.

"Come on, we need to find the princess before the High Councilor throws us in that damn human prison where they're locking everyone up."

They'd locked everyone up in a human prison? What the hell are they doing?

The doors closed again, and the guard's footsteps faded down the hall.

I breathed a sigh of relief and slumped back against the cold stone wall, the anxiety of the enclosed space temporarily forgotten.

Am I looking all over this place for nothing? Maybe I would have had better luck finding help in the village?

There was likely very little hope I'd find loyal survivors still in the castle. What had I been thinking? Why hadn't I just run to the village and asked someone to sift me back? Though, that would have been equally as dangerous. Ronaldo had eyes and ears everywhere, and I wouldn't put it past the common Fae to turn on me in return for a reward, if it came down to it.

Taking a different route, I followed the passageways through the castle to the kitchens. What was normally a bustling space with staff everywhere was now cold and silent.

He's gotten rid of the kitchen staff? What is his play here?

Was he planning to simply take over the castle, or did he intend to give it to one of his cronies after he locked my father away forever? Ultimately, it didn't matter one way or another. What was for sure and certain was that I was going to be stuck in this realm until I could find someone to help me, so I needed food.

Pots and pans hung from hooks around the marble island that still had a dusting of flour on it as if they were told to leave in the middle of cooking. I crept into the pantry where they kept the fruits and vegetables and found several small canvas bags that were used to take produce to and from the markets.

Grabbing two of the bags out of the pantry, I filled one with what I thought I would need in case I didn't get out of this mess soon, and the other I placed the book gently inside. At least that got it out of the waistband of my pants. I needed that book, and I couldn't imagine what would happen if I dropped it and lost it.

It would most likely mean the end of everything. Grey would be stuck in the human world forever, along with my father and those loyal to him. I couldn't accept that reality. It would break me. Now that I'd found my fate and been reunited with my long-lost family, there was no way I was losing them all over again. Not while I still had breath in my lungs and blood pumping through my veins.

"She must be here somewhere," someone said, walking into the kitchen.

I backed up into the deep royal pantry against the far wall as quietly as I could, feeling for the lever I knew was there.

"What if she's not? What if she went back to the human world after the Shifter King and the High Councilor has us wasting our time searching for her?" another voice asked.

"It's not our job to ask questions, idiot. You know what happens to those who dare to question him."

Finally, just in the nick of time, I grasped the lever and pulled it without hesitation. The back wall swung me in a half circle and deposited me in the hidden room behind the pantry. It was sort of a secret panic room the kitchen staff could use if the castle was ever under attack.

Why didn't they use it?

Or did they? The panic room was connected to a tunnel that led to the castle grounds. They could have already made a run for it.

"Did you hear that?" the voice asked from the other side.

"Yeah, it sounded like gears grinding in the pantry!"

Shit. I need to get out of here before they figure it out.

On silent feet I raced down the passage, my breathing short and labored when I hit a fork. One way would take me out of the castle but on the opposite side from where the village was, but it would be harder to get to the village from there without being spotted. It added a significant distance to how much ground I'd have to cover to achieve my goal.

The other way would take me back through the castle. Neither were great options, but I had a better chance of remaining hidden inside the castle than I did outside its walls.

With a heavy heart I took the left-hand side and chose to stay within the castle. There were a few others who would know of the passageways, but not many.

Could one of them be hiding out down here too?

It was a long shot, but one I needed to take. If someone else was hurt by the Council and holed up down here, and I could prevent further harm from befalling them and chose not to, I would never forgive myself.

Keeping a steady pace, it wasn't too long until I made it to the library and slipped inside. The space was exactly as I remembered. There were shelves as tall as the ceiling as well as shorter display shelves in neat rows throughout the massive area.

"I want her found!" Ronaldo roared as he slammed open the doors. "Search for the castle's passageways and find her!"

Startled, I scampered back behind a shelf to hide and waited for them to leave. I couldn't risk going back into the passageway with Ronaldo so close. They'd definitely hear the tell-tale grind of ancient gears.

He may have been a scummy, oily bastard, but he wasn't entirely stupid.

"Some of us have heard odd sounds like grinding gears or metal on stone. That might be her entering those passageways," the man from the kitchen said.

"And you didn't think to look for a secret exit? This is a castle. They have those kinds of protections built into them to protect the royal family and its servants. Idiots!"

"We did look, sir, but there was nothing out of the ordinary in the girl's room or the kitchens," the man said.

"You didn't look hard enough, obviously! They're hidden for a reason. They aren't supposed to be obvious, or they would be pointless, wouldn't they?" Ronaldo slammed his hand on one of the tables with a loud *thwack* that vibrated in my ears despite the distance between us.

Panic rose up inside me.

This isn't good at all! Shit. He could find me here any second. I need to think!

How was I going to get out of this without him finding the passages?

"Sir, we *will* find the girl. We will scour the entire castle for its passages."

"Start here in the library," Ronaldo commanded. "There are always passages leading into the library." Then he waved a hand, dismissing them from his sight in frustration at their apparent ineptitude before exiting the chamber.

Shit. Fuck. Shit!

My eyes widened in fear as the two men went over to the nearest shelves and started pulling books off, as if they might find a secret lever hidden amongst them. They threw them on the ground, discarding them when they weren't what they were looking for.

I wracked my brain for anything that I could do to stop them from finding me once I closed the hidden door but came up empty. There was no way to hide the sound of the ancient gears grinding against one another when they were so perilously close. My magic tingled beneath my skin, giving me an idea.

One of the men turned the corner at that precise moment and spotted me.

Shit.

"Were you spying on us, Princess?" the man asked loudly, alerting his colleague.

"I don't know what you're talking about," I said curtly as I slowly backed through the still open door to the passage. I needed the time and room to swing it closed, but the Fae guard was still advancing on me.

In response to my peril, Shadows appeared, writhing on my skin.

On instinct, I thrust my hand out in his direction, my heart hammering in my chest. The magic shoved him back just enough that I was able to slam the door in his face. My hands pulsed with energy as I laid them upon the door, sealing it against everyone but me.

I needed to find a way out of there. Ronaldo would know soon enough that I had been spotted, and they would be combing the entire castle looking for me. My time was quickly running out. I jumped, startled by a deafening *boom* that sounded from the other side of the sealed passage door.

They were prepared to destroy the entire library to get to me it seemed. Those monsters were destroying books so that Ronaldo could capture and torture me again, before killing me for all the world to see.

Another *boom* rattled the stone walls, and pieces of rock and dust from the ceiling rained down on me. I backed up before turning left and right.

Which way should I go? Back the way I came, or further down the passage?

More debris rained down on me, and I turned to the left. I needed to go further. They would probably be searching the kitchens next, looking for me since they'd spotted me in the library and had heard the gear grinding in the pantry.

I sprinted down the passage until I was sure I was in a completely different wing of the castle and stopped to catch my breath, not used to so much running. I rested my hands on the walls searching for the button I knew to be hidden there. It was the exact same stone as the rest of the wall, perfectly blended to be indistinguishable from the naked eye. There were no seams or anything to even hint that there was a possible exit in the vicinity.

A second later my heartbeat quickened, and my breathing became ragged as an arm wrapped around my middle and a hand covered my mouth. Whoever it had taken me by surprise tugged my back against their chest.

"Do not scream," a male voice whispered harshly in my ear.

In blind panic I kicked my leg, aiming for what I knew would hurt most, trying to get the stranger to loosen his hold on me.

He grunted in pain, but only held me tighter, refusing to relinquish his hold. "Stop!" he urged as he shook me.

I opened my mouth to bite him, because there was no way I was going to scream and alert Ronaldo as to where I'd escaped to.

"Fuck, you play dirty." He grunted again. The man was strong and yanked me back into a different passageway, all while keeping his hand firmly over my mouth.

Where is this fucker taking me?

With all my might, I dug my heels into the ground, unwilling to give up. I would fight with everything I had, for myself and for those I loved. Those who were relying on me to come to their aid.

But he lifted me easily despite my frantic efforts, and dragged me down the dark passage.

What the hell do I do now?

I was clearly overpowered and outmatched in the physical strength stakes department, and whoever it was had taken me completely by surprise. I hadn't even heard him approaching until it was too late. What was he planning to do to me?

He wouldn't have cared if I screamed if he was one of Ronaldo's goons... so who is he and what is he doing in the castle? Is he on my side? Is he loyal to my father?

My heart raced, and my head swam as I hyperventilated. But an even better question was, would I live long enough to even learn those answers?

CHAPTER 4

They led us into the prison with guns at our backs instead of the swords they had previously utilized. Electronic doors buzzed before swinging open for us, and I was shoved roughly inside.

"What the hell are we doing in a human prison?" I asked.

The guard behind me shoved me against the wall. "I said, no talking, mongrel."

"I'll show you a fucking mongrel," I bit out, my hackles rising at the sheer nerve of his canine insult.

He pressed the barrel of his gun into my temple, hatred burning in his eyes.

But another guard intervened before things escalated, stepping up to pull it away. "The High Councilor wants this one *alive*," he stressed.

"He's got a smart fucking mouth for someone in magic-blocking cuffs," the first guard retorted and shoved me again, slamming my face into the wall.

"You can rough him up if he doesn't follow the rules or throw him in the hole, but you're *not* to kill him!" the newer guard barked back. "Orders are orders."

Each guard grabbed one of my arms and led me further into the prison. There were several, austere, concrete levels in the area where they housed the inmates.

"Are you okay?" Fenrick whispered so low I almost didn't hear him.

I nodded imperceptibly so as not to piss off the guard who clearly wanted me dead. We needed to use this opportunity to figure out what was happening with the supernaturals, then find a way to escape.

The guard shoved me to the left as the others were escorted elsewhere.

I stopped short, digging in my heels, refusing to budge.

Two men grabbed my arms and tried to pull me forward.

I yanked my arm free of one of them. We couldn't let them separate us. That would be the worst-case scenario in this place.

How will we get out if we aren't together?

I spun around on the other guard and kicked him in the gut, taking him by surprise.

The guard bent over with a groan, clutching at his middle.

The other guard recovered from the impact first and tackled me to the ground.

My head hit the concrete and bounced off, stars dancing behind my eyes as I tried to gain my bearings again.

"Where are you taking him?" Fenrick bellowed, struggling against the guards who held him.

The guard leading him sneered. "You should worry about your own life, traitor."

As soon as the other guard recovered, together they pulled me to my feet.

I shook my head to clear it and continued my struggle, the beast within me refusing to give up the fight and lose ground.

The guard who stopped the other one from killing me only minutes ago squeezed my arm subtlety.

I glared back in defiance before a lightbulb clicked on inside my foggy head.

Wait! Did he just shake his head at me?

The gesture was so minute, I could have *almost* imagined it... but I wasn't about to question my instincts. "Where are you taking me?" I roared as I struggled to get free again even though it was futile. If something was afoot, I wasn't going to let on.

The Shadow King tried to get to me, his expression one of unbridled anger and authority.

The guard at his back pulled him away as he yanked at his arms, twisting them behind him.

"That's my daughter's mate. You will not separate us!" he declared.

"You don't make the rules here, *King*," the guard shot back with a chuckle of dark mirth.

Without warning, Fenrick pulled out of his guard's hold and launched himself toward me.

Just as fast, one of the other guards pointed his gun at Fenrick's head.

Fenrick stopped and stood deadly still, his throat working as he held the guard's gaze unflinchingly.

"There are no orders to keep the rest of you alive," the guard who saved me from brutality earlier said. "I would be *very* careful in your choices if I were you."

I wrenched my arm from his grasp, ready to knock the gun away with everything I had. Those were *my* people, and I would do anything to keep them safe.

"No!" Magna screamed, shattering the tense stand-off and shocking us all. "Don't resist, Grey."

I glanced at her and the terror on her face was real. Something terrible was going to happen if this continued. It was clear as day that Magna had foreseen this particular situation's outcome. With utmost restraint, I scanned the faces of the others, noting their deadly stillness.

This wouldn't end well. I could almost feel death in the air as it hung over us, waiting for someone to tip the scales of fate.

The guard cocked his weapon, which was trained on the loyal Fae.

Fenrick stared him down, a vein in his temple pulsing as he kept himself in check by a mere thread.

With a heavy heart I nodded my understanding of Magna's warning and relaxed my shoulders. I wouldn't struggle again, no matter what. I trusted Magna's visions. She'd never let me down or led me astray. "Stand down, Fenrick," I ordered, eyeing the Fae who'd fast become a valued friend. "There will be no death today. Don't give them what they want."

"But..." Fenrick sighed and took a step back, obeying.

The guard lowered his weapon and grabbed me roughly around the biceps again.

"Fine. Take me to whatever fresh hell you have planned for me," I said and let them yank me down the hall and away from my family and friends.

"You're going to wish you'd struggled harder, Shifter King." The guard to my left chuckled.

"And you're all going to wish you chose the winning side when I come for you in the end." I couldn't help the words as they rolled off my tongue. They weren't idle threats, they were an iron-clad promise. One way or another, I was going to end all the traitors to the crown.

"You keep saying that, but look where you are. I don't think you'll have such a cocky attitude after your session." He shoved me forward.

The halls were long as we walked and painted a drab gray, probably intended to sap and destroy any and all hope the inmates here might have. Cells lined the walls on either side, and people stared out from little plexiglass windows at me as I was shoved past them.

An electronic buzzing met my ears as we reached another door that needed a keycard to enter. The guard on my right flashed his badge over the scanner and the *click* was ominous.

I didn't want to go in there, but what choice did I have? If I fought them, I would probably die or worse... they'd take their vengeance on those I cared about, and my mate would never forgive me if something happened to Fenrick, her father, or Magna. Whether I liked it or not it was abundantly evident that there was no escaping whatever this was, so I just had to accept it.

The guards walked me through what appeared to be a secure medical unit, but everything felt wrong.

This wasn't a place of healing and recovery. This is something else entirely!

The sterile scent of rubbing alcohol tainted the air and there were people hooked up to machines while others in white lab coats poked and prodded them like they were experiments. At that moment, one of Aurelia's greatest fears flooded back to my memory and my eyes widened in sick realization.

The people struggled against their bonds as they were strapped down and gagged. They weren't on those gurneys willingly. They were being tested on like lab rats. How could it be that it was our own kind doing it to each other?

What the fuck?

I was dragged into a room with a bed that was similar to those in the hall and braced myself for whatever they were going to do to me. Whatever this was, I obviously survived it. Magna had warned me off resisting. I had to hold onto my faith that she wasn't wrong. Now was not the time to doubt the sage and seer.

The guards strapped me down, the cruel cuffs still hindering any use of my inherent shifter magic.

When they were finished, Ronaldo stepped into the room. A hint of madness gleamed in his eyes as he smiled gleefully at me. He was the last person I expected to see, given we'd been sent here by him from Faery. "You will tell me all your secrets, Shifter King."

"The fuck I will."

This isn't about experimenting on me. This is a torture session. Great.

"How the hell am I going to be of any use as your slave if I'm being tortured?" I scoffed.

"You'll heal," he assured me as he picked up a scalpel and sliced through my shirt, nicking the skin in several places,

Despite the fleeting pain, I didn't flinch. There was no way I was going to give him that kind of satisfaction.

"Tell me where the princess is," he demanded.

"Go to hell," I said through gritted teeth. I wasn't playing his game. I would simply endure the same way my own father had endured during his centuries long incarceration.

He jabbed me with the tip of the scalpel and blood squirted from the wound in my chest.

Pain flared like fire, but I still refused to react. That was exactly what he wanted. He was the kind of sick fuck who fed on people's screams, and I would die on the damn table before I ever made a sound. It would take far greater men than him to draw forth that kind of submission from me.

He stabbed me again on the other side of my chest and blood spurted everywhere as it jetted out under pressure.

But still, I didn't flinch or react.

He started getting frustrated, as evidenced by his pinched brows and his snarl of anger as he sliced through my skin.

I may just die on this table. No, don't think like that! You're going to survive this, kill them all, and be reunited with Aurelia—our princess!

My wolf howled in my mind, taking most of the pain from me into himself so I could hold my ground.

But I knew we wouldn't last forever with Ronaldo hacking away at us the way he was.

"It can all stop if you tell me where the princess is hiding," Ronaldo purred.

"Fuck you." Wise or not, it was the first thing that sprung to mind. There would be no dulling my defiance, that was for damn sure.

"Give me the little hammer." Ronaldo waved to the guard.

The guard handed him a small surgical hammer obediently and without hesitation.

I didn't need to be told what that was for—it was for breaking bones.

I'm not sure how long we will last without screaming if he does what I think he's about to... damn it.

"I'm going to break all the bones in your hand one by one until you tell me where the princess is." Ronaldo grinned like a devil.

I balled my hands into fists, my jaw clenched.

The guard gripped my wrist, hitting the one pressure point that made my fist open on reflex.

Ronaldo gripped my pinky finger with one hand and lifted the hammer over his head before slamming it down on the second knuckle with enough force to shake the whole table.

My back arched as blinding pain tore through my hand, but I didn't make a sound. Still, I reacted, and that was more than enough motivation for the sadist to continue his torture.

"Don't want to tell me where the princess is? Then we can change the topic of conversation," Ronaldo said. "Where is your Facility? I know you have people. Where are they?"

"I'm not telling you anything, asshole. Break the bones in my hands —go ahead—but before the end of this, I will see you dead."

"Wrong answer." Ronaldo grinned before slamming the hammer down on my ring finger.

I panted through the pain, not willing to give in and scream.

I won't. Fuck him!

He broke three more knuckles before he grabbed the scalpel again and dug it into my left pec.

I couldn't see what he was doing but the cuts and pain were definitely forming a pattern along my skin. Blood dripped down my side, sliding along my skin in warm rivulets. I clenched my good hand into a fist, my nails biting into my palm. That little bite of pain helped to relieve some of the pain in the other hand and made it remotely more manageable. "You're wasting your time. I told you, I won't tell you anything."

"You misunderstand what this is, Shifter King," Ronaldo spat the word *king* at me as if it dripped with poison. "This is simply fun for me."

I already knew that, but the evil grin on his face was deranged in a way I hadn't seen before. He was getting high causing pain. A sadist in the truest sense.

How much does he enjoy the suffering of those people he's experimenting on? Do I even want to know?

"You can stop the pain and ruin my fun if you just answer my questions, mutt." Blood ran continued to down my sides as he continued to carve something into my chest.

I squeezed my eyes closed and panted through gritted teeth.

I will not break. I will not break.

My people and Aurelia meant more to me than my own life. I would never tell this monster where to find them. "Do what you want to me. I won't tell you shit."

"I hope you enjoy the marks I've etched permanently into your skin then." Ronaldo sat back and admired whatever the hell he'd done to my chest. "Without your magic, this will scar nicely before it gets the chance to heal." He grabbed a mirror and pointed it at an angle I could see my chest.

I shouldn't have looked. I knew I should have kept my eyes closed but curiosity got the better of me and I glanced at the mirror with disdain and anger. *Shifter Trash* was carved into my chest in crude, blocky handwriting.

I'm going to destroy this motherfucker!

Ronaldo's laugh grated on me as he picked up the hammer once more.

I wasn't going to make it out of this unscathed, so it didn't matter what he carved into my skin. Whatever scars I bore from this day forward, I would wear them with pride. They would remind me of my strength and resilience, of surviving this hell hole, and of conquering my enemy when all was said and done.

I closed my eyes and waited for the pain to come. The anticipation was almost worse than the pain itself. I forced myself to relax my muscles and breathe through my nose, so I didn't make it worse. If I tensed up waiting for it to happen it would cause more pain. That was why people in car accidents who saw the impact coming and tensed were always the ones with the worst injuries.

I nearly screamed as my thumb caught fire and white spots danced behind my closed lids. A grunt of pain escaped me despite my best efforts, and my back arched off the gurney as the blinding torment tore through my hand and traveled up my arm to my elbow.

"Tell me where *she* is!" Ronaldo screamed. Without warning or waiting for my answer, he slammed the hammer down again and again.

I lost the battle and bellowed my agony. Shame didn't even get a chance to take root inside me. There was no time to think—merely react.

Ronaldo laughed and slammed the hammer down again, shattering the last solid bone in my hand.

Black overtook all my senses and pain swallowed me alive. Without any say in the matter, I passed out hard, the sickening blood loss and soul-crushing weight of oblivion too much to bear.

CHAPTER 5
Aurelia

The scream on my lips was muffled by his hand as the stranger took me through another passage into a dark chamber.

Could I be wrong about him not being a part of the Council's guards?

I thrashed against him, and the kiss of metal armor met my skin. If he wasn't with the Council, why was he wearing armor? My father's army had already been rounded up by the Council and their minions.

How likely was it that the man who was abducting me was able to escape the Council on his own? But then why was he trying to keep me quiet if he was on their side? If he was with the Council, the first thing he'd want to do is alert the other guards. There was no doubt a reward for the man who managed to bring me to Ronaldo himself...

Who the hell is this?

"Shut up, Princess," my abductor's gravelly voice whispered next to my ear. "I'm going to remove my hand, but bear in mind if you scream, we are *both* completely fucked."

And there's my answer.

This man had either pretended to join the Council to find me himself, or he was able to hide without them catching him. Either way, I didn't really have any choice but to listen to him when he put it so bluntly. Screaming was a terrible idea, given the Council had men all over the castle searching for me, but still, could I trust a stranger in the middle of the lion's den?

No. But maybe we can help each other if he answers my questions.

I nodded my head in understanding against his palm.

He released me and took a step back, giving me some space to whirl around and confront him face to face.

"Who are you?" I demanded suspiciously as I glanced at the armor he was wearing. I recognized it as the armor my father's army wore, but I had never seen this particular man before, not even in my childhood memories that had so recently been restored.

"My name is Kiernan," he answered calmly, "and I was in your father's militia—his elite force that was sent to find you when you were abducted from your bed all those years ago."

"Then why weren't you there when Fenrick found me at the portal? I don't remember seeing you there." I crossed my arms over my chest and allowed my magic to seep into my palms discreetly.

"I was in the human world pretending to be a warlock and looking for you, Princess." He bowed his head in subservience.

"Then why have I never seen you before? And how did you escape the Council? How do I know you're not a spy?" I asked the questions in rapid fire.

"Whoa, Princess. Take it easy on the questions. I'll answer, but you need to breathe." He raised his hands in surrender.

I arched a brow at him, waiting for an answer, magic at the ready in case he wasn't who he said he was.

"The Council came in unexpectedly not long after you and your parents escaped from their fucked-up meeting." He ran a hand over his head. "I had just been called back because you resurfaced, and I was in the castle. They didn't know I was even here."

"And how long have you been hiding?" I asked.

He held up a finger. "They attacked the barracks first and had men on the inside. They brought everyone to the courtyard, and I watched from that window as they gave them all a choice. They either swore allegiance to the Council, or they were sent to the dungeons." His eyes were haunted before he squeezed them tightly and blew out a resigned breath. "I need to find a way to get them out of the dungeon so we can take back our kingdom and stop their evil plans for world domination."

"But there's no one in the dungeons," I whispered.

"What?" His eyes narrowed at me.

"My father and my mate, along with Fenrick and a friend, were arrested by the Council. They're still searching for me, so I went to the dungeons to release the men that were still loyal to my father, but the dungeons were empty." I sighed and flopped down into a dusty wingback armchair.

"They're not there?" he asked. "Then where are they?" He planted his hands on his hips and paced back and forth.

"I don't know. I wish I did, because that was my only hope for saving my father and mate." I tilted my head back and blinked away the tears of hopelessness forming in my eyes.

How has this all become such a mess?

"Do you know where the king was taken?" he asked.

"No. I think they were all taken back to the human realm, but I'm not certain." I clenched my fists at my sides, still unsure if I could trust Kiernan.

He'd said he was part of my father's elite militia, but he still didn't say why I'd never seen him before and had gone on to completely ignore my spy question.

"But why would the Council take them to the human realm? They hate it there. They loathe the humans!" Kiernan rubbed his chin, deep in thought.

"They have some kind of deal with the humans, we think. We've already been outed to the humans. Our lives are no longer secret. The world of myth and magic has been exposed. They have some kind of chemical that forces shifters to go into a rage and shift beyond their control. It was caught on camera and has been all over their media ever since."

"Shit," Kiernan swore, pressing his palm to his forehead.

"Yeah, it's pretty fucking bad," I admitted. "We've never experienced anything of this magnitude before. And I need an army, but I can't even sift back to the human realm to get help! I've been wandering around the castle, but every second I stay here is one second closer to them catching me and doing gods know what to me. I suspect no matter what I do, the outcome will be my demise."

"You can't sift?" he asked as if taken aback. and

I glared at him.

Like I need to be reminded of that right now! It's not like I was raised in Faery. I was abducted to the human realm and treated like a slave...

Kiernan grimaced at my reaction. "Ah, that's right, you're a young one."

"Yes, but I'm not dumb or naïve. How do I know you're not a spy for the Council just trying to gain my trust and any information I have before you turn me over to them?"

"You don't," he admitted. "And you're smart for not trusting me just because I wear your father's armor. Some of those men were right there with the Council guards rounding everyone up. Keeping your wits about you will keep you alive."

"Fair enough." I nodded.

At least he seems transparent and honest enough. He's not trying to sway me and he's not encouraging me to trust him blindly.

"I wouldn't trust anyone, Princess, especially those who tell you to trust them. They are the worst." He flexed a hand at his side.

"What are we going to do, then?" I asked, choosing to ponder Kiernan's jaded comment later.

"I don't know. What was your reason for wandering around the castle?"

"After I realized the army wasn't in the dungeons, I was trying to find someone to sift me back to the human world and not get caught by Ronaldo and his guards." I sighed.

"Why the human world?" he asked frowning. "If what you said earlier about us being exposed is true..." he trailed off.

"We have a sizable army there that can help us, and I'm the only one who can get them back into Faery." I chewed my lip nervously. It was a hell of a plan, but it was the best shot we had.

"Then let's go get your army." He held out a hand to me.

I hesitated, still not sure I could trust him. What if he was a spy looking for the location of the Facility and Grey's people? What if I led him to our army and was responsible for ruining everything?

"I can see the indecision in your eyes. You don't trust me." He nodded calmly, like he expected as much.

"This whole *nice guy here to save the day* thing could be an act to get me to tell you where the Facility is so that the Council can attack and destroy what little hope we have left of reclaiming Faerie." I raised a haughty and suspicious brow at him.

"Good girl," he said before dropping to one knee and resting his sword openly across his hands.

"What are you doing?" I asked, taken aback by the sudden and seemingly genuine subservient gesture.

"I swear to the gods and on my honor to protect and serve Princess Aurelia of the Shadow Kingdom until my dying breath," he announced, before he bowed his head.

Magic tingled in the air, wrapping around me and squeezing my chest, binding us together in a way that was unmistakably solemn and true. He'd just made a magical vow to serve and protect me.

I did not see that coming.

"Well, that was unexpected," I said, swallowing hard, not quite knowing what to say at moment such as this. The weight of his vow was a tangible thing and demonstrated the sanctity of the trust and loyalty he'd just invested in me.

"I won't tell you pretty lies but will give you the truth, always, Princess. I won't tell you that you can trust me—but I will prove myself the best way that I can, with my vow."

"What about your vow to my father?" I asked, wide-eyed.

"It's because of my vow to your father that I have made this vow to you. He would want someone to be by your side while he can't be here himself. He is my king, and you are his daughter—my allegiance is as much yours as it is his," he finished, still kneeling on the ground.

I had a feeling he would remain there until I told him otherwise. "Okay, for what it's worth, you've proved your point, and I appreciate your loyalty to my family. You can get up now." I waved a hand awkwardly for him to move.

"If people bowing to you makes you uncomfortable, you are going to have a very hard time being the princess you were born to be," Kiernan said with a chuckle as he rose to his feet once more.

"Trust me, I'm all too aware, but it was more your whole vow to protect and serve me that what made me slightly uncomfortable," I admitted as I stood from the chair. "Believe it or not, I'm not entirely okay with people risking their lives for me. I'm not used to being treated this way. It feels new and strange despite my upbringing in the castle before I was abducted."

"Fair enough, Princess. You were away a long time, and I imagine whatever you've been through has shaped who you have become. Our experiences forge us like a blacksmith's anvil. We can't deny what we have been through. But believe me when I say, you can handle this. You are the Shadow Princess."

I blew out a relieved breath, and my shoulders slumped, grateful that he understood where I was coming from and buoyed by his faith in me, even when I didn't feel it myself.

What are we going to do now? I have a guard from my father's militia sworn to me and we are still behind enemy lines...

"Would you be comfortable taking me to this army of yours now?" Kiernan asked.

"It's not so much of an army in the traditional sense," I corrected. "But they are a force that will fight for Grey and for the chance to get back into Faery." I adjusted the bags on my shoulder. The book felt warm through the canvas, comforting me that it was still in my possession. I needed it more than almost anything else. There was something inside that could help us with the Council.

There has to be. I just need time to find it.

"Can they fight in a battle or are they civilians?" he asked.

I chewed my lower lip before answering. "They're basically elite mercenaries." It was the only way I could think of to describe the people at Grey's building. They used a ring to decide disputes and worked whatever jobs they were told for pay. It was a bit barbaric and transactional for my liking. But at least I hadn't seen another fight since Layla had tried to drag me into combat.

"Mercenaries?" he scoffed, seemingly affronted by the suggestion. "Why would the Crown Princess work with a group of criminals?"

"I didn't always know I was a princess," I retorted as I planted my hands on my hips, meeting his gaze and daring him to say more. He didn't have the right to judge me or the people at the Syndicate. They may not have liked me all that much in the beginning, but they would do what needed to be done when the time came. I was sure of it. If nothing else, they were loyal to Grey, and I was his mate.

"Forgive me, Princess. I did not mean to insult you." He bowed his head in apology.

"It's fine. Trust me, I'm used to it. Just don't judge them. They've been looked down on by the Fae their entire lives and won't take kindly to it from you when we go back there without Grey. So, keep your tongue in check, okay?"

"Understood. So, how do we get to this place?" he asked.

"We will need to sift," I said. That was going to be the hardest part of this plan. I needed to trust him enough to put the image in his mind.

"That's going to be a problem, Princess. The castle is warded against sifting in or out. Unless we make it onto the grounds beyond the main walls, we can't do it." Kiernan ran a hand down his face.

"Fuck!" I practically yelled.

Kiernan flinched and scanned the chamber and the dark passages beyond for any threats.

Shit! I forgot we were being hunted down like dogs. Good job, Aurelia.

"I know of a concealed place in the woods that we could sift from without anyone seeing us," Keirnan offered, refusing to comment on my faux pas.

"Yeah, the only problem with that is getting there without being seen," I huffed in frustration. It felt like my plan was falling apart at the seams already.

"I guess you don't know *all* the passages in this place then, do you, Princess?" Kiernan grinned. He turned to the passageway he'd dragged me through only minutes ago.

We hurried through the tunnels to a part of the castle I'd never seen.

"There are passages that lead to the barracks?" I asked in a whisper.

"They were built in case of an emergency. They allow us to get to the king faster. Only a few of the king's most trusted soldiers know they exist at all."

"That's a fantastic idea. My father is tactical and practical man it seems." I nodded.

"That he is," my guide and rescuer agreed.

We crept along silently for what felt like forever until light filtered in below a door that I hadn't seen before.

How long have we been walking?

Nothing was familiar here, so there was no way of knowing or measuring the time.

Kiernan tapped on something, and stone ground against metal, and cogs and gears worked together.

I flinched at the loud sound and held my breath until the door swung completely open and my breath caught in my throat.

We're in the woods!

I could scarcely believe it. My heart sang with triumph and hope at the sight of the tall trees that towered over us as we rushed from the passage. There were verdant shrubs and tall grasses all over the area, and when I spun around, I found we'd just walked out of what appeared to be a small cabin.

"There's no time to waste, Princess," Kiernan said as he grabbed my hand.

With a resolute nod, I closed my eyes and gave him the image in my mind.

The world lurched, and we spun through time and space before our feet landed on solid ground once more. We'd landed on the soft grass just right outside the Syndicate's wards.

"Let me do the talking," I said, breathing a sigh of relief. "They can be temperamental." I took a step forward and crossed the wards.

"Stop!" someone yelled, and scarcely a heartbeat later guns were squarely pointed at my face.

My heart hammered in my chest, and I put my hands up in the air, showing that I was no threat. "It's me, Aurelia," I explained quickly. "Grey's in trouble, and we need your help."

A man I'd never seen before stepped forward. "Grey's not here. Now, I'm in charge. Make one false move, and I'll shoot, princess or not."

Who is this?

My mind ran rampant with possibilities as the two of us stood surrounded.

Shit! Has the Council somehow already taken over the Syndicate?

We were royally screwed if they had, and that was the understatement of the century.

I think I've just walked headlong to my own death. Fuck!

CHAPTER 6

"What did they do to you?" Fenrick yelled, aghast.

I blinked my eyes open, barely able to see the blurry outline of the Fae guardian who had quickly become a trusted and loyal friend.

"Watch it, traitor," the guard carrying me snapped before dropping me on the cold concrete of a cell.

I gasped as pain burned my back and my joints popped as I crashed to the floor.

One guard stomped from the cell, his disdain for us abundantly clear.

But the other watched us closely. "I'll be back later," he whispered and closed the cell.

Why did he whisper? Is he on our side?

He was the same guard who had squeezed my arm earlier in warning. Could it be that we had someone on the inside without even being aware? I groaned, pushing the thought aside for now, my head fuzzy and sore. I squeezed my eyes closed tightly and willed the room to stop spinning around me.

Fuck this.

"What is that on your chest?" Fenrick growled, intuitively moving to attend to me.

"Ronaldo's parting gift." I coughed and curled in on myself, bracing against the renewed onslaught of agony triggered by the impact of being dumped in the cell. It wasn't that I didn't want Fenrick to see the damage —I didn't care if he did—but I needed to protect myself. My body instinctively curled so my wounds weren't on display, a distinctly wolfy trait.

"I can't heal you with these cuffs on," Fenrick said regret filling his tone.

"It's okay, I can't shift to heal myself either." I shook my head and winced again when a fresh wave of pain sliced through it.

Did they kick my ass once I passed out? Why does my head hurt so badly? I don't remember anyone punching me in the head...

"They did a number on you and want you to suffer. How are we going to mix with the rest of the population and get a look around this hole when you can't even stand?" Fenrick sighed.

"Maybe that's the point. He wants to torture me and then starve me because I can't move." I moaned as I tried and failed to sit up.

"That guard whispered that he would be back. He's the same one who stopped the other guy from shooting you. Do you think he meant he would come back to help?" Fenrick asked with a note of hope in his voice.

"We can't trust anyone here, Fenrick. They are *all* from the Council. They are the enemy," I said, gritting my teeth against the throbbing pain in my mangled and broken hand.

"But this guard doesn't seem to want you dead. His expression when the other one dumped you on the ground was murderous for a second, I swear, before he schooled himself completely blank."

Not a moment too soon my oversensitive shifter hearing picked up the sound of boots stomping down the hall just outside our cell. I shushed Fenrick before the door opened again.

Speak of the devil...

The very same guard we'd been talking about came through and closed the door behind him. He crouched in front of me with wide eyes, his emotion on full display. "I can't heal you completely or they will know someone on staff helped you," he apologized.

"Why are you helping me?" I gritted out, wary as all hell.

"Dan sent me," he explained quietly. "He knew something major was going on when you all took so long to come back to the Syndicate." He placed his hand over mine and green healing magic spread through me, popping my bones back into place.

I nearly screamed at the instantaneous pain but locked my jaw so I couldn't open my mouth and alert anyone.

"What are you doing?" Fenrick accused under his breath as he approached the man defensively.

"I'm healing his crushed fingers. They used a hammer and shattered his damn bones," the guard said. "You can heal. You *know* exactly how painful it can be for a patient." He removed his hand a minute later.

Relief flooded me, and I flexed my still stiff and sore hand. It hurt, but it wasn't broken anymore, and I was thankful as fuck for that. "What are you? How are you able to heal?" I asked.

"I'm half Fae. It was the only way I could be a guard in here." The half Fae moved his hand over my chest next.

"So, basically the half Fae children they abandoned to a cold new reality are welcomed back if they do Ronaldo's dirty work? Got it." I shook my head. Ronaldo really was a piece of shit. I would be dealing with him soon. Just as soon as I got out of this hellhole. His name was at the top of my shit list.

"Basically, but it's good for us because now I can get word to Dan about where you are, and they can get a team here to rescue you." The guard pulled his hand from my chest, having relieved some of the pain with a look of apology.

"I get it, no stress. Your life is on the line if they find out you've healed me. I'll survive. Thank you for what you've done." I dipped my head to the man and pulled myself up into a seated position, propping myself against the cold wall. I was still stiff, and pinpricks of pain hit me if I moved a certain way, but at least I could move.

Ronaldo will be pissed.

I grinned at the thought of the belligerent old man being enraged and flummoxed as to how I managed to heal so quickly. Every little win counted against that man, even if meant I was being petty.

"I have to go now, but I'll help whenever I can," the guard whispered and left our shared cell.

I glanced at Fenrick with a raised brow, wondering how in the hell that just happened. "Did that really just happen?" I asked in case I was in some kind of delusional pain-induced nightmare and was still, in fact, broken.

"It did. But how on earth did Dan manage to get a plant in here so quickly?" Fenrick shook his head is genuine wonder.

"Dan is fucking resourceful. He also knows just about *everyone* in the supernatural community in Dallas. He always gets the job done. I'll give him that." Could I truly dare hope that Dan would find a way to get us out of here? Every guard I'd seen so far appeared to be Fae.

What's happened to the human guards who worked here before?

"Well, despite what he did to Aurelia, I'm glad he's on our side." Fenrick held out a hand to help me get up from the ground.

"Same. He didn't really mean for all of that to happen, though. He's a good man at heart, and I've already punished him for what went down." I grabbed a plain gray shirt that lay folded on the bottom bunk on the opposite side of the cell and pulled it over my head, wincing as I did so. The marks on my chest weren't entirely healed, but I didn't want everyone to see that I'd been marked in the first place, unwilling to give Ronaldo that satisfaction.

I flexed my hand and winced when it was still a bit sore, pain radiating from the joints. The guard was right. If Ronaldo found out that I'd healed completely already there would be an investigation, and we would lose the only advantage we had. It was a great turn of events to have a guard on our side, and I wasn't about to squander it.

An electronic buzzing sound filled the cell, irritating my ears as the door swung open. I glanced at Fenrick in question.

He shrugged. "They do that when it's time to go to the mess hall." He stepped out of the cell into the throng of people rushing from their cells.

"How long did he have me chained to that table?" I asked.

"I've been here for three solid meals already, so I'm guessing a full day?" He nudged me when I stopped walking.

Shit. No wonder my head is fuzzy. Shifters need a lot of energy, and I'm running on empty!

"Okay, show me the way." My stomach growled at the thought of food. When I'd been preoccupied by pain, I hadn't realized how hungry I was, but with the mention of food, my stomach rumbled, and even my wolf whimpered in my mind, starving as well.

I followed Fenrick and the horde of prisoners down the maze of cells to a large room. There were no windows, and a buffet-style line had already started in the far corner. There were human guards mixed in with the Fae guards, which I found interesting. I raised an eyebrow at Fenrick.

He shrugged and grimaced. "They have some kind of arrangement," he whispered as he handed me a scratched up metal tray.

There were workers serving behind a plexiglass barrier, dishing out some kind of disgusting-looking slop. I sighed, but my wolf whined his dire need for whatever the hell it was they were feeding us as we moved down the line.

"We already guessed that much, but the humans look distinctively uncomfortable being in the same room with the Fae," I said, scanning the guards discreetly one by one.

I pitched forward as I was shouldered unexpectedly in the back. I nearly busted my face on the plexiglass but caught myself at the last second before I spun around to find the man already striding away.

What the fuck was that about?

I turned back and retrieved my tray of food and followed my friend.

Fenrick strolled over to a table in the corner.

Relief flooded through me as I spotted two familiar faces at the table.

They're okay!

The Shadow King nodded as I sat across from him.

Magna smiled. "You didn't struggle," she said with what sounded like genuine relief.

"No, I let him carve those awful words into my chest and break my hand instead," I growled under my breath.

Magna winced, tears filling her eyes at my snide declaration.

I shook my head and pursed my lips.

I don't need tears. I need revenge and a way out of this fucking cesspool.

"Sorry," I said, catching myself after a moment. There was no need to be a smart-ass to Magna. She'd been nothing but good to me and the Syndicate. "Sometimes I forget that you see too much." I set my tray down on the table and picked up my fork to take a bite of whatever the gruel was that they'd served us when I noticed the odd separation of the guards.

The human guards were clearly confused about what was happening and why. They whispered to each other, probably unaware that the Fae guards could hear them without trouble.

"The humans are scared and confused," I whispered, leaning into the others and keeping my voice low. "We can probably use that to our advantage." I put the spoon to my lips and grimaced. The slop on the end of it didn't even smell appetizing in the slightest, but I shoveled it into my mouth, nonetheless. I couldn't be picky when eating was the difference between life and death. It was fuel, and that's all that mattered.

"Look what we have here," a deep voice echoed through the now silent mess hall.

I turned to see a huge shifter that I'd never seen before staring directly at me. He had to be some kind of bear, and we wolves never really got along with the bears in nature. "And what is that?" I asked, turning to rise from my seat and stand at my full height.

"The great Shifter King was caught by the Fae? Your father must be rolling over in his grave right now." The shifter laughed. He obviously thought he was at the top of pecking order here.

Wrong thing to say, asshole.

He was the first but wouldn't be the last to challenge me in this shit-hole. It was the way of the world in prison—you always took out the biggest motherfucker first.

I can handle this.

"What grave?" I asked. "He wasn't dead until a few weeks ago, and I doubt the *High Councilor* gave him the courtesy of a proper burial."

The shifter sneered, not caring at all that his barb didn't stick, or the information that my father had been alive or in prison for centuries bothered me.

"Hey!" a guard shouted. "Do we have a problem over here?"

I lifted a brow at the shifter in question. "I don't know. I don't have a problem, but this guy clearly does."

The shifter's face turned red as he took a threatening step forward. "You have a big mouth, Shifter King. Someone should do something about that." The shifter balled his fist, preparing for a fight.

I felt more than heard the chairs screeching across the tiles behind me. I waved Fenrick and the Shadow King off, not wanting them to get into trouble along with me as I stared down the grunt in front of me. "So, you are going do something about it?" I taunted. "Or is it you who is all mouth and no bite?"

The shifter growled and predictably swung a meaty fist at my head.

I ducked easily despite my injuries, seeing the blow coming from a mile away.

The shifter spun around, but not fast enough.

I kicked out a leg and sent him sprawling to the ground in a heap. He fell hard, hitting his head on a nearby table and bumped into a warlock.

The warlock growled as he turned on me with a glare, clearly pissed.

I wasn't the one who'd bumped into him, but apparently everyone had a chip on his shoulder in this place.

In the next instant chaos ensued, a riot breaking out in red-hot minute just as the warlock punched me in the face, and everything turned black.

CHAPTER 7
Aurelia

"You're not in charge. Where's Dan?" I yelled, demanding answers.

They surrounded us with guns drawn, serious and menacing.

I didn't recognize a single one of them, but then, I hadn't met everyone in the Syndicate. It was a large organization, after all. I glared at the man in front of me. Was he a lackey of the Council's? Could they have broken through Grey's protective wards and taken over the place in his absence?

No, that's not possible.

I'd felt Grey's wards as we stepped over them. They were still firmly in place and functioning. This was something different. Were they simply idiots on a power trip perhaps? Was this a simple play for power within the Syndicate and nothing more? Either way, this was bad. How was I going to get the help I needed for those I loved if they locked us away in a cell? A moment later, a gun dug into my back.

A shifter shoved me forward roughly, clearly not giving a shit about who I was to Grey or Faery at large.

Where is everyone? Where the hell are Dan and Asher? They would be able to put a stop to this.

"Dan is gone," a shifter whispered behind me, the voice distinctly feminine.

I glanced over my shoulder at the woman whose brows were pinched in confusion, though she didn't hesitate in shoving me forward.

"Gone where? He's in charge here, not you," I growled back at her before I glanced at Kiernan.

His sword was still in its scabbard, but his hand gripped the hilt, just waiting for the opportunity to wield it.

"Stop asking questions," the man in charge said in a gruff tone. "*You're* the damn reason the boss left us in the first place, and I will see to it that you punished for his disappearance, wicked Fae!"

"It's always going to come back to that, isn't it?" I fired back. "This has nothing to do with Grey at all, but your own prejudice against the Fae. It was our corrupt Council that fucked us all over—not the royal family and not me. And incidentally, they're the very same Council bastards we're trying to fight against right now!" I threw my hands up in frustration and anger.

The action set everyone into uneasy motion. They steadied their guns, ready to take me out on a heartbeat's notice.

"I have no problem shooting you, Princess." The asshole in charge got right up in my face with a sneer. "But if you come with us quietly, you won't end up a stain on the concrete right here and now."

"Where are the Riders of the Hunt?" I demanded. "Dan should have left one of them in charge in his absence. This is *ridiculous*."

He refused to answer my question, and instead one of his lackies prodded me in the back to move.

Kiernan placed a hand on my shoulder and squeezed it in support. "They won't kill you, Princess. I won't allow it," Kiernan whispered.

I nodded, grateful for it. Our magic was probably faster than bullets if we were forced to fight or defend ourselves.

Maybe.

Kiernan would know better than me, but it wasn't something I could ask him at the moment. Not to mention, I *really* didn't want to test that theory.

They steered us to the parking garage, a force surrounding us on all sides.

I groaned, secretly hoping I didn't get thrown in a cell next to that crazy bitch who screamed all the time.

Wouldn't that just be poetic justice?

I frowned and turned to peer at Kiernan, wondering what he was thinking about all this.

Without prelude or warning Asher burst from the elevator. "What the fuck are you morons doing?" he bellowed as he stomped toward us, his face red with his rage, the guards' impending deaths reflected in his eyes.

Finally, someone who can talk sense to these people!

My heart skipped a beat, and I breathed a heavy sigh of relief. We were going to be okay.

"The Fae are a problem," the man who'd claimed to be in charge sneered. "They cannot be trusted!"

"Grey will do worse to you then he did to that backstabbing bitch if you don't let his Fated mate go. Do you have any idea who she actually is?" Asher asked, his voice like gravel as he got right up in the shifter's face.

"Yes. I know she's the reason Grey is gone and she's the reason the Council has gone murderous. She's the reason they are taking over the fucking world and rounding us up like rabid dogs!" the shifter yelled.

"Excuse me?" I snarled, my temper rising anew. "What' the fuck is this about the Council rounding everyone up?"

"Don't talk to me, Fae whore," the man spat with venom.

Asher took a swing at the guy, his enormous, meaty fist flying through the air with deadly precision.

At the exact same time Kiernan drew his sword.

The asshole was thrown to the ground, sailing backward with the power of Asher's punch.

Kiernan had nicked the man's throat and advanced on him, his blade tilting the shifter's chin up from his place on the concrete as he looked down upon him. "If you ever speak to the future queen of Faery that way again, banishment will look like a walk in the park," Kiernan hissed with a deadly calm.

Asher clenched his fists at his sides, ready for the shifter to argue so he could indulge in the pleasure of laying him out again.

I shook my head and pressed my hand to my forehead with a grimace. "I've finally figured out a way for us *all* to go home, and this is the reception I get? Un-fucking-believable."

The rest of the Riders of the Hunt blocked the elevator doors, on guard, ready to have their brother-in-arms' back.

Zeke winked at me.

They were intimidating, sure, but I was tired of being protected by intimidating men. I was a future queen, and I had every intention of proving myself. A queen needed her subjects, but she had to show that she was *worthy* of being followed, of ruling those under her protection. And getting my people home and rescuing those I loved was my top priority in doing just that.

"Home to Faery?" someone whispered behind me.

I chose to ignore it.

"It doesn't matter what she says!" the shifter now on his knees bellowed. "She's the reason the boss is gone and she should be punished."

"Your boss is gone because he was helping me find what we needed to send everyone home to Faery!" I shouted.

I am so done with this bullshit.

Asher stomped forward, picking the shifter up off the concrete. "*She* is your boss' mate and deserves the same respect you've shown him."

"It's fine, Asher. Grey has always ruled with fear, so maybe I should have started with that." I let my hands glow with my magic and stepped around the man to stand next to Asher.

The rest of the guards shifted nervously from foot to foot, fidgeting with the safety mechanisms on their guns, most likely unsure of what they should be doing, or on whose side they were on.

Shadows pulsed up my arms as I stared down on the asshole.

He gulped, his pulse fluttering erratically at his neck, and fear was thick in his eyes. "I'm in charge while Dan is gone!" he argued despite his predicament.

"You will *never* be in charge!" Asher roared as he lifted him by his shirt and shook the man violently.

The rest of his brothers created an imposing wall of pissed-off Riders of the Hunt in front of the elevator as they closed ranks.

"Put your guns down," Zeke ordered all those present, his tone lethal.

What could the Riders have ever done that scared everyone so much? Ever since they helped Grey rescue me from Malcolm, they had been nothing but kind and respectful to me. Seeing the murderous side of them was different and more than a little humbling, and I was glad they were on my side and loyal to a fault.

The group surrounding us glanced between one another and the man who was leading them, and then finally holstered their weapons.

"Now, *move*." Asher dropped the man to the concrete and shoved past several of the shifter guards still circling me.

The guards scattered like ants.

I glanced up at Asher's murderous expression. He was a big softy when he wanted to be, but he could scare the life out of someone as well. "Asher, it's fine." I sighed, letting my magic recede into me.

"Come on, Princess. We need to know what's happening. Your mother is beside herself with worry." Asher wrapped an enormous arm around my shoulders protectively.

"What about *him*?" someone shouted behind me, referring to my newest traveling companion. "He could be a spy!"

"He's with me," I said with more calm than I felt. "He saved me and swore a magical vow. *No one* is to touch him." I spun on the group still surrounding Kiernan, my eyes blazing with challenge.

"You heard the princess, *now move*!" Asher took a threatening step toward the group.

They all backed away from Kiernan, hands up in surrender despite their sour expressions.

"That's a neat trick." Kiernan smirked.

"These idiots piss me off to no end," Asher explained. "I don't usually throw my weight around like that, but with Grey and Dan both gone, it's been getting a bit ridiculous around here." The Rider shook his head as he led me to the elevators.

Zeke nodded his head as he stepped out of the way. "Glad to see you're safe, Princess. We were worried about you," he said earnestly.

"I was worried there for a bit myself." I chuckled.

Kiernan jogged up next to me. "Did you say the queen was here?"

"Yes, she's here and more than a little worried about her family disappearing on her," Asher said, shooting me a pointed look.

"Later," I commanded. "I don't want everyone to hear this." I glanced around the parking garage warily. I couldn't trust any of these shifters in Grey's absence, it seemed. I stepped inside the elevator.

The Riders along with Kiernan all followed me inside.

Asher hit the button for the top floor, and we rode up in silence.

I blew out a relieved breath when we reached the top floor and grinned. This place felt like home, and I was gladder to be back here than I'd expected to feel. I rushed down the hall to Grey's office and forgot for a second that he wasn't there. The space smelled like him. I spun around in a circle just breathing it in for a second before noticing Asher's look of amusement.

"Did you miss this place?" he asked, chuckling.

I shrugged. "I guess I did. It's a thousand times better than hiding out in the dusty passageways of the castle and running from Ronaldo's guards."

"That's fair enough." Asher bowed his head to me.

"So, how long has Dan been gone?" I asked as I sat down in Grey's chair behind his desk, glancing between the Riders of the Hunt. They were all huge, imposing figures, though I'd only gotten to personally know Asher and Zeke.

"He's been gone a couple days now. We aren't sure what he's plotting." Asher ran a hand down his face.

"Grey and my father, along with Fenrick and Magna, have all been captured by the Council," I said, dropping the bomb no one wanted to hear.

"Fuck," Asher cursed.

"Yeah, my thoughts exactly. We need to find them because I have no idea how long they will let them live at this point, especially if they try standing up for themselves." I chewed my lip nervously.

"Do you know where they've taken him?" Asher asked. His body was coiled tightly, and he kept clenching and unclenching his fists at his sides.

I hadn't asked how they knew each other or what kind of relationship the Riders had with my mate. It seemed there was never time. "No. I'm guessing somewhere in the human realm, because they dragged them to the portal after they were captured." It was the only thing that made sense, but at the same time… it didn't make sense.

Why drag them through the portal instead of to the Council chambers or the castle dungeons?

Zeke sat at the conference table and pulled out his laptop, searching for any clue as to what was going on this side of Faery and where Grey might have been taken.

"I think we might need to talk to that shifter again. What jail was he in?" I asked.

There had been something very clearly wrong with the place they had kept him. He should have been able to use his strength to get away, but he couldn't.

"I want a sample of whatever they dosed him with," Zeke said, never looking up from his laptop.

"What good will that do?" I asked, drumming my fingers on the desk.

"If we know what it is, we may be able to find a way to counter it. The shifter said it was chemical and felt like bottled rage. That's a terrifying combination when working with shifters." Zeke continued tapping away on the keys.

Asher sat in the chair next to him with a huff. "We need to work on one thing at a time. We need to be focused."

"Agreed," I acknowledged. "Hey, Kiernan," I said looking to the Fae.

"Is there anything you remember from your time in the castle that might be of use?"

"I heard a great many conversations about the human government, but you already seem to know that they're working together," Kiernan said.

"It's the only thing that makes sense. They used a chemical on the shifter so he would shift into his wolf on camera." I shook my head. "It's like they're aligning their prejudices, but to what end?"

"That stunt caused a lot of civil unrest. Plus, there were Fae guards in the human jail," Asher pointed out.

"We don't know how deep this alliance goes, though. Were those guards just planted there, or did the human government allow them to be brought in? How much do the people in the prisons know about what's actually happening there?"

"Those are all very good questions that we do not have the answers to." Asher slammed his fist on the table in frustration. It was clear the Syndicate's inaction in mine and Grey's absence had been testing him. Without answers or information, they hadn't been able to do anything of consequence besides bide their time.

"We need to get them out and soon. Every day that Grey is in their clutches could be his last." I laid my forehead on the cool desk and blew out an unsteady breath.

The Fates can't take him yet. He's mine and if I lose him, it will break me beyond repair.

CHAPTER 8
Grey

I howled as something hit me in the back, and electricity burned beneath my skin, rippling like living wildfire. My body twitched uncontrollably as I flopped about on the ground like a fish out of water.

Fuck. That hurt!

Hands gripped my arms, hauling me to my feet, but my knees buckled under me, and I would have crashed to the ground again if it weren't for the guards holding me up.

"Picking fights in here is a *very* bad idea," the guard who'd helped me before whispered.

"I didn't pick that fight. He attacked me." I tried to shrug him off, but I was still sore from the torture session and the electrified baton had just radiated pain throughout my entire body.

"It doesn't matter. That's not what the guards saw... You're going in the hole," he said loud enough so that everyone heard.

That is not the place I want to be. Damn it.

I glanced over my shoulder at the others' worried faces and subtly winked, letting them know it would be okay. At least for now I wasn't going to get another torture session.

"Let this be a lesson, new people!" The guard holding me up turned his glare on everyone in the room. "If you fight, you will get Tasered and sent to the hole for a full day. If you do it again, it's a week." He shoved me out the door for good measure. Everyone was watching, after all. "You just made things exponentially more difficult for us," he whispered so low, only a shifter could hear.

"That wasn't my fault. I don't go around picking fights," I said. "I'm not an idiot."

He yanked on my arm to get me to move faster as he dragged me through the halls. Cells lined each wall, but there was no one inside them. Everyone was in the mess hall, eating garbage and probably gossiping about the fight that just broke out.

"Some of the guards seem uncomfortable," I said, changing the subject.

"The humans are scared of us. They know they aren't strong enough to take us down without their special batons. It's why they were given those when witches and shifters were brought in."

He was sharing information, but I had a feeling he would keep up the act no matter what went down. Even though he'd healed me, I couldn't trust the guy.

Not completely.

If it came down to getting us out of here or his life, he would choose his life, and I couldn't fault him for that. We were all just creatures that wanted to live, after all.

He led me to a heavy metal door that had a distinctively ominous feel to it.

I reared back, not liking the looks of it at all.

He swiped his badge across the scanner and that electric buzzing echoed through the hall as the door slid open.

I understood now why they called it *the hole*. There were no lights in the four-by-four cell. It was cramped as fuck, and there were no windows to let any light in, either. I was going to be sitting in the dark for an entire day, completely alone and uncomfortable.

Just fucking great.

"If this happens again, it's a week, Grey. You need to be careful in here," he whispered before closing the door and blocking out all light.

The box was so small I couldn't stretch my legs out when I sat down. Guards passed by every so often, their words the only company I had.

"We're going to be getting even more of the crazies," a guard said. "They're rounding them all up."

What the fuck? They're really going that far?

I had thought the country was founded because of persecution and on the concept of being free, and now they were doing this just because they were scared?

"Not all of them are going to prison," another voice said. "They have special intake facilities to see if they're a threat to humanity."

I call bullshit. I doubt anyone comes out of those facilities alive. They are just saying that so they can have an excuse to test on my people. I need to get out of here. My people are in fucking danger, and I'm stuck in this fucking box!

"Do you really think they'll let any of them go? You're an idiot, if you do," the first guard scoffed. "They're too dangerous."

"Locking them all up forever doesn't make a lot of sense though, either. They're a drain on our resources locked in prisons and facilities. There's got to be another way, right?"

"Are you becoming a bleeding heart, Thomas? You saw that brawl in there. If they didn't have those cuffs on, it would have been *a lot* worse."

"I'm not a bleeding heart," Thomas grunted back.

The hall went quiet after that, and I had no clue how long I'd been cramped up on the floor of the tiny cell when more voices filtered in.

"I don't know why we have to listen to that guy," a new voice said, reaching me from the hall.

"He's got an *in* with some high-profile people, including the Department of Justice," someone responded.

"So, he can just take over? I had friends that were fired so his freaks could come in and run the place."

"I would watch your tone, man. I get it, I do. But there's something seriously off about that guy. He has his own room in the medical unit, and people have heard screams coming from it," the new voice warned.

"You think he's torturing people? That's not even legal," the second voice huffed.

"Are they even people, though? Do they get the same human rights we do when they aren't even actually human?"

"No, you're right. They aren't human, so our laws don't apply to them. That's why they can all be rounded up and dealt with. No activists will care that strange, magical creatures are being treated like animals."

I shifted my position on the floor and clenched my hand into a fist, shaking with rage. These assholes really wanted to be gutted by a wolf's claws. They were fucking begging for it. And how I wished they could be mine. But I couldn't do that. If I killed a human guard, the punishment would be far more severe than a day or a week in the hole. I doubted that Ronaldo would let the humans sentence me to death though. Without doubt, he wanted my death for himself.

"That's a pretty fucked-up view, man." The first guard chuckled.

"You saw the video of the guy who turned into a raging wolf! That's the shit we're dealing with in here. I do *not* get paid enough to have to worry about getting mauled by a fucking rabid werewolf or whatever."

"The President of the United States said Homeland Security is handling it," the first man said.

"Yeah, *handling it* means they become our problem."

The assholes were seriously pissing me off. They had no care for the fact that despite us not being human, we were still intelligent people with families and innocent children. We had just as much of a right to peace, freedom, and life as they did. I tuned out after that before I ended up raging in the tiny cell and got myself stuck in there longer.

I must have fallen asleep at some point because I blinked my eyes open to the harsh, LED lighting flooding through the open door.

"Learned your lesson yet, mutt?" Ronaldo's wheezing voice was like claws on a chalkboard.

I kept my mouth shut as I stood. My bones creaked, and I cracked my neck. Sleeping sitting up when I couldn't shift was murder on my back. I stared down the High Councilor, waiting for him to tell me why he was releasing me from the hole rather than a guard. He didn't disappoint.

"You have one last chance to tell me where the princess is hiding, or I will use other means to find her." Ronaldo warned, glaring at me.

"I'm not telling you shit, asshole." I crossed my arms over my chest defiantly.

I couldn't tell him even if I wanted to, not that I do or would. —She's my Fated mate. I have no idea where she is or if she's even still alive. No, don't even think that way. She has to be alive. I would have felt it if she'd died...

"Fine. I gave you a chance." Ronaldo waved a hand to the guard behind him. "Take him back to his cell."

The guard grabbed my arm roughly, squeezing it hard. He wasn't the same one who'd been helping me, but he wasn't one of the scared humans, either. He was Fae, and if his attitude was any indication, he'd bought right into Ronaldo's bullshit rhetoric. The guard shoved me when he could, pushing me into the wall and just all around manhandling me. It was to be expected that when we got back to my cell, he shoved me against the bars.

"You're filth, and we will eradicate you from the realms. We have already started the process." He shoved my face between the bars.

Fenrick stood with his hands balled into fists, wanting to protect me.

I shook my head as much as I was able. We didn't need anyone else to end up in the hole.

We need to get the fuck out of here.

The guard finally swiped the keycard over the scanner, and the door slowly swung open. He shoved my back, hard.

I stumbled into the cell, still aching from my time in the cramped cell.

The guard slammed the door closed behind me. "You'll get yours, shifter scum!" he called over his shoulder as he strolled away.

"You make friends everywhere you go, don't you?" Fenrick shook his head with a lop-sided smile.

"It's part of my charm, I guess." I chuckled.

"Where did they take you?" Fenrick asked.

"The hole, just like he said. It's a tiny cell that's pitch black and boring as all hell. But I got some information from some stupid human guards who didn't realize I could hear them through the steel door."

"What is it?" he asked warily.

"They are rounding all of us up and throwing away the keys," I huffed and dropped down onto the cot.

"Genocide. Fuck. I didn't even think the Council was *that* evil." Fenrick sat with his elbows on his knees on the cot opposite me.

"Look who runs the Council... the guy took pleasure in carving *Shifter Scum* on my body. Of course, they're *that* evil." I fell back on the cot, thankful I could stretch out my legs finally and get proper blood flow back.

"You're right—" Fenrick started to say.

I shushed him. The sound of several pairs of footsteps making their way toward us reached my ears, and I stood abruptly. There had only been one time that I had to be escorted by more than one guard, and that was when they took me to Ronaldo's personal house of horrors in the medical wing. I wasn't ready for another damn torture session.

This isn't good at all. Is Ronaldo making good on his threat from earlier? Fuck!

Two guards stepped up to our cell and sneered at Fenrick through the bars. "You're coming with us, traitor."

"The hell he is!" I stepped in front of Fenrick, acting like a shield for my friend, but knew it was futile.

"Don't get yourself in even more trouble, shifter scum. Do you want to go back to the hole already?" the guard on the right said. He swiped his badge over the scanner and stepped inside with one of those electrified batons all the human guards wielded. He flicked it on, and the *buzz* of electricity met my ears.

"Where are you taking him?" I asked, throwing my hands up in surrender. Getting in the shit wouldn't help Fenrick or any one of us, for that matter.

"The High Councilor wants to have a chat with him."

"Fuck, no. Take me instead." I took another step forward.

The man thrust the baton at me.

I was forced to step back.

"Boss' orders were to bring in the traitor. Now, you can get out of my way, or you can have electricity flood your system, and then I'll kick the shit out of you."

"It's okay, Grey. Stand down. I can take it." Fenrick patted my shoulder as he took a step around me.

I lunged at the guards, but before I could get close, Fenrick shoved me back on my ass. "Stop, Grey. It'll all be okay in the end."

"He better come back from this!" I roared, my blood boiling. "I'm already planning each of your bloody deaths. If he doesn't return, I'll torture you so slowly when I get out of here that you'll wish a wolf would just tear your throats out!"

The guards didn't even spare me a glance as they took a resigned Fenrick from the cell and marched him down the hall.

Hopelessness ate at my insides as the door closed behind them, locking me in with no way to help my friend. I gripped the bars and watched until they were out of sight, my knuckles white and my heart racing.

Please let him come back.

CHAPTER 9

The TV in the corner of the room blared with the carnage that was the current landscape of Dallas. Humans were terrified in the knowledge that supernaturals existed and were acting out everywhere. It wasn't just local now either, it was on a global scale.

One picture after another of people being beaten by gangs of humans who thought they were supernaturals flashed across the screen. The death toll was rising steadily, and people were being accused left, right, and center without proof of being magical.

"It's a bloodbath," I whispered to myself. "It's like the Salem Witch Trials all over again—only worse. Don't people ever learn?"

"No, Princess," Asher said softly. "They let their fear of the unknown rule them, while some use it to their advantage to seek vengeance on those they feel have wronged them."

"He's right," Zeke chimed in, never looking up from his screen as his fingers flew across the keyboard. "There are reports of people being beaten who had not a single drop of magical blood in them. They were merely pointed out by jealous fools who wanted what they had, so they seized on an opportunity among all this chaos."

"Or the hatred in their hearts made them so angry that they were willing to lash out in any way they could to do the most damage possible." I sighed.

Why do people have to be so cruel?

Why couldn't they stop their hatred of the unknown? We were in an era where they were supposed to be getting past all the bigotry and hatred of centuries gone by, but every time something came along that they didn't understand, they lashed out, acting on pure emotion and fear, without a thought for the carnage or consequences their actions might cause.

The scene changed on the TV to a bunch of people throwing bottles at storefronts. My eyes widened as I realized they were outside a potion shop on the witch side of Dallas. I'd been there. "What the hell are they doing?" I whispered, my eyes glued to the screen.

Asher ran a hand down his face, not for the first time today. "It's been like this for a couple days now, Princess. They've been looting and rioting, causing general calamity."

"But, why? What does that accomplish?" I asked, my brows furrowed and my head aching.

"Absolutely nothing," Zeke groaned beside Asher. "They are tearing their own neighborhoods apart out of fear or just because they can. They're acting like mindless animals..."

"Humans make no sense," Asher grumbled.

"A witch just got mugged in broad daylight and nearly beaten to death." Zeke never looked up from his laptop. "Instead of taking her to the hospital, they're holding her in one of those special facilities to be tested on."

"That is so much bullshit!" I leaned forward.

I was right. I've always thought we'd be tested on one day like lab rats...

"Did the people who hurt her at least get arrested?"

Zeke glanced at me over the screen and shook his head, his lips pursed. "The police said she started it and let them all go."

"How can they do this? These are people we're talking about, not monsters. Innocents are being treated like criminals out of fear and the real monsters can do stuff like this and get away with it!" My hands tingled with my magic, and I clenched them into tight fists. I couldn't let my anger get the better of me and trigger my magic in a way I'd struggle to control. I was better than that, and the guys here didn't deserve the hassle of cleaning it up in the aftermath.

"Look at that sign!" Kiernan said with a shake of his head. "*Animals Belong in Cages*. Complete bullshit when *they* are the ones acting like animals."

I peered at the sign and growled. Why did people have to be like that? This was all the Council's doing. I was certain humans wouldn't react this catastrophically if they hadn't been egged on by corrupt Fae propaganda and manipulation. In that moment, I made a promise to myself and the realms I held dear to end their oppressive rule. "This is what the Council wanted from the beginning. It will be easier to round up the supernaturals with the humans' fear thick in the air," I said. "They're just using the humans. They have no more tolerance for them than they do shifters, witches, or anyone else who isn't pure-blooded Fae. They just have something to gain at the moment."

I knew how Ronaldo thought. He was the worst of all the supernaturals I'd ever met. The way he was planning this and executing his vision was beyond deplorable—it made me sick to my stomach.

"What do we do?" Kiernan asked, his eyes full of fire. "How do we stop this?"

"We don't," Dan's voice sounded from the office door, startling me.

"Dan! Where have you been?" I jumped from my chair.

Dan had black circles under his eyes and his dark hair was sticking up at odd angles as it matted with blood. He limped into the room and dropped into a seat next to Asher. "They're rounding up our people.

Innocents with kids and families are disappearing into thin air." He ran a hand down his face and sighed heavily.

"The government called for those actions," I said.

"I know, but two days ago I got a tip that an influential shifter family was on the chopping block. It was something about a political rival accusing them of being supernatural. They were going to be raided. This is the only safe place for us in the realm now."

"Nowhere else is safe?" I asked in horror.

How are we supposed to enact a plan to rescue my mate and move if there is no safe harbor to be found?

I glanced back at the TV screen, watching the people riot and loot once again. They didn't care that they were harming others. They were hurting other humans, supposedly to get back at supernaturals… and for what? What was the purpose of any of the senseless violence?

We are so fucked.

"Shifter side is completely deserted. They're all gone, and I don't know if it's because someone tipped them off, or if everyone simply fled when the raids started happening." Dan tilted his head back and huffed out a breath of frustration. The feeling of powerlessness was getting to everyone it seemed.

"What about the witches? This must be fucking terrible for them," I said, running a hand through my long hair.

"The witches have been hiding. Their side of town looks abandoned, but only because it's like a no man's land now. Someone informed them where to find the communities of supernaturals, and that's where they went first."

"Shit! *Malcolm.* He's lived here long enough to know where the communities are and who the big players are. He would have tipped them off." I shook my head, clenching my fists anew at the thought of that bastard.

"Malcolm." Kiernan turned sharply to me. "Your betrothed?"

I held up my hand to ward off that conversation. "Don't even start with that. I will *never* marry that creep. I have a mate."

Kiernan nodded and turned back to the TV, thankfully ending that subject.

I didn't want to ever speak of it again. I had my mate, the Shifter

King, my beautiful Grey. And no one was going to tear us apart. Not if we had any say in the matter!

"Yes, I believe Malcolm tipped them off about quite a bit. But we are extracting as many as we can when we get a tip telling us who might be next," Dan said. "It just takes a lot of manpower to make shit happen with all this going on and danger at every turn."

"Is that why you left those idiots in charge?" I asked with a raised brow.

Dan flinched. "I'm sorry about that, Aurelia. They know better now than to do anything like that to you again. I told them I would let the trolls have them for punching bags...and worse, if I ever heard such disrespect out of them ever again."

"Grey would have lost his mind and done something similar to what happened to Layla." I said and shuddered at the memory of her horrific and gory—but much deserved—demise.

"About Grey," Dan said slowly.

"Do you know where he is?" I gasped, jumping from my chair again, my eyes locked on his face.

"I do. I have a man inside the maximum-security prison they've taken over, and he has eyes on Grey and your father."

I flopped back into my chair, slumping in my seat, my heart thumping so hard it hurt to breathe. They were in prison here in the human realm and no doubt they were in a similar set-up to the jail they broke the shifter out of. "How are we going to get them out?" I asked, swallowing the lump in my throat.

"I don't know yet, but at least we know they're alive, Princess." Dan patted my hand.

There was a time I would have recoiled and probably slapped him for having the nerve to touch me after what he'd done when we first met on witchside, but that had passed with all the help he'd given me and my mate ever since. "He probably thinks I'm dead," I whispered. Tears burned behind my eyes, and I hated it. The last thing I wanted to show was weakness, but the thought that my mate might have been hurting because he thought I had died absolutely gutted me.

Like he's not in enough pain and danger already!

Asher glanced at me from his spot at the table going through reports. "I'm sure he can tell you're still alive through the bond you share."

"How can you know that?" I asked.

Asher just shook his head.

Was there a story there? Did the big man have a mate in the past? If so, what happened to her? I wanted to ask the questions out loud, but something gave me pause.

Asher's eyes hardened, a ghost of pain or anger behind them, and he returned to trawling through his papers.

"It's just a shifter thing," Zeke offered in the prevailing silence. "Shifters have Fated mates, but some of us do not."

My shoulders curled in on me as I peered down at my lap. This was not the conversation we needed to have.

Damn me and my big mouth.

I'd gotten us side-tracked. We needed to be focused on getting Grey out of that prison. Straightening myself, I tried to be the princess they needed me to be. I could lament my shortcomings in the future.

If I ever have that luxury.

"Anyway, we need a plan or something to get Grey out of there." I crossed my arms over my chest. "How hard can it really be for people like us to break into a human prison? Surely, with enough of us, we could storm the place and take them by force if need be?"

"That's the problem, Aurelia. The warden fired half his men so that Ronaldo's own guards could be installed alongside the humans. It's the *only* reason I have eyes in there." Dan looked away from my hopeful expression as it fell.

"How can Ronaldo have so much influence that he can just get away with all of this?" I threw my hands up in the air and stood, opting to pace the room as I wracked my brain.

Zeke glanced up from his laptop. "Think about it. The human government knows that shifters are stronger than humans, and that witches have powers unthinkable to them." He sat back and waited for his words to sink in.

"They can't lock us all up because we're more powerful, so they need traitors like Ronaldo to move against his own kind in return for a promise of safety or some fragile peace where they don't perish entirely."

"Bingo. It wasn't about Ronaldo's influence. It was about the human government's need to have security for the humans, and this is what they came up with. They made a deal with the Devil, so to speak." Zeke rubbed his eyes with his thumb and forefinger.

"You're the smart one, aren't you?" I grinned.

Asher scoffed. "If *he's* the smart one, then I'm the *sexy* one."

"Right." Zeke coughed a laugh.

I rolled my eyes, but Asher's comment hit its mark, and I chuckled along with them. I still didn't understand how anyone could be scared of the giant teddy bears that were Asher and Zeke. Forcefully returning my thoughts to the matter at hand, I licked my lips, before chewing on the lower one. "I bet the human guards aren't happy about losing their jobs, and it's adding fuel to the fire." I pointed to the TV, where a sign talked about supernaturals taking over the world and making humans slaves.

"That is definitely Ronaldo's long-term plan, but I don't get how he's going to pull it off." Zeke glanced at the screen before turning back to whatever research he was conducting.

"He doesn't just want the humans as slaves, though. He wants everyone to be slaves to the Council, and too many Fae are jumping on his bandwagon. If we don't do something, we're going to lose this war and possibly everything we love." I sighed. The thought was too dire to consider.

"We need to come up with a plan to stop him. No matter what, he can't be allowed to enslave everyone in the realms." Dan leaned forward on his elbows, his expression darkening in thought.

"You didn't see what I saw in Faery when he captured Grey and the others. He took over my father's entire castle. If the knights didn't swear an oath of allegiance to him, they said they were imprisoned—but when I went to the dungeons, no one was there. They were empty." I covered my face with my hands. It seemed hopeless, and I fought tooth and nail against the feeling of despair that threatened to swallow me whole.

Asher slammed his hands down on the table, startling me. "We're looking at this the wrong way. We need to tackle this *one* problem at a time. We can't fight this war on all fronts."

I gasped when I glanced at the TV, seeing what had Asher riled so suddenly. They had a little girl of no more than eight years old crying for her mother as they shoved her in the back of a cop car for no crime or reason other than having the apparent misfortune of being born a shifter.

"That's barbaric! She's just a child." I jumped from my chair, clenching my fists angrily at my sides as my temper flared along with my magic.

"Until we can figure out how to stop this, we need to figure out how we can protect the innocent. They don't deserve to be locked in cells and tested on. They don't understand what's happening here. We're soldiers. We're magical. We're in positions of authority and power, no matter how bad this all looks. We can do something! We have to." Asher turned his angry gaze on Zeke.

"I'm on it," he said, his screen capturing his attention once more. "I can hack into their systems and find out whoever they are going after next." Zeke tapped away at his computer. "And with any luck, we can get to them first."

I tried to calm my racing heart and hoped he could do what he said. If we could get the innocent supernaturals caught in the crossfire to safety, it would be a start and a step in the right direction. My heart broke for that little girl as she stared hopelessly from behind the windows of the police car as it drove away from the cameras. She reminded me so much of myself that it rattled me to my very core.

These are my people. I can't fail them!

CHAPTER 10

W*here the fuck is Fenrick? It's been too long. Why isn't he back yet?*

I had nothing to do but pace the empty cell anxiously and wait for any news regarding what had become of my friend.

If Ronaldo's killed him, he will suffer my wrath!

My shoulders slumped in defeat. The uncomfortable feeling of impotency was eating me alive from the inside out and was frustrating the shit out of me. I was an Alpha and used to taking action and making things happen. But instead, I was neutered, at least for the time being. I couldn't do anything to the damned corrupt Councilor while locked away in a cell with these damn magic cancelling cuffs on my wrists.

And I sure as hell wouldn't plan any kind of escape until I knew Fenrick was safe. He would be getting out of this with us. There was no other option. During our adventures together, united by the common thread of Aurelia, we'd become close and trusted allies. And I didn't leave men behind.

I tugged at the ends of my unwashed hair as I continued to pace. Who else had Ronaldo been torturing? And were the king and Magna okay? What lengths would Ronaldo stoop to in order to get his hands on my mate and the Facility? Aurelia and the Syndicate were likely the only ones who could help us bring an end to Ronaldo and his reign of terror.

Slow, methodical footsteps sounded, coming down the cell block, and I tensed. There was only one man this time, so it wasn't them bringing Fenrick back from his torture session with Ronaldo.

What now?

The same guard from before stopped just outside my cell and stared at me with a raised brow. "Time to go to the mess hall," he said.

My stomach rumbled as if on cue, and I grimaced. How long had it been since I'd eaten anything? I couldn't even remember. I didn't get a chance the last time we were there. Not that I would call what they'd served in the mess hall food. It was scarcely enough to sustain life and repugnantly tasteless fare at that.

He swiped his badge, and the buzzing of the door as it opened echoed through the cell.

Reluctantly, I emerged from my shared cell and followed him.

He grabbed my arm roughly, pulling me into his side to speak more covertly, though from the outside it likely looked like he was roughing me up a bit. "I don't have to tell you again what will happen if you start more fights, right?" His gaze flicked up to the security camera at the end of the hall and then back to me with a warning look.

"I told you, I didn't pick that fight. I have no intention of going back to the hole." I played along, yanking defensively at my arm in his grip.

"I also said last time that it didn't matter *who* started it. You will be sent back to the hole, and if your rumbling stomach is any indication of how hungry you are, you won't last the week-long sentence." He yanked on my arm again in a show of force.

"Understood," I growled. He wasn't wrong. There was no way I would survive another day without food. I wasn't stupid and I had no intention of dying in this shithole of pain, death, and deprivation of liberty.

"Are you trying to start something with me now?" He sneered, committing to his role in front of the cameras. He was really good at pretending he hated my guts and everything I stood for.

"No. You were supposed to be taking me to the mess hall, *traitor*." I spat the last word for effect. I had called every other Fae guard on duty some version of that the insult, so it would be suspicious if I didn't treat him the same.

He yanked me back, so we were nose-to-nose and my back was to the camera. Then he slipped something into my pocket.

I stiffened but kept my glare firmly in place for the cameras on the opposite end of the hallway.

"I would watch who you call a traitor in this place, *Shifter King,*" he snarled.

"Everyone in this place will get what they deserve before the end of this. *Everyone*," I said as both a promise and a threat.

This particular ally was helping as much as he was able to undercover, so he wouldn't face my wrath… but every other Fae and human in this hole who assisted in keeping us chained and imprisoned simply because we were different, would.

He moved around me and pushed roughly against my back, shoving me down the hall. With his mission complete, he had to continue with the charade and return to his regular routine to avoid raising any suspicions.

I didn't dare risk taking note of what was in my pocket until I was back in my cell. It would likely get us both in serious trouble. I did, however, notice that none of the other inmates had an escort through the prison, and I narrowed my eyes at the guard.

He shrugged and tugged me along. "You're a flight risk and a troublemaker," he explained gruffly. "We have been told to have eyes on you constantly when you're outside your cell."

That makes sense.

Ronaldo knew me better than I thought, because I *would* escape at the first opportunity if given the chance. What he had failed to realize though, was that I had a man on the inside, and as long as it was safe to do so, the guard was going to continue to help us work towards making an escape.

I snorted derisively. "Troublemaker? Yeah, that's me all right." I strolled through the doors to the mess hall, parting company with the guard, and got in line for whatever it was they passed off as sustenance in this purgatory.

I scanned the room casually, as if I didn't give a shit about anything, careful to remain nonchalant and aloof. There were groups of inmates clustered around tables, as usual, but I quickly realized there was a distinct divide. The groups without cuffs on their wrists were clearly the human criminals who belonged there originally, and there weren't many of them.

Had they shipped the majority of the humans off to other prisons to convert this a supernatural prison? If so, then why did they keep human guards around? Was there some kind of deal going on behind the scenes between Ronaldo and the human government? Or was it as simple as they didn't have enough Fae to do the job? Whatever the answer, it remained to be seen.

The line moved fast, and I easily found Magna and the Shadow King at a table off to the side, by themselves. "What the hell happened to you two?" I asked.

Magna had a prominent black bruise around her eye, and her shoulders were hunched as if she were a shrinking violet, a wallflower trying not to draw attention to herself.

The Shadow King wasn't much better off. Beneath the collar of his shirt thin red lines were visible, like he'd been sliced open. "That bastard, Ronaldo, took great pleasure in slicing me up," the king confirmed, adjusting his collar.

I dropped my tray on the table with a loud clatter and growled low in my throat. That bastard was going to pay for what he was doing to us. We were being treated with more cruelty and less respect than common animals!

"Where's Fenrick?" the king asked, glancing up and searching the mess hall.

"He's probably in the same place you both were. It was maybe an hour after they released me from the hole that he was taken to Ronaldo, and I haven't seen him since." I ran my hand down my face and dropped down onto the bench seat across from them.

"He's making his way through all of us then." The king sighed. It was abundantly clear he was struggling with a sense of futility too.

"What questions did he ask?" I prompted as I poked at my food, keeping my voice low.

"He asked me where the passageways in the castle led and if I knew where Aurelia was. One of his guards had said he'd spotted her in the library—but they still haven't found her. He also asked about the Facility's location." The king picked his fork up and grimaced at his plate's meagre offerings.

My heart leapt with the news that someone had seen her.

My beautiful mate!

My inner wolf howled with preemptive joy.

Could she really be alive? Was she presently running from the Council? "So, they think they saw her?" I asked, not daring to hope, but despite my best efforts to suppress my elation, my heart felt lighter.

My wolf perked up his ears and whimpered, wanting his mate back with him. He wasn't the only one, but we had to get out of this damned place to find her.

"Yes, but that's not entirely good news either, I'm afraid. If they saw her, that means she's stuck in Faery. She can't sift yet." The king took a bite of the tasteless gruel, his lips twisting in an almost comical mix of disappointment and disgust.

"Shit. I hadn't thought of that. And they probably have guards all over the castle looking for her." I turned to Magna. "What did he ask you?"

"It was strange," she said. "It was like he knew who I was and what I could do. He's asked me a lot of questions about the future. He also asked me about Aurelia." Her eyes became glassy for a moment.

"How could he know about your secret? That is something we've carefully guarded for years." I grabbed the stale bread roll off my plate and tore it in half, my heart thumping in my chest.

"He knows far too much for my comfort," Magna agreed.

"I think he's starting to get frustrated that no one will tell him what he wants to know." I grinned. "He expected someone to break by now."

"That's dangerous, though." The king eyed me over his fork. "Frustration and anger lead to recklessness, and he could go too far... and he's with Fenrick."

I tightened my fist around the roll and squashed it. "His death will be mine either way, but if Fenrick doesn't come back to the cell, I will ensure that I torture Ronaldo slowly before I end his miserable existence."

Magna blinked at me as if awakening from a dream, then glanced over at the huge shifter I'd had an altercation with the other day. "Befriend the bear," she said cryptically.

"What?" I asked. "You want me to befriend the damn shifter who got me Tased and thrown in the hole?"

"It's important, Grey. You need to befriend the bear shifter."

"Magna, you *do* realize how crazy that sounds, right? If I go over there right now, he's just going to get aggressive again, and I'm going to get a whole week in the hole. None of us can afford that." I shook my head, unconvinced.

The Shadow King glanced over his shoulder and frowned at the big shifter.

He glared at me with hate filled eyes.

"Those are not the eyes of someone who wants to be friends," the king agreed, shaking his head as he turned back toward us.

"You *need* to befriend the bear," Magna warned again with no further explanation, but her tone was one of quiet urgency.

"Can I at least eat first?" I asked. "Last time I didn't even get a chance to eat before I was thrown in the hole." They never gave me shit all to eat in the hole, and despite how disgusted I was with the food in the mess hall, I couldn't go much longer without fuel. My stomach rumbled angrily as if attesting to the fact.

The king chuckled as he met my gaze. "I'm genuinely surprised you aren't rabid already. With your shifter metabolism, you need to eat *a lot* more than the rest of us. You're much stronger than anyone is giving you credit for, Grey." The king popped a piece of crumbly, stale bread roll into his mouth.

"Well with these cuffs on, I can't shift. I think it's the only thing that's kept me from losing my shit completely. They're keeping that side of me suppressed, so I don't think I'm using the same amount of energy I normally would."

The king nodded at me in understanding.

I didn't need my shifter metabolism if I couldn't shift, and for the first time, I was grateful not to have my magic. If I'd had it, I never would have survived the hunger. I would have burned myself from the inside out trying to sustain myself and it would have all been for naught.

I sighed, ending the conversation, and ate in silence until everything was cleared from my tray. It wasn't nearly enough, but it would get me through.

Magna smiled and handed me her roll. It was like she read my mind.

I grimaced and nodded my thanks and bit into it with a savage hunger. It had little to no nutritional value, but it was something, and that was better than nothing. "We need to figure out a way out of here," I whispered. "And the sooner, the better. They are calling me a flight risk, so I have a guard watching me at all times. It's fucking suffocating."

"I noticed that. There are several of them at the moment. They're all tense now, watching your every move," the king observed over my shoulder.

"I don't know how, but we *need* to make it happen. We can't let Ronaldo take over the damn world." I steepled my fingers in front of my lips, wracking my brain for a solution, but any tangible answer remained elusive and infuriatingly out of reach.

"Befriend the bear," Magna said again, breaking the silence between us.

"Do you really think that will help?" I asked. How could befriending a psychotic shifter who wanted to fight me help us get out of the hellhole we were in? It didn't make sense, but that was all the information I was getting from Magna. She always was cryptic, though I was starting to understand that not all of it was intentional. She might be a mystery and enjoy her riddles on occasion, but she was also a conduit for the future and the unseen powers, and that *had* to be taxing.

"Yes, it's the catalyst. Befriend the bear, Grey." Magna nodded to the shifter who was still glaring daggers at me.

"Fine, I get it. The future must unfold as it will." With little choice, I pushed myself up off the bench and walked toward the shifter.

The room fell eerily silent as the entire mess hall stared. Everyone was holding their breath to see what the hell I was doing.

I approached the shifter's table with more outward confidence about the situation than I felt and grinned at him. Regardless of the odds, I was a king, and I wasn't going to cower from my fate if this was the path forward.

The bear frowned and growled at me like he was more bear than man, even in his cuffed form. "What do you want?" he asked, clenching his hand into a fist as he stood from the bench.

In a red-hot second, I was surrounded. Ten shifters circled around me, boxing me in like a solid wall of muscle and rage.

The guards stepped away from the walls, batons drawn, all of them on edge. It seemed they were waiting for the inevitable, just holding out until someone was stupid enough to make the first move.

Despite Magna's strange, esoteric prompting, I couldn't help but feel like I was about to get mauled and beaten the shit out of by a pack of angry shifters. And then I'd be locked in the hole again to rot, just to add insult to injury—the proverbial cherry on top.

Just fucking great.

CHAPTER 11

"Aurelia!" my mother yelled as she burst into the office. Her frantic eyes scanned the room, and her face fell when she didn't find who she was looking for.

"I'm sorry," I said, a lump developing in my throat. It was clear she was looking for her husband, my father, the king of Faery. "They're alive but being held in a human prison."

My mother erupted into tears and hugged me to her. It still felt awkward, but I was getting more used to her affection now that I had my memories back. She nodded against my shoulder in acknowledgement of the bad news. "I'm just glad you're safe." She sniffled.

"We're going to get them back, Mother. We have to," I promised as I patted her back. I glanced around at all the men assembled in the room. They were the best shot we had at planning a prison break into a maximum-security facility. And one thing was for sure and certain… no matter what, they would have my back every step of the way, and I was grateful for that.

"I know you will, sweetheart. You are so strong and determined. Is there anything I can do to help?" she asked, taking a step back and swiping away her tears.

"I need you to stay here and help with the people we rescue. There are families with children being brought in, and they need to know where they're not allowed for safety reasons. This isn't a facility meant for children, and we will need to block off any rooms that house weapons."

It was the only thing I could think of to give my mother a sense of purpose without endangering her. The queen was strong, that went without saying, but given the trauma of recent times and now the absence of my father, I didn't think my mother was presently up to the task of a prison break. We only had one shot at this, and we needed the best of our team to pull it off.

"I can handle that." She nodded firmly, shadows lurking behind her eyes.

Good.

I'd been afraid she was going to argue about coming with us on the rescue mission. Then I would have been forced to get one of the guys to back me up on my reasoning… or lock her away somewhere, but thankfully she seemed to know her own limits and was grateful to be useful in the capacity I'd suggested. —She was a mother and family woman herself, after all.

I knew that if it were me, and they were telling me I couldn't go, they would definitely have to lock me up to keep me away.

Because one way or another, I'm getting my mate back.

I turned back to the group with a determined frown. "Okay, where were we?"

Zeke turned his turquoise eyes on me. "I think I can get into the mainframe but the supernaturals there aren't listed. I'm looking at the government's lists too, but Grey and Fenrick aren't on that list either. It's like they never existed."

"How can Ronaldo get away with this? He can just lock them up in a prison without so much as a trace. It shouldn't be allowed!" I sank down into a chair wearing a scowl of frustration. How the hell were we supposed to even attempt to get them out if we didn't know where to look in the first place? The place was likely huge, heavily fortified, and filled with armed guards.

Ash scrubbed his hand down his face. "He has friends in some very high places if he can pull something like this off."

"There are laws against this sort of thing for a reason. He could be doing *anything* he wants to them because according to the rest of the world, they aren't even there." I slammed my fist on the desk, my temper flaring. My shadow magic rose up and swirled angrily around my arms. It was coming easier to me lately. Though, it also got out of control more easily, like now when I hadn't even called it. But emotions were running impossibly high, and I wasn't exactly an experienced magic user, so it was to be expected.

Zeke glared at his laptop screen. "They don't see us as human, that's the problem, so their laws don't apply to us. There are no protections legally in place for our kind."

"Oh?" I asked with a sudden, wicked grin. "If their laws don't apply to us, then they can't bloody detain us."

"I would say that as well," Asher said, though I could hear there was a *but* coming. "But if the Council has declared themselves our governing body, we would have to abide by the Council's rules, and they *can* detain us."

"Why'd you have to burst my bubble so fast?" I asked with a defeated pout. I thought I had found an obvious loophole in their idiotic reasoning, but of course, the Council had named themselves our government as soon as they overtook my father's castle and taken out Nicholas, my mate's father, the original Shifter King.

"Sorry, Princess," Ash chuckled humorlessly. "It's unfortunately what makes the most sense."

"I know it makes sense," I replied. "But I was getting all sorts of ideas. There must be some people out there reacting differently to this, right? Are any civil rights attorneys standing up for us?" I asked, turning back to Zeke.

"There have been some people speaking out in support, but they are being sidelined and labeled as sympathizers. Some of them even have supernatural spouses or children, and it's making life really difficult for them right now." Zeke turned his screen to face me.

The article was a political hit piece talking about shifter sympathizers being arrested for speaking out against the government and hiding their loved ones. "This is fucking insanity," I whispered.

"It is, but this is our life unless we do something about it." Asher clenched his fist, his gaze hard on mine.

"We are going to stop this, no matter what it takes," I told him passionately. "The Council *will* be ended. I'll fucking end them myself, if I have to," I growled.

Dan rushed into the room, his eyes wild as his gaze found mine. "Turn on the TV. They're about to make an announcement!"

"What kind of announcement?" I jumped from my chair and raced to the television, turning it on, forgetting entirely that there was a remote for the damn thing.

"They're making a presidential statement about the existence of supernaturals and what the government plans to do about the *problem.*" Dan planted his hand on his hips, his breathing heavy.

"Problem?" I hissed. "Our people have been living among them peacefully for centuries, and now we're the problem?"

"It's fear, Aurelia. That's all it is." Dan patted my shoulder.

"I don't care about their fear. There are countless lives on the line!" I narrowed my eyes at the screen.

The podium stood empty as we waited for the President to address the nation. There was a box live-streaming in the corner, showing more of the lawlessness in the major cities around the country. It was all being blamed on us, like we'd just shown up out of nowhere and started trouble.

"The looting and rioting aren't us. It's the humans' reaction to us. They're using us as scapegoats and taking advantage of the chaos. How is that our fault?" I asked, the anger in me deflating a little.

"It's not, but the government is in a tight spot with so many people demanding regulations on supernaturals around the globe." Zeke rubbed his neck.

Dan stepped forward, shushing us and pointing to the screen.

A group of people filed into view behind the President of the United States.

"Good morning to all Americans. Some troubling news has come to light in recent weeks. Be assured that we are doing everything to protect the American people. Not to be confused with the beings we have recently discovered that live among us." The President paused and held up his hand to quiet the reporters in the crowd. "I will take questions after I'm done with my statement. This very troubling news has a silver lining. We can learn from these creatures to better the human race."

"You mean by testing on us, you piece of shit!" I snarked at the screen, my chest rising and falling with each heavy breath.

"All supernaturals must be registered with the Department of Homeland Security and will be sent to our intake facilities where they will be evaluated to find out if they are safe to live among humans in this country. If they are deemed unsafe, they will be remanded to maximum-security prisons around the country."

"I bet those *intake facilities* are labs, and no one ever leaves once they are there," I growled. It seemed like everything I feared as a child was becoming cold, hard reality. Testing on supernaturals was going to happen, if it wasn't already...

"The Department of Justice will be conducting random raids on any individuals suspected of being supernatural. It will be better for everyone if you all turn yourselves in, rather than making us waste valuable time and resources to track you down. The consequences will be severe, and assets you own may be seized if you do not comply with the new laws," he finished, before he opened the floor to questions.

I turned terrified eyes on the guys, my insides trembling. "This is so much worse than I could have imagined."

"It's like Nazi Germany all over again. They are moving backward instead of learning from the past." Ash stood and went to turn the TV off.

I stopped him. "Wait. I want to see if anyone asks the right questions."

The President pointed to a woman in the front.

She stood, notebook in hand as she addressed the nation's leader. "Isn't this a bit extreme?" she asked. "They have obviously been living among us long enough to have homes and families and businesses, and there hasn't been any cause for concern until now."

They turned the camera back on the President. "No, this isn't extreme," he denied. "Have you not seen the protests and fights that your station broadcasts on repeat? These creatures *are* dangerous, and until we can explain more about them, they should be registered as supernatural. These actions are about keeping American citizens safe."

"But, Mr. President, this looks a lot like Germany before World War II. Shouldn't we be morc understanding of individuals who are different, rather than just locking them up?"

"Are you sympathizing with these creatures?" he asked the journalist, a dangerous warning tone in his voice.

She gasped, her eyes wide as she backtracked. "No, I just wonder how far down this slippery slope you're willing to go? Do human Americans who don't fit into your societal norms have to worry about this happening to them too? How will these suspected supernaturals be identified? Can just anyone with a grudge report someone? There are too many variables to consider."

"I'm glad you asked that question. We will have reporting centers open at all local police stations. There will be a verified staff member there who will have the ability spot the lie and should someone falsely accuse another of being one of these creatures, they will be penalized under the new laws."

"They are going to have Fae at the police stations to tell when people are lying? Bullshit." I bit down on my inner lip and flopped back in my chair, over this façade of a press conference.

The President called on a man in the front next.

"Mr. President, do you have any words for the human individuals who are rioting and looting in the streets over this tricky situation?"

"I want my fellow Americans to know that the conduct that we have seen in our cities over the last few days is unacceptable. I am prepared to send out the National Guard to stop these people from behaving this way. All violators will be punished harshly under the law. Stop the rioting and looting. We are taking care of the problem. Remain alert but peaceful."

"Wait!" I yelled spotting something out of place and turned, fumbling for the remote. I rewound to the correct place. A flash of magic filled the screen, and I paused. "What the fuck is he doing with the President of the United States?" I pointed to the corner where Malcolm stood behind the President, his eyes sparking with his magic.

Everyone in the room broke out into a litany of curses that would have made a sailor blush. Is that what Ronaldo had meant in the dungeon of the castle about the human government? "Is mind control an actual thing?" I turned to my mother.

She nodded. "It's not done, though. Fae children are taught at a young age how to shield themselves from it so there was never really a point in trying."

"Humans don't know that it exists, nor do they have the power to shield their minds even if they did. Fuck." I groaned. I tilted my head back and squeezed my eyes shut. This was fucking bad. I couldn't even hate on the President or call him prejudiced because this wasn't him. He was being controlled by a sadist who wanted to take over the world.

The only sound in the room was Zeke's rhythmic tapping on the keyboard in front of him. "This doesn't really change anything," he offered.

"Doesn't it?" I asked, turning my gaze on him.

"Not really, no. Regardless of the chaos going on at large, we still need to get Grey and the others out to stop the Council's crazy." Zeke shrugged.

Dan leaned down on the table, locking eyes with me. "I think we're looking at this all wrong."

"What do you mean?" I asked, my lips turning down.

"Knowing this might not be the President's agenda at all, but rather the agenda of the Council itself, all we would have to do to stop the registration of supernaturals is to cut off the Council's influence." Dan's eyes were wide.

"I don't know. What if we cut off their influence, and to save face the President continues or decides on an even worse plan?" I chewed my lip, wracked with anxiety. "What if instead of testing on us, he decides full blown genocide is the better option?"

Though no one wanted to give voice to the dark truth, it was a very real concern. The human population was infinitely bigger than ours. How could we hope to fight and prevail against armies of millions and win? My heart lurched and I fought every intrusive thought that reminded me of Murphy's Law.

No! There must be a way we can survive this. There just has to be...

CHAPTER 12

I dropped into a fighting stance and spun around, eyeing the shifters around me. I didn't recognize any of them, especially because of the direction they were facing.

The bear shifter growled and took a menacing step forward.

The others closed ranks around me, boxing me in further.

What the hell is going on here? Are they protecting me from the bear? I don't need protection.

"Look, I don't want to cause any trouble. I thought we could be allies," I said, but the snarling of the wolves around me drowned out my voice.

"You want to be allies?" The big shifter laughed. "Why would I want to be allies with the disgraced Shifter King's brat?"

"Because he *wasn't* disgraced. He was set up by the same people who locked us in here," I said as I eyed him. He wasn't going to buy it, and that was fine. I could at least tell Magna that I'd tried.

The guards inched closer to us with their batons at the ready.

I scanned the room warily. I didn't want them to hear what I had to say to the supernaturals in the room.

"What's going on here?" the guard from before shouted.

My shoulders stiffened as I turned to face him. I was not picking a damn fight this time. I had no idea why the shifters surrounded me.

"Nothing. I'm simply trying to make amends." I put my hands up in surrender, not wanting to get another electric shock like last time.

Out of the corner of my eye, the Shadow King stood, ready to jump in and help if needed.

I shook my head.

Magna tugged on his arm to make him sit down.

What is she up to?

She obviously saw everything taking place and knew it needed to be done, but I was confused as fuck. The entire mess hall was silent again.

The guard jerked his head toward the snarling shifters around me that had yet to take their gazes off the bear shifter.

"Stand down, brothers. You don't want to go to the hole. Trust me!" I barked at the shifters.

The ten shifters all whimpered, and their shoulders slumped at the reprimand. They stepped back from the bear with their necks bared to me in subservience. They really *were* trying to protect me when I walked up to the bear. They weren't on his side at all.

"See?" I waved a hand at the gathered group as well as the guards. "No problems here."

The bear sat back in his seat and crossed his arms over his chest.

The guard raised an eyebrow at the bear.

The shifter shook his head and grumbled, "We were just having a chat."

The guard took a step back and waved a hand to the other guards to step back against the wall to their usual watchful positions.

The shifters around me shuffled their feet, their heads still down and necks bared.

"What the hell were you all doing causing a scene like that?" I asked.

The biggest one who stood directly in front of me turned, and I recognized him as someone from the Syndicate.

"Sorry, Boss. After I saw you get Tased the other day, I couldn't let it happen again. I know you of all people will have a plan to get us out of here." The shifter's eyes shone with his inner wolf.

"I'm working on it," I answered. I hated having all their hopes resting on my shoulders, but I would figure something out. We would not be there long. I would make sure of it. That was the duty of a leader and king, after all, to protect and safeguard his people.

"You have a plan?" The bear shifter sat forward with his elbows on the table in front of him, his curiosity piqued.

He didn't seem like much of a team player. When I'd seen him in the mess hall initially, he had been sitting on his own, glaring at anyone who dared come too close.

"I said I'm working on it," I confirmed. "You will *all* know when it's time to go." With a final nod of acknowledgement at my people, I spun on my heel and stomped back to Magna and the Shadow King.

I glared at Magna, but there was no heat in it. I couldn't stay mad at the woman. She'd been very helpful over the years, and she never did anything without reason.

"Was that so hard?" She smiled knowingly.

"Considering I thought I was about to get Tased again if I couldn't defuse the situation? *Yes*," I said.

"Grey, we need all the help we can get for when the time comes," she whispered.

Apparently, the shifters who'd stood up to protect me had followed me because they filled in the seats at the table around me.

"You are the most powerful shifter in this whole damn place, Shifter King. That's why Brutus attacked you. His bear felt threatened. They're solitary creatures, so he felt he had to make a stand." The shifter I'd recognized from the Syndicate ducked his head.

The one next to me stared at me with hopeful eyes. "We request protection. Some of the warlocks have been raging on us, saying it's our fault this happened and there are many more of them here. They don't fight fair, and attack in groups while the guards aren't looking."

"If you're requesting my protection, why try to protect me?" I asked. "That doesn't even make any sense." I ran a hand through my hair and stared at Magna and the Shadow King.

They were doing their best not to burst into laughter at my discomfort as several other shifters came up behind me offering their rolls and whatever else they had, requesting protection.

Shit. This is stupid.

Why couldn't they just stick to packs instead of pinning all their hopes on me? The mantle of leadership was a heavy burden, and though it was one I was naturally equipped for, it didn't feel like any less of a weight on my heart.

The shifter from the Syndicate huffed. "You're our best chance of escaping and waging war on the Fae. I told them all this because you have the Syndicate, and your army there is loyal to you. These shifters will be loyal as well. We just have to figure out a way out of here first."

"I'm working on it," I said for what felt like the thousandth time.

If only I could work on it a little faster.

My tray was full once again, and instead of arguing with them, I accepted their tokens of loyalty and promised them whatever protection I could give. Shifters weren't to blame for outing supernaturals to the humans. The Fae Council was, and I would be letting the warlocks in the prison know that immediately. We weren't enemies, but we *did* have a common enemy, and I would use that knowledge to get the warlocks off the shifters' backs. "Where are these warlocks?" I asked the shifter next to me.

He nodded to a table in the opposite corner of the mess hall.

Shit. That's less than ideal.

If the guards saw me walking over there after the scene I'd just made, I could end up in the hole again, but the supernaturals in this place needed to stick together not bully each other. I rose from my seat and noticed several guards around the walls tense as I walked around the room to the warlock table.

The man in the middle of the table smirked at me as I leaned over.

"You've been harassing my shifters. Why?" I asked with a growl.

"A shifter is the reason we're in this place in the first place," the warlock said.

"It could have just as easily have been a witch or warlock that was caught. The Council selected the wolf specifically for achieving the most dramatic effect. Think about it. Why are the Fae in this building holding us prisoner?" I asked.

The warlock arched a brow and scratched his chin. Maybe this was the first time he'd listened to sense about this and not his own raging thoughts at being sent to prison for what he was.

"My people broke the shifter out of jail, and he told me that he smelled something chemical before he lost control. I know that the Fae are working with the humans to make us all their slaves. I've spoken to the *High Councilor* myself. The man is like any superhero villain, he's all endless monologue about his plans for world domination."

The warlock leaned forward, studying me like he thought I was lying, but something in my expression must have told him the truth. "We've been lied to and persecuted before. Why should we trust a shifter?" he asked.

"Because I have the means to get us out of here and take the Council down. Ever heard of the Syndicate?" I asked, and shocked gasps echoed around the table.

"You're not the boss of the Syndicate." The warlock sneered.

"You believe I'm the Shifter King, but I couldn't possibly be the owner of the Syndicate?" I smirked.

"I wouldn't believe that either, if all the shifters hadn't been whispering about it since you arrived," the warlock said.

"Honestly, I don't care what you believe, but we need to stick together in here, not torture each other. Ronaldo does enough of that as it is." I shook my head.

The warlocks glanced warily between each other as I said the High Councilor's name without his title.

"The High Councilor is torturing people?" one of the warlocks whispered.

"Yeah, only *every* day. We're being carved up like Christmas hams and broken like wishbones. A friend of mine was taken to him yesterday and he's yet to come back." I glanced between the warlocks, letting them see how serious this was. I wasn't lying about the fact that we all needed to stick together and that I was going to get us out of here.

"Okay," the warlock in the middle said. "You said you were going to get us out of here?"

"I can't tell you how or when, just stop harassing my shifters and be ready." I leaned forward on my elbows, meeting their gazes unflinchingly.

"We'll leave the shifters alone." The warlock nodded.

"Good." I pushed up from the bench seat and moved back to the table with Magna, the Fae king, and the rest of my loyal wolf shifters. I sat down in my seat and nodded to everyone. "They won't harass you anymore or they're getting left behind when we get out of here."

"You're really planning to break us all out?" one whispered.

"Yes, we *must* stop the Council. They can't be allowed to continue what they're doing." I clenched my hand on the table.

"Shifter King!" someone called out in warning.

I turned to find the guard standing behind me.

"Time to go back to your cell," he ordered.

No one else moved, but I stood from the bench, pocketing a couple rolls as I did, and let the guard manhandle me out of the mess hall while everyone else watched on in silence.

"That was reckless," the guard whispered. "Making alliances and deals right under the guards' noses."

"It wasn't. I have a seer on my side who told me to do it," I said shaking my head.

"She shouldn't be able to see through the cuffs." He squeezed my arm as we stomped between the cells on our way back to mine.

"Well, she's half Fae, half witch, so I don't think even Ronaldo knows how to handle her." I yanked my arm away from him.

"Interesting. You've already surrounded yourself with people who are extremely useful." The guard nodded as if his approval carried some weight.

I snorted. "It's how I made my fortune in this realm, and it's how I'm going to get us all out of this mess when the time is right." I didn't tell him my mate was really the one who was going to be responsible for getting us out of this. We all knew she was the one that was destined to take down the Council. It was her destiny to bring peace and justice to Faery as the Shadow Princess.

When we got back to my cell, he swiped his badge, and the cell buzzed as the door swung open.

My shoulders slumped as I sighed and trudged into the empty space.

"Try to keep a low profile from now on," the guard warned as he closed me in.

"How do you expect me to do that when I have shifters actively requesting protection?" I asked and scanned the cell hoping I'd been wrong, and Fenrick was really there.

No Fenrick. Where the hell is he? What is that sadist doing to him, and how the hell are we supposed to get out of here when he's disappeared? I'm sure as hell not leaving without him.

CHAPTER 13

"We need to call a meeting," I said to Dan and the rest of the guys.

"Why?" Dan asked.

"We need to lock down the building. Only authorized personnel should be able to leave and only those that can spot a tail. We can't risk leading any of them back to us."

"Smart." Ash nodded. "They are targeting supernaturals, and anyone not trained to watch for someone following them could lead the government right to our doorstep."

The sound of Zeke tapping away on the keys of his laptop filled the silence that stretched between us all. "We've been managing to get to most of the innocents before the government has, but what happens when the building reaches capacity?"

"I don't know," I admitted. I hadn't even thought that far ahead yet. "We might have to think about having the witches and warlocks build more temporary housing. That will be harder to control though..." I leaned back in the chair and sucked in a steadying breath. With every day that passed I missed Grey more and more and prayed to whatever gods that might be listening that he was okay. I needed to get him out, but I had to secure the building and the people we were helping first, or he would have nothing to come back to.

"Okay," Dan said, taking the lead voluntarily. "I'll call a mandatory meeting, but we have teams out in the field so not everyone will be there."

"That's fine. This doesn't apply to the extraction teams anyway, they're already some of the best we have." I nodded.

Dan rushed from the room to call the meeting with all the residents. The Facility was getting seriously crowded, but we were beating the Council more often than not when it came to hiding the people the government was chasing.

"I think I got something!" Zeke shouted above the distant growing din of voices.

"What is it?" I asked, a spark of hope flaring in my chest. I jumped from my seat and rounded the table to peer over his shoulder.

"Schematics," he said. "They'd been deleted from the prison's server recently, but I was able to recover them."

"Why would they delete something as important as that? Don't they have to keep them by law?" I asked, my brow furrowing as I peered at the screen.

"I guess since they're making it a supernatural prison the same laws don't apply." Zeke rubbed his eyes, agitation clear in his body language.

"Bastards," I grumbled. "They don't want to risk the supernaturals getting hold of any information that could be used to orchestrate a break in. They know it won't keep us all out of there. How are they even keeping them in there?"

"I found something that might explain it," Zeke mumbled as he hammered away on the keys. "There is a patent for a new type of cuff in the US Patent Office. It apparently blocks magic."

Ash's head snapped up to his brother, his gaze blazing. "They patented magic-blocking handcuffs? When was it filed?"

"Six months ago."

"Shit. They've been planning this a long time." Ash clenched his hands into fists on the opposite side of the table.

I deflated and sat heavily back in my chair. "How are we going to do this when they've been planning it for so long? They've likely got fail-safes already in place for any trouble that might arise."

"Because we have the one thing they can't control." Ash grinned at me.

"And what's that?" I asked, hoping he wasn't about to say what I thought he was going to.

"You, Aurelia! You're the one thing that they couldn't control no matter how hard they tried. They literally had you kidnapped as a child so you wouldn't be able to stop their plans. So, while yes, they have been planning this longer than any of us could have guessed, you are the one thing that can stop them."

"I was afraid you were going to say that. No pressure." I sighed. I was being thrust into a leadership and savior role regardless of whether I was ready for it or not.

Fuck me. Being the Shadow Princess has knobs on it!

Dan ran into the room panting. "All right. Everyone is gathered for the meeting."

"That was fast," I acknowledged, before nodding to Zeke and Ash.

We all filed into the elevator down the hall. "Is there a way to alter the wards—to keep everyone in?" I asked.

"The only one who can make changes to the wards is Grey," Dan said, hanging his head.

"Well, at least we can use that to our advantage. Those coming in will have to be escorted through the wards by someone who's authorized to be here. And if anyone leaves without permission, they won't be able to return." I leaned back against the wall of the elevator, feeling slightly more relieved, but anxious all the same.

The elevator dinged when we got to the first floor. I rolled my shoulders back and straightened my posture, following Dan into the last room I had ever wanted to enter again, but it was where they held meetings as well as fights. I blew out a nervous breath and followed him to the center of the room.

The bleachers were full of stunned supernaturals. There were even people standing along the walls, glancing around with trepidation, clutching children to their chests protectively.

"Thank you all for coming on such short notice!" Dan yelled over the top of the whispering crowd. "We have an announcement to make." He nodded to me.

I exhaled deeply and took a step forward, steeling my will. "Many of you know the dire situation in which we find ourselves. Most of you were extracted from your homes before the government could arrest you and take you to their testing facilities or lock you up in a prison cell."

People nodded but started fidgeting nervously like hens surrounded by foxes. It was an uncomfortable topic and there was no easy way to broach it.

"From now, until we stop the Council and return home to Faery, the Facility is on lockdown. I understand this may be concerning to some of you, but it's for the safety of everyone here. We will still be sending extraction teams to retrieve supernaturals before the government can get to them, but only those teams are allowed to leave."

The whispers turned to grumbling and a few called out that our safety measures were bullshit.

Dan and the Riders stepped up on either side of me with their arms crossed over their chests, acting as my muscle and back-up.

"Anyone who doesn't like this new ultimatum is free to leave now and never return. You can take your chances with the testing facilities and the human government!" Dan barked.

The crowd fell silent.

Zeke pointed at a man in slacks and a button-down shirt. "Are you trained to watch for a tail?"

The man frowned and shook his head, clearly uncomfortable with having been put on the spot, but he answered quickly and honestly. "No."

"If you left and came back, you could potentially lead the Council or the human government to everyone here, yourself included. This is for your safety as well as everyone else here."

Dan cut in, clearing his throat, "This has *never* been a civilian facility. We have highly trained operatives we send out into the world on various jobs. They are experts in their fields and at making sure they aren't being followed. No one leaves except for authorized personnel. If you leave without permission, you will not be able to return. No second chances."

Ash gripped my shoulder, lending me his strength and friendship. "And if you think this is a joke and leave anyway and lead someone to our wards? Retribution will be swift and brutal. You'll wish the enemy had gotten to you first! Do not put the lives of innocent people on the line because you think you're better than the rest of us or somehow entitled to special treatment. I will not be lenient if we are found."

"You're all dismissed," added Zeke with his booming voice, ending the meeting.

I glanced at Ash with an imperceptible frown. What he'd said was going a little overboard, but the crowd didn't argue, and I was thankful for that as we turned on our heels and stalked from the room and back to the elevator. "Do you think they'll listen?" I asked when the doors closed behind us.

"Most of them will, but I noticed a few cocky assholes in the crowd who will probably try to leave to test us. But don't fret, Princess, they'll be handled." Ash crossed his arms over his chest and glared at the wall, allowing his anger to bolster his will.

"They will just be less people to worry about, Aurelia," Dan added.

"I know we can't save everyone," I agreed. "I'm just worried they'll lead the government right to us."

We wandered into the office, and the TV was still blaring with the news we almost constantly had on stream now. It was pretty morbid. And I shouldn't have allowed myself to watch it so much, but I needed to know what was happening. My desire to be informed and abreast of current events overwhelmed any emotional response. There was just too much resting on my shoulders to fall to pieces now. Faery itself depended on me.

"Are supernaturals finding a place to hide?" the newscaster asked.

"Three sting operations to capture these creatures came up completely empty yesterday here in Dallas."

I grinned and glanced between the guys. Their smiles were smug. "They're noticing that it's not just coincidence."

"The Department of Justice put out a statement early this morning warning that anyone caught aiding supernaturals will be brought up on charges of aiding and abetting a felon and placed in prison."

"They would have to catch us first." Ash chuckled.

I sat in the chair behind the desk and shook my head. "They would put us in prison or a testing facility either way. If I am going to go down, I rather it be for the crime of saving innocents, at least."

"Maybe we should think about that as an opportunity to break into the prison. Are we looking at this the wrong way?" Zeke mumbled, his shoulders hunched as he lost himself in thought.

"What do you mean?" I asked.

Is he seriously suggesting we get ourselves arrested and hope they send us to the correct place?

"I've been looking at these schematics day and night and I can't find a way in except through the front door." Zeke scrubbed a hand over his face.

"But we don't even know if they would take us to the correct facility if we got arrested," Ash said, voicing aloud what I was thinking.

"It's too risky," I agreed. "We might end up in some black hole site, miles from anywhere, let alone Grey or allies."

"This whole mission is too risky, but we're still doing it," Zeke argued back.

"How do we do that and ensure we're going to the right place though? We can't. We have no idea how they choose who goes where, and we only have one shot at this." I tilted my head back and squeezed my eyes shut.

None of this is going to be easy it seems. Freedom is always hard won… that's just a historical fact.

"We can't. I say if there's only one way in, we blow the doors wide open and go in guns blazing," Ash suggested as he flopped in his seat.

"You always were the *blow shit up and ask questions later* kind," Zeke huffed.

"Do you have a better idea?" Ash snarked and threw a wadded-up piece of paper at him. "And not the one where we all get arrested and possibly split up to be tested on and caged like fucking animals."

Zeke hung his head. "No, but if we just go and blow shit up, we're going to need a large team to evacuate at multiple entry points, and there's only one way in and out."

Dan sat forward, his gaze intense. "We have specialized teams for operations just like this. The team that got the shifter out of jail when he was exposed to the human world was quick and efficient."

"And what about your guy on the inside? Will he be able to help at all?" I asked.

We hadn't heard much from the half Fae man reporting to us, other than being updated occasionally that Grey was still alive. Apparently, he'd been locked in solitary for a day because of a fight with a shifter, but other than that, they were all surviving.

"He might, but that's not something I can just ask over the phone or via text. He's too careful to let them figure anything out. They could trace the call to me. Not to mention he's searched randomly, including his phone. The Fae don't trust him."

"Because he's a half breed," I snarled.

"Exactly. They weren't exactly kind when they found out a half Fae was already a guard in that prison when they took over, but they let him stay on, likely thinking it gave them strength in numbers."

"Figure out how you can get word to him and pick the teams. We'll definitely have to come up with a better plan than blow shit up and ask questions later." I cocked a brow at Ash. "We might end up blowing some of our own people to hell."

He just chuckled. "Aw, come on, Princess. It's a solid plan," he defended himself with a scoff. "And if we take out a few traitorous Fae fucks in the process, I'm not going to be mad."

He wasn't wrong there. I didn't care what we did truthfully as long as it got us to Grey and the others. I wasn't in the business of caring about what happened to turncoats and traitors. All those following the Council were disloyal to the Crown, to the Shadow Fae family and I wouldn't stand for it. But every day our loved ones rotted away in there was a day too long as far as I was concerned.

We needed to get them out, one way or another. I was afraid of what Ronaldo and the other Fae might do to them, given the luxury of too much time. But one thing was certain... I would kill them all and laugh while doing it if *anything* happened to Grey and my friends!

CHAPTER 14
Grey

I shot up from the cot when the electronic buzzing of the door sounded in my cell.

Two guards threw Fenrick's unconscious body on the concrete floor without an ounce of decency for his injuries.

He was a mess of bruises and bloody cuts all over his chest, the word *Traitor* was etched in his skin and still bleeding. They'd cut obscenely deep.

I winced internally. "Fuck! What did he do to you?" I raced to him, dropping to my knees on the hard concrete floor. Blood was flowing from his wounds far too quickly for my liking and it didn't appear to be stopping anytime soon. I howled in anguish when all I could find in the cell was my own wadded-up shirt.

"Grey? What is it?" the shifter in the cell next to ours asked as more howls filled the cell block.

"They fucking tortured him and the bleeding isn't stopping. I need something to stop the flow, but all I have is my shirt!" I growled. The stench of blood was overwhelming, the whole block could scent it on the otherwise sterile air. I pressed my shirt to the worst of his wounds, but it was quickly soaked in a stomach-churning amount of blood. I could barely recognize my friend's face for all the bruises and beatings he'd obviously endured. His lips were split on both sides of his mouth, and his eyes were black and swollen shut.

"Here!" the shifter called out and handed me a piece of cloth around the bars. "There's more coming."

"What do you mean, more?" I asked, my brow furrowing.

"All the shifters in the block are tearing their shirts and whatever else they can find to help him," the shifter answered.

I grabbed the cloth from him and quickly wrapped it around the worst wound on his side—it had been cut open with a blade. It seemed almost like Ronaldo was personally offended by Fenrick. Maybe he was. Ronaldo obviously thought all Fae should be loyal to him and the Council, even above and beyond King and Crown.

More and more pieces of fabric in the form of torn shirts and ripped sheets came around the bars until I had all of Fenrick's bleeding wounds tied off and bandaged. "Do you all see what I mean now? None of us in this place are safe from whatever whims Ronaldo has. He can torture or kill us at any time, and there is nothing we can do to stop it!" I yelled for the entire cell block to hear.

"We have to get out of here," someone whispered. "We have to fight back."

"Yes, but we have to be smart about it. We can't just fight back without a plan." I wanted them all to know that we were getting out but warn them not to go crazy and get themselves thrown in the hole or encourage torture with their behavior.

We have no choice... we still have to play along for now.

I sat with my arms around my knees as I watched Fenrick's steady breathing. At least he was breathing normally now, and the flow of blood was slowing.

"Blood, death," Fenrick muttered in his sleep.

Shit.

What the fuck was he dreaming about that those words would come out in his sleep? It was a little too ominous for my liking.

A whimper from the cell next to mine met my ears. "Is he awake? Did he hear something when he was being tortured?" they asked.

"No, he's still out cold. I don't know why he said that. It could be a trauma response to torture. We won't know until he wakes up." I checked his wounds again and redressed them, but they seemed to be healing. Fenrick was Fae, so at least his healing abilities were working better for him than mine had.

"Days..." Fenrick groaned.

I couldn't tell if he was waking up or still dreaming because his eyes were still swollen shut. He gripped my arm to pull me closer to him, his grip like an iron vise.

"Fenrick? Holy shit. Are you okay?" I breathed. I didn't know what I was thinking to ask something so mundane. Of course, he wasn't okay. He looked like he'd been put through a meat grinder.

"Grey, murdered," he mumbled.

"No, I'm right here," I assured him as I clutched his hand. It was about the only place on his body that wasn't beaten or bloody.

"What's going on?" the other shifter asked.

"I think he's waking up but he's not coherent. He said something about me being murdered."

"Three days." Fenrick groaned. He cracked an eye open, but his pupil was blown wide.

Does he have a concussion? It's more than likely.

"What about three days?" I asked, no more enlightened.

"Death, blood," he said then passed back out.

"I don't know if I'm understanding him correctly, but whatever he's saying doesn't sound like it's going to end well for us."

Whimpers and growls from the other shifters in the cell block filled the air, and I couldn't exactly blame them. I rested my head back against the wall, my arms propped up on my knees as I waited for Fenrick to wake up again.

A hand nudged me, and my eyes shot open. I must have dozed off.

Fenrick was blinking his eyes at me. The swelling had lessened enough for him to see.

I shot to my feet, and gently pulled him into a sitting position, taking care not to put pressure on the worst of his injuries before they were fully healed.

Fenrick still winced at the movement.

"What happened?" I asked him. "You were mumbling something about three days and death and blood."

"Fuck!" Fenrick shouted and jumped to his feet as fast as a bolt of lightning, but with his blood loss and swelling, he stumbled and nearly crashed back down to the floor.

"Gods, Fenrick, take it easy. You've lost a *ton* of blood." I steadied him and helped him sit down on the cot.

"You don't understand. We have to get out of here. Everyone is going to die." He turned to me wide-eyed, fear apparent in his bloodshot gaze.

"Are you sure you don't have a concussion?" I asked, peering at him, trying to assess just how aware he really was.

"I overheard some of the guards talking about moving people to the testing facilities. They were saying they couldn't wait until this place was rubble." Fenrick gripped my arm.

"Are you sure? You may have heard wrong. You were pretty beat up when they dropped you in here." I sat next to him, pursing my lips.

"I *know* what I heard, Grey. They left me in there for dead, thinking I wouldn't make it so there was no reason for them to bother being quiet around me. They planned for me to die in front of you." He ran a hand through his hair and winced.

"Fucking hell. Tell me everything," I growled, my rage blazing within me. They had intended to take one of my closest friends and allies from me... My vision became tinged with red, and I cracked my knuckles as I clenched them into fists.

"The plan was never to make us their slaves but to test on anyone that could be useful to their plans and then eradicate the rest." He hung his head.

"Test us for what? What are they trying to do? I never thought the facilities were for the Fae but for the humans. I thought that was part of the agreement. The Council hands over some of their slaves to the humans for testing, and they did what they wanted. What am I missing?" I leaned forward with my elbows on my knees, my chin resting on my fists.

"The Council has been using human technology to create bioweapons to use against all who oppose them." Fenrick moved to jump up again, having clearly not learned from his first failed attempt at standing.

I put a hand on his shoulder to keep him seated. "What kind of bioweapons are we talking about here?" I asked.

"For one thing, they developed a mind control serum. Fae can already read minds, but the scale they want to control people on is truly terrifying."

"So, that's what the testing facilities are doing... streamlining the development of this serum." I shook my head, disgusted to my very core.

"They let a lot of information out in front of me they probably shouldn't have, but like I said, they don't expect me to ever leave here alive." Fenrick grimaced.

"What else could there possibly be?" I asked, not exactly sure if I really wanted to know.

What he's already revealed is terrifying enough.

"The shifters are resistant to the serum, and they have no clue why," Fenrick said, rubbing his eyes.

"So, that's why the shifters are being taken in for testing, rather than just being imprisoned across the country," I mused.

This is precisely what Aurelia feared all along...

"And what about the rubble comment?" I pressed.

"In three days, everyone in this place is going to be cannon fodder. They're going to kill us all."

"Fuck. That's not enough time." I ran a hand through my hair, my heart thumping in my chest as the stakes continued to rise at an exponential rate.

"How the hell are we going to plan and execute a prison break in three days?"

"We have people to help now, but it's still going to be a stretch," I said. "But we need to find a way to get these damn cuffs off."

"Grey?" the shifter in the next cell whispered low.

"What is it?" I asked.

"We might be able to get close to a guard. My cellmate is an accomplished pickpocket."

"That's a good start," I agreed. "As long as he doesn't get caught and thrown in the hole."

"Who are you talking to?" Fenrick asked with a frown.

"A lot happened while they were torturing you. A bunch of shifters have requested protection. That's how I got the stuff to dress your wounds."

"What did he say?" Fenrick asked.

Boots stomped down the hall along the cell block, and I grimaced. "Later."

The guard who'd been helping us stepped into view.

My shoulders relaxed, and I breathed a small sigh of relief.

"They expected you to die in this cell," he said as he nodded to Fenrick.

"I'm stronger than I look." Fenrick growled, despite his disheveled and beaten state.

The guard swiped his badge on the scanner and the door opened. "I'm here to take you to the showers. You need new clothes before you go to the mess hall. You both do, apparently."

We followed him out of the cell and down a hall I hadn't been in before. A huge communal shower stood at the end of the hall.

"You have five minutes to get cleaned up. There are new clothes in the lockers over there." He pointed to a bank of lockers and then turned his back on us.

Fenrick's body was stiff as he moved to unravel the makeshift bandages on his chest.

I turned away, unwilling to waste a single minute of the short time we were being given for the shower.

"So, what did that shifter say?" Fenrick muttered beneath his breath as the roar of water from the shower filled the air.

"His cellmate can get us a key." I held my arm up to bring his attention to my cuffs.

His eyes widened. "That's pretty fucking useful."

"Yeah, but will it be enough?" I scrubbed my hair and tilted my head beneath the spray of the shower. It felt so good to get the grime, sweat, and blood from my body after so long. I'd almost forgotten what it felt like to be clean. Maybe clean was an overstatement, but I was definitely getting cleaner. It seemed like such a luxury now.

"It's a start, but if it's only shifters against the guards, we don't stand a chance," said Fenrick.

"I have an understanding with the warlocks," I revealed. "But I'm not bringing them in on the plan when we make it. I've just told them to be ready." The guard didn't give us any soap or anything to wash with, so I scrubbed as best as I could with my hands. The end result wasn't perfect, but I felt at least a bit more refreshed.

The water ran cold, so I turned it off and headed to the lockers the guard had indicated. The shirts and pants in there all looked the same, just different sizes. I grabbed a set in my size and pulled them on quickly.

Fenrick walked up beside me. "What are the odds we might come across some of the guards' uniforms and can get out that way?"

I glanced down at my own bulk and then raised an eyebrow at him. The Fae were naturally lean and tall, but there wasn't a guard in the place whose uniform would fit me, let alone any of the others. "Even if we could, it wouldn't work. The shifters are all too large to fit in those uniforms." I shook my head. It was a nice thought. Too bad it just couldn't be that easy.

"Let's go!" the guard yelled, ensuring he played his part convincingly.

Despite the fact I knew he had to keep up appearances so as to not be discovered as a mole, I was really getting tired of being ordered around. It was against my Alpha nature to let people boss me around and I'd had enough.

We trudged back to the guard, but he didn't move.

He peered down the hall to make sure we were alone. "You have two days to get yourselves and the shifters out of here. They are moving all the shifters to the official testing facility before this place is taken out. They want you specifically, Grey. You need to get out."

"I know, Fenrick overheard them." I crossed my arms over my chest.

"Fuck," Fenrick cursed. "That moves the timeline up and we are still no closer to a feasible plan."

"We'll do whatever it takes to stop this from happening. They want me alive as the King of the Shifters. But I won't be their damn guinea pig... I won't go down without a fight."

The guard nodded and escorted us back to our shared cell before locking us in.

We'll get out of this or die trying.

I didn't want to think about which option was more likely. I was the King of the Shifters and boss of the Syndicate, I had to remain strong and appear in control, even if I felt like the world was crashing down all around me. Death was coming for us all, and I had a feeling none of us would make it out of this unscathed.

CHAPTER 15

Aurelia

"Where are they?" I asked for the thousandth time as I paced the empty parking lot.

Dan huffed. "They'll be here."

It was hard enough to commandeer a prison van, but now the guy tasked with bringing it to us with enough explosives to level the place was missing. "What if they were caught? Our entire plan hinges on us getting that van past security." I clenched my fists at my sides, my heartbeat skipping erratically.

Ash patted my shoulder. "Let's not put that kind of thinking out into the universe."

Zeke stepped up on my other side with a smirk. "It *will* work out, Princess. Don't worry."

"What are you up to?" I asked, narrowing my eyes at him. "You're altogether too confident."

"Why would you think I was up to something?" he countered with a mockery of innocence.

"Because you're smirking at me like this is all part of the plan, and this was definitely not part of the plan that I was involved in. Smash and grab, remember?"

"I remember." He grinned at me again.

"Ash, why is he doing that?" I asked.

"You're adorable when you're wound like a top." Ash chuckled.

"So not helping," I huffed, my nerves practically already shot.

The rest of the teams walked up to us, then looked about in confusion at the lack of a transport van.

Yeah, I'm confused too. We only have one shot at this, and it looks like it's getting blown to smithereens...

"Stop fidgeting," Dan whispered. "They'll be here."

"Are you sure? Because they should have been here already."

"Maybe they got stuck in traffic," Dan suggested, but he didn't seem so confident anymore.

"Close ranks, we may have a problem," Ash said as he peered at something over my shoulder.

I spun around and gasped as sirens blared and several black prison vans sped up the street. "Shit. Someone betrayed us."

"Be calm. Fight them, but in the end, surrender," Zeke muttered under his breath.

I turned, glaring at the rider of the hunt. "Oh my gods. What did you do?" I gasped, wide-eyed.

"I got us in the prison under our terms and without bloodshed." Zeke shrugged.

"Can I kill him?" I turned to Ash, magic lighting my palms.

"Not today, Princess. Not until we know the plan." Ash pushed his brother.

Zeke stepped back and raised his hands. "Just follow my lead. We need to get in, and I'm getting us in. We don't have much time before they eradicate everyone in the place."

"What?" I hissed as the vans drew closer. "You could have started with that instead of going behind our backs and coming up with your own plan!" Could I get away with smacking a Rider of the Hunt? I sure hoped so, because even though I really liked Zeke, I preferred being informed when there was a change in plans even more.

"All the shifters are being moved to the testing sites and everyone else is going to blow up in an explosion, which is set to go off in three days."

"Why did that change the plan, though?" Asher growled.

"Because they will be expecting a simple smash and grab. Just follow my lead." Zeke glared at Ash.

"Fine. But what happens when they see me and realize who I am?" I asked. The vans were almost on us, and I really wanted to punch Zeke, but he wasn't wrong. They would probably be expecting someone to try to break in and make a last-ditch rescue effort.

"You will most likely be taken to the medical unit, so use that to your advantage," Zeke mumbled.

The vans surrounded us, and my magic thrummed beneath my skin. Shadows pulsed with excitement at the thrill of the fight. Guards flooded out of the vans like a swarm of ants with guns raised.

I flicked my wrist, and magic and shadows mixed, blasting through several guards. I didn't care about Zeke's bullshit plan. If there was going to be blood paid, it was theirs. I certainly wasn't going to make it easy on them after all the horror they'd inflicted on our people.

"Princess, behind you!" Ash shouted in warning.

I spun on my heel and blasted the group of guards raising their guns at me.

They flew back into one of the vans with a thud.

"They just keep coming," I growled.

Arms wrapped around me from behind, and I flipped the man over my shoulder and flicked my wrist, sending him skidding to the others where his head smacked into a hubcap.

"Take her alive!" one of the guards yelled, pointing at me.

"Shit," I said, spinning to Zeke with a glare. "There are too many of them."

Three guards rushed me, but Ash and Zeke got to them first, leveling them with a powerful blast of magic. The ground rumbled beneath my feet, and everyone but me stumbled to the side.

My magic buzzed beneath my skin angrily.

Am I doing that?

The ground beneath one of the vans split in a wide chasm and it crashed inside, exploding in a fiery ball of flames.

"Aurelia, tone it down!" Ash yelled. "You're taking out ours along with theirs."

I heaved in a breath and did my best to control the magic pulsing from me, but it wouldn't stop. The strength of my power was overwhelming as it came out to protect me from the threats.

"I'm trying!" I screamed as another chasm opened beneath two guards who were racing toward me. It swallowed them up and closed over their heads.

But still more guards flooded the once empty parking lot.

Where were they all coming from? It didn't make any sense until I scanned the area and glanced at the man who ordered them to take me alive. He had a phone in his hand and was talking to someone. "Take him out," I said, pointing. "He's calling for back-up." I took deep, controlled breaths, and finally the ground stopped shaking.

Several of my team went after the leader.

I spun around as a grunt sounded behind me.

Dan stood there with a gun in his hand and a guard knocked out on the ground. "Keep your eyes open, Princess. The cowards keep trying to sneak up behind you," Dan said and fired the gun in his hand. He had my back, which would have surprised me before, but he was loyal to Grey, and that made him loyal to me as well.

"Enough. You're surrounded. Surrender now!" the lead guard bellowed.

It went against everything inside me to surrender. I glanced at Zeke warily.

He better know what he's doing.

I nodded imperceptibly to Zeke and Dan.

They ordered everyone to stand down.

"If I get tortured again, I'm going to kick your ass," I growled under my breath.

"Trust me," Zeke whispered as we were swarmed.

Three guards grabbed my arms, clamping cuffs on my wrists behind my back.

Then the leader sauntered up to me wearing a sickening grin. "I'm going to be rewarded for bringing you in." He ran his index finger down my cheek.

Repulsed by his intrusive touch, I snapped my teeth at him and glared.

No one touches me like that but Grey!

Ash, Dan, and Zeke struggled against the guards that were holding them.

"Don't fucking touch her!" Ash bellowed. His power glowed behind his eyes as he raged against the guards.

"You don't have the power here, criminal. Those cuffs block your magic." The man grinned, clearly pleased with himself.

"Please don't evil villain monologue," I groaned.

"You're feisty. I like that. Maybe the High Councilor will let me play with you when he's got what he wants." The leader's eyes glittered with lust.

All the guys struggled against their bonds, trying to get to me or tear him to shreds.

I wasn't sure which was more likely, but probably the latter. I shook my head at them, accepting my fate. I would see Ronaldo in the prison, and he'd probably torture me again before he killed me—but at least the others would get Grey and everyone else out before the whole damn place blew.

I stared Zeke down, still unimpressed with the sudden and unexpected change of plan.

The leader yanked on my arm to move me to one of the transport vans.

His plan had better be a good one, or he's going to be in some serious shit!

Anger pulsed within me, and shadows curled around my fingers lazily, just letting me know it was there.

Wait. I still have access to my magic?

I snapped my gaze back to Zeke.

He shook his head, eyes wide as he stared at my fingers.

How did I still have my magic? The cuffs were supposed to block it.

Do they just not work on me?

Either way, I needed to hide it, or they would find another way to block my magic. I banished the shadows quickly before anyone saw and raised my brows at Zeke. Was this part of the amazing plan he didn't tell us about, or was this yet another way I was simply different from everyone else?

The back door to the van opened to two bench seats, one on each side. There were no windows, and the vehicle had practically been gutted. The guard yanked me up into the van in front of him and pushed me forward.

I fell heavily on the seat at the end closest to the front panel, grimacing as I righted myself.

The leader sat down next to me with a leer, and my skin crawled as he rested a hand on my thigh. There was nothing I could do with my hands bound behind my back, and he knew it.

Asher shoved in and sat in front of me. He lunged forward to get in the leader's face but was hit in the back of the head with the butt of the gun in the guard's hands that sat down next to him.

"You will behave as a prisoner should, or we will not be lenient!" the leader barked.

"Get your filthy, fucking paws off the princess, traitor," Ash gritted out between his clenched teeth.

"Again, you don't make demands here. You're my prisoner, just as she is, and I can do as I please." His hand inched up my thigh even more.

Dan eyed that hand like he could cut it off with only the power of his mind and loyalty to Grey.

I shook my head at them. I didn't want them getting knocked out, or worse, because the Fae bastard was getting handsy.

The leader squeezed my thigh so hard I would have bruises later.

I flinched, practically plastering myself to the wall to get away from him. I needed to stay calm and not telegraph the fact that I still had access to my magic. It was going to be difficult if the man kept putting his hands on me.

He fished his phone from his pocket and pressed a button. "We got twenty incoming. Tell the High Councilor to meet me in medical. I come bearing gifts." He grinned, glancing at me through the corner of his eye.

Fuck. I knew he'd get Ronaldo in there right away to deal with me.

I stared at Zeke with both a warning and a threat in my eyes.

The big bastard grinned at me. Yes, he'd been right about where I would be taken, but that wasn't a good thing. Ronaldo wasn't going to let me out of his sight once he got me into the medical unit. He certainly wouldn't risk putting me with everyone else. I wouldn't have the opportunity to see Grey or even find out what Zeke's ultimate plan was.

Damn. I wish I could read minds.

It fell silent in the van, none of us willing to give the guards a reason to punish us. I wasn't about to talk and possibly make the guards suspicious, either. The road leading to the prison was bumpy, and I jostled around trying to keep myself from touching the traitor, but other than that, the journey was uneventful.

Before long the tall, imposing building came into view and filled me with dread. We had to go there. Now that I was seeing it with my own eyes, I realized our original plan had been foolish, anyway. There was a solid brick wall surrounding the building and five guards at the gate waiting to check the identification of the guards and usher us through.

How had I ever convinced myself that we could pull that off? I just hoped that Zeke's plan was better than mine... because if not, we all might die in there.

CHAPTER 16

"Why would anyone try to break in?" a shifter whispered within earshot.

My inner wolf's ears pricked up, and I swallowed the lump that instantly developed in my dry throat. "What?" I asked through the bars.

Fenrick raised a brow at me, wincing afterward, the result of his extensive bruising and swelling. Poor guy had taken a legendary beating.

"A large group was brought in last night. The rumor is they tried to break into the prison but were betrayed and caught," the shifter said, raising his voice louder this time.

"Fuck... you don't think?" Fenrick asked, leaving the question unspoken.

"That it wasn't a break-in, but rather a rescue mission? Yeah, that's exactly what I think." I covered my face with both hands and released a deep sigh.

Shit.

"Who do you think it was?" Fenrick pressed.

"My money is on Dan and the Syndicate, but I wouldn't put it past the Riders of the Hunt to do something like that as well." I peeked between my fingers at him. That was monumentally stupid of them to try to break into the prison like that.

And if it was them, then who is running the Syndicate?

"How many?" I asked the shifter, trying to push my rising adrenalin down.

"I don't know exactly. I just heard through the grapevine that the group was big. Around twenty, I think, was the word."

"If it's who I suspect, they probably left the damn place unguarded. Damn it!" I jumped to my feet, my agitation winning over, and paced the length of the cell.

If this was Dan, then we are in deeper shit than we thought.

"Easy, Grey," Fenrick said, trying to soothe the beast that was rising within me. "We already planned to get everyone out anyway. And if it *is* your guys, at least they are well-trained to assist us in our escape."

He was right, but the whole thing still left me feeling uneasy. They weren't supposed to come after me if I ever got caught. Who could have convinced them to risk an extraction like this?

Growling echoing down from the end of the cell block caught my attention just before a set of boots stomped down the hall toward us.

I spun to the door and waited for the guard that usually helped us with my hands on my hips. But it wasn't him.

A different guard stood by the door and sneered at us.

"Where's my usual guard?" I asked, my brow furrowed.

"Shut up, mutt!" the unfamiliar guard barked back, opening the door with his badge.

I glanced at Fenrick, a surge of dread pooling in my gut.

Did we get him killed? Fuck!

"Let's go. I don't want to wait around all day to escort filth to the mess hall!" the guard roared, clearly running low on patience or filled with far too much hate.

We stalked out of the cell together, shoulder to shoulder, as we followed the asshole guard to the mess hall in tense silence.

Were these new prisoners our allies? And why would the guards take them into custody here if they were just going to level the place in two days? I had so many questions and no answers. My mind spun, and my brain ached.

We pushed through the doors to the mess hall and got in line.

I scanned the faces of everyone in the room, and my gaze landed on a distinct pair of turquoise eyes. "Fuck," I grumbled under my breath.

Fenrick spun in the direction of my stare and straight onto the Riders of the Hunt. "Well, that answers that question," he said.

We grabbed our food and made our way to the table in the back.

Magna and the king sat with Asher and Zeke, along with the rest of their brothers.

"What the fuck, Ash?" I dropped my tray on the table, leveling him with a glare.

"What can I say? Shit went south. It all got fucked up." Ash shrugged and waved his hands as if to say 'c'est la vie'.

"I would definitely say it all got fucked up if you're sitting across from me in this hell." I shook my head and grimaced.

"It *didn't* all get fucked up," Zeke grumbled in opposition.

"You fucked us all over," Dan said hissed.

"I'm telling you that it's better this way," Zeke growled back. "This'll work in our favor."

"Yeah, it's better eating fucking gruel and waiting for the hammer to drop on our heads. So much better." Dan clenched a fist around his fork, his temper fraying.

I glanced between the men who were all glaring at Zeke.

What the fuck did he do?

He was the reason they were all there, I was sure. Dread sank into my stomach like a stone. Who was here, and what was happening back at the Syndicate if everyone I trusted in a position of authority was in prison? I sat heavily on the bench. "Okay. Who else is here?"

"Dan brought in three teams along with us and your mate," Ash said slowly.

"Aurelia is here?" I asked scanning the mess hall to no avail. "Where the fuck is she then?"

Relief that she'd survived the fall in Faery filled me with temporary relief, but it was quickly squashed when I processed what he'd just said. She was in the prison with us. She'd tried to break in and rescue us all and was caught. And now, my mate was far too close to Ronaldo's sadistic ass for my liking, being locked up in here.

"They immediately separated her from us, and we haven't seen her since." Zeke shook his head.

Fuck. My mate is alive but hidden somewhere in this gods' forsaken hellhole?

"You never should have brought her here," I growled, my inner wolf's hackles rising.

"Right. Like she would let us leave her behind," Zeke scoffed.

He wasn't wrong. They would have had to lock her in a cell to get her to stay behind. So, either way, she would have been locked away. "Fine, I get it. She never would have stopped." I didn't like it, but I understood why they'd brought her along. I'd have done the same and worse to retrieve my mate were the shoe on the other foot. "What's going on outside?" I asked. "It's been a while since we heard anything." In fact, we'd gotten zero information since being locked away.

"The human government is rounding up all suspected supernaturals for testing and making them register as a supernatural." Ash clenched his fist around his roll and turned it to powdery dust.

"It's such bullshit." I picked up my fork and stabbed the mushy substance that the prison passed off as food.

"Obviously, but what do you mean, Grey?" Ash frowned.

"They're out to execute everyone who isn't useful. That's why I'm so freaked out about Aurelia being here. The prison is going to blow in two days, and sometime tomorrow they are moving all the shifters to a more official, permanent facility so they can test their mind control serum on us. Apparently, we shifters aren't as prone to it as other supernaturals."

Zeke shook his head. "Fuck. I knew they were going to blow the place up, but I thought it was a ploy to kill off all the royalty from Faery so their new regime couldn't be challenged."

"Nope. As the Shifter King, I'm prime testing material. Think about it… the royalty of Faery, regardless of caste, are usually among the strongest, so it'd make sense they want to keep us until we cease being of use to them." I grimaced and shoveled food into my mouth, swallowing without tasting it.

"We all need to get out of here. Ronaldo is probably coming in his pants with excitement at the mere thought of having us all locked away in here." Ash wiped the crumbs from his hand and grabbed the roll from my tray, tearing into it with his teeth.

A shifter reached over and handed me his own roll without a word.

Zeke raised a brow at that but didn't comment. The other shifters were constantly giving me gifts in return for protection. And all I'd done so far was tell some warlocks to back off. Zeke drummed his fingers on the table. "So, we need to get out of here tonight?"

"That would be ideal, but we don't have a way," I said as I glanced at Dan. "Your man on the inside disappeared. They gave us a new guard this morning."

"Fuck. Was he discovered?" Dan asked and rubbed his hand down his face.

"I don't know, but I hope not." I sighed.

Maybe he's just been reassigned elsewhere?

"This isn't good. I was hoping that we had him on the inside at least." Dan hung his head. "Damn it."

"Don't worry." Zeke patted Dan's shoulder. "It doesn't change the plan. It's going to work out, you'll see."

"The plan you refuse to share with the class?" Dan grumbled.

I snapped my gaze to Zeke. What the fuck was he planning?

The rider shook his head and smirked, remaining tight-lipped on the subject.

Magna placed a calming hand on my arm. "Don't. This is for the best. Trust in your friends, Grey."

"What did you see?" I asked, my curiosity getting the better of me.

"You know I can't tell you that." She shook her head with an apologetic smile.

"I know, but I hate being the last to know the plan." I tilted my head back, squeezing my eyes shut.

How am I supposed to lead if I'm left in the dark?

"Your shifter is coming," Magna said quietly. "He has something for you."

I turned just as the shifter that worked for the Syndicate bound up to me.

He had a grin on his face and went to reach into his pocket.

I growled like a rabid beast in warning. "Not now. If that's what I think it is, the guards are *always* watching me here," I whispered so low only a shifter could hear.

His eyes widened, and his gaze flicked around the room, noting all eyes on us. Especially since we were currently sitting with the supernaturals who'd tried to break in. "No problem, boss." He nodded, then glanced at Dan. "Shit. What are you doing here?"

"We were framed. They thought we were breaking into the prison for some unknown reason, and they brought us in," Dan lied easily.

"You really think I'd believe that?" the shifter questioned, raising a brow at Dan.

"I don't care what you believe. We have eyes on us, and that's the only thing I'm telling you," Dan snarled and stared the shifter down.

He bowed his head in submission. Dan mightn't be a shifter, but he was my second in the Syndicate, so carried significant authority. Any shifter would be wise to abide his word—unless they wanted to deal with me and my wrath.

"Sit down," I said to the shifter, pointing at a spot next to the Shadow King.

He'd been uncharacteristically silent upon hearing the news that Aurelia was in this hellhole with us. He was probably worried that she was in the hands of Ronaldo.

As her mate, I was just as worried, but needed this information to help us all. We had to get everyone out of here and we needed to do it sooner rather than later. I glanced over my shoulder at the guard who'd replaced the one that'd been helping me.

His eyes gleamed with malice. He was going to be a tough one to get past. He may not make it out of the prison, and I wasn't sure that I gave a fuck, because he was definitely drinking the Council's Kool-Aid.

I glanced at the shifter as he sat next to the Shadow King and then back at Zeke. "We only have one shot at this. Are you going to be ready to go tonight? And how do we get Aurelia out?"

Magna nudged my shoulder, her eyes swirling with her mysterious seer magic. "We *are* ready and able to get out tonight. Your shifter has what you need, and your mate will be ready. Trust me, Zeke is right. This will work."

I did trust Magna. Her visions had never failed me. She always seemed to point me in the right direction, even if she couldn't tell me everything I needed to know. A lot of the time it *was* better for her to keep things close to her chest. We didn't want to change the outcome or compromise the hand of Fate if she was pointing us in the right direction.

"Okay, I get it. I'll play along," I agreed for Magna's sake, glared at Zeke all the same. "I don't like being left in the dark, Rider. And I hate that my mate is probably being tortured right now."

"I know, but we can't just talk about this out in the open. You never know who might be listening," said Zeke as he scanned the room.

"Shifter hearing would be an issue if all the shifters here weren't loyal to me."

"Loyalty can be bought with freedom. Though it would be a lie, and we all know it. The kind of loyalty that can be bought isn't forever." Zeke clenched his fist on the table.

"Anyone who betrays us in this place can rot!" I said loudly enough for all to hear.

"That was subtle." Ash smirked and shook his head.

"They need to know what the stakes are here. They need to know that there will be *no* mercy for betrayal." I shrugged, not giving a shit.

"Well, you are definitely giving off *I'm going to kill you* vibes, so there's that." Zeke chuckled.

Something shoved me roughly in the back, and the shifters at the table growled.

I turned to the guard behind me. The new bastard with malice in his eyes.

He sneered at me. "Time to go, mutt." The guard poked me in the back with his baton again.

I nodded to the others, urging them to stand down, and stood from my seat with Fenrick at my side. I still didn't know what the plan was, but it seemed neither did anyone else. Zeke was keeping it quiet, but he had Magna's backing, and that was enough for me. I would be ready. Ultimately, I didn't have a choice, because if I wasn't ready for *anything*, then whatever plan Zeke was hatching wouldn't end well for any of us—least of all my precious golden-haired mate.

CHAPTER 17

"Stay in here." The sleazy leader of the guards shoved me into a sterile white operating room.

The click of the lock as he closed the door was like a gunshot to my ears. I was going to kill Zeke for this. That damn Rider was a pain in my ass. My rage instantly plummeted to the pit of my stomach when I realized the only thing in the room in which I was being held captive was an operating table... and there were no windows. I wanted to ask what the hell Ronaldo used this room for, but I was afraid I already knew. After my experiences in Faery, the most obvious truth was that he'd been torturing my people.

My only saving grace was that Dan's man on the inside had told him that *they* were still alive—my mate, my father, and my dearest friends. If it weren't for that knowledge, I would have already lost control.

Please let them be okay.

I paced the small room, wringing my hands together. Keeping my shit together was harder than I'd expected it to be.

This is stupid. Why did I let them take me instead of fighting harder?

My hands shook, and I wiped the sweat from my palms on my jeans as I tried to steady my breathing.

Something buzzed before the door was pushed open, and Ronaldo stood there with a smug grin on his face and several guards flanking him. "Princess."

"Ronaldo," I answered with a sneer. "You won't get away with this."

"But I already have, Princess. You'll have no one left, and after tomorrow, you will *all* be dead or under my control."

He snapped at the guards, and they advanced on me.

I struggled slightly, maintaining my charade, but let them strap me to the operating table. No matter what happened, I couldn't let him know that I still had access to my magic. I had no idea what Zeke's plan was, but I was sure that it wasn't underway yet and I needed to bide my time. "You think you can control me?" I scoffed.

"I will have no problem controlling you, girl. You're nothing but a nuisance." He took a threatening step towards me.

"Then why are you so obsessed with me?" I laughed. The Councilman had a sick obsession with hurting and controlling me, and though I did kind of understand his reasoning, there was still so much about the prophecy I didn't know.

"You are in my way," he said simply. "You were the only one who could have ended this before it began... but not anymore. Now, I have you exactly where I want you, and you won't be getting away again."

Chills rolled down my spine at Ronaldo's evil grin despite my brave face. "You're sick and twisted. If you hadn't turned the Fae against the supernaturals in the first place, there would be no need of a prophecy. You were drunk on that power and wanted more. And now you want to rule humans, which is insane since they outnumber us by a great deal."

"I tire of your mouth. Maybe when I have you under my control, I will give you to Malcolm, and he can make use of it. He has always had a soft spot for his *betrothed.*"

Real terror snaked through my chest, and my stomach plummeted.

He can't really control the minds of the Fae... We Fae have shields. We can't be controlled...

A moment later Ronaldo returned, wheeling a cart laden with medical tools.

I flinched. Was he going to torture me so I would drop my shields, the same way he had tried to torture my shadow magic out of me? How long could I hold out against his torture without using my magic to defend myself? Could I defy my own instincts? How far did *mind over matter* truly go? "You'll never control me," I said through gritted teeth. Regardless of what lay ahead, there was no way in hell I was showing this prick an ounce of fear.

Ronaldo's sadistic laugh filled the small space as he picked up a syringe and gripped my arm.

Magic tingled beneath my skin, but I held it back by sheer force of will. I refused to show signs that I had my magic. It would be catastrophic. It'd ruin everything and endanger those I loved.

He pushed the syringe in my arm and the cool liquid plunged into my veins, leaving an icy chill in its wake. The tingling of foreign magic in my veins started at my arm and arched up through my body to my head. "In just a few seconds you will be completely under my control." Ronaldo grinned.

My magic battled with whatever he'd just injected me with, and I shivered. Whatever the substance was, it was powerful and threatened to overwhelm me. My back arched involuntarily as my magic turned molten in my veins.

Ronaldo's grin dropped from his face as my entire body started shaking. "What's happening?" he asked, taking a step forward and leaning over me. "She shouldn't be able to fight it off. It should be working already!"

One of the guards stepped forward. "She's powerful. Maybe the magic blocking-cuffs only mean that she can't use magic outside her own body?"

I held back a scream as my magic boiled me from the inside. It was excruciating, but whatever drug Ronaldo had used on me was burned up within seconds. I slumped back down on the operating table with relief, my breathing heavy. But my respite was short lived.

"Get me more!" Ronaldo barked at a guard. "Double the dose. She can't fight it off forever."

"Sir, that much could kill her," the leader that brought me in said as he stepped forward. "You promised I could play with her once she was under your control, before you give her to Malcolm."

"Well, she won't be under my control until we can stop her magic from fighting the serum, will she?" Ronaldo yelled back, a vein in his temple throbbing.

He's really going to do this.

My shadows tried desperately to free themselves and protect me from the threats in the room. I held them off as best as I could, unwilling to reveal my hand just yet.

"If she dies, she will be of no use either, sir." The leader crossed his arms over his chest.

"She's good for nothing but to please my men," Ronaldo retorted. "She's already been sentenced to death for her crimes against Faery. What do I care if the princess dies? Everyone who would care is in a cell and will be joining her in death soon enough."

I gasped at his words. It hadn't been entirely real until I heard it from his lips. He really was out to destroy all supernaturals. He never had a plan to enslave them... he was only ever going to destroy them.

"If you're planning on killing us all, why bother experimenting on us?" I spat.

"The humans believe they're in control and required testing facilities to learn more about us. They are a particularly stupid breed. The mind control is simply a failsafe for any who manage to avoid capture and death." Ronaldo shrugged.

The other guard rushed back into the room with a tray in his hands. The syringe was even bigger this time. Electric blue liquid sloshed about inside it.

I yanked at my arms, trying to get free physically. My magic had a mind of its own when it came to protecting me from that crazy shit, and it hurt like a bitch. I clenched my fists and tugged on the straps, but they were so tight I wasn't getting anywhere.

Ronaldo clamped a hand down on my arm and held me still as he brought the syringe down on my arm.

My magic swirled within me, and shadows danced behind my eyes as I screamed in pain. My magic heated up and became an inferno in my body once more, trying to burn away the much larger dose. Convulsions wracked my body, and I even frothed at the mouth. I had no idea how I was managing to keep my magic under wraps, but it was costing me a great deal. It pulsed away inside of me, burning away the toxin, and soon the convulsions eased, allowing me to slump back on the table in fatigued relief.

"No!" Ronaldo roared, squeezing my arm harder as he raged.

I closed my eyes and did my best to calm the magic that was waging war inside me, just dying to get out and have its vengeance.

Without warning, he pulled the shining medical cart full of implements closer to him and a crazed grin spread across his lips. He was going to torture me. "How are you doing that?" Ronaldo growled. "That dose would have killed a grown man, and you are a small slip of a girl!"

"Fuck you," I sneered. I didn't care. He could torture me all he wanted. The wounds would heal probably faster than he would expect, and then I would get the fuck out of there at my first opportunity. We'd danced this dance before, and I was ready.

He grabbed a scalpel and held it up for me to see, turning the gleaming blade over dramatically. "I carved the words *Shifter Scum* into your shifter with this scalpel. It seems only fitting I use it to carve into your pretty flesh as well."

The gleam in his eyes would have scared the piss out of a grown-ass man, but I knew what was coming. We'd played this game already, and I refused to take the bait. It wasn't shocking that the sadist had tortured Grey, but it hurt all the same. I'd have my revenge.

We all will.

"It doesn't matter what you do to me. I'm *still* going to be your end." I smirked.

"The traitor screamed so beautifully for me as I practically bled him dry. He wasn't supposed to make it out of here alive. Oh, well, there will be plenty of time to torture him at the testing facility."

He planned to send Grey to a formal testing facility? He wasn't going to kill him here with the rest of us? That fate would destroy Grey more than any torture possibly could.

No. I can't think like this. We are all getting out of here and then taking the Council down once and for all!

The scalpel pierced my arm as Ronaldo dug it in as deep as he could into my skin. Fire burned in my veins as blood trickled down my arm and pooled on the sterile table beneath me. I locked my jaw against a shriek of pain. The worst part though, was the expression of euphoria on the High Councilor's face. He was absolutely getting off on torturing me. If that wasn't utterly sick and twisted, I didn't know what was.

"Tell me how you keep burning through my influence, and this all stops," he crooned. "I'll take you to a cell where you can heal until the explosion."

"Fuck off!" I gritted out.

He slashed at my arm, cutting across the other cut to create an *X*.

I squeezed my eyes shut and held back a whimper of agony. My skin burned with pain even as my magic rallied to heal my injuries. It was the only thing I could allow it to do as I kept it in a stranglehold. This was the exact place Zeke wanted me to go, and I needed to figure out *why* before they put the escape plan into action. I just had no idea how to do that with Ronaldo slicing me up.

He moved from my arm with a scowl and pressed scalpel into my cheek, but not hard enough to break the skin. His angry gaze pinned me to the table. "How are you healing so quickly?"

"I don't know," I hissed, meeting his gaze with daggers of my own.

"Did someone tamper with her cuffs?" Ronaldo asked over his shoulder.

The leader of the guards who'd taken us in stepped forward. "No, sir. I put those cuffs on her myself, and no one has touched her since."

"Hm. I may just have to keep you around at the testing facility after all if your magic is leaking through those cuffs," Ronaldo mused. "You're much stronger than I gave you credit for, Princess."

"With all due respect, sir. I don't think that would be wise. Even though subjects are strapped down, they are less secure, and she could escape with the shifter."

Without warning, Ronaldo dug the scalpel into my cheek.

I gasped at the pain so very close to my eye. Hot blood trickled down my face to my lips, painting a bloody smile as I collected some of my own blood in my mouth and spat it in Ronaldo's face.

"You may be right," he said with a sigh. "She's too wild to trust in the facility. She will just have to die along with the rest of them. What a shame." Ronaldo swiped the blood off his face and slashed my cheek again. Without a trace of remorse or humanity, he kept slashing at my face and arms until I gave him something.

With my brow furrowed, and my heart racing, I let out a scream of agony at the assault. My back arched and blood drenched me and the table to which I was strapped, but my magic worked swiftly to heal the worst of my injuries.

"I will be back for you, Princess," he warned. "This time I will make sure you die like you should have in the Council chambers you destroyed."

"Fuck off, Ronaldo," I said, spitting the words at him like venom.

He was the scum of the Earth, but he held my life in his hands. How exactly did he plan to make sure I died this time? Despite my faith in my family and friends, and my rebellious spirit that persevered… I wasn't sure I wanted to find out.

Zeke… Grey… please hurry!

CHAPTER 18
Grey

The electric buzzing of the door woke me, and I jumped to my feet, staring at Dan on the other side. My eyes practically bugged out of my head. "How did you get out?" I asked as I moved to the door.

Fenrick followed close behind.

"Zeke is a smart bastard, let me tell you. He somehow planned it right down to which cuffs they would put us in. He refused to tell us anything, but our cuffs are useless. They don't block shit." He held out a hand with a characteristic grin.

I reached out and let him grip my wrist, turning it to place a small key in the hole and unlocking them. My wolf lunged to the surface as magic rushed through me in waves. I nearly stumbled. I'd almost forgotten what normal felt like—to feel like an actual shifter, and not a creature stunted and shut off from the core of its very being.

Fenrick doubled over at the waist, probably feeling the same sense of relief and connection to the core of his being like I had.

I walked over to the cell next to mine and handed the shifter the key, the one who had been whispering to me all this time. "Get this to everyone on the cell block. They all need to unlock their cuffs as fast as possible," I said, before turning back to Dan. "What's the plan?"

"Follow me." Dan took off down the hall that led toward the showers.

I shrugged at Fenrick before jogging after him.

"Where are we going?" Fenrick asked.

"There's a control panel down this hall that will open all the cells in the prison. I need to get to it before anyone realizes we're out." Dan turned down the second hall.

Six guards stood around in a circle talking in hushed voices when we skidded around the corner.

Reacting on pure instinct and the innate desire in all things to be free, Fenrick blasted one of them with his magic.

At the exact same moment, I rushed one, crouching low and taking him to the ground. "Dan!" I shouted in warning.

But our friend was fine, he already had two others pinned to the ground with his magic.

I gripped the guard's baton and flicked the electricity on, hitting him in the neck with it.

He grunted before his eyes rolled in the back of his head, and he was out for the count.

I glanced up at the others, but they had already taken care of the other five guards.

"Let's go." Dan wiped his hands on his pants and turned down the next hall.

Fenrick ran his hand down his face, a concerned grimace flitting across his features. "Are we stupid for leaving them alive? Is this going to come back to bite us in the ass?"

"It might, but they were just humans... and despite what they are doing to us right now, I don't like killing humans," I said. "There's no honor in it."

"It won't matter in a minute!" Dan called over his shoulder as he raced ahead.

"Why is that?" I asked almost bumping into him.

He skidded to a halt in front of me. "Because there are about to be *a lot* more of us than them." He grinned. The black panel on the wall had a keypad on it, keeping it locked. Dan held a hand over it, and then there was a loud *pop,* and sparks flew from the damn thing before the panel popped open.

"What are you doing?" I asked with a frown, keeping a wary eye on the intersecting halls.

"Getting back-up." He flipped a switch, and the lights flashed red as a siren sounded. The cells all buzzed, and the sound of grinding metal filled the air. Dan whooped, fist pumping the air.

Without delay, we raced back to the cell block to see shifters stumbling out of their cells, their cuffs no longer binding their inner animals. Howls of excitement flooded the hall as they jumped all over each other.

I was as relieved as the next guy to be free, but there was no time to waste. I grabbed the shifter that worked for me by the scruff of his neck. "We aren't out of here yet," I warned him. "There are six guards in the back hall. They probably all have cuff keys. I need you to get them for me."

He nodded dutifully and grabbed another shifter, taking off in the direction I'd pointed.

The rest of the shifters stopped celebrating and stood at attention, sobering as they waited for instructions.

I turned to Dan with a raised brow. "Do you know where the other supernaturals are being kept?"

"They're all in this block as well as the next block over, where they had me." He pointed down the hall in the opposite direction.

"Good." I grabbed the shifter that was by the next cell. "Do you still have the keys?" I asked, my gaze firm.

"Yes," he said, nodding and swallowing hard.

"Go take the cuffs off the warlocks and others. I'll send help when they get back."

The shifter nodded again, and several others took off with him to the next cell block to get the rest out of their cuffs. Everyone was going to need full access to their magic if we were going to make it out of here before it blew.

"Where are the Riders?" I asked Dan.

"They're busy holding off the guards until we can get everyone out of their cuffs."

I jogged down the hall and nearly ran into the shifters that were sent to get more keys. "Go on, meet up with the others and help get the warlocks out of their cuffs!"

We raced to the end of the other block and past the warlock who'd been bullying the shifters before I came in.

He nodded as he got his cuffs removed. "What's the plan?" he asked.

"The plan is to get the hell out of here without dying." I shrugged. I didn't even know what kind of plan Zeke had cooked up in that crazy head of his, but whatever it was, it was working swell so far.

"That's not much of a plan," remarked the wizard.

"You're out of your cell and the cuffs, right?" I asked, hiking my brow at him.

"Fair enough," he agreed. It was a taste of freedom and that was more than we'd had mere minutes ago.

I stopped next to Ash and Zeke as we came up on them. "Okay, liar, how are we doing this then?"

"That was harsh," Zeke said, "but not untrue."

"You can tell us the plan now, dipshit!" Ash barked, his temper ever short.

"Someone is going to have to blast the doors open. But we need Aurelia to get out of the medical unit before we can leave."

"We're sitting ducks right here. How long do you think we have before they call for back-up or try to blow this place to smithereens early?" I asked, scrubbing a hand down my face.

"Probably only a few minutes," Zeke admitted.

"Fuck. That's not exactly helpful." I sighed, keeping myself in check through sheer force of will.

We're too close to fuck it up now.

"We can hold them off," the warlock said as he clapped me on the shoulder. Magic lit his other palm, answering his summons.

I grinned. Damn, it felt good to have all our powers back. I scanned the group of men gathered around.

We can do this.

We could get out of here, I truly believed it now, but what were we going to do once we did? "What was the state of the Syndicate when you left?" I asked.

"Overcrowded but fine. Why?" Zeke answered.

"We'll need somewhere for everyone to go in the aftermath."

"That's what we've been doing this whole time. Gathering anyone who is outed as supernatural and giving them space at the building. We'll figure it out once we get there."

"Let's go, then." I jogged off to the other end of the cell block to the heavy metal door locking us all in.

Dan raced up with a badge in his hand and swiped it on the keypad. The alarm continued to blare in my oversensitive ears and the panel on the door flashed red. "Fuck, it's not working." Dan grunted with an immediate frown.

"Can you override it?" I asked, turning to Zeke. He was the resident hacker, and I'd never seen a system he couldn't break into.

He has to be able to do something.

Zeke rushed to the panel on the door and typed a few codes, but shook his head. "Shit. The overrides aren't working."

"Fuck." I slammed my hand on the door.

We're so close!

"Can you get around it? What if you just blow the electronics inside like before?" I asked Dan.

"I could try that, but I'm not sure if it will open it or stay closed permanently." Dan leaned his forehead against the door, concentrating on channeling his power, then placed his palm on the scanner. Magic lit his hand in a green glow. There was a *pop* of electricity and then nothing. The door didn't move so much as an inch.

I shoved Dan out of the way in frustration and desperation and pushed the door, but it was too heavy for me to move on my own. "Ash, Zeke, help me push this," I demanded.

The two loyal Riders and several others lined up on either side of me and we pushed the door until our muscles strained with burning pain. It creaked and groaned beneath our weight and considerable force before finally sliding open. The supernaturals around us cheered as they flooded out of the main cell block to the front of the prison.

Guards flooded the area with their electric batons at the ready, barking orders to one another, but no one listened. Their show of force descended in chaos and panic as shifters tore their clothes off and shifted like lightning. Wolves and bears tore into guards all around me, their inner animals rejoicing at being free for the first time in gods only knew how long.

Blood sprayed across my face as I rushed to lend my strength to the fray. My wolf prowled in my head, wanting out. It had been too long since I gave in to my beast, but I had to hold back until we got the hell out of here.

One of us has to maintain a clear head for fuck's sake!

The other shifters had no such thoughts. Letting their animals tear through the guards without mercy, they painted the prison red.

I ducked just as a guard swung his baton at my head, punching him hard in the gut.

All the air rushed from his lungs as he doubled over, unable to withstand the power I packed as a supernatural.

I took the baton from him and clouted him over the head with it, knocking him out cold.

Something slammed into my back, and arms circled my neck in a pathetic attempt at a chokehold. I lunged forward, throwing the guard over my shoulder, breaking his grip, and slammed the baton into his skull with more force than I'd intended.

"Grey, we're surrounded!" Ash yelled over top of the chaos.

He was covered in blood from head to toe, most of it I was sure wasn't his. The shifters weren't taking prisoners, that was damn sure. They were getting their revenge.

"Shit." I spun around, ready to defend myself.

Eight guards were circling the two of us.

Ash glared at the one standing in front of the rest, apparently their leader.

"You want his death, brother." Ash clapped me on the shoulder and pointed at the man.

"And why is that?" I asked with a grin.

"He put his hands on your mate."

The grin slipped from my face, and I felt the blood inside my veins both simultaneously boil and freeze.

He did what now?

"I'll make it slow and painful then," I threatened with dark glee as I took a menacing step toward him, twirling the baton I still had at my side.

"Yeah, that was me, mutt. And once the High Councilor figures out how to control her, he's going to give her to me to play with before he palms her off to Malcolm." The man's eyes glowed with undeniable lust for my mate.

My wolf beat at the cage I had him locked in, trying valiantly to take control, to defend his mate's honor and tear this bastard a new asshole. "I'm *definitely* going to kill you now," I growled.

With a flippant hand motion, the entire group descended on us at once. We were overwhelmed, and everyone else was in the middle of their own battles, literally fighting tooth and claws for their freedom.

I snarled at the leader of the guards, my wolf howling behind my eyes as I let my hate rise.

If something doesn't even up this playing field soon, we're royally screwed.

CHAPTER 19

Having recovered from my torture, and been temporarily freed of my bonds, I paced the small operating room when the lights flashed red, and an alarm blared in my ears. The door to the room swung open wide, hitting the wall behind it and surprising the shit out of me. "What the hell are they doing?" I whispered to myself as I took several tentative steps toward the door.

Chaos reigned outside as people in white lab coats scattered like frantic ants. They raced for the doors I'd been brought through, muttering all the while about getting locked in with the animals if they didn't hurry.

Of course, they think we're animals. Do they want to see what kind of animals we really can be?

My magic formed a ball in my hand, and I threw it at a cabinet. It was immediately engulfed in flames. Several shrieks filled the room, and I rushed to the other tables I came across on the way, removing restraints from a man tied to a bed.

He quickly got up, but he stumbled to the side haphazardly as if he were still weak or injured.

I steadied him, but I needed to help the others as fast as I could, before smoke filled the room and choked us all out.

"Go. I'll help," the man urged and steadied himself on the bed.

"Thank you." I nodded to the man, not knowing what type of supernatural he was, and raced to the other beds. Some were better off than others, but at least after a few moments they could walk on their own.

"Get to the main prison as soon as you can! There should be a rescue party nearby. I have something else I need to do." I spun back to the hall in which the room I'd been tortured in was, and rushed through the medical unit, searching for the serum he'd used on me. If I could find their supply and destroy it, they wouldn't be able to use it on others. I had no idea if it was the only batch or not, but it would hurt the Council regardless.

I glanced through the doors on both sides of the hallway, finding offices with computers. My magic swept through the room, frying every device in each office before moving on. Small *pops* of electricity followed in my wake as I destroyed the evidence of our being here and any test results they might have logged on us.

Maybe I should have thought this through better. I'm going to have to come back this way.

I raced to the end of the hall and threw open the double doors using my magic. There was obviously a reason they didn't have that connected to the prison's evacuation system. I stepped inside the room and growled low in my throat. It was another lab, but there were people hooked up to tubes and machines that seemed to be keeping them alive.

What the fuck do I do? I can't just leave them!

"Fuck!" I shouted.

"What is it?" a man's voice asked behind me.

I spun, ready to throw magic until I recognized the man I'd helped earlier. "I can't get them out of here. I don't even know if they're alive, or which ones are capable of surviving being shifted…" I shook my head in frustration and dismay.

"I was an ER doctor before they started rounding us up," said the man as he stepped forward. There were two beds with people strapped to them close by, and he got to work checking their vitals and muttered to himself. "Neither of them has any brain activity." He frowned. "I don't even know why they are keeping them alive."

"What the fuck?" I asked, a pit forming in my stomach. "Why would they keep them alive without brain function? It's sickening…"

"The experiments they're doing here are vile. Maybe they want to be able to control something that doesn't have the free will to interfere or resist."

"That's fucking terrifying. I think I would rather be dead for good than have my body used like I was some kind of walking zombie." I shivered.

How could they do this to us? Their own people? Supernaturals just like them…

Allowing the rage of injustice to fill me, I licked my lips and straightened my shoulders. "They're gone. I'm going to light this place up before the fires spread and trap us back here."

The man took a step back with a nod. Just like me, I had no doubt he viewed what I was about to do as mercy.

Magic flooded my system, and I prepared myself for what came next.

I'm doing them a kindness.

I unleashed my magic, and it flew at the shelf on the wall. There were vials of electric blue liquid there that had to be the same as the serum Ronaldo injected me with. I could only hope that those were the only doses left and that the computer files I'd destroyed weren't backed up somewhere else. The glass vials exploded into a noxious vapor that filled the air, and I coughed. "Get out of here," I warned. "You might not be strong enough to fight it."

"What about you?" he asked, worried, his expression strained and torn by indecision.

"I'll be fine. I've fought it off before more than once. Go!" I waved at him to hurry.

With one last unsure glance, he nodded and raced away.

Three more shelves were stocked with vials of the blue liquid, and I torched them all, along with a couple of computers that dotted the room. A single tear tracked down my cheek as the machines keeping hearts beating *popped* with electricity and died.

Ronaldo and his Council were monsters in the truest sense for testing on my people, and I would make them pay for it. I raced from the room as an explosion rattled the ground beneath my feet. Making my way to the next room, I found there were shelves upon shelves of the vile stuff. I let my magic go wild. Glass shattered and rained down on the floor as vapor hissed before being sucked up into the vents in the walls and ceiling.

Shit. I hope that doesn't affect the others' escape.

A ball of fire flew at me as several more combustible medical supplies exploded, one after another in a chain reaction. I hurled myself to the side just as the whole wall came down. With practiced ease, I rolled back to my feet and sprinted down the hall.

I think that's enough destruction for one day. The fire should spread to the other rooms on its own. I don't need to add to the danger.

What kind of chemicals were being stored in that room? That had been a bigger explosion than I was expecting.

All around me the entire medical unit sounded like a battlefield as electronics caught fire and solutions of various sizes and colors exploded. I dodged several more errant fireballs as I directed my magic at the main room where the prisoners had been tested, frying the last computers still standing as well as any other vials of that foul serum as I raced away.

The ground rumbled beneath my feet again as I rushed out the main door to the medical unit and slammed it behind me.

Gods, I hope no one else was in there. Those poor people were already dead, but please don't let anyone else be stuck in there!

I slammed my fist into the wall, furious that Ronaldo and his Council were just using people for their own gain, as if they were baser animals or mere produce to be harvested. I fucking hated it. The floor rolled suddenly beneath my feet as a deafening roar surrounded me. I pitched to the side and clutched at the wall, the breath almost knocked from me.

I must keep moving. I can't get caught up in the explosions or risk being discovered by the Council's goons.

I picked my way through debris and burning embers as I shuffled through the hall to the central portion of the prison. That was the only part of the plan Zeke had told me. We were to meet at the front of the prison so that we could get the fuck out of here.

He's probably not going to like the detour and chaos I've caused. Oops. Oh, well! He'll just have to deal with it, considering he did this to us. Not to mention I was fucking tortured—again.

I rounded the corner and stopped dead in my tracks, my breathing hard as my heart thumped behind my ribcage with exertion.

Ronaldo stood in the hallway with a sneer on his face, with two guards standing at attention at his back.

"What have you done?" Ronaldo roared.

I grinned. "My magic may have taken exception to the atrocities happening here. I guess I blew some shit up."

He glanced down at the cuffs still on my wrists. "Impossible! You have the cuffs on. You can't possibly have your magic. They were designed to keep it tamped down."

I called magic into my palms where it swirled and writhed like a living thing, an inherent part of me.

Ronaldo's eyes widened in shock. Now, he had irrefutable proof I wasn't lying, and it clearly rocked his damn world.

"You were saying?" I smiled sweetly.

"How is that possible?" He turned furious eyes on his guards as if they were somehow to blame.

"I'm more powerful than whatever you have in these things." I shrugged.

"You are becoming more of a nuisance than I had ever imagined you could be, Princess. Stop this! You don't know what you're doing!"

"No," I growled, letting the magic build in intensity in my palms.

"I will kill you, Princess," Ronaldo hissed and took a threatening step forward.

"You've already threatened to do that countless times, Ronaldo." I smirked. "It's kind of losing its effect."

"Foolish, insolent girl!" Ronaldo bellowed back. "You could have still been queen if you had just fallen in line with what we had planned!"

"You mean keeping dead people alive for your own nefarious purposes? No fucking way, thank you." I shook my head and lobbed a ball of magic at the three men. I was done with their shit.

Enough is enough.

They all dove out of the way and my magic blasted the wall behind them, shaking the building around me. The whole place was going to go up in flames soon. I needed to get the hell out, but Ronaldo and his goons were still blocking my exit. They weren't going to give up so easily, it seemed.

"Enough of this!" Ronaldo hollered. "I wanted to execute you publicly if it came to it to make an example of you to all of Faery, but you are proving yourself to be far too much of a thorn in my side." He turned to his men. "Kill the princess. *Now!*"

The men with Ronaldo drew their guns, aiming them squarely at my chest.

Does he really think those are going to hurt me? Human weapons...

I smirked. "You are too cocky for your own good," I spat, cocking a prominent brow.

"No, Princess, *you* are. Do you think mind control is the only weapon I have been working on?" Ronaldo chuckled. "That would have been very shortsighted of me, wouldn't it?"

"What are you talking about?" I asked, summoning more magic as we faced off against one another, three against one. I worried my lip at his smug expression and the flames licking up the walls all around us. I needed to get out of here, preferably without bullet holes in my chest.

"After we get rid of the supernaturals, the humans will clearly be next. I couldn't have them possessing better weapons than us," Ronaldo scoffed as if the answer were obvious.

I eyed the guns a little more warily. What the fuck was in them? I didn't want to find out if I could avoid it. "You made bullets that will kill us?" I gasped.

The sick and twisted, power-hungry bastard was using human technology and mixing it with magic. It was a lethal combination that would end disastrously if someone didn't stop him.

"We have many weapons now. More than you could ever imagine, but you won't live to see us use them on your rebellious friends."

"Rebellious? Are you kidding me? You're trying to eradicate them after exiling them for centuries! Why even come here and start this when you had Faery to yourself?" I threw my hands up.

This prick doesn't make any sense. He already had everything...

"Because of you, Princess. Your birth signaled the end of that era, and we had to find a way to ensure that we could keep what we had."

I took a step back when he moved closer. I was not about to let him get his hands on me again—*ever*.

The guards at his side cocked their weapons unflinchingly. Whatever those guns were loaded with, they were confident in it. They were facing down the Shadow Princess herself, and they didn't seem concerned.

Shit. What am I going to do now?

I could use my magic, but what were the bullets in those guns capable of? Was Ronaldo bluffing to save his skin, or was he telling the truth? Would they kill me or hurt me so gravely my magic couldn't heal me, or was there something in them that would do something to my magic? I glanced around the hall again. Thick, black smoke rose into the air and flames danced along the walls. My situation was growing increasingly more dire.

The ground rumbled with another explosion, and I stumbled to the side.

The guns followed me as I went, the guards maintaining their aim despite the turbulence.

"Kill her now, before the entire place comes down on our heads!" Ronaldo commanded. "I want to see her draw her last breath with my own eyes!"

I'm out of time. Fuck!

My stomach dropped and my heart sank as I thought of Grey. I was never going to see my mate again. Ronaldo was about to win. He was ordering my death, and there didn't seem to be anything I could do to stop it.

CHAPTER 20
Grey

"What the fuck?" I yelled, as an explosion rumbled through the prison, shaking it to its very foundations.

Have they decided to blow it up early?

We were still surrounded by guards. They wouldn't purposely blow up their own people, would they? I caught myself with a dark, internal chuckle.

Of course, they would. Ronaldo only cares about himself.

Several guards stopped advancing and glanced at one another, probably wondering the exact same thing.

"Get them! The High Councilor wants the shifter *alive*!" the leader screamed, his face reddening as he scowled at me.

The others still wore wary expressions, unconvinced. They shuffled their feet and glanced at the door longingly. They were the smart ones, but they were torn between their duty to their superiors and saving their own lives.

The other guards fled the room the moment they had the opportunity, having the right idea, unwilling to die for people who didn't give a shit about them.

Some of the supernaturals looked to me for guidance. With the guards fleeing their fights, they were free to run themselves, and I didn't blame them if they did.

"Go!" I said, waving them off, taking the burden of duty and choice from their shoulders. I was still outnumbered with just Ash and myself up against eight of these assholes, but I didn't want anyone dying for me.

"No, stay and finish this!" the leader hollered as several men who stepped toward the door.

"Is pleasing that jackass worth your life?" I asked. "This place is about to blow sky high, and you'll all be dust."

The men all took a step back except for the leader of the group.

He stepped forward. "You're all cowards!" he roared. "I'll be rewarded when I bring this mutt to the High Councilor."

"Wrong answer," I hissed with dark amusement. "Why do the bad guys always say stupid shit like that?" I asked, glancing at Ash. "Honestly, it's ridiculous."

"I think it's in the Evil Villain Rule Book. It says they must be morons." Ash rolled his shoulders back and cracked his knuckles.

"You're probably right." I smirked.

"Who are you calling a moron, mutt? At least I was smart enough to choose the winning side!" The leader grinned.

The men who had shown up with him were slowly backing away toward the door while his attention was firmly locked on me. They were definitely the smart ones.

I would be getting the hell out of here the second I had my mate safely in my arms. "You really think this is what winning looks like?" I waved my hand at the chaos around us—the bloodshed, the fire, thick smoke, and crumbling buildings coming down around our ears.

Ash chuckled. "I mean, it does look like someone is winning, but it's not you."

The leader scowled anew and held up his baton threateningly.

I dropped into a fighting stance now that it was a fair fight. My wolf howled in my head, desperate to be free. We needed to take care of this asshole, find Aurelia, and get the hell out of here before it was too late.

The leader of the guards lunged with his baton, nearly catching me in the shoulder.

I jumped back and crouched even lower, my eyes gleaming with my inner wolf. "Is that all you've got?" I taunted. I wasn't about to let him put one over on me. My wolf was seeing red and wanted this idiot's blood.

Magic grew in the man's palm as he lunged for me yet again.

I dodged the ball of magic, and it hit the wall with an ominous crack. It wasn't enough to do a ton of damage, but with the explosions already wracking the prison, it was enough to be a concern. How much could the foundations take before they just gave way? "You're weak," I said.

His eyes flashed and glowed with hatred, but before he could throw more magic, he was swept off his feet by a gust of air.

I glanced at Ash and grinned.

He's such a cheeky shit.

"You call me weak, but you can't even fight fair," the leader snapped back. He swung again wildly, letting his rage and emotions get the better of him.

I ducked below the baton and wrapped my arms around him, tackling him to the ground. With lightning quick reflexes, I gripped the wrist that held the baton and smashed it against the floor until he let it go, and it rolled away, the threat of electrical torture eliminated. My hands shifted to claws as I wrapped them around his neck. They pierced the skin, blood gushing from him as he desperately tried to punch me in the kidney.

I grunted in pain as he landed the blow, but refused to let go. This man had touched my mate and threatened to use her as a *plaything*. Unwelcome images of what he could do to her filtered into my mind, repulsing me to my core, but I shoved them aside. I was not going to stand for it. I'd promised many of the assholes in this place death, and his would be the first.

The man's skin paled as he clutched at my clawed hands. His blood soaked my skin. I'd nicked his carotid artery, and he would bleed out within seconds. The last thing he saw was my face.

I am his end. I am his death.

The thought was exceedingly satisfying. "I told you that I would kill you for touching her," I snarled venomously as the light went out of his eyes. I retracted my claws, my human hands returned, and I sat back on my haunches. One down, but how many to go? I scanned the room for any others who I'd made that particular promise to, but didn't find them.

The guards were fleeing for their lives from the explosion, and in their haste had left the doors wide open.

A hand was thrust into my view, and I took it, letting Ash pull me up. "That was pretty gruesome."

"Have you looked around? This whole scenario is pretty fucking gruesome." I wiped my bloody hands on my pants without a second thought. The roar of another explosion met my ears, and I spun in a circle, looking over the area for my mate, but there was still no sight of her.

Dan jogged up to me. "Come on, Grey, we've got to run." Dan tugged at my arm to get me moving.

I resisted. "Where is Aurelia? I don't see her anywhere," I growled. My wolf paced in my mind as I searched every face for her but came up empty. I turned to Zeke with a glare.

His fucking plan looks like it's going to leave me mateless.

Dan tried again to nudge me to the door. "We have to go before more guards come. I'm sure they will, they're like an army of ants."

"They're blowing this place up early. There's no way. There are no more guards, and the ones that have fled aren't coming back." I shook my head.

"That's not what this is!" Dan argued. "They would have just blown it up in one massive explosion. We have to go before they realize that and come back to find the cause. Some of them have more balls than the others and are still loyal to Ronaldo." Dan ran a hand through his hair in frustration. My second-in-command was desperate to get me to safety, but it wasn't happening—not yet.

"I'm not leaving without my mate!" I roared and brushed his hand off my shoulder. "Where is she likely to be?"

"Medical unit," Zeke said without hesitation.

"You guys get the hell out of here. Get everyone back safely to the Syndicate. I have to go after Aurelia," I barked, issuing what could be my final orders. I wouldn't have them all wait for me and die in the process. They needed to run, because even if Dan was right and they didn't blow the place early, *something* was happening... and I had a sinking suspicion it was originating from the medical unit. I turned on my heel and ran through the hall, not caring one bit for my own safety.

I'm coming for you, Aurelia. Hold on.

Ash jogged up beside me and kept glancing over his shoulder warily.

"You got my back?" I asked without stopping.

He nodded.

I turned the corner to the medical unit, and flames licked up the walls in an uncontrolled inferno. The bright orange flames cast the white-washed, normally sterile environment in an eerie, apocalyptic glow.

What the hell happened here? Is my mate okay?

Thick, black smoke billowed through the hall, and a horrid chemical scent mixed with the oxygen-depleted air, causing a racking cough to tear through me.

Fuck. Did she blow up the whole lab?

Ash and soot covered the floor, and I kept to the middle of the long hall, acutely aware that the walls were burning, but otherwise, I didn't care. I needed to find Aurelia and get us all out. I refused to live in a world without her. I wouldn't even entertain the idea. I would follow her in death as well as life, no matter the price. She'd become everything to me, and I refused to fail her now.

I pushed through the main door that led to the unit and stopped in my tracks.

Aurelia stood there, magic pooling in her palms as she faced off against Ronaldo and two guards who both had guns pointed at her chest. Flames grew ever closer to her by the second and the haze of smoke thickened in the air.

"Grey!" she called out, her gaze a mix of raw bravery and that of a woman stricken by the trials she was being forced to confront.

I lost control of my inner wolf as he lunged forward violently, completely taking me off guard. He snarled at the men who turned wary eyes on me, momentarily distracted from their original target.

Ronaldo took a step back, a touch more cautious. A flicker of fear was visible in his eyes now. "Kill the girl," he ordered, "and get me the wolf alive!"

The men cocked their guns, taking aim at my mate once more.

Ash flicked his wrist, the hulking Rider reacting instantly, sending a brutal gust of wind at them.

The men stumbled to the side, thrown off balance.

My wolf took over completely then, the change ripping through me as I jumped in front of Aurelia, growling low and menacingly. He wasn't about to let them get away. He could end this madness once and for all if he could just get to Ronaldo. My wolf stalked forward on silent paws, ready to rip their throats out for threatening his mate.

One of the men raised his gun to shoot me.

Ronaldo hissed at him. "No, you fool. I need him alive!" His plans for domination really were more important to him than anyone doing his dirty work, that much was blatantly apparent.

It almost made me feel sorry for all the fools who were loyal to him —almost. A heartbeat later, my wolf lunged at the man, taking his wrist between sharp teeth and sinking them into his arm.

The man cried out as blood sprayed from his wrist. He dropped the gun on the floor, disarmed and helpless.

I flicked it toward Ash with my paw.

"Careful!" Aurelia warned. "The bullets can kill us."

"Shit," Ash cursed as he picked up the weapon and flicked the safety on.

I shook my head from side to side, digging my fangs into the man's arm. My wolf craved more blood, more devastation for all that had befallen us and our mate.

The guard screamed in agony again before passing out cold from the pain and blood loss.

I dropped him to the floor, discarding him like garbage, and snarled my rage at the other man.

He was still holding his gun, but his terrified expression told me he wouldn't be testing me the way the other guy had. He crawled back on his hands, trying to put distance between us as an arc of magic shot above my head, aimed for Aurelia.

She ducked it easily and dove out of the way, sending her own blast of magic back at Ronaldo.

My wolf howled a battle cry, the sound clawing it way up from my very soul before we jumped in front of Aurelia, desperate to protect her.

Ash sent another turbulent gust of wind at Ronaldo.

The corrupt wannabe-dictator deflected it and laughed. "You're all fools! You think you can beat me, but I've already won."

"Look around you," Aurelia scoffed. "Your prisoners are escaping, and your Frankenstein lab is going up in flames. You haven't won *anything*. Your plan has gone to shit."

So, she did blow up his lab. My mate is a badass!

"Frankenstein lab?" Ash asked.

"They had people with no brain function hooked up to machines. I think he was trying to create some kind of magically controlled undead army or something. It was creepy as fuck." Aurelia shivered. "I put the poor souls out of their misery, rather than see him succeed."

I nudged Aurelia with my hip and crouched down on the floor as I snarled at Ronaldo.

What a fucking psycho!

If it hadn't just spilled from my own mate's lips, I never would have believed anyone could stoop to such disgusting and depraved evil against their own kind.

Ronaldo lifted a hand to attack us,but fortunately for us, Ash was a faster draw.

He blasted him back with another gust of air and sent him flying into the wall with a vicious *thud*.

"Get on his back, Princess. We need to go!" Ash yelled as he held his hand out, pinning Ronaldo to the wall with the constant stream of his magic.

"I can finish this now," Aurelia argued, her eyes flashing dangerous. "If I kill him, we can end this once and for all."

"This place is about to blow sky high after what you did with your magic. Live to fight another day, Princess," Ash gritted out.

I nudged Aurelia with my nose. The fire was getting perilously close, and we had no idea what horrors she may have missed when destroying the place. My instincts were overwhelming me despite my desire for vengeance and blood. They were telling me that we had to get the fuck out of there and *fast*.

Aurelia ran her hand over the silky fur on my neck, hesitant to leave business unfinished. I understood he'd caused her so much pain, but we couldn't linger.

I shivered at her touch, and my wolf nearly purred with excitement and contentment at her closeness, but we couldn't get complacent. Not now.

We need to go.

"Now, Princess," Ash commanded.

Aurelia pulled a face at the Rider, but finally climbed onto my back and dug her fingers into the soft fur at my neck.

I needed to shift with her more often when we weren't running for our lives. My wolf absolutely loved having her soft hands in his fur. As soon as she was safely mounted on my back, my wolf leapt over the man lying unconscious on the floor and past a fuming Ronaldo.

He was spitting curses at Ash, who still held him immobile with his magic.

We raced from the hall, but it was too late. I skidded to a stop as the building shook violently and a deafening boom ripped through the space, drowning out all other sound. Without any other available option, I crouched as close to the ground as I could get.

Aurelia lay flat on my back, clinging to my fur as an explosion tore through the hall, the blast wave sending us both flying.

Flames licked at my fur, and a howl of agony and anguish tore from my wolf just as I slammed into the wall and the air was driven from my lungs. Debris and chunks of brick rained down on my head.

Fuck. I've failed my mate and now we are all going to die...

The finality of my last conscious thought broke my heart as the chaos all around us faded to black.

CHAPTER 21

I blinked my watery eyes open, wiping them free of grit and dust, only to be welcomed back by more billowing black smoke. A racking cough exploded from my lungs, the flesh inside me burning in pain and protest. Drywall covered my lap, huge pieces of it having fallen on me from the ceiling, and fragments of brick from the walls lay everywhere.

"Fuck."

Where's Grey?

I scanned the smoke-filled hall, my stomach lurching when I found the vague outline of my wolf mate against a now half destroyed wall.

Thinking only of my mate, I threw the dusty plaster off my lap and crawled over to him, heedless of the debris on the floor as I went.

Grey was lying prone on his side, a gash on his wolfy snout. His eyes were closed, but his chest was thankfully still rising and falling with rattling breaths.

Swallowing my fear and the overwhelming sense of devastation plaguing my heart, I held my hands over his chest. The green glow of my healing magic rushed from my body into his in a steady stream. "Please, please," I begged. "You *have* to be okay." I repeated the words over and over again, praying to the gods that he would be all right. But no matter how much magic I poured into him, he didn't open his eyes.

I sat back on my heels, staring at him through the smoke, hot tears pricking at my eyes, until a groan met my ears.

Fuck, Ash is here!

I threw my gaze over the room until I found him and rushed over, turning his big body. I almost couldn't move his bulk, but after a couple of attempts, I finally rolled him onto his back.

He groaned again.

"Are you okay? That explosion was horrific," I said, my brow crumpled with concern.

Ash blinked up at me. He had a gash on his forehead and a piece of debris was sticking out of his side. It looked incredibly painful. "I need a healer," he coughed.

"I need to get that piece of wood out of your side, so I can heal you." I shot him an apologetic smile, my heart hurting for him.

This is going to hurt like a bitch.

I had to be fast before he lost even more blood. I counted down from three in my mind before yanking it out in the direction of its entry and tossing it aside. Without delay, I placed my hands over the wound, pouring my green healing magic into Ash.

He seemed much better off than Grey. He was at least awake and coherent, but I didn't want to miss anything I might not be seeing.

Asher patted my hand, his eyes becoming more focused now that the healing magic was washing through him and mending him from the inside out. "Where's Grey?" he asked, forcing his immense Rider bulk to sit up.

I pointed to the large, black wolf that still lay in a heap and frowned. "He won't wake up. My magic doesn't seem to be enough. How are we going to get him out of here?" The knot in my stomach twisted as the heat of the flames around us grew more intense with every passing second.

"Easy there, Princess. It's going to be okay. I'm stronger than I look." Ash winked at me, revealing that his rebellious and cheeky nature was still well intact.

I rushed to Grey and felt for his pulse again. It was a little stronger and his breaths weren't rattling the way they had been. It was a good sign, but I was still worried sick. His injuries were healed, but he wasn't waking up. It made no sense.

What's wrong with you, Grey? I wish you could tell me...

"It will be okay, Princess. He'll make it through this." Asher clapped me on the shoulder in encouragement before bending at the knees and hefting Grey's great wolf body over his shoulder.

"We really need to get out of here." I coughed and held my hand over my mouth and nose. The level of black smoke filling the shaken building was becoming critical. There wouldn't be much breathable air left soon.

"You first. Grey would kill me if I didn't have your back, even if I was lugging his heavy ass at the time."

"You don't have free hands, *I do*. I can watch all our backs," I argued. "You go ahead, I'll be right behind you."

"Fine, but if you ever tell Grey I let you watch my back, we're going to have a serious problem." He raised a brow at me.

"I won't tell him. Go!" I slapped his back, urging him to move it.

He took off at a jog, a monster of a man considering he was running with my mate in his shifter form.

I glanced behind me at the flames, my eyes searching the flickering, hungry fire. Was someone else back there? Could I dare hope that Ronaldo was burning in those flames? He was a slippery bastard, though. And my gut instincts told me it was likely he was still alive. Pushing that thought temporarily from my mind, I followed quickly behind the Rider, making sure to keep an eye on our backs all the while.

Walls crumbled around us as we ran, the fire was so terrifying close now that it licked at my skin as we ran. I winced, but the pain didn't last long as my natural healing abilities as a Fae repaired the burns almost immediately.

"Almost there!" Asher shouted ahead of me.

Relief flooded me as I coughed again. Having no other option if I wanted to continue to live, I heaved in a breath of chemicals and smoke. My poor lungs burned like they were on fire, and they very well could have been with all the foul and industrial strength toxins in the air.

Asher burst through the doors of the medical unit as another explosion nearly blew us off our feet. "Why the fuck are they still here?" Ash growled as he surveyed the scene before us.

Shifted animals took on several Fae guards in a brutal scrap.

Fenrick was loyally fighting by my father's side as just the two of them battled against six more men.

"We all need to get out of here before it's too late!" I wheezed. The air out here was much clearer than in the medical unit, and I took in several gulps of fresh air.

More guards flooded the space surrounding the group.

My magic pulsed beneath my skin, the shadows of my birthright writhing over my arms and hands in response.

The guards swarmed my father and Fenrick.

"Aurelia!" Dan yelled, suddenly noticing me among the violence and bloodshed. "They found Aurelia! Retreat!" he called.

They were too late though. The guards blocked the door, creating a physical barrier between us and freedom.

Shifters snarled and bit at the men, attacking without mercy in their animal forms as magic flew from the magic users in the room. It was absolute chaos. No one seemed to hear Dan call for retreat as they continued to fight for their lives, unaware of the dangers they faced.

I took a step forward to warn them, to help in any way I could.

These are my people!

Ash grabbed my arm, keeping me behind him. "Ronaldo wants your head. He probably sent these guards in so they can kill you," Ash warned.

"I'm not weak, Asher," I growled. "I can take care of myself! I'm stronger than I look," I added, reminding him of his own truth.

"And Grey will have my head if something happens to you. Just stay behind me while I get you both out."

"I can't promise you that." I shook my head. I had friends and family out there fighting for their lives, and if they needed me, I was going to help them, no matter what Asher said.

He knew that just as well as I did, if the frown on his face was anything to go by. "I know, Princess, but I had to say it to save my own skin."

We hustled out into the mayhem and dodged guards left and right.

Several of the bastards rushed us, presenting a united front.

Even with Grey slung over his shoulder, Ash was able to use his elemental magic to gust air at them and throw them against the wall some ten feet away.

"Aurelia?" my father shouted, his eyes wide with relief as our gazes met.

I watched in horror as someone came up behind him with an electrified baton.

The man was grinning like an evil mastermind as he swung the baton at my father's head.

I screamed, unleashing my magic, the only thought on my mind to protect my father. My shadows burst from my body in a swarm of darkness, writhing around the room, it surged forward with a mind of its own.

People froze in confusion, too stunned to get out of the way of the mass of black that was flooding the prison.

"Run!" I yelled, my eyes wide as power surged through me, making me more alive than I'd ever felt.

Would my shadows let the supernaturals go unscathed? Could they tell the difference between friend or foe, or was this destined to be a bloodbath? I didn't know. I couldn't answer that. I wasn't in control of the shadows as they wrapped around guards, flinging them about in every direction like ragdolls.

The shadows flowed and pulsed around the shifters, and I took the opportunity to race to my father as the guard who'd threatened his life was thrown into the wall with a loud and sickening *thwack*.

"We need to move!" I screamed, trying to make eye contact with my friends and allies. My shadows swirled through the space and finally became more placid and calmer as the guards were all either pinned to the wall or lying in bloody heaps on the floor.

"Princess, what did you do?" Fenrick asked me with wide eyes.

"I may have blown up their lab, and if we don't get out of here soon, that won't be the only thing on fire." I glanced around the room, then to the door.

Innocent prisoners flooded from the room now that the guards were all taken out and the way seemed clear.

Ash jogged up to my side with Zeke and Dan hot on his heels.

"You were supposed to leave," Ash griped at the men.

"Did you really expect us to just leave the boss behind?" Dan raised a brow.

"Can we argue about this later?" I threw my hands up in frustration.

Bricks fell down around us, and plaster and drywall crumbled, falling on my head as we ran for the door. I didn't even notice the guard at the entrance until the last moment.

He stood directly in front of me, rage in his eyes as he slashed at me with a sword more reminiscent of Faery than the modern human world we were fleeing from.

I reacted instinctively, bending my back like an acrobat or dancer. A breath of air whispered across my nose—that was how close it got to slicing through me.

Fenrick roared behind me, ever loyal to the royal family, and lunged at the guard.

But my shadows were already taking care of the scumbag. They flung him back ten feet into a solid brick wall, his head smacking against it. The *crunch* that followed the impact turned my stomach.

Even with such a devastating injury, he wasn't dead, because he was Fae, but he was going to have some problems if he didn't get healed quickly enough.

Arms wrapped around me from behind, catching me unawares.

I turned sharply in the embrace to find myself face to face with my father.

"You're okay," he whispered with relief.

"No time for that, Dad. We need to get out of here before the whole place explodes!" I grabbed his hand and tugged him along with me, glad to see the people I loved still alive.

"You called me Dad." He swallowed hard, his eyes watering.

"I told you, I remember now." I glanced around. Panic warred inside me as I scanned the doors. There were still far too many people inside.

They need to run!

"Aurelia? What happened to you?" Fenrick asked, pointing at my side.

I glanced down as I stepped outside into the cool night breeze and gasped as pain tore through me at the realization. There was *something* sticking out of my side. Blood oozed from the wound that wouldn't heal because of the foreign object piercing my skin.

How did I miss that?

I dropped to my knees, a blazing fire burning in my side and moaned in pain, my breath hitching on a whimper.

Someone caught me before I fell completely into the dirt, and strong hands cradled my body. "Where did that come from?" Fenrick whispered as he touched the piece of splintered wood.

I screamed, agony lancing through my side even with the soft brush of Fenrick's gentle touch. "I didn't even feel it," I gasped. "I don't know."

"We have to remove it, daughter," my father said.

"I know. I just can't," I cried.

Fenrick held my arms pinned to my sides as he cradled me to his chest. "The faster we get it out, the faster you can heal, Princess."

I understood that logically, but the pain was making it impossible to see reason as I tried to pull away from him. I didn't want it to come out. It would hurt even more. What if my healing didn't help fast enough?

Was this how Ash felt?

"I'll heal you the second the piece is out." Fenrick squeezed me tighter. He kept my arms trapped so I couldn't call my magic.

"No," I said on a moan, my heart racing with panic and exhaustion.

My father's face swam into view. "Yes, daughter. We need to get that wood out, and we need to get back to the Syndicate where it's safe for you to rest and recover."

"Grey is still unconscious, Princess," Fenrick reminded me. "But I fear trying to sift you with the wood in your wound."

"Aurelia," Ash growled from nearby. "I will hold your ass down. You just pulled a piece like that out of me without an argument. Now, let them do it, or *I* will force you."

"Fine," I croaked through a dry throat.

Fuck. Gods help me.

I braced myself against Fenrick, turning my face away and burying it against his chest.

Zeke stepped closer. "This will be quick, Princess, I promise."

My vision dotted with white spots the moment Zeke moved into action.

He gripped the piece of wood and didn't even count.

My back arched and a scream tore from my lips as the wood was pulled out of my body. Blood gushed from the wound like an overflowing sink, soaking my pants and shirt through before healing magic flooded me.

Even with Fenrick's magic surging through me, my eyes rolled into the back of my head.

Will his magic be enough?

My last conscious thought left me trembling with uncertainty before blackness engulfed my vision and I gave in, passing out. My time at the prison was done.

CHAPTER 22
Grey

Pain lanced through my body as I shifted back to my human form.

What the hell happened?

Blinking my eyes open, a sterile white room greeted me.

Where am I? Did Ronaldo catch us?

I panicked when I realized something was holding my arm down. I turned to find Aurelia's golden head on my shoulder, sleeping away peacefully. Thank the gods she was there and safe! Memories of what happened cleared as I continued to blink away the confusion. The last thing I remembered was the explosion and debris falling on me.

How did I get here?

I ran my fingers through her hair, committing her to memory all over again. I felt like we'd been apart for a lifetime.

She groaned in her sleep, shifting her body closer to mine instinctively.

She was so fucking beautiful it hurt to look at her sometimes. There would never be a day when I wouldn't be grateful and in awe of the fact she was mine. Licking my lips, I sent my awareness through my body, from my head and right down to my toes, checking for injuries or anything out of the ordinary. But now that all the pain seemed to be gone, my body felt *amazing*. Better than it had in days, weeks... months, even.

"Grey?" Aurelia asked, blinking her eyes open.

"Hello, mate." I grinned, kissing her forehead.

"You're okay?" she asked, searching my eyes, her heart so painfully obvious behind her concerned gaze that it made my soul ache.

"I'm better than okay now that I have you back in my arms. I thought you were dead, beautiful." I reached out and pulled her body flush with mine in the bed.

"I couldn't get you to wake up," she explained, her voice hitching momentarily. "I healed you, but you were still unconscious throughout our escape." She buried her face in the crook of my neck, shamelessly nuzzling and inhaling my scent.

"I'm fine, my love," I promised as I kissed her temple.

She squeezed me tighter, unwilling to let go.

My wolf howled in my head. I needed to reconnect with my mate. It had been way too long since we were together. I needed to prove to myself she was really here, *alive*. I pulled her onto my chest and kissed a blazing trail down the side of her neck.

Aurelia squirmed in my arms, a small smile creasing her lips. "Grey, what are you doing? You were just *unconscious*."

"Need you," I growled. I couldn't get any more words than that out between kisses. My wolf was riding my ass to get closer to her and reconnect on a primal level—the only level he understood. He was all instinct, and that was all that mattered to him.

"I don't think this is a good idea," she moaned, but her hands fisted in my shirt, pulling me closer.

I chuckled before flipping us over, so she was on her back. I pinned her to the bed beneath me and stared into her striking eyes. "I thought you were dead." I gripped her chin between two fingers, my brow creased with a sense of intensity that overwhelmed my mind and flesh.

"I'm right here, Grey," she soothed as she ran her hands up my chest and around my neck and through my hair. She pulled my head down to meet her lips in a claiming kiss.

I groaned, and my cock hardened against her thigh. This woman was my everything. The simple act of just pulling me into a kiss could make me hard as stone for her. I had never felt anything like what I felt for her with anyone else.

Her tongue teased my lips, her gaze inviting me to commit to what I'd started.

I opened my mouth immediately to her, our tongues dancing languidly in an exploration of each other. The kiss was breathtakingly passionate. It felt as if we were finding ourselves again, together.

Breaking the kiss, I trailed my lips down her neck once more, tasting the sweet and salty flavor of her skin.

Aurelia's fingers tightened in my hair, her body tensing beneath me.

I kissed lower, nipping her collarbone before pulling the strap on her tank top to the side. Her nipples formed delicious, rosy peaks where my chest was pressed to hers. The only thing between us was the scrap of fabric that comprised her tiny sleep shirt. "Why do you have clothes on?" I groaned, pulling up the shirt and releasing her breasts. Without waiting for an answer, I licked my lips and reached out, rolling one tasty nipple between my fingers.

Her nails dug into my scalp, and her chest rose as she pressed herself up and against me.

Accepting her unspoken invitation, I leaned forward and took the other nipple in my mouth.

"Grey," she growled under her breath, a hint of desperation to her lovely voice.

"You didn't answer my question, my love. I *need* these off." I untangled her fingers from my hair and sat back on my heels, pulling her up with me.

Her long golden hair was deliciously mussed, and her eyes glowed with undeniable lust. She was just as hungry for me as I was for her.

I tugged the hem of her shirt up and over her head and pressed my lips to hers, before whispering against them. "I'm going to worship every inch of your body before I push inside you and make you come on my cock," I promised. Gripping her hands in mine, I laid her back on the bed, pinning her hands above her head and kissing my way down her bountiful chest.

"Keep your hands there or I'm going to edge you so hard, you'll be a sobbing mess, begging me to let you come," I warned as I stared into her eyes, waiting for her nod or give me some indication she understood my terms before I let her hands go. My fingertips stroked down her arms with a featherlight touch that had her squirming beneath me. I clamped a hand on her hip to still her. My cock was already hard as granite beneath her, and if she didn't stop moving, I was going to explode far too soon.

"Grey, I need you," she whined, her gaze equal measure lust and plaintive innocence all at once.

"Not yet, mate." I shook my head, denying her request. I pressed a kiss to each of her breasts and moved lower, nipping at her hipbone on my way to where I *really* wanted to go. "Spread those pretty thighs for me."

Her legs fell open wide on my command, a moan tumbling from her lips.

A strangled sound escaped my throat at how wet she already was through her lace panties, mirroring her desire. Shifting one hand to a claw,I tore them off her, throwing the slimsy fabric scraps over my shoulder in my haste. I breathed deeply and shivered in anticipation as the scent of her arousal filled the air. My wolf howled in my mind, thrashing to get to his mate and mark her once and for all as ours, but I held him back.

This isn't the time for that.

"You smell like heaven," I said, returning to my planned assault. I gripped her inner thighs with both hands, holding them down on the bed, giving me unobstructed access.

"Grey," she whimpered, her eyes burning with need as her chest heaved with panting breaths.

With a wicked smile, I leaned forward and ran my nose down her thigh slowly, close to her pussy, but not where she wanted me most. I wanted to tease her until she couldn't take it anymore, but between her intoxicating scent and beautiful body, I didn't know how long *I* could hold out. I was practically edging myself as much as I was her. My wolf howled in frustration, demanding I sink my fangs into her and make her officially ours, but I refused the urge.

"Stop teasing me," she said, frustration lacing her tone as she attempted to wiggle her hips and close the space between us. She couldn't move though, and her attempts were in vain.

My fingers dug into her thighs, holding her firmly in place. They were going to leave pretty red marks on her beautiful flesh for a minute when we were done. Unable to deny either of us the pleasure any longer, my wolf growled in my head as I licked up her pussy to her clit. I sucked the most sensitive part of her into my mouth and stared up at her. as Aurelia's back arched in ecstasy and her arms, which had been over her head, came down slightly.

I backed away, denying her for breaking my command.

"Grey!" she cried out in anguish and quickly threw her arms back over her head.

"Good girl." I smirked with unbridled lust as I licked at her again.

Her arms strained with the need to move, but she held them where I commanded. She was obedient, even if she was a rebellious Fae princess.

I sucked her clit between my teeth, nibbling and nuzzling at the precious bundle of nerves with pointed attention.

My mate screamed, her hands fisted in the sheets above her head, her knuckles white as her shadows swirled around her. She blinked at them and then glanced down at me with a devious grin.

"What are you plotting, love?" I asked, noticing her wicked expression.

Her shadows danced behind her eyes. "I think it's time for a little payback," she said, biting her lower lip in the most incredibly sexy way.

What is she up to?

Shadows wrapped around my wrists and raced up my arms. They

went higher and caressed my shoulders before tweaking my nipples and traveling lower.

"What are you doing, mate?" I asked dangerously.

"I told you... I'm getting payback," she purred, completely undeterred. Her hands were still obediently above her head, but her shadows writhed across my skin and down my rippling abs.

"Aurelia."

"What's wrong?" she asked innocently, batting her long eyelashes at me.

"You know what," I growled, attempting to swat away the shadows making their way down to my already rock-hard cock. My hands passed right through them, unable to affect or deter their descent.

My mate grinned. She clearly loved teasing me in the same way I teased her. "I have no idea what you're talking about," she mocked apologetically. Her shadows moved down my body and wrapped around my cock, stroking it softly.

With nothing else for it, I pushed two fingers deep inside her pussy as I unsuccessfully tried to chase away her shadows again. My balls were *aching* for a release that I refused to give them until I'd wrung a couple of orgasms out of Aurelia, first. "Stop," I said in a strangled tone.

"Stop what?" She giggled.

"Don't play games with me. I'm hanging on by a thread here, mate." I curled my fingers inside her, hitting that spot I knew made her writhe without fail.

"Gods, Grey!" she shouted, her back arching dramatically. Her body convulsed as her shadows became even hungrier. They tormented me, licking and stroking me without reprieve.

Fuck. I'm not going to last if she keeps that up.

I gripped her thighs harder and pushed forward, removing my fingers and lining up my cock. "Is this what you want, my love?" I ran the head of my cock up and down her wet entrance, circling her clit as she came down from her peak.

"Yes!" Her head thrashed back and forth, and her back arched for a second time as her body shook.

I pushed forward and thrust my cock inside her hard and fast. My wolf howled at the connection to our mate, and my balls drew up, ready to explode. I managed to hold back my orgasm by sheer force of will, stilling inside my mate all the while managing to maintain my hold on her.

Aurelia attempted to squirm, but my grip was unrelenting.

I couldn't let her move, not even an inch. If I did, this would all be over before I was ready, and it had been far too long since I'd connected with her for this to end so soon. "I need a second," I grunted.

"Grey, I need you to move," Aurelia groaned. "Please, fuck me! I need to feel you."

I leaned my forehead against hers and took a deep breath, squeezing my eyes closed to calm myself.

Her shadows pulsed against my body, making it harder and harder for me to control myself. They writhed and caressed me, obviously directed reacting to how Aurelia was feeling. The way they touched and lavished me with affection was merely an extension of her.

"Call them back, mate. I can't do this—I can't hold on. I'm going to come if you don't pull them back," I grumbled.

If anything, the shadows' actions and attentions had become more insistent and even wilder than before. They lavished my skin with Aurelia's desire, and when they painfully tweaked my nipples, it was over.

It was impossible to hold myself back anymore. I felt like a frazzled fuse, the flame of my soul like a hair-trigger on a million pounds of dynamite.

It's too much!

I thrust forward, burying myself to the hilt.

Aurelia's fingers tightened in the sheets above her head as she whimpered. Her chest heaved with the force of her panting breaths, and her thighs quivered around me.

I leaned forward, returning the pleasure torment she was inflicting upon me by taking a nipple into my mouth and sucking on it *hard*.

"Gods, Grey. I'm going to come," Aurelia moaned, a strained note of panic to her voice.

"Then come for me, mate," I said and bit her nipple.

Her entire body shook violently as her body milked my cock like it was her last meal.

I lost all control and pistoned my hips into hers, chasing my own orgasm like a madman. My hands tightened on her thighs as I thrust deeply inside her for the final time. Tingles raced down my spine right down to my balls, the backs of my thighs lighting up with a blazing heat as I moaned out her name. My wolf howled in my mind, urging me to mark her for real. He begged me to make her mine. My mouth filled with the sharpened fangs of my shifter, but I refused to mark her for life yet.

I slumped to the mattress, falling beside Aurelia and pulled her fuck-sated body into my arms, resting my chin on her shoulder, just waiting for her to catch her breath. "I missed you, Princess. I thought you were dead." My voice cracked at the end, and I closed my eyes against the visions of what might have happened to her at the prison, let alone what I felt when she'd fallen into the earth in Faery as we were taken hostage.

"I'm okay, Grey. I promise." She kissed my chest just over my heart. "I'm not going anywhere."

"What happened back in Faery?" I asked, because that was what I still didn't understand.

How is she here and safely in my arms when I watched her fall into that gaping hole? How did she survive?

"The trees did that to help me get the book," she said simply. "They had it all covered, my love. If it wasn't for them, I never would have found it."

"I'd wondered briefly if it could have been the trees," I mused as I squeezed her tighter.

My mate was amazing. Her connection to the shadows and her bond with nature was unparalleled, even by her father and mother—the King and Queen of Faery. Which, as it turned out, was a good thing, because my golden princess was going to have to be stronger than ever before to get through the challenges that still lay ahead of us.

We've won this battle... but I have a feeling we aren't going to get through the war unscathed.

CHAPTER 23
Aurelia

I squirmed in Grey's arms and sighed. We were finally back together, and I couldn't help but smile at the sheer sense of relief and happiness it brought me. But despite being reunited with my Fated mate, I was acutely aware we still had work to do. I couldn't just lay around when I knew chaos was reigning beyond the safety of the Syndicate. "Grey, we need to go," I groaned into his chest.

"Not yet, beautiful. You're naked in my arms. I need more time." His strong, familiar arms tightened around my body, holding me close.

I grimaced. "Grey, Ronaldo got away, and somehow Malcolm is controlling the human government. We need to make a plan. We can't hide while the world burns." I wiggled against him.

Bad move. His body hardened against me, responding to his wolf's carnal need after our considerable time apart. "That's not helping the situation." He grinned, his eyes flashing with desire.

"Grey, come on. Seriously." I slapped at his chest and fussed some more, impatient to *do* something, anything that could make a real difference. Finally, he let me up, and I raced to the bathroom to prepare for the day. I was excited to see the rest of my friends who'd been imprisoned. I'd seen some of them as we'd narrowly escaped with our lives but hadn't been able to talk to anyone.

Arms wrapped around me.

I turned the shower on and glanced back over my shoulder. "None of that, Grey. Not now. We really need to call a meeting."

"Fine," he said, clearly disappointed, but took it in stride as he stalked from the bathroom.

I hurried through my shower and got quickly dressed.

Grey was waiting in the bedroom for me, fully dressed in one of his crisp suits. He looked absolutely delicious, and he was all mine.

I strutted up to him and went up on my toes for a kiss.

Grey leaned down, brushing his lips against mine. "If you want us to leave this room and get on with it, I suggest you *not* look so damn sexy when asking for a kiss."

"Fine," I pouted, showing him that I wanted him just as much as he wanted me, even if I was eager to get the ball rolling on our next plan of action. I smiled and turned to leave.

Grey gripped my hand and pulled me back into the circle of his arms, grinning as he led me from the room.

When we got into the hallway, worried faces looked at us with relief.

"Aurelia," my father breathed.

"Dad," I said, smiling.

His eyes widened at the word, just as they had when I'd said it at the prison, and a small grin lit his features with happiness, then his eyes misted with tears.

I left Grey's arms and wrapped my father in mine. "I thought they were going to kill you in that place." I sniffed, a fresh mist of tears pricking at my own eyes.

"Me? No, dear daughter, I'm stronger than that." He chuckled and squeezed me closer, patting me on the back all the while.

Grey's hand was still lingering around my waist, preventing me from going far. It flexed against my hip, like he was unwilling to let me go.

I understood what he was feeling, not wanting to let him go either. What would I have done if I thought he was dead? I couldn't say that I wouldn't be behaving the exact same way. "We need to call a meeting," I said, directing my announcement to everyone gathered. "We need to figure out a way to stop Ronaldo once and for all."

"He was in the medical unit with us, right?" Grey asked, frowning.

"He was, but I doubt he was killed in the blast. We couldn't get that lucky. It would be too much to ask." I rolled my neck back on my shoulders, trying to relieve the tension there.

I do wish he had died in that explosion. It would have made our lives so much easier...

"You're right. The last thing we want to do is underestimate that corrupt bastard." Grey nodded in agreement. He pulled me along behind him to the office that had been my home for the last few weeks. He sat in his office chair and pulled me down onto his lap.

"Grey," I said, wiggling to stand.

Grey's hands tightened around my waist. He wasn't going to let me up, and if I kept wiggling, there would soon be a bigger problem on his mind. "Stop, mate. Let me hold you." He pressed a lingering, soft kiss to my neck.

"Okay." I sighed and leaned my back against his chest, submitting to his need to simply hold me. To be comforted after all the trauma we'd been through.

His arms were like possessive but loving bands of steel around me, so it really didn't matter if I agreed or not. He was in control. His Alpha nature had risen to the forefront in a big way since he thought he'd lost me.

Dan stepped into the office, cleared his throat, and turned the volume up on the TV. The explosion was caught on camera along with a flood of inmates leaving the scene and magic swirled on the screen.

I saw my own image there and grimaced.

Damn it.

"Supernaturals that were deemed too dangerous to remain within the community at large caused an explosion at the maximum-security prison outside of Dallas yesterday," said a reporter on the scene. "The President is about to make a statement regarding the breech shortly."

"Where did they get video footage?" I asked, straightening in Grey's lap, my breathing slowing as I consciously forced myself to remain calm.

"I'm sure they had surveillance cameras all over the prison. They probably took it from there." Grey rested his chin on my shoulder, seemingly not perturbed in the least.

I stared at the screen as the building burned and people fled. The words at the bottom of the screen caught my attention.

Many dangerous supernaturals at large in Dallas after grizzly prison break. Death toll is currently unknown.

"Dangerous," I scoffed in disgust. "We didn't become dangerous until they made us that way. It's their fault people died. We were just trying to survive and protect our loved ones."

"I know, love, but they don't see it that way." Grey kissed the other side of my neck, as if the touch of his lips could ease my growing anxiety.

It would be really nice if they could, but until this is all sorted out, I won't feel at ease ever again.

"They can't see past their own fear," my dad said, watching the screen from the doorway.

"So, how do we stop this witch hunt?" I asked, casting my gaze between our allies, family, and friends.

Everyone grimaced and then shrugged. No one knew what to do.

It was going to be up to me, ultimately. The burden of this mess, given I was the princess of the prophecy, was mine to figure out. I glanced down at the desk. The gold book was still sitting right where I'd left it when we went on the mission to rescue the supernaturals in prison.

Can the book help me with the humans as well as the Council? It can't hurt to try.

"I don't know, but we will figure something out. We always do." Grey squeezed my hip.

"Shhh," Dan waved a hand at the TV.

The President stood in front of the podium to address the nation once more.

I sat forward, hoping that he wouldn't incite more violence against us, but I wasn't hopeful when I glanced behind him and found Malcolm standing there.

"My fellow Americans, it has come to our attention that a tragedy struck just yesterday outside of Dallas. The National Guard has been mobilized to remedy this situation. The dangerous supernaturals who committed this egregious act against humanity will be swiftly brought to justice."

"That's *so* much bullshit. What was a crime was the horrible things they were doing to the people inside that place," I snapped, my temper fraying.

Grey shuddered beneath me.

Had he been subjected to the same treatment in that hellhole I was? I glanced at him over my shoulder with concern and empathy.

He shook his head, his eyes haunted. He obviously didn't want to relive his experience or talk about it right now.

"I am calling for anyone with information on the whereabouts of the rogue supernaturals to come forward so they can be tried for their crimes."

A singled-out picture of my face flashed on the screen, and I gasped. "What the hell?" My hands tightened into white-knuckled fists on the desk.

"This is the mastermind behind the prison break," said the President. "And she is considered extremely dangerous. Do *not* approach her. If you see her, call the police immediately. There is a reward for information that leads to her arrest."

"And... that was my plan," Zeke grumbled under his breath.

He'd planned to have me targeted and specifically arrested? Ugh!

"And it almost got us all killed!" I glared at him. "Seems like the plan didn't go quite the way you imagined..."

"And now Aurelia is public enemy number-one." Grey tilted his head back and squeezed his eyes shut. "Fuck me."

"Did you see Malcolm behind the President again?" I asked, changing the subject. There was no point dwelling on Zeke's cock-up.

He'd gotten us in and Dan's contacts had gotten us out, that's all that mattered and it was in the past. What mattered was what we did moving forward—now.

"Yeah," Zeke sighed, obviously quietly relieved I wasn't boxing his ears in for getting my image to the human media and putting a giant nationwide target on my back. "There has to be a way to stop all this."

"Wait, *Malcolm*?" Grey asked, doing double-take.

"We think he's controlling the President, but before we got into the prison, we weren't exactly sure how. Now, we know that they've been testing a mind control serum. They have probably been using it on all the world leaders... but for how long?"

Zeke tapped away at his keyboard, the resident hacker jumping into action. "We're safe here for now though, as long as they don't know where we are. We just need to bide our time and figure out a way to get to Malcolm."

"Malcolm is mine," Grey said, growling.

"It's not just about me anymore, Grey. It's about *all* supernaturals. He needs to be taken out by any means necessary." I shook my head. I appreciated how protective my mate was, and I loved that the growly, possessive Alpha wanted to kill anyone who dared to hurt me...

But I'm not a damsel in distress.

I was destined to stop this mess, and come hell or high water, I would—but I would need help. Grey needed to understand that if someone else had the opportunity to take Malcolm out, they *had* to take it. This wasn't a mere revenge fantasy; too much was at stake.

We may never get another shot.

"Who is this girl?" the host on the TV asked, pulling me from my thoughts.

Another video of me played on the screen, shadows dancing around me as my hair blew in the wind.

That's not good.

"I don't know, but from that video, she looks like some kind of demon. Are demons real?" the other host asked with a gasp.

I shook my head. "Fucking idiots."

"The President has a meeting today with the UN to discuss the global supernatural problem," another reporter said, then video cut off and showed the UN building with all the world's top leaders shaking hands.

"Do you see that?" I asked, pointing to Malcolm in the background.

"Fuck!" Fenrick said, his eyes wide and filled with disgust.

"What?" I asked, gazing over the people on the screen to see what had triggered that response.

"They are *all* Fae. The men talking with Malcolm are all there to control the human leaders!" Fenrick ran his hand down his face. "They're all loyal to this corrupt cause."

"So, it's not just Malcolm using the serum on them?" I asked.

That would make things exceedingly more difficult on our part. How could we free all the world leaders if there were multiple Fae controlling them? The only time they were ever all in the same place was at the UN Council meetings. We didn't have the resources to track leaders and corrupt Fae all over the world.

"This is a bigger problem than even we realized. How many Fae do they have controlling humans?"

"If I know Ronaldo, he'll have a back-up for every Fae he has watching the world leaders. He's been planning this for far too long. He won't be taking any chances. He can't risk failing," Fenrick said.

"So, then, just taking Malcolm out wouldn't work on its own. Damn it." I slumped back into Grey's chest. The magnitude of our predicament felt crushing.

Grey rubbed his thumb in soothing circles over my hip. "We'll figure this out, beautiful. We don't have any other choice. We'll find a way."

"I know, but I can't just sit here doing nothing. The world's leaders are about to hold a meeting to decide the fate of all supernaturals, and there's nothing we can do about it. What if they decide to wipe us all out?"

"They probably will try to do just that, but they won't succeed," said Grey confidently.

"How can you be so sure?" I asked, my heart thumping in my chest with frustration.

"Because even if they knew where this place was, they can't get through my wards, even with their weapons." Grey shuffled, adjusting in his seat beneath me.

"Ronaldo could, though. He's been developing more than just a mind control serum. The guns that they had pointed at me were Fae made, combining human tech *and* magic. For all we know, they could already have something that can blast right through magical wards."

"How is that even possible?" Grey asked. "Metal and magic don't mix. Are you sure they were magic?"

"Ronaldo was so smug. He was telling me all about how those weapons were strong enough to kill me. I'm not sure how he pulled it off, but there was no iron that I could sense in them. They were imbued with magic somehow."

"Either way, they have no idea where we are. If they did, they would be here instead of calling for blood with their human puppet."

"Right. So, we don't have to worry about that just yet, though I think it's best we all remain cautious and vigilant." I turned to Dan. "Is the site-wide lockdown still in effect?"

"Yes, no one leaves. We aren't even sending extraction teams out anymore because it's too risky. We've saved who we can, anyone else still left out there is going to have hide or protect themselves, unfortunately." Dan crossed his arms over his chest with a grimace.

"We were almost at capacity before the prison break, so we probably have even less room now," I said, my gut sinking.

What if there *were* still other innocents out there that we could help? What if more supernaturals were put in the position of being annihilated because we weren't able to provide our assistance? What if people died just so we could remain safe? I wasn't sure I could live with myself if I knew people had perished like that.

They're my people after all... why should I be protected, simply because I was born to royalty?

"Hey..." Grey soothed, sensing the thoughts that were plaguing me. "We will help as many as we can, okay?" He squeezed me closer reassuringly.

"But how?" I asked. "This place at capacity, and we can't let the Council and their weapons find us, or everything will have been in vain. All the suffering and the lives lost will be meaningless if we let them find us." I swallowed hard and licked my lips, raising my gaze to our most trusted gathered in the office. "It will end in the death and torture of all supernaturals across the world, not just in America."

Gritting my teeth, I squared my shoulders and pursed my lips in thought.

No. I will die before I let that happen! Supernaturals are not going to become extinct on my watch. Not as long as I still draw breath.

CHAPTER 24
Grey

I held Aurelia to me, not caring that we were in the middle of a meeting to plan how the hell we were going to stop the Council and their dastardly plans for the Fae and humanity alike.

"I think I've found a way to get to the President!" Zeke shouted, his eyes lighting up in a *eureka* moment.

"What is it?" Aurelia asked, sitting forward, snapping the golden book closed.

"He's going to be at a gala in Dallas tomorrow night. It's a last-minute addition to the war on supernaturals." Zeke frowned.

"There shouldn't even *be* a war on supernaturals. We have lived here for centuries without a problem," I said with a heavy sigh. My wolf howled in my mind. We had protected the humans from the worst of our kind, and this was the thanks we got for it. Bullshit fear was the only reason we were being targeted after all this time. People became stupid and resorted to the mob mentality when they didn't understand something.

"Be that as it may, they're raising money to fund their agenda and let people know they are safe." Zeke continued to tap away at his keyboard.

"They have been relatively safe from us for *centuries.* We have even protected them from supernaturals who have wished them harm. But because they never saw the good done, they're focusing on their fear and the fact that we are more than they are."

Dan cleared his throat. "I hate to give an unpopular opinion here, but what happens if we release the President from the mind control, and it just makes things worse?"

"What do you mean?" Aurelia asked.

It was nice to see her interacting with Dan after he'd inadvertently gotten her foster mother killed. Or at least that's what she thought.

I never thought the two of them would get past that.

"Right now, they're being controlled so they only attack the innocents, the ones they know about..." He held up a hand when Aurelia opened her mouth to argue. "What the Council is making them do is disgusting—there can be no doubt—but what happens if we release him from that control, and he in his human fear encourages the government to go full Nazi? What if we tamper with the situation and it inspires a complete genocide?"

"According to them, we're animals," I reminded him. "It wouldn't be genocide to them. It'd be considered culling or simply eliminating a threat to humanity. I imagine the cause might even seem heroic in their eyes." I shifted uncomfortably in my chair and clutched Aurelia close, drawing strength from my Fated mate and her passion to set things right.

Would they really do that?

I thought the world had learned from Hitler. Weren't we supposed to learn from history and not make the same mistakes again? Wasn't that the saying? The events of World War II were devastating for all involved. War never achieved anything. Communication was key, it always had been, but when corruption got involved and the waters became murky, things became far more complicated and most, not just humans, resorted to violence.

The right of might.

The sentiment was as old as time itself.

"Are we entirely sure that's not the Council's idea? Maybe the human leaders are just scared and unsure? Ronaldo was the one talking about getting rid of the supernaturals he didn't desire—shifters, witches, you name it. It seemed the only ones he wanted left in Faery, and in control, were pure-blooded Fae. So, it certainly couldn't hurt to get rid of the Fae controlling them." Aurelia tilted her head to the side in thought. "Maybe once we eliminate the control, they can be reasoned with?"

It was clear Aurelia felt the same way I did regarding the unnecessary violence and bloodshed. She wanted this to be over with as little death and destruction as possible, even if it was her own people suffering. Aurelia had proven time and time again that she was strong and a natural-born leader, but she was no dictator or despot. She abhorred the thought of completely unchecked control just as much as I did.

"Do we want to risk that, though?" Dan asked. "I say we cut the head off the snake. We should be making plans to get rid of the Council before we even worry about the humans, controlled or otherwise."

"I see your point," I said as I nodded. "But if we are walking into an all-out war with the Council, how will we fight the humans in the aftermath? We'd be spent."

"We may not have to if these aren't their actual policies." Dan shrugged.

"Then why not get the mind control link broken and *then* go after the Council?" Aurelia asked.

"If we go after the humans first, then we may be fighting a war on two fronts. One against the humans, and one against the Council. It would spread us too thin, too fast, and we don't have much of an army as it is to begin with," he answered.

Dan wasn't wrong. Our army was small and consisted mostly of mercenaries and people whose discipline was bought and paid for. They didn't fight for a cause. The people who worked for me at least were highly trained and personally loyal to me, but there weren't a lot of them. The Council had taken over the Shadow King's army on top of having their own guards. We would be screwed if we had to fight both the Council and the humans.

"He may have a point, Princess," I sighed.

"What?" Aurelia sat forward on my lap and turned to me sharply. "The humans shouldn't be denied their free will. If we can stop the mind control, maybe they'll realize we aren't the enemy they think we are!"

Zeke's hands flew over his keyboard. "With all due respect, Princess, that's a bit naïve. No, they shouldn't be without their free will, but do you honestly think their gratitude will outweigh their fear? The protestors, the looters, and the violence in the streets haven't been ordered through mind control. Those are ordinary, everyday American citizens acting the way humans do during times of fear and uncertainty."

Aurelia deflated instantly, her shoulders slumping as she saw the wisdom of the Rider's words. "You're right." She sighed.

I glared at Zeke over my mate's shoulder for upsetting her. She didn't deserve the *naïve* comment. She had shown time and time again she was stronger than anyone gave her due credit for, and she was going to be the one to save us all. The pressure of that knowledge weighed heavily on her, I knew firsthand. And more than anything, I wished I could take that burden from her, but it wasn't mine to bear. It killed me.

"I agree the fear will still make the human government take action against the threat, namely us. Even if the President doesn't agree that we're a danger, he will be pressed to act against us no matter what because of the Council's actions."

Aurelia moved to stand.

My arms tightened around her, unwilling to let her go.

"I don't care if they come for us. We shouldn't let them continue to be controlled! It's sickening. We're better than that."

"You're too good for supernaturals, love." I kissed her cheek. "They made us their enemies, remember that. I would just assume the wisest course of action is to deal with one opponent at a time."

"So, we are imprisoning them the way they are doing to us? How is that right?" She crossed her arms over her chest and sat stiffly on my lap since I refused to let her move.

My wolf was being a possessive fucker. He didn't like the idea of my mate moving to anyone else in the room despite knowing they were no threat to our claim on her. "Not at all. We are only holding off on helping them until we neutralize the bigger threat, love. They will get their free will back, I promise you that. But I don't think it's wise to do it yet."

Ash took a step forward. "With all due respect, Grey, I agree with the princess. They may only be acting in a way the Council wants them to and may actually be an asset in the war against the Council. The humans could potentially be our allies. We could show them that most of us are here in peace."

Aurelia glanced over her shoulder at me with a glare. She agreed with him clearly, but what would happen if they were even more aggressive in their need to get rid of us or test us further? It could become ten times worse.

I sat back and thought about Zeke's statement. The Fae Council was trying to eradicate us, and there wasn't a whole lot we could do about it without getting rid of them, which we still didn't know how to do.

Maybe it's best we get rid of Malcolm's mind control and then see where the chips fall with the humans? It stretches our resources thin, but it doesn't spill blood—not yet, anyway.

"Okay," I said, having made up my mind. "I think we should take the chance and do everything in our power to stop the mind control of the President. The American government could be an asset, and honestly, my kind-hearted mate is right. No one should have their free will stripped from them. The sooner we right that wrong, the better."

Aurelia turned to me with wide eyes and smiled, obviously taken aback by my turnaround.

My wolf preened at the thought that she was no longer mad at us.

"Now that's settled, let's get that information on where the President will be tomorrow!" Aurelia clapped her hands, rearing for action.

She really was the best of us despite the burden Fate had rested on her shoulders.

No matter how long I held her, kissed her lips, or claimed her body, I still couldn't believe this woman was mine.

"He'll be at a fancy restaurant downtown campaigning for the arrest of all supernaturals and calling for more regulations. That's what the gala is raising money for." Zeke growled.

"They are literally raising money to have us turned into lab rats, no doubt so they can study us to make super-human soldiers." I shook my head. It was disgusting. How could they do this to people who had never harmed them? We'd lived among them and protected them. Why was it now that they knew we existed they had a problem with their neighbors and friends?

We had been part of many communities and had human friends, but just because they now knew we were different, we couldn't be trusted. It was, at its core, a race war. It was purebred Fae against all the other supernaturals, and humans against all supernaturals. I imagined that we seemed like evil sci-fi aliens to them. We'd invaded their world—their safe space—and now that they knew it, they wanted us gone.

"I'm guessing that's *exactly* what the human government wants, but the Council is controlling how much information they get at this point." Zeke typed a few more things on his keyboard as he spoke.

"So, how are we getting into the gala?" Aurelia asked. She leaned back into me again, finally not trying to leave the protective circle of my arms.

My wolf loved it. He didn't want his mate too far from him after the distance while we were in prison.

"I've already hacked the guest list and gotten all of us invites under fake names. There's only one problem," said Zeke, glancing around at all of us.

"What is it?" I asked, pulling Aurelia back.

"Aurelia is public enemy number-one," he reminded us as he raised an eyebrow at her.

"Shit," she groaned and leaned her head all the way back on my shoulder to stare forlornly at the ceiling.

"What are we going to do?" I asked.

The Shadow Queen walked into the office with a glint in her eyes. "I have a talent that may be able to help with that," she said with a knowing smirk.

"Mother? You can help?" Aurelia perked up, giving her full attention.

"I can pull off exceptional glamours. Even better than what you do for your own wings, sweetheart." She glanced pointedly at Aurelia's glamoured wings, which were nowhere to be seen.

She still hadn't learned to use them effectively, but then she was taught to hide them from the world at a young age for her own protection, so I couldn't blame her for that.

She needs to learn though.

We would have to make it a priority after the war. She needed to be stronger than even she knew she could be, to be the queen. She was already the strongest woman I'd ever met after the things she'd endured, but Faery needed her operating at one hundred percent.

"Can you change all of our appearances?" I asked. That would prove extremely useful and help us get into the gala.

And if we can get to Malcom, we can kill him, eliminating the mind control on the President.

"I can only do five at a time," she admitted. "It takes an exceeding amount of power. I have tried more in the past, but it ended badly. So, choose your top five," the queen suggested as she eyed us all.

"Well, obviously, I'm going," Aurelia said, brooking no argument.

I growled, scooping her up in my arms and stomping through the office into the hall beyond so that we could have a modicum of privacy. "Aurelia, *please* don't do this. They want you dead more than anyone. I can't risk losing you." I cupped her cheeks and backed her up against the wall, my eyes searching hers.

"I have to, Grey. I can't let this happen. Malcolm, Ronaldo, and the Council need to be stopped." She shook her head at my pleas and tried to pull away.

I wouldn't let her go, though. I couldn't. She was mine. I couldn't handle it if something terrible happened to her. My wolf would go rabid. He would lose his shit, and we would have to be put down if anything happened to her. I would never be the same. "But you don't,"

I argued back. "You could stay here, safe, until the actual war comes to pass. You're the one destined to end this madness. If something happened to you too soon, then everything could be lost," I said. "And it would destroy me."

I pulled her close and pressed my lips to hers, infusing the kiss with all my heart.

I can't survive without her.

All I could hope for was that if something happened to her, I'd die too... because without her, I had no life to live for.

CHAPTER 25

The dress they helped pour me into for the gala was too tight. I could barely breathe against the corset strapped around my torso. "How the hell am I going to fight in this?" I asked with a grimace, turning to the men in the room.

They all stared at me with stunned expressions, their eyes wide and their mouths ajar.

"Stop it!" Grey barked, glaring at the others. "You're making her nervous."

"They're making me slightly uncomfortable, not nervous," I said as I stepped into the entryway.

"Well, they need to stop that too," Grey grumbled. "You're mine. They need to stop looking at you like that."

In a way, I can't blame them. It's probably more shock than anything. This is the most princessy *I think I've ever looked...*

Grey wrapped his arm around my waist as we all made our way to the parking garage.

Zeke, Ash, and Dan followed behind us.

My mother had glamoured us so everyone we met would see something different, but we still saw each other as we truly were. It was a very clever trick, and I hoped it was one that I could one day learn to master. It certainly came in very handy!

"You remember the plan?" Grey asked me as he helped me into the limo.

"We make plans all the time, but they always seem to go to shit," I responded.

"I know, but we don't know exactly what we're walking into, so I wanted to make sure we were all on the same page." He settled into the seat next to me and rested a possessive hand over the form-fitting dress on my thigh.

"I get it," I said as I sat back, already filled with anxious energy.

What am I doing? Really?

Was I going to get us all killed by thinking that I could take Malcolm out? He deserved it, and I wanted nothing more than to be the one to end him for the hell he'd put us all through. It was more than that though. He was behind the human government's imprisonment and testing of supernaturals. Whether it was tonight or a year from now, I would see him dead before the war was over.

We arrived at the red carpet, and the guys all piled out of the car.

Grey offered his hand for me to take.

My form-fitting emerald dress flared out at the bottom, and my hair was done in an elegant up-do on top of my head. I felt like a peacock, though it was nice to feel pretty for once. I'd spent so much time wearing fighting attire or covered in filth, that I'd almost forgotten what it felt like to take care of myself. Realistically, it was a luxury I hadn't had since I was a child and was abducted from Faery.

"You look beautiful, love," Grey whispered in my ear.

"You look good yourself," I responded. "But we aren't here to have fun." I scanned the red carpet behind him, trying to appear as casual and nonchalant as possible. I couldn't see Malcolm anywhere yet, but that didn't mean he wasn't puppeteering the president.

Grey wrapped an arm around my waist and led me through the doors and into the grand ballroom.

The entire space was majestic, filled with an opulence I wasn't used to.

The others fanned out around the room, but they kept their eyes on us as we swept through the area.

"The President isn't here yet. He will probably be the last to arrive and no doubt surrounded by security," Grey muttered.

"So, what do we do then?" I asked, sucking my painted bottom lip into my mouth.

"We can dance. It will give us a better view of the room and we can see if we can get eyes on Malcolm."

"What if he doesn't show up?" I asked, worry lancing me in the heart. Everything hinged on Malcolm being at the gala with the President, but what if he wasn't? What would we do to stop the atrocities happening to the supernaturals? I would have done anything to stop the ruthless madness. But I couldn't stop anything if Malcolm didn't show up.

Grey twirled me around the dance floor with an elegance that took my breath away. He was an Alpha, a lethal shifter, my Fated mate, and an incredible dancer!

I scanned the room, but no matter how hard I looked, I didn't catch sight of the slimy fucker, Malcolm.

Just then, the main doors to the ballroom opened, and a flood of men in black suits surrounded someone in the middle. The President had finally arrived, his wife on his arm in a flowing, royal blue gown. She looked elegant and sophisticated. Too bad her husband might be a world class asshole.

"Let's see if we can get close to them," I whispered.

"No need. Zeke moved around the seating chart online and got us a spot at his table." Grey smirked.

"Of course, he did. That man never does anything by halves. I shook my head with a casual smile.

When it was announced that dinner was being served, Grey led me to the table and pulled my chair out for me.

I sat down primly next to the First Lady and my eyes widened at Grey.

Zeke really wasn't playing around when he set this all up!

"Hello," the First Lady acknowledged, nodding to me before turning back to her husband.

"This is all for such a great cause. I'm so pleased to be able to donate," I said loudly, opening conversation. The words tasted like bitter bile on my tongue. It was not a great cause at all. It was a death sentence for *so* many, if not all of us, but I needed to get the President's attention.

"I'm glad to meet a fellow American who believes in this amazing cause," the President answered and nodded.

"I anxiously await the day that we have them all rounded up," Grey added smoothly.

"Yes, the recent devastating attack on the prison here has set us back slightly, but they will be found and brought to justice for their crimes," the President said with confidence.

Their crimes. He really just said that.

I still couldn't see Malcolm anywhere in the room. From how far away did the mind control work? Was this just the mind control serum talking, or did the President really believe what he was saying?

"The extremists say that the prison was set to explode anyway, and that it was just a safe place to round up supernaturals so they could be exterminated," Grey commented.

The President's eyes flashed with warning as he narrowed his eyes at Grey. "That's ridiculous. We are just protecting the American people from dangerous beings who shouldn't be here in the first place."

"And rightly so," I said, glaring calmly at Grey to cool down.

He was going to blow our cover if he wasn't careful. We hadn't found Malcolm yet, and it looked like this whole mission was for nothing anyway, because the President fully believed in his prejudice whether it was of his own design or not.

What the fuck are we supposed to do now?

I locked gazes with Zeke and widened my eyes at him.

The President caught on surprisingly fast and glanced between me and Zeke.

My stomach lurched.

Shit. I think our cover was just blown.

The President stood up so fast his chair toppled to the ground, and he pointed at Zeke and Ash. "They are supernatural. They are the ones who blew up the prison. Get them!"

A hand clamped around my arm unexpectedly and dragged me up out of my seat. Without anything else to do, I screamed in the Secret Service agent's face before cocking my arm back and punching him. "Don't touch me!" My knuckles cracked against his nose, and I shook my hand out. I spun around to find Grey.

His body vibrated, his wolf precariously close to the surface. Claws replaced his hands as he stared down the two men approaching him. They were also wearing dark suits like the Secret Service.

"If you resist, it will be worse for you," the President announced loudly.

"It can't get much worse than the Council trying to blow us all up," I sneered. There was no point maintaining the ruse any longer. The jig was up.

"That's a lie!" The President slammed his fist down on the table.

The other people backed away from the spectacle, leaving the five of us alone with the President and his Secret Service agents.

"It's not. We were all locked in that hellhole, tested on, and tortured!" I yelled. I needed the people in that room to hear me, but as I stared into the President's eyes, they were strikingly clear. He wasn't being controlled right now. He believed in what he was doing. That was even worse than the alternative.

No one would be safe in the mortal world with the human government out to get us. Arms wrapped around me from behind, squeezing me like a vise. The man lifted me from my feet.

I kicked back into his shin with my pointy heel.

A bellow of rage filled the room as Grey slammed a clawed fist into one of the men before him.

My shadows pulsed beneath my skin as my magic writhed. It wanted out. It wanted to protect me from the imminent threat. But if I succumbed to using my magic against them, I would be playing directly into their hands and showing them that we *were* monsters they made us out to be. That wouldn't help matters or our cause. All it would do is create more fear and chaos. I didn't want to be the reason for that.

Shadows swirled over my arms angrily, and I took measure of the dire situation in which we found ourselves.

People gasped and backed away from me.

"That's her, the woman that blew up the prison!" several people whispered.

Fuck. The shadows are a dead giveaway. That or my glamour has dropped!

"Get her!" the President roared.

Suddenly, Zeke was in front of me, protecting me with the mass of his immense Rider body. I hadn't even seen him move. "What are you doing?" I hissed at his back.

"You have to be protected." He grunted as magic filled his palms.

"Zeke, no! We can't use magic against them, or we are exactly what they think we are," I warned.

"We are protecting ourselves. That's all we've ever done. It's why we hid for centuries among them. I'm not letting them take you to Ronaldo."

"You can't use your magic!" I growled. It would ruin everything and play right into their hands.

"Fine," he snapped, dropping his magic, but didn't move out of my way.

I glanced around the room.

Grey was fighting against two Secret Service agents, but they were no match for him. He took them down with his fists alone, but his claws punctured his palms and blood dripped from them as he fought hard against his primal urge to shift. "We need to go. Right now!" Grey bellowed.

Zeke backed me up to Grey, and the others created a protective barrier around me as Zeke put up a shield. They wouldn't be able to get to us through his ward.

"Do not let them leave." The President took a step forward. "They need to pay for their crimes!"

Several of the agents pulled guns and pointed them at us.

Still, Zeke kept backing us toward the door. The men were all protecting me like I was precious or fragile.

I hated it. They needed to protect themselves too, but would it do any good to tell them that? A gust of wind blew through the room and pushed the guards farther back. I peered over at Ash with a raised brow. "I said no magic!" I growled.

The agents lifted their handguns at us. "Just surrender and no one gets hurt," one of them urged.

"We aren't doing anything. We haven't done anything to deserve this treatment in the first place. Just let us go!" I shook my head.

"Don't move," another agent said. He pointed his gun at my head, ready to take me down by any means necessary. If those firearms housed Ronaldo's deadly supernatural bullets, we were all fucked.

Zeke's magic flared as he once again stepped in front of me, blocking me from the agents' view, then a loud shot cracked through the air.

Arms grabbed me from behind, turning me into a hard chest and spinning me around.

I screamed and thrashed in those arms, but Grey's warmth soothed me. I peeked around him just in time to witness Zeke falling to the ground in a puddle of blood.

No. Not Zeke. As much as he's pissed me off, I didn't want to lose my friend!

I lunged for Zeke. I wanted to heal him, to at least try! My magic flared in response to my desire and emotions.

Grey held me back as I struggled in his arms. "I know, love, I know. But his sacrifice will be for nothing if we don't leave *now*." Grey lifted me off my feet and threw me over his shoulder as he raced to the door.

The others shot magic at the agents until we were all on the other side.

Tears poured down my cheeks as we made our way outside and into the humid Dallas air.

Grey put me down, but held tightly to my hand.

Zeke is gone. I can't believe it...

I looked up to Ash.

His face was stricken but determined at the same time. “We can mourn him later, Aurelia. We have to go. That’s what he would want,” he said gruffly, his gaze holding mine for a breathless moment.

My heart broke as we ran for our lives. How could we just leave one of our own behind?

Dan ran right next to me so that I was flanked on both sides. “Live to fight another day, Princess,” he breathed between strides.

Live to fight another day…

But how many of those did I really have left? Only time would tell.

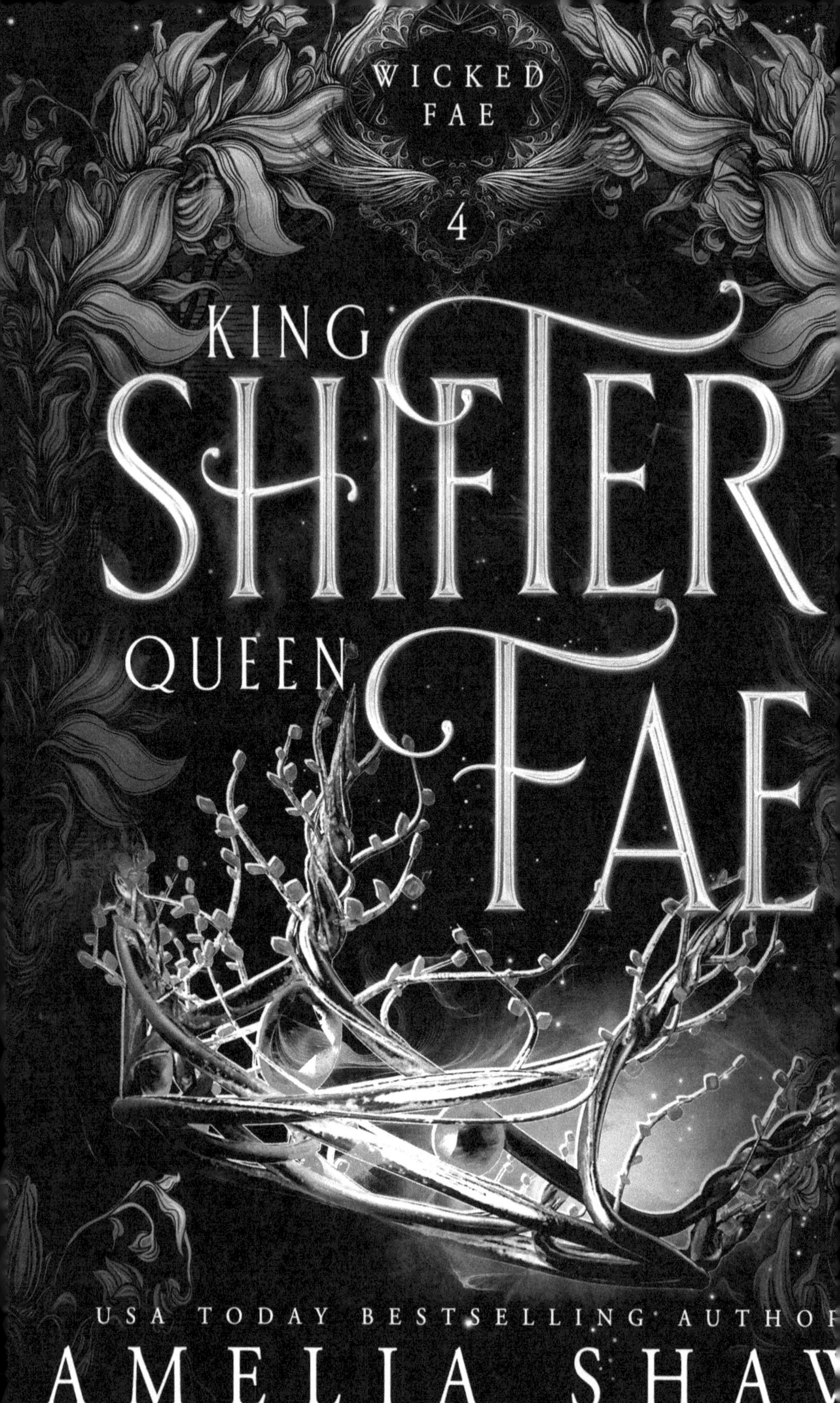
WICKED
FAE
4
KING
SHIFTER
QUEEN
FAE
USA TODAY BESTSELLING AUTHOR
AMELIA SHAW

King Shifter and Queen Fae

CHAPTER 1

Aurelia

The crushing weight of losing Zeke bore down on me as heavy and physically painful as enduring the crushing cascade of an avalanche.

Grey skidded to a stop, our escape halted. "Damn it!"

I spun instinctively to see the problem, trusting my mate's actions.

Secret Service agents pursued and surrounded us like a swarm of hornets, their hands on their weapons, ready to lay fire. They weren't going to let us get away.

I stared one of them down, but there was something unnervingly off about the man's gaze. It seemed oddly blank… vacant. I glanced back at the doors we'd come through just moments ago, and my shoulders slumped. We were leaving behind Zeke. He'd pissed me off more often than not, but ultimately, he was my friend, someone I could trust, and I hated having to abandon him, even in death.

Asher clamped a strong, firm hand on my shoulder. "He would want us to get out of here, Aurelia."

"I know." My voice wobbled.

"Then stop looking back when the fight is in front of us. You've got survive this, or his sacrifice will have been in vain." He nudged me forward.

"But how are we going to get out of this?" I asked, glancing around.

Grey ran his hand down his face in frustration. "I don't know how we can without using magic against the humans."

"It's our only option," Dan said, his tone steadfast although tinged with regret.

One of the agents stepped forward, his eyes glassy and strange like all the others. "Come with us quietly and no one else will to get hurt."

"Yeah, right," I growled. "Your bosses plan to murder us all, the same way you did Zeke!" Magic pooled in my palms. It wasn't the solution I wanted at all. I *hated* the idea of using magic against humans.

But we need to get out of here, and I won't let Zeke's death be for nothing!

I peered over at Grey, my chest heaving with emotion and the sheer willpower it took to hold back my shadows.

He nodded his head in confirmation, approving the only option we had available to us. "I don't want to use my magic on them any more than you do, but it's the only way." He clenched his hands into fists as if steeling his nerves.

The men surrounding us took aim but didn't move to shoot us.

"Using magic against us is illegal. You will be tried and put to death," the agent in front said in an eerie monotone as he took another step closer.

Grey growled low in his throat, and his eyes glowed, revealing his inner wolf. Together, Grey, Ash and Dan formed a tight circle around me, even though I was the most powerful among them.

"Overprotective men," I whispered under my breath, even though a part of me would always appreciate their chivalry and protective natures.

Grey shot me a quick wink. His oversensitive wolf hearing picked up everything, including my mild annoyance at the men protecting me.

I took a step forward, ready for action.

Grey blocked me. "What are you doing?" he snarled low, as if admonishing me.

"Fighting! We need to get out of here before even more of them show up." I rolled my eyes at my Alpha lover and nudged him to the side.

I'm not helpless. I can do my part.

"Stop." That voice was one I knew all too well.

How did he manage to evade us inside the event?

I spun on my heels to face Malcolm.

He stood at the top of the steps at the exit of the building from which we'd fled. "I need them alive!" he barked, offering me a sinister smile.

The Secret Service agents holstered their weapons and lunged for us as one, limited to their physicality to take us.

My shadows writhed up my arms before flooding to my hands. They shot out at in streams of darkness toward the leader as he rushed me, trapping him in chains. "How did we miss him in there?" I called out. "I didn't see him anywhere—not once."

"It doesn't matter," Asher grunted. "We just need to get out of here." He tossed the man he was grappling with over his shoulder.

The man gasped as he landed on his back mere seconds before two more men rushed Ash.

With a roaring battle cry, he roundhouse kicked them both, one after the other.

"Aurelia, behind you!" Grey yelled.

Receiving the warning just in time, I ducked and spun around in a low, sweeping kick, taking my attacker off his feet, and jumped back up into a fighting stance. The Secret Service agents outnumbered us four to one. The odds of us getting out of this situation without using further magic on the humans were terrible. Sheathing my shadows temporarily, I let my natural purple magic fill my palms and prayed to whoever might be listening that what I wanted to do would work, then flung the magic at the men closest to me.

The magic hit the first man in the chest, and his eyes rolled back in his head. He fell into the man next to him. He was out like a light. I just hoped I'd only knocked him out and hadn't killed him instead. But there was no time to worry about that, as three more men rushed forward to take his place.

Ash stepped up behind me and plastered his back to mine. "You need someone at your back, Princess. They seem to be gunning for you specifically."

"Yeah, I think that's Malcolm's influence," I mumbled, and threw another sparkling ball of magic at the men encircling me.

One agent dove out of the way just in time for the ball to miss him, but it struck the man fighting Grey in the back, and he toppled over.

Please don't be dead.

Magic, I'd learned, was about motive, and I had *no* intention of killing them. I only wanted to disable them for the moment, so that we could make our escape. I had to believe they were simply unconscious, trusting in my inherent talent, learned skills, and instincts, because I was *not* a cold-blooded killer. I never would be!

"Get her! I don't care what you do with the others, I want her alive!" Malcolm bellowed.

He just doesn't fucking get it. I will never be his!

"He's still an obsessed psycho," I muttered and shook my head. I blasted more of the agents with my magic, one after another, but the first ones I'd struck were already starting to wake up.

Fuck! That didn't last nearly long enough.

The men wasted no time in taking Malcolm's declaration to mean that he didn't care if everyone else died. Several of them drew their weapons once more, pointing them at Grey and the others.

Ten agents surrounded Ash and me as we fought back-to-back. My magic pooled even faster in my palms, answering my dire need, and I threw it as quickly as it appeared. In short order I'd knocked out enough of them that I could at least maneuver and escape the tight circle in which they'd surrounded us. "Ash, go help Grey!" I yelled as three agents attacked Grey from all sides.

"No! He'll be *pissed* if I leave you unprotected," Ash said, before his voice broke off in a pained grunt.

I turned at the sound to see a man holding a long, sharp blade dripping with Ash's blood. I screamed and launched myself at the man without thinking, my hands glowing with a chaotic mixture of purple magic and shadows.

I refuse to lose anyone else!

"You stupid man!" I roared in frustration and anger. "You took a knife for me, didn't you?" I glanced back at Ash. There was a rip in both his shirt and jacket and a small line of blood dripped from the thin laceration.

"Aurelia, watch out!" Ash bellowed, his expression distraught.

The distraction cost me. The blade-wielding attacker took the opportunity and stabbed me before I could even think to move.

Pain lanced through my gut, seared up through my chest, and a burning agony lit all my limbs on fire.

The man grinned at me with genuine malice. He wasn't being controlled or under some kind of magical influence like the other agents. His will was free, and his eyes were cold and cruel. He yanked the blade from my stomach just as my magic erupted, striking him in the chest. He screamed as he flew back, the shadows eating away at his skin with a vengeance. It was gruesome to behold. They burned away the fabric of his uniform, then melted through his skin until bones and bleeding tendons could be seen under his charred flesh.

I fought the urge to puke and forced myself to my feet, lurching away from the true horror my magic could unleash upon another being.

I did that.

My head spun, and I swallowed hard as I clutched at my gut. My magic was something truly terrifying, or at least it could be, but I didn't have time or strength to break down over what I'd just done. I'd wanted the man to hurt just as badly as he'd hurt me.

Does that make me a terrible person? Could I be a cold-blooded killer?

I shook off the grim thoughts. This was war and we were fighting for our lives. I could unpack that mess later. Blood dripped down the front of my dress, seeping through my fingers, but I wasn't too worried despite the pain—my wound would heal soon enough. I turned to find more agents wielding long blades. They clearly weren't human at all, but rather Fae pretending to be Secret Service.

One of them slashed out wildly at Grey, and I saw red.

Thankfully, he jumped back unharmed.

Pain distracted me, echoing in the wound left behind by the traitorous Fae guard in my belly. It pulsed to the beat of my heart and blood continued its steady stream from the wound.

It should have started healing already...

Perhaps the adrenaline of the fight was keeping the blood pumping out of me. Maybe I needed a breather to allow my magic to catch up, but it was a luxury I couldn't afford. I couldn't stop. I had to keep fighting, no matter what. We had to get out of here, push through. Everything depended on us escaping this mess alive, but we were still heavily outnumbered, and more agents continued to flood the streets like a virus.

I'd lost sight of Grey and Dan in the commotion as I spun, kicking out at a guard. Blood gushed from his side as my stiletto, which had seemed appropriate for the gala event, pierced his skin. I shoved him away from me and searched for Grey and Dan, but there were just too many enemies and barely any allies.

How the hell are we going to get out of this?

Without warning, something hit me like a battering ram and shoved me to the side. I blinked up at Ash from where I'd landed on my ass, stars dancing momentarily before my eyes.

He punched an agent in the face, and a *crack* filled the air as the man's nose gushed blood and he fell to the ground, limp.

Ash reached out to me, his knuckles cracked and bleeding. In an instant he pulled me to my feet.

I nodded gratefully as I fought to catch my breath and banish the stars. A second later, a sharp pain sliced through my back. I instinctively arched and screamed as I tried to evade the agony cutting through me. Blood gushed from my back as I stumbled gracelessly forward into Ash, my face contorted.

He shoved me behind his impressive bulk, shielding me with his body from further harm, and disarmed the agent in a swift maneuver before slicing the blade across the man's throat with a bellow of rage.

Tears pricked at my eyes, my breath hitching in my throat as I pressed my free hand to the gash on my back. It came away slick with blood. I stumbled sideways from blood loss. I wasn't healing as fast as I should have been.

Why am I not healing? I don't understand.

Arms banded around me from behind, locking my arms to my sides. Whoever had taken me hostage lifted me from my feet.

I kicked back desperately with the pointy heel of my shoe, catching him in the shin.

"Stop fighting!" the man hissed.

I kicked him again and again as I thrashed in his hold like a worm on a hook. My shadows writhed along my arms in response to my distress and slid like tar onto the man where his arms held me tight. He screamed as they burned away the cloth of his suit jacket and melted his skin beneath.

"Aurelia!" Grey roared.

The agent dropped me to the ground as he batted at the shadows and continued to scream.

Even though I was losing an obscene amount of blood and in agony, I still hated to witness the wrath of my magic. I hated having to use it this way. And though I could justify the brutal use of magical force as we fought for our lives, I didn't have to like it. I stumbled back to my feet with considerable effort.

Grey was fighting to get to me, but there were too many guards rushing toward me. He'd never make it through alive.

Dan appeared instantly at my side, a blade in each hand. He must have stolen them from the agents he'd fought and bested. He handed one of them to me.

"Thank you. I hate using my magic like that," I gasped as I took the blade and twirled it in my grasp. With what strength I had remaining, I slashed at anything that came too close to me.

But the only agents who would venture near the blades were the ones with blank eyes. The others very carefully and consciously kept their distance.

Without warning, my head spun suddenly and violently. I pitched to the side, directly into Dan.

What is happening to me?

I blinked, trying to clear my head and vision, but the ground was uneven, and the night sky swirled around me in a chaotic and haphazard kaleidoscope of color and darkness.

"Aurelia, are you okay?" Dan asked, gripping my shoulders to steady me.

"I'm dizzy," I managed, but my words were slurred and my tongue felt thick in my own mouth.

"Shit," he swore. "You're not healing!" He glanced down at the hole in my stomach, blood still openly flowing from it.

"But why am I not healing?" I shook my head in denial. It didn't make sense.

"You were stabbed," he said, his gaze shifting to the daggers we both held. "The blades might have been coated with something to stop the healing process."

"Twice," I said and stumbled again, the world spinning.

"What?" Dan asked, searching my face.

"I was stabbed twice," I slurred as I dropped to my knees. "Well, stabbed *once* and then slashed from behind." But why was I being pedantic? The point remained that I was injured, and my strength was failing me at an alarming rate.

Who do I feel so tired?

My knees gave out, unable to hold me anymore. I fell to the side, heavy and uncontrolled, like a dead-weight. My head slammed into the concrete sidewalk, pain exploding behind my eyes so fiercely it stole my breath away.

"Grey!" Dan roared. "The princess is injured."

Darkness swirled in and out of my vision. I slapped at the ground unwilling to accept defeat, desperate to get up. I needed to help them—to get to my feet and continue the fight—but my limbs were *so* heavy.

And I'm so tired...

Unable to hold them open a moment longer, my eyes fluttered closed, and darkness engulfed me completely.

CHAPTER 2

Grey

"Grey! The princess is injured!" Dan's words hit me like a sledgehammer in the gut.

I spun to face him with a bellow of anguish. My wolf exploded out of me without my consent, ripping through the agents gleefully and without mercy as he raced to his mate's motionless form.

Aurelia was pale and her eyes were closed.

Please, gods, let her be okay!

My wolf nudged her with his nose. She felt cool to the touch, which disturbed him deeply. I stood over her protectively, snarling in my black wolf form. No one would get to my mate again. I wouldn't allow it. My wolf howled.

Ash materialized next to me.

My wolf overtook me, growling a warning at the Rider.

"Easy, now. We need to get out of here. Let me carry her for you." Asher raised his hands in surrender.

He's a friend. Let him help! I commanded my wolf, asserting my authority. It went against everything my wolf stood for to let someone else touch his mate, but Ash had proven his loyalty time and time again to me and my future queen. My wolf nodded his furry head in agreement, then snarled again at the encroaching agents. He crouched down, ready to pounce on anyone that dared to get too close to us.

All around us guns were drawn again and pointed squarely at my wolf.

"Give up, Shifter King!" Malcolm cackled from his observation point on the stairs. "You're surrounded. It's over. Shift back and they won't kill you all."

Ignoring the pompous ass, Ash secured Aurelia in his arms and glanced down at me. "Are you ready to mow them down, Grey?"

I nodded, since it was the only way I could communicate with others while in my wolf form. My wolf howled with rage-fueled glee and launched up from his crouch, crashing into the first row of agents with the force of a cannonball.

Guns were fired, one after another, cracking like thunder in our ears, but Ash's magic prevented the rounds from hitting us. He tossed the bullets away with his powerful breeze, as another gust of wind pushed back the second row of agents trying to advance.

They fell like dominoes into one another, providing us with a small window to escape.

"No!" Malcolm bellowed. "Get up, you fools. They're getting away!"

Vacant-eyed men scrambled in response and a hand grasped my leg.

I tripped over my own paw and landed heavily on the man's chest. A *crunch* sounded beneath me.

The man screamed, but the sound was short lived, and his hand went slack.

Damn. My weight must have broken a rib.

Not that I gave a shit. He was merely an obstacle between me, my mate, and freedom. So, without a backward glance, I bound away from him.

"Where are we going?" Dan asked through heaving breaths as he joined us a second later.

"We can't let them follow us back to the building. There are innocents there," Ash said, adjusting his hold on my precious mate.

"We need to get to the car so Grey can shift!" Dan answered and picked up his pace, jogging down a dark alley.

We'd known going into this that things could end up going south, so we'd organized a back-up plan for just such an outcome. All we had to do was make it to the SUV. Thundering steps sounded from behind us, and my wolf growled low in my throat.

They are following us.

I'd known they would. We had to move faster. I rammed my head into Asher's thigh and nudged him forward faster.

Dan opened a door at the end of the alley, and it creaked, the sound like a gunshot to my oversensitive shifter ears. The human agents were still fairly far off, so hopefully they wouldn't have heard it.

I bounced into the dark room, which was likely a storage closet. The four of us barely fit inside the small space, but we weren't intending to stay there long.

Dan closed the door quietly behind him and clicked the lock into place. The businesses in the alley had all been owned by shifters until we'd been outed to the world. Now, they provided places that shifters or other supernaturals could go to hide if the need arose unexpectedly.

We'd always had a contingency plan... until the Fae Council came along and ruined everything. We had never planned for this level of madness, but we were doing our best to keep it together on the fly.

Dan flicked on a light and threw a bundle of dark clothes at me.

I shifted quickly and dressed to leave. We still needed to get to our vehicle. "There were agents following us," I informed them. "We need to get to the SUV, but we can't risk everyone." I ran my hand through my hair in frustration.

This is all so fucked!

I reached for Aurelia, still unconscious in Ash's arms. The only way I knew she was alive was the faint beating of her heart. "What the fuck happened?" I asked with a scowl as I followed Dan out of another hidden door and into what used to be a thriving restaurant.

"Those knives the Fae agents had... they must have had something on them to prevent healing."

We followed him through the dead establishment and out into the cool night air on the street that ran parallel to the alley.

Dan clicked the front door shut behind us.

"We need to get her somewhere safe. She's lost too much blood," I said as I pulled her carefully from Ash's arms and to my chest.

Ash sighed. "The Compound is heavily warded and there's no one there, with my brothers helping at the Syndicate."

"Okay, let's go." I gripped the door handle and pulled it open, climbing up into the backseat with Aurelia curled in my lap. I pressed my lips to her cool forehead, praying that we would figure out a way to save her in time.

I need her. The entire supernatural world needs her...

"Fuck!" Dan yelled as a gunshot exploded in the air nearby.

He dove into the driver's seat and slammed the door quickly behind him as a hail of bullets pinged the metal. Thankfully my SUVs were all bulletproof, which was why I insisted we bring one of them instead of the mission-ready SUVs the Syndicate used.

"Drive!" I shouted as bullets continued to ping off the vehicle's armor.

Dan sat up in his seat and pushed the button to start the vehicle and threw it into Drive.

We tore out of the abandoned parking along the street as quickly as possible while men in suits chased after us, shooting the entire time.

"Take as many turns and side streets as you can before going into the woods east of Dallas," Ash instructed.

Dan tore down alley after alley, but our evasive path was taking too long to get us where we needed to go.

Aurelia's respiration was getting lighter the longer we took to get to the Rider's Compound.

"We need to get there, *now*," I stressed. "I think we've lost them." I pulled Aurelia's head to my shoulder, squeezing her tighter.

"Are you sure?" Dan asked and glanced at Ash from the driver's seat.

"Yeah, I think Grey is right. We've lost them, and the princess needs healing." Ash clenched his fist. He glanced back at me holding her with a grimace.

Meanwhile, Dan's knuckles were white. He was gripping the steering wheel too tightly. "There's just one problem with this plan," he announced. "None of us are healers." His eyes widened in the rearview mirror at me as he spoke.

"We'll worry about that when we get to the Compound," Ash said, but his tone wavered, as if he seemed genuinely scared for Aurelia.

My mate inspired loyalty in nearly everyone she met. The gods couldn't take her from me. She had to survive these wounds.

She has to.

My wolf whimpered in my mind at the thought of losing his mate. His power was stronger than that of almost any other supernatural. If he lost his Fated mate, I didn't know if I would be able to rein him in, or that I would even want to.

The world will burn if she dies... and I will light the match.

Dan maneuvered my SUV through the city streets, avoiding unnecessary detours, and in no time, we were driving down a dirt road and into the forest.

The road was bumpy as fuck, and I shielded Aurelia from the jostling motion as best I could.

She didn't open her eyes once the entire drive, but at least she was still breathing.

Ash pulled something from his pocket and hit a couple buttons when we got to the wrought iron gate that surrounded the Compound. The gates creaked open in response, though far too slowly for my liking.

I shifted in my seat. This was taking too damn long. How much blood had Aurelia already lost? We needed to get her inside safely, and then get a healer there quickly.

Dan hit the gas hard as soon as the gate opened and followed the curved driveway that led up to a state-of-the-art garage which was already open and waiting.

As soon as the SUV was parked, I threw my door open. "Get Fenrick on the phone *immediately*."

"I'm on it, Boss." Dan pulled his phone from his pocket and raised it to his ear.

Ash ushered me through the door in the garage that led into the main house.

I didn't even so much as look at the place as I followed him down a long hallway.

Dan was hot on our heels seconds later. "How's Fenrick going to get here?" Dan asked me, as we turned a corner into a spare bedroom.

I laid Aurelia on the bed.

"The King of Faery has been here before. It was a *very* long time ago, but he should still be able to sift to the gate."

I ran my fingers tenderly through Aurelia's golden hair as the two men spoke quietly in the corner about Fenrick's impending arrival. They would figure it out and get him here. I knew they would. They'd never let me down before. My wolf whined in my head, begging to be let out, to curl up around his mate like a furry shield, but I couldn't lose control right now.

After she's healed, I promised.

Once Fenrick arrived and healed her of her injuries, I could shift and sleep by her side until she woke. I didn't want to be apart from her any more than my wolf did, and I knew he could feel that and knew it to be true.

"Fenrick and the king will be here momentarily," Ash said, interrupting my discussion with my inner wolf.

I glanced up from my mate and noticed that Dan was gone, and Ash had pulled a chair up on the other side of the bed. I peered back at Aurelia, not wanting to take my eyes off her for another second.

Her heartbeat had slowed significantly since we arrived, even though the bleeding had finally stopped.

She's probably running on empty.

It was a grim thought, but she'd lost so much, I imagined it wasn't too far from the truth.

"I think you need to get cleaned up, Grey," Ash suggested with a grimace.

I was covered in blood—mine, Aurelia's and the gods only knew who else's—but I couldn't bring myself to care. I wasn't leaving Aurelia's side until she was healed. I just couldn't. "No."

"Grey, you're covered in your mate's blood and the blood of the men you killed tonight," Ash said.

"You're covered in blood too," I retorted, never taking my eyes from Aurelia's pale face. I leaned down and kissed her forehead, pushing every bit of love and devotion I had for her through my lips, willing her to feel it, to absorb it, and draw strength from it.

"I know, and as soon as Dan gets back to make sure you don't shift and tear Fenrick apart while he heals Aurelia, I'm going to go get cleaned up." Ash shook his head, one heavyset brow hitched.

"I have no intention of hurting Fenrick," I huffed back.

"I know you don't, but your wolf nearly maimed me earlier for getting close to the princess." He shook his hand out, trying to relieve the pain of having clenched it through most of our drive over.

"You got too close to his injured mate, but I calmed his ass down." I brushed the hair away from Aurelia's face. "What do you think is taking them so long?" I asked.

"We're here," Fenrick announced from the doorway. He rushed inside the room and cursed when he inspected the wound in her stomach.

"It's not healing. I need you to heal her," I mumbled, my heart in my throat.

What if he can't heal her? Are we about to lose our mate even after all of this?

"I'm going to try my best, Grey, but I need you to move." Fenrick patted my shoulder.

"I can't. I have to stay close." My hand tightened around hers.

Dan gripped my other shoulder much more firmly than he would have ever dared before. "Move, Grey. She needs a healer now or she's going to die. I will move you *myself*, if I fucking have to."

He's right. I need to move.

But how could I force myself away from her when she was injured? My wolf howled in my mind and butted against my barriers with all his might as I stood. He didn't want to be too far from his mate.

We're not going far.

I held my hands up in surrender and backed away from the bed slowly. Every step away from her was painful, like walking on glass with bare feet. My heart cracked in my chest with each footfall, but I stepped back all the same. I needed her to be okay. I needed it more than my next breath. "Just fix her," I whispered, my voice betraying my fear.

My hands clenched into fists at my sides even as my wolf howled and whined and attempted to break free. I needed her to be healed. I had to keep it together just a little while longer... because there would be no world left for me if she died. I would incinerate it all, and every single fucking person responsible for her death would pay dearly. I would make sure of it.

CHAPTER 3

Aurelia

My body burned painfully on my left side, and I grimaced, sucking in a quick, deep breath to avoid the hiss that wanted to escape from between my teeth.

Why am I so hot?

I lazily threaded my fingers through soft fur, and not two seconds later, did a mental double take.

What?

My eyes blinked open instantly to a sterile, white room and a white wolf fast asleep, practically on top of me.

What the hell happened? Where are we?

The white wolf was obviously my beautiful Grey, but what had happened to us? Nothing in the room seemed familiar. We weren't at the Syndicate, that was for sure. I sat up gingerly, wincing at the pain in my gut as memories flooded back to me of the fight with the human agents and the disguised Fae with their poisoned blades—and me being injured.

I ran my fingers over my abdomen with hesitant fingers where the blade had cut through my skin. It was no longer bleeding and there were mercifully no puckered scars or visible damage left behind by the serrated blade.

Did the Council capture us?

I shook the big wolf's body next to me and tried to wake him, but he didn't budge.

Did they do something to my mate?

My chest fluttered with anxiety and fear. Was that why I couldn't get him to wake up? What was going on? This room wasn't the best by any stretch, but it also didn't remind me of how the Council treated their prisoners. No... this was something else. I just didn't know what.

"Grey," I croaked, my voice hoarse. I needed water in the worst way. It felt like I'd chewed glass the night before and swallowed it, the jagged edges cutting all the way down. I nudged Grey again, my anxiety growing with uncertainty.

His wolf whined in his sleep but still didn't open his eyes.

"Grey, wake up. What's happened? Where are we?" I shoved his flank harder.

His wolfy tongue lolled out of his mouth.

Under any other circumstances I would have found that adorable, but my hands were shaking, and my imagination was running wild. If we weren't being held prisoner by the Council, had we been captured during our daring escape and handed over to the humans? Was this a room in another testing facility?

The wolf whimpered and turned blinking blue eyes at me before that same tongue licked up the side of my face with a *yip* of excitement.

"Hey, wolfie. I'm glad to see you too, but I need to talk to Grey." I buried my face in his fur, surreptitiously wiping the wolf drool off my face.

His wolf whined but seconds later, a very naked Grey pulled me into his arms. "You're alive," he breathed.

"We have to find a way out of here," I whispered harshly. "What happened? How did they catch us? Where are we?" I asked rapid-fire. I tugged out of his grip and grasped his hand in mine to pull him out of the bed, but he was immovable.

"Stop. We're safe, Aurelia. What are you talking about?" Grey frowned.

"Where are we then, Grey? I've never seen this place before." I chewed my lip, my chest rising and falling as my heart pounded like a racehorse at full gallop.

"We couldn't go back to the Syndicate because we were being followed. This is the Riders' Compound. We're safe." He kissed my temple, trying to ease my stress. "I promise, we're safe."

Safe? Are we really safe anywhere?

"The Riders' Compound?" I asked, my heart cracking in my chest at the memory of Zeke.

They had lost their brother because he was helping me, and now I was taking refuge in their secret space. How was that even fair? They had all done nothing but help us with our Fae Council problem, and I was grateful to them for it, but now guilt gnawed at me. There was no replacing Zeke. No matter what I did, or how we succeeded, life would never be the same without the burly Rider who excelled at hacking.

"Hey, don't think like that," said Grey, interrupting my thoughts. "I can already see and smell the guilt *all* over you. Helping us helps all supernaturals, and Asher would be happy to help you heal." Grey wrapped his arms around my waist and pulled me into his naked body despite my initial resistance.

"How the hell can you smell my guilt?" I asked with a defeated sigh.

"I'm the Shifter King, mate. My nose is better than anyone's." He rested his chin on the top of my head.

"We're really safe and at the Riders' Compound?" I asked. I trusted Grey with my life, but I still needed confirmation for my peace of mind with everything that had happened. I just couldn't believe that they'd actually gotten us away from the President's Secret Service detail. There had been so many of them, and the last thing I remembered was being overwhelmed, and then darkness...

"Yes, but now I need to ask how you're feeling, Princess," he responded with a subtle smirk. "You didn't heal. They stabbed you, and you weren't healing. It drove me and my wolf to madness thinking you were going to die."

"I feel fine," I assured him as I turned my gaze up to his and kissed his chin. There was a shadow of a beard there that tickled my nose, and I giggled with relief. Resting my head on his chest, I allowed myself to simply listen to the sound of his heart thumping beneath my ear, steady and strong. He was solid, and I was so thankful. I could always rely on Grey, and that thought gave me a great deal of comfort regardless of what peril faced us.

His fingers trailed over the line where the knife had sliced my stomach, but there was nothing there. Only the memory of that wound still existed between us, the same as with the slice to my back. I was practically good as new.

"Should we get dressed and figure out what our next steps are?" I asked with a lopsided smile.

Grey's arms tightened around my waist like he didn't want to let me go.

I understood the sentiment, because I would have been the same if the roles of our situation were reversed.

"Not yet," Grey said with a growl. His wolf was riding him. His eyes glowed as the wolf lunged to the surface.

I raked my fingers through his hair and nuzzled into his neck, pressing my lips to his skin, just breathing in his scent before speaking again. "I think everyone might want to know that I'm okay."

"Fuck everyone else. I'm your mate and I'm not ready to give you up to the rest of the world yet," Grey growled again.

It was so strange after all the years that I'd had no one, to now know that I had a mate and parents who loved me. I also had wonderful friends who trusted me and needed me. I felt out of my element when I thought about my past.

Who is this new, beloved, magic-wielding warrior princess?

The idea of how much I'd changed and grown almost made me

chuckle. Life was beyond strange... I could never have imagined living and walking the path I was now. It was like a dream, yet it was very much my reality. The sheer volume of love and pain I'd endured since meeting Grey was testament to that.

Grey's arms tightened around me briefly again, and then he sighed, the man understanding what his wolf could not. "You're right. We need to go so they all know you're okay, or I'll never hear the end of it."

"We're going to have to come up with a plan," I mumbled into his chest, a part of me lamenting that we had to return to the proverbial and literal front so soon. It seemed like quiet moments like this were far and few between lately.

Things were unfortunately worse now than ever before. The agents' eerily blank eyes flashed in my memory, and I shuddered on Grey's lap. They weren't normal. Malcolm had been controlling them, of that much I was sure. And if we didn't do something about it, we were going to find ourselves in a lot more trouble than we'd bargained for.

Malcom needs to be removed from the board. His influence is toxic. A disease that spreads wherever he goes.

Consciously retreating from the darkness of the Fae who'd once been my betrothed, and back to the light of my mate, I grinned. "You should probably get dressed first," I said, suppressing a giggle.

Grey glanced down at his naked body.

His sudden reaction drew my own gaze.

Do I really want him to get dressed?

With all that tanned, toned skin was on display, he looked mouth-watering. I shifted next to him and winced in pain.

Damn it.

I sighed. There wouldn't even be time for a quick roll in the sheets. I was still too stiff and sore, even though someone had gone to the trouble of healing me. Though I showed no outward wounds or scars, the internal pain was still very real and present.

Grey pushed me gently back to the bed and got up, grabbing a pair of sweats from the chair next to the bed. "You're still sore," he said, not wanting to injure me further.

"Only a little..." I said and pouted. Though "a little" was an understatement, I didn't want my gorgeous mate to think I no longer desired him, because I did. And as soon as I was back to one-hundred-percent strength, I'd be seizing the first opportunity we had to prove it!

"Come on, let's go tell the others you're awake and figure out how we're going to stop the Council once and for all." Grey held a hand out to me, a wry smile on his lovely lips.

I glowered momentarily but gingerly got up from the bed. Someone had changed me from my blood-stained gown into a comfortable pair of sleep shorts and a tank top. I was pretty sure that would have been Grey, so I squeezed his hands in unspoken thanks. No matter how much I trusted my friends, I didn't want anyone else seeing me so vulnerable or changing me, and I'm pretty sure my mate felt the same way.

Grey opened the door, trailing me behind him.

A heartbeat later, Fenrick fell inside the room, toppling over from his seated position on the floor. He blinked his eyes open rapidly and jumped to his feet, suddenly alert. "What's going on?" he asked as he scanned the hallway. His shoulders hunched, and his hands clenched into fists at his sides while he searched for a threat that wasn't there.

"Everything's fine," I said and smiled at Fenrick. "I think we just woke you."

His eyes widened, and he blew out a relieved breath. "Yes, sorry. I was on guard," he explained. "I didn't want to go too far. You scared us, Princess."

"I kind of scared myself." I chuckled.

"Never again," Grey growled, his eyes flashing.

"None of us can promise that," I answered. "All we can do is try not to let it happen again. And I promise to do *my* best, so it doesn't." I stepped forward feeling a little more myself with each passing moment. "Now, we need to come up with a plan. This has gone on long enough."

"You're right, Princess," Fenrick muttered as he led the way down the hall. "I picked up Zeke's laptop in case we needed it before I came to help heal you."

So, it was Fenrick who healed me!

I would have to thank him, but not now. I hung my head, and a single tear leaked from my eye.

Zeke.

He'd been shot, and I'd left him behind.

Grey squeezed my hip as he no doubt felt and smelled my guilt over the loss of the Rider through our mated bond.

What does Ash think of me? It's my fault his brother is gone.

"It's not your fault, mate," Grey assured me as he squeezed me again.

"Isn't it, though? That was my plan. I'd wanted to take Malcolm out, and then we couldn't even find him." I shook my head.

"You can't blame yourself, Aurelia. We forced you to leave him behind. You're the future queen of Faery. Your life and safety were paramount, mate. It's what he would have wanted." Grey pulled me down the hall.

"Are you sure about that?" I asked, my heart in my throat. "I hate that we had to leave him... You all made sure that even though I was injured to the point of near-death, that you brought me back to be healed. My life isn't worth more than anyone else's."

Overhearing our conversation, Fenrick turned sharply and scowled at me. "It's not? You are the one who is prophesized to save the supernaturals and usher in a new era. How can you say your life isn't worth more? You are meant to rule and save us all."

"But why?" I threw my hands up in frustration. "Because some seer two hundred years ago said it was true? I haven't done anything so far but screw up and get people I care about killed."

Both men stared at me with equal expressions of disbelief.

What were they thinking? I couldn't even begin to guess. I certainly hadn't saved anyone. Zeke had died because he was protecting us—because he was protecting me.

"You were the one who organized the people at the Syndicate to rescue the supernaturals being targeted by the government. Or did I imagine that?" Fenrick asked slowly.

"It was just the right thing to do." I crossed my arms over my chest. "They were all innocents and didn't deserve to be persecuted."

"Indeed. But not only that, you helped destroy a prison that was holding and running tests on innocent supernaturals, *and* on top of that you destroyed much of the Council's research into mind control."

Fenrick had a point, but I still wasn't sure what it was. "That was selfish," I said. "I needed Grey and the rest of you back. It was entirely for me. I needed my family. I couldn't lose you all after having just found you. As for the others that were released? Well, that was a happy coincidence." I glared at him in frustration.

"They were all innocent. None of us committed the crimes we were accused of. There weren't even any logical crimes, really. Simply existing is the crime they accused *you* of as well, Princess." Fenrick crossed his arms over his chest, looking every bit as defiant as I felt.

"Ugh! I know. I mean... I just don't think I've done all that much to inspire this kind of loyalty. When we've saved Faery and everyone can return home, I might feel worthy. But until then, we need to get a plan together to get rid of the Council once and for all." I stepped past Fenrick to the door behind him.

People were whispering on the other side, and my shoulders slumped as I recognized Ash's voice.

Does he hate me? How can I even face him when I let his brother die?

I squared my shoulders and pushed through the door.

My father was the first to glance up at me, and he was on his feet before I could even take a step into the room. His arms wrapped around me, and I blew out a relieved breath. "I'm so glad you're okay, daughter," he said.

"I'm not exactly sure I am," I admitted, though I embraced him in return. "What information do we have that can help eliminate the Council and stop the humans from targeting supernaturals?" My voice was robotic even to my own ears.

"We know the location of one of the facilities where they are holding more supernaturals. We could rescue them—they can help us in the coming war," said Fenrick.

"How?" I asked, my brow furrowing.

"Zeke was searching for them. He left us all we needed to know." Fenrick hung his head, his voice thick with emotion.

He must have heard what happened to Zeke.

A tear rolled down my cheek as shame and self-pity overwhelmed me, but I nodded for him to continue. My throat practically *burned* with grief, and if I knew that if I tried to talk, it would sound unrecognizable.

"He found one that we could infiltrate. From what I can see, we have a real chance of rescuing these people."

"Given that he's gone now, I think he would want us to go after them. It's the least we can do in his memory. Let's make a plan and free them before more lives are lost," I said with a conviction I didn't feel.

We were going to save the supernaturals... and then we were going to destroy the Council. Zeke deserved that from us.

CHAPTER 4

Grey

I pulled Aurelia against my chest and heaved a sigh of relief, relishing in the feel of my mate's curves and her delicious, familiar scent. It was late—we'd been strategizing all day, trying to figure out how to infiltrate the facility Zeke had located. Weariness tugged at the fringes of my consciousness. The last twenty-four hours had been an emotional and physical whirlwind. "We need to rest and recharge, beautiful," I suggested as I brushed a lock of golden hair from her eyes.

"But I don't want to wait to save them," Aurelia said, suppressing a yawn.

"You almost died less than a day ago," I argued back quietly against her ear. "You need sleep, and I need to hold you.".

The others in the room we'd been deliberating with clearly heard me, but none of them moved or acknowledged our conversation.

Dan cleared his throat, drawing attention to himself with a curt nod.

Good, old, reliable Dan.

"I need to make some calls and organize supplies. I think it's best if we wait. We don't want to go in half-cocked or ill-prepared, not with innocent lives at stake. Let's call it a night."

Aurelia leaned forward as if to rise to her feet, unhappy with the notion of waiting, even if it presented our best chance.

My arms tightened around her. I wasn't letting her off my lap.

She cast a tired and unimpressed glare at me over her shoulder, then proceeded to wiggle her hips.

If she really thinks that's going to be incentive for me to let her up, she is sorely mistaken.

"Stop it, mate," I growled in her ear. "Rest is going to be the last thing on my mind if you keep that up."

Her breath caught in her throat, and she bit her lip.

I squeezed her thigh, rubbing my thumb in slow circles as I held her down against my hard cock. I was always hard when she was near me, but with her wiggling in my lap, it was even more torturous. I needed to show her how much I needed her and soon. She'd almost died, and ever since, we've been planning our next course of action. I had to prove to myself and to my inner wolf that she was still here, that this wasn't all some strange fever dream, and my mate wasn't dead.

"Fine," she huffed. "I don't want to fuck this up. We will go in tomorrow night and rescue them."

I stood in one fluid motion and tossed my mate over my shoulder as if she weighed nothing at all.

Aurelia squeaked in surprise and slapped my ass in playful objection as she hung upside down. "Grey, I can walk!" She pummeled my back with the flats of her palms.

I nipped her ass cheek and continued strolling out of the room to the sound of muffled laughter from the others. I didn't give a fuck. I needed my mate. *Now*. Once out of sight, I raced down the hall to the room that Asher had given us for our stay and kicked the door shut before tossing her on the bed.

"Grey, what are you doing? I thought you wanted to *rest*," she emphasized as she leaned back on her elbows, one prominent brow raised.

"There's plenty of time for that." I pulled my T-shirt over my head with one hand and smirked with a bone-deep satisfaction.

Her gaze followed my movements, her teeth worrying her lower lip.

She is so fucking perfect, and she is all mine.

With a knowing smile, Aurelia sat up on her knees before me and reached for the button of my jeans.

I batted her attempt to undress me away and wrapped her wrists in one of my hands behind her back. My wolf howled and battled to the surface at the knowledge that we had our mate at our mercy. My fingertips shifted to claws, but I was careful not to let the one encircling her wrists scratch her milky skin.

"Grey?" She peered into my eyes. "These don't belong to me."

I traced the back of my claw along her collarbone to the thin strap of material holding the tiny tank top on her body. "I'll buy them new clothes," I growled. Without further discussion I cut both straps and leaned over, licking a hot path down her neck, to her shoulder, and finally to the confluence of her throat where I planned to mark her as mine forever. I nipped the skin there, tasting her.

Aurelia moaned as the tiny tank pooled around her waist, revealing her beautiful, full breasts to my hungry gaze. "I want to touch you too," she protested, struggling in my grip to no avail.

I wasn't letting her go. I would never let her go again. "Lean back and grab the headboard, gorgeous. If you're a good girl, I'll let you touch me all you want."

Her eyes lit up at my words.

Licking my lips, I released her wrists, enjoying the vision before me.

Aurelia pulled the ruined tank top off along with the small sleep shorts, and lay back on the bed, gripping the headboard as she'd been instructed.

"Fuck, you're perfect, mate," I praised, leaning over her and taking her nipple into my mouth, swirling my tongue around her rosy bud before nipping it with just the right amount of force.

Aurelia's back arched, and her breathing grew heavy, but she dutifully refused to let go of the headboard. She knew the rules. We'd played this game before, back at the Syndicate.

I stared up into her eyes, relishing the fact they were already blazing with need. With a devious smile, I plucked at her other nipple with my fingers, teasing as I kissed my way toward it. Then, sucking the nipple into my mouth, I lavished it with the same affection.

"Grey, I need you," Aurelia panted desperately, squirming beneath me as she sought friction. Her hips bucked up to meet mine, but were met by the stiff, fabric barrier of my jeans.

"Patience, my love. You're such a good girl. I want to reward you." My tongue darted out, licking its way down her body to the sensitive spot where I knew she needed me most. I gripped her inner thigh, rubbing my thumbs across all her creamy skin as I pushed her legs as far open as they would go. "I'm going to fuck you with my tongue until you're dripping wet for me," I murmured against her soft stomach. "You're going to be so mindless for me, but you won't take your hands off the headboard will you, my good girl?"

She shook her head in acknowledgement, but didn't answer with words.

"I need you to tell me you won't let go," I said, my tone one of warning.

"I won't let go! *Please*," she begged.

"Please what? What do you need, mate?" I crooned, my breath whispering over her flesh.

"I need you, Grey. I need my mate!" she gasped.

I growled against her stomach, my cock stiffening more than I ever thought possible. My wolf surged to the surface again, responding instinctively to her breathy tone. I barely managed to hold him back from biting her, from making her ours entirely.

I blew out a breath to calm myself and locked the wolf down before running my finger up her slick pussy. "You're already *so* wet for me."

"Yes, Grey," she moaned.

I pushed a single finger inside her and curled it in a way I knew would have her climbing the heights of ecstasy in mere seconds.

She arched back and her head thrashed, nonsensical whimpers tumbling from her lips like fervent prayers.

Pumping my finger inside her, I added a second before circling her swollen clit with my rough thumb.

"Grey, oh, gods!" Aurelia screamed, convulsions wracking through her body. Her walls tightened around my fingers almost painfully as she spasmed repeatedly with her first orgasm. Wave after brutal, rippling wave slammed over her beautiful body, leaving her gasping in their wake.

I stroked her inner thigh as I waited for her to come down. The urge to taste her and the need to feel her wrapped around my cock was overwhelming. My cock throbbed with a life of its own, literally begging for attention. Raising my gaze, I looked up at Aurelia with a grin.

She was still holding on to the headboard with a tight, white-knuckle grip. Her breaths came in shallow pants as she squirmed, driven to desperation by oversensitivity. "Please... I need to touch you." She pouted.

"Not yet, my love," I drawled, eager to draw out her pleasure as I leaned in and lapped at her juices, satisfying my inner wolf.

She groaned low in her throat and wiggled her hips, still blatantly needy even after her first orgasm.

I adored that about her. As a lover, I'd noticed she was never truly satisfied until my cock was buried deep inside her. Knowing everything leading up to that moment was mere foreplay for her, I allowed my tongue to circle her overstimulated clit.

She screamed, the sound swallowed by the room.

Fuck.

Her breathy pants, plaintive whimpers, and lustful screams were everything. Taunting her, I sucked her clit into my mouth and suckled hard and fast, assaulting and worshipping her all at once.

Aurelia's thighs locked around my head, holding me where she needed me as her second orgasm blasted through her. Unable to catch her breath, she screamed my name, her voice breaking in the most beautiful way imaginable, so raw and pure.

I chuckled against her clit, the vibration of my laughter only prolonging her euphoria.

She clenched her thighs harder, her arms straining as she gripped the headboard for dear life, and she came in a great gushing wave.

I supped upon every single drop before her thighs went slack.

With a growl of frustration, she took back control. "Enough! Fuck me, mate," she commanded, her tone oozing royal authority.

It was the sexiest thing I'd heard in my life. Obeying my beautiful future queen, I sat up and got off the bed, tearing at the buttons on my jeans. I needed them off. I needed to be inside her.

She sat up on her knees and clenched her hands repeatedly, getting blood flowing again, before reaching for my open jeans and gripping me through my boxers.

"Fuck, Aurelia," I snarled, my eyes closing momentarily. "I don't know if I can handle you touching me right now..."

"Too bad," she snarked as she rose higher on her knees, leaning in and kissing me hard—tasting herself on my tongue as she rubbed my cock with a feather-light touch. Her free hand explored, running down my shoulder and over my chest.

I shuddered under her attention. "What are you doing to me, Princess?" I groaned.

Aurelia squeezed my cock harder and grinned as she kissed a burning trail down my neck to my shoulder, nipping it lightly before moving further.

My knees buckled, and I twisted to fall back on the bed, pulling her down on top of me.

"I'm going to slowly torture you... the way you did me." She took my nipple between her teeth and smirked. Pain mixed with pleasure as she slowly ran her fingers over my still-clothed cock. She kissed, nipped, and sucked her way down to the waistband of my jeans, a woman on a mission.

I sucked in a sharp breath at her touch, flesh against flesh.

She reached inside my boxers and shoved them down so my cock sprang free.

"Aurelia, stop," I pleaded, but my request lacked any conviction. "If you put your mouth on me, I'm not going to last. I'll be done for. You're too perfect."

With another grin, she refused to listen and ran her tongue up the underside of my shaft, before swirling it around my sensitive, gleaming head.

I growled out her name, reached down and gripped her under her arms, then pulled her swiftly up my body. I meant what I said. I wasn't going to last. I kissed her hard and rubbed my aching cock along her soaking slit.

Despite her desire to torture me in return, her hips bucked against me instinctively, and a soft moan escaped her lips.

"If you want to be in charge, you can, but you're going to do it while riding my cock." Hissing through my teeth at the heady sensation, I pushed her down on my dick, all the way to the hilt.

She tilted her head back in response, her long hair tickling my thighs as she squeezed her eyes closed and simply reveled in the connection between us.

By the gods...

I hadn't realized how much I truly needed her until this moment. My cock twitched inside her, alive with yearning.

My mate held perfectly still as we became one.

I adjusted my hips, my lower lip slack, hitting that sacred spot inside her with the tip of my cock.

Moaning, Aurelia took back control. She circled her hips, before sitting back and raising herself up, bouncing up and down on my shaft.

Fuck me. She is fucking heaven!

"I feel so full, Grey," she whispered huskily. "Fuck, it feels *so* good." She circled her hips again, stoking the fires of my soul, taking her time.

"Baby, I needed you to move." I gripped her hips and lifted her off me almost to the point I was no longer inside her and then slammed her body back down.

Both of us cried out, overwhelmed by the brutal intensity of our shared pleasure.

Aurelia dug her short nails into my chest, leaving angry, red, crescent-shaped marks on my chest.

The little thrill of sharp pain titillated me, drawing out my inner

Alpha even more aggressively. She could mark me as often as she wanted, whenever she wanted.

I am hers.

I lifted her over and over again—using her luscious Fae body like a cock glove—until tingles started in my balls and ran up my spine like tingles of hot lightening. I thrust my hips up into her wildly, pumping furiously as my impending orgasm shook me to my core. At the very last second, I flipped us over in one fluid motion, so that she was beneath me, and threaded my fingers through hers on either side of her head.

I fucked her hard and fast as my cock ached and my balls grew tight, drawing up. A roar exploded from my lips, my voice joining hers as my orgasm stole the wits from me, leaving me seeing stars. I came harder than I ever had before, spurred on by the ecstasy of Aurelia's third release.

Leaning down, I kissed her with a savageness that consumed me and collapsed on top of her, before rolling off to the side and pulling her into my arms.

Aurelia's lust-glazed eyes glowed with love as she stared up at me, her chin resting on my chest.

"I think that was exactly what we needed," I whispered, pressing a gentle kiss to her forehead. "We need to remember what's important now, more than ever. We need to remember what we are fighting for."

Aurelia cleared her throat and licked her lips before answering. "And what if I've forgotten what that is?" she asked, glancing away, her lower lip trembling.

I gripped her chin and turned her back to face me. "What do you think we're fighting for?" I asked, my gaze searching hers.

"Right now, it feels a lot like vengeance," she whispered.

"No, my beautiful girl," I said, brushing her hair aside and trailing the backs of my fingers down her flushed cheek. "We aren't fighting for vengeance. We're fighting for the right to live and be free, to love who we want without persecution. And when the time is right, we *will* defeat the Council because they are fighting for nothing but greed and power. Their cause is corrupt, while ours is just, Aurelia. We will prevail because our very lives depend on it."

Aurelia sighed and nodded against me, a single, glistening tear leaking from the corner of her eye. "We have to fight," she agreed, "for all those who aren't strong enough to fight for themselves—and for those we've already lost."

CHAPTER 5
Aurelia

Anxiety and nervous energy thrummed through me. I was fidgeting… I knew it, and everyone else did too, but I couldn't help it.

Grey wrapped his hand around both of mine to stop me with a subtle, empathetic smile.

"The last break-in didn't go so well," I mumbled by way of explanation.

We lost Zeke. He's dead because shit went south.

"Plans were changed on the fly last time. It was unavoidable, Aurelia. But we have planned this from start to finish, and no one here is going to change those plans. I promise you we're prepared this time." Grey squeezed my hand, offering me his silent strength and support.

"A million things could go wrong," I argued anxiously as I chewed my bottom lip, fighting my anxiety within myself like it was a physical beast to be slayed or shoved back down into the pit from whence it came.

"It could also go smoothly, baby. Now, more than ever, you must have faith that we're exactly where we are meant to be." He leaned back in the driver's seat of his SUV as we waited for the signal.

"What about Dan and Fenrick? They have to set it off."

Ash patted my shoulder from the back seat, his hulking figure offering a semblance of comfort in his brother's absence. "Stop worrying, Princess. They're both skilled warriors. They won't fail you."

It almost sounded like they were doing this *just for me* and not the good of all supernaturals, from the way he said it. And I didn't know how I felt about that. I didn't want them to fail—it was the very last thing I wanted. But if they did, they wouldn't be failing me... they'd be failing us all. We were here for everyone, after all, not just a special few.

Grey tensed noticeably.

My senses immediately became hyper-aware in response. I turned to him just as an explosion rattled the windows of the SUV. Fire and smoke rose from behind the building we were watching, and I shoved open the door, breathless as I drank in the sight.

We all scrambled from the vehicle, ready to execute our plan.

Fenrick appeared in front of us with a grin. "Time to go." He placed a hand on my shoulder, the other on Grey's, and sifted us into the building.

I stumbled slightly as the word lurched.

Grey reached out, his hand on my arm steadying me as we appeared in a dark room.

Dan stood in front of us, his gaze far off as he stared at something I couldn't see.

"Dan?" I asked, my voice catching in my throat.

Something is wrong.

He spun around, his eyes wide and glistening with emotion.

I gasped at the glimpse I got from behind him. "No!" I gasped, my stomach convulsing inside me, rebelling at the gut-churning sight before us.

"What?" Grey asked, his brow furrowed. He marched forward to peer around Dan and stopped still. "What the fuck are they doing?" he breathed.

The scene before me was like something straight out of a horror movie. The large rectangular window Dan stood in front of was a viewing window. Ultraviolet lights glowed in the room beyond. Beds lined the walls in rows and supernaturals lay in them, unconscious, with countless tubes coming out of them as IV bags pumped a bright blue liquid directly into their veins.

"What is going on?" I asked in shock, the sour taste of stomach acid in my mouth. "Is this a testing facility?"

"It is," Fenrick growled. "But I never even imagined it would be like this, though. They're not testing anything... they're just killing them,"

"This is fucked! How are we supposed to get everyone out when they're hooked up to tubes? And how do we even know if we disconnect them, that they'll survive what they've had forced into their bodies, already?" I hugged myself and hung my head.

We didn't think this through. We weren't prepared for anything! How could we rescue these people when we didn't even have enough help?

"The facility is huge. Maybe the Shadow Warriors are in a different section," Fenrick said as he patted my shoulder.

"They're all shifters," Grey said, sniffing the air and engaging his keen senses. "They aren't going to last much longer in here. We need to get them out *now.*"

I squeezed Grey's hand in comfort despite how physically and emotionally sick I felt. As the Shifter King, and their ultimate Alpha, I knew he could feel their torment. This had to be the hardest on him.

"Fenrick, can you go and get my parents? We need as many Fae that are on our side to sift these people out." I glanced at my childhood protector, my eyes beseeching him.

Fenrick nodded dutifully and sifted from the room in an instant.

Something doesn't feel right. How are we able to sift in and out at all, let alone undetected? It doesn't make sense.

“Is the Council getting sloppy?” I wondered aloud.

“Why would you think that?” Grey asked, cracking his knuckles one by one.

“Doesn’t this seem too easy to you? We sifted in undetected, and despite the explosion, there’s no alarms, no swarms of guards?”

“Maybe they think the human government got to us first? They may have assumed their facilities were no longer in need of maximum security.” Grey folded his arms over his chest.

Fenrick popped back in a minute later with both my parents and the Shadow Guardian who’d helped me get out of Faery when I was trapped there.

I sighed in relief. They were here to help get these people out of here and in this instance, it was a case of “the more, the merrier”. I rushed to the door next to the viewing window and wrenched it open, not wanting to waste another minute. A siren blared as soon as I stepped through the door, and I froze.

So much for no security...

“Fuck!” I shouted over the blaring noise. “We need to get them all out of here immediately!”

My parents and the Guardian jumped into action, unhooking the slew of shifters as quickly as possible and sifting several of them out at once.

“Come on.” Grey gripped my hand and dragged me through another door at the other end of the room. This room was more of the same, and I deflated. We had our work cut out for us. How on earth were we going to get everyone out of here with the sirens blaring and guards most likely closing in on us? I spun in a circle, searching for someone—anyone—who could help us get some of the shifters out.

A man sat up in a bed at the other end of the room, catching my gaze. His eyes glimmered with hope as he stared at me.

“Grey, the Fae are in this room!” I ran to the man and pulled the wires from his arms and unbuckled the straps around his wrists and ankles. “Can you walk?” I asked breathlessly.

“Princess Aurelia, I knew you would come.” The man bowed his head to me.

"Less bowing and more getting the fuck out of here," I grumbled, still hating the bowing and scraping thing.

I don't think I'll ever get used to that! Ugh.

Grey chuckled apologetically. "She doesn't like that. We also don't have a lot of time. Is everyone here Fae?"

"Yes," he answered. "Mostly guards from the Shadow Kingdom who refused to fall in line." The man jumped from the cot and stumbled slightly, holding his head as if he felt woozy or disoriented.

"Easy, there. You've been tied to that bed for a while, I'm guessing." Grey reached out and gripped his arm, helping to steady him.

"I've been here for a long time," the Fae grumbled. "I just need a second to get my bearings."

"We may not have a second. Can you sift?" I glanced back at the door with growing apprehension. The deafening sirens continued to wail as I scanned the room. I glanced up at the ceiling and groaned. In each corner was a dome with a blinking red light on it.

They're recording everything that happens here. Fuck!

"We're being watched," I warned them. "They're probably waiting to ambush us at any second." I straightened my spine, on edge.

Grey rushed over to the next nearest gurney where another man was struggling, and helped remove the tubes from his body.

The man stood quickly, seemingly having fared a little better than the first man we assisted, and the two of them went to work on the rest of the men in the room.

"Come on! We need to keep moving, or there's no way we'll get everyone out of here!" Grey urged, running back and reaching for my arm.

We moved through the room, making good progress, to find another door, unfortunately locked.

I shoved against it, but it wouldn't budge. "Stand back," I said to Grey. Without waiting, I let a small trickle of magic fill my palm and flung it at the door. A deafening boom filled the space a heartbeat later.

Grey launched himself at me, tackling me to the floor, shielding me with his body as debris sailed over our heads and smoke billowed from the now open doorway.

"We could have thought of a better way, Aurelia," Grey chided.

"We don't have time for all that," I grunted beneath him. "There could be more that need saving!"

His big shifter body was too heavy for me to move, so he rolled to the side and hopped to his feet, reaching a hand down to me.

Dan pushed through the main door we'd entered, his eyes wild. "What happened?" He stared at the burning rubble that was once a door.

"That was me." I grinned.

Grey grabbed the fire extinguisher and blasted the door with it until the flames died down, and we could walk into the next room. Even more beds filled the room, supernaturals lying in them unconscious.

How many of my people are being held in this awful place?

The door at the other end of the room flew open, and men flooded through it one by one in tactical attire.

I backed up into Grey and turned to him, my stomach dropping, and my heartrate increasing tenfold.

His eyes were widened in the opposite direction, at the door we'd just come through. "Fuck," he growled.

More Council soldiers were blocking our exit, and we weren't any closer to getting the others out. There had to be *hundreds* of beds in this room. It was easily ten times larger than the ones before. "What are we going to do?" I asked, panicking. "None of us can sift!"

I would be able to sift eventually, but I had yet to learn how.

Is now the time to experiment? Probably not...

But if we couldn't figure something else out before we were captured, then I would have to try my best and pray to the gods it worked.

The guards filed in with batons in their hands, raising them threateningly as they lit up with electricity.

Fenrick popped in and cursed before gripping onto two of the gurneys and sifting right out again a mere second later.

We are on our own. Fuck! We're in so much trouble. What the hell are we going to do?

I pooled magic in my palms and scanned the crowd of about twenty guards on my end. Another twenty were poised for action on Grey's side, and there were only three of us. The odds were well and truly stacked against us.

"You need to try to sift back, Aurelia!" Grey grabbed my arm and turned me to face him, his expression one of utter and bereft seriousness.

"I can't!" I shook my head, my chest aching with the pressure.

The man nearest to me smirked.

I recognized him as one of the men who'd captured us outside the prison. He wasn't the asshole who'd wanted to keep me as a toy, but he was just as bad. From what I'd heard, Grey had personally killed the man who tried to lay claim to me. But I wasn't losing sleep over that. He'd deserved to die for his crimes against his own people. I only wished I could have been there to see it.

Shit. Maybe I'm becoming bloodthirsty when it comes to the Council... Oh well.

More magic pooled in my hands as I gazed around the room at all the supernaturals they were keeping in stasis or slowly killing. How was I supposed to get them out of here when I couldn't sift? Dan and Grey couldn't either. Dan was only half-Fae and Grey was a wolf shifter. We were completely stuck.

"Give yourselves up and no one gets hurt!" the Fae guard roared in warning, not humoring us any longer.

The others fanned out around him and held up their batons. There was nowhere to go.

Power buzzed beneath my skin as I held my ground.

I'm not leaving without my people, asshole.

The guard smirked like he knew whatever I was planning wasn't going to be so easy.

It wasn't. I couldn't let it be easy for them. They'd hurt too many of us and caused chaos in the human world. If they were going to catch me, they were going to have to work for it! Shadows writhed around my arms as more magic than I had ever used before built inside me, buzzing like a swarm of angry bees.

The men attacked as one, but they were too late.

A blinding light mixed with swirling shadows shot forth from my palms in a beautiful and terrifying cacophony of magic.

The guards screamed and ducked, but it was to no avail. Every last one of them was burned to ashes in seconds.

Frantically, I turned to Grey and Dan, but they were fine. I breathed a painful sigh of relief, but the magic writhing inside me was like a living thing. It knew we wouldn't be safe until we got everyone out of here. I closed my eyes tightly and focused with all my might, imagining the infirmary at the Syndicate.

I need everyone out of this building and healing!

Magic erupted from me in a blinding wave that knocked the breath out of me, and I swirled through time and space as I sifted for the first time! I stumbled as my feet hit solid ground, and strong arms wrapped around me, keeping me upright.

"You are truly incredible, Aurelia," Grey said, squeezing me to the comfort of his solid, warm, and sturdy chest. His eyes weren't on me, though. They were on the hundreds of Fae and shifters that had still been in beds in the facility.

I slumped into Grey's chest, but my relief was short-lived as complete and utter exhaustion took over, stealing the legs from under me. If Grey hadn't been holding me, I would have slumped to the ground and passed out. Instead, I blacked out, safe in his arms instead, one last thought flashing through my mind with beautiful, crystal-clear clarity.

I did it.

CHAPTER 6
Grey

"A couple hundred warriors are great," I said as I ran a hand down my face. "But they still won't be enough. Not by a long shot."

Aurelia was fast asleep on my lap, wiped out from her overuse of incredibly powerful magic.

Fenrick checked her over to make sure she wasn't in distress or injured.

I was more than thankful for the Guardian. He cared about her almost as much as I did. Or maybe he loved her every bit as much as I did, but just in a different way. He'd cared for her and known her since she was a child.

"They won't be well enough to march into battle for a couple days," Fenrick warned. "They've been through a lot."

"What are we going to do?" I asked with a hint of frustration. "The Council soldiers still outnumber us."

Dan tapped his index finger on the golden book, his brow raised in query. "Did Aurelia end up finding anything that could help us get rid of them yet?"

My mate stirred in my arms temporarily and sighed before laying her head back on my shoulder, drifting off once more.

"Not yet," I conceded. "She's been looking but hasn't found anything concrete." I shifted her slightly in my arms, so she was more comfortable.

Aurelia's body suddenly stiffened, and she shot upright in my lap, nearly headbutting my chin. Her eyes wild and alert, she panicked. "Where are they? Did we get them all out?"

"Easy, love," I soothed. "They're all in the infirmary, recovering." I rubbed her back in comforting circles. "You got everyone out and turned the guards responsible for maintaining that hellhole to ash."

Her shoulders slumped, but she relaxed against me.

I wasn't sure if it was in relief or guilt for killing the guards.

It's probably a bit of both.

"What were you just discussing?" Aurelia yawned. She was still exhausted.

I hated that she wouldn't take the time for a proper rest after expending so much magic. I didn't even bother suggesting it because I already knew what her answer would be. She was stubborn, determined, and just wanted to end the Council's reign of tyranny against our people every bit as much as I did.

"Even with the Shadow Warriors recovered from the facility, we don't have the manpower to take on the Council. We still need more help." I squeezed her hip affectionately with a grimace.

"Shit," she breathed. "What do we do? We could break into the other facilities Zeke had on his radar, but those people aren't warriors, they're civilians." She tapped my hand and moved to stand.

I held her firmly in my lap, unwilling to let go just yet.

"We need to come up with a plan. We need more help," she said, reiterating what I'd said moments before.

A knock sounded on the door to the office. "Come in," I called out to whoever waited on the other side to come in. Everyone knew not to disturb us unless it was vitally important, and by the scent reaching me, I had to guess it was Magna.

Has she had some kind of vision?

Sure enough, Magna pushed through the door a second later with a glint in her eye. "I've got a possible solution," she announced. "But it's not going to be easy."

I scoffed and chuckled, shaking my head. "When is anything ever easy?" I asked, a single eyebrow raised.

"Do you want to know the solution, or are you going to just snark at me?" Magna asked, mimicking me with a prominent brow of her own.

"Sorry, yes," I backtracked. "Tell us, what's the plan?" I knew Magna wasn't one to beat around the bush, even if she was as mysterious as the dark side of the moon.

"There is a group of rebels in Faery and their numbers are growing every day. With the rebels' help, we will have enough people to take down the Council." Magna sat heavily in the chair from which Dan had stood.

Dan ran a hand through his hair, pursing his lips. "You want us to go to Faery?" he asked.

"The two of us are needed here," advised Magna with a shake of her head. "You need to work with our recovering army to get them ready."

"Who did you see going to Faery?" Aurelia asked, sitting up straighter on my lap, her gaze focused on the seer.

I wished like hell that she would stay behind where it was the safest, but I knew that would never happen. My strong-willed mate would never let us go off into danger and leave her behind to babysit the operation here.

"Your father must go," she said. "So, that means Fenrick will volunteer. The two of you must also go, of course, so Asher will likely volunteer his protection."

She wasn't wrong. Ash had become very attached to Aurelia. He protected her just like Zeke had. I'd never seen the Riders of the Hunt care about something or someone other than their bikes and each other, but they definitely cared about the princess.

Ash crossed his arms over the massive bulk of his chest. "You would be right about that. I'm not letting the princess go back into enemy territory without me again."

"It turned out just fine last time, Ash," Aurelia said, grinning.

"You were *lucky* last time," he countered. "This time, you'll be protected at all costs." He glared down at her, not taking *no* for an answer.

"I don't need a babysitter, but fine," Aurelia answered. "If Magna has seen that we all go together, I won't stop you from coming with us."

"All right, then," I said. "Everyone go and grab what you need, but not more than you can carry. We'll likely need to change into Fae clothes once we get there to blend anyway." I squeezed Aurelia and helped her stand.

We're going back to Faery. What could possibly go wrong?

With our plan to keep it light, we didn't need to grab clothes, and Aurelia was a weapon in her own right, but I still grabbed a dagger and a weapon belt for her to wear while we were in Faery. Everyone there had magic and likely wouldn't hesitate to use it, so having additional protection couldn't hurt.

"Do I really need this?" Aurelia asked, her nose scrunching. "You've seen what I can do..."

I clipped the belt around her waist. "Better to have it and not need it, than need it and not have it."

The others met us in the garage not long after I got her sorted. "Are we ready to go?" I asked. There was no point delaying if Magna had already seen events unfolding. It was obviously what needed to happen, one way or another, if we were to stand a chance of defeating the Council.

All our friends and allies nodded.

Our minds made up, we trusted our future to Fate and raced out past the wards surrounding the grounds of the Syndicate.

Aurelia frowned. "How did I manage to sift us into the building?" she asked.

"I don't know," I admitted as I squeezed her shoulder. "I guess you're even more powerful than the wards. You are the Shadow Princess, after all."

"That's only slightly terrifying." She groaned.

"Why?" Ash asked from next to me. "It's a good thing you're powerful enough to take care of yourself."

"Power corrupts," she countered. "Just look at the Council. I don't want to be end up corrupted like them." She shook her head and swallowed hard.

"The mere fact you're worried about that possibility tells me something, mate." I said, glancing at her drawn features.

"What does it tell you?" she asked.

"That you could never be corrupted," Ash answered before I could.

I glared at him with a hint of humor.

That was my line.

She could never become corrupt like the Council. She was too pure, and the fact that she was worrying about having too much power for good and honest reasons proved it.

"He's right, my love. I was just about to say that exact same thing."

"Are you sure?" Her expression was skeptical, her tone uncertain.

"Absolutely," I said when we made it through the last, and strongest of the outer wards.

Aurelia didn't shudder like she usually did when she passed through them. She frowned in confusion. But it made sense that if she was stronger than the magic holding the wards in place that she wouldn't feel the effects of walking through them anymore. She'd truly come into her power, and when she learned to harness it completely, she'd be the greatest force to be reckoned with all of Faery

Fenrick lay a hand on my shoulder and his other on Aurelia's.

The king placed his on Ash.

It was time. We had a mission, and it was time to execute it with or without a plan. We needed to get to Faery and try to recruit the rebels to our cause. The goal seemed simple enough, but the means of achieving it remained elusive.

I swirled through time and space as we sifted to Faery once again, breathing out a sigh when we landed in the forest just outside the Shadow Kingdom.

"There's a small village close by where we can get information," Fenrick said, jumping straight into action.

"Then let's go," Aurelia announced and waved a hand for him to lead the way.

We picked our way through the forest and around the brush on our journey.

Aurelia occasionally laid her hand upon a tree, smiling softly as it spoke to her through her inherent bond with the land. When we were just inside the tree line, she stopped and frowned. "Something isn't right," she warned. "The trees want us to stop and go in the other direction."

"Why?" I asked as we came to a temporary halt.

"Danger," she answered simple and shook her head. "Their method of communication is beautiful, but very basic. All they know is that the town is dangerous to us."

"Should I glamour myself and take a look?" Fenrick asked, unwilling to place the princess in danger.

Aurelia tilted her head to the side as if she were listening to them. "They don't like that idea either, but it's worth a shot."

"I'll go with you," I said, determined to get eyes on the situation myself. "If you can glamour me too?"

"I can do that. Princess, you stay here with Asher and your father. We'll be right back." Fenrick stared at Aurelia, likely expecting her to argue.

Instead, she nodded. "Good idea. Go scope it out. No one goes alone. We need to stick together."

Fenrick's eyes widened in shock when she didn't argue, but the expression was quickly replaced with one of determination. The Guardian turned his stare on me.

Magic tingled along my skin, making me shiver. "Is it done?" I asked. My voice sounded lower and rougher than I'd ever heard before. I'd had no idea a glamour could change the pitch of my voice as well as my appearance.

He inclined his head. "It's done. Let's go see what we can find out." Fenrick stormed across the tree line, ever the dutiful Guardian.

I jogged up next to him and crossed my arms over my chest.

What are we even looking for in this tiny town? I seems unlikely the rebels would have their base set up in such a small place.

Fenrick squared his shoulders and marched to the town like he was still a soldier working for the king. Having that kind of attitude in unknown territory could be dangerous if he wasn't careful. We needed to blend in with the locals, after all, not give them a reason to turn us over to the Council.

Unexpectedly, something drew my attention. "Shit," I cursed.

Fenrick turned to me with a frown.

I pointed at a sign in the town square. Wanted posters were plastered all over the town's message board. I strolled up to the board as casually as I could while dread coursed through my body like liquid ice.

"What are they?" Fenrick whispered as he glanced at the board as well.

"They're wanted posters. They have rewards out for us even here," I mumbled.

There was a picture of me that must have been taken without my knowledge when I was at the prison, and one of Fenrick, and the king as well. Aurelia's picture, meanwhile, was hand drawn and looked like it could be just about any pretty female in Faery.

"Can you read what they say?" I asked quietly.

"Basically, if any of these people are spotted in Faery, they are to be turned over to the Council guards immediately. The reward is no taxes for a full year." Fenrick clenched his fist.

"What do you mean, no taxes?" I asked. "I didn't think the kingdoms believed in taxation. They have enough land to remain powerful and employ the common Fae to tend to it all."

Is this the Council's doing? Are they taxing the citizens of Faery to keep them weak and under their control?

"The king never taxed his people. So, I don't know what this means, but we need to find out and stop it." Fenrick spun on his heel and stomped back to the tree line.

I followed close behind him, fuming as I made sure to avoid unnecessary eye contact. Even glamoured, I didn't want us to draw attention to ourselves.

How can the Council just start taxing the people when they've never been taxed before?

It was disgusting. And then to add insult to injury, the reward for turning the true good guys of Faery over was a return to their normal way of life for a year.

We burst through the trees, ready to relay what we'd learned.

Ash tensed, stepping in front of Aurelia like a mountain of man before he realized it was us in glamour, and relaxed.

"The Council is even more corrupt than we realized, Your Majesty," Fenrick revealed and hung his head.

"What is it now?" the Shadow King asked, his brow creased with concern.

"They are *taxing* the citizens of the Shadow Kingdom," Fenrick growled.

"Taxing?" Aurelia questioned. "Don't taxes just help keep a kingdom running?"

"No, my daughter," said the king. "That's just what the humans claim. The Fae have never taxed their people. We help keep our people fed by employing them to tend the land and giving them opportunities to be productive with what skills they possess. This is disgusting and a betrayal of our ways."

"Also," Fenrick said with an apologetic grimace. "They have bounties on all our heads. The most desperate will try to hand us over to the Council for the reward."

"So, what's the bounty?" Ash asked, folding his arms over his chest. "What are the Fae willing to betray the royal family for?"

"One year of no taxes," I growled.

"So, we basically need to treat everyone in this realm as if they are an enemy, or we could get captured by the Council?" Aurelia chewed her lower lip, the delicate skin whitening where her teeth pressed down.

"This development has just made our lives a hundred times harder," Fenrick bemoaned as he scrubbed a hand down his face.

"So, everyone needs to be glamoured, and no one goes anywhere alone, just like Aurelia already suggested. We need to stay on our toes.

Desperate people do desperate things, and we don't want to be casualties of a war before it's truly begun," I said with a huff.

This is fucking bad. How are we going to find the rebels while dodging desperate Fae? If any of our glamours slip or our plan gets tripped up...

The outcome didn't bear thinking about. It was far too dire to even contemplate.

CHAPTER 7

"We still need to go into town," I reasoned. "What if the rebels are there and we miss them?" I shuffled my feet anxiously. We couldn't just skip the town because there were signs plastered on the noticeboard asking for information on us... even if they were putting bounties on our heads. We needed information, no matter how dangerous it was to obtain.

"I doubt the rebels will have made this tiny village their base of operations," Grey said skeptically as he peered around the forest.

"They most likely didn't," I agreed. "But shouldn't we at least check it out before making assumptions? It will save us time in the long run. We don't want to miss anything that could prove vital." I crossed my arms over my chest. I wasn't going to back down on this issue. We weren't going to make progress if we started doing things in a half-assed manner.

If we're all in, then we're all in, and that's that.

"Okay," Grey conceded. "But we all need to be glamoured before we go in. Desperate people do desperate things, and they can't be held responsible for those actions. Faery is living in tyranny, and the people are panicked." Grey ran his hand down his face, revealing his frustration.

"Glamours? Is that all? That, I can do!" I grinned. I had been glamouring my wings for as long as I could remember.

How hard can it be to change my appearance?

I closed my eyes, focusing on what I wanted, and allowed a trickle of magic to pour from my core to my limbs to coat every inch of me like a shimmering, magical, gossamer blanket. I imagined red hair and brown eyes to mask my blonde hair and blue eyes. When I was certain I had achieved my goal, I opened my eyes, everyone's shocked expressions meeting mine.

"Very good, daughter." My father nodded with approval.

"You look completely different!" Grey grinned. "You're really getting a hang of your magic instinctually now, beautiful."

Despite the serious nature of our mission, I couldn't help but feel my cheeks flush with heat at his comment. It felt good to have my growing skills recognized and praised. "And what about Ash?" I asked, pushing my butterflies back down. "He's not Fae. How is he going to blend in?"

"I'll glamour him," Father said, turning to Asher. "If he will allow me."

"Of course, Your Majesty." Ash nodded, turning to the king.

It was the first time I'd ever heard the Rider show deference to my father as the Shadow King. He called me Princess all the time, but I couldn't remember him ever addressing my father that way. I glanced between the two of them with a shrug.

The Shadow King summoned his power forth and poured a strong glamour over the huge Rider, disguising him with ease. Next, he glamoured himself. It was amazing to witness. My father and Asher looked nothing like their true selves at all. There was no way they could possibly be recognized.

Grey wrapped an arm around me, and we looked like a completely random Fae couple from the lower, working class. We picked our way through the underbrush and crossed the tree line into the little village.

"This town mainly consisted of people who once worked the fields for the palace," my father said as he casually glanced around.

"And now they are doing what?" I asked, keeping my tone low and conversational.

"I don't know," he admitted. "But if the Council is taxing them, then they are basically indentured slaves at this point." He clenched his hands into fists by his sides, keeping his royal anger in check.

"They need to be stopped," I whispered back. My father might be trying to hide it, but I felt a unique connection with both my parents, not dissimilar to what I felt with my mate, and I knew how they were feeling even if they were presenting a poker face to the rest of the world. My dad was like a bomb about to explode, his lethal rage simmering just below the surface, and I understood why. Seeing our people like this was difficult, to say the least.

We strolled through the town, peering at the drawn faces of all those around us. This isn't how I remembered this small village. When I was little, it had always been lively, with smiling Fae and an atmosphere of friendliness. Now, everyone glared at one another with suspicion.

What's happened to them? Is the Council truly so abominable as to keep its own people as slaves?

Who was I kidding?

Of course, they are.

As we walked through the town, whispers started to follow us. The gazes of the suffering townspeople were distrusting and accusatory. They brooked no compassion.

I imagined they had none left to give if things were as terrible as they seemed.

"Shit," my father breathed from behind me.

That does not sound good.

I don't think I'd heard my father ever curse until now. I turned my shocked gaze on him. "What?" I asked, my gaze roaming over the growing crowd.

He nodded to a man standing in a nearby doorway. "Thomas can see through glamours."

"How?" I hissed, but there was no time for explanations.

"My King," the man mumbled, stepping forward. "How could you abandon us like this?"

My father's shoulders slumped at the accusation. "I didn't abandon you," he tried to reassure the disgruntled Fae. "Hold onto hope, my friend. We are here to fix everything."

"There is no hope left," Thomas said flatly, shaking his head. "They are making us work your fields and are giving us just enough in return to sustain one person—even those of us who have families. Everything else they take for their army. They take *everything.*"

"We're going to stop them," I said evenly, stepping toward Thomas with a placating gesture.

"I'm sorry, my king," he apologized, "but I have to feed my family." Thomas glanced away, his lips pursed.

"What are you talking about?" I asked, my brows furrowing as I searched his face.

A moment later Thomas made a hand signal and suddenly we were surrounded by Council guards. "Forgive me."

My father nodded to the man, at a loss. He couldn't blame him. He certainly understood but had hoped to be afforded the chance to set things right.

Swords were drawn all around us, but there was something off about these guards I noticed quickly. Their eyes were blank, just like the human Secret Service agents that attacked us outside of the ball.

"I thought Fae were taught to shield their minds from a young age?" I asked, glancing between my father and Fenrick.

"They are," Fenrick said, stepping up to my side, ever ready to defend me.

"Then how are they being controlled?" I hissed. Magic pooled in my palms in response to my hammering heart rate and the danger surrounding us. I controlled my magic, but in dire circumstances it seemed to have a mind of its own.

Without warning the guards rushed forward.

Ash used his elemental magic to shove them back, but it didn't work for long. There were ten of them and only five of us. We'd survived far worse odds before, but we'd always been in the human realm.

Now, we were surrounded by innocent Fae and everyone in the village had magic. And as Grey had highlighted earlier, it was more than possible that any of them would do whatever they could to capture us, if for no other reason than to simply be able to feed their families. The scent of desperation grew thick in the air, pungent and choking. The promise of a year without taxes and more food to feed those they loved was too tempting for people who had been starving.

"What do you mean, they are being controlled?" my father asked.

"Their eyes are just like the Secret Service agents' in Dallas. They aren't just soldiers following orders, they've been robbed of their free will!" I threw a small ball of magic at the encroaching guards.

They dove out of the way before the magic could hit them.

Grey slid in front of me and growled, my beautiful, fierce, and powerful mate. My protector. "We can't worry about that. *We* need to get out of here."

"We've drawn quite a crowd," Fenrick observed with a grimace.

I glanced over my shoulder to find a small sea of angry Fae staring at us like they wanted to kill us all.

Well, isn't that just fucking great?

What were we going to do now that we were surrounded by even more enemies? And I was using the term enemies extremely loosely. Most of those now baying for our blood were our poor people merely trying to survive. They felt used, hurt, and betrayed, and more than anyone, I understood that feeling all too well. "I don't want to hurt them." I sighed. "They're just desperate Fae that need our help."

"We can't help them if the Council get their hands on you again, Princess," said Fenrick, clapping a hand on my shoulder.

"I don't know how much longer I can hold them off, Princess," Ash grunted as he continued to use his elemental powers to hold the guards at bay.

"We're going to have to fight our way out, Aurelia. It's the only way," Grey said over his shoulder.

My shadows pulsed and writhed along my arms as I allowed magic to pool in my palms. I couldn't help but wonder what might happen if the guards were no longer under the control of the Council. Would they be on our side, or would they still come after us? "Let them come, Ash," I said heavily. "We aren't getting out of here any faster this way."

Ash dropped his magic begrudgingly and raised his fists, ready for hand-to-hand combat.

The guards rushed forward like a swarm of angry wasps.

Grey pulled the sword from his side and rushed the nearest guards. My loyal men, my family, friends, and allies formed a circle around me, swords drawn—creating a shield of bodies—and began battle with the Council guards.

My magic pulsed in my hands, bright and glimmering, while my shadows writhed down my arms, mixing together to form a huge sphere of sparkling shadow. I blinked down at the magic, my heart racing and gut wrenching, unsure if I should use it.

What will it do to the desperate and innocent Fae around me?

The memory of my shadows and magic melting the skin off the guards who'd assaulted me at the facility returned to me, and I grimaced.

No! I don't want my magic to do that. I want to help these people. They are not my enemy. They are my people!

With my intentions clear, I sent a silent prayer to the gods, and magic shot from my body in every direction like a blast wave. It knocked every enemy on the ground, but my friends immediately around me remained standing. I stumbled at the magical toll on my body and covered my eyes, hoping against hope that I hadn't just made a terrible mistake and incinerated the entire damn village.

I could never live with myself if I'd hurt all the innocent people in this place. A town I used to frequent and play as a child... a town where there was once joy, prosperity and love. I covered my face with my hands, not daring to look upon the possible carnage. BScreams of anguish and agony never came.

Someone grabbed my hands, and my breath caught in my throat, but I'd recognize Grey's presence anywhere.

He pulled my hands away from my face and grinned at me, his expression one of wonder. "What did you just do?" he asked, standing directly in front of me, most likely so I couldn't glimpse the silent carnage I'd unleashed upon the town.

"Are they all dead?" I choked out, my heart tangibly aching in my chest as if someone were squeezing it and purposely digging in their nails.

A groan met my ears, and then another, and another.

What the hell have I done? Are they all dying cruel, slow deaths?

I couldn't take not knowing a moment longer. I needed to know what I'd done to these poor people. I moved to the side and glanced over Grey's shoulder, my throat tight with tension.

The guards were all blinking as if dazed and confused and were holding their heads.

"What happened?" one of them asked. "My head's all... fuzzy."

I blinked back at the Fae man. His eyes were no longer blank. They were alert and showed a presence of mind, though they were very evidently confused.

Did I actually lift their mind control?

I dropped my glamour and stood directly in front of him, stepping around my mate to speak with him. "Do you know who I am?" I asked.

He instantly dropped his face to the ground in a deep bow.

The rest of the guards, his comrades, all followed suit.

"Your Highness..." he breathed. "What's happened? They told us you were dead."

"I'm sorry to be the bearer of bad news. They had you under mind control." I shook my head in dismay and motioned for them all to rise.

The Fae guard's eyes widened, and he met my gaze with a horrified expression. "I remember now! They put us in prison for refusing to join their ranks. We refused to stand against the royal family. But how did we end up here?" He glanced at the others,

The small contingent all shrugged, none the wiser than he.

"They somehow figured out how to mind control the Fae despite our learned mind blocks. It's extremely concerning," I answered.

"How many of the guards here are actually working for the Council of their own free will?" Grey asked, interjecting in the search of knowledge.

"I don't know." Fenrick peered around at the townspeople. "But we need to get out of here before these Fae call more guards."

"You have a choice to make," I said to the guards. "We're leaving here, now. Are you with us or the Council?"

"We want to take those snakes down," the same man said, looking to his fellow soldiers.

"Then we need a way out of here without these Fae following us. Do you know a place that's safe, at least for a time?" I asked.

"We don't know what's safe anymore, Princess. And what's worse? We can't remember what atrocities we may have committed while under their control. We're so sorry, Princess," he said speaking for them all. "We have failed our kingdom." He hung his head.

The other guards mirrored his remorse, clearly in agreement.

"None of that's your fault," I said, "but we really need to get out of here." I glanced around the village. There were so many Fae...

"I think I know a place," Grey growled with a frown. "That is, if it's still even there and warded after all these years."

"Are you helping us or the Council?" I asked the ten men around us. "You need to decide *now*. We aren't taking anyone with us who intends to assist the Council."

The men all dropped to their knees again and bowed to me.

"I swear fealty to the Princess of the Shadow Court," said the first Fae guard. "I swear my sword and my protection to any monarch to come after Princess Aurelia and her Shifter King."

The others echoed his oath, awaiting my command.

I was stunned but breathed out a relieved sigh.

They're actually on our side!

Things were starting to look up if we were already adding more trained soldiers to our ranks and cause.

Was it possible that there were others in Faery who were also under the Council's poisonous influence? And if we found them, could I lift the mind control on all of them the way I had these men to build ourselves an army?

"Please, rise now. We need to run. The locals are getting restless." I peered around at the villagers and swallowed. They didn't want to hurt us, I was sure, but their survival was more important than their morals.

The Council had the realm right where they wanted it. The Fae would do anything to survive, and I had a feeling that was exactly why Ronaldo had started taxing them. It was disgusting, and I had every intention of destroying him for it. He'd already earned his death by my hand a hundred times over—but this was going *too* far. Making starving innocents choose between their loyalty to their benevolent monarchs or their very own flesh and blood? It filled me with a rage so cold, I even frightened myself.

"Let's go." Grey wrapped a hand around my wrist and pulled me away from the soldiers.

"Wait!" I pulled against my mate and turned back to the Shadow Guards. "Can you sift us out? Perhaps to somewhere in the forest, where the townspeople won't be able to follow?"

"Yes, Your Highness," the same man said, bowing his head as he held out his hand to me.

Grey got there first. "You take us together, and do *not* touch my mate," he growled low in his throat.

I stared up at Grey with wide eyes. He was always possessive, but why was he acting like this with new allies? The guard had sworn fealty to me as had the others. They weren't going to hurt me. I seriously needed to have a talk with him and the others about the overprotective bullshit they were constantly pulling. It was getting stifling, especially when we all knew *I* was the key to stopping the Council. I couldn't do whatever it was I'd eventually need to do if they kept me locked within the suffocating bubble of their protection.

The loyal Shadow Guard simply nodded in response and took Grey's hand without complaint or question.

He's sworn fealty to Grey and our future children as well… that's good enough for me.

Apparently, Grey wasn't as easily convinced. He pulled me into his arms, and we were sucked into a swirl of time and space.

I had to trust we'd be safe with these Fae, even though I had no real idea where the hell they were going to take us.

Please don't make me regret this!

CHAPTER 8
Grey

The world spun like a kaleidoscope of colors and chaos before dropping us into the middle of a forest. It was dark and gloomy, and I recognized it instantly. "This isn't the same forest we were just in previously," I said, drawing my sword from its sheath. "Why did you bring us here?"

"You mentioned you might know of somewhere to hide out," the Fae guard said. "So, I brought you to the Dark Forest."

"What's your name?" I asked, my blade still at the ready.

"Talon, Your Majesty," he answered and bowed his head.

I flinched. I wasn't the Shifter King yet, and I was no one's "majesty", and wouldn't be even after this was all over.

It's not who I am.

I may be the next rightful Shifter King, but that didn't mean I wanted everyone to bow and scrape at my feet. I felt very much like my mate, Aurelia, in that regard. Being a leader was one thing, but being royalty wasn't something that sat well with me.

"Talon, I'm Grey, and you *will* address me as such. I'd recognize the Dark Forest anywhere. It was just outside of my original home, long ago—but where are the others?" I peered through the blackened, gnarled trees, but none of the others had sifted in yet.

I don't like this.

I pulled Aurelia behind me, still not trusting the Fae, even after his oath. It hadn't been made in blood, and I *never* trusted an oath not sealed with blood. We couldn't exactly spill blood in the village for an oath when we were running from the Council, though...

"The others are right behind us, I'm sure," Talon said.

I narrowed my eyes at him, not convinced. "How can you be sure?"

"We have a shared mind link. The king enacted it himself to ensure his men could always communicate effectively during battle. But when we were under the Council's control, I'm not sure if it still worked or not. Or whether the Council did something to sever that bond. I'm hoping they got my message."

"So, we're waiting here, just hoping that the others got your message?" I threw my hands up in frustration.

Aurelia placed a calming hand on my back.

I took a deep, cleansing breath. I still didn't like this, but at least we were close to shifter territory and a place I could protect my mate.

I hope.

"We are. They will be here soon, I'm sure of it." Talon looked over the forest with a hopeful expression.

I crossed my arms over my chest as I waited impatiently.

This had better not be a trap. I will not hesitate to shift and rip this fucking Fae apart with my bare teeth!

I bared my teeth at the man, uneasy. Sifting was an instantaneous form of transport. What was taking them so long?

Aurelia stepped around me, her expression calm. "They will be here,

Grey. I know he's not lying to us." She rested her hand on my biceps, meeting my gaze.

"How can you possibly know that, Aurelia?" I asked. "You trust far too easily. I love that about you, but it also scares the hell out of me." I closed my eyes and tilted my head back. I needed to protect her, but how could I do that when she was constantly getting into situations just like this? She was too trusting, almost bordering on naive.

Talon watched us warily as another guard popped into existence in the Dark Forest.

My shoulders tensed, and I reached for my sword before I realized the guard had Asher with him. "Where are the others?" I asked Ash as I took a step closer to him.

Ash smirked. "Worried about us, were you?" he asked with a chuckle. "They are being transported. But the moment you and the princess left, the villagers sort of went a little feral and tried to attack us."

"What?" Aurelia shrieked, her eyes wide and her expression aghast.

I pulled her into my side to comfort her. "They're all warriors, mate. They will be fine."

"How can you possibly know that?" She retorted, throwing my question right back at me as she clenched her fists in the fabric of my shirt. "There were *so* many people there—they would have been horribly outnumbered!"

Ash shook his head. "The people in that village are not trained in combat. They don't stand a chance against trained warriors, Princess. Your father and Fenrick are fine."

"Then where are they? Why aren't they here with you?" she shrieked, revealing the depths of her level of attachment to her father and her childhood protector.

I pulled her against me with my hand on the back of her head in reassurance. "They *will* be fine, my love, and if they aren't here in the next five minutes, we'll go back for them. I promise."

She blinked back her tears as she stared up at me. "They better be here in five minutes *unharmed*, or the Council is going to have a battle on their hands much sooner than they ever expected."

"There's my bloodthirsty mate." I chuckled and kissed her forehead.

I would personally make sure that the Council paid dearly if anything happened to the king or Fenrick. They had become important to me simply because they were important to Aurelia. It was a new feeling, one I hadn't felt in more than two centuries. The Shadow Princess was like a bulldozer as she came into my life, changing every fucking thing.

But I have no regrets. I love her and she's worth it.

"I'm not bloodthirsty," she growled back. "I just want to protect those I love!"

Ash cleared his throat. "All right, it's been long enough. I want to go back and help them."

"No need." Fenrick's voice sounded behind me.

I spun with Aurelia still tucked into my chest to find Fenrick, the Shadow King and the rest of the previously mind-controlled guards standing behind me.

"Thank the gods," I sighed, my heart flooding with relief. "Okay, let's get a move on. We need to find shelter."

"I thought you knew of a place?" Fenrick said with a raised brow.

"I do, but we were waiting for you to show up. Took you took long enough." I winked, just glad to see them after what Ash had revealed to us.

"Those people were crazy," the Shadow Guardian bemoaned. "I get that they're starving, but they were like animals, and we didn't want to hurt them, so yeah, it took a bit longer than expected to make a clean break." Fenrick turned his gaze on my mate.

She was the sole reason they had shied away from hurting the villagers.

She wouldn't have liked it one bit.

We were in the midst of a realm-wide war, and she was still too kind-hearted for death and destruction. She was the same way with the Secret Service agents. How were we going to defeat the Council once and for all if she refused to use her magic to harm others unless they absolutely deserved it? That was why we continued to protect her. We couldn't afford her kindness-inspired hesitation when it came down to her life or someone else's.

I would burn the realms to the ground if they hurt her because she'd wavered. I would not hesitate to destroy everything, because *she* was my everything. As I stared at Ash, the king, and Fenrick, I realized they would do the same. We didn't even need to discuss it to know we were all on the level.

I sniffed the air and peered around the forest to get a grip on my bearings. My sense of direction wasn't as great as it once was. I'd been away far too long, so I leaned into Aurelia. "Can you ask the trees where we are?"

Aurelia nodded and pulled away from my arms to set her palm on the nearest trunk. She flinched slightly, her brows scrunching as she communed with the tree. "We are about a mile west of the Shifter King's castle." She stared at me.

"Good. We should be able to get to the safe house quickly then." I nodded and headed towards the castle. My own personal hideout as a pup wasn't far away. I'd had wards set up and I hoped that they were still there, and the Council hadn't taken over my secret space. I'd had an extremely powerful witch set them, so I held out hope.

Will Aurelia be able to get through them?

I guessed she would because the wards at the Syndicate were strong, and she got past those just fine. It would help my mate to be able to pass through them in a time of crisis, especially if she needed to sift there.

"Where is this place?" Aurelia asked, observing the terrain as we kept a brutal pace.

"Shifter territory." I wrapped my hand around hers.

We raced through the woods like the Riders of the Hunt were on our asses, but of course they weren't, because Asher was with us. We burst through the tree line to the perimeter of the house I'd left behind more than two centuries ago.

Everything looked exactly the same as I'd left it. I raised a hand to the wards, and they buzzed briefly beneath my palm. They were still there, which meant that no one had crossed without my knowledge in my absence. Well, at least no one who wasn't stronger than the witch who'd cast them in the first place.

"It doesn't appear to have been tampered with, but I'd still like to do a perimeter sweep before we assume it's safe," I said.

"Agreed." Aurelia nodded.

"You're not sweeping the perimeter. You're staying with your father and Fenrick, where it's safe." I glared down at her.

"Oh, I'm not? And who made that decision?" Aurelia crossed her arms over her chest.

"I did," I growled. "I'm your mate and I can't even begin to explain what the fuck I would do if something happened to you. You are *mine*, and I will not back down where your safety is concerned."

"You all have got to be kidding me!" She threw her hands up in the air.

Her father and Fenrick had discreetly taken up positions on either side of her, flanking her as I spoke the words that would probably damn me with her for eternity.

I refused to let her become a casualty. She wasn't just my mate, she was the Shadow Princess, future queen, and the key to the prophecy. My safe house might be warded, but I wasn't taking chances when it came to her life.

She is the key to everything.

If the Council had gotten inside my protections to ambush us and I didn't check first and lost her, we would all be doomed. The others more than me, because I would become the monster the Council thought I was. I would become *the* threat of Faery and destroy them all.

She glanced between Fenrick and her father, tapping her foot on the grass all the while.

They both looked to her with pleading eyes, willing her to listen to my wisdom.

Aurelia finally sighed. "Fine! I'll stay here for now, but you can't protect me from this war. You can't protect me from everything. I'm the key to saving Faery and I *will* have to fight."

I ignored the wolf in my head that growled angrily, not wanting our mate anywhere near the impending war. All he knew was his mate was in danger.

Is that why I'm lashing out now?

My shifter was being a massive pain in the ass and pushing me to hide her from everyone and everything in a bid to keep her safe. But Aurelia was right, neither of us could shield her forever. Pushing that thought from my mind for the moment, I took off and ran the perimeter in wolf form, searching for anything that could possibly harm us while we stayed, but I found nothing.

I can't believe it's really been fully warded for all these years!

When I got back to Aurelia, I shook my onyx head, indicating the immediate surroundings of the safe house were free of threats.

My mate dug her fingers into my fur, rubbing between my ears with a smile.

I shifted quickly, much to my inner wolf's protests. "I didn't find anything problematic," I said and shook my head. "The wards have held steady and strong. I think we could make this our hideout."

"We aren't hiding from the Council," my mate countered. "We are simply biding our time until we can take them down." Aurelia shoved at my chest playfully, but her tone was serious. "We're not fucking around."

"I know that, my love, but we *need* to lay low for a while. Just until we can figure out what to do." I allowed my gaze to wander over the clearing.

"That may be, but you don't need to treat me like a liability." She crossed her arms over her chest and marched past the wards, clearly unhappy with my attempt at placation.

I glanced at the others and grimaced.

They all shrugged.

What the hell was going on? She wasn't being reasonable. She didn't even know if the house she was walking into was safe or not.

"You're not a liability, you're my life!" I shouted at her back, unwilling to let it go.

"Then maybe you should remember that I'm not a baby or a helpless female!" she called over her shoulder.

"You're neither of those things," I said as I stomped toward the house. If she was going to be angry and walk away, I was going to follow her and make her realize what was really going on. I would do *anything* for her. Anything to keep her safe, no matter the consequences for the world.

And that's the truth, whether she likes it or not!

She was mine, and I didn't care how mad she got about my need to protect her. I would do it a thousand times over, and she couldn't stop me.

Not a hope in hell, mate.

"Aurelia, stop!" I yelled. "I haven't checked the house yet."

"No!" she argued back. "I don't answer to you or anyone, Grey. My life is my own."

"But we don't know if it's safe," I growled.

"I don't care! I'm strong and capable and I can take care of myself. I'm tired and need to crash, so either give me the benefit of the doubt or leave me the fuck alone." She turned to me with a glare, her eyes hard. "You're suffocating me!"

Shit.

Had I crossed too many lines with my mate? Was she done with me? I moved faster toward her, ready to pull her into my arms... but was she right?

Am I being an ass?

We couldn't defeat the Council if we were busy fighting amongst ourselves. I needed to make my mate see that there wasn't a problem. She needed to realize I was on her side, no matter what. But if she wanted me to give her space—to let her walk into what could be her certain doom—for the sake of some misguided sense of independence in all this chaos? Well, I wasn't sure I could do that.

We all just want to protect you, Aurelia... You're our only hope.

CHAPTER 9
Aurelia

I stormed toward the beautiful old house fuming. Why did he have to behave like that? What made him think I couldn't take care of myself? Anger bubbled up within me as I pushed through the double doors and stepped inside. Dust puffed up in my face, and I coughed. It was old and had been sitting unused for centuries, but the amount of dust was slightly off-putting.

I waved a hand in front of my face and stepped further inside.

It would be beautiful if it was cleaned up.

There were a few worn sofas under high, vaulted ceilings, but otherwise, there were no decorations of any kind.

"Aurelia, where are you going?" Grey shouted from behind me.

I stomped through the house and down the hallway. I didn't want to be in the same room as that overbearing asshole right now. "I'm going to find somewhere to sleep. *Alone*!" I yelled back. Maybe I was being slightly dramatic, but I was empathically tired of everyone thinking I was helpless. I was the one who'd stopped the mind control on the guards outside, not any of them! I was also the one that transported hundreds of innocent men from their medical beds in the facility!

I've done my fair share to demonstrate I'm capable, for fuck's sake!

"We don't know if it's safe," Grey called again.

"And I'll be the most powerful person in the room, so I'll be fine!" I waved a hand over my shoulder.

I trudged to the end of the hall and shoved the door open. A huge bed with bedside tables awaited. It was the perfect place for a nap. I strolled inside, but the heat at my back let me know I wasn't alone.

An angry shifter was right behind me.

Great. Couldn't he just give me a little time to myself?

I spun on him and poked a finger into his chest. "I *said* I wanted to be alone."

"And my father always taught me to never go to bed angry with your mate, so we're going to have this argument *now*." Grey crossed his arms over his chest and crowded closer.

His woodsy scent filled my nose as I sucked in a breath. That wasn't going to help me stay mad at him. My shoulders slumped. "What do you want, Grey? I'm tired."

"We need to check it's safe before you sleep," he said as he reached for me.

I backed away, tired of proving myself and demonstrating I was different from everyone else, only to be coddled and treated like a child. I didn't need a cuddle. I needed to be trusted and respected. "Then check the house already. I need rest. Do you have any idea how exhausting that magic was for me?" I shoved at his chest. It was the wrong move. I knew it the second I touched his sculpted pecs.

He pushed forward and crowded me until my hands were pinned between us. "Do you have *any* idea what I would do to the world if something happened to you?" He cupped my cheek.

I turned my face away so I couldn't see the fire in his eyes and did my best not to breathe through my nose as I glared at the floor. "You're treating me like a helpless damsel in distress when we both know that I'm anything but! I saved you from the Council prison, remember?" My gaze clashed with his.

"I would be the monster the Council expects me to be if anything happened to you, Aurelia. I would burn down the world and anyone who ever hurt you or looked at you wrong. Know that. You. Are. Mine. Mine to love and mine to fucking protect."

I gasped at his words and the glowing intensity of his eyes. He was deadly serious. He would actually *destroy* the world for me. "Don't do that. I just need you to see me as an equal. You and the others are constantly surrounding me in fights, guarding me like I'm some kind of porcelain doll that needs protection in case I shatter. How do I prove more than I already have that I'm *not* going to break?" I threw my hands up in the air in frustration.

"I do see you as an equal. Hell, you're better than me in every way, Aurelia. You are the one who made it possible for any of us to go home. You're everything to me, and the idea of losing you makes me crazy," Grey growled. Without warning, he slammed his lips against mine in a brutally passionate kiss.

I tried to push against his chest, but my fingers gripped his shirt and pulled him closer instead. He was mine as I was his. I just wished he'd give me the same consideration I gave him. I didn't coddle him the way he did me... but a moment later all thoughts tumbled out of my head.

He wrapped his arms around me and plastered his chest to mine. "I love you, mate. I will do anything for you. I'm sorry for upsetting you. I will try to be better," he said between heated, breathless kisses.

"I love you too, but sometimes the overbearing Alpha bullshit pisses me off." I pulled back just enough to glare at him.

Grey gripped my ass, pulling me impossibly closer. "Then how about we fuck all that anger out before our nap... together."

"I told you, I am taking a nap alone."

"Then I guess I have to grovel a bit to get you to let me sleep with you again." His sexy grin alluded to all kinds of dirty promises.

"And how do you plan on doing that?" I shoved him back, successfully this time, allowing myself to catch my breath.

"You'll see." He grinned as he crowded me until I was backed against the wall.

"What are you doing?" I protested.

"I'm showing you how I'm going to grovel." He pressed his lips to the hollow of my neck.

I shuddered under his touch. I couldn't deny him—even angry.

He is mine.

His lips trailed down my neck and his tongue poked out to lick at the spot where he would mark me for *real* one day. Every bite and mark before then were simply love-bites, they weren't the final truth of our union I'd wear on my flesh for the rest of my life.

I squirmed but couldn't move, finding myself firmly pinned against the wall. "Grey," I moaned, his name like a prayer on my lips.

He gripped my ass and pulled me even closer, until the hardness of his cock pressed against my belly. "What do you want, mate?" he asked, his hot breath fanning over my neck.

"I want you," I groaned, my heart racing. "But I also want you to see me for who I really am, and not as some princess who needs to be kept in a tower."

"I know that's not you, Aurelia. I love every part of you, even the stubborn parts." He chuckled against my skin as his lips traveled lower, squeezing my ass again and rubbing his cock over my thigh.

"Then prove it," I challenged, my skin tingling with anticipation.

"Gladly." He grinned and lifted me off the ground.

I wrapped my legs around his waist, reveling in the strength of his muscular form.

He carried me to bed, laid me down on the dusty comforter, pulled my shirt off over my head, and stared down at my heaving chest.

My skin prickled with heat as his gaze roved.

He kissed down my body and his fingers trailed over my shoulders, pushing down the straps of my bra.

I shivered under his attention, quickly reaching back to unclasp my bra before letting it fall to the bed.

Grey groaned and pinched one of my nipples between his fingers, then swirled his tongue around the other.

I arched my back into him, allowing him better access.

His fingers trailed down my body to my core, and he slid his hand beneath my pants, not even bothering to take them off before he circled my clit with his thumb.

I gripped his shoulders as the intensity of my pleasure grew and squirmed beneath him.

"I love the way you grip me like I'm everything in the world to you, mate," Grey growled against my breasts.

My nails dug into his skin even harder as the vibrations of his voice and the feel of his hot breath assaulted me. I was going to come while half-dressed… just from this.

How does he do this to me?

How did he make me feel both treasured and desired at the same time? "Grey," I moaned breathlessly. "What are you doing to me?"

"I'm about to make you scream, Princess." He glanced up at me with a devilish smile before pulling his hand from my pants and popping the button.

I whimpered at the loss of him where I needed him most.

No! Please, it's too soon!

The bastard just chuckled darkly as he sat back on his knees, his eyes hooded with lust as he stared down at my heaving body.

I wiggled my hips, inviting him to take action.

Instead, he continued to peer down at me.

The experience would have been unnerving if it'd been anyone but Grey. I ran my hands over the swell of my breasts and down my belly. If he was just going to stare, I'd give him a show. I shoved my hand inside my pants and circled my clit with fumbling fingers, a breath rushing out of me.

A strangled moan escaped him as his eyes glowed with his inner wolf, and he flew into action, unable to contain himself. He gripped the waistband of my jeans and pulled them down hard, his gaze zeroing in on where I was touching myself. Without prompting, he gripped my thighs, pushing them wide for a better view.

"You're wearing too much," I said, my breath catching in my throat as I witnessed his hunger.

Grey jumped off the bed and flung his shirt over his head before ripping his jeans off in seconds. All his tanned, toned, skin now on display—just for me.

My gaze roamed over every inch of him, my need to feel him inside me reaching frustrating heights.

He stalked back to the bed and his hand pumped his cock slowly as he watched me.

My back arched as tingles raced down my spine. "Grey, fuck. I need you." I wasn't about to give myself an orgasm when I had him *right* here.

He smirked and kneeled on the bed, edging closer. "What do you need, mate?" he asked.

"I need you to fuck me." I reached up and gripped his shoulders in an effort to pull him down on me, but he was too strong. I huffed in annoyance when he resisted.

But the next second, he gripped my thighs and pulled me closer. He lined his cock up with my entrance, but didn't push inside. Instead, he teased me, rubbing his cock up my slick slit and over my swollen and over-sensitive clit.

Stars burst behind my eyes as he continued with his game, and my head thrashed.

"You're so fucking responsive, my love," he praised before finally burying himself inside me.

The forceful intrusion was just what I needed. My walls gripped Grey's shaft as he filled me, and it felt like heaven.

He growled as he pulled out and slammed back in, hitting *that* spot hard.

A rainbow of colors danced behind my eyes, and I screamed as white-hot euphoria blasted through every inch of my body. My ears rang, and I barely heard his curses over the white noise in my mind. I was floating. There were just no words to describe the intensity of the ecstasy flooding me from the crown of my head to the very tips of my toes.

By the gods...

With a final roar, Grey thrust into me harder and faster, hitting that sensitive spot again and again, before emptying himself inside my pussy and collapsing on top of me. We were both breathing heavily as he rolled to the side and pulled me into his chest. His hands rubbed soothing circles on my back as he kissed my forehead with something akin to reverence. "It's not in my nature to let my mate jump headfirst into danger, my love." He rested his chin on the top of my head. "But I'll try to stop being so overbearing and protective if it makes you happy."

"We aren't going to have a choice soon, my love," I echoed. "The Council is coming for us all, and I'm the only one who can stop them." My hazy thoughts roamed.

Why would the Fates rest this mammoth task firmly on my shoulders, alone?

It seemed impossible, but it was something I had to do... no matter the consequences.

CHAPTER 10

"The house is secure," Fenrick said just as we walked out of the bedroom. "Though there *are* two centuries worth of dust caked everywhere."

"That's to be expected." I shrugged.

"I still think we should look for more Council guards that are under the Council's control," Aurelia said, crossing her arms in the hallway.

"I don't want you going after the Council's guards just to see if you can do for them what you did with your father's men. It feels like an unnecessary risk."

My wolf growled in my head in agreement. He was riding me hard to keep our mate protected, but after the conversation I'd just had with her, I knew that wasn't a practical approach. She was part of this, whether I liked it or not. My wolf was just going to have to learn to get over the fact his mate was stronger than him and accept it.

"I'm not going in without a plan or setting myself up as bait, Grey. If you would just listen..." She glared at me, the relief and pleasure of our hot sex already forgotten.

Shit. I'm fucking everything up!

"Sorry, my wolf is being a total pain in my ass," I apologized.

"It's fine." She sighed, clearly making a concerted effort to rein in her temper. "I personally think the guards should return to their posts and pretend like they are still under the Council's influence. They can get inside information and send word whenever they discover a new group of blank-eyed guards so I can try to heal their minds and get them on side."

Ash stepped forward, grinning. "That's a good tactical plan that puts you in as little physical danger as possible, Princess. I like it."

He's not wrong.

The plan *was* solid, and while the guards were out searching for others, we could still work on tracking down the rebels.

Fenrick nodded. "It makes sense. We could divide and conquer, with both groups looking for something different. And if we both succeed, we might actually stand a chance against the Council and increase our numbers."

"Agreed," I said, nodding.

Aurelia's gaze snapped to mine. "You're agreeing? Even though we have no idea if I will be able to free the others of the mind control?" Her gaze flicked back and forth between my eyes, searching for *something*.

"My love, we all know you'll be able to do it again. You're the only one who is unsure. We all believe in you. We have all along." I wrapped my arms around her.

"Then why fight it?" she asked, her brows furrowed.

"I thought you were planning on taking unnecessary risks. You kind of have a track record of doing that..."

"Ugh! Only to save *you*, you big, dumb wolf!" She laid her head against my chest and sighed.

My heart thumped harder. It scared the hell out of me and made me proud in the same breath that she'd risk her life for me. I leaned down and kissed the top of her head again. "As much as I appreciate your courage, my beautiful mate, no more risking yourself, especially for me," I whispered into her golden hair.

"I'll make no promises on that, wolf." Her words muffled against my chest.

I still heard them. How could I make this woman see there was *no* life for me without her in it? There was no life for anyone without her... well, none that anyone wanted. If the Council won the upcoming battles, they would enslave everyone.

We have to stop them before their greed dooms us all.

"Let's get back to the plan," Ash said, clapping me on the back with a crooked smile. He was right. This wasn't a conversation for mixed company.

The guards peered at us with amusement, like watching their princess spar with the Shifter King was the highlight of their day. It probably was, since they couldn't remember much since being under mind control.

Aurelia turned to the guards and straightened, rolling her shoulders back as she peered at every man in turn. "Do you think you can do this? Can you pretend to be under their control? What about the villagers who saw you run off with us? What do we do about that?"

The leader of the group stepped forward and bowed his head to us both in turn before he spoke. "It would be our pleasure to deceive the Council and save our fellow warriors from their insidious influence. We will gladly accept this task."

"And what about the villagers?" Aurelia pressed again, chewing her bottom lip.

"We will tell them that we followed you to apprehend you, but you escaped us." He clasped his hands in front of him.

"It's a smart plan." Fenrick nodded.

"Okay, but if the Council suspects anything, I want you to get out of there immediately. I won't risk people. I just can't." Aurelia wrung her hands together.

I bet she's still dwelling on Zeke...

"On your order, Princess. If we are found out, we will abort the mission." He bowed again and placed a fist over his heart.

The men filed out dutifully to fulfill their new orders.

I wrapped my arms around my mate once more. "You're going to be the best queen," I assured her.

"Someday, but only if we can conquer the Council. The only way to beat them is to find the rebels... which is obviously easier said than done." She sighed.

There's a town a little larger than the village we were in on the other side of the Dark Forest. We could start over by checking there," Fenrick suggested.

"Hopefully, there's no one who can see through glamours there." I rubbed my eyes.

That had been a total fucking cock-up. What were the chances?

"We'll need different disguises this time, since the Council will probably be on the lookout for us." Aurelia huffed. She stepped away from me and closed her eyes.

She was so beautiful, it took my breath away. I still couldn't believe she was mine or that she'd forgiven me for the mess with Dan and her foster mother. It was a miracle we were all here. Her body transformed before my eyes, and I grinned at the black-haired beauty standing in front of me.

Fenrick gripped my shoulder, and cool magic washed over me in a wave as my own new glamour slid into place.

I was just lucky shifters weren't allowed back into Faery yet, because they would sniff me out a mile away. "So, are we all good, then?" I asked, my voice raspy and rough. It still amazed me how far Fae glamours could go. They could change you into an entirely different person.

"We are good to go," Fenrick confirmed as he gripped both mine and Aurelia's arms.

At the same moment, the Shadow King held out a hand to Ash and we were all swirling through time and space in a matter of seconds.

My feet hit the soft, packed dirt a heartbeat later, and I caught Aurelia before she stumbled and fell. The chattering of Fae met my ears from the other side of the tree line. Fenrick had sifted us to the other side of the Dark Forest.

"The Fae have already heard that the Shadow King is back somewhere in Faery. But the excitement doesn't appear to be because they think they're going to be saved… It sounds like several of them are openly discussing the reward. We need to be wary." I clenched my fists at my sides.

"We'll be careful," Aurelia promised me and patted my arm.

"I know you will be…" I held my hand out to her.

She placed her hand in mine with a smile.

"Because you're not leaving my side," I finished.

Aurelia rolled her now green eyes but didn't comment further.

I was grateful for that, because her lack of argument meant she would listen to me just this once.

"Let's try the local pub," Fenrick suggested. "We can enjoy a meal and hopefully garner some new information." He strode toward the village with the rest of us in his wake.

I kept my hand in Aurelia's the whole way as we walked past the Fae.

All chatter died away as they saw us striding through their little town.

Are they simply wary of strangers?

Several older Fae glared in my direction, while others just scurried into their homes, slamming their doors shut behind them.

"I'm not getting a welcoming vibe here," I whispered.

"They're scared," Aurelia said under her breath. "The Council has taken everything from them, and newcomers must be suspected now."

"The Council has spies everywhere," Fenrick agreed. "Any strange people in town are suspicious. It makes sense, but it's going to make this twice as hard."

The Shadow King squeezed Fenrick's shoulder. "That's why we're going to the pub. People get drunk and let things slip out in mixed company."

Fenrick's plan was solid, but as we rounded the corner to the pub, whispers floated to me. The word rebellion caught my attention, and I flinched, stopping in my tracks. "You all go ahead. I'm going to check something out, really quick." I squeezed Aurelia's hand before I let go.

"I thought we were sticking together," she said.

"It's probably nothing, but I overheard a whispered conversation. I just want to check it out. I'll be inside in a few minutes." I strode away from the group and rounded the corner of the pub.

Two men stood at the back of the stone building with their heads together, whispering about something I couldn't quite make out.

"You're part of the rebellion," I whispered so only they could hear me.

Both men flinched openly and spun on me, magic flaring in their hands. "There is *no* rebellion. What nonsense are you speaking?"

"I was told by a powerful seer to seek out the rebellion. That's you, right?" I was still whispering so as not to draw unwanted attention to the conversation.

But the men before me had no such issues. "Your powerful seer was wrong, or maybe you're a spy for the Council." the same man spoke, crossing his arms over his chest, his bushy eyebrows pinched down in a scowl.

"I'm not a Council spy." I laughed. I couldn't help it, that was the farthest thing from the truth.

The other man took a threatening step forward. "If you're not a spy, then you're working against them... and there's a hefty reward available for any Council dissenters."

"Give us one good reason why we shouldn't call the guards, and have you arrested for questioning," the man with bushy eyebrows said.

"Because we both know it won't just be for questioning. The Council is on a massive power trip." I planted my hands on my hips. "Plus, I could take you both of you down before you could even open your mouth to call for the guards."

The men glanced at each other warily and then back to me as if assessing their options.

I held my hands up in the air. "But I don't want to do that. We're on the same side, I think, but I won't be taken by the Council again... so make your choice." I clenched and unclenched my fists at my sides. My wolf was snarling in my head. He wanted to be let out, to prove who the Shifter King really was.

I can't shift though, it'll blow my cover.

"What do you want?" the bushy eyebrowed man asked as magic

filled his palms again. He didn't believe me, that much was clear, and he was ready for a fight.

I couldn't blame him. His life would be on the line if he was found out by the Council. "I just want to talk. I need to locate the rebellion."

"I've already told you the rebellion doesn't exist. We've all been thoroughly beaten into submission by the Council. We couldn't rebel even if we tried. Why don't you take *that* back to the Council," he snarled.

The other guy stepped forward, magic pooling in his hands too. They were ready for a fight, and clearly convinced I was working with the Council.

How bad would it be if I shifted in this back alley and showed them once and for all that I definitely wasn't working for the Council?

No. If I shift, they'll know who I am and I can't let that happen until I know for sure they are rebels.

Whether I liked it or not, it looked like I had a fight on my hands. I just hoped this scuffle didn't destroy any chance we had of enlisting the rebels aid in the war ahead.

CHAPTER 11
Aurelia

"Where is he?" I asked, chewing my lip nervously. Grey was taking too long, and it was making me twitchy.

Is my mate, okay? Maybe I should have gone with him.

"He'll be fine, Daughter." My father patted my shoulder reassuringly.

He couldn't know that for sure though. We had no idea what Grey was facing behind the pub. What if the men he'd confronted had called the guards and I wasn't there to clear them of their mind control? What if he was attacked? Could he stop his wolf from shifting and betraying his glamour? I shifted uncomfortably in my seat.

A woman brought over five bowls of hot, fragrant stew and a round of drinks for us all, but Grey still wasn't back yet.

"I need to go check on him," I grumbled.

"You're not going anywhere alone." Ash gripped my arm lightly in warning. "He'll have my ass if I let you go out there."

"You're a bunch of cavemen," I huffed under my breath, trying to maintain a low profile and not raise suspicion.

Why can't any of them sense something is off?

"She's right," Fenrick said with a sigh. "He's been gone too long. I think we need to check."

"See? It's not just me." I glared with pursed lips at Ash and my father. "Fenrick and I will go take a look while you two stay here."

"No, we aren't splitting up again. We all go or none of us." Ash crossed his arms over his barrel of a chest.

"Fine, together then. But what about the food?" I asked. "We still need to eat, and we've already been served."

"We'll come back as soon as we find Grey," my father said and waved to the woman behind the bar and handed her some coins when she approached.

Her eyes widened in surprise.

"Give these bowls to anyone in need. We'll be back to eat once we find my daughter's mate."

The woman nodded and dropped the coins in her pocket before hurrying to clear the bowls from the table and shuffled back behind the bar.

"That was nice," I said, grinning at my father, feeling a touch uplifted by his gesture.

"I hate seeing what the Council has done to my people," he growled under his breath.

"We'll fix this, don't worry." I stormed out the door,

The men grumbled in my wake.

I rounded the same corner that Grey had and gasped at the scene in front of me. Two men were standing in front of Grey, glittering magic pooled in their palms.

"What's going on here?" I asked as I strode closer, ready for action.

Grey's shoulders bunched up at the tone of my voice, and he

glanced at me over his shoulder. "Go back inside, love. I have this under control."

"No. I'm not going back inside. They are threatening you." I took a step closer to the men.

No one threatens my mate.

My shadows appeared instantly on my arms in response, writhing with anger.

The men's eyes widened in horror as they stepped back.

"You're a Shadow Fae?" the one to the left with big eyebrows whispered.

"I am." I grinned. "Now, do you want to tell me what is going on here, or do I need to make you talk?"

"You're in league with him! We'll tell the Council that you're dissenters and we will be rewarded," he said too loudly for comfort.

My father gripped my arm and pulled me back.

I glanced over my shoulder to see his head cocked to the side.

"Teo, is that you?" he asked, his brow furrowed.

"How do you know that name?" the man asked in return.

"Bram!" he said a moment later, recognizing the other stranger too. "What are two of my best guards doing in this little town?" My father dropped his glamour for just a second, revealing who he truly was.

Both men cursed.

"You know them?" I asked, frowning at my father. "For fuck's sake, Dad. You could have led with that!"

"We can't talk here," said Teo glancing up and down the empty alley. "How did you get here? Where have you been all this time?"

"Not here," I said, meeting their gaze evenly. "You already said it's not safe."

"We're looking for the rebellion," Father whispered.

Bram and Teo glanced at each other and then glared at Grey.

"You vouch for *him*?" Bram sneered.

I edged closer to Grey, my shadows still swirling along my arms, begging for a reason to put them in their places.

My father pushed me gently toward Grey and stepped in front of me. "Of course, I vouch for him. He's my daughter's mate and the rightful Shifter King." He raised a brow at the men.

They both cursed again and glanced at Grey with wide eyes.

"And you're the princess? Shit," Bram said softly.

"We need get you out of here," Teo interrupted. "The town is crawling with Council guards." He waved for us to follow him further down the alley.

"Dad, are you sure about these guys? They threatened to take us to the Council," I whispered.

"Yes, daughter. They were just keeping themselves safe against strangers and traitors. They don't want to wind up in the Council's grasp any more than we do. They are two of my most loyal warriors."

"Okay," I said with a heavy sigh and followed the two Fae. I hoped I wouldn't follow them to the destruction of the realms, because that was what it felt like.

Can my father really trust these Fae after everything that's happened? What if they're leading us into a trap?

I gripped Grey's hand in mine, willing myself to remain calm and in control of my emotions.

Asher and Fenrick closed in on us from both sides, my Shadow Guardian next to Grey and the Rider at my elbow.

When did their loyalties shift?

I glanced up at Ash warily.

He winked at me. "I take my promises seriously, Princess. I will protect you until the end of this war and until you stop requiring my protection."

"My magic could put you on your ass, you know." I raised my brow. A gust of wind hit me from the side, and onyx hair flew into my face in a stream of darkness.

Ash chuckled and called his magic back.

Smart ass.

I stuck my tongue out at him and willed my shadows to shove him back.

He stumbled but he righted himself quickly. "You play dirty, Princess. I like it."

"Don't ever forget it," I snarked with a playful wink of my own.

Teo and Bram stopped in front of a decrepit building. The door was barely hanging on by a single hinge.

I shot them a dubious look. This wasn't what I'd expected the underground hideout of the Resistance to look like. "Are you sure this is where we want to go?" I asked. "This feels like a trap."

"It's not a trap, I swear it," Teo said, shooting my father, the king, a look that said, *trust me*. "It's just a safe place to talk."

I glanced at my father for confirmation.

The Shadow King nodded. For better or worse, he trusted these Fae men.

It's now or never, I guess.

If we wasted this opportunity, we may never find it again.

Grey squeezed my hip in reassurance. "It'll be okay, mate."

The two men who meant the most in all the realms to me said it was safe, so I suppressed my anxiety and followed the warriors into the gloom.

Bram lit a small oil lamp once we were all inside and away from the door.

Teo walked around the room, his palms facing the walls as they glowed a soft yellow.

Is he putting up wards? I need to learn how to do that if it's something Fae are able to do.

"It's safe to speak now," Teo said as he took a seat next to Bram.

Bram waved a hand for us to sit around the wooden table and get comfortable. "This conversation may take a while, so you might as well sit."

We took the seats offered, and I ended up sandwiched between Ash and Grey. They were never going to stop being the cavemen who always had to protect me.

"How did you get out of the castle?" my father asked, starting the conversation. "Everyone was either sent to the cells or mind controlled if they didn't willingly join the Council's side."

"Can you drop your glamours?" Teo asked, frowning. "It's weird talking to strangers when so many of them have been Council plants lately."

I dropped my glamour, feeling the subtle magic slough off me to reveal my true appearance.

Both men bowed, cursing themselves for the way they'd behaved before.

"Princess, please forgive us. We didn't know who you were!" Bram practically laid his head on the table in front of him.

"I was glamoured. It's fine. Please continue." I glanced around, shifting uncomfortably in my seat.

I'm never going to get used to this royalty shit.

"Tell us how you escaped the Council."

"We weren't at the palace when everything went down. We were here visiting with family," Bram answered.

"A few days after the Council ransacked the castle, word reached us that the king was in prison and the Council now ruled Faery. We were set to head back to the castle but hid out here until it was safe to return and search for survivors." Teo shook his head in dismay as he recalled the Council's betrayal.

"We found a couple men huddled in the passageways under the castle, practically starved and brought them back here."

I gasped at his words. I'd been in the castle but had only encountered one person.

Did I not search hard enough?

I hung my head as tears burned the back of my eyes.

I could have helped them... but I didn't look hard enough.

Grey pulled me to his side, sensing my emotions and rubbed my back.

I buried my face in his neck to stop anyone from seeing my weakness.

"Princess, what is it?" Teo asked, leaning over the table.

"I could have saved them." I sniffled.

"What? No. This was early on in the Council's uprising, Princess. You weren't at the castle at that time. There's nothing you could have done." Teo shook his head. "Besides, even if you had been, they were well trained to hide in the tunnels if the Council ever turned on the royal family."

Of course, he's right. I didn't make it into the castle's tunnels until after my father, Grey, and Fenrick were taken captive when we returned!

Relieved, I sniffled again, wiping away my burning tears.

Bram straightened and stared at me with kind eyes. "Those men are alive, today, Princess. They went through hell, but they *are* alive. You did not fail them by not finding them when you came. They are much improved now and remain on our side."

"All right, I'm glad to hear it," I said, pulling myself together and returning the conversation to the task at hand. "We need to find the rebels. We need an army. I'm working on it, but we just aren't sure we'll have enough men to take them down." I ran a hand down my face.

"The rebels definitely want the monarchy back," said Bram. "They just don't think it's possible with the king in prison or possibly dead as far as they know. The Council has spread many rumors and lies to sew unrest among the people." Bram clenched his hand into a fist.

"The king is right here," my father said firmly. "And I'm disgusted with the taxes and the slavery the Council has subjected my people to. We had to flee the village closest to the castle because they are basically slaves there, and the Council isn't giving them enough to survive on. It's horrific."

"Most of the people there tend the fields," Teo said, rubbing his chin.

"Yes, and they still are, but they are only being given enough rations for one person even though many have families to feed. They are starving and desperate. They need our help, and the only way we can do that is to take down the Council down once and for all... and the only way we can do that is with the aid of the rebels." My father slammed his fist on the table.

"We'll take you to the rebels as soon as we can, but I just want us all to get on the same page first," Bram said, leaning back in his chair.

"It seems like we're all on the same page already." I crossed my arms over my chest, wondering what they were getting at or not revealing.

"How did you get out of prison?" Teo asked my father.

"Aurelia busted us all out." He nodded to me with a hint of fatherly pride.

"Zeke helped a lot, too," I mumbled and glanced at Ash. I hoped that by mentioning our lost friend I didn't bring up a bunch of bad shit for him. The memory of the night when Zeke was shot blasted through my mind, and my shoulders slumped. The loss was still too fresh. It had only been days since we'd left Zeke bleeding on the ground.

My father took over the conversation, obviously realizing I needed a minute to compose myself. "They got us out of the prison even if it was in a most unconventional way."

"I may have blown a few hundred gallons of their fucking mind control serum sky high." I shrugged with a smirk. I was glad I'd done that, but Zeke was still on my mind, and it hurt.

Ash seemed to realize it, placing his hand on my shoulder and squeezing it gently.

I nodded my thanks for his silent support. "Okay. I think we're all caught up. Now, can you please take us to the rebels? We don't have time to spare." I grimaced as I stood.

"Yes, Princess. We'll take you to the rebels now," Teo said, rising to his feet also.

I smiled briefly, thankful things were finally falling into place. Hopefully, the rebels would help our cause. Because if they didn't, I had no idea what else we would do.

I'm powerful, but I'm not a one-woman army...

And I sure as hell hoped I didn't have to be.

CHAPTER 12

"Okay," Bram said as he pushed up from the table. "Let's go to the rebellion."

Instead of taking us back the way we came, he moved through the room to a different door shrouded in shadows.

Where are they taking us?

I wrapped an arm around Aurelia's waist and followed.

The men opened another door. It was dank and cold as they led us down the corridor.

What the fuck is happening? Why am I following these Fae into dark tunnels without any real assurance that we will be safe?

The king trusted them, but was that enough? The king had blindly followed the Council for centuries. Was this going to be more of the same?

I pushed Aurelia behind me and nodded to Ash and Fenrick.

Neither of them needed further instruction to close ranks at her sides.

Aurelia huffed with an exasperated sigh.

I glanced back just in time to see her roll her eyes. "Don't argue," I warned under my breath.

"I have no intention of arguing," she replied in the darkness with a grin.

"Good." I nodded and continued to follow the two Fae men who'd accosted me in the alley. They had been assholes, and I still didn't trust them. No matter what the king said, I would have my guard up when it came to Aurelia's safety. Her security always came first, and the king knew that as well as I did.

We traveled through the tunnels to gods know where, and the longer we walked, the more wary I became. All of this could have been an elaborate trap set by the Council and the guards Aurelia had freed with her magic. We had no way of knowing who was loyal to our cause without proof—and the proof would be in action.

Are they really in on it with the Council? Are they trying to figure out exactly how far my mate will go to help her people?

"Here we are!" Bram yelled and threw his arms out wide. "Welcome to the Resistance."

Were the dramatics necessary? The entire room fell silent. The sounds of swords clashing subsided as everyone turned to stare at us.

There were people of all walks of life in the huge space into which we strolled. I even noticed some Shadow Fae with shadows writhing over their arms. They were trying to learn from the centuries-old Fae how to wield them, even though my mate had all but mastered them in a few short months.

A man on a dais stood as he saw us walk through the passageway, glaring at our group.

I didn't like the look he was giving us. Were we going to be handed over to the Council after everything we'd been through? Was this an elaborate ruse?

We didn't have our glamours on, so the whispers from those on the ground all spoke of the kings and the princess. Some even recognized Fenrick as Aurelia's guardian. They knew who we were, so why weren't they welcoming us? We were obviously on the same side.

"Santori!" the king boomed, taking a step toward the man on the dais. "Is that really you?"

"My king? It can't be!" The man mirrored the king's approach. "How did you escape the Council?"

The king turned to Aurelia and nodded with pride once again. "My daughter saved us all, and she's going to save the realms as well."

"That's little Aurelia?" The man cocked his head to the side as he rushed to us from his spot on the dais. "You're so big!" he exclaimed.

"I'm an adult now, yes," Aurelia said, crossing her arms, a prominent brow raised.

"Yes, of course. I apologize. I simply meant you've grown up. The last time I saw you was... when you were nine." He shook his head.

"Before Malcolm kidnapped me," she confirmed as her shoulders slumped.

I didn't know if that would ever stop being an issue for her. She'd lost out on so many memories as a child because of it. I pulled her closer to my side and kissed her temple. Things had to work out exactly as they had, unfortunately, or else I never would have met her, and we never would have set out on this journey together to save the realms.

"Right," Santori said. "Malcolm. Has anyone taken that bastard's head yet?"

"No." I growled. "But I plan to at the first opportunity."

Santori glanced at me and cocked his head to the side as if confused by what I was doing here.

I rolled my shoulders back and stared the Fae down. He was one of the king's friends, but that didn't mean he wouldn't have the same bias as the other Fae.

"You're the Shifter King?" he asked.

"Yes," I said, even though I didn't feel like much of a king as I fought for my life against the Council.

"How did you get into Faery?" It was a general question, not an accusation.

I pulled Aurelia a little closer. "My mate is incredible," I answered before kissing the top of her head.

"Mate? Oh, my. Things *have* been happening. Come, I want to hear everything!" Santori spun on his heel and barked orders at the people that were now standing around gawking at us.

"Get back to work. We need to be in top shape to defeat the Council!" One of the trainers bellowed as we passed.

"We need your help," Aurelia said at my side, speaking directly to Santori. "We have a small army, but it's not enough to defeat the Council. Their actions are unforgivable, and they must be stopped."

"We have the same goal, Princess. Let's go eat and discuss how we can help each other." Santori grinned as he opened a door that led into yet another series of tunnels.

It seemed that everything the rebels did was literally underground. It would drive my wolf mad to constantly be underneath the earth and not feel the sun on my skin or the breeze in his fur. But these were dark and dangerous times, so I understood their need to hide.

We followed him into the tunnels and to a large dining area. It was empty, but could easily seat a hundred men.

Santori yelled a bunch of orders.

Several women bustled out of the kitchen with platters of food.

Well, that's convenient.

"What's been happening here?" the king asked, approaching Santori.

"When the Council announced that they'd arrested you for treason, I was suspicious. I could see no reason you would commit treason against your own people. A few of your guards were here on leave, so I sought them out. They said that Aurelia had been found and sentenced by the Council to death and you all fled..." He eyed our group. "Is that true?"

"Yes, after Ronaldo tortured me to get my powers to ignite." Aurelia folded her arms.

She hated talking about her time in the castle dungeons, and I knew it wasn't because of the torture. That was where she'd befriended my father, and he'd died trying to protect her. My father had been many things, but that was what I was most grateful to him for. He'd protected my mate when I couldn't.

"We fled and were looking for something to defeat them with when Aurelia was sucked down a hole. The rest of us were captured and taken to a human prison to be tortured and killed," the king said. "Aurelia and Asher ultimately helped us escape."

Santori eyed Ash. "You're a Rider of the Hunt, yes? Why do you care about what the Council is doing?"

"Faery was once my home too." Ash shrugged, but his body was rigid, as if he were expecting a fight. "Despite that, I have alliances to uphold, and the longest running friendship besides my brother's is with Grey. He needs help, and so I'm here for him."

"Likewise, brother." I clapped him on the shoulder.

With that, we all dug into the delicious food set before us. I hadn't realized just how hungry I was until I'd started eating.

"We have somewhat of a plan in place, but we're not sure of anything after gathering allies," said Aurelia as she sat up straighter in her chair.

"And how do you plan on gathering these allies?" Santori asked with a raised brow.

"We encountered a group of soldiers with strange, blank eyes. I realized they were under the influence of the Council. I was able to remove the mind control, but we suspect that the Council has even more of the Shadow Warriors controlled in the same way. Those warriors I freed are searching for more guards that the Council has under their power. If they're successful in finding them, I can remove the control from them as well."

Santori sat back in his chair and gripped his chin between two fingers. "The soldiers only come out to police the people. If you want to find them, you're going to need bait."

I stiffened at his words, not liking the sound of that at all. I glanced at Aurelia at my side and shook my head, already knowing what she was going to propose. "No. You're not going to be bait." I clenched my hand into a fist.

"Not just me. Isn't there a bounty on all our heads?" She grinned.

"I'll be bait then, and you stay here."

"I can't! I have to be the one to release them from the mind control, Grey. You know that." Aurelia crossed her arms and glared at me.

She wasn't wrong, but I couldn't help my instinctual desire to protect her. She was my mate. I needed to know she was safe. I tilted my head back and squeezed my eyes shut. My wolf was banging against the cage inside my chest like a rabid beast. He wanted to shift and show her who the true Alpha was. He wanted to snarl at anyone who got close enough to harm a single hair on her head.

I took a few calming breaths and pushed him back down. His instincts to protect his mate were right, but she didn't see it like that, and I had to *try* to stop the caveman shit, or I'd drive her away.

"Fine," I conceded. "You glamour yourself like someone from the town, and *I'll* be bait. Ronaldo wants me alive to experiment on." I shot her a pleased look, but I already knew it was no use.

"No. We all act as bait. It's the only way we can explain all the back-up we'll have when they bring us in." Aurelia shook her head.

I sighed in defeat. "How many men can you gather to take us to the guards?" I asked Santori.

"There are five of you, so I would think ten would suffice." He shrugged like this was no big deal.

What if something went wrong though? What if this plan didn't actually save anyone, and instead walked us to our doom?

"It's fine, Grey." Aurelia squeezed my hand. "We will have plenty of back-up, and I'll hopefully be able to free more guards from the Council's mind control."

"But what if we're wrong, and there aren't as many controlled Fae as we think? We could be walking into something we can't escape," I said. "Ash, Fenrick, what do you think?"

"I think it's risky," Ash admitted. "I would much rather the princess stay behind, but I understand why she can't. We have to remember they're looking for us as a group, now, and will be suspicious if she's not with us."

I clenched my hand into a fist. I hadn't thought of that, but he was right though. The Council would never believe they'd caught us without her. They'd known she was with us when they grabbed us outside the portal. Where we were concerned, she was never far, and it was true. "Fine. What do we need to do?" I sighed in resignation, hoping against hope that I didn't just doom us all with my begrudging agreement.

CHAPTER 13

“Is this necessary?” Grey grunted as one of the rebels tied rope around his wrists in front of him.

“They aren’t tying it tightly. It’s just to make the guards think we’re under their control.” I bumped my shoulder into his. My hands were already bound in a similar way as we got ready to make the drop. Well, maybe we weren’t making an actual drop, but the Council thought we were being handed over, and that was what really mattered. We needed more warriors if we were to stand any chance of winning the war for Faery, and this was the perfect opportunity to obtain them.

Santori and his men ushered us through the tunnels to the drop point.

We were surrounded by grim faces on all sides, though a few sent me nervous glances of concern. It seemed like they didn't want me to do this. I was their princess and would one day be their queen if we managed to stop the Council, so I understood their apprehension.

I have to do this, though. No one else can do it but me.

Santori came to a stop in front of us and glanced at me over his shoulder. "Are you ready, You Highness?" he asked.

"As ready as I'll ever be." I shrugged.

"You can still change your mind, love," Grey said, his eyes pleading with me.

"And do what?" I hissed back quietly. "Stay behind and let the men fight? Get captured by the Council? Again." I twisted my arms in the ropes. They were very loosely tied so I could get out of them easily.

"That was a low blow," Grey said as he flinched at the memory. "I thought you were *dead*."

"I'm sorry," I added, unable to hide the exasperation in my tone. "I'm just tired of people expecting me to sit back and be the damsel. I'm *not* the fucking damsel in this story, I'm the hero—or at least, I will be." I stomped my foot, my lips set in a hard, grim line of determination.

Everyone stiffened at the unexpected noise when it echoed off the walls around us.

Santori nodded his head at our ranks, then opened the door. Bright sunlight filtered into the tunnel.

I took a deep, shuddering breath and rolled my shoulders back.

It's now or never—and never isn't happening.

It was time to face the Council guards. With any luck, I'd hopefully be able to bring them out of their mind control.

We marched through the Dark Forest silently, surrounded by the rebels. They would shove one of the guys occasionally, just to make it look genuine, in case we were being secretly watched.

The gnarled and twisted canopy of trees above blocked the sunlight from reaching us, leaving our party in an eerie and oppressive state of gloom as we trudged along. These dark trees didn't speak to me in the same way the others in the realm could, though I wasn't sure why.

"Here!" Santori barked as we came to a halt in a clearing.

There was no one here yet, but the guards would be arriving soon, I was sure of that much. There was no way in hell Ronaldo would waste an opportunity to capture us again. We remained the biggest threat to him and his grand, corrupt plans to dominate Faery as well as the mortal realm of Earth.

"They're coming," Grey whispered in my ear under his breath. "They're trying to surround us."

A lone man stepped through the trees dressed in the armor of the Council. His eyes glittered with malice and were completely clear of mind control.

Fuck. He's a traitor because he wants to be!

"Shit," I whispered back between gritted teeth. "He's not being controlled."

More men stepped from between the trees, following the first. There were probably twenty in total, and only half of them had the blank, tell-tale expression I'd come to recognize as someone being under the Council's mind control.

"Are you sure?" Grey mumbled out of the corner of his mouth as he eyed the armored Council guards.

"We can save the ones that are being controlled, but this is going to be bad for Santori and the others." I chewed my lip. "If any of the Council soldiers get away, they will talk, and all of these good Fae will be labeled dissenters."

Ash glanced at me. "So, we make sure none of them get away then."

Santori stiffened. He didn't like the thought of killing the men of Faery any more than I did, but it was becoming quickly apparent that we didn't have a whole lot of options.

"Let's just play this one move at a time," I said, eying the approaching group.

The man with the cruel smirk stepped forward and bowed mockingly. "Your Highness, we've been looking for you."

"And why is that? So, you can take me back to your master and have me murdered?" I raised a defiant brow. My fingers itched to ditch the ropes around my wrists, but I had to time my actions perfectly. I let my magic build up beneath my skin and tingle down my spine while keeping it concealed.

"You think the Council wants your death, Princess? On the

contrary! You will be the most prized slave of all once they have control of your mind." The traitor laughed.

"I know Ronaldo wants me dead," I spat back.

"No, you're wrong. With all that untamed magic running through your veins, you will be the ultimate weapon. The High Councilor wants you under his thumb, doing his bidding, not under the ground."

I glanced at the others as a growl sounded behind me. We needed to stop talking, and soon, because the overprotective men in my life were all about to lose their shit in a serious way.

The traitorous fool had just openly admitted in front of all these witnesses that the Council used mind control.

Is he stupid, or just overly cocky? Probably both.

I clasped my hands together, and the ropes fell away from my wrists. The magic under my skin blasted out of me, the healing tendrils of my shadows seeking the men who were being controlled.

They all dropped to the ground as they were released and granted their freedom once more. Holding their heads, they groaned, seemingly disoriented and dazed.

The Council guard in charge laughed maniacally and drew his blade as if thrilled by the challenge we presented. "I knew this wasn't going to be a simple drop. Do you think your Resistance is secret? *Nothing* is hidden from the Elders." He stepped forward dramatically and swiped at Santori.

Santori jumped back just out of the blade's reach.

Grey freed himself and the others on our side with the help of his partially shifted claws and then gripped the sword at the belt of the closest rebel. It was exactly as we planned.

Shadows writhed along my skin and mixed with my natural purple magic, ready to answer my will.

The men who had been mind-controlled blinked rapidly before rising to their feet. They were obviously confused, which was understandable, but we didn't have time to waste.

We have to act—now!

The traitorous leader swiped his blade out once again and the *clang* of metal against metal met my ears.

Grey faced off against him with furious ease, a seasoned warrior in his own right as the head of the Syndicate and rightful Shifter King.

A powerful gust of wind blasted through three other Council guards, throwing them back into the trees on the other side of the clearing with brutal force.

There was only one other person outside of me that could have been. I turned to Ash.

The Rider was wielding his sword and his magic at the same time. He winked at me and then slashed at his next opponent.

"Kill them all! I need the princess alive!" the asshole fighting Grey bellowed as he sliced into my mate's side with his sword.

Grey grunted in pain as he stumbled back.

My magic exploded from me like a shockwave of sparkling purple and snaking shadows. Someone was screaming, the shrill tone clawing my ears. It took me almost a full second to realize the anguished sound was coming from me.

The guards who were previously mind-controlled came to their senses and jumped into action, forming a circle of protection around me.

I shook my head and shouted at them, "Help him. My mate needs your help!"

The guards glanced at each other before peering at my father for guidance.

"Your princess has given you a command. Do it!" the Shadow King roared. He was fighting two of the Council's guards at once using his magic and a stolen sword.

"We need to get out of here!" I yelled, my gaze fixating on Grey's bleeding side.

One of the Shadow Guards I'd just freed turned in my direction. "Go, Princess, we'll hold them."

I didn't like the sound of that plan, but with Grey injured, there didn't seem to be much choice. The Rebels shouldn't have even been there, but they'd come to help me. I thought it would be easy. I was going to use my magic on the guards, and they would all fall in line. But we were terribly wrong. They hadn't all been under mind-control for starters, and now innocent lives were in danger.

The guards unsheathed their swords in unison and attacked our enemies.

The man who stabbed Grey took a step back as the one of the freed warriors who spoke lashed out at him.

"What? That's impossible!" He looked over the group of Fae that were now on our side with wide eyes and parried another blow from my new friend.

"It's not impossible!" I answered him "And it's the very reason Ronaldo will never be able to control me." I glared at the idiotic fool as I rushed to Grey's side.

The guard lunged at me in a rage.

I twirled to the side, just out of his reach, instinctively throwing shadows in his face as I did.

He grunted but he swung again and again.

I didn't have a sword, only the small dagger on my belt that Grey had insisted on.

Oh, gods, Grey. I hope beyond hope you're okay!

Fenrick was next to me in a breathless second, ever reliable. He slashed his sword at maniacal guard, acting once more as my personal protector, just as he had when I was a child.

The Fae man jumped back, a grin plastered on his face. "The traitor!" he announced with glee. "Your head alone will bring me power with the Council." He laughed mockingly.

"You have never been a better swordsman than me, Malichai," Fenrick warned as he held his borrowed weapon higher.

"No? I think you're remembering things backward, old friend. I was chosen for the Council's guard, while you were chosen to babysit a princess." Malichai laughed.

"I was chosen for the highest honor!" Fenrick spat back. "It was my duty to guard our future monarch, while you were nothing but a cog in a corrupt machine. You were a grunt and no more, a power-hungry, corruptible servant chosen to do the Council's dirty work!" Fenrick snarled.

As I held my ground just offside to Fenrick, I glanced over at Ash.

He was still battling a Council guard when two of the warriors I'd freed rushed to intercept the guard attacking him.

"What are we going to do, Princess?" one of them called back.

"We need to get out of here," I asserted again as I took the opportunity to rush to my mate, leaning down to inspect his wound. Something didn't look right about the stab wound. I peered at Grey. His skin was ashen, and his breath rattled in his chest. I ran my fingers over his face, my heart in my throat.

He blinked up at me in confusion before he recognized who I was. "Go. You need to go on without me," he urged as a cough wracked his body.

"No," I said, firmly putting my foot down. "I'm not leaving you behind!"

He leaned up on his elbows and tried to roll to his knees, straining with the effort.

I pushed him back down. There was no way he was moving like this, not under his own power.

Fenrick stood at my back, the clash of swords ringing in my ears.

What do I do? I have to do something!

All the Council guards were fighting with the Shadow Warriors I'd freed from their mind control, and Santori's men formed a wall around us. Two men rushed forward and picked Grey up more gently than I would have thought possible for trained warriors.

"We can't go back to base. If they follow us, then we will doom everyone," Santori warned as he stepped forward, his eyes on the fray of battle.

"Agreed. We have a place, but sifting is still difficult for me... and I'm afraid with his injuries it will be too much." I wrung my hands together as I stared at my mate.

"Go, Princess! Go, now!" one of the warriors shouted. "We'll hold them off."

"Do you know the way to the house?" I asked Fenrick.

"Yes." He nodded.

"Let's go, then!" I waved a hand for him to lead us back to the house.

It wouldn't hold everyone for long, but we could get away from the assholes trying to kill us. We followed behind Fenrick, and I prayed to whatever gods might be listening that the men we left behind would be okay.

I had so many others to worry about, it was overwhelming. I had to worry about the realms as well as my mate. He couldn't leave me now, just when we were coming to the crux of the war.

I need you, Grey.

I glanced at him, as the two warriors carried him.

His eyes bored into mine. "You should have left me behind, my love. I am nothing but a burden right now."

"Stop it. We aren't leaving you behind, you self-sacrificing idiot," I said I jogged beside him.

"Why the fuck would we leave *you* behind?" Asher roared from behind and shook his head.

"I'm only slowing you down," Grey rasped.

"Shut up," Fenrick growled and rushed ahead.

"I don't care if you slow us down. We will fight if we need to. I refuse to let you die out here. It's you and me against the world, remember? Just hold on!" I rushed past him to catch up with Fenrick. I couldn't take another word of Grey's self-sacrificing bullshit. I needed him just like he needed me. I was pretty sure I'd proven that again and again. But I would prove it a million more fucking times over if it meant he would be sitting safely by my side when the time came.

The only problem was no one was safe. Not really. Even if we got back to Grey's hideout in time, *something* wasn't right, and I had a deeply unsettling feeling nothing ever would be again.

CHAPTER 14

They were being unreasonable as they trudged through the dark forest, carrying me—a damn burden. They needed to sift back to the house and lose the Council, but Aurelia refused to sift because it might be too much for me in my current condition.

"Leave me behind!" I demanded, but they had all stopped listening to me about ten minutes ago.

Aurelia didn't even turn at my order. Her shoulders stiffened, but she continued to stomp forward. She would sooner die than leave me behind.

"Maybe we should just knock him out. His hollering to be left behind is probably bringing attention we don't want," Santori chuckled.

"No one hurts my mate," Aurelia said with a growl, flashing him a warning glare.

"But he's being a pain in the ass," Santori mumbled.

"I don't care. Ignore him!" She grumped at me over her shoulder. "No one is leaving you behind. It's not an option, so just stop it."

"You would already be safe at the house if you had," I retorted as I narrowed my eyes at her. My wound wasn't healing, and I didn't know how much time I had left. It would kill Aurelia to watch me die, and I couldn't stand that.

"We're almost there, Grey. Stop with the bullshit!" Fenrick barked, adding his authority into the mix.

I hated being weak, but I couldn't deny that the pain I was experiencing was visceral. Agony sliced through me every second. The wound inflicted upon me itself had stopped bleeding, but it still wasn't knitting and mending like usual.

There was something terribly wrong. The wound was turning an ugly shade of greenish black. I suspected poison, but I couldn't be sure. It had been centuries since I'd been back to Faery, and the Fae could have developed gods-only-known-what since then.

The rebel warriors carried me across the tree line, stopping just outside the wards to the house where we were staying.

I groaned as they walked across the wards and a thousand fire ants lit me up from the inside out. It wasn't *actually* fire ants, but rather the way the wards affected me as we passed.

Since we'd made it safely without incident, I finally stopped arguing as I was carried into the house to the bedroom Aurelia and I had shared. Only the two men who carried me and my friends followed inside.

Aurelia wrung her hands as I was put down on the bed, her face etched with concern.

I reached a weak arm out to her. Despite my state, I yearned for nothing but to comfort her. To take the sadness from her eyes.

She sat on the edge of the mattress next to my hip, worrying her lip. "What's wrong? Why isn't he healing?" she asked, her voice a breathless whisper.

The king stepped forward and bent at the waist to check the wound. His expression turned grim. "You knew?" the king snarled at me.

"I had an idea, yes," I said, glancing at the wall. His accusing stare was too much. He knew as well as I did that there was only one way to stop the poison coursing through my body.

"*That's* why you were so adamant about being left behind!" The Shadow King crossed his arms over his chest, his lips a thin line.

"What's going on? What aren't you telling me?" Aurelia asked. Tears pooled in her eyes, and she placed her hands over the wound in my side. A green glow lit her palms as her power rushed through me.

She's wasting her energy.

I reached for her hands.

She batted mine away and kept pushing more magic into me.

"Aurelia, stop," I whispered.

"Fenrick, help me," she begged, turning to the Fae guardian.

"You're the strongest of us, Princess. If you can't do it, then I certainly won't be able to either." He hung his head.

"No, I don't accept that. What's wrong with him?" Aurelia turned her pleading gaze on her father.

The king stared at me.

I begged him with my eyes not to put this on her. I didn't want it to be like this.

Why can't the Fates give me just one good thing that isn't shrouded in sadness?

"The blade had poison on it, Aurelia. A poison that's resistant to healing magic. That's why he's not improving," he said, glancing down at the blackened wound.

"Poison? What kind of poison? How do we cure it? There must be a way to save him." She jumped to her feet and paced, her mind already working through a million possible scenarios to save me.

"No," I said as I reached for her hand and pulled her back down on the bed next to me. "Let me go. You can be happy again after you defeat the Council. I don't want it to be this way."

She only resisted a little bit, finally sitting down and glaring at every man in the room. "Someone better tell me right now how to fix this."

Tears stained her cheeks as they slid down in rivers, her gaze landing on mine.

I reached up, wiping them away as my chest burned with agony.

This will destroy her.

Was I being selfish by not telling her the only known antidote to the poison?

"I've only ever heard rumors about this working... and there's a cost involved." The king glanced at me, before returning his attention to Aurelia. "Doing this could put your life at risk as well, daughter."

"I don't care!" she said, her voice raised. "I will do *anything* to save him. Just tell me what I must do." She squeezed my hand.

"It's all just rumors and speculation, but from what I have heard, the blood of a Fae is the only way to heal that poison. Grey would have to bite you and tie himself to you in a completed mate bond."

"I won't do it! Not like this," I growled.

"But it will save your stubborn ass." Aurelia threw her hands up in frustration.

"We don't know that for sure," I growled. "Your father didn't tell you the risk. If the rumor isn't true and your blood can't save me, then you will die along with me. Your fate will be tied to mine, and everything will have been for nothing if you die, and the Council succeeds." I winced as the black veins from my wound to my stomach spread a little more. Pain pulsed through me, but the anguish in my heart was worse. My chest cracked wide open at the mere thought of leaving Aurelia behind.

But it's the hand I've been dealt.

"I don't care!" she screamed, her tight grip on her temper fraying under duress. "I will not lose you. Let the fucking world burn for all I care." Her shadows pulsed and writhed angrily on her arms as she stared me down with a fire I didn't know she possessed.

In that moment, I saw her for who she could have been if the Council and Malcolm hadn't gotten away with her kidnapping.

"Aurelia, think about this," Fenrick whispered, beseeching her to see reason.

"I *have* thought about it," she snapped as she rolled her shoulders back and pinned him with her stare. "I don't want to live in a world without him in it. Is that selfish? Maybe! But I have been running around the realms trying to stop the Council for everyone else. Grey is mine. I think I'm allowed to be selfish this once."

Fenrick's shoulders slumped in defeat. He knew as well as I did she wasn't going to budge on this. She called me stubborn a lot, but she was even more stubborn than I was when she got something in her head.

"She's not wrong," Ash said, speaking for the first time since we arrived. "If anyone can survive this, it's the princess. You said so yourself, Fenrick, she's the strongest of us all."

"See? I can do this! I can heal him. If *he* does what *he's* supposed to." She glared at me.

"It's not a risk I'm willing to take. You're meant to be queen. You're meant to save the supernaturals, and usher in a new era for them all. You can't do that if you're dead." I flinched in pain, grimacing as I shifted on the bed.

"Everyone out," Aurelia whispered, her voice deathly fierce. "He won't do this with everyone here watching."

"I won't do this at all, so they might as well stay."

"Get! Out!" Aurelia roared, rising from the bed to face them all, her shadows going ballistic all over her.

I shook my head. There was no reasoning with her now.

The others obediently filed out of the room, closing the door firmly behind them.

Traitors.

Though, I probably would have done the same if that anger had been directed at me...

"You *will* do this, Grey." Aurelia clenched her fists at her sides.

"No."

"If you don't, I'll follow you right into the beyond. I will let the world burn, regardless." She placed her palm on my chest over my heart defiantly.

My wolf was eerily silent throughout the entire argument. He didn't really understand what was happening or why he felt so weak. His emotions were more of an impression in my mind than an actual feeling.

"You wouldn't let everything be destroyed, my love. I know you're a better person than that." I shook my head and placed my hand over hers.

"Please, Grey. Don't make me live without you. Try, please?" she cried.

Pain, sadness, and anger warred inside of me that it had come to this.

Aurelia leaned her head down on my shoulder, her hot tears dropping on me one after another.

I didn't dare wipe them away. If our roles were reversed, would I be begging her the same? I would do anything to keep her safe, and in my arms, yet I was denying her that same right.

But I'm not the one who's meant to change the world. She is.

If she died, all would be lost. We would be in the beyond together though, and we wouldn't have to live in the world without each other. My own selfish desires argued with my need to fix the world, and the longer she sobbed over me, the harder they were to fight. "I didn't want our actual mating to be a time of sadness, of a desperate need to save me," I whispered and wrapped my arm around her.

"We won't have a mating at all if you don't stop being so bullheaded!" She sniffed.

I chuckled and then groaned as the pain seared through me more deeply. It was getting worse, and I was getting weaker. If I didn't make a decision soon, I wouldn't be able to. That authority would be denied me. "Okay," I said, relenting.

Her head shot up from my shoulder, her eyes full of hope.

"I'll do it."

"This will work, Grey. It has to!" Aurelia grinned as she helped me sit up in the bed.

I winced as the black veins crawled up my abs toward my heart.

She pushed her hair away from her neck and tilted her head to the side, offering me *everything* in that one moment. This selfless, beautiful, perfect woman was mine and was providing me yet another chance to prove I was worthy of her.

I wasn't worthy of her, but for every second I continued to breathe, I was going to do my best to show her how truly perfect she was, and that she was mine. I kissed her neck in the spot where I intended to claim her.

My mate gasped at the contact but only leaned closer to me. "I love you, Grey. Please, make me yours for eternity," she whispered. "I can't do this without you."

My wolf howled in my head. It was the first sound he'd made since I'd been stabbed, and my teeth elongated in my mouth. I kissed her neck again, hoping I didn't hurt her when I claimed her as mine.

Aurelia fisted the sheets at my sides as my teeth grazed her skin, not in a bite but a tease.

I needed her to relax. This was meant to be a euphoric experience, but since we were in a dire situation, I wasn't sure how it would go. I prayed to whatever gods might be listening that I wasn't about to doom the realms as I closed my eyes and sank my fangs into her throat.

CHAPTER 15
Aurelia

As Grey held me close, his nose trailing over my skin, he plunged his teeth into my throat, hard.

A scream tore itself from my lips. White-hot euphoria blasted through me and rainbows danced behind my eyes in a dizzying kaleidoscope of flashing light and swirling, geometric patterns. I couldn't comprehend how anything that felt *so* good and *so* right could have inspired such fear in my mate.

He's truly my mate now.

The bond snapped into place in my chest, and my body shook with unparalleled pleasure. "Grey," I breathed, my breath rushing out of me as I relaxed.

My mate pulled back and licked my neck with a sensual groan.

I blinked away, clearing the fog in my brain and grinned at him. "We're linked!"

"We are, and we didn't die." He glanced down at the puncture wound in my throat, but it was already knitting itself back together.

I gasped as my eyes fell on his injury, my heart filling with relief and hope. "You're healing." I reached for him and ran my hand over the healing skin. It was rejuvenating, the toxic black veins clearing and vanishing before my eyes at an amazing speed.

"You don't usually recover this quickly," I said with awe.

"I took on some of your healing abilities," he explained before he brushed my hair out of my eyes and leaned forward, kissing me hungrily. "You are truly perfect."

"I told you this would work."

Grey wrapped his arms around me and pulled me into his chest. "Yes, you're apparently smarter than me too."

"I'm glad you're seeing that now," I snickered, biting my lip with a smile.

Grey cupped my cheek and kissed me again, not waiting a second before he was seeking entrance to my mouth.

I pulled back and frowned at him. "You're still healing!" I protested. "You nearly died. We can't do that right now." I shook my head.

"It's part of the bonding, love. We must." He kissed down my throat over the mark he'd just left on my skin.

I shuddered under his touch. "We can't," I groaned. "We're not alone in this house..."

Grey ignored me as he rolled us, so he was pinning me to the bed. "I don't give a fuck. I need you, Princess. *Now.*" He ripped my shirt over my head with a growl of hunger and tweaked a nipple through the fabric of my bra.

I wiggled my hips even as I tried for a third time to slow things down.

But Grey wasn't having any of it. A claw extended from his finger, and he sliced through the thin material between my breasts as if it were butter. He flung the scraps off the bed and attacked my breasts with vigor, sucking a nipple into his mouth and teasing it between his teeth.

My back arched, pressing into his mouth even more aggressively. Grey growled against me, sending tingles dancing over my skin. I ran my fingers through his silky hair, pulling him down closer instead of pushing him away.

"I can't wait another second to taste you, sweet mate." He licked down my stomach, to my jeans, and growled.

"I didn't exactly have time to get undressed," I breathed as I reached between us.

Grey slapped my hands away impatiently. "I'll do it."

"Don't rip—" I stopped when he did exactly that. The sound of ripping fabric tore through the room, and I flinched.

He was tearing all my damn clothes!

I won't have any left.

"Grey, I'm not going to have anything else to wear," I groaned.

He wasn't listening as he spread my legs wider, picking up my calf to place a kiss there before moving higher.

I shivered, anticipation thrumming through me.

Grey's eyes glowed with his inner wolf as he watched me and licked my inner thigh.

I squirmed, wiggling my hips, needing something tangible. A part of me both loved and hated how easily Grey got under my skin, setting me ablaze with the faintest of touches.

I need him.

"I need you naked," he growled as his gaze roamed over me. He leaned down and inhaled deeply through his nose.

What the hell is he doing? Is he smelling me?

"Mine," he growled possessively and licked his lips. In this moment, he was more wolf than man.

Is his wolf taking control?

All thoughts fled my mind as he continued his delicious assault on my body.

He licked all the way up my slit and circled my clit.

My back arched and the crescents of my fingernails dug into his scalp. "Grey!" I cried out to the ceiling, my head thrashing.

Oh, gods! Everyone in the house will have heard that!

He circled my clit faster, before sucking it into his mouth. His fingers dug into my inner thighs, holding them spread wide.

I bucked up into his mouth, unable to deny myself the pleasure he offered so willingly.

His gaze found mine and the glow of his eyes brightened further. With his lips, teeth, and tongue, he ate me savagely.

My hands tightened in his hair, my spine tingling with the beginnings of my first orgasm as my body shook with tremors. I didn't know how much longer I could last, given the way he was devouring me.

He growled against me, causing my hips to buck. "Not yet, mate. You will only come when I'm buried inside you." Grey backed away from me, clucking his tongue with a devilish wink.

A strangled groan escaped my lips when I realized what he was doing. He was edging me.

Oh, hell no! Not now.

"Then fuck me already and seal the mate bond!" I gripped his shoulders with a strength I didn't know I had and pulled him closer.

Grey fell over me, but his hands snapped out to either side, keeping him from crushing me with his weight. He leaned down and took my lips with his.

I kissed him hard, tasting myself on his tongue as my hips bucked against him.

Grey just chuckled into my mouth. "You're a needy little thing, aren't you, mate?" he whispered against my lips. He tweaked my nipple between his fingers before running his hand down over my belly only to sink two fingers inside me. My body clenched around them as he curled them inside me, hitting my G-spot and setting off my orgasm.

"Grey!" I shouted, the sound of my voice strangled as fire tore through my veins. My whole body shook with my release as white light filled my vision.

Grey chuckled darkly and continued thrusting his fingers inside me hard and fast, prolonging the orgasm as he kissed my neck where his mate mark was etched into my skin.

"I need you to mark me, mate," he groaned. "I need your mark on my skin more than I need breath in my body. Make me yours."

"I'm not a wolf, Grey. I don't know how to do that," I said as I came down from the high I rode.

"It's an instinct, my love. Just do what feels natural to you." He rolled onto his back and pulled me along with him, so I ended up on top. "The bond won't be fully formed until you do. We must bear each other's mark."

I straddled his waist and stared down at him in silent contemplation. He was already mine, but how did I mark him to prove it to the world? I didn't really care about proving it to anyone else, but with the way Grey was staring at me, he needed this more than anything, and I understood more than most when I allowed myself to think about it. I proudly bore his mark and waited forever for it.

I had to think of a way to mark him... even if I couldn't shift my teeth and bite him like he'd done to me. Biting my lower lip, I reached between us and gripped his cock in my hand, pumping him slowly and methodically while I searched my instincts for a way to mark him.

Grey gripped my wrist and moaned as he pulled my hand away and wrapped it around his throat. "I know my cock belongs to you, love, but I would rather you mark me for the world to see. I'm yours for eternity."

"I'm yours as well, mate." I leaned down and kissed his lips. My hand around his neck tingled as I scooted further down his body.

His other hand tightened on my hip, and he grimaced. "I'm the luckiest man in the world, but I won't be able to hold myself back from flipping you over and fucking you until you're screaming for me if you keep going the way I think you are."

"Why would you want to hold yourself back?" I asked with a sly grin. My hand on his throat heated as I shimmied down his body. Lining my entrance up with his cock, I grinned as I rubbed myself against him.

A strangled moan escaped Grey, his eyes closing briefly.

I wiggled my hips wickedly.

A moment later he hissed, surprising me and shocking me all at once.

A golden light seeped from my hand around his throat like an aura of sunshine. "What's happening?" I asked, wide-eyed as I sat up and sank myself down on his beautiful cock.

"It feels like fire, but in the best possible way!" he said, breathlessly. "I think you're marking me, mate."

"But how?" I groaned as the light grew brighter and I circled my hips seductively, grinding into him to heighten my own pleasure. His cock hit that spot inside me again, and I screamed just as the light beneath my palm grew to blinding levels.

Grey reached up, holding my hips down so that he could buck his hips up into mine. "Come for me, mate. Seal the mate bond for eternity!" he yelled.

Unable to stop it, I came again at his command. My whole body shook and trembled with ecstasy as his seed filled me. Until the brute force of my release subsided, leaving me gasping. My glowing hand—which had been fused to his neck only moments before—finally dimmed. I removed it as I collapsed on his chest with panting breaths as the aftershocks of my orgasm continued to ripple through me.

The golden cord that had formed between us strengthened as I stared at his neck, where a dark black ink-like blotch that resembled the humans' depiction of a simple fairy silhouette was etched into his skin.

That's my mark.

I trailed my fingers over the blackened skin in awe, pleased my instincts had served me. I'd marked him in return, just as he'd desired.

He groaned even as he was spent. "What does it look like?" he rasped as he pulled me down.

"It's a black fairy," I explained, "like a Shadow Fae." I smiled at him, my heart full.

"Perfect." He grinned back at me and pulled me to his side.

I laid my head on his chest, listening closely to the strong beat of his heart. He was here, and we were connected. I didn't have to worry about him dying anymore. "You know, we should probably get up and do something..." I shifted in his embrace, but his arm banded tighter around me.

"Not yet," he whispered and kissed my forehead. "I'm not quite ready to face the world yet after our mating."

I glanced up at him with a frown. "So, what does this bond mean for us exactly? You healed faster than ever. You said something about adopting some of my abilities?"

"I don't know what it means entirely," he admitted "I just know there will be changes in both of us over the coming days and weeks." He peered down at me with pure adoration in his eyes.

My heart swelled with love for the man holding me.

He is worth every risk.

I just wished he'd realize it more than he did. I never again wanted to have another argument like the one we'd had. It pained me to know that he truly believed in his own mind that risking everything for me was acceptable, but me doing the same thing for him was not. "I hope you understand *now* that we are in this together, no matter what. If you can risk your life for me, then I can do the same for you." I poked him in the chest with a defiant smirk.

"You are literally the only hope to save the realms, my love. I'm sorry if I don't want to jeopardize that along with your life, especially when we both owe Ronaldo a gruesome final death." He rubbed my back as he spoke.

I understood where he was coming from. I had no intention of dying. We were fighting a war against oppression, it was important...

But how good will victory actually feel if I don't have him there, by my side, to share it with me?

With that thought, I spoke my mind. "I don't care about anything if you're not there to share in the victory." I kissed his chest over his heart. "We're in this together, Grey—for eternity. Our bond is a promise, an oath that neither of us can break."

"Fine. No more decisions without consulting each other first, and I will try to contain my wolf instincts as long as we can try to come to a *mutual* agreement where your safety is concerned."

"We're linked now, Grey," I answered. "Our life forces are tied together, so your safety matters just as much as mine."

He opened his mouth to protest.

My hand covered his mouth. I wasn't having any of it. "No arguments. I know you feel the connection as strongly as I do. If something were to happen to you, I would die too. So, no more unnecessary risks for either of us. We need to be smart if we're going to win the war for Faery."

"Very well, mate. But there's no way in this realm or any other that I won't *always* worry about your safety. I will protect you with my last breath," Grey said. "Even if that means it's yours as well."

CHAPTER 16
Grey

"I think it's time to go back," Aurelia announced to the others. "We need to start planning for war."

Santori ran a hand over his face. "Are your supernaturals ready for war?"

"They're some of the best trained fighters I've ever seen," I said with a nod. Some of my people had been with me since I first opened the Syndicate. They had been training for centuries to take down the Council.

They are ready. They have to be.

"What about your people?" Aurelia asked with a frown. "I saw many just learning how to use their shadow magic."

"When the time comes, the rebels will use whatever they have at their disposal to take down the Council," Santori assured her.

Fenrick leaned forward in his seat, eyeing us all. "Are we sure about this?"

"What do you mean?" I asked. "We don't have a choice but to take them down."

"No, no. That's not what I'm asking. I'm just wondering if we're moving too quickly. We only have one shot at taking down the Council, and I don't want to blow it because we weren't prepared."

"We're as ready as we're ever going to be," I replied. "And I think we need to move before any of their experiments are successful. Currently, their mind control serum doesn't work on shifters. But what if they figure it out? They could take control of over half our army during the height of battle, and then all would be lost."

"What about the rest of the controlled warriors?" Fenrick drummed his fingers on the arm of his chair. "Some of them were manipulated from the start. They didn't choose a side."

"They will be freed as soon as the Council is gone. They might already be onto the fact I can free their guards, so I agree with Grey. It's best we move quickly now," Aurelia said.

"It depends on the possibility the mind-controlled guards that fought against those assholes in the forest let any of them get away. We have to operate under the assumption that the Council does know what you can do." I squeezed Aurelia's hip, drawing her nearer.

"Okay, then. When do you leave and how will you contact us when the time is right?" Santori asked.

The man was obviously ready for a fight. I couldn't blame him. After seeing for myself the destruction the Council was bringing to the Fae, I was ready for this battle as well. I glanced at my mate, and a thread of nervousness tore through our shared bond.

What will happen to us during this war?

War was violent, and there was never a real winner. People were always lost on both sides and lives were changed forever. We were fighting for our survival, though—not just our own, but that of the entire supernatural population of both realms. The fact we were fighting for our very right to exist gave me hope that we stood the better chance. We had a reason beyond power to fight.

"We will leave as soon as possible. If you could allow Fenrick to sift into the tunnels, he will send word directly when it's time to fight." Aurelia sat up straighter in her chair, her posture rigid and regal. She looked every inch the queen she would one day become, though her doubts continued to trickle through the bond.

I glanced over, flexing my fingers on her hip to get her attention as I poured all my confidence in her and our armies into the bond.

She peered at me with a small smile.

"I'll ensure the wards permit Fenrick's passage," Santori agreed with a nod.

"Okay, I guess it's time to go back and rally everyone together." I stood, pulling Aurelia up at my side. I didn't like returning to the human world having been in Faery, but hopefully once we defeated the Council, that wouldn't be an issue. I scanned the old house, imagining a whole different life for myself and my mate. One where we could make the place a home. It wasn't realistic. We were both royals, and the house wasn't well defended, but it would still be ours.

Fenrick clapped us both on our shoulders and grinned. "Ready to get back?"

"Let's go. The faster we do this, the faster we can end the Council for good."

We swirled through time and space, and the landing wasn't as difficult this time as my feet crunched the gravel as I touched down. Aurelia didn't even stumble. Were we just getting used to sifting, or was it the bond that made things easier? I was stronger now than ever before, and power thrummed beneath my skin, but I didn't dare use it until I knew what it did.

We landed outside the wards of the Syndicate, and I immediately stepped in front of Aurelia at the scene that played out before me. The wards to the building were surrounded by human military.

What the actual fuck?

Guns were drawn when they caught sight of us, and blank eyes stared us down.

"Fuck it. We're in trouble," I mumbled under my breath.

Malcolm stepped out from the crowd, a smug smile on his face.

"I can save them the way I did the Fae guards," Aurelia whispered behind me, though she didn't move to stand next to me.

I was grateful for that. She was letting me protect her. "They're just humans. What if you break their minds?" I asked. Even the Fae she'd saved had been affected by her breaking the control over their minds. It wasn't painless, and humans were far less resilient than even the weakest supernatural.

"What else can we do?" she asked. "We're outnumbered."

Ash and the Shadow King stepped up next to me with their swords drawn.

"We're going to have to fight and let Aurelia at least try," said her father.

"All right, but Malcolm is mine," I growled.

Aurelia spun me toward her and kissed me hard. "I'm going to try to break the control and then I'll race across the wards to get help."

"That's a good plan." I nodded and turned back to the military.

If Dan grabbed some of the others who were trained to fight, then we could even the playing field out a bit.

How long have they been outside my wards, waiting to ambush my people?

"Malcolm!" I roared. "Fight me."

"Why would I do that when I could just have the humans kill you and bring the princess to me?" Malcolm planted his hands on his hips.

"You mean my bonded mate?" I asked with a grin.

Malcolm's expression became murderous as his face turned red. "You lie." Malcolm unsheathed his sword.

"Why would I lie about that?" I crouched into a fighting stance.

He stalked forward, his face coloring almost purple with rage. "You would lie to avoid death! You think I won't kill you if it means her death." He slashed his sword at me, brazen and full of rage.

I jumped back, bringing up my own weapon to block the blow. We were evenly matched. We'd fought several times before, and the slippery bastard had always gotten away. I lunged forward and sliced at his midsection, but the clang of his sword meeting mine filled the air. Magic bubbled up inside me, begging for me to unleash it. But I didn't know how to use magic. I was a shifter, and the only thing I'd ever learned to do was shift.

Malcolm swung his blade, going wide with his sweep.

I parried with my own blow as static electricity crawled up my arms and tingled at my fingertips. My sword glowed blue with power, and I swiped out at Malcolm again.

The electricity hit his blade, and he cursed, dropping the weapon. The scent of charred flesh burned in my nose as he glanced down at his blackened hand. "You really did bond with the princess," he hissed as his good hand pooled with magic.

Fuck. He's going to fight with magic now.

I didn't even know how I'd allowed power to flow into my sword. The magic seemed to have a life of its own. I gripped the sword in both hands, unsure what I was going to do next.

More and more magic filled Malcolm's palm.

"I told you I had. You're the one who didn't want to believe it." I shrugged with a nonchalance I didn't feel. "All this time you've believed Aurelia was yours to claim—but she's mine!"

Enraged, he threw the ball of magic at me with a wild battle cry.

I swung the blade at it like a human baseball bat, running on pure instinct alone. When the magic connected with the blade, it soared back toward him with the strength of my strike and blasted Malcolm square in the chest.

Malcolm screamed as his own magic burned a hole right through his chest. With a horrified, twisted expression on his face he dropped to his knees.

I stalked forward with my blade. "I told you, one day I would have your head," I growled and swung the sword still crackling with magic in a wide arc. His head tumbled from his shoulders and rolled away like a gory game ball.

The human military stopped battling with the supernaturals that Aurelia had brought out to help and they all blinked at each other in confusion.

I scanned the battlefield, only caring about finding one person.

Aurelia was several feet from the wards, squaring off with a human

He stopped mid-attack, his weapon falling from his grasp as he blinked at her, confounded as to the predicament in which he found himself.

She held her magic, summoning it back at the last second before spinning on her heel. A brilliant smile lit her face up with relief and pride when she glanced at the body at my feet. "You did it!" she yelled and ran into my arms, letting her guard down. "He's finally gone."

"Aurelia!" the king bellowed.

I spun just in time to shield her from the man that rushed us.

"What did you do to us?" the man shouted. He held his gun at the ready, with his finger on the trigger, willing to take us out if necessary.

Aurelia squared her shoulders and rose up to her full height as she stared the human down. "We did nothing but save you from being controlled by that monster."

"You're *all* monsters. But that man was helping us round all of you up!" This soldier had obviously been drinking the Kool-Aid before his mind had been controlled.

"These *monsters* have been living among humans for centuries, and you never knew it. They have been your neighbors or possibly even your friends, and you turn on them so suddenly because they were born with magic?" Aurelia said.

"They were biding their time, waiting to enslave all humans," the soldier spat back.

I scoffed. "Yeah, because we sat back and waited for human technology that could literally destroy the world before we were ready to attack you and take you out. We watched the human population grow to an unimaginable size that outnumbered us a hundred to one before we decided it was time. Do you even hear yourself right now?"

"He's completely brainwashed, Grey, even without the mind control. There's no reasoning with him." Aurelia turned to Dan. "Lock him in the cells. He's a danger to us."

"Are we sure that arresting human soldiers is the best idea, love?" I asked but nodded to Dan to do as she said.

Dan stepped up to do as commanded.

The soldier swung the butt of his rifle straight for Dan's head in response.

But Dan's supernatural reflexes kicked in at the last second, and he gripped the gun as it came at him, tossing it to the side before he tackled the idiot.

More soldiers raced forward, but the majority hung back to see what was going to happen. They weren't shooting at us, so we still had an advantage.

One moron raced toward Aurelia.

My heart thumped in my chest, and before he could get there, magic buzzed beneath my skin and suddenly, without having taken a single step, I was in front of her, blocking the blow of his weapon with my forearm. I reached up and ripped the gun from his hand and turned it on him, hitting him right in the face.

He crumpled to the ground, unconscious.

"Grey, did you just sift?" Aurelia whispered behind me, excitement and wonder in her tone.

I glanced at her with a smirk. "I think I did." I turned back to the chaos. All the men who'd rushed us were being carted away by my team. The remaining humans still stood around, a mixture of awe and trepidation painted on their faces.

"We are no threat to you," Aurelia called out to the soldiers. "The Fae who have wormed their way into your government are the real threat. All we want is peace."

A man dressed in all black tactical gear stepped forward and glanced at Malcolm's headless body with a frown. "We can't have peace. Now that supernaturals are known to the world, I fear there will never be peace between us."

It was the fear I'd harbored for centuries. It was why we'd worked so very hard to stay hidden all this time. As long as we were in the human realm, no supernatural would ever be safe again.

CHAPTER 17

Aurelia

The soldiers milled around the battlefield outside the ward. Most had no memory of anything that had happened during the last few weeks.

How did the Council control them so thoroughly that their memories were wiped clean?

"Are we sure letting them go is a good idea?" Ash asked. "What if they lead the government right to us?"

"The troublemakers are in the cells now, Ash. I can't hold the human army in prison because we're scared."

"She's right. They will see it as an act of war," Grey agreed as he wrapped his arm around me. We hadn't had a chance yet to talk about the new powers he was displaying. He'd sifted right in front of me.

I hadn't even learned how to control that particular power yet. It only worked when my emotions were running high. "We don't need a war with the humans." I sighed. "Once we defeat the Council, everyone can return to Faery and leave the humans alone once and for all."

"It won't end there, love. Humans know we exist now. They will always be looking for us." Grey pulled me in close.

The soldiers wandered away in groups, speaking frantically to each other in hushed tones, but at least they were leaving.

All except the man in the black tactical gear who'd spoken before. He stepped up to me with a nod. "You're the princess everyone is looking for," he said.

"I am."

"I remember more than the others it seems. I'm a Secret Service agent. I'm not even supposed to be working with the army..." He shook his head.

"You were at the gala," Grey informed him, narrowing his eyes on the man.

"Yes, I don't remember everything, but most of it. I have some information you might need. Is there somewhere private we can talk?" the agent asked.

I glanced at the building, unsure if I should even suggest it. He'd been the one to say we would never have peace, and now he was asking for a private place to give us intel. I wasn't sure if that was the best idea.

"Why should we trust you?" Grey asked. "You said yourself that we will never have peace."

"The information I have is what you want, and I'm risking everything, including my life, to give it to you. I can't talk out in the open like this." He scanned the clearing, but all the soldiers had already left.

"How important is this information?" I asked. "Are we talking life or death?"

"It could be, for a lot of people." The agent glanced between us.

I didn't know if we could trust him, but he was sticking his neck out on the chopping block just by having the conversation with us. What if we dismissed him and the intel he had could have ended the war in our favor? "I think we should go inside, Grey. We should hear him out, especially if what he has to say may save innocent lives." I chewed my lip.

"Fine, but I hope you understand we'll need to take your weapons, and you will be guarded the entire time you're inside the wards." Grey stepped forward, waving a hand.

Dan and two other shifters stepped up, flanking the man.

"I understand," the agent replied and held his arms up.

"Search him. Take any weapons he has, or any kind of listening devices, and then we'll step into the building," Grey said to Dan.

The man had an impressive arsenal of weapons strapped to his body. It was a little terrifying. I never would have checked some of the places where they'd found guns and knives.

"Take off your boots," Dan ordered.

He untied the laces and took them off one at a time.

Dan pulled two small daggers and a handgun out of each.

"They also have compartments in the heels," the agent told Dan and clicked a button. A blade shot from the back of the heel of the boot.

I gasped.

Holy crap. That's cool.

Dan wrenched it out of the heel and handed the boot back to the man before doing the same with the other. "These certainly aren't standard military-issue," Dan grunted.

I counted fifteen weapons pulled from various places on the man's body, but they found no listening devices.

"Use your magic, Dan," Grey commanded.

"What magic?" I asked. I knew he was half-Fae, but I'd never seen him use any powers before.

Dan's hands glowed midnight blue.

"He can detect and disable electronics. So, if there are any hidden devices on him, they won't be recording anymore." Grey crossed his arms over his chest.

"I told him where the blades in my boots were. Why would I do that if I was hiding listening devices?" asked the agent.

"You may not even know they're hidden on you. You were being mind-controlled, remember?"

"That's fair." He nodded and allowed Dan to continue his search.

"I found something," Dan said with a growl. "It doesn't matter now, though, it's completely fried."

"All right then, let's go." I stomped forward with purpose. I was probably too curious for my own good.

What information does he have for us, and why is he risking his life by giving it to us in the first place?

He was Secret Service, and the President wasn't exactly the biggest fan of supernaturals. In fact, the complete opposite, as far as we knew.

My shoulders slumped as I followed the men into the garage. It was hard to think back to the gala. We'd lost Zeke that night and been forced to leave him behind.

We all got into the elevator, and Grey pushed the button for the interrogation floor. That was on the same floor we'd just had all the unsafe humans sent.

"Are you sure this is a good idea?" I asked him.

"We need to make it look like he's on their side, and we're locking him up too for the time being. But they will all be released to the authorities once we get a witch to wipe the memory of our location from their minds." Grey grasped my hand.

"You have a tactical mind." The agent nodded subtly. "I appreciate you taking these steps to protect my life."

"Like I said before, we aren't the monsters we've been made out to be," I answered, shuffling my feet as I waited for the *ding* of the elevator. The wait was torturous, even though it was probably only a minute.

The elevator doors finally opened, and Dan shoved the man out into the large room where magical cells lined the walls.

Lydia screamed obscenities at us.

Ah. Just another day at the Syndicate.

"You can't leave me in here with humans!" she yelled.

"You're lucky I didn't put any *in* the cell with you," Dan barked back. "Now shut up before I cut your rations."

Lydia closed her mouth and sat back against the wall, glaring at us—specifically me. She hated me after what'd happened when I'd first come to the Syndicate. Both she and Grey's second-in-command at the time had involved themselves in some shady dealings with Malcolm in an attempt to get rid of me.

She deserves to be locked up. She's a traitor.

"Don't bother with her. I forgot she was even here." Grey waved a hand as we continued past the cells. "Put him in the box. We need to have a chat," he said aloud. Grey glared at the men in the cells as he walked past them. They had attacked us of their own free will. They thought we were monsters, but *they* were. They were the ones rounding up supernaturals and persecuting them for simply being different.

Have they learned nothing from their own history? Apparently not.

We followed Dan into the box with the Secret Service agent. It was a twelve-by-twelve room with no windows. It had a single metal table in the middle of the room that was bolted to the floor.

I closed the door behind us with a soft click and turned to the agent. "This is the most secure place in the building besides my floor. You can speak freely here."

Grey sat in the chair in front of the table and pulled me down on his lap.

"You're the ones who've been rescuing the supernaturals from the prisons and the intake facilities," the agent said. It wasn't a question.

"Yes," I said. "Why is that important?"

"Well, there's a secret facility that no one but the President and a few of his top advisors know about."

My shoulders slumped. "We haven't been able to get to all of them yet." I wanted to, but there just wasn't space here, and we had to gather an army to march on the Council. The fact that so many supernaturals remained incarcerated and were still being tested on weighed my spirit down.

"This place isn't on any list you may have. It's top secret and only for the high profile supernaturals that the High Councilor wants for special projects."

"And why are you telling us this?" Grey asked.

"You said you've been breaking in and getting people out. I'm giving you the top-secret location of one of these places so you can continue to do just that." The man sounded frustrated as he growled the last word.

"You lost someone." I cocked my head to the side, a bubble of empathy forming in my chest.

"My wife is a witch. They somehow figured it out and detained her *and* my nineteen-year-old daughter. They have been holding them there, over my head, so I'm forced to do their bidding." He rubbed his eyes with his forefinger and thumb.

I glanced away from him and swallowed the lump forming in my throat. "I'm sorry about your wife and daughter, but we have a war on the horizon and more people already here than we can deal with. Once we defeat the Council, we'll try to get everyone out of those facilities, and hopefully even make a treaty with the President. But until then, we are spread too thin." I hung my head. Tears clogged my throat and burned the backs of my eyes. I hated leaving people in those facilities even a day longer than they needed to be. It broke my heart and left a horribly sour taste in my mouth.

"You don't understand," the agent replied. "I'm not just asking for them. There's someone *you* love there as well." His gaze bored into mine.

"What are you talking about?" I sat forward on Grey's lap with a frown.

"The man with you at the gala. The one who was shot? He didn't die from that wound. He's still alive and being held prisoner."

Ash's fist slammed into the man's shoulder, toppling him over in his chair.

The agent grunted but didn't fight back, simply raising his hands in surrender.

"You think you can get us to save your family faster by lying to us?" Ash growled low and threatening as he leaned over the man with a snarl.

Dan clapped him on the shoulder. "Ease up. There are ways to find out if he's lying, man," the half-Fae said.

Ash straightened to his full height. His body was rigid, and his expression contorted with rage, but he backed off the agent.

"I'm not lying. I was ordered to stay with the President after you all fled, and what I saw was terrifying. The man who was shot lay there bleeding, but a few minutes later, the bullet popped loose from his side all on its own and the skin healed! I was forced to knock him out again, and they took him out through the back."

My eyes widened, and hope flared inside me.

Could it really be true? Was Zeke really alive? I glanced at Grey.

He was staring intently at the man, keeping his cards close. "How do you know he wasn't taken to a different facility?" Grey asked.

"Malcolm ordered them to take him to the secret facility. I was there. I heard the command. He's there right now with my wife and daughter. They knew he was important to you, so they didn't want to risk putting him in a lower-level facility." He stood and brushed off his clothes.

Ash's eyes watered, but he held his emotions in check. "Zeke's alive," he said softly as his gaze met mine across the room.

A grin tugged at my lips.

Fuck yeah! We're doing this. There's no question.

"Where is this facility, and how do we get them out?" I asked.

He wrote down coordinates and handed them to Grey, but his expression was still grim. "One last thing. You need to hurry, because Ronaldo almost has his mind control serum perfected. Once he does, they will be the first ones he uses it on."

My breath rushed out of me as I nodded at my mate.

Once more, we were fighting against the clock.

Why can't anything ever be simple?

CHAPTER 18
Grey

"This could be a trap," I said once we were back in my office, away from prying ears.

"He certainly dropped a bomb on us. Was it simply so we would hurry up and free his family? That being said, we can't risk giving the Council the opportunity to complete their serum." Dan ran a hand down his face.

Fenrick pulled Zeke's laptop closer and powered it on, gripping the coordinates in his other hand.

How do we even know if this place exists? The guy could be lying through his teeth about everything to lure us into the clutches of the government.

"If Zeke's alive, we have to do something," Aurelia said, arms folded. She held an insane amount of guilt bottled up inside of her for what had happened to Zeke.

I wish I could take it away or soothe it somehow.

"It's in the Nevada desert, according to these coordinates, but there's nothing there from what I can see... just sand." Fenrick frowned at the screen.

"Could they have them in an underground bunker of some kind?" Ash suggested as he leaned over Fenrick's shoulder.

"It's possible." Fenrick tapped a couple keys. "There's no surveillance. It's also a no-fly zone. It seems suspicious as fuck. What is this place?"

"You have got to be fucking kidding me," I said and rubbed my chin, my mind whirring.

"What is it?" Aurelia asked, glancing up at me.

"You don't think..." I sighed. "No, it's too crazy to even fathom." Everyone in the room would laugh if I said what was thinking, but the rumors surrounding the location suggested it was some kind of weird alien testing facility the humans had set up decades ago.

Could it have been real all along, and now they're using it to test on supernaturals like us?

"What are you thinking?" Ash asked.

"Nope, nothing. It's stupid. I want a tactical team out there immediately. We need to see firsthand just how good their security is and where the best entry and exit points are." I turned on the news and sighed. Just like every other day, the camera showed supernaturals in magic-blocking cuffs being shuffled onto buses. It made me sick to my stomach.

"I'm on it, boss," Dan said as he typed something on his phone.

"Even without the Council controlling them, this is still going on." Aurelia gestured at the television and slumped down in her seat.

"We don't know who else they have keeping them under control. I doubt Malcolm was strong enough to control all the humans. There are still a lot of unknowns here, beautiful, but we'll figure it out."

"I have a team of five heading out in five minutes. The Fae warrior guy that the princess brought back from Faery is going to transport them," Dan said, still staring at his phone.

"Good. The sooner we get some intel on this place, the better. I refuse to go in blind and risk everyone." I squeezed Aurelia's hand. Her worry for Zeke flooded the bond, and I pulled her into my side. I was worried about the Rider as well. I'd thought along with the rest of them that he was dead. It was a massive relief to find out he was alive... but was it all an act? Was the human government trying to draw us out?

The news droned on in the background, like nothing else was going on in the world other than the "supernatural infestation", as they called it. Other countries had followed the United States' lead and began global witch trials, locking up anyone with a drop of supernatural blood.

"New developments in science today," the newscaster said brightly. "Scientists are one step closer to identifying and creating a blood test to check for supernatural heritage. This breakthrough will be a huge win for the war on supernaturals."

"They can do that?" Aurelia gasped, her expression one of horror.

"I would assume it's similar to those DNA kits that they use to check paternity."

This was not good news for the supernatural population. We'd become adept at hiding in the shadows for centuries, but you couldn't hide your blood. If they made everyone take these blood tests, even more supernaturals could be revealed and rounded up—possibly even those with such diluted blood, they didn't even know they had any supernatural heritage in them.

"We are well on our way to a national database for supernatural species," the news presenter continued. "It's a huge victory, and to be honest, I can't wait to take this test to prove that I'm human! It will be a relief to have that piece of paper to show everyone that I'm not a monster. I'm sure others will feel the same." The woman flipped her hair over her shoulder and smiled for the cameras.

The man next to her put a finger to his ear and held up a hand. "It seems we're getting word that the President is about to address the nation. We'll take you to the Rose Garden, live."

"I wonder what this is about?" I groaned.

"It can't be anything good." Ash straightened, crossing his arms over his bulky chest.

The camera flipped to the Rose Garden, where the President walked out to the podium, his expression grim. If this was about the new breakthrough, he wouldn't have looked like that.

Dread pooled in my gut, but it wasn't all mine. Aurelia's feelings rushed through the mate bond as well.

"Hello, America, I have a heavy burden to bear today. Ten American soldiers have been declared missing in action. Yesterday they were sent to a supernatural stronghold to detain everyone in the building, but they were ambushed with magic. Some of the men who managed to return to us said they were knocked out and detained by these supernaturals." He paused dramatically as if to let that sink in.

"I had a feeling that was what this was about. Any word on a witch that can erase the humans' memories of where they've been?" I asked Dan.

"We don't have a witch here that can do it, and the ones from the outside I called didn't answer. I'm hoping they haven't been rounded up like the others." Dan hung his head.

"These are dangerous criminals," the President went on. "There is body cam footage of a shifter beheading a trusted ally of the American people. He will be sorely missed." He paused again.

"Not likely," I grumbled. "Did you check all the men in the cells for body cams and listening devices?"

"Of course," answered Dan promptly. "But that was during the fray..."

"The good news is that I have been informed these supernaturals are the very same ones who blew up the Dallas prison, and we have a powerful alliance that will eradicate them. We are also only weeks away from a federal mandate that will make testing for supernatural blood mandatory for every American citizen."

The crowd of reporters around the President all started shouting questions at once, vying to be the one chosen for their question.

He held up a hand for silence, but it didn't do a thing to stop them all from yelling. Mandatory testing was a controversial topic apparently, and not welcome by all.

"We must do something. There's no space here, but we can't just leave people in those testing facilities." Aurelia clenched her hands into fists on the table, her lips thinning into a grim line of determination.

"There has to be something we can do other than sit here and watch this vitriol," Ash grumbled in agreement. He was itching to get Zeke back just as much as we were, probably more. They were Riders of the Hunt and had been brothers for millennia.

"There isn't much we can do but research the other facilities and work out a plan of attack. You all don't have to be the ones who go into every single one of them to rescue people. I can send tactical teams so that you can focus on the war with the Council," Dan said.

"No, we need to keep everyone we can here. We need them training and ready for war when the time comes. I'm only sending one tactical team out to scout that place for a reason," I said.

Fenrick peered closer at the computer screen. "We can still do the research for after the war. I don't think humans are going to suddenly stop persecuting supernaturals just because we win this war."

"I agree," Aurelia said. She was still staring at the TV, where more and more lines of supernaturals were being herded like cattle onto buses.

I wanted to turn the thing the damn shit off but couldn't. We needed to keep tabs on what was happening in the world, especially when it wasn't pleasant. "Don't watch it, love. It's only upsetting you more," I suggested as I rubbed her back in soothing circles.

"I can't just turn a blind eye to it, Grey," she answered with stoic grit. "I have to watch it. If I don't see how the people are suffering, how can I hope to be a leader that will end that suffering for them?"

"But it's hurting you, Aurelia. I can feel it through the bond how much." My chest tangibly ached with the pain she was feeling.

My mate is going to be an amazing and most empathetic queen.

"I'm sorry, I don't know how that works. I can't shut it off." She frowned.

"I don't want you to turn it off. I like knowing how you're feeling," I said.

"It's hurting you too, though." She glanced at me with watery eyes.

"Only because you're hurting, love. I'm strong. I can handle it, I promise."

"Um, Grey?" Fenrick frowned, interrupting. "I think there's some truth to what the agent said."

"Why? What did you find?" I got up from the table and stalked around to look at what he'd come across.

"I hacked into the database for one of the testing facilities we have yet to hit… and found some videos of test subjects."

Aurelia rounded the table and was at my side in a second. "What's happening to them?" she asked.

"Don't look, Princess. Some are pretty gruesome." Fenrick shuddered.

"I have to look. I must know. I already told you all not to try to shield me from this." She crossed her arms defiantly. "These are my people."

Fenrick glanced up at me for approval.

I shrugged. I wasn't here to tell her what to do. As far as I was concerned, we were equals—except when it came to her safety.

Fenrick turned back to the keyboard and typed a couple of commands before a video played on the screen.

"This is test subject seventy-seven and we may just have a breakthrough today," the scientist on the screen said almost giddily.

The woman on the bed was blonde and had catlike features. She must have been some kind of cat shifter. Her eyes were closed but her face was contorted in pain as her body convulsed on the bed.

The scientist turned to her, and a look of horror crossed his face as he screamed. "No!"

Foam frothed from her mouth as the convulsions that wracked her body became even worse than before. She was dying. It resembled a human overdose.

How much of that damn serum have they given that poor woman?

Pain sliced through my chest as I watched with bated breath.

Her hands shifted into black claws and then back again. It was clear that she was a jaguar shifter, and they were rare.

I wished I had known she was out in the world. I would have brought her to the Syndicate to train. That's why I started the Syndicate. I collected and protected rare supernaturals and gave them a purpose. She'd fallen through the cracks though, and I felt sick.

The machines hooked up to her flatlined and the scientist screamed in apparent frustration as he grabbed some paddles to try and restart her heart. I hoped for the woman's sake that he was unsuccessful. She wouldn't suffer in the beyond.

"That poor woman," Aurelia whispered, her voice shaking. "We have to stop this. They are killing supernaturals in the name of science."

"There's more," Fenrick said as he clicked another video regretfully.

"After the unfortunate incident yesterday," the scientist started speaking, "we are going to try something different today."

"Do I even want to know?" I asked.

"Probably not." Fenrick shuddered.

"This is test subject eighty-two. She is a known witch, and we are going to practice transference."

"What the hell? Is that what it sounds like? Are they trying to remove her magic?" I stared at Fenrick, wide eyed.

The brunette was tied to a table with tubes and electrodes riddling her frail frame.

The scientist flipped a switch and waited.

The woman gasped as electricity flowed into her and magic pooled at her fingertips.

The giddy scientist brought over some kind of suction device and attempted to literally suck the magic into a canister connected to itbut it wouldn't work. "Release your power to me and the pain stops!" the scientist barked at the girl, but no matter how hard he tried, he couldn't suck away her magic.

"This is disgusting," I growled. "I don't need to see any more to know we have to do something. The question is, how?" We'd have to wait on tenterhooks for the tactical team to report back, because there was no way we were going in half-cocked or blind.

If there's any chance of saving Zeke, we're going to make damn sure we don't leave without him. Not again.

CHAPTER 19

"Sit down, Ash." I glared at him. We were all frustrated, but my face softened when I saw the worry in his eyes. We'd all been affected by the horrific videos of the testing facility. I shuddered as I remembered the witch dying on the table as the scientist lost his temper and turned up the voltage of his machines. Supernaturals weren't people to him, they were merely inhuman test subjects. It was soul-destroying, and I prayed to whatever gods were listening that Zeke could survive long enough for us to get him out of there.

"I can't!" Ash bellowed. "Where is the tactical team? It's been *two* days of complete radio silence. We need to go in!"

"We don't have any information on the place, Ash. We could be walking to our deaths if we try our luck without any kind of recon," I reminded him for the hundredth time. I glanced back down at the book in front of me. It was the golden spellbook I'd been searching for, but so far it hadn't given me any insight into how to defeat the Council.

Have I been wrong all along? Is the book not important?

Had I been banking all my hopes on a book that didn't have a way to stop them? I'd been poring over the book for days now, but nothing in it had called to me. We'd risked our lives for this book.

There has to be a reason for it. There has to be something...

"Where's Magna?" I asked Dan.

"She's helping with rations today. Why?"

"I need to speak to her about this useless book." I pointed to the gold book with a huff of frustration. Why had she thought this was the key?

"I'm sure it's not useless if Magna sent you to find it, knowing she would end up in prison and tortured after, Princess." Dan raised an eyebrow.

I slumped back in my chair. He had a point. Magna was a powerful seer, so she would have known what would happen when we went to get the book, but the sneaky woman never told us all the facts. It could mess up the future. She'd told us *that* all the time.

The news played in the background as I continued flipping pages. They were all still excited about the breakthrough that had been made in identifying supernatural DNA via blood. It was a lot more complex than human DNA apparently, and had taken scientists a while to figure it out... but now they had it narrowed down and were working on getting the test mass produced.

The lengths they were going to simply to eradicate us from existence were terrifying. We would be gone, nothing more than fairy tales come to life only to disappear into obscurity, if I didn't find a way to defeat the damn Council. I glanced back at the book, feeling flat, and continued flipping through the pages.

"Magna will be here soon," Dan informed me. "Don't be harsh with her. She carried a heavy burden. She also went through hell in that prison," he said as he sat next to me at the table.

"I would never be harsh with her," I responded. "Magna is my friend even if she is frustratingly cryptic half the time." I flipped to another page, but I was barely paying attention.

"You asked to see me, Princess?" Magna said as she glided into the room.

"What's with the *Princess* shit? You've never called me that before." I crossed my arms over my chest, my brows furrowed.

"I figured I should get used to calling you by your title." She grinned, winking at me, and sat down on my other side.

"You're just screwing with me," I huffed. "You already knew I was going to get frustrated and ask to see you today, didn't you?"

"Of course, I did. I know all, remember?" She chuckled.

"Sadly, you don't know all," I said as I shook my head.

I wish she did. It'd make all of this so much easier.

How could she be so lighthearted when everything seemed so bleak? I was drowning in misery and responsibility. There were so many things I needed to do. I needed to free the supernaturals from the testing facilities and defeat the Council, but I had no idea how I was going to do any of those things realistically.

"There's nothing in here." I stabbed my finger at the page of the book. "I've gone through it a hundred times, and I'm still not finding anything that can help us stop the Council."

"Are you sure? Maybe you're not looking for the right thing." She raised a brow as if prompting me to think more deeply.

"You're telling me... what? That I need to put my intentions into scanning the pages?" I scoffed.

"No, but perhaps it's the spells you're looking for that are the problem."

"I'm looking for something that can defeat the Council!" I threw my hands up. "What else would I be looking for?"

"If you're looking for a death spell, then you definitely won't find what you're looking for in that book." Magna tapped the golden pages knowingly.

"How else am I supposed to defeat the Council then?" I asked. They wouldn't stop coming after us all until they were eradicated. How could I possibly win the war and not kill them? That didn't make sense. War was war. One side had to pay the price.

"When one army defeats another, is the other army always slaughtered?" she asked in her usual round about riddles.

"No… the survivors are usually spared, but in this case the Council *must* atone for their crimes. You didn't see the videos of the experiments they had human scientists performing." I shuddered.

"Yes, they need to pay," she agreed. "But why does a book of light magic need to be the answer? How do you stop them and then try them for their crimes? Isn't that the real question you should be asking, Princess?" Magna grinned.

I sat back in my seat and glanced over at Dan, exhaling my frustration as I did so.

He was typing away at his phone, pretending he wasn't listening, but I knew he was.

"So, I can't kill them in battle, or I would be unjust?" I asked.

Magna nodded sagely.

How is that just, then?

I'd watched videos of supernaturals dying because of the experiments they were performing on them. How many had they murdered in their quest for ultimate power?

"I can see the wheels spinning in your head, Princess," Dan said, never glancing up from his phone. "You will be a just ruler, we all know that. But I think what Magna is saying is that if those assholes die in battle, the people of Faery won't get the closure they need. That's why it would be unjust."

"When did you become a philosopher? It had to have happened after you shot me with a sedative dart and put all this into motion," I snarked back at him.

Dan grinned at me.

We'd become fast allies since that happened. I didn't exactly know when we had, but he was a good person, and I knew he'd just been following Grey's orders. No one could have foreseen that act would start this whole mess in which we found ourselves.

Well, except for probably Magna.

"You're still going on about that?" He laughed. "I thought we'd moved past that, Princess."

"Never." I bumped his shoulder with mine and turned back to

Magna. "So, this book will give me the answers I need to defeat the Council as long as my goal isn't their death in battle? It wants me to seek due process?"

"Correct," Magna said and rose from her chair.

"Where are you going?" I asked.

She walked back to the door. "Grey will be here soon with news, and I am still needed elsewhere. You know what you're looking for now, Princess. You don't need my help."

I slumped back in my chair, unsure if I really knew what I needed. The way to defeat them wasn't death. It couldn't be. I glanced back down at the book, and something on the open page snagged my attention. I leaned in closer, my brows furrowing as I read. It was a binding spell.

Well, I'll be fucked!

"Did you find something?" Dan asked with a grin. "I know that face."

"That crazy seer led me to the exact spot I needed without me even noticing," I grumbled.

"Did you expect anything less from her? She may speak in riddles, but she always leads you to exactly where you need to be, precisely when you need to be there." Dan laughed.

I ignored him mostly because I didn't want to tell him he was right. I scoured the pages, mentally devouring the binding spell. It was the first flicker of hope we'd had and could be used to bind the Council's powers forever and make them... basically human. It wasn't until I got to the last page of the spell that I noticed there was a stark warning.

This spell should only be used in the direst of circumstances, and only by a powerful, Royal Fae. If the gods don't deem the caster worthy of binding, all will be lost. Binding Fae is almost as gruesome as death. They will become human without their magic. Heed this warning. The penalty is death if the gods don't approve.

Chills raced down my spine upon reading the words. I was a powerful Royal Fae, probably the most powerful in the realm, and the Council deserved a hell of a lot more than just becoming human. The warning still chilled me to the bone, though.

What if the gods don't deem me worthy of performing the spell?

What if they decide I'm not worthy of the throne? Will using this spell kill me?

I chewed my lip nervously as I mulled it over, my gaze fixating on Ash.

He continued to pace, walking back and forth across the room with glassy, unfocused eyes. He hadn't paid any attention to the conversation we'd just had, so he wouldn't know that the spell I'd just found was dangerous.

I decided then and there that I wouldn't tell anyone about the warning in the book. I had to keep it to myself. I had no doubt whatsoever that they would stop me from using it if I revealed the potential toll it would demand.

"What did you find?" Dan asked with a raised brow, braking into my thoughts once more.

"Something that could turn the tide in this war with the Council, but if I told you, I would have to kill you." I closed the book so no one could see the page I was on.

It was written in Fae, and even though Dan was half, he'd never been taught to read the language. My secret was safe from him, but I didn't want my father or Fenrick potentially seeing the page it had been open to. They would tell Grey in a heartbeat, and all would be lost.

This has to begin and end with me.

Just as Magna had said, Grey came rushing into the office a moment later, his eyes wide with worry and anger.

"What is it?" I jumped from the chair and rushed to his side.

The expression on his face was grim as he glanced between the three of us. "The scouts are back, and the news isn't good at all."

"What do you mean? What happened?" I asked and wrung my hands together.

Please don't tell me they're all dead. Please don't tell me we're too late to save Zeke.

It was my fault he was taken in the first place. If I had fought harder against Grey and Ash, we would have seen he wasn't dead. We could have dragged him out of the gala, and he never would have been in that place at all!

"The place is fortified and guarded to the extreme. My scouts barely made it out with their lives," Grey said as he wrapped his arms around me.

"Did they manage to get inside?" Ash asked.

"No, it was exactly as I suspected. The humans have been using that base for years, but everyone thought it was an urban legend."

"What are you talking about?" I frowned.

"The place they took the supernaturals that only a few people know about?" he began. "Is none other than the site where it was rumored they were testing on aliens. It's top-secret and a no-fly zone. No one's ever thought it really existed, but we know it does now. Our high profile supernaturals are being taken to Area 51."

"You have to be joking!" I said.

How the hell are we supposed to get into Area 51? It was supposedly the highest security military base in the entire world!

Hopelessness tore through me. The human—and potentially alien—technology securing that hell hole would be far too advanced for us to just walk in and rescue people. Even with the best tactical team the Syndicate had on its payroll, we were totally fucked!

CHAPTER 20
Grey

I grabbed Aurelia's hand, and we rushed to the elevator. I hadn't seen the tactical team yet and I couldn't bring myself to tell my mate the news I knew in my gut, already…

We can't get Zeke out. Not yet, anyway.

My mate's hopelessness flooded our bond. It seemed I wouldn't have to voice what I was thinking, after all. She knew as well as I did that we couldn't go busting into fucking Area 51 to get people out. It didn't seem possible, even for supernaturals.

"Let's talk to the scouts," I suggested, "and then we'll see if we can come up with a plan." I rubbed her shoulder.

"Okay," she said softly.

The elevator doors opened to the infirmary, and I scanned the beds. "I thought you sent a team of six," I said to Dan, my brow furrowed.

"Shit. Where are the others?" Dan cursed, his expression fraught.

"This is all that made it back?" Aurelia asked, covering her lips with trembling fingers as she walked over to the bed nearest us.

I recognized the Fae warrior she'd brought back from the castle. He lay there, beaten, bloody, and barely conscious.

"Ambush," he said weakly.

"It was a trap. The agent lied to us!" I clenched my hand into a fist, my knuckles cracking. Anger pulsed through me. I wanted to go down to the cells and beat *him* bloody.

The warrior pushed himself to sit, wincing in pain all the while. "I don't know if he lied or if they were just ready for any possibility. We were scouting the area for an entire day before we were ambushed by the military. There are definitely people being taken there, though."

"Did you get close enough to see any entry or exit points?" I asked. Even though we weren't going to be able to go in and get them *now*, it didn't mean all the information we could gather wouldn't be useful.

"No, they must have high-tech sensors or something, because the second we were past a certain point, we were ambushed." The Fae warrior shook his head.

Fenrick crossed the room and held out his hands, ready to heal the survivor.

The warrior shook him off. "No, I'm Fae. I'll heal. Save your strength."

Aurelia cocked a brow at him, her lips pursed. "Don't be stubborn. Let Fenrick help speed up the healing process."

"Yes, Your Highness." He smirked briefly, clearly remembering her dislike for royal protocol.

"You look half dead and you're still acting like a smart ass." She rolled her eyes but offered him a warm smile.

"So, you saw them bringing people in?" I asked, getting the conversation back on track.

"I did. The same buses that've been all over the news were coming and going on that first day."

Dan stepped up next to me, his face pale. "And the rest of the team?" he ventured.

"Either dead or captured. I tried to get us all out of there, but they closed ranks on us and split us up. I couldn't get a handle on everyone. I thought Duke was the one with the worst injuries, but I was stabbed in the gut right before I sifted us out."

Four more casualties in a war we never wanted to fight.

If they were in the testing facility there, we were going to have to get in and free our people. I just didn't have the faintest idea how.

"Is there a chance they're still fighting or were left out there to die?" Dan ran a hand down his face.

"I tried to go back but before I could, the scouts manning the wards here brought me in. I don't think I could have done much anyway. I passed out the second we got inside."

"No, you did what you could," I said, clapping him on the shoulder with a somber nod.

"We need to speed up the timeline on this war." Aurelia sat down in the chair next to the Fae's bed. "Maybe if we establish the new rule of law in Faery, we can reason with the humans... they might let our people go home to Faery? I mean, ultimately, they want to be rid of us, so pulling off a mass exodus home would achieve that end."

"You think that's remotely possible?" Dan asked. "Right now, the Council is controlling the testing, and I'm sure they're controlling what the humans can access."

"But if we take them out, the humans will still have free rein to test on anyone in their custody," I said as I gripped the back of Aurelia's chair.

"I need to believe they can be reasoned with. We don't want to go to war with the humans, but by the same token, they can't detain our people like this either." Aurelia glanced up into my eyes, her lips pulled down in a worried frown.

"We'll figure it all out when the time comes, love." I patted her shoulder and leaned down to kiss her forehead.

Aurelia licked her lips, pausing to take a sharp breath before she whispered, "I think I found a way for me to defeat the Council." Her unease pulsed through our bond. She didn't want to tell me what she'd found, at least not the whole story.

What has her so freaked out?

"How?" Dan asked.

"The golden book," she said, shaking her head at him. "You were there when Magna told me I was looking at this all wrong."

"Yes, Princess, but you didn't tell me *how*." He crossed his arms, eyeing her as if trying to figure out what was going on in her head.

"It's complicated," she answered. "I'll need to get close to them." She chewed her lip.

There's definitely something she isn't telling us. Even Dan can sense it.

"It's too dangerous going anywhere near the Council," I countered.

"Grey, you know I have to do this. It's always been me." She stood from her chair and faced me, her chest rising and falling with each anxious breath.

"No. Whatever this is will be too dangerous. We just need to take them out and be done with it."

Dan was shaking his head before I even finished my sentence. "Magna said that approach won't work."

"That's how I was looking at everything—all wrong." Aurelia tipped her head toward Dan. "The book doesn't kill. It's a book of light."

"So, how the fuck do we defeat the Council without killing them?" My knuckles turned white as I gripped the chair hard.

"They need to be tried in front of the people. If we don't, we will ruin our relationship with them. I will be seen as unjust if I set out to kill them. I won't be worthy of the crown if that's the path I choose to walk, Grey. My people won't respect or follow me if slaughter is the best solution I have to offer."

"This is war, Aurelia. People die in war," I said.

She hung her head, not meeting my eyes. She *knew* how dangerous this plan of hers was.

Is she expecting she won't survive?

"I understand that more than you know, Grey."

"We're not discussing this any further. We'll figure out another plan that keeps you safe," I growled.

"Oh, we're not discussing it? And suddenly I don't get a say? We're bonded, Grey, but that doesn't mean you get to make decisions for me!" Her face turned red, and anger flared through our bond.

Shit. I've really stepped in it, now.

I sent my regret through the bond to her. I'd promised at my hideout in Faery that we'd always discuss matters as equals, and at the first mention of a threat to her life, I broke my word.

She wasn't having it and glared at me in return.

Like the idiot I am when it comes to her wellbeing, I doubled down in the face of her wrath. "Aurelia, we *have* to do this my way. I can't lose you!" I hung my head. Aurelia was my one weakness, and it was plain as day for one and all to see.

"You're not hearing me!" she snapped. "You're letting your stubbornness rule your damn brain again. We *can't* kill the Council." She threw her hands up in the air.

"I don't care what Magna said, or what the people of the realm think!" I roared right back. "I care about your safety."

Dan planted his hands on his hips with a grimace. "Killing the Council *is* the safest option, tactically. You are the princess of the realm and meant to rule, regardless of what the people think or feel. We have to consider your safety above all else, Princess."

"You too?" she scoffed, rounding on Dan, her temper flaring anew.

"You shouldn't even be fighting in the war," he said.

It was totally the wrong thing to say, and I flinched in sympathy for him even as he tried to back me.

Aurelia poked him in his chest. Then clenching her hand into a fist, she pulled her arm back to punch the idiot.

Fenrick grabbed her arm at the last second and pulled her back behind him. "The royal family of Faery has boasted many proud warriors over the centuries, and Aurelia is no different. She has proven time and again that she is more than capable, yet you all still doubt her? Shame on all of you."

"Thank you, Fenrick," said Aurelia, glaring at me and Dan in turn.

"I'm not done yet, Princess," Fenrick said, raising a brow at her over his shoulder. "At the same time, you need to remember that their worry comes from a place of love and respect. Everyone wants to return to

Faery, but they want to go home to the place they remember. You are the only one who can give them that, and as such, you must be protected. You are the golden daughter of prophecy. Without you, Faery has nothing."

Aurelia instantly deflated, her expression souring. "Fine. We need to find a compromise then."

"You're going to put that secret plan yours into action whether I like it or not, aren't you?" I asked.

There was no way my stubborn mate was about to back down. I knew her too well to ignore that fact. She was as stubborn as me.

But what if I can convince her to at least accept guards while she executes it? Surely, she can't reject such a reasonable compromise?

The Riders of the Hunt loved her like a sister. I'd bet they would willingly take up positions around her and protect her while she got close enough to the Council to enact her plan.

A commotion in the hall ensnared my attention, dragging me from my thoughts. I spun to the door to the infirmary.

Fenrick and Dan moved almost as fast as I did to block the possible threat to Aurelia.

She rolled her eyes.

A shifter burst through the door with heaving breaths. He was a scout entrusted to watch the wards, and no threat to her.

I sighed with relief as I waited for him to catch his breath.

Did he run up the stairs to get to the infirmary?

"You have something to report?" Dan asked.

"Yes... sir," he wheezed.

"Give him a second to catch his breath." I shook my head at Dan.

"If it's so important he ran all the way here, we may not have time for that," Dan said.

"Council," the scout breathed.

"The Council? What about them?" Aurelia asked, her eyes wide.

"Here," he answered, still gasping.

"Are you telling me the Council are inside the building?" I growled, my inner wolf rising.

"No... wards."

"Shit. They've found the Syndicate?" I asked.

The man nodded, relieved he'd delivered the message.

I grabbed the remote for the TVs and switched it to the surveillance footage from outside the building. It seemed they were bringing their attack to us. Half the people in the infirmary were on the Council's most wanted list… and now we were out of time.

"How did they find us?" Dan asked, though he didn't appear to expect an answer.

"Were you followed?" I asked, turning back to the warrior still in the bed.

"It's possible. I have heard that the Council has the power to follow the signature of sifting, but I thought it was just a rumor."

"It's not," Fenrick confirmed. "But the person has to be in *close* proximity during the sift to follow it, so there were Fae there when you sifted out. And now they've alerted the Council to our location."

"Fuck," the warrior said, hanging his head. "I have failed you, Princess."

"It's not your fault. You couldn't have known," Aurelia said with unexpected determination. "We wanted to move up the timeline so we could get our people out of the testing facilities. This might have just given us what we already wanted."

I glanced at my mate warily. Her determined gaze ate away at something inside me. She wasn't going to listen to reason, and that announcement had gotten us out of our argument without a solution. I glared at the surveillance footage. The Council had their entire army at our wards and were using magic to try to get past them. They couldn't, of course, which offered some relief. "We need to sound the alarm. War has come for us," I said resolutely, "whether we wanted it or not."

Aurelia turned to the scout with a frown. "Get all the civilians to a safe place, now. Everyone else needs to get to the garage."

The man glanced briefly at Dan.

He nodded to do as she commanded.

Aurelia growled low in her throat, her eyes flashing as she made her displeasure known.

Dan glared at the scout. "Do not defer to me when the princess of our realm gives you an order. She outranks me."

A deafening boom rocked the wards, and I stumbled. It seemed if they couldn't get in with subtly, they were going to use brute force.

Fuck.

The war was inevitable... and it was happening *now.*

CHAPTER 21
Aurelia

Rage poured through me, but I couldn't act on it. I had to keep it in check and use it when it benefited us most.

But right now, we need to get the army together.

As soon as the elevator doors opened, I was racing through the garage, searching the myriad of faces for my father. He needed to find the warriors we freed from mind control, while Fenrick went to warn our rebel army.

"Fenrick, follow me!" I waved a hand at him.

Fenrick fell into step and kept pace with me.

I continued my search for my father. He had to be there with everyone... He was a warrior king. Like Fenrick had said, we came from a long line of warriors. He would not be sitting this battle out. I finally spotted him in the back corner of the garage where weapons were being handed out to the army. I waved a hand high above my head to get his attention.

Spotting me, he nodded and made his way over to us. He raised a brow in question at me as he approached.

"I need you to go to the house in the Dark Forest and alert the warriors we freed that war is starting," I said.

My father grinned. "Why don't you go alert your army, and I'll fight the Council in your place?"

I bristled at the thinly veiled attempt to keep me out of battle. All these overprotective males were going to turn me prematurely gray. "Nice try, Dad, but we all know I have to be the one to end the threat of the Council." I squared my shoulders, holding his gaze.

"It was worth a shot." He chuckled and kissed my forehead. "Don't put yourself at unnecessary risk, daughter."

"Any risk I take will be calculated and necessary. I can promise you that." I hugged him hard.

My father gasped like I'd shocked him and when he pulled away, tears shined in his eyes. "I'm so proud of you, Aurelia. Give them hell! I know our future is safe in your hands."

I didn't know if I would ever see him again. The binding spell was complicated and could result in my death, but at least the Council would no longer have their magic, and my parents could try them for their crimes. They could usher in their own new era without me if that's what the Fates and gods decided. "I will," I said with tears streaking down my face. I wiped them away and turned to Fenrick.

He was the friend I'd tormented as a child. The one person I could play hide and seek with, even though he hated it. He'd never figured out how I always managed to hide so well from him.

I smiled softly as the memories of laughter and smiles came back to me.

"Don't do that, Your Highness. You're not sacrificing yourself. Promise me." Fenrick choked on his words.

"I'm not sacrificing myself," I told him. "I'm doing everything I must to take them down." I rolled my shoulders back, mentally preparing myself for what was to come.

"Why do you look like you don't expect to see me again then?" He gripped both my biceps in his hands, his gaze searching.

"This is war, Fenrick. There are always going to be casualties in war." I sighed.

Not even I can see all ends here… if anyone can, it's Magna and she's the one who advised this path.

"If I come back with the rebels and find you took unnecessary risks to protect the realms, I will be so angry with you, Princess," he choked out.

"We need the rebels here, now, Fenrick. I don't have much of an army without them. Just go. Please don't make this harder than it already is." My heart deflated like a balloon, but I nodded at him with what resolute courage I had. I didn't want to disappoint anyone. It was the last thing I wanted, but the truth was, I didn't even know if I would survive the binding spell. These goodbyes weren't what I would have liked them to be, but I needed to make sure my loved ones understood I wasn't being reckless.

I'm making sure they all live.

I would do whatever it took so they would be free of the Council's atrocities and be able to rescue our people from the human detention centers. We needed to save our people no matter what, and when I said *we*, I knew deep down in my bones that it would all come down to *me.*

I've always known it.

"I'm going to the rebels now. Be careful, Your Highness." Fenrick bowed his head, stoic and formal as he sifted from the garage.

Why is he suddenly being so formal? Was it something I said?

Strong arms wrapped around my waist from behind, and I stiffened. My anger bubbled to the surface, and I attempted to break the hold.

"My love, I'm sorry." Grey spun me around in his arms.

I glared at him.

In the next instant he leaned down, taking my breath away with a hard, desperate, and passionate kiss.

I gripped his shirt in an attempt to push him away, but my hands didn't get the memo, and instead they pulled him closer.

When he deepened the kiss even further, it was like our souls connected on some primal and celestial level. Grey growled into the kiss, the vibrations pouring through me. "I just need you safe, love," he said when we parted.

The army was all around us. We didn't have time for another argument.

"Grey, we always knew from the beginning that this was going to come down to me, and the fact you don't think I can do what I'm destined to do hurts beyond belief." I shook my head, biting my inner lip.

"What?" he said, his brow creasing. "This has nothing to do with your capabilities, my love. It's the fact that we just bonded, and we're supposed to spend eternity together. I want a good deal of that time spent on this side of the Veil. I want little princes and princesses we can spoil rotten. I want a life with you. I'm afraid there's a chance we won't get to share that. It's never been about how strong you are, Aurelia. We all know that if anyone can do this, it's you."

Tears streaked in rivers down my face at his words. That was the future I wanted for us too, but it was up to Fate now. I had to do this. I had to defeat the Council and ensure they were tried for their crimes.

And the only way to do that is with the binding spell.

"No, love, don't cry." He leaned his forehead against mine.

"If the gods deem it so, then that's what we'll have. It's everything I want for our lives too, Grey. But the realm needs to be safe first, and the only way to make it safe is to win this war and defeat the Council my way." I stared directly into his eyes, hoping he would finally listen.

"Fine," he agreed. "But not alone. I will be leading the army, and you'll hang back until you can get a look at the Council and do your thing."

"I just sent my father and Fenrick to get our allies in Faery. They can surround the Council guards, and we can win this fight faster than we first thought possible."

Especially if my plan works. It has to work.

The book wouldn't have opened to the page with the binding spell unless it was the only way. Magna had said I needed an option that wouldn't be fatal, and it was definitely that.

I stepped out of the garage and into the bright sunlight. It shouldn't have been a beautiful sunny day when there was a battle about to take place. Were the gods laughing at us, mocking us with one last picturesque day as we fought for our own survival? Is that why it was a perfectly pretty and warm day when blood would water the earth in untold volumes?

The army all stared at me with trepidation. Most of them worked at the Syndicate and knew how to hold their own, but many were those we'd rescued from regular lives among the humans. They weren't trained, but they wanted to help and had been working hard to make a difference. I was proud of them.

We were still far enough away from the wards that Ronaldo and his army of assholes wouldn't see or hear us as I turned to face the crowd. I held up a hand, and the chattering stopped as all eyes focused on me. "I was an orphan, or at least I thought I was," I began. "Even so, from the age of nine, I have been working toward this day... the day we would take down the Council. Those we once trusted have betrayed us and want to enslave us."

The crowd roared, and a figure among them stared back at me.

What the hell is Magna doing with the warriors? She shouldn't be fighting.

A sprite zipped around her shoulders.

I gasped in surprise. It seemed like an eternity since I'd last seen her. I couldn't hear my little pixie friend over the crowd, but I could guess she was cursing the Council with all her heart and calling for their deaths to avenge her sister. I smiled at them and nodded. They had their reasons for wanting justice, and who was I to deny them that chance?

I held my hand up to calm the crowd. "We are about to go into battle. We aren't going into this for the same reasons the Council is, though. We aren't even at war for the same reasons the humans have warred among one another for centuries. We go to war now for our very survival!"

Grey stepped forward then, addressing them all. "The Council wants to control us and if they can't control us, they would see us all dead. I've seen the videos of the experiments they have been performing. And if we don't defeat them now, we may never stop them." Grey wrapped an arm around my waist and pulled me closer.

Another cheer came from the large crowd. They liked the fact that we were presenting a united front, even though I wasn't quite sure how long it would last. There was no way to know if either of us would live to see the end of this day, let alone a future ruling Faery together.

"King and Queen! King and Queen! King and Queen!" the crowd chanted.

I wasn't the queen of Faery yet—my parents were still alive. And even though Grey was technically the Shifter King already, I couldn't be the Shifter Queen...

I'm not a shifter.

"The army is letting us know who they're fighting for, my love." Grey said as he sensed my inner turmoil through our bond, before kissing my temple, and pulling me closer.

The crowd roared louder, their cheering full of genuine heart.

"But I'm not a queen, Grey," I whispered as I stared out over them.

"You're a princess—Fae royalty—and bonded to the Shifter King, your Fated Mate. You may as well be queen." He raised a hand to silence the masses and addressed them once more. "The Council is trying to destroy everything, including our way of life. We won't let them take that from us, will we?" Grey roared.

Our army stomped and screamed their enthusiastic agreement,

I was sure they could be heard all the way back to Dallas' city limits, they were going so crazy! Seeing Grey and me together obviously gave our army hope. I just prayed they would still have that same hope after I did what I had to.

Dan stepped up beside me and handed me my bag.

I glanced inside and saw the golden book. It was exactly what I needed.

He winked at me, then nodded and squeezed my shoulder. That was all the affirmation I was going to get from him. Even though he'd voiced his concerns earlier, he was still behind me.

It warmed my heart.

"So, are we ready to win this war?" Dan roared, riling the army up again.

The warriors went insane, banging on anything and everything they could get their hands on, while still stomping their feet. "Get into position and let's show the greedy Fae Council who gave them their power in the first place!"

With that, the warriors roared one final time, then dispersed into their positions.

Grey spun me around once more. He kissed me hard, and his arms wrapped around my waist.

My heart broke in half. It felt like a goodbye. Tears streamed down my cheeks.

This can't be goodbye. It won't be.

Why did the Fates have to be so cruel? I couldn't have even a year with my mate before everything went to hell? "Grey, I love you. No matter what, please remember that, okay? No matter what happens..." I kissed him softly in return.

"You're making me want to put you in the cell with Lydia until all this blows over." He leaned his forehead against mine, his eyes momentarily closed.

"I think that might be worse than facing the Council," I snickered with a frown.

"Whatever you do, love, don't die. Promise me," Grey pleaded.

"I can't promise you that any more than you can promise me. But I will do everything in my power to come back to you. In this life and in any other. That I can promise, my love." I called him my love for the first time, like he so often did to me, because that was exactly what he was. Grey was the love of my life, and even if I didn't survive this day, I would always fight to come back to him in the next life.

We would be together for eternity, even if taking out the Council killed me. I would make sure of it.

CHAPTER 22

As I pulled away from Aurelia, her words made me feel uneasy. They sounded romantic and passionate, but I could read between the lines...

Is she planning on dying in this war?

The mere thought was completely unacceptable. She had to survive. She was meant to usher in a new era. That was what the prophecy said. But now that I was thinking about the prophecy, I cursed myself in my head. It said she would usher in a new era for supernaturals, but it never specified whether she would live to see that era for herself. Was she destined to die? I couldn't bear the possibility.

She'd promised not to take unnecessary risks, but what was the spell she'd found in the book? She hadn't divulged its purpose, other than the fact it would stop the Council but wasn't of a mortal nature.

I turned her in my arms and cupped her cheeks. "I need you to promise me you'll stay back a safe distance to complete the spell on the Council. I need to know you're at least *somewhat* safe."

"I will stay back as far as I can to complete the spell," she promised. "But I have to do this, Grey. I *must* complete this spell, or everything will have been for nothing."

"I know, love. Just be safe and come back to me," I said just as I spotted Magna. I wanted to have a conversation with the seer before we went to war. Kissing her one last time, I tore myself away from my mate with a regretful gaze and made a beeline for Magna. "What is she about to do?" I asked.

"I don't know what you're talking about, Grey," she said far too casually.

"Yes, you do. What is she planning? You told her we couldn't kill the Council in this war. I want to know what you showed her," I growled.

"The Book of Light doesn't contain death spells," the seer answered. "She was searching in earnest for something that wasn't the correct answer. I simply pointed her in the right direction."

"Does the right direction end in her death?" I asked, crossing my arms, my pulse racing in my ears as I tried to maintain my outwardly stoic and grouchy demeanor. If Magna said *yes*, then I didn't know what I was going to do or how I was going to cope. We'd been allies for centuries on Earth, but if her directions resulted in me losing my mate, I didn't think I could ever forgive her.

"Every decision the immortals make shows me a different timeline, Grey—a different fragment of a possible future—one of many. You know this. We have discussed it many times. I cannot be certain if this time the decision to use the spell will end in her death... but the depth of your love her for her, and the love of those closest to her, makes it highly improbable."

"That's not good enough for me," I snarled under my breath.

"I knew you were going to say that, Grey. We have had this same conversation in my head a hundred times." Magna smirked. "You need to trust in your mate and your family. That's how you make sure you both survive this battle."

"Family?" I scoffed. "I have no family, Magna, and *you* know it."

"You don't?" she asked, hurt lacing her tone as she regarded me. "So, the found family that you have been working with for centuries doesn't count? We mean nothing?"

"That's not what I meant, and you know it, Mags. I'm sorry. I'm just lost and confused. I just need direct, solid answers, not riddles." I sighed.

"They're not riddles. Trust your gut and the people closest to you. They won't let you down. They would rather die than see the princess fall. Trust in us. Together we are stronger than you know."

Ash and the other Riders were huddled in the corner, watching Aurelia like they knew something was up, which concerned me.

I nodded to Magna. This was happening, whether I liked it or not. "I trust you all with my life, but I would give that up for her to live."

"Trust that we all know that and would do the same. I wouldn't have helped her if it wasn't the only way." Magna lowered her gaze.

"And just how many futures have you seen, and how many does she die in?" I asked.

"I have seen infinite futures, some more terrible than others. But out of those where she enacts this plan, there's more that end with her alive than her death, Grey. Trust your people and trust yourself." She nodded and then walked away.

What the fuck am I supposed to do with that?

Again, there were more riddles than truth. Magna hadn't told me exactly what the plan was, but the odds were higher this way that my mate would live. Only if the right decisions were made, though... which left a hell of a lot of room for error. With that, I stalked toward the Riders. They were a somber bunch now that Zeke was possibly locked away in a seemingly impenetrable bunker in Nevada. I made eye contact with Asher, tipping my head to one side in a *join me* gesture.

He broke off from the group of his brothers to speak to me.

"You love Aurelia like a sister," I said, beginning the conversation.

"Is that even a question?" Asher asked, a heavy eyebrow cocked.

"No, it was a statement," I clarified. "She agreed to hang back and take down the Council with the spell she's casting. Meanwhile, I need to be on the front line to lead our troops. So, I need someone to protect her. I don't know exactly what she's planning or how it works... but I do know there's a chance she won't survive it."

"How do you know that?" Ash asked, his tone one of anger, like the thought of Aurelia not surviving the battle made him murderous.

Believe me, I feel the same.

She had to survive, and if I couldn't be right there with her to make sure of it, there was no one else I wanted more at her back to ensure her safety than Asher and his brothers.

"Magna said there is a chance she might not survive—but free will and our choices always play a part in how Fate's hand plays out. She said to trust myself and trust in my family, so I'm trusting in my brothers. The Riders of the Hunt will protect Princess Aurelia... even from herself."

"You have my word as a Rider, Grey. I will do everything in my power to keep the princess safe. I would have done it even if you hadn't asked. She is our hope for a new world." Ash shook his head and held out his hand.

I took his hand in mine and nodded in return as relief flooded through me. I trusted Ash with her life. He'd protected Aurelia on numerous occasions, even from me when that was what she needed. He would watch out for her, and that meant my focus wouldn't be divided in the upcoming battle.

We will emerge victorious, even if the Council thinks they have us cornered.

War was bloody, and we would have our fair share of casualties, but in the end, the Council would fall. I would make sure of it.

I have to.

With Aurelia's safety secured, I raced out of the garage to the front lines with our warriors. They were beating their swords against their shields, and many of the shifters had already shifted into their animal forms. My gaze followed Ash and his brothers.

They made their way to Aurelia and circled her, creating a shield of burly flesh and ready magic.

Aurelia's irritation flared through the bond. She said something to him that I couldn't hear.

Ash shrugged and pointed in my direction.

Fucking traitor.

He was selling me out to my mate, but I didn't have time to think about that. Besides, she'd promised to accept a reasonable compromise.

Ronaldo's high-pitched squeak of laughter grated on my ears. "You think you can defeat my army that has been fighting for centuries with that pathetic, rag-tag group?" Ronaldo laughed again.

"We have something they don't!" I roared to my warriors.

"And what is that?" Ronaldo asked mockingly.

"We are fighting for our right to live! We're fighting for our families and our children. We're standing today so they don't have to fall. So they aren't oppressed or sent to testing facilities to be lab rats and casualties in the Council's quest for ultimate power over all the realms! They are fighting for greed. But us? We are fighting for our lives, and that makes us far more dangerous!" I bellowed, amplifying my voice with the power of my inner wolf.

Our army roared, and I even spotted Aurelia's *whoop* of encouragement at the back of the throng. The Riders of the Hunt surrounded her, and her irritation continued to flood our bond over that fact, but she was also impressed and inspired by my speech.

"For life! For a new dawn for Faery!" I bellowed as I turned and raced toward the wards with my army at my back. How long would it be before Fenrick and the king returned with reinforcements? We needed them to win this thing, and I'd hoped that my and Aurelia's speeches would have given us enough time.

The Council hadn't been able to get through our wards, so all they could do was wait until our ranks crashed through them and into their soldiers.

I wondered where Aurelia was as I began to cut down Council guards. "Avoid the ones with blank expressions!" I yelled at the last second. Those who were under the Council's mind control would still come after us, but if we could detain them instead of killing them, it would be beneficial for everyone in the future. They were mere puppets at this point.

Several shifted warriors leaped up in front of me and took out the guards with their arsenal of teeth and claws.

I recognized them as shifters from the prison, the ones we'd liberated. They had as much of a vendetta against the Council as I did. They hadn't been experimented on, but the only reason they weren't was because of my mate. She'd saved them from that fate.

They were loyal men, but I didn't need to be protected. I could take care of myself. I flinched at the thought. Aurelia had said something similar, and now when it came to it, I was getting angry I was being protected. I internally chastised myself. I was the Shifter King, and I needed to realize people would try to protect me above all else... just like I expected my mate to understand.

Shit. I've been an ass.

How could I expect people not to protect me, but get mad when she felt the same? I'd been a major hypocrite, and if we lived to see another day, I'd have to make it up to her. I sent apologies through the bond to her, but nothing came back in return. Terror flooded me as I realized I couldn't get a read on my mate's emotions. What was she doing that she wasn't pouring her feelings down the bond? She didn't know how to shut them off as far as I was aware.

Is she already casting the spell?

I roared out a battle cry in rage and frustration, and my sword sliced through a Council guard. His eyes were clear as he fell, which meant he agreed with their greed. He'd committed to this war and the atrocities of the Council willingly and knowingly. Did he think they would be on the winning side? If so, he was sorely mistaken. My army fought for the right to tomorrow, because if the Council won, we would be eradicated. We all knew this was our final stand, and we were going to make sure hell it counted!

As we plowed forward, my sword clanged against a guard's with blank eyes. I spun around him and hit him on the back of the head with the hilt of my dagger. He wasn't here of his own free will. He was just as much a victim as the rest of us. I only wished I had Aurelia's power, so that I could release them from the mind control.

Their numbers would certainly swell our ranks.

My fingers tingled, and magic whispered up my spine as I had a thought. My heart pounded in response. Was it possible I had that power too now that we were properly mated and bonded? I didn't even really know how magic transferal worked, or what happened when a Fae mated with a shifter. It rarely happened.

With nothing to lose, I raised my palm at the next blank-eyed warrior I came across and let the magic simmering within me fly. The blast hit him square on the forehead.

He crumpled to his knees on the ground with a groan. "What happened?" he asked as he blinked up at me in confusion.

"Whose side are you on?" I asked as I pointed my sword at his throat.

"What do you mean? Are you at war with the Shadow King?" he asked, his eyes darting from side to side as he surveyed the battle raging around us.

"You were fighting with the Council a second ago *against* the Shadow Kingdom and the rest of the supernaturals," I growled. "So, whose side are you on?"

The man's eyes widened, and he shook his head as he brought his fist to his chest. "My allegiance is to the Shadow Kingdom! I told the Council to go fuck themselves."

"Good," I said and helped the man up. "That's what I was hoping to hear."

He pushed me out of the way just in time to block another sword coming at my back.

Fuck, that was close.

I grinned at the man before we stood back-to-back. A circle of clear-eyed guards and mind-controlled guards formed around us.

"Did you free me of whatever they did to me?" the warrior asked over his shoulder as he kept his eyes on our enemies.

"I did," I said.

"Then free them too. We can turn the tide of this uprising." He pointed to the others around us.

"I don't know if I can do it again," I admitted. "I wasn't even sure how it worked on you."

"You need to try, or we're all screwed, and even more people will die," he said.

I had to admit he was right, but how could I do it? There was only one way to find out. "I'll do what I can," I called back, "but I can't make any promises!"

CHAPTER 23

Aurelia

"Where do you think you're going, Princess?" Ash grabbed my arm and pulled me back.

"I'm going to find the Council." I ripped myself from the Rider's grasp, my irritation flaring.

"You're going to find the Council... Princess, you do realize what a bad idea that is, right?" he asked.

"I have to end this before too many people die!" I argued as I turned to leave.

Asher's brothers staunchly blocked my path.

"You're going to get close to the Council and do what? I was asked not to leave your side, and I need to know what we're getting into here." Ash crossed his arms defiantly.

I gripped the book in my hand more tightly as I looked over the battlefield for a place I could start casting the spell. "I don't need to be super close to them, but close enough that I can see them and perform the spell."

"Fine," he agreed. "We can make that happen, but I want you out of the way of the fighting. We'll protect you—even if that means we have to protect you from yourself."

Compromise, Aurelia. You might be the one the prophecy foretold, but it's going to take a team to make this happen!

With a small grimace, I nodded. "Thank you, Ash." I flipped the book open to the page I needed as I ran behind the Riders of the Hunt.

They were a formidable shield wall, but one by one they broke off from the group as Council guards attacked them with their swords.

I glanced up at the *clanging* of metal and into the blank eyes of a Council guard. My heart lurched with empathy. I knew I shouldn't risk it because the spell to defeat the Council was already going to take almost everything I had... but my magic swirled inside me, yearning to rid the man of the mind control he was under. I flung my magic, and it struck him in the face.

He crumpled to the ground at Ash's feet and groaned. He blinked up at us from the ground in confusion before his eyes widened in understanding.

"The Council was controlling your mind. We're at war for Faery." I shouted. "Go!"

The soldier scrambled to his feet, weapon in hand and sprinted toward the Council guards to champion our cause.

I sprinted to a less chaotic spot, and the trees moved to give me cover as I read from the book.

"Princess, you can't use that spell!" Ash appeared at my side once more and reached for the book in my hand.

I dodged him, keeping hold of the golden book. "You can read it?" I asked in shock.

"Yes," he growled. "And that spell is *too* dangerous, even for someone as powerful as you. It's meant to be a last resort. It's meant to require everything the caster has."

"I know that" I retorted. "This *is* our last resort, Ash. Don't you see that? We don't have any other option. I scoured this book from cover to cover for something to help us, and this is the only way forward." I shook my head, willing him to understand just how dire our circumstances were. "Victory for Faery hangs on a knife-edge, Ash..."

Ash deflated, knowing with a soul-crushing certainty that this was what I had to do. "Do what you must," he said as if each word pained him. "I will protect you until my last breath."

The battle raged on around us, and more Council guards poured into the forest near the Syndicate's headquarters by the second.

I couldn't risk using any more of my power on the ones that were still being controlled. They would have to wait until the spell was complete.

A great battle cry filled the air all around us.

I glanced up, my heart jolting in my chest with hope.

Fenrick and Santori, charging the enemy from the back of their ranks with a roar. Our reinforcements had arrived.

Thank the gods they made it in time!

Our people from the Syndicate were more than capable of holding their own, but they'd been outnumbered at least two to one. The battle raged on, supernaturals fighting against each other for the very right to exist. I hated that it had come to this, and that I was thrust into the middle of it.

"You're not going to let me talk you out of this, are you? Does Grey know?" Ash asked with a sigh as he placed a hand on my shoulder and leaned down to read more of the spell.

"He knows I have something that will stop the Council, but he doesn't know what it is. We fought over it earlier." I glanced away, my eyes prickling. I let my gaze rove the battlefield for any glimpse of Grey, but he was in the thick of the fight and not visible to me. I sent up a prayer to the gods.

Please let him be okay. Afford him the opportunity to live up to the title of Shifter King for a long time to come.

I turned back to Ash, my expression solemn. "I'm doing this. If I don't, then all is lost, and the Council will continue with their tyranny until every last one of us is a lab rat or a slave."

Ash snapped the book closed in my hands, his inner fears and personal feelings for me getting the better of him. "You're not if I take this from you, Princess. You didn't tell Grey what a dangerous spell this was."

"I don't have to run everything past him just because he's my mate. We've all known from the beginning that defeating them was going to fall squarely on my shoulders. And it has. I must do this."

A scream tore through the battlefield, ringing out over the clanging of metal, sword on sword, and sword against shield.

I turned to see a shifter in their tiger form tearing through an enemy soldier. There was so much blood and death, it threatened to drown the landscape in crimson.

I'm the only one who can stop this carnage.

I had to do or say something to convince Ash that this was my decision and the right thing to do.

His hands still trapped mine around the book. He wasn't letting go, no matter how hard I tugged on it.

"Don't make me waste my magic on you, Ash. I have to do this. We both know my magic might not be enough as it is, so I can't afford to waste any more. This *has* to work," I said, glaring at the Rider with desperation thrumming through every fiber of my being.

Ash growled, his lips tight and pursed, but then his gaze softened, and he sighed, hanging his head. He finally released the book and stepped away. "You better survive this, Princess. They call us Riders of the Hunt for a reason. We can ride anywhere, and we will ride straight across the Veil and drag you back if we have to!"

I took a huge breath and opened the book. The pages fluttered instantly to the one I needed.

This is it.

A loud voice boomed over the sounds of the battle. "We can stop this right now. Just hand over the princess!"

Ronaldo thought he could bargain with us? I almost snorted in derision. It wouldn't change the ultimate outcome of this battle. If they handed me over to the Council, they would all still be eradicated, one way or another. The idea that he thought this war was something we could or would just give up on was laughable.

I turned away from his voice and asked the trees to lift me up into the air so I could get eyes on the Council.

They resisted at first, knowing from my mind what I was about to do, but finally a branch wrapped around my waist, and lifted me high.

I could see the entire battle from this height. The Council guards were surrounded by the supernatural army and the Fae rebels. I couldn't make out anyone's faces, so I had no idea how my family was doing.

Are they still alive?

Grey's reassurance flooded through the bond. He was still there. He was still fighting with his people. He would protect my family from the Council to the best of his ability.

I sent back all the love and regret in my heart. Confusion returned to me and then his terror. I did my best to shut down the link between us so I could focus. It wasn't anything I'd learned, but more an act of instinct and trust. There was a definite possibility, just as Ash had said, I might not make it out of the spell alive... but I had to do it.

I have to try!

It occurred to me that perhaps it hadn't been the best idea to distract my mate while he was in the heat of battle. I looked out over the battlefield again but couldn't pinpoint him. But I knew he was still out there—somewhere—fighting for us, and my heart swelled with pride. Our mate bond was strong, and if by some twist of Fate the spell didn't kill me, I would tell him just how much I loved him and how proud I was that he was mine.

The book flared with magic as I began the difficult and intense chant. It was intimidating, but I did everything I could. I'd been practicing the words inside my head all afternoon to get them right. Magic poured from me in an incredible stream of power as I stared at the Council members surrounded by their guards. They had a protective shield around them, but it wouldn't stop the binding spell from hitting them with its full force.

I started the chant at a whisper, but my words subtly grew louder as the spell called for it. And with each and every moment, as the crescendo of ancient magic blossomed, I never took my eyes off the Council.

The weakest members began to fidget and were shuffling their feet nervously. They knew something was happening. They could feel it.

I would have smirked with satisfaction, but I couldn't spare the breath. I was shouting the chant to the heavens now, pouring every ounce of magic I possessed into the spell.

Ronaldo's eyes widened in terror, and the expression on his face was priceless. He knew exactly what I was doing. I was too far away to hear his whispered words as I continued my chanting, but I thought he mouthed *the book*.

He turned in my direction and glared at me with all the hate and loathing in his black heart.

I continued chanting, the raw power building to impossible heights.

Why is it taking so long?

Several of the Council Elders dropped to their knees, but not Ronaldo or the main assholes from my trial. They remained standing and huddled together, whispering to one another.

Did they seriously think they could stop me now? The chant was almost complete, and they would be bound until they faced trial for their treason, very, very soon.

"Get her!" Ronaldo's voice echoed over the battlefield as he pointed to me.

Our armies had already formed a wall around the Council's army, and I was safely outside it.

I glanced down at Ash, the words spilling from my lips by rote now.

The Rider was fighting off a glassy-eyed guard who must have slipped through our army's defenses.

Then the tide of the battle inexplicably shifted, and the guards charged toward me.

I continued the incantation, watching as if from afar, not afraid in the least. I knew the trees wouldn't let anyone get to me. By the time they did get close, the chant would be done. I poured all my heart, soul, hope, and magic into the words, my voice becoming a keening prayer to the gods, until something incredibly fragile cracked inside me, and pain like a bolt of lightning lanced through my chest. Breathing hard, I stared Ronaldo and the others down.

They wailed in defeat, their hate and thirst for power pitiful in the face of hope and love, as they dropped to their knees.

I leaned against the trunk of the tree and slumped to my ass on a branch. I placed a hand on the trunk but couldn't hear anything. My lips trembled.

I can't talk to the trees anymore.

The realization was crushing, but I'd finished the spell to stop the Council and their villainy without murdering them all in the name of justice. I blinked several times as I tried to focus, tried to make out Grey's face in the sea of Fae and shifters, but I couldn't keep my eyes open. They were just too heavy, and I was exhausted beyond mortal understanding.

The pain in my chest eased as my eyelids fluttered closed, and I floated away into the clouds of eternity. At least if I was dying, I was content in the knowledge that I'd done it. I'd stopped the Council once and for all. My father was a good king and would be able to try them for their crimes and usher in the new era we were promised.

In the darkness of my fading consciousness, I felt my valiant heart slow its steady rhythm, but I felt nothing but peace. I'd succeeded, and the realms would be safe. Those I left behind that lived—my family—would help make it so. I knew that with a soul-deep certainty.

As the last tangible connection I had was severed, a smile tugged at the corners of my lips and a tear slid down my cooling cheek.

We'd did it, Grey. It's over. I love you.

CHAPTER 24

Grey

A Council warrior lunged for me but stopped short before his sword hit mine and crumpled to his knees, holding his head. He gritted his teeth, clenching his eyes shut as if he were in sudden and unfathomable agony. All around me, warriors were reacting the same way, their swords clattering to the ground as they nursed some unseen anguish.

Ronaldo screamed, his voice rising above the others.

But was it with pain, frustration, or fury? And why did they all suddenly fall? The few Council guards that remained standing ran, closing ranks around the Council, but it was no use, because one by one, the men on the ground got to their feet and turned on the Council, who was soon vastly outnumbered.

Did Aurelia do that just now? Was that the spell? That can't be right...

I knew she could release the influenced warriors from their mind control without the need for some epic spell from the golden book though, so that couldn't be all she did.

What the hell is going on?

I wanted answers and one way or another, I was about to get them. I stalked toward the Council, barely bridled rage boiling just below the surface.

It seemed their warriors realized something was amiss and they began sifting out one after another. Fleeing to save their own skins, they left the Council to deal with their own fates alone.

"My magic. She stole my magic!" Ronaldo roared, his fingers curled like claws of despair. He thrust out his palms to blast me away, but nothing happened.

My heart swelled with pride. My Aurelia must have done that. That's what the spell to defeat the Council was for. It'd somehow left the Council completely powerless and bereft of their magic. I grinned at Fenrick.

He strolled up next to me with a smile as wide as my own.

"My mate is a total badass!" I laughed as I clapped him on the shoulder. "She did it!"

"That she is," he agreed. "But where is the princess?" He glanced around, surveying the sea of faces around us.

"Ash is with her," I assured him. "We need to arrest these assholes."

Dan rushed over and tossed me a backpack. "That should hold them until we can get them in the cells," he said confidently.

I opened the bag to find several sets of magic-binding cuffs inside like those used in the prison. It was probably overkill, considering they had no magic anymore, but I wasn't going to take any chances.

The previously mind-controlled warriors had their swords at the ready, having recovered after their release, and were surrounding the Council as they waited for orders.

"I've got this," I said as I stepped in front of Ronaldo, the absolute worst of all the Council members, and shoved him to his knees. "I should kill you here and now for all the atrocities you've committed."

"Do it, then," Ronaldo goaded me, his head still high even while he was on his knees. The truth was, he'd probably rather be dead than magicless, practically human...

But I'm not going to give you that much mercy.

"The very least I should do is kill you for the imprisonment and torture of my father for centuries, but my mate is right. The people deserve justice above all else, and that's why you're under arrest." Seizing his arms, I clapped the cuffs on his wrists behind his back.

Fenrick grabbed another set of cuffs and secured another male Council member.

"These are useless!" Ronaldo laughed. "Your mate probably died binding our magic with that book."

I hit Ronaldo in the back of the head, letting out some of my frustration on his cruel ass and smart mouth.

He fell to the ground, his face in the dirt.

I reached out for the bond, but it was eerily quiet. It hadn't been silent since we'd formed it. I looked over the battlefield for any sign of her, but she was nowhere to be found.

She can't be dead. She wouldn't have performed that spell knowing it might kill her, right?

"Where is she?" I asked Fenrick, keeping my tone even and unemotive. "Do you see her?"

There were wounded warriors everywhere, from both sides, but I couldn't think about them now.

I need to find my mate.

"Get cuffs on all the Council members and get them to the cells," I ordered Dan as I stalked away.

I passed a group of shifters standing over a Fae warrior. He had a slash through his side, and they were trying to help him stop the bleeding. Now that the war was over, my people were helping the wounded without discrimination. That was what I liked to see. Continuing in my search, I stomped past them toward a larger group of supernaturals. "Have any of you seen Aurelia?" I asked.

They shook their heads but parted for me like a wave.

The sight that greeted me had me rushing over and dropping to my knees.

The king lay wounded on the ground, his chest rattling with every breath.

"Poison," he whispered, looking up at me. "The blade was poisoned."

"Shit. Where's the queen?" I turned to the group of shifters.

"She stayed back to keep the young ones calm," one of the witches said.

"Someone go and get her, now!" I barked. Emotions clogged my throat. The king couldn't die. Aurelia would be devastated! She would be, because she was definitely alive.

I gripped the king's hand, offering him comfort as one of the men shifted and ran back to the Syndicate building to do as I'd commanded.

"Where's Aurelia?" The king coughed, blood staining his lips.

I wiped them clean and swallowed hard. He was really dying.

What the hell are we going to do without the king?

"I don't know. I was looking for her when I came across you." I pursed my lips and took a deep breath before continuing. "But Ash is with her. He'll keep her safe." I had to believe that. No other outcome was acceptable. She *had* to be alive.

"You two will have to rule," the king whispered as another round of blood-choked coughing wracked his body. He was fading fast.

Fenrick rushed to me and dropped to his knees. "What happened?"

"Poison," I said grimly. "The Council must have ordered the king's death and sent an assassin into the battle to take him out."

"Fuck," Fenrick growled as he tried in vain to pour green healing magic into his king. It wasn't working. "Where's the queen?"

"I sent a shifter to get her from the bunker, but I'm not sure she's going to make it in time." I clutched the king's hand. I wouldn't allow him to be alone in his final moments. I'd never been good with showing this kind of emotion. It was difficult, but losing the king hurt in a way I never expected it to. It was going to devastate my mate, and that only made the pain that much worse.

The queen ran toward us, crying out the king's name, hair streaming behind her, and tears streaming down her face.

I turned away and coughed to disguise the lump building in my throat. The king had become not just a good friend, but a part of my found family.

Was this how Aurelia felt when my father died in front of her?

The crushing despair wracked me, and hot tears burned the backs of my eyes.

The queen wailed as she fell to the ground at the king's side.

His eyes cracked open, and he smiled at her.

I couldn't take any more of this. It felt far too personal to watch their final goodbye. I stood up and gazed over the battlefield again. Many of the previously mind-controlled Fae were leaning over supernaturals, using their healing abilities to help the wounded. The sight gave me hope, but I still couldn't find or sense Aurelia through our bond. "Where the hell is she?"

I rushed back to the wards. She was supposed to stay back behind the battle lines. I'd made sure she wouldn't get close enough to the Council, but did she listen? I couldn't know—she was just as stubborn as I was. A crowd had formed at the wards, and I prayed to whatever gods that were listening that they weren't crowded around my mate's body.

I grabbed a supernatural that was running past me.

He stopped in his tracks and bowed his head to me.

"Have you seen the princess?" I asked breathlessly.

"No, my king. I haven't seen her since before the battle." He glanced at my hand.

With a nod, I released him, spinning back toward the crowd.

The mass parted to reveal and a somber Ash kneeling in front of me.

My body buzzed with electricity, and my wolf whimpered and howled in my head. I glanced down at the bundle he carried gently in his arms. I'd recognize that golden halo of hair anywhere. The world spun around me, and I bellowed with rage as I dropped to the ground. What had she done? No, this couldn't be the way this ended. It couldn't.

Not the king and his daughter!

Magic pulsed beneath my skin. We were bonded... if she died, I was supposed to be taken with her.!

Why am I still here? How?

What kind of cruel trick had Fate dealt me that she was so still in Ash's arms? "No, no," I breathed. "This isn't right. It's not supposed to be like this."

"I'm so sorry, Grey," Ash whispered. I'd never seen so much emotion on the Rider's face before, not even when we'd had to leave his brother with the Council at the gala. A wetness pooled around his eyes and a single, fat tear slid down his cheek, Aurelia still cradled in his arms.

The magic in my veins roared inside me, desperate to get out. What would happen if I let it out? I would burn the world. I'd told her that if I lost her, the world would have a new monster to deal with. I tugged her out of Ash's lap and fell back on my ass in the grass. I inhaled deeply through my nose, filling my keen senses with her beautiful scent. Then burying my face in her hair, I broke down.

My chest burned with regret, anger, despair and probably a few emotions I couldn't even name. I squeezed her close and rocked us on the grass as my magic forcefully pushed at the boundaries of my chest. It wanted out, but I was sure there was nothing it could do in this situation. Magic couldn't bring back the dead. Aurelia's eyes were closed, her expression peaceful, and I kissed each lid softly.

The magic building inside of me trickled out through my palms where I was touching her and glowed bright gold against her skin. I glanced at the magic, shocked it had managed to slip out of me. I panicked and tried to pull it back, but it built within me like a great deluge between one breath and the next and rushed out with the stream of my emotions to flood Aurelia with warmth.

"I told her I would ride across the Veil and bring her back if she died..." Ash choked out the words. His head was down, and he swiped his eyes. Was the Rider crying like I was? He was so distracted by his grief, he didn't notice the golden magic pouring out of me and into her until the light grew so shockingly bright, everyone everywhere for miles must surely have been able to!

The magic continued to flow into my mate, swelling like a glittering river of pure sunlight, bold and strong. I couldn't have stopped it even if I'd wanted to. It simply poured like a broken faucet, from one vessel to another. Then, like a fountain, it erupted from her chest, forming a sparkling dome of pale gold that shimmered above us like a bubble before it began to dissipate. Her skin warmed, and her usual healthy glow returned before my very eyes.

My mate gasped for breath, startling me as her eyes shot open. "Grey?" She lifted a hand to caress my tear-stricken face.

My mouth hung open, and words escaped me as I stared into her beautiful eyes. The bond flared back to life with a vengeance, and her relief and love filled every part of me.

"You're alive!" I sobbed and pulled her closer, never wanting her to leave my sight again. The emotional trauma was too much to bear. How the hell had my saved her? Magic couldn't bring people back from the dead... and my magic hadn't even so much as reacted to the king's death. Why had it reacted so violently and desperately to hers?

"What happened?" she asked as she gently laid her head on my shoulder. "Did we win?"

"Yes, Princess," Ash chuckled as he swiped away a fresh curtain of tears. "But if you *ever* do anything like that again, I'll lock you in a padded room for the rest of your days!"

"Agreed," I said as I nuzzled her neck where my mating mark was.

"So, it worked? The Council's magic is bound, and you brought me back?" Aurelia cupped my cheek as she eased back to look at me. "How?"

"I don't know," I said honestly. "I was lost in my grief, and my magic flared. It just poured into you. There was an epic eruption of golden light... and then you woke up." I shook my head in wonder. "It's like the power of our love brough you back..." I breathed, my heart in my throat.

It sounded crazy when I said it out loud, but there was no other real explanation for it. She was alive, and we'd won the war. The Council would be tried for their crimes, and we could figure out a way to work with the humans.

Aurelia smiled. "And where are the others? My father—is he okay?"

Fenrick jogged over with a frown and dropped to his knees. He bowed his head, but his eyes were red and glassy. "The Shadow King is gone, Your Majesty."

Aurelia gasped and tried to tear herself from my arms.

I held her to me even more tightly. I wasn't ready to let go of her yet.

"He can't be gone!" she cried, sobbing in my arm. "No! Don't you dare call me Your Majesty, Fenrick." She was the same Aurelia she'd always been.

"I'm sorry, Aurelia, but before he departed this world for the beyond, it was his final wish that you would rule together, as King and Queen of Faery." Fenrick nodded in my direction.

The Shifter King mated to the Fae queen... maybe that's how we're going to usher in a new era?

Our people would all be safe in Faery and free from oppression, regardless of whether they were Fae, shifter, half-blood, or any kind of supernatural in between. We'd lost a great and noble king this day, but the future was looking brighter than ever before...

As long as we can find a way to work with the humans.

CHAPTER 25

"Why are we doing this now?" I asked over my shoulder.

"My queen, we have been over this. The people need some light after all the dark." Magna grinned.

Grey stepped next to me in a suit that looked sinful on him and kissed my cheek.

"Right after the coronation, we have a meeting with the world leaders in the human realm. You want to be seen as the magnanimous queen you are. And not everyone knows I'll be your king. We need to show a united front."

"Not everyone agrees with your decision to let the other supernaturals and the half-breeds return. They need to see that they're wrong, and bigotry will not be tolerated." Magna nodded.

"I understand." I sighed as I stood in front of the mirror in a gold gown that would have been all the rage in the regency period. The crown was in the throne room on a dais, waiting for the ceremony to begin. We'd brought some technology to Faery and were going to livestream to all the towns so they could see the event without being physically present. It had taken us weeks to get everything set up, but it would be worth it.

A part of me secretly hated it though, because technology only served to remind me that every day that passed was another day that Zeke, our hacker, and the others were still trapped in human detention facilities.

I need to bring our people home.

Grey walked up behind me and placed his hands on my bare shoulders. He must have sensed my anxiety through our bond. "It will be okay, my love. We just need to get through the ceremony and then have a chat with the humans." He squeezed my shoulders and pressed another supportive but chaste kiss to my cheek.

"It's time." Magna grinned.

"Finally. Let's get this over with," I groaned.

"The king needs to go out first. Asher and Fenrick will escort you," Magna said, shooing Grey out of the room.

Grey winked at me over his shoulder as he left our room.

Magna closed the door firmly behind him and smiled.

"This is what you were leading us to, wasn't it?" I asked the seer with a subtle shake of my head. "Was this the plan all along?"

"Not quite, but we're almost there," she said with a twinkle of mischief in her eyes.

"There's more?" I asked with a sigh.

"Not for you, Princess. Your story has its happy ending, but others are just beginning."

"You and your riddles. Honestly, woman!" I shook my head with a chuckle.

The doors opened, and Fenrick stood in front of me and bowed deeply.

I scowled at him, then rolled my eyes. "Stop that," I scolded. "You know how much I hate this pageantry."

Fenrick stood with a laugh and a shake of his head. "Are you ready to be escorted to your coronation?"

"I would rather be getting our people out of the testing centers... but sure, let's get this over with."

Magna rolled her eyes but followed behind me to make sure the long train on my dress fanned out just right.

"The ceremony won't take long, I can assure you." Fenrick held his arm out to me.

I looped my arm through his and smiled at Ash as I did the same with him. "Let's just get this done with so we can save our people."

"Agreed," Ash said. He'd been the only one who'd agreed with me that we needed to secure our people *before* the coronation. He wanted Zeke back as much as I did, if not more, but we were overruled by the needs of many.

I could see their point, but I also didn't like the idea of my people suffering unnecessarily for the sake of formality. If I could help them quickly, I wanted to do it.

"You know the human government won't take you seriously unless you are the actual queen by law," Fenrick reminded me, squeezing my hand.

I huffed out a breath. This was the same argument we'd been having for weeks, and I *got it*. I did. It made sense, but it didn't make me happy.

Supernaturals and Fae alike lined the hall leading to the throne room and when they saw me, everyone dropped to one knee, their heads bowed.

I am never going to get used to this.

And it was especially weird when we got to the rest of Ash and Zeke's brothers, and they were kneeling as well.

"Get up," I whispered to the Riders. "What are you doing?"

"They are showing respect to their queen," Ash whispered in my ear.

I nodded with a small smile, though it irked me to no end, and allowed Ash and Fenrick to lead me into the throne room where Grey stood at the door. We'd been practicing this procession and ritual for weeks. I just had to promise to uphold the laws of the realm and protect my people, and then I would be crowned. It was simple enough and would only take a matter of minutes, but it was tradition and mattered to the people of Faery.

I took a cleansing breath and smiled at Grey as brightly as I could muster.

He reached for my hand, sending me his love and confidence through our bond all the while.

Together, we both made our way down the aisle lined with friends and family until we arrived at the steps of the dual thrones of Faery.

We knelt and said a prayer to the gods that they would bless our reign before standing once more before taking our seats side by side.

The high priest asked us to give our vows to our people and then we said another formal prayer to the gods for their blessing before the crowns were placed on each of our heads. The crowd exploded with cheers and applause as we smiled and waved. Then, with the pageantries aside, we hurried from the throne room into the surveillance room we had prepared off to the side just for this occasion.

We're certainly going to be a much more modern monarchy, that's for sure!

"Are the world leaders on call yet?" I asked the tech.

"They aren't, but you are a couple minutes early." He grinned and passed a small, sleek microphone to Grey.

Grey clipped it carefully to my dress before attaching his own.

The shifter tech handed us both a set of earpods to secure, then he clicked a few more buttons, and we were ready for the video call.

A few moments later, the President came on the screen. "You." He pointed a finger accusingly but did a double take when he saw the crown atop my head.

"Mr. President. You have something that belongs to me, and I want them back." I said confidently, remaining calm.

"I have something of yours? I don't have anything that belongs to you. *You* were supposed to be tried for the explosion of the prison. How are you suddenly wearing a crown?"

"I would mind your tone and show respect for the new queen of Faery if I were you," Grey growled smoothly.

The President glanced at Grey next to me and his eyes widened.

"Look, before this meeting devolves any further, you have my people locked in your testing facilities, and I want them back," I said placing a hand on Grey's arm.

"No," the President said obstinately.

"No?" I asked, cocking my head to the side, my brow creasing in surprise.

"I have citizens of the United States locked in detention facilities. They are *mine* to punish as I see fit."

"Your citizens to punish? What crimes have they committed? Didn't you detain them because they weren't human, and as such had no human rights... but now you claim they *are* your citizens, and you can punish them as you see fit?" I asked and glanced at Grey. "Am I hearing this correctly?"

"You are, my love. It's the most hypocritical bullshit I've ever heard spewed in my life." Grey sat forward, glaring at the President.

"We need to come to an agreement," I pressed. "All supernaturals are welcome back into Faery, but I will not force them to. Some still have families in the human realm, and I need to know they will be safe to return there without persecution."

"Monsters will *always* be labeled monsters. They will never be welcome to live among humans." The President slammed his fist on the desk in front of him. It seemed he wasn't going to budge on his stance.

I glanced at Grey.

He nodded, knowing exactly what I was asking without words.

"If you don't release my people from your detention centers, I will have no choice but to attack those centers and free them. I will send as many teams as necessary, and they will make the explosion at the Dallas prison look like a bonfire."

"Where is the High Councilor?" the President barked. "I will only deal with him."

"He is currently on trial for his crimes against my people. I expect to sentence him to death any day now." I smirked.

"Who gave you the authority to sentence him to death?" The President's face became an ugly eggplant color of rage.

"My people and the gods, of course, themselves, who just witnessed my coronation." I grinned. "As the Princess of the Shadow Kingdom, I was naturally next in line when the Council assassinated my father on the field of battle."

The President went suddenly pale. "I didn't know the Fae had royalty... I thought the Council..." he stuttered.

"You were given wrong information," I informed, cutting him off. "The Council used you and controlled your peoples' minds to do their bidding. They will be punished, but that's not why I'm talking with you now. The matter at hand is that I want my people released from your detention facilities *and* I want you to pass legislation to make sure that any supernatural who decides to stay in the human realm is recognized as a citizen. They are to be afforded rights and not be subjected to any more scrutiny than any other natural born citizen."

"That's not possible! The American people are terrified of the threat the supernaturals pose. We cannot just let them roam free on the streets." He slammed his fist on the table again as another world leader popped onto the screen.

I glanced at Grey for guidance. I didn't know who the woman was.

"Hello, Mrs. Prime Minister," Grey greeted her warmly. "Have you had a chance to look at the proposal we sent over?"

The Prime Minister smiled at Grey and nodded. "It was all very reasonable. If the supernaturals in the UK cause unrest, they will be sent back to Faery to be tried for their crimes. We will release everyone in our custody to you, but they will have the option to stay or go as they like."

"And has your parliament decided on a plan of action?" I asked.

The President scoffed in background, but I ignored him. The British Prime Minister seemed much more reasonable and pleasant to talk to.

"We have decided that we would rather work with you than start a possible war with the supernaturals. We will agree to your terms," she said succinctly and nodded.

I sighed with relief. If only the other world leaders were so easy to work with. I glared at the screen with the President.

He'd overheard the entire conversation with the British Prime Minister, and his purple complexion grew even darker.

"You, Mr. President, have my family locked in your testing centers, and I refuse to leave them there to die, but I don't want a war with the United States. It was my home for the majority of my life... but be warned. I *will* take out every one of your facilities if it comes down to it. So, I'll leave the decision in your hands. Make your choice."

The British Prime Minister gasped. "Carl! Let her people go. They aren't a threat to you," she advised.

"No. I will keep her people and any other supernaturals found on US soil. They aren't human, and we need to know more about them, Bridget. I'm surprised you gave into their demands so easily!"

"We don't want war with these people, Carl," the Prime Minister hissed at him. "They might be different, but they are still people. We're all in this world together, different realms, different countries... it doesn't matter. Bigotry and division have never achieved anything!"

Maybe that was exactly what the President wanted—war—but we would avoid it at all costs. Somehow, we would get our people out of those centers.

We have to.

"We don't want to start a war either. Too many lives have already been affected and lost. Simply give us back our people and we can come to an agreement we can both live with," I offered with a raised brow.

The President grumbled into his microphone and started consulting with people off screen.

We'd saved the supernaturals and the realms from the Council and outright disaster, but we still had a long way to go for a lasting peace. I just hoped Asher could hold out until then and didn't go rogue and attempt to release Zeke...

That could start a war we really aren't ready for.

But I'd been through my trial by fire, and I knew that no matter what the future held, I could handle it—as long as I had those I loved by my side.

Epilogue

GREY

5 years later...

A scream tore through the castle, setting my nerves on edge. I clung tightly to my son, Christian, as I raced through the empty hall. "Do you think it's time?" I asked.

"Time." Christian nodded seriously. The future king of the realm was a serious little tyke, much like his grandfather had been. He frowned and his bottom lip quivered as another wail pierced my eardrums.

"Aurelia!" I called out, my stomach twisting with worry as I turned the corner.

"Grey?" Her whimper came from our bedroom. My beautiful mate was doubled over, holding her rounded belly in the doorway.

"My love, get back into bed!" I said as I set Christian down on the floor.

He toddled over to his mother and rested his little hands on her stomach. "Sissy."

"Yes Christian, but we need Mommy to lie down for sissy to come out." I ruffled his blond hair and kept my tone calm.

Bright blue eyes blinked up at me, before he glanced back at his mom. "Rest," he instructed sagely.

Aurelia forced a small smile to her lips, even though her breathing was labored. She winced as pain tore through her again.

I wrapped my arm around her back and bent forward, picking her up in a bridal hold to carry her back into the bedroom.

Christian followed close behind me and jumped on the bed.

I laid Aurelia down gently and helped her get comfortable.

He snuggled next to her with his tiny hand on her huge belly.

"I need to call the healer, now," I said, glancing down at Christian. "Protect mommy and sissy until I get back."

He nodded seriously again, his understanding of what I needed from him showing once more that he was much older than his years suggested.

I turned around and raced from the room, almost running into Fenrick who stood in the hall on high alert.

"What's happened to the queen?" he asked, his eyebrows snapping together.

"It's time for the babies to come." I ran a hand down my face, trying to keep it together.

"The first set of twins in the history of Faery is going to be a celebration. Why do you look so uneasy?" he asked.

"I'm always uneasy when she's in pain," I said with a shake of my head. When Christian was born three years ago, I was a complete wreck; and today was no different.

"Everything will be fine, Grey. She's strong." Fenrick clapped me on the shoulder in a friendly effort to comfort me.

"I know, but that doesn't stop the wolf inside me from pacing around and causing my stress to double. I need to find the healer." Leaving Fenrick to guard the queen, I raced down the hall.

The healer should have been ready and waiting by Aurelia's side. We'd known the birth would be any day now. We'd found out just how short a hybrid pregnancy could be with Christian's arrival. She'd been pregnant for only five months instead of the expected nine, and with twins we knew that would be even more accelerated.

I pounded on the door to the healer's room.

How can they not hear my mate screaming when everyone else can?

"Can I help you, my king?"

I jumped and turned around, finding the healer rounding the corner as she walked calmly toward me.

"Where have you been?" I roared in frustration. "The queen is in labor, and you are supposed to be there!"

"I'm sorry, my king. I needed to go to the village for more supplies." She bowed her head and hurried off to find the queen.

I groaned and marched after her.

Fenrick grabbed my arm as I tried to push past him. "You need to calm down, Grey." Fenrick said, slapping me on the back.

"I can't calm down when I can *feel* her pain." I clenched my fists at my sides.

"If you act like a raging bull to the healer in there, I will remove you," Fenrick said curtly. "Then you need to be stronger. Your mate needs a calm presence at her side, not whatever the fuck this is." He huffed at me, crossing his arms to show me he was serious.

A fresh wave of pain stole my breath away as my mate bellowed her agony from the bed. I raced into the bedroom.

"Grey," Aurelia gasped out, then whimpered again. "It hurts."

"I know, my love, but you're doing *so* well." I sat on the bed next to her and brushed the hair away from her forehead.

The healer cleared her throat and met our collective gaze. "It will all be over soon, my queen. Just like last time, with Christian, I need to lock onto their energies so I can bring them out into the world. Now, brace yourself."

We'd watched some videos of human births when Aurelia was pregnant with Christian, thinking they would prepare us better for what was to come. But we couldn't have been more wrong. Human labor was *nothing* like Fae birth!

For starters, they weren't bloody magical!

The Fae healer rested both her palms on Aurelia's stomach and hummed to herself, her brow furrowing in concentration as she locked in on the baby's unique power signature. "Got her!" she announced brightly.

With a burst of green magic and light, the first of the twins appeared in the healer's arms. With a satisfied smile she passed the squalling infant to me.

The precious little thing was a wriggling, wet mess, but she was also incredibly beautiful. I stared down at her, cradling her tight against my chest to keep her warm. Her hair was a beautiful, soft chestnut color, and her big blue eyes—just like her mother's—stared up at me.

"Sissy!" Christian called out, crawling over to me across the bed excitedly. He placed a kiss on the baby's rosy cheek. He was going to be such an amazing big brother to our girls.

I couldn't wait to see them all grow up together. With a heart full of love, I turned to Aurelia and presented the newest addition to our growing family.

Her eyes glowed with love for the tiny infant. "Dahlia," she whispered, reaching out to brush the backs of her fingers against the girl's cheek.

"One more to go," the healer said. "Brace yourself again, my queen," she warned as she placed her hands on Aurelia's stomach. aShe began humming once more, eyes closed as she sought the second twin's signature.

My mate winced, her brow creasing deeply as she sucked in a shallow breath. Fae babies mightn't come out the way they did for humans, but it was clear it was still a painful process in its own right.

I glared at the healer, ever protective of my precious mate.

She didn't pay any head though, and got on with delivering our second daughter. Another ripple of bright green magic and light pulsed through the air and then the other twin appeared, nestled in the healer's arms. She moved carefully up the bed to present her gracefully to our queen, before placing her in her arms.

"Kenzie," Aurelia said breathlessly, pressing a kiss to the girl's hair.

The twins were identical and absolutely perfect. With a giddy heart, I heaved a solitary sigh of relief before the worries of the future came flooding in. What kind of mischief would the two of them get up to? I couldn't even imagine. "We are going to have our hands full with these two beauties." I said, shaking my head.

"Maybe when they get older it will be easier to tell them apart," Aurelia said, staring lovingly down at the baby in her arms.

"Hopefully," I grumbled, already afraid of what was to come. I had no doubt whatsoever they'd have fun at some point tricking us and pretending to be one another... I stood up from the bed and rocked Dahlia in my arms.

The healer returned to the rest of her birthing duties, namely using her magic on Aurelia to heal any internal damage the babies may have caused, as well as removing the afterbirth.

Dahlia stared up at me, my precious princess. She scrunched her nose up as if she could hear my thoughts.

"We make some beautiful babies, mate." I turned my grin on the love of my life, the incredible woman who'd helped me save our world and our people from tyranny and corruption to usher in a new era of peace, beauty, and prosperity. Aurelia was my equal, and match in every way, and I couldn't wait to spend the rest of eternity with her.

* * *

Aurelia

Five years even later...

"Those girls are as impossible to catch as you were," Fenrick grumbled aloud.

"You asked to be the twins' guardian, Fenrick." I grinned back at him. "What did you expect?"

He ran a hand down his face and sighed. "I expected they would stay the sweet little princesses they were as babies. But this? This a reign of terror."

Christian stomped into the throne room his eyes blazing with anger. "Where's Dahlia?" he demanded in a huff.

"She and Kenzie are off somewhere causing chaos again, why?" I asked him.

"She broke my tablet! And I know it was *her* because I have to tell her ten times a day that it's mine and she can't play with it!"

"I did not break it." Dahlia jumped out from behind my throne, crossing her little arms and glaring back at Christian.

"Well, it didn't just end up broken by itself," Christian argued back.

"Enough," I interjected, struggling not to roll my eyes. "You have your own tablet, Dahlia, sweetheart. You know you're not supposed to touch other people's stuff without asking first." My children were as willful as they were stubborn, but with Grey and I for parents, I should never have expected anything less.

"I didn't break it, though," Dahlia repeated.

I actually believed her, but they needed to be allies, not enemies. "How about this... we'll get you a new tablet," I said, directing my gaze at my son. "And your sister won't touch it, will you?" I finished, glancing at the chestnut-haired little spitfire.

Dahlia was only five and already she and her sister were a complete handful. They really needed a guardian each, but Fenrick desperately wanted the honor. And even as one of the best in the realm, he had trouble keeping up with them. Not that I didn't have full faith in his ability to protect them when it was called for. They were just typical twins!

The doors to the throne room burst open and Ash stepped through the door with his arms out wide. "Where are my favorite princesses?" he boomed.

And right behind him, Zeke.

My heart swelled with happiness to see him. It'd taken some serious diplomacy to get our people back, including our favorite hacker, but it had been well worth the effort. The Riders of the Wild Hunt had their brother back. I'd never take that man for granted again.

"Uncle Ash Uncle Z!" Dahlia yelled.

A moment later Kenzie popped up on the other side of my throne and rushed toward the hulking duo too.

They so rarely were able to see Ash and Zeke these days, since they'd chosen to live in the mortal world. So, when they did come back to visit the kids, they were filled with excitement.

I stood up and rested my hands on my hips as I watched my girls.

They chattered incessantly at their honorary uncles, like tomorrow wasn't promised.

Both of them wore genuine, grins on their faces, listening with the patience of saints as they were regaled with all they'd miss since they last visit.

Even though Ash and the other Riders of the Hunt weren't technically blood family, they were all like brothers to me regardless, especially Zeke. What'd happened to him had really hammered home the old adage 'no man left behind'. It's something I'd ensure would never happen again.

We've always been our strongest when we're together...

Arms wrapped cheekily around my body from behind and pulled me into a familiar broad chest. "You're all smiles," Grey observed as he kissed his mark on my neck.

"They were fighting again, then Ash and Zeke came in saved the day. It's like it's completely forgotten." I leaned my head back on his shoulder with a contented sigh.

"I doubt it's *completely* forgotten." Grey chuckled, gesturing toward Christian's stormy face.

He was shooting subtle glares at the twins whenever the Riders weren't looking.

I shook my head. Moments like this would probably get mentioned every time he got mad at his sisters for the rest of eternity...

Poor little man. He's outnumbered.

"You're right, but at least for this moment we have a little peace." I turned in his arms and stared up into his gorgeous face. Even after all these years, I ached for his touch.

"I wouldn't change a thing," Grey said as he pulled me closer to his hard chest. "Our girls are chaos gremlins and will be a force of nature when they grow up, but they are perfect. Christian's a little broody, but he's mine... so that was to be expected."

"You were definitely broody when we first met," I agreed with a grin before pressing a teasing kiss to his lips.

A chorus of youthful "ew's" filled the throne room, egged on by a certain pair of uncles.

My giggle was lost as Grey deepened the kiss, infusing it with passion and love. When he finally pulled away again, he didn't leave. Instead, he pressed his forehead to mine. "I *was* broody," he agreed. "But a strong-willed Fae princess changed me for the better. One day Christian will find someone too, and he'll become the best version of himself as well."

"Let's not get ahead of ourselves." I didn't even want to think about the day my babies moved on and spread their wings to follow their own paths. "They're still children," I said, "and I want to keep them small as long as I can."

"Of course, my love," Grey soothed, kissing the tip of my nose with a grin.

Our life was chaotic and messy sometimes, but it was also amazing beyond words. Growing up, sleeping on the dirty carpet inside an old wardrobe... those days seemed so far away now—no more than a distant memory. But they'd helped forge who I was destined to be and taught more than a few important lessons.

I'd never take my babies, or my mate for granted; and my found family was every bit as precious to me. I wouldn't change them for anything in the world. They were mine—perfectly imperfect as a family could be—and no matter what challenges we faced, we'd protect each other always...

Because that's what families do.

THE END.

www.ingramcontent.com/pod-product-compliance
Lightning Source LLC
Chambersburg PA
CBHW071744210726
48292CB00012BA/13
9781923446724